# Rocket Raccoon and Groot

## TALL TAILS

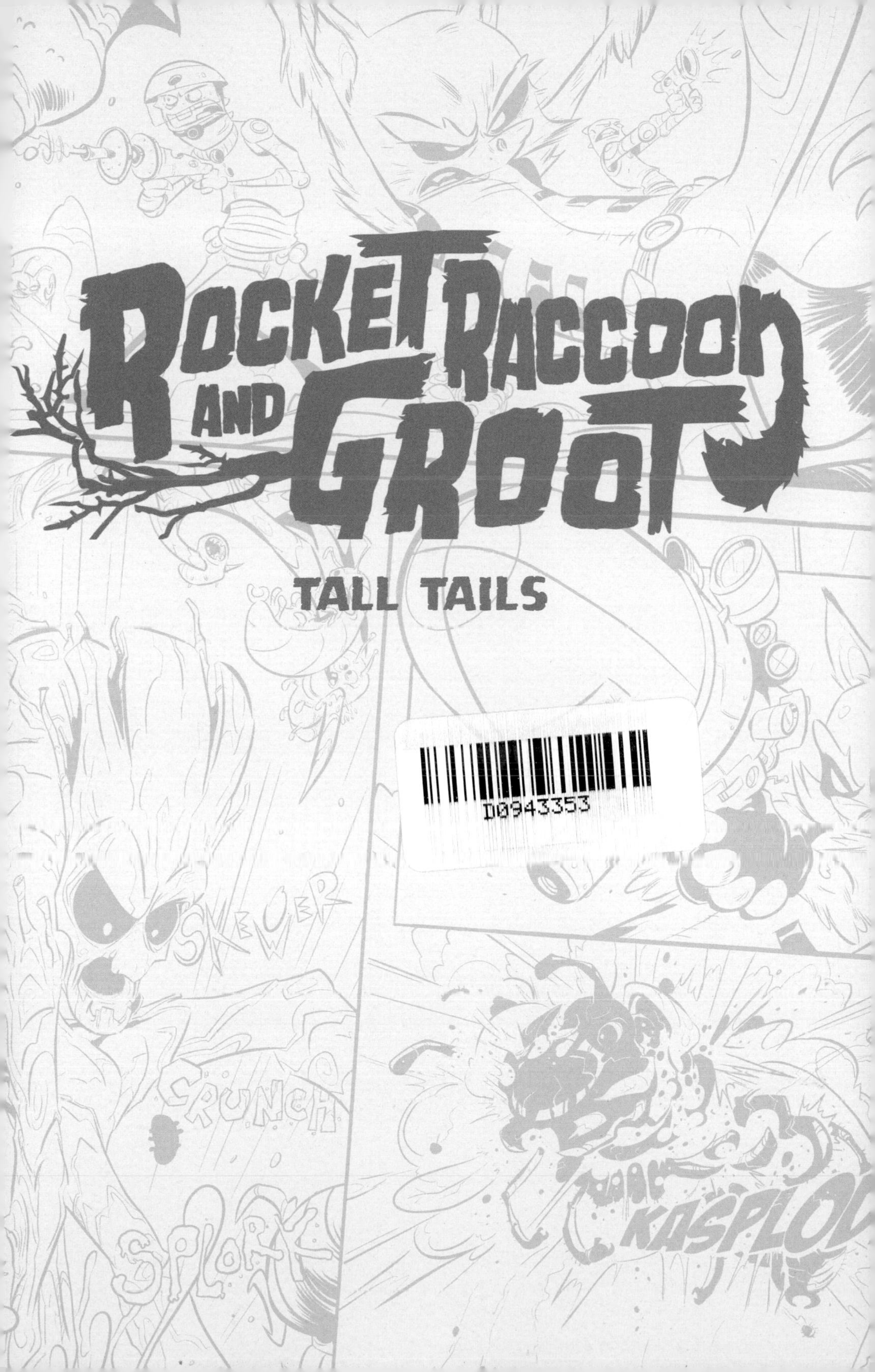

SKEWER
CRUNCH
SPLORK
KASPLOO

# CONTENTS

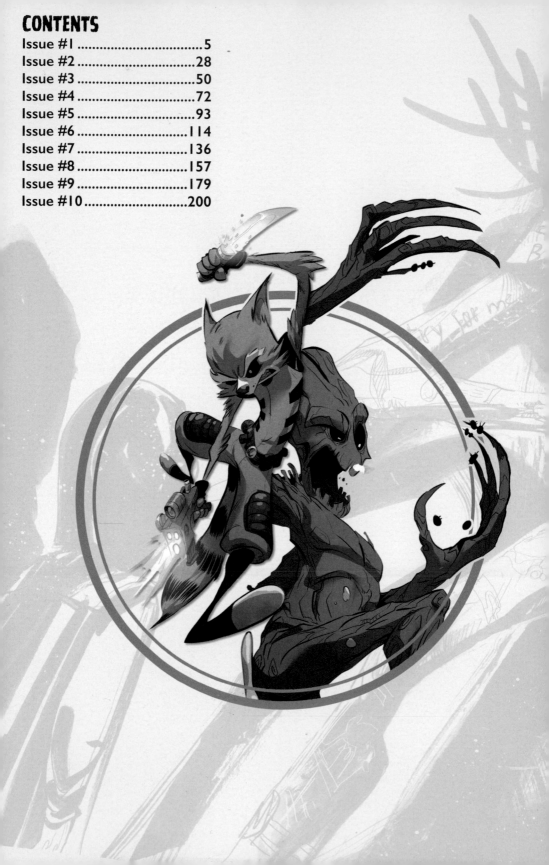

# ROCKET RACCOON AND GROOT

## TALL TAILS

WRITERS
### SKOTTIE YOUNG (#1-6) & NICK KOCHER (#7-10)

ARTISTS
### FILIPE ANDRADE (#1-3), AARON CONLEY (#4),
### JAY FOSGITT (#5), BRETT BEAN (#6) & MICHAEL WALSH (#7-10)
WITH JOSH HIXSON (INKS, #10)

COLOR ARTISTS
### JEAN-FRANÇOIS BEAULIEU (#1-6),
### CRIS PETER (#7) & MICHAEL GARLAND (#8-10)

LETTERER
### JEFF ECKLEBERRY

COVER ART
### SKOTTIE YOUNG (#1-6) &
### DAVID LOPEZ (#7-10)

ASSISTANT EDITOR
### KATHLEEN WISNESKI

EDITOR
### JAKE THOMAS

Groot created by STAN LEE, LARRY LIEBER & JACK KIRBY
Rocket Raccoon created by BILL MANTLO & KEITH GIFFEN

collection editor JENNIFER GRÜNWALD
assistant managing editor MAIA LOY • assistant managing editor LISA MONTALBANO
editor, special projects MARK D. BEAZLEY • vp production & special projects JEFF YOUNGQUIST
vp licensed publishing SVEN LARSEN • svp print, sales & marketing DAVID GABRIEL
editor in chief C.B. CEBULSKI

ROCKET RACCOON AND GROOT: TALL TAILS. Contains material originally published in magazine form as ROCKET RACCOON & GROOT (2016) #1-10. First printing 2020. ISBN 978-1-302-92115-6. Published by MARVEL WORLDWIDE, INC., a subsidiary of MARVEL ENTERTAINMENT, LLC. OFFICE OF PUBLICATION: 1290 Avenue of the Americas, New York, NY 10104. © 2020 MARVEL No similarity between any of the names, characters, persons, and/or institutions in this magazine with those of any living or dead person or institution is intended, and any such similarity which may exist is purely coincidental. Printed in Canada. KEVIN FEIGE, Chief Creative Officer; DAN BUCKLEY, President, Marvel Entertainment; JOHN NEE, Publisher; JOE QUESADA, EVP & Creative Director; TOM BREVOORT, SVP of Publishing; DAVID BOGART, Associate Publisher & SVP of Talent Affairs; Publishing & Partnership; DAVID GABRIEL, VP of Print & Digital Publishing; JEFF YOUNGQUIST, VP of Production & Special Projects; DAN CARR, Executive Director of Publishing Technology; ALEX MORALES, Director of Publishing Operations; DAN EDINGTON, Managing Editor; SUSAN CRESPI, Production Manager; STAN LEE, Chairman Emeritus. For information regarding advertising in Marvel Comics or on Marvel.com, please contact Vit DeBellis, Custom Solutions & Integrated Advertising Manager, at vdebellis@marvel.com. For Marvel subscription inquiries, please call 888-511-5480. Manufactured between 1/17/2020 and 2/18/2020 by SOLISCO PRINTERS, SCOTT, QC, CANADA.

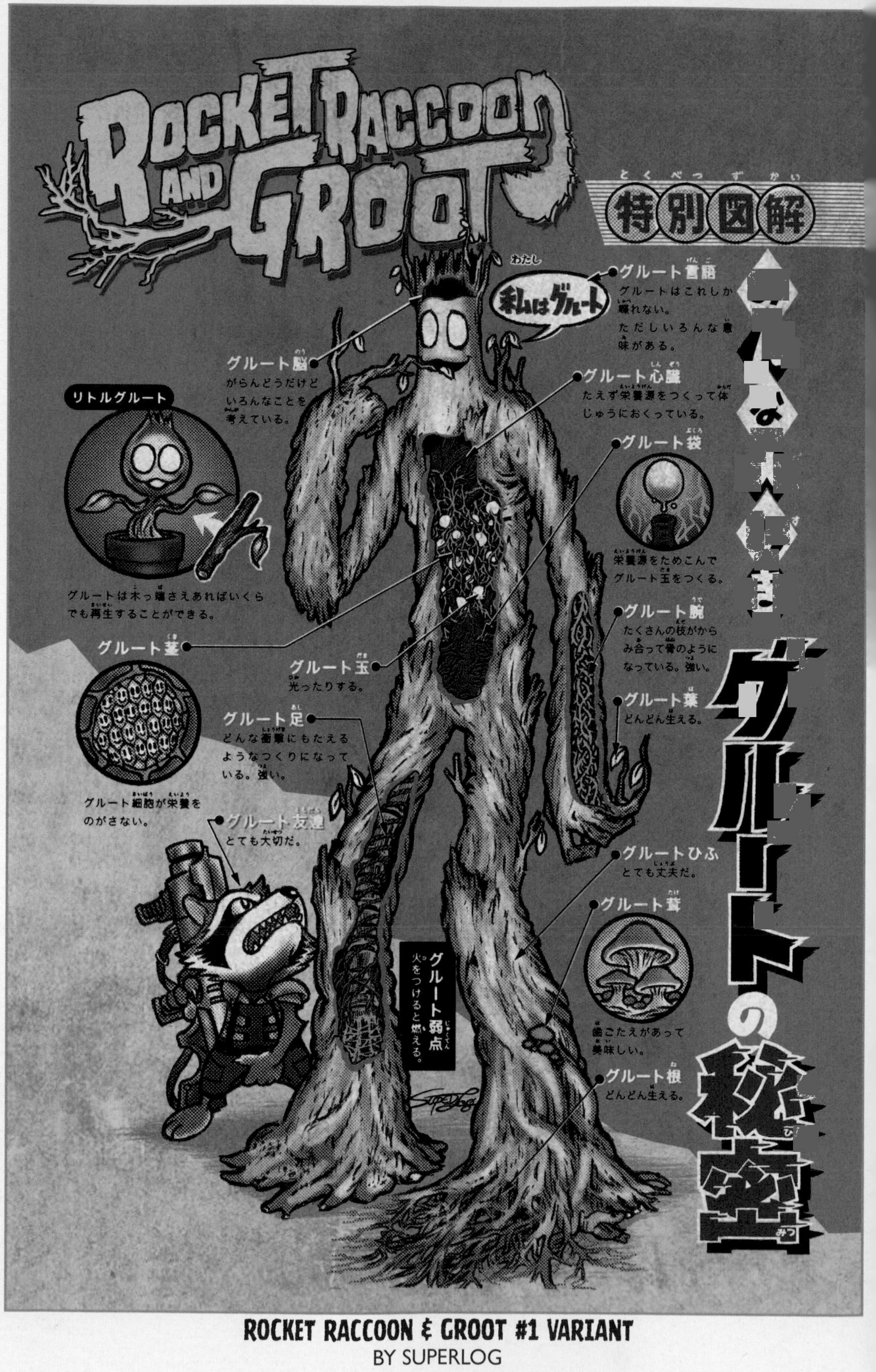
ROCKET RACCOON AND GROOT
特別図解
グルートの秘密
私はグルート
グルート言語
グルートはこれしか喋れない。
ただしいろんな意味がある。
グルート脳
がらんどうだけどいろんなことを考えている。
リトルグルート
グルートは木っ端さえあればいくらでも再生することができる。
グルート心臓
たえず栄養源をつくって体じゅうにおくっている。
グルート袋
栄養源をためこんでグルート玉をつくる。
グルート腕
たくさんの枝がからみ合って骨のようになっている。強い。
グルート葉
どんどん生える。
グルート茎
グルート玉
光ったりする。
グルート足
どんな衝撃にもたえるようなつくりになっている。強い。
グルート細胞が栄養をのがさない。
グルート友達
とても大切だ。
グルートひふ
とても丈夫だ。
グルート茸
歯ごたえがあって美味しい。
グルート弱点
火をつけると燃える。
グルート根
どんどん生える。

**ROCKET RACCOON & GROOT #1 VARIANT**
BY SUPERLOG

# 1

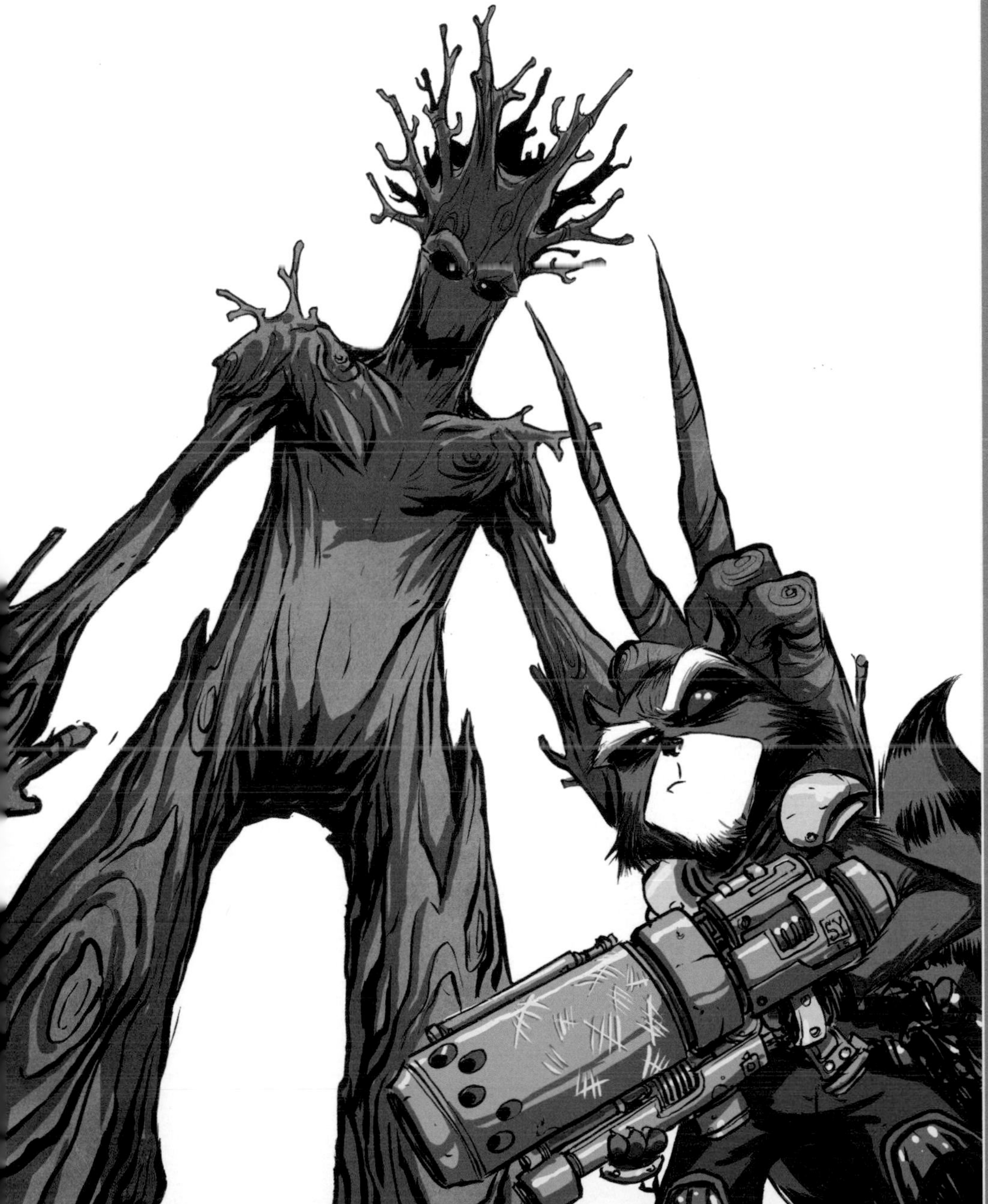

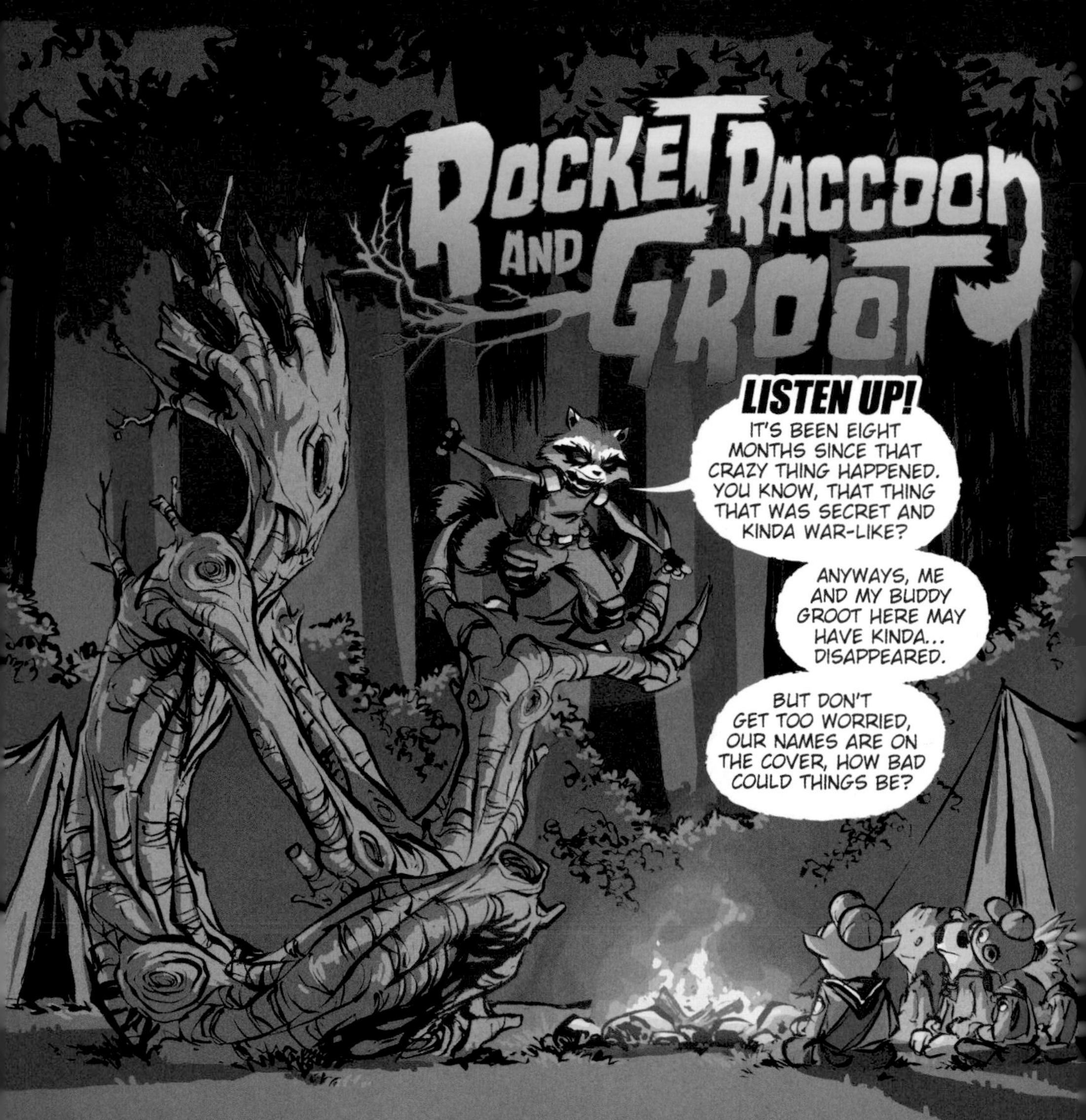
ROCKET RACCOON AND GROOT
LISTEN UP!
IT'S BEEN EIGHT MONTHS SINCE THAT CRAZY THING HAPPENED. YOU KNOW, THAT THING THAT WAS SECRET AND KINDA WAR-LIKE?
ANYWAYS, ME AND MY BUDDY GROOT HERE MAY HAVE KINDA... DISAPPEARED.
BUT DON'T GET TOO WORRIED, OUR NAMES ARE ON THE COVER, HOW BAD COULD THINGS BE?

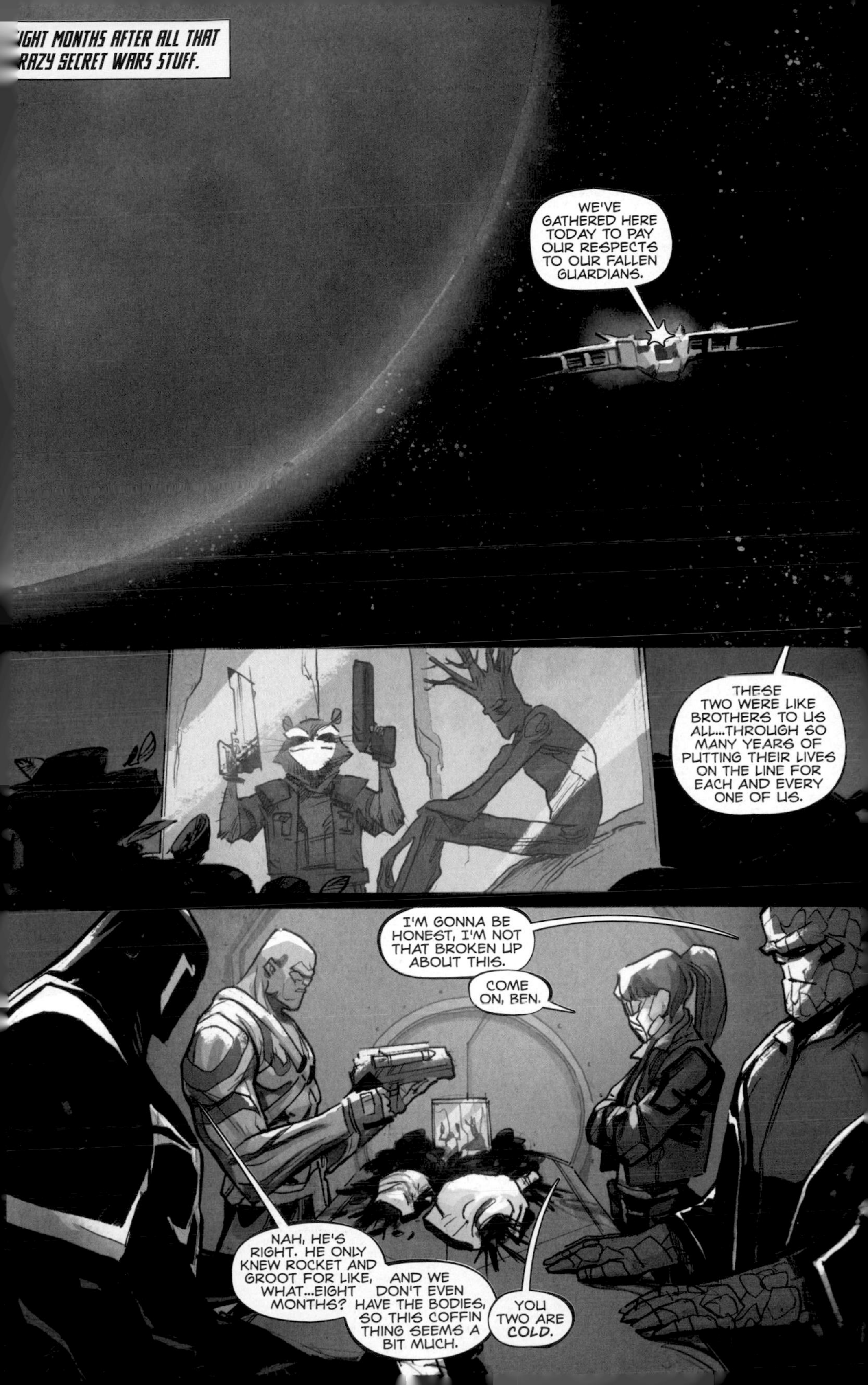
IGHT MONTHS AFTER ALL THAT RAZY SECRET WARS STUFF.
WE'VE GATHERED HERE TODAY TO PAY OUR RESPECTS TO OUR FALLEN GUARDIANS.
THESE TWO WERE LIKE BROTHERS TO US ALL...THROUGH SO MANY YEARS OF PUTTING THEIR LIVES ON THE LINE FOR EACH AND EVERY ONE OF US.
I'M GONNA BE HONEST, I'M NOT THAT BROKEN UP ABOUT THIS.
COME ON, BEN.
NAH, HE'S RIGHT. HE ONLY KNEW ROCKET AND GROOT FOR LIKE, WHAT...EIGHT MONTHS?
AND WE DON'T EVEN HAVE THE BODIES, SO THIS COFFIN THING SEEMS A BIT MUCH.
YOU TWO ARE COLD.

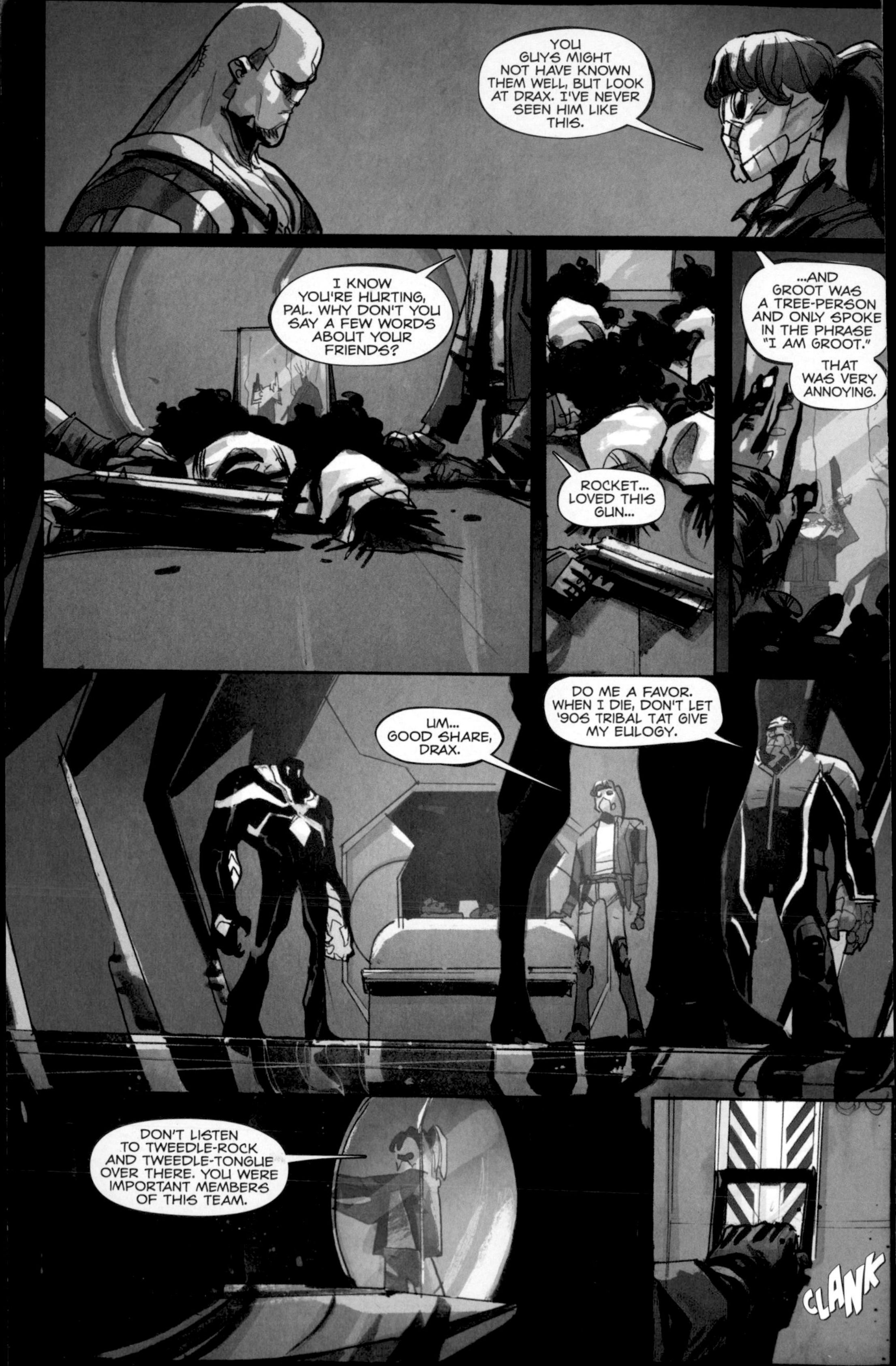
YOU GUYS MIGHT NOT HAVE KNOWN THEM WELL, BUT LOOK AT DRAX. I'VE NEVER SEEN HIM LIKE THIS.
I KNOW YOU'RE HURTING, PAL. WHY DON'T YOU SAY A FEW WORDS ABOUT YOUR FRIENDS?
ROCKET... LOVED THIS GUN...
...AND GROOT WAS A TREE-PERSON AND ONLY SPOKE IN THE PHRASE "I AM GROOT."
THAT WAS VERY ANNOYING.
UM... GOOD SHARE, DRAX.
DO ME A FAVOR. WHEN I DIE, DON'T LET '90S TRIBAL TAT GIVE MY EULOGY.
DON'T LISTEN TO TWEEDLE-ROCK AND TWEEDLE-TONGUE OVER THERE. YOU WERE IMPORTANT MEMBERS OF THIS TEAM.
CLANK

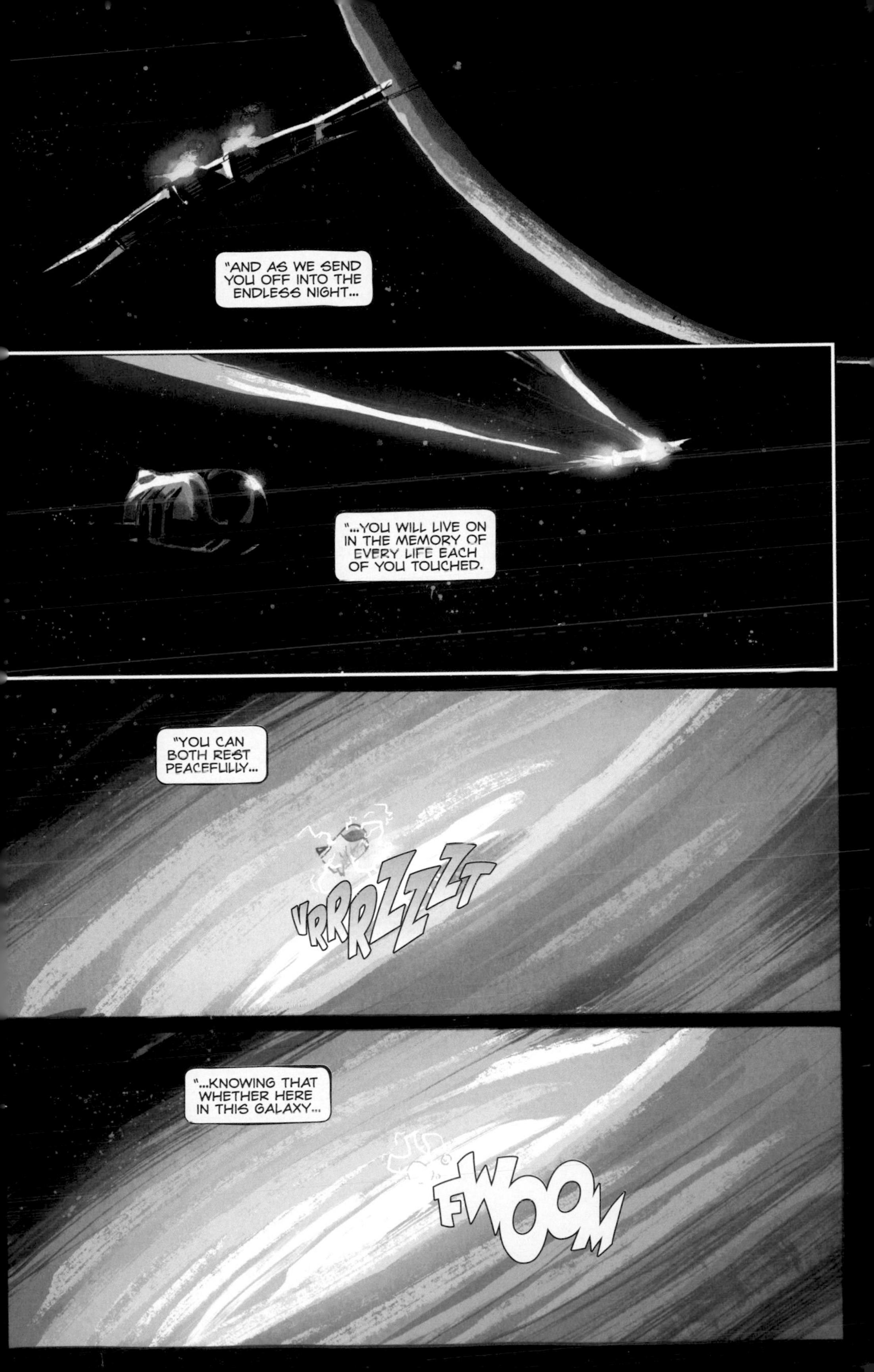
"AND AS WE SEND YOU OFF INTO THE ENDLESS NIGHT...
"...YOU WILL LIVE ON IN THE MEMORY OF EVERY LIFE EACH OF YOU TOUCHED.
"YOU CAN BOTH REST PEACEFULLY...
VRRRZZZZT
"...KNOWING THAT WHETHER HERE IN THIS GALAXY...
FWOOM

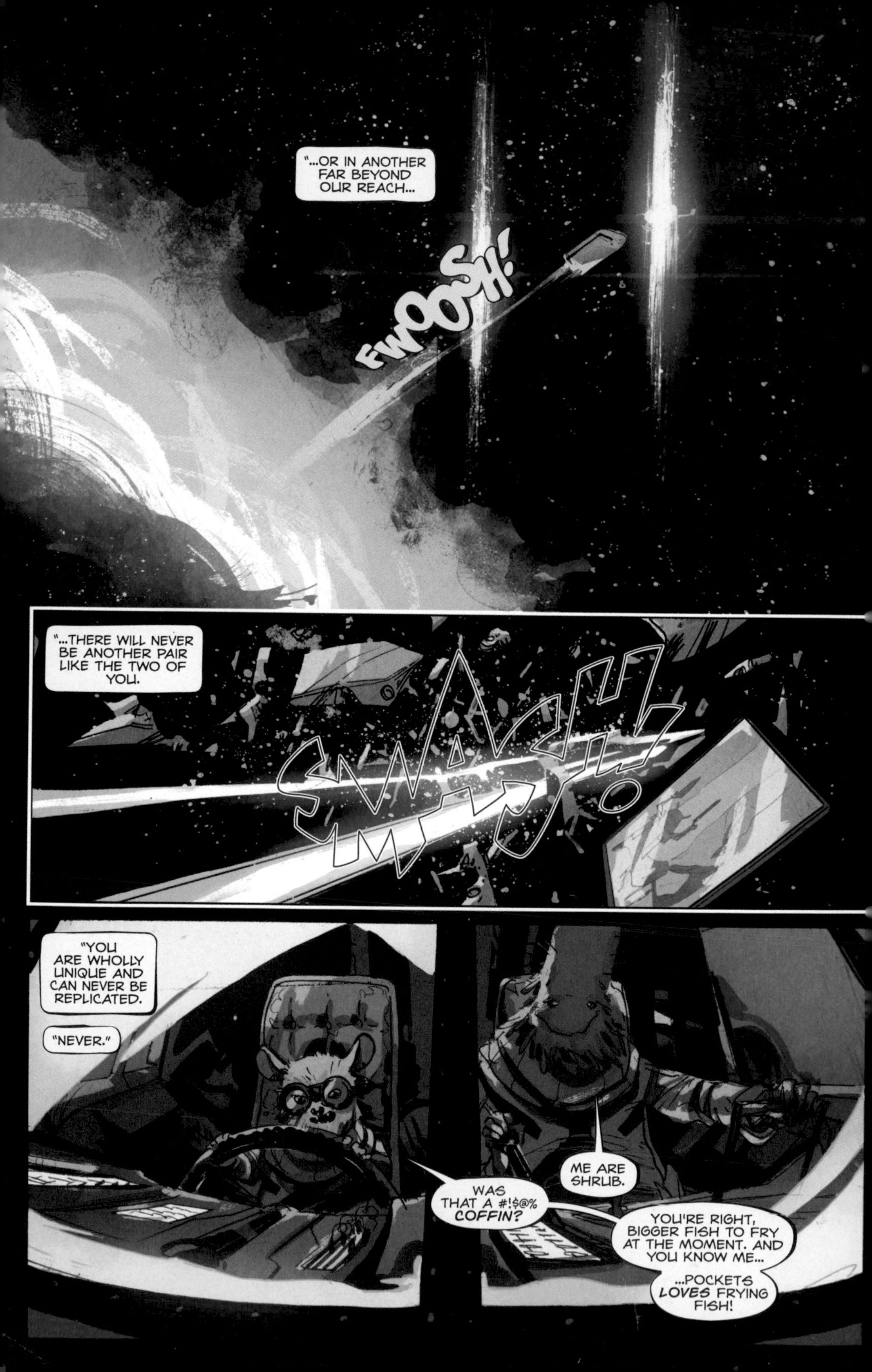
"...OR IN ANOTHER FAR BEYOND OUR REACH...
FWOOSH!
"...THERE WILL NEVER BE ANOTHER PAIR LIKE THE TWO OF YOU.
SWAAASH!
"YOU ARE WHOLLY UNIQUE AND CAN NEVER BE REPLICATED.
"NEVER."
WAS THAT A #!$@% COFFIN?
ME ARE SHRUB.
YOU'RE RIGHT, BIGGER FISH TO FRY AT THE MOMENT. AND YOU KNOW ME...
...POCKETS LOVES FRYING FISH!

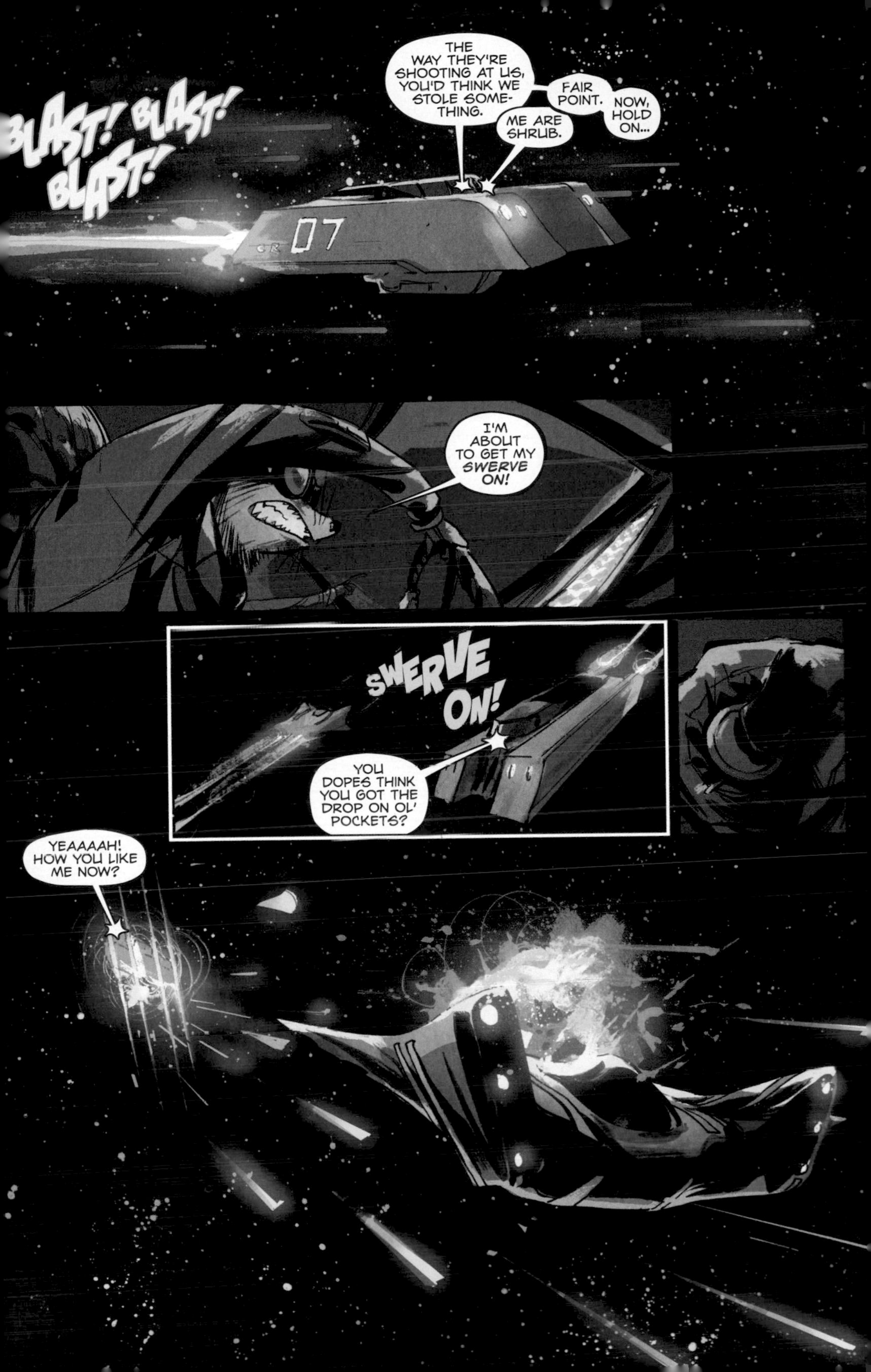
BLAST! BLAST! BLAST!
THE WAY THEY'RE SHOOTING AT US, YOU'D THINK WE STOLE SOME-THING.
ME ARE SHRUB.
FAIR POINT.
NOW, HOLD ON...
I'M ABOUT TO GET MY SWERVE ON!
SWERVE ON!
YOU DOPES THINK YOU GOT THE DROP ON OL' POCKETS?
YEAAAAH! HOW YOU LIKE ME NOW?

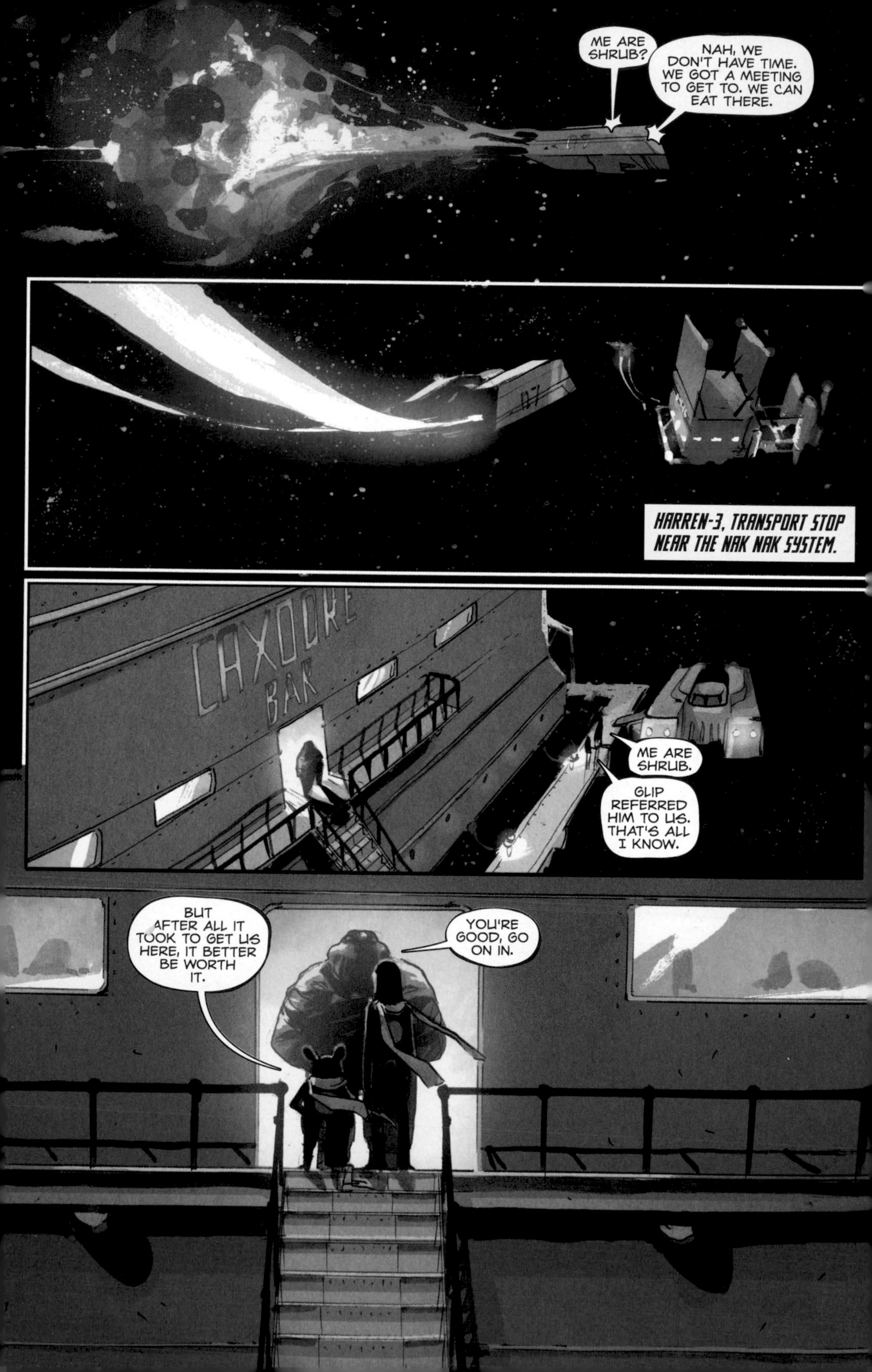
ME ARE SHRUB?
NAH, WE DON'T HAVE TIME. WE GOT A MEETING TO GET TO. WE CAN EAT THERE.
HARREN-3, TRANSPORT STOP NEAR THE NAK NAK SYSTEM.
CAXOORE BAR
ME ARE SHRUB.
GLIP REFERRED HIM TO US. THAT'S ALL I KNOW.
YOU'RE GOOD, GO ON IN.
BUT AFTER ALL IT TOOK TO GET US HERE, IT BETTER BE WORTH IT.

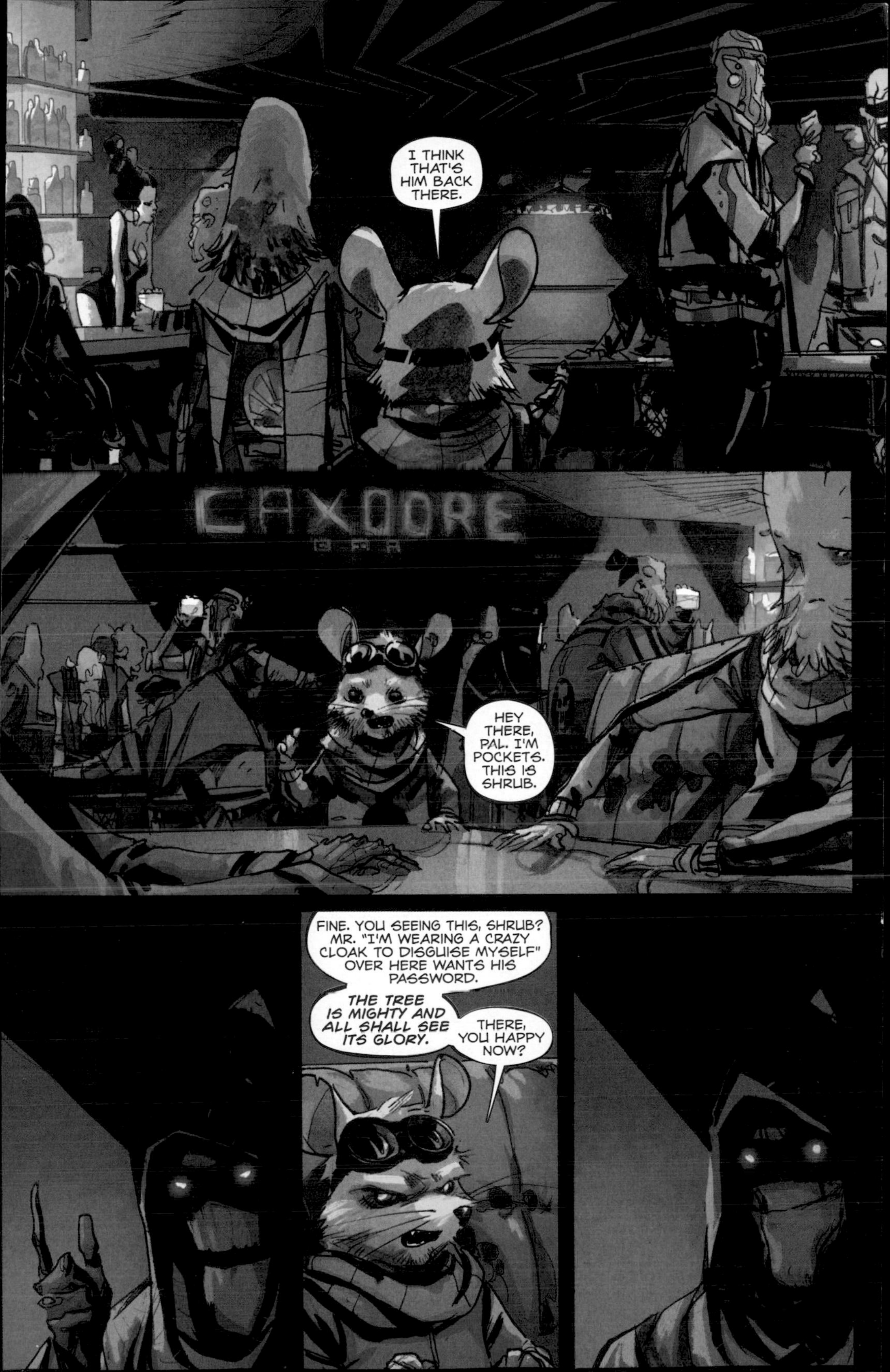
I THINK THAT'S HIM BACK THERE.
CAXOORE
HEY THERE, PAL. I'M POCKETS. THIS IS SHRUB.
FINE. YOU SEEING THIS, SHRUB? MR. "I'M WEARING A CRAZY CLOAK TO DISGUISE MYSELF" OVER HERE WANTS HIS PASSWORD.
THE TREE IS MIGHTY AND ALL SHALL SEE ITS GLORY.
THERE, YOU HAPPY NOW?

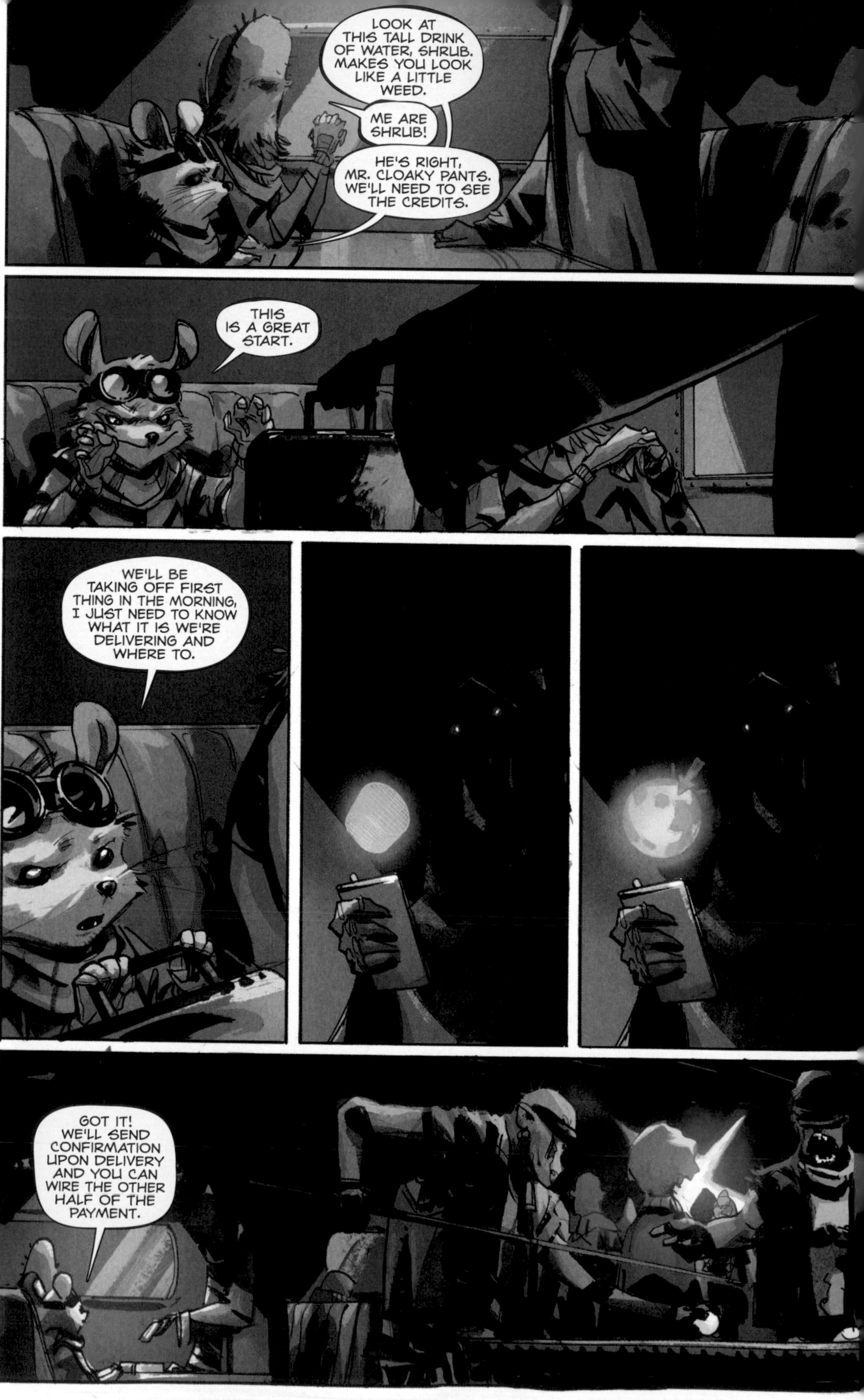
LOOK AT THIS TALL DRINK OF WATER, SHRUB. MAKES YOU LOOK LIKE A LITTLE WEED.
ME ARE SHRUB!
HE'S RIGHT, MR. CLOAKY PANTS. WE'LL NEED TO SEE THE CREDITS.
THIS IS A GREAT START.
WE'LL BE TAKING OFF FIRST THING IN THE MORNING, I JUST NEED TO KNOW WHAT IT IS WE'RE DELIVERING AND WHERE TO.
GOT IT! WE'LL SEND CONFIRMATION UPON DELIVERY AND YOU CAN WIRE THE OTHER HALF OF THE PAYMENT.

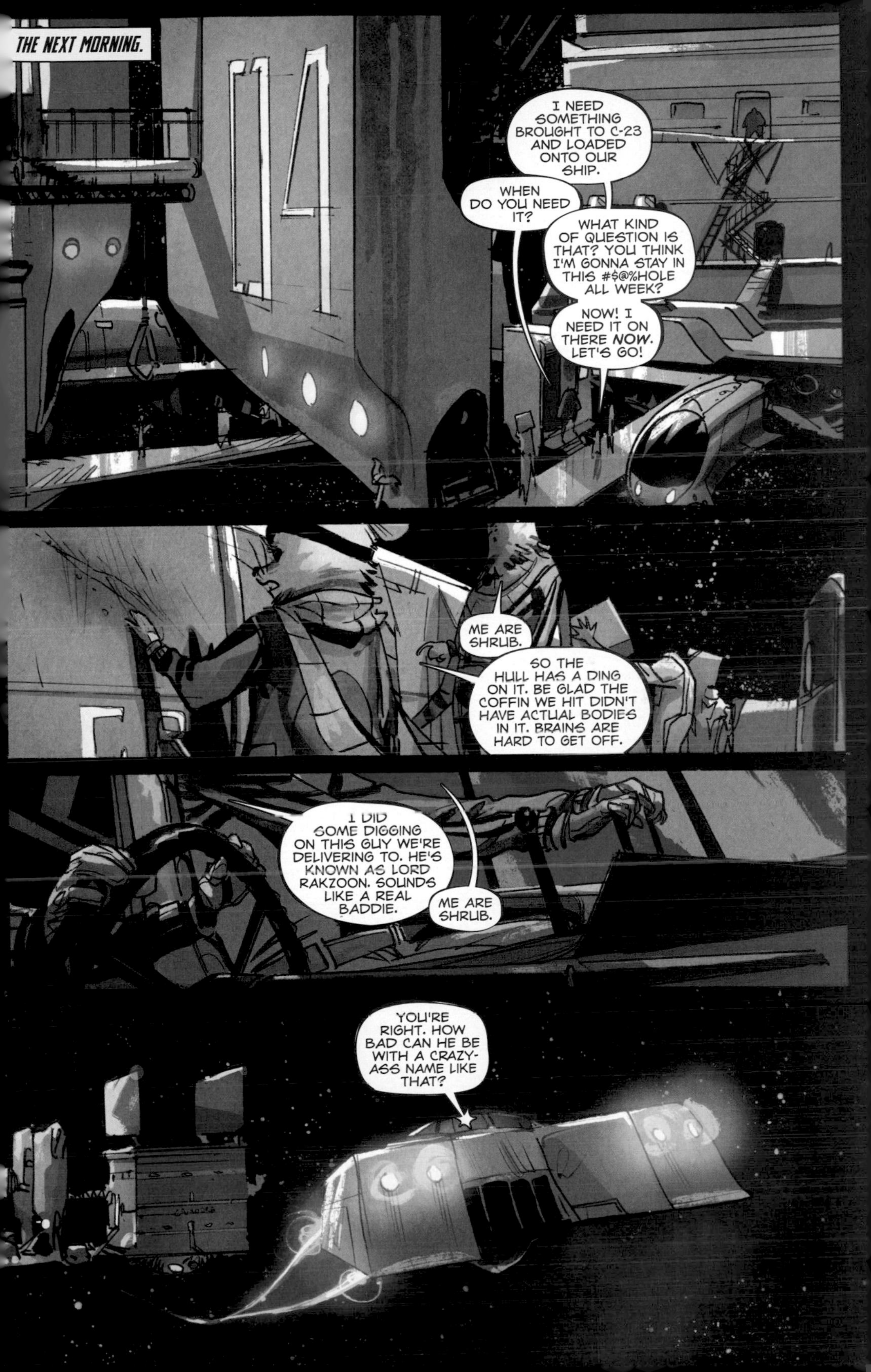
THE NEXT MORNING.
I NEED SOMETHING BROUGHT TO C-23 AND LOADED ONTO OUR SHIP.
WHEN DO YOU NEED IT?
WHAT KIND OF QUESTION IS THAT? YOU THINK I'M GONNA STAY IN THIS #$@%HOLE ALL WEEK?
NOW! I NEED IT ON THERE *NOW*. LET'S GO!
ME ARE SHRUB.
SO THE HULL HAS A DING ON IT. BE GLAD THE COFFIN WE HIT DIDN'T HAVE ACTUAL BODIES IN IT. BRAINS ARE HARD TO GET OFF.
I DID SOME DIGGING ON THIS GUY WE'RE DELIVERING TO. HE'S KNOWN AS LORD RAKZOON. SOUNDS LIKE A REAL BADDIE.
ME ARE SHRUB.
YOU'RE RIGHT. HOW BAD CAN HE BE WITH A CRAZY-ASS NAME LIKE THAT?

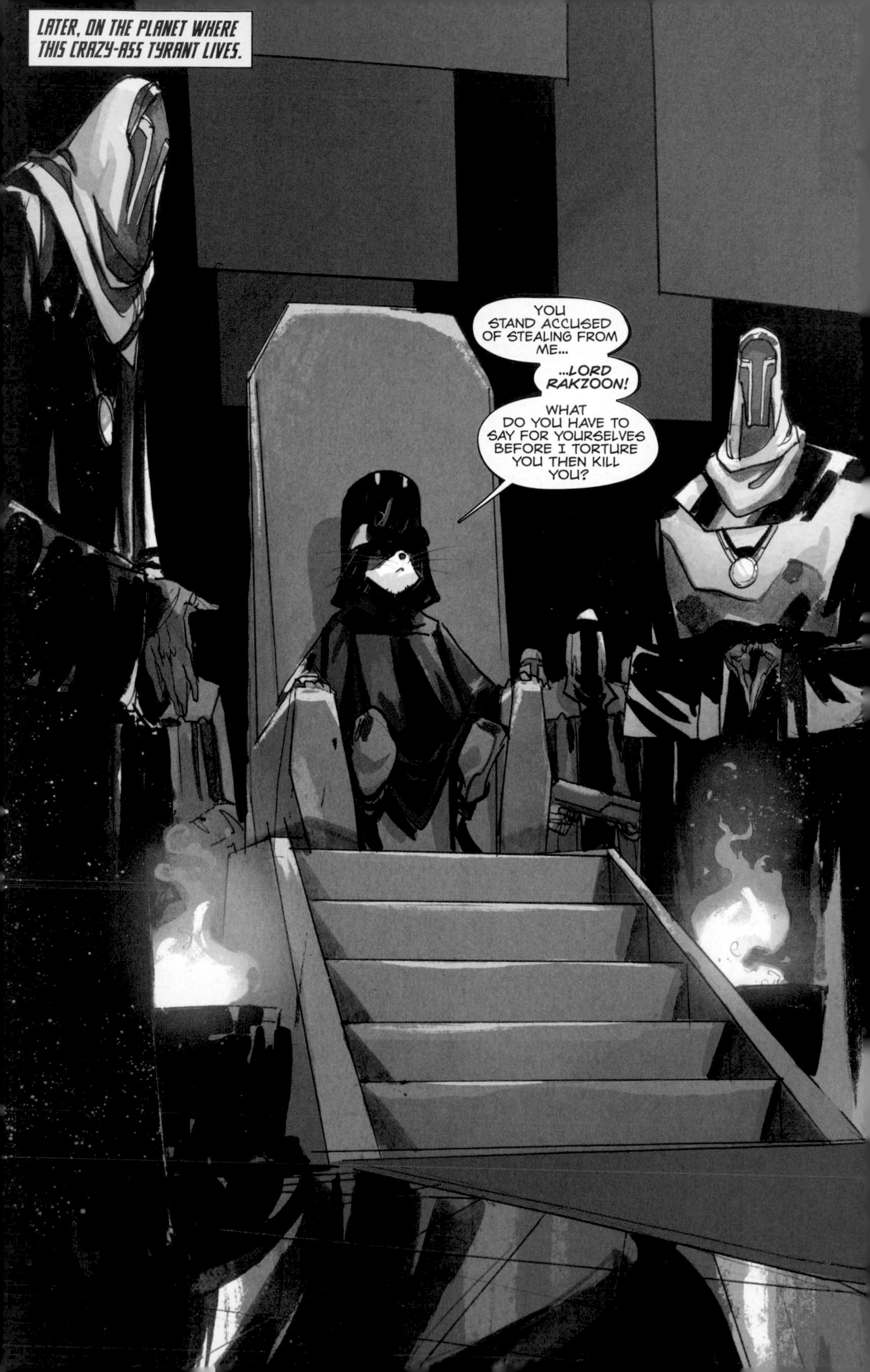
LATER, ON THE PLANET WHERE THIS CRAZY-ASS TYRANT LIVES.
YOU STAND ACCUSED OF STEALING FROM ME...
...LORD RAKZOON!
WHAT DO YOU HAVE TO SAY FOR YOURSELVES BEFORE I TORTURE YOU THEN KILL YOU?

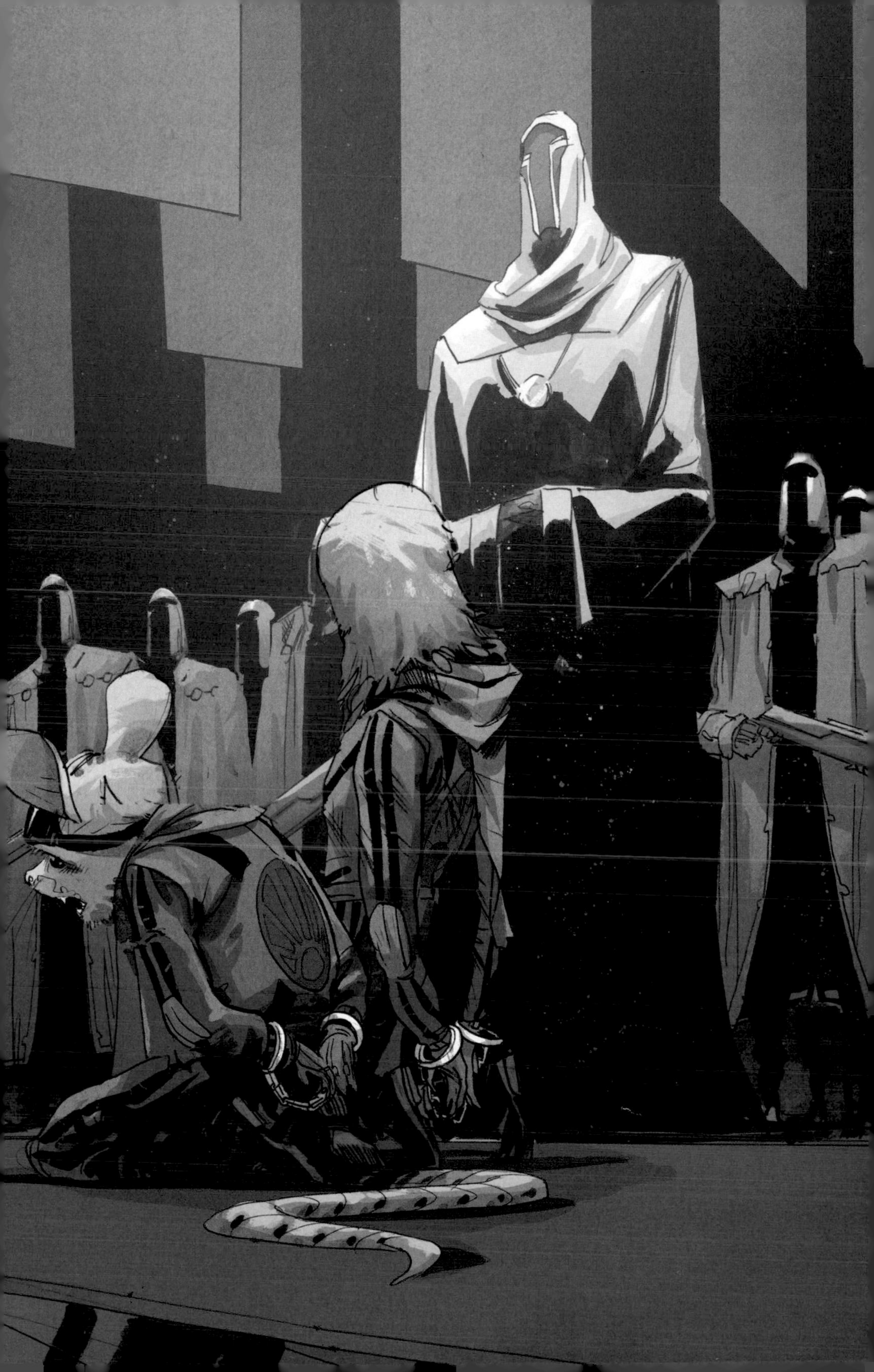

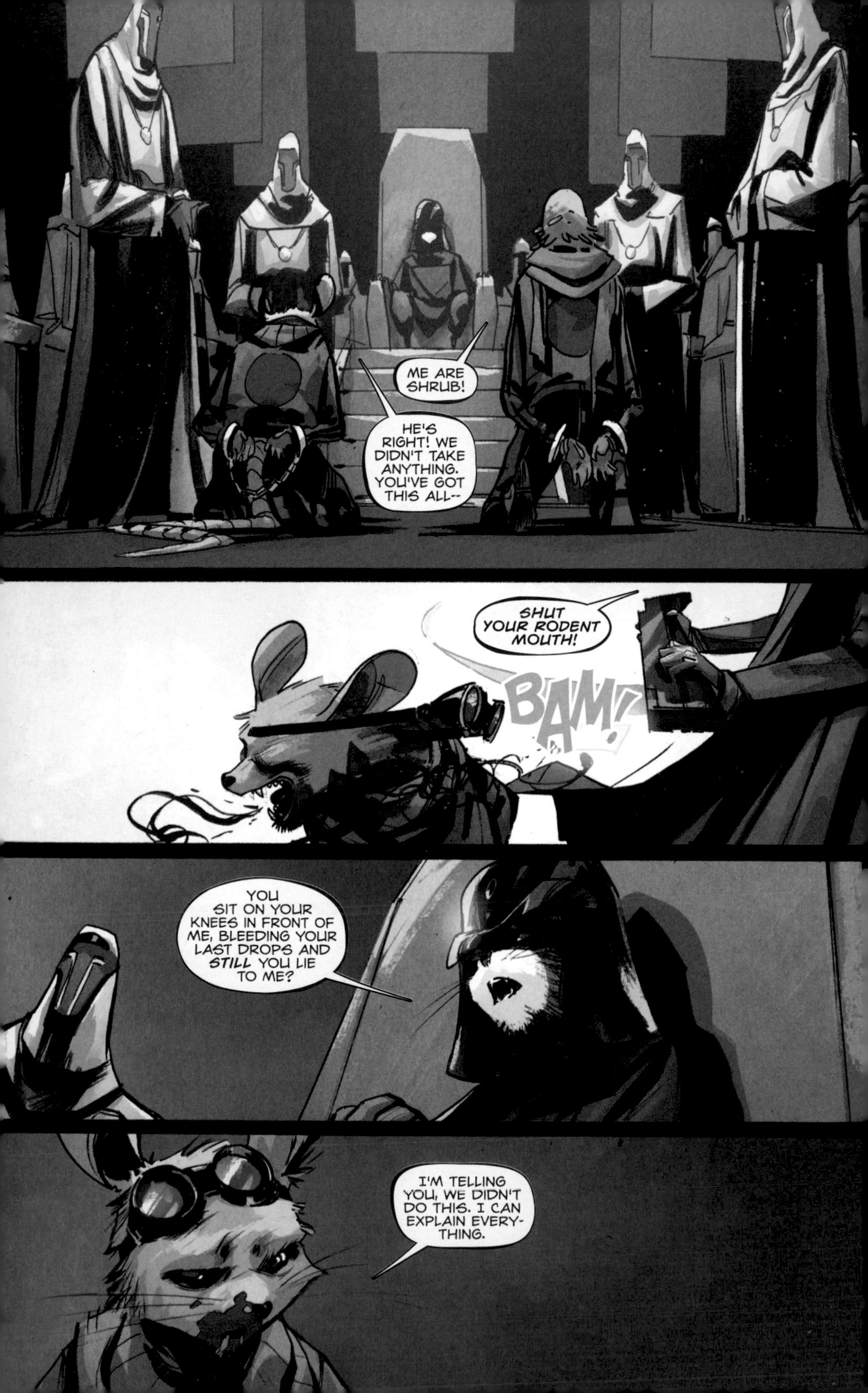
ME ARE SHRUB!
HE'S RIGHT! WE DIDN'T TAKE ANYTHING. YOU'VE GOT THIS ALL--
SHUT YOUR RODENT MOUTH!
BAM!
YOU SIT ON YOUR KNEES IN FRONT OF ME, BLEEDING YOUR LAST DROPS AND STILL YOU LIE TO ME?
I'M TELLING YOU, WE DIDN'T DO THIS. I CAN EXPLAIN EVERY-THING.

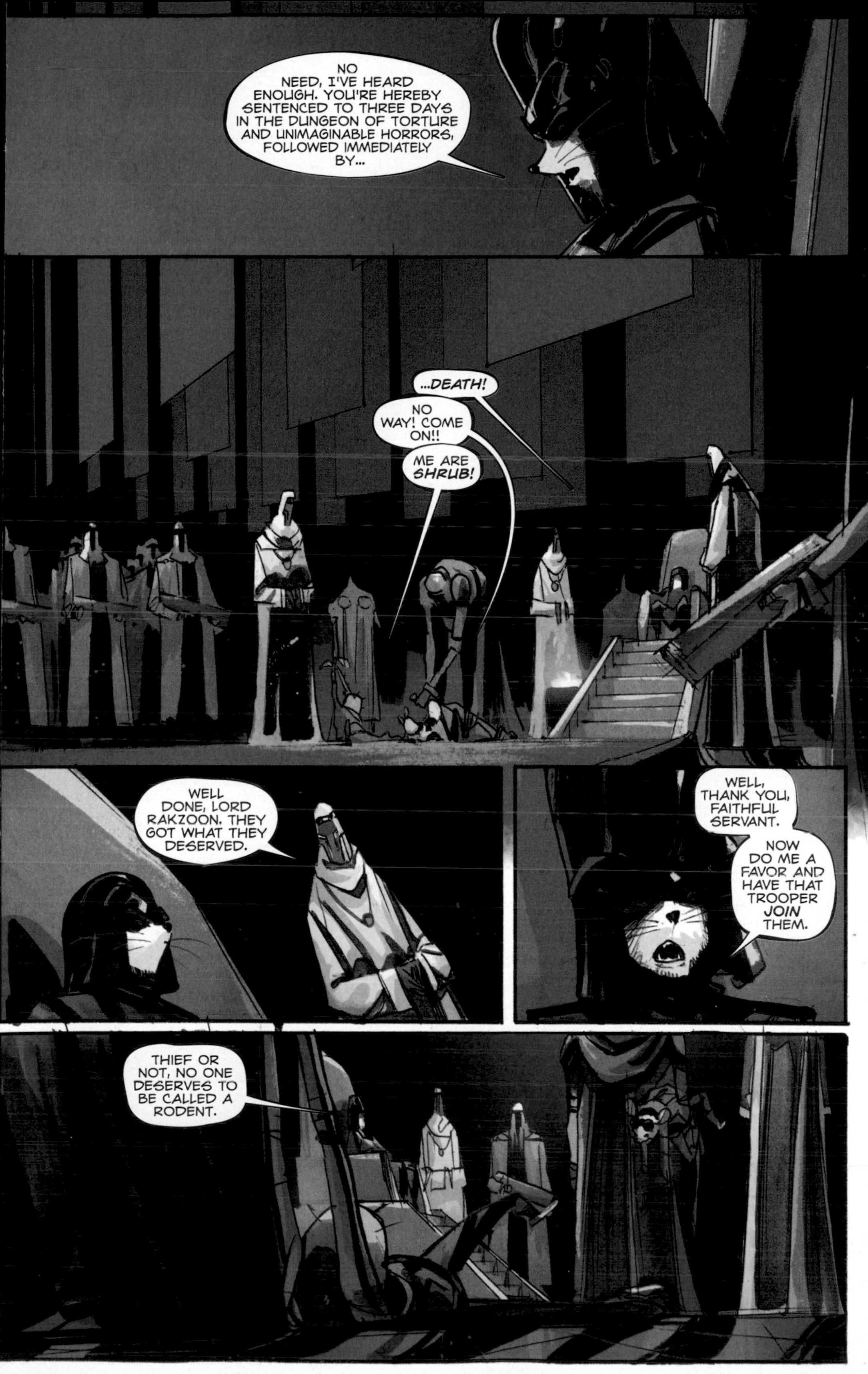
NO NEED, I'VE HEARD ENOUGH. YOU'RE HEREBY SENTENCED TO THREE DAYS IN THE DUNGEON OF TORTURE AND UNIMAGINABLE HORRORS, FOLLOWED IMMEDIATELY BY...
...DEATH!
NO WAY! COME ON!!
ME ARE SHRUB!
WELL DONE, LORD RAKZOON. THEY GOT WHAT THEY DESERVED.
WELL, THANK YOU, FAITHFUL SERVANT.
NOW DO ME A FAVOR AND HAVE THAT TROOPER JOIN THEM.
THIEF OR NOT, NO ONE DESERVES TO BE CALLED A RODENT.

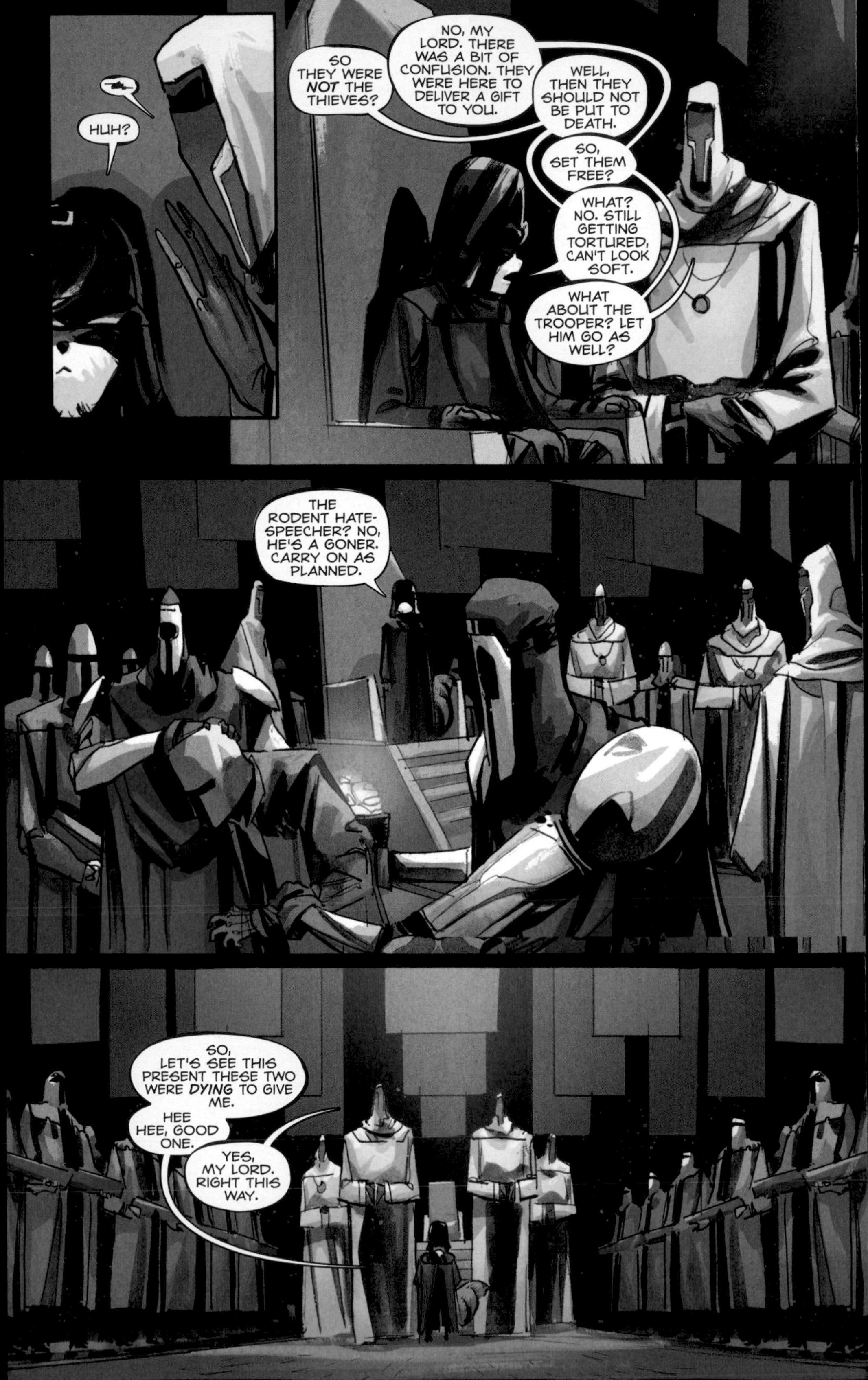
HUH?
SO THEY WERE NOT THE THIEVES?
NO, MY LORD. THERE WAS A BIT OF CONFUSION. THEY WERE HERE TO DELIVER A GIFT TO YOU.
WELL, THEN THEY SHOULD NOT BE PUT TO DEATH.
SO, SET THEM FREE?
WHAT? NO. STILL GETTING TORTURED, CAN'T LOOK SOFT.
WHAT ABOUT THE TROOPER? LET HIM GO AS WELL?
THE RODENT HATE-SPEECHER? NO, HE'S A GONER. CARRY ON AS PLANNED.
SO, LET'S SEE THIS PRESENT THESE TWO WERE DYING TO GIVE ME.
HEE HEE, GOOD ONE.
YES, MY LORD. RIGHT THIS WAY.

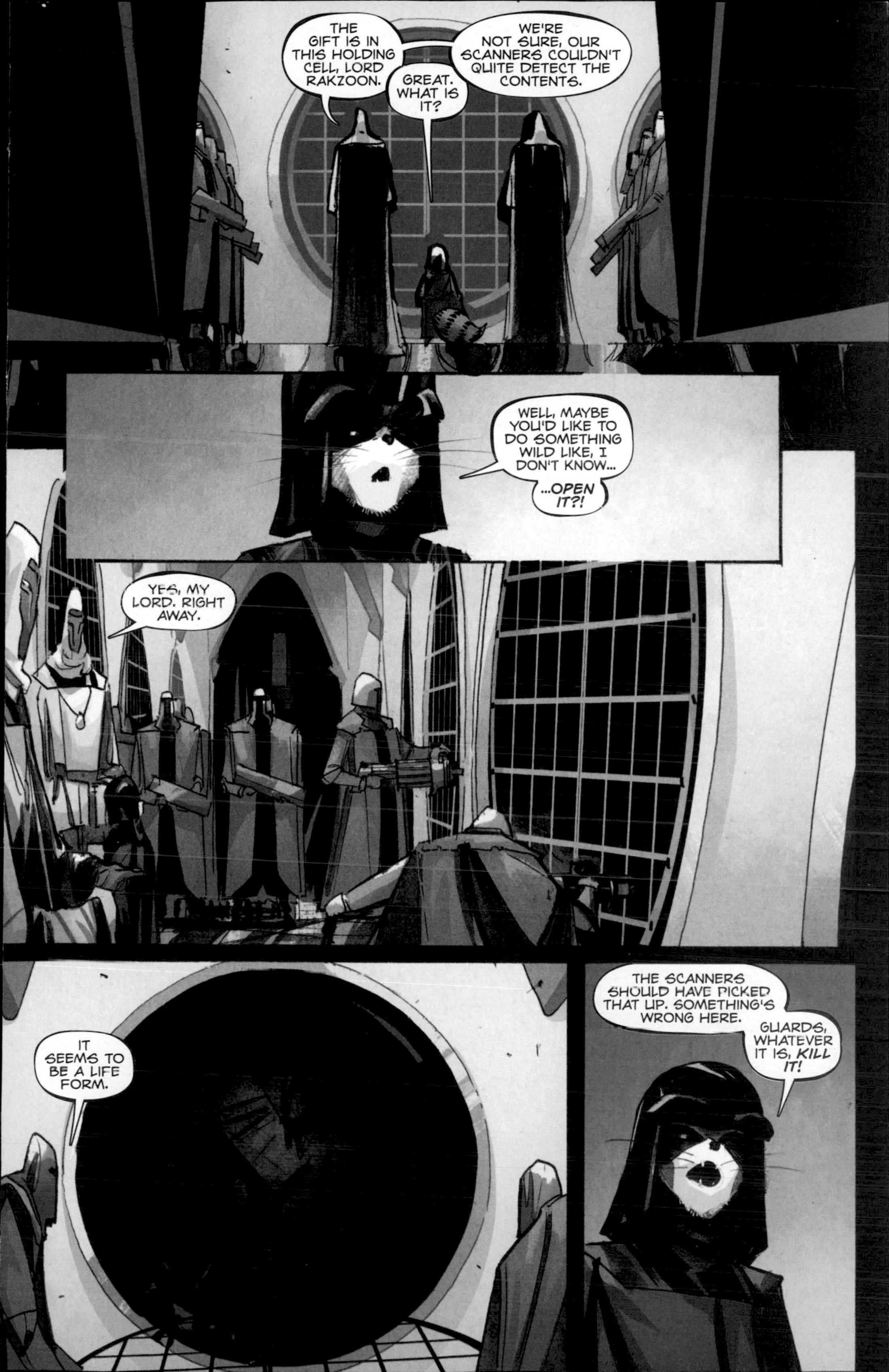

THE GIFT IS IN THIS HOLDING CELL, LORD RAKZOON.
GREAT. WHAT IS IT?
WE'RE NOT SURE, OUR SCANNERS COULDN'T QUITE DETECT THE CONTENTS.
WELL, MAYBE YOU'D LIKE TO DO SOMETHING WILD LIKE, I DON'T KNOW...
...OPEN IT?!
YES, MY LORD. RIGHT AWAY.
IT SEEMS TO BE A LIFE FORM.
THE SCANNERS SHOULD HAVE PICKED THAT UP. SOMETHING'S WRONG HERE.
GUARDS, WHATEVER IT IS, KILL IT!

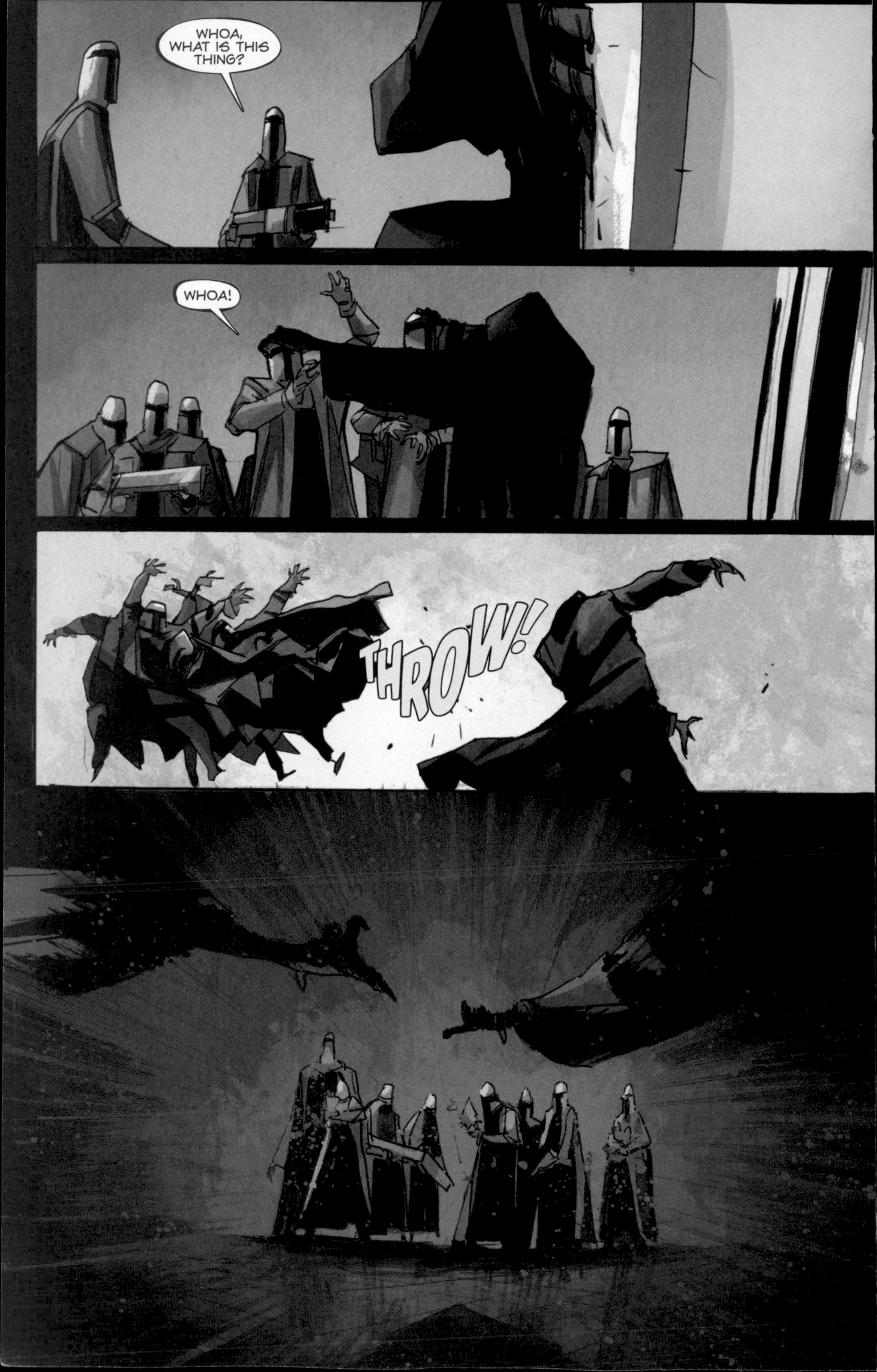
WHOA, WHAT IS THIS THING?
WHOA!
THROW!

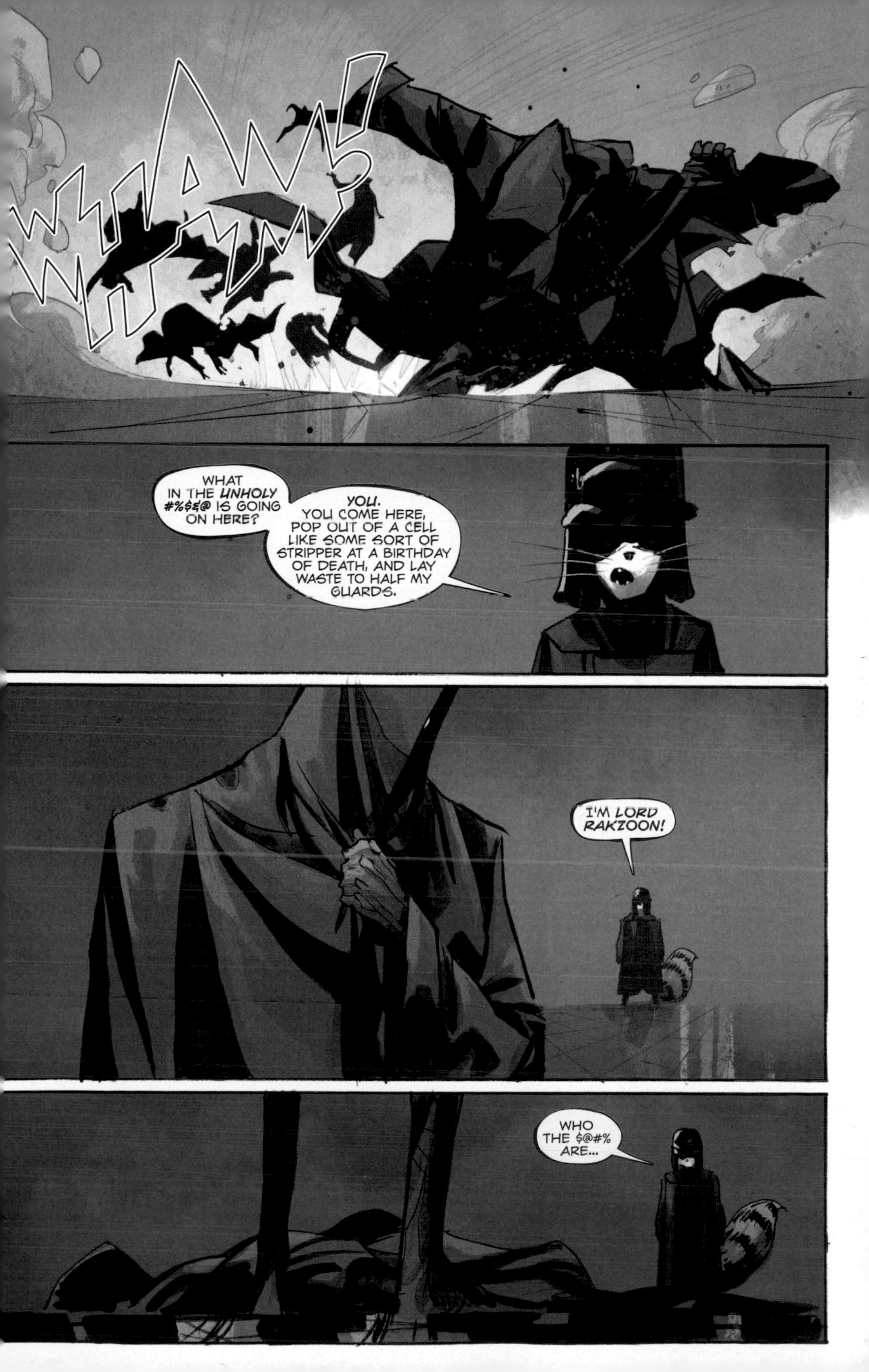
WHAM! WHAM!
WHAT IN THE UNHOLY #%$&@ IS GOING ON HERE?
YOU. YOU COME HERE, POP OUT OF A CELL LIKE SOME SORT OF STRIPPER AT A BIRTHDAY OF DEATH, AND LAY WASTE TO HALF MY GUARDS.
I'M LORD RAKZOON!
WHO THE $@#% ARE...

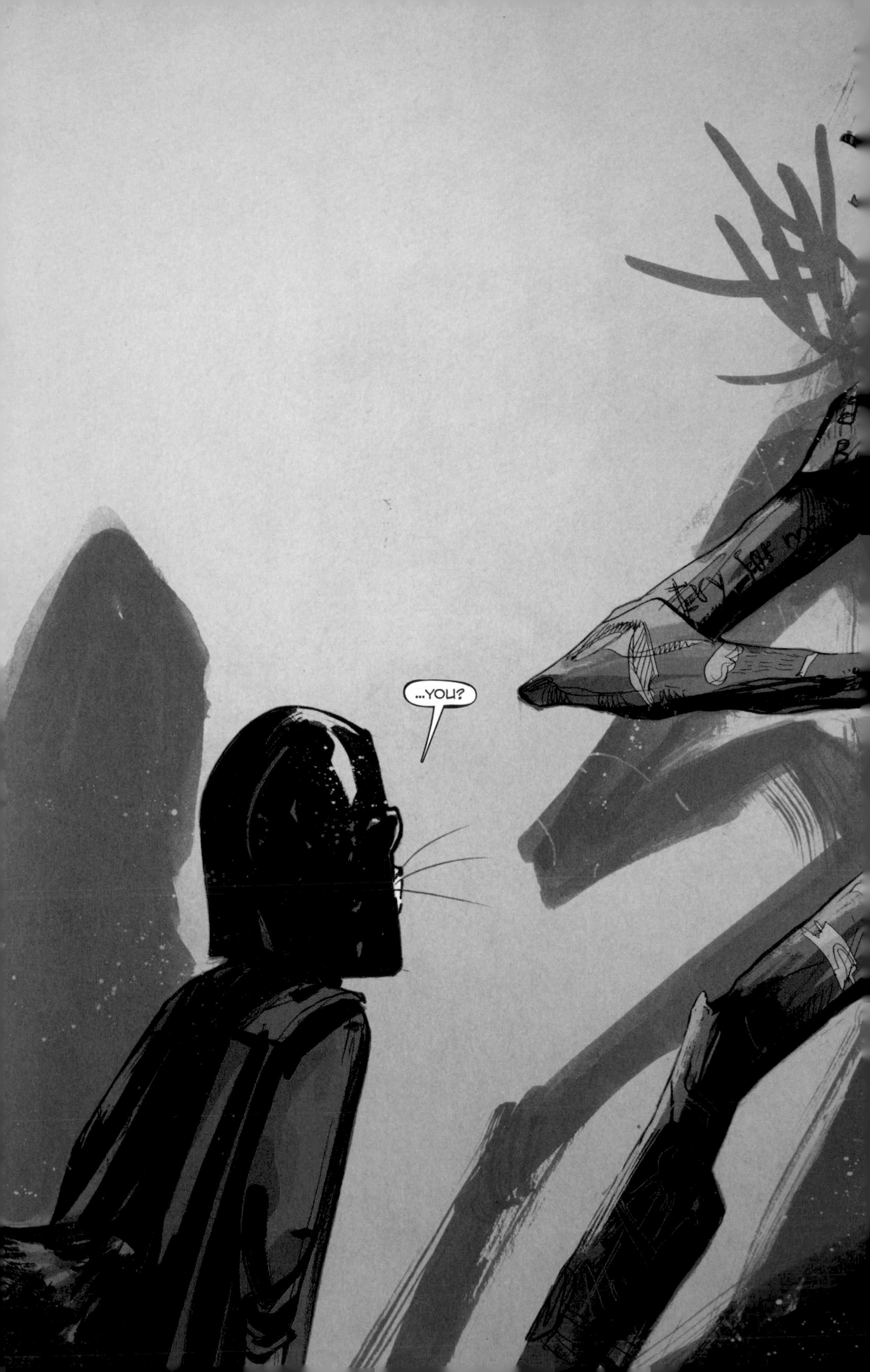
...YOU?

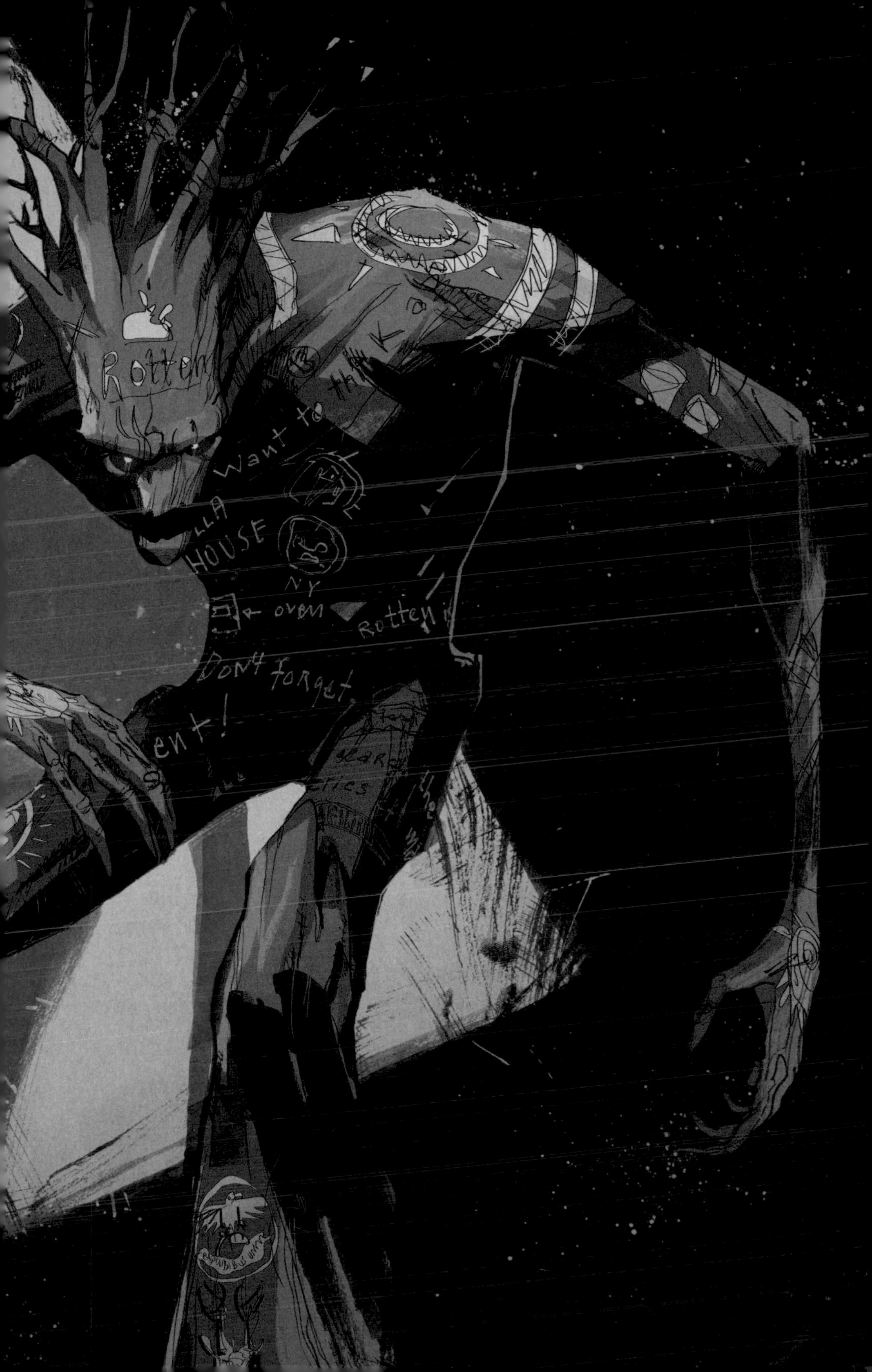

Rotten
Want to
HOUSE
NY
oven
Rotten
Dont forget
ent!

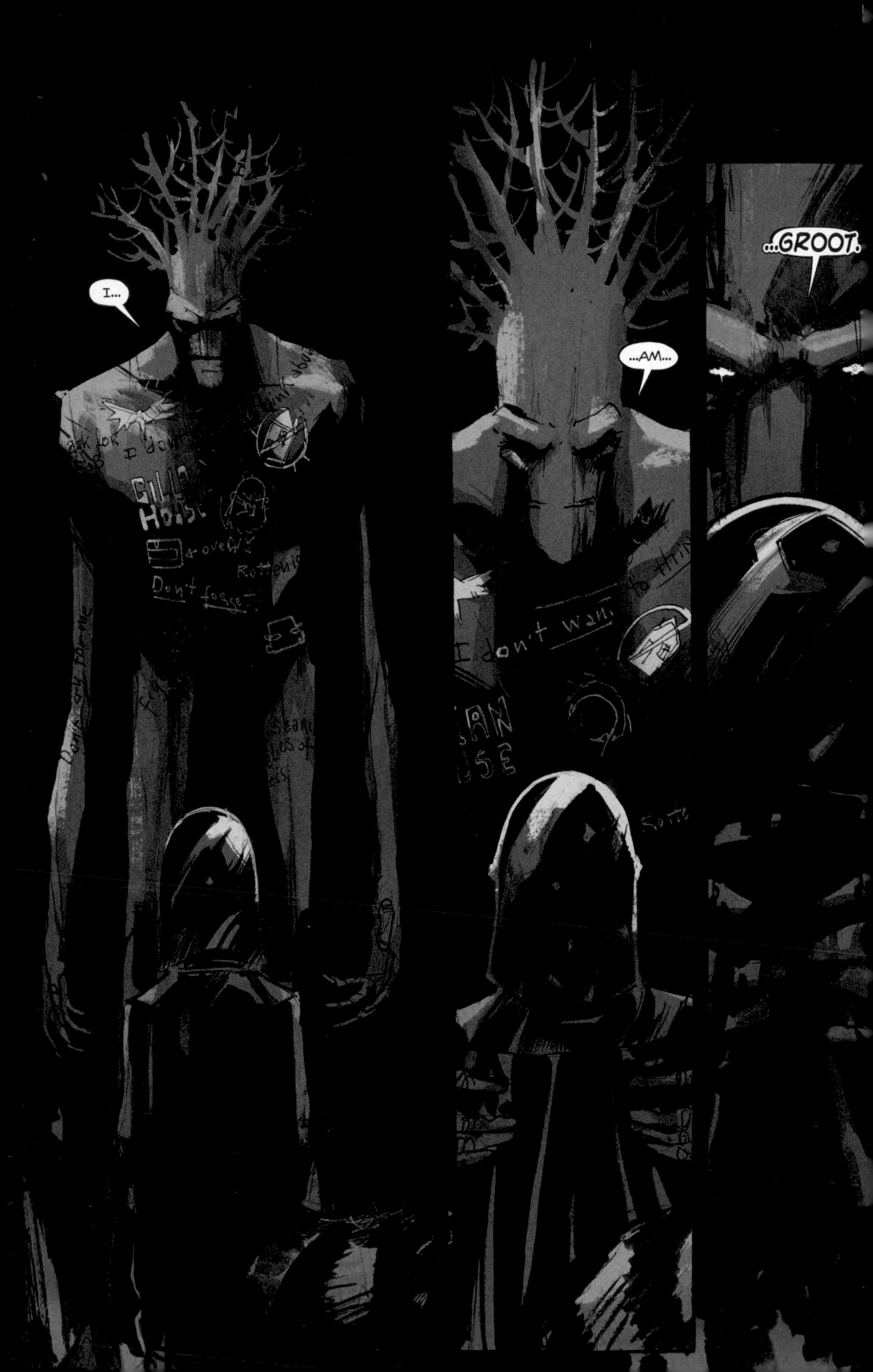

I...
...AM...
...GROOT.

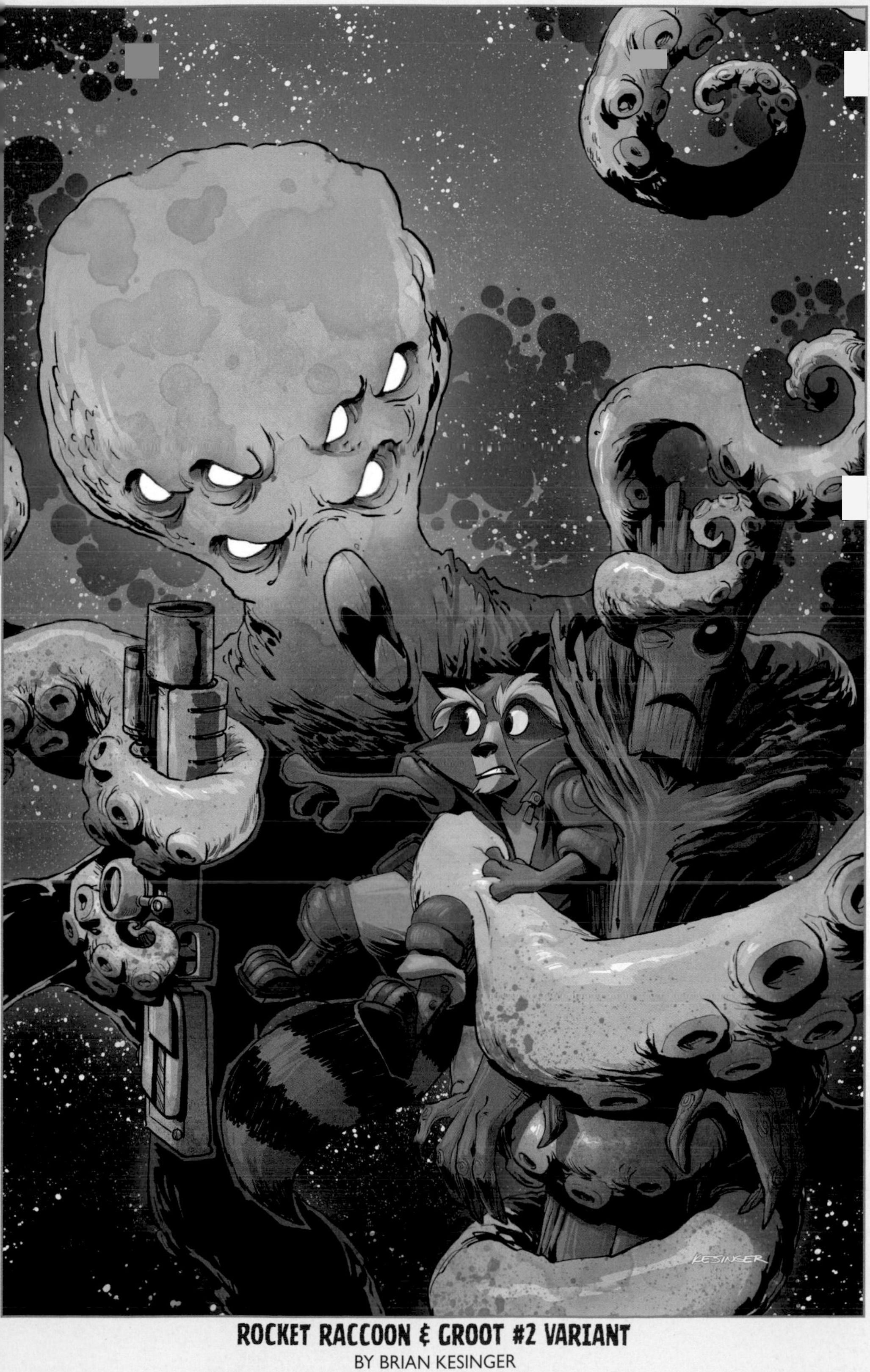
KESINGER

**ROCKET RACCOON & GROOT #2 VARIANT**

BY BRIAN KESINGER

2

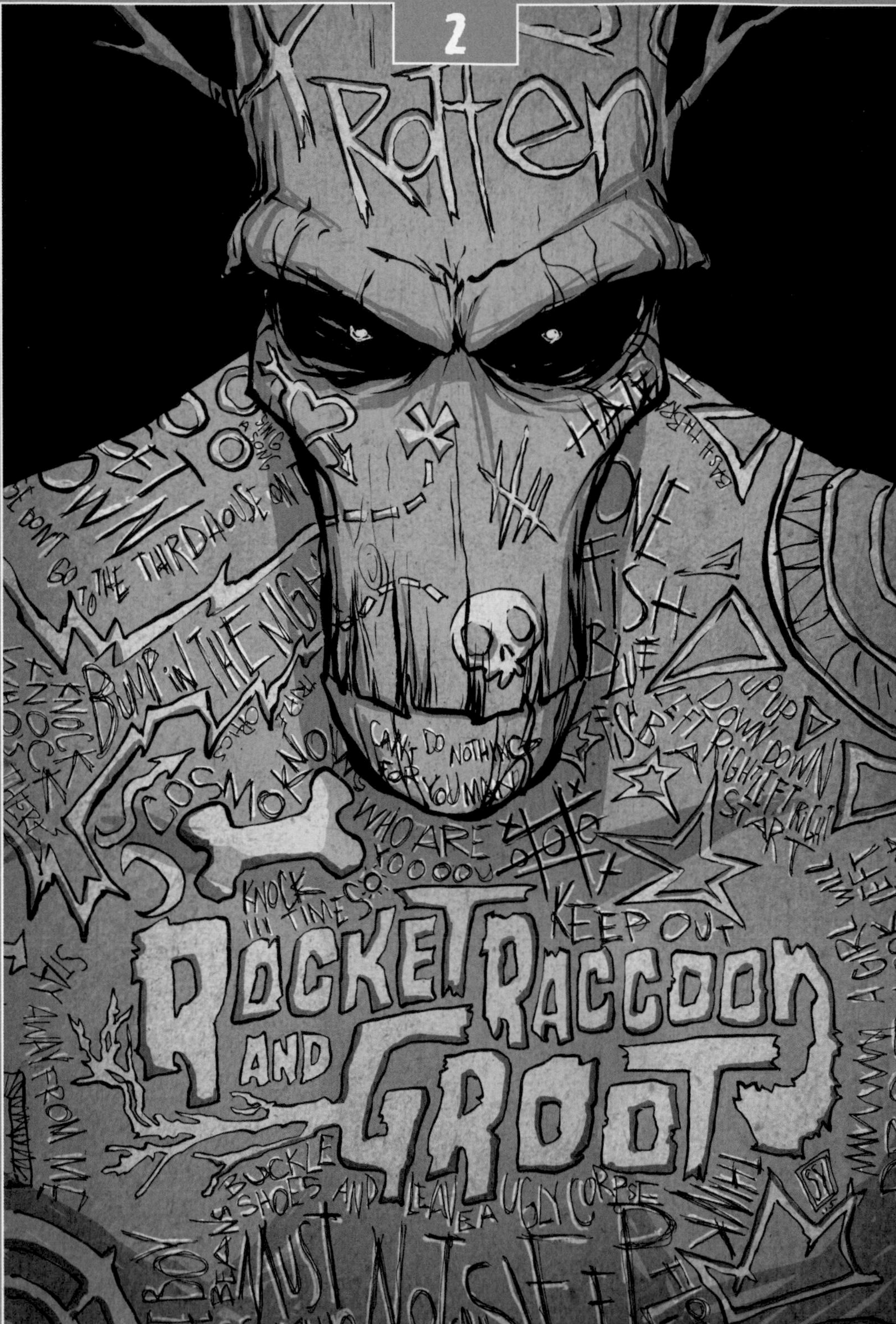
Rotten
TO THE THIRDHOUSE
BUMP IN THE NIGHT
KNOCK KNOCK
COSMO
CAN'T DO NOTHING FOR YOU MAN
WHO ARE YOOOOOU
KEEP OUT
UP UP DOWN DOWN LEFT RIGHT LEFT RIGHT B A START
ROCKET RACCOON AND GROOT
BUCKLE SHOES AND LEAVE A UGLY CORPSE
MUST NOT SLEEP

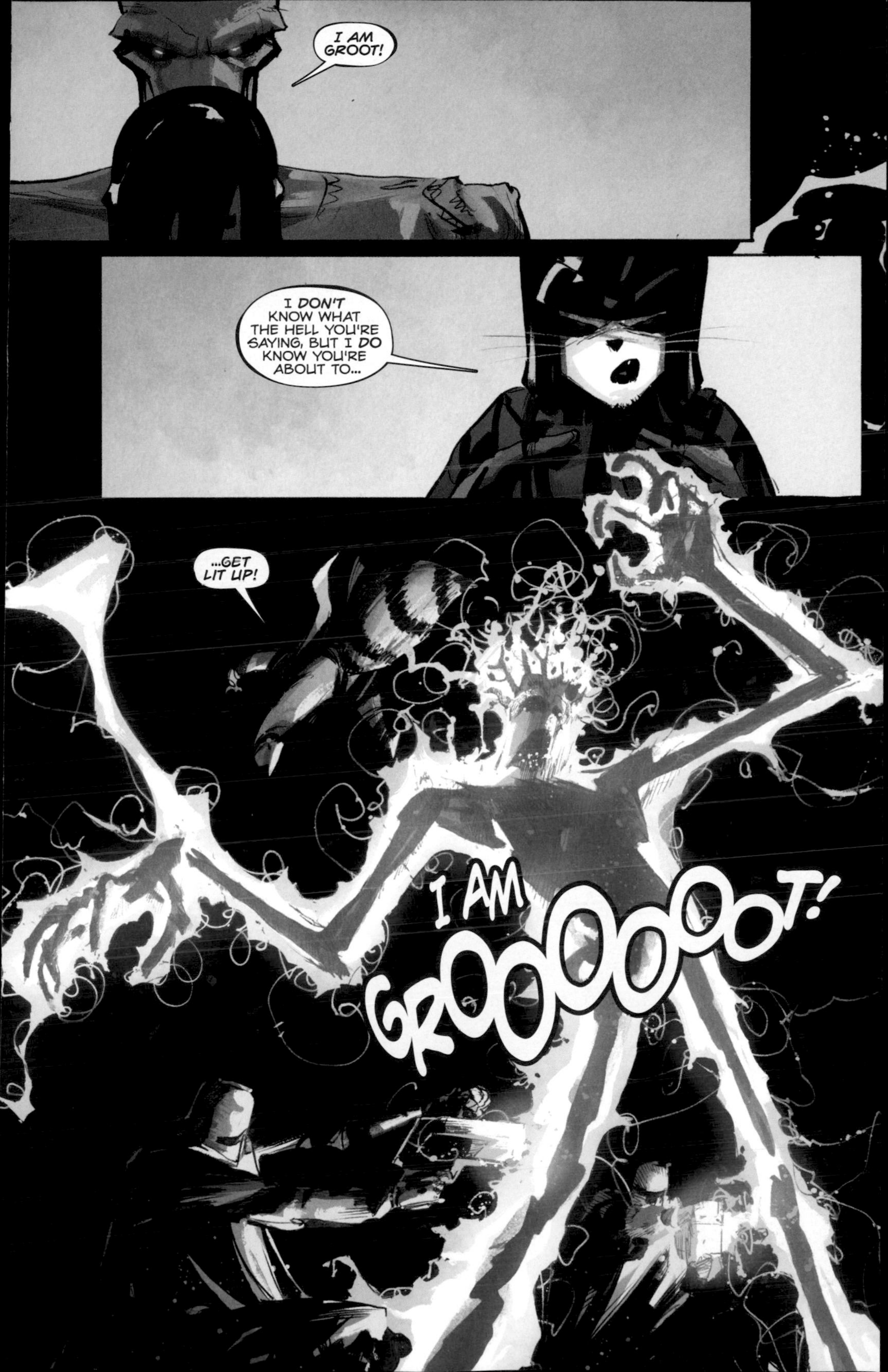
I AM GROOT!
I DON'T KNOW WHAT THE HELL YOU'RE SAYING, BUT I DO KNOW YOU'RE ABOUT TO...
...GET LIT UP!
I AM GROOOOOOOT!

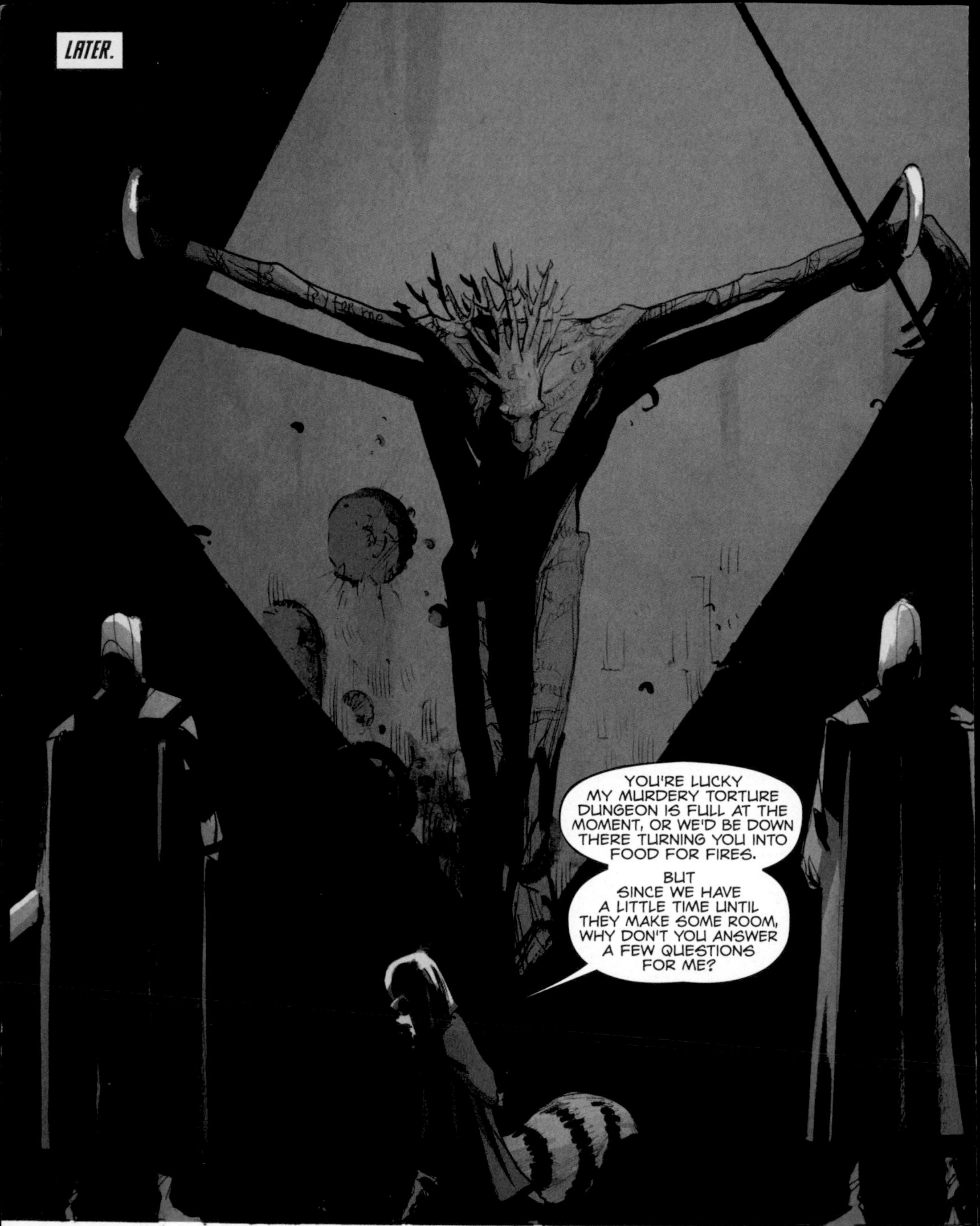
LATER.
YOU'RE LUCKY MY MURDERY TORTURE DUNGEON IS FULL AT THE MOMENT, OR WE'D BE DOWN THERE TURNING YOU INTO FOOD FOR FIRES.
BUT SINCE WE HAVE A LITTLE TIME UNTIL THEY MAKE SOME ROOM, WHY DON'T YOU ANSWER A FEW QUESTIONS FOR ME?

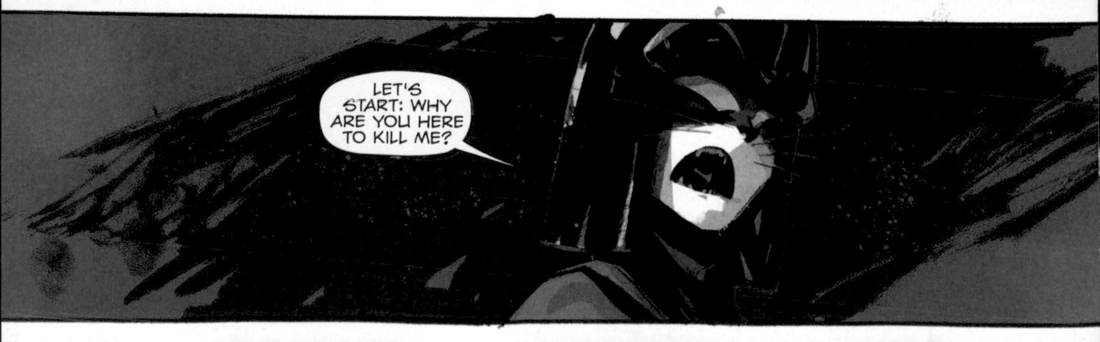
LET'S START: WHY ARE YOU HERE TO KILL ME?

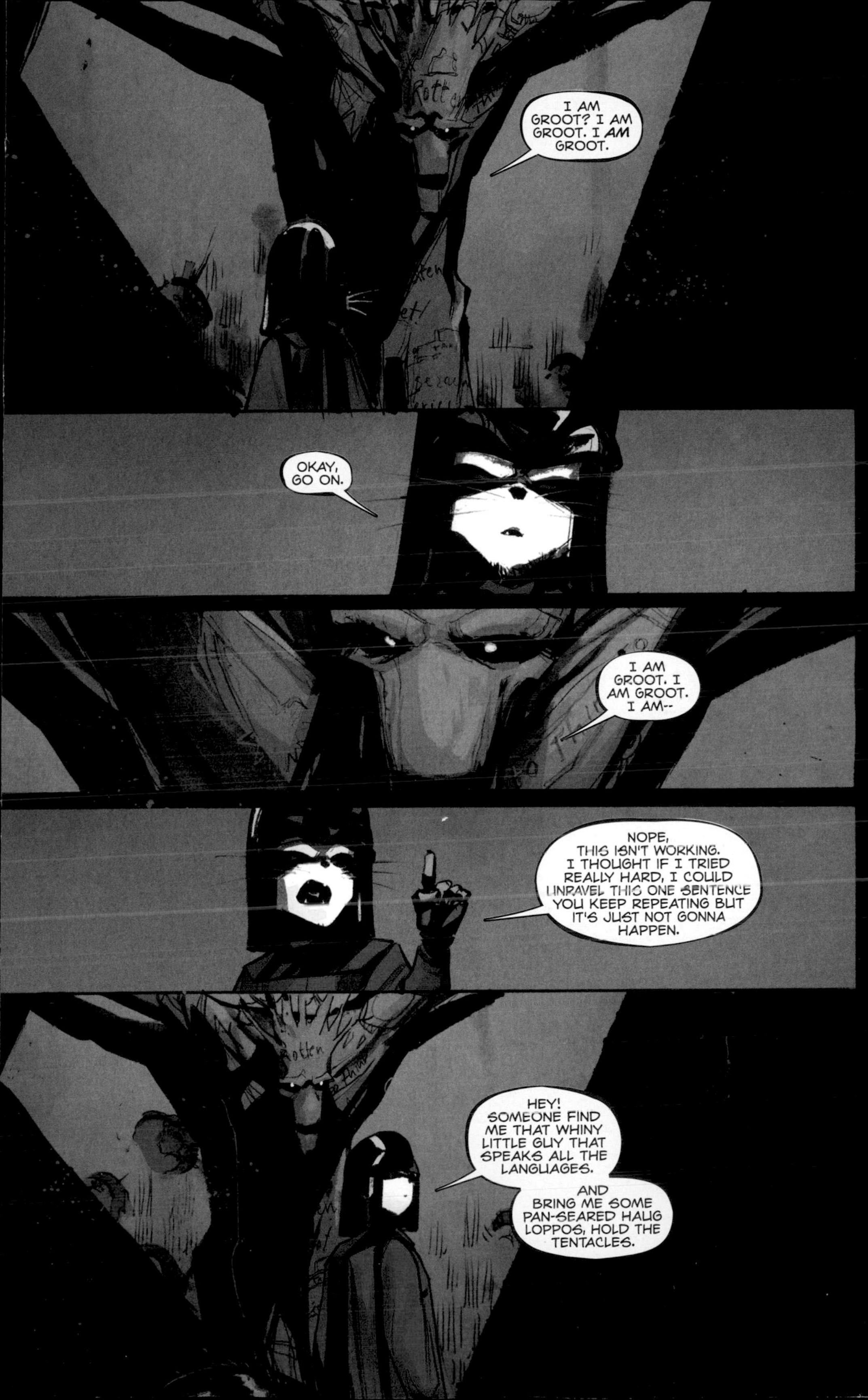
I AM GROOT? I AM GROOT. I *AM* GROOT.
OKAY, GO ON.
I AM GROOT. I AM GROOT. I AM--
NOPE, THIS ISN'T WORKING. I THOUGHT IF I TRIED REALLY HARD, I COULD UNRAVEL THIS ONE SENTENCE YOU KEEP REPEATING BUT IT'S JUST NOT GONNA HAPPEN.
HEY! SOMEONE FIND ME THAT WHINY LITTLE GUY THAT SPEAKS ALL THE LANGUAGES.
AND BRING ME SOME PAN-SEARED HAUG LOPPOS, HOLD THE TENTACLES.

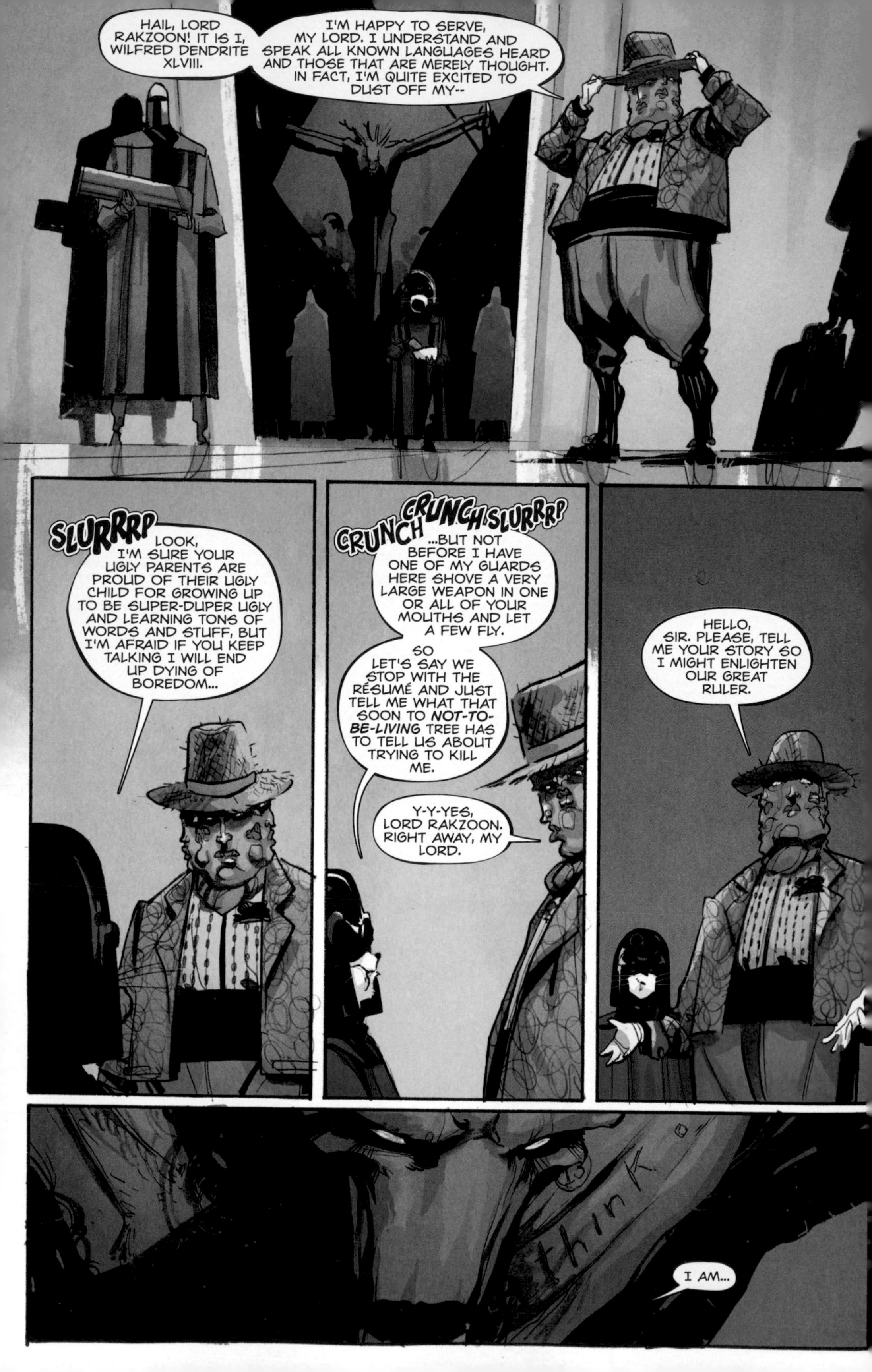
HAIL, LORD RAKZOON! IT IS I, WILFRED DENDRITE XLVIII.
I'M HAPPY TO SERVE, MY LORD. I UNDERSTAND AND SPEAK ALL KNOWN LANGUAGES HEARD AND THOSE THAT ARE MERELY THOUGHT. IN FACT, I'M QUITE EXCITED TO DUST OFF MY--
SLURRRP
LOOK, I'M SURE YOUR UGLY PARENTS ARE PROUD OF THEIR UGLY CHILD FOR GROWING UP TO BE SUPER-DUPER UGLY AND LEARNING TONS OF WORDS AND STUFF, BUT I'M AFRAID IF YOU KEEP TALKING I WILL END UP DYING OF BOREDOM...
CRUNCH CRUNCH SLURRRP
...BUT NOT BEFORE I HAVE ONE OF MY GUARDS HERE SHOVE A VERY LARGE WEAPON IN ONE OR ALL OF YOUR MOUTHS AND LET A FEW FLY.
SO LET'S SAY WE STOP WITH THE RÉSUMÉ AND JUST TELL ME WHAT THAT SOON TO *NOT-TO-BE-LIVING* TREE HAS TO TELL US ABOUT TRYING TO KILL ME.
Y-Y-YES, LORD RAKZOON. RIGHT AWAY, MY LORD.
HELLO, SIR. PLEASE, TELL ME YOUR STORY SO I MIGHT ENLIGHTEN OUR GREAT RULER.
think
I AM...

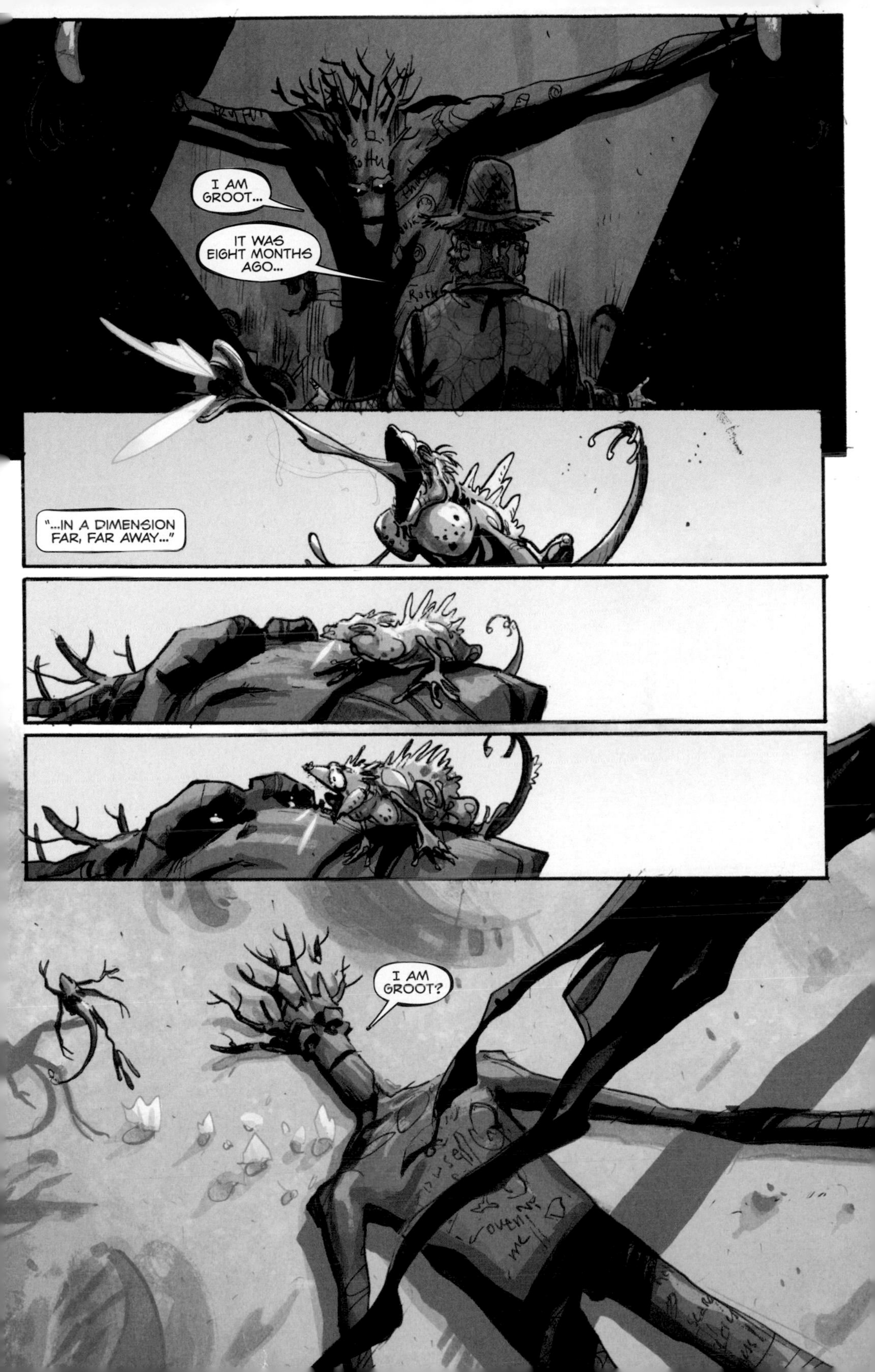
I AM GROOT...
IT WAS EIGHT MONTHS AGO...
"...IN A DIMENSION FAR, FAR AWAY..."
I AM GROOT?

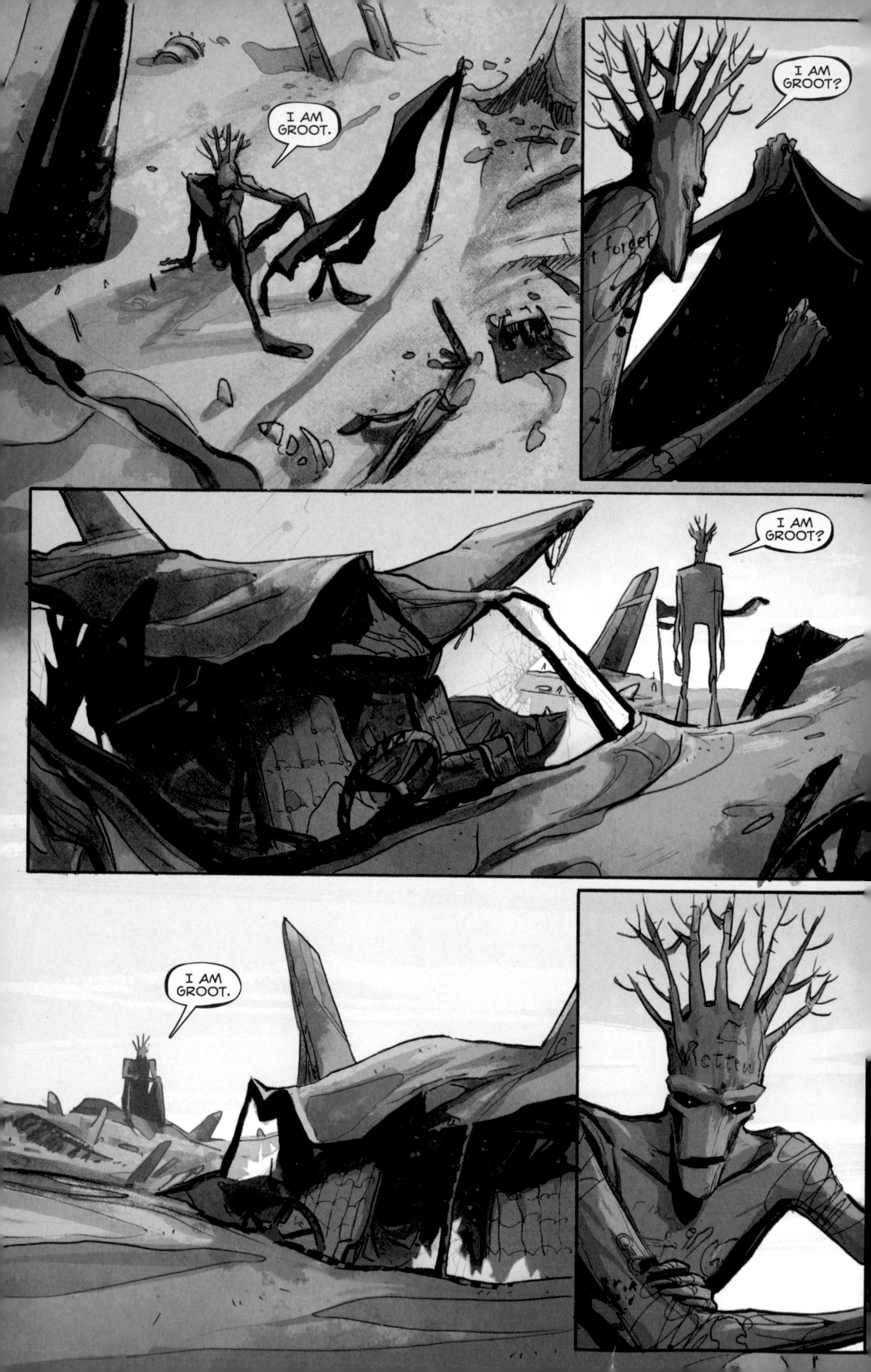
I AM GROOT.
I AM GROOT?
I AM GROOT?
I AM GROOT.

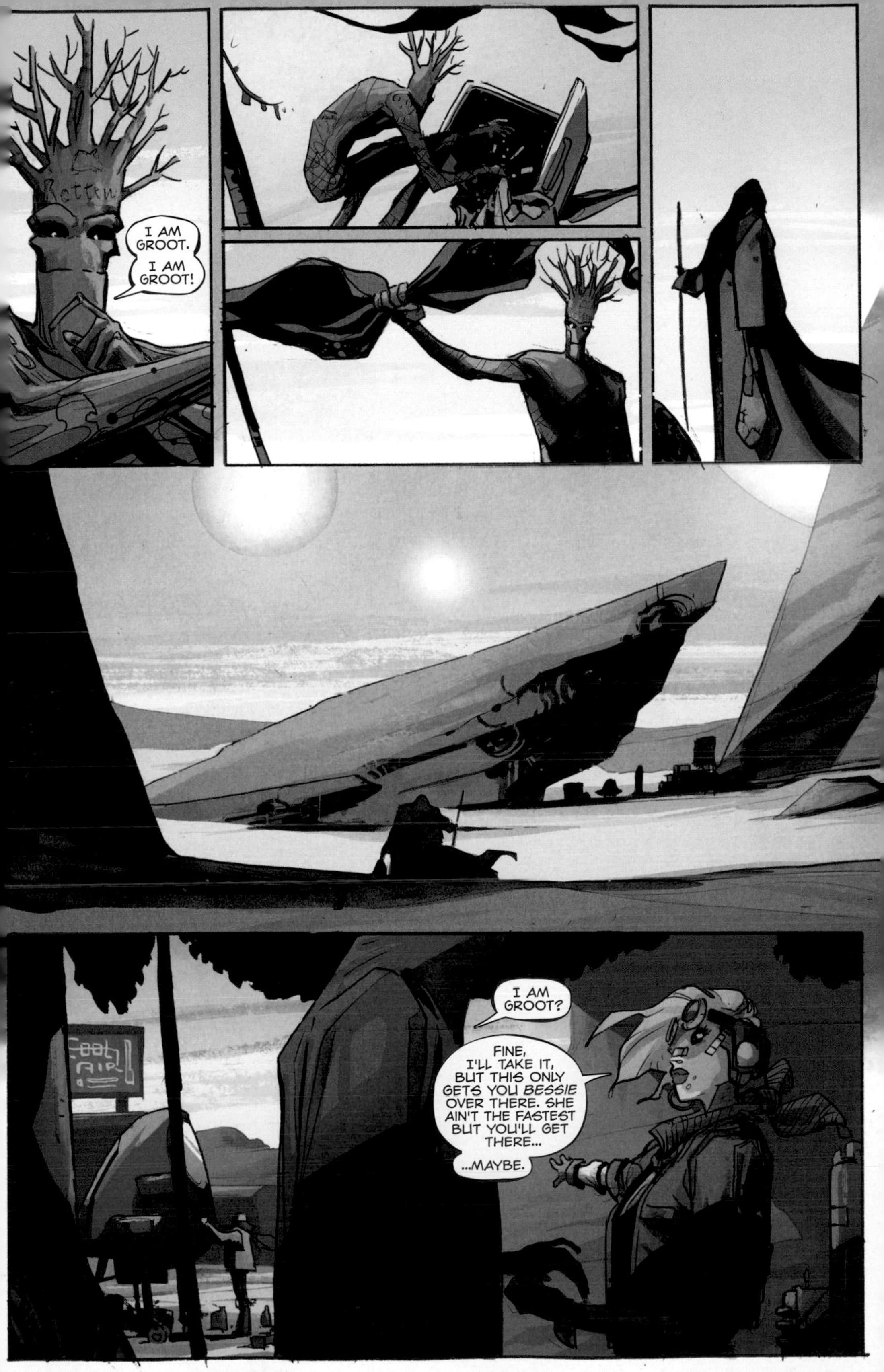
I AM GROOT.
I AM GROOT!
I AM GROOT?
FINE, I'LL TAKE IT, BUT THIS ONLY GETS YOU *BESSIE* OVER THERE. SHE AIN'T THE FASTEST BUT YOU'LL GET THERE...
...MAYBE.

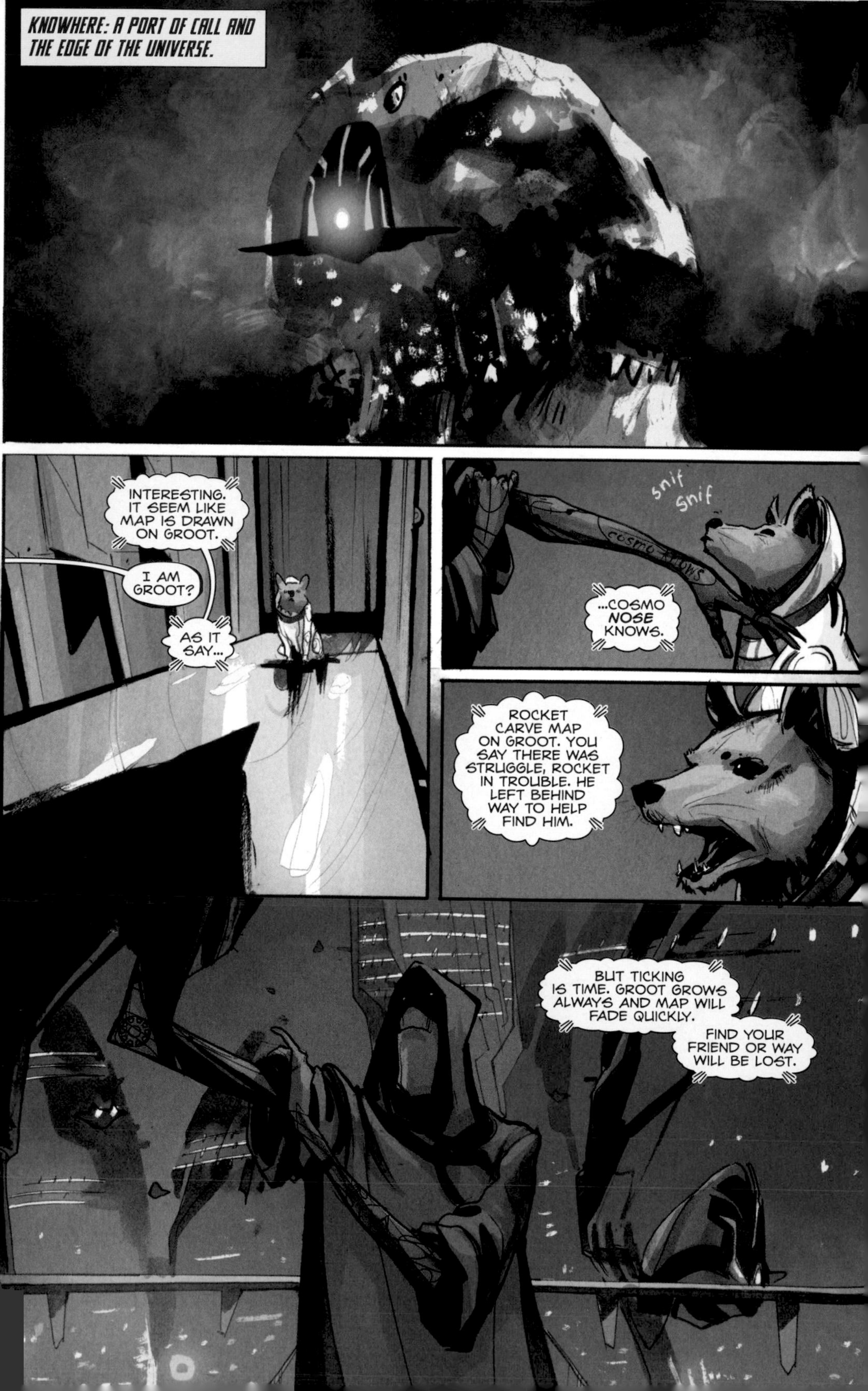
KNOWHERE: A PORT OF CALL AND THE EDGE OF THE UNIVERSE.
INTERESTING. IT SEEM LIKE MAP IS DRAWN ON GROOT.
I AM GROOT?
AS IT SAY...
snif snif
cosmo knows
...COSMO NOSE KNOWS.
ROCKET CARVE MAP ON GROOT. YOU SAY THERE WAS STRUGGLE, ROCKET IN TROUBLE. HE LEFT BEHIND WAY TO HELP FIND HIM.
BUT TICKING IS TIME. GROOT GROWS ALWAYS AND MAP WILL FADE QUICKLY.
FIND YOUR FRIEND OR WAY WILL BE LOST.

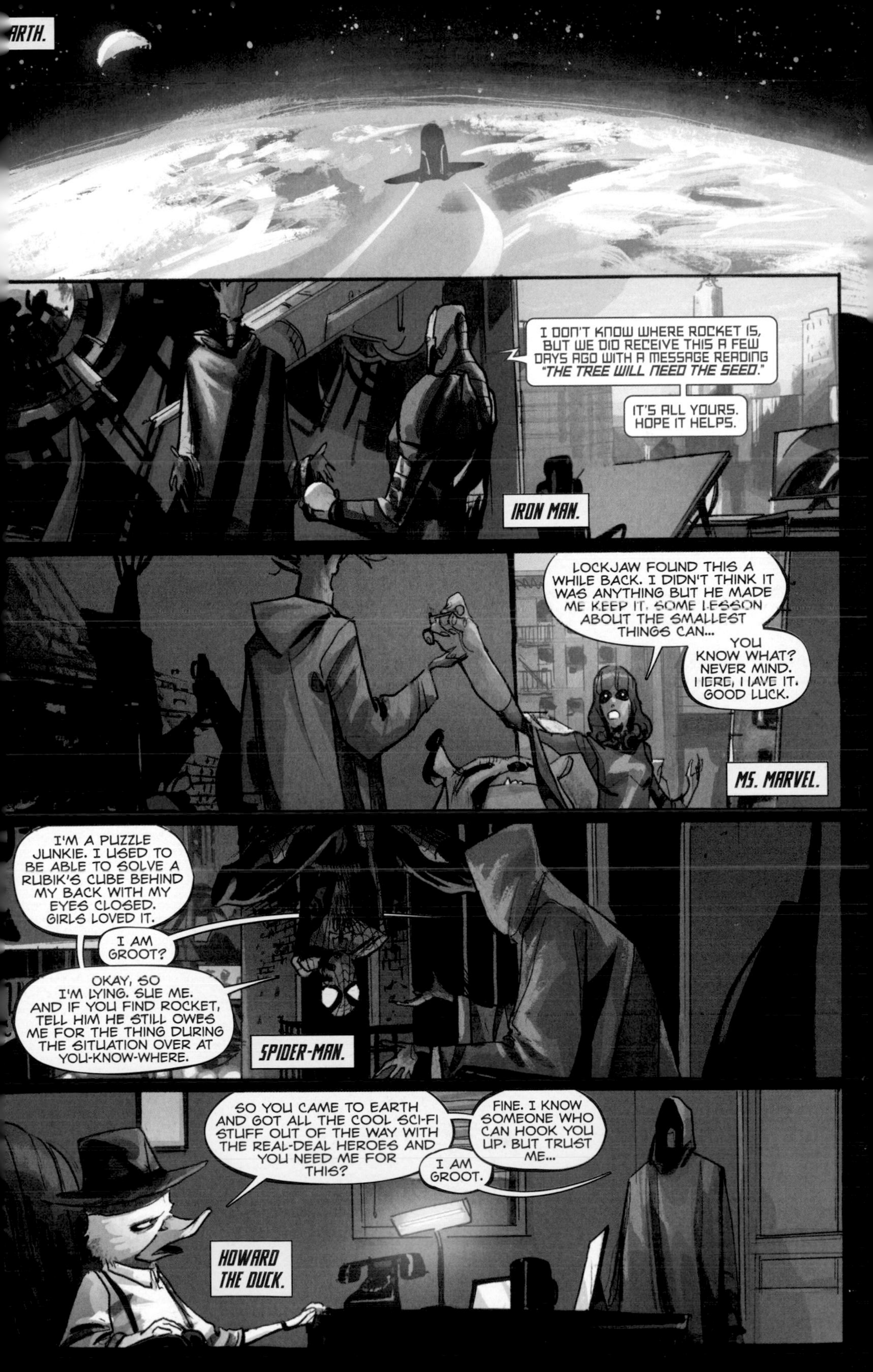

ARTH.
I DON'T KNOW WHERE ROCKET IS, BUT WE DID RECEIVE THIS A FEW DAYS AGO WITH A MESSAGE READING "THE TREE WILL NEED THE SEED."
IT'S ALL YOURS. HOPE IT HELPS.
IRON MAN.
LOCKJAW FOUND THIS A WHILE BACK. I DIDN'T THINK IT WAS ANYTHING BUT HE MADE ME KEEP IT. SOME LESSON ABOUT THE SMALLEST THINGS CAN...
YOU KNOW WHAT? NEVER MIND. HERE, HAVE IT. GOOD LUCK.
MS. MARVEL.
I'M A PUZZLE JUNKIE. I USED TO BE ABLE TO SOLVE A RUBIK'S CUBE BEHIND MY BACK WITH MY EYES CLOSED. GIRLS LOVED IT.
I AM GROOT?
OKAY, SO I'M LYING. SUE ME. AND IF YOU FIND ROCKET, TELL HIM HE STILL OWES ME FOR THE THING DURING THE SITUATION OVER AT YOU-KNOW-WHERE.
SPIDER-MAN.
SO YOU CAME TO EARTH AND GOT ALL THE COOL SCI-FI STUFF OUT OF THE WAY WITH THE REAL-DEAL HEROES AND YOU NEED ME FOR THIS?
I AM GROOT.
FINE. I KNOW SOMEONE WHO CAN HOOK YOU UP. BUT TRUST ME...
HOWARD THE DUCK.

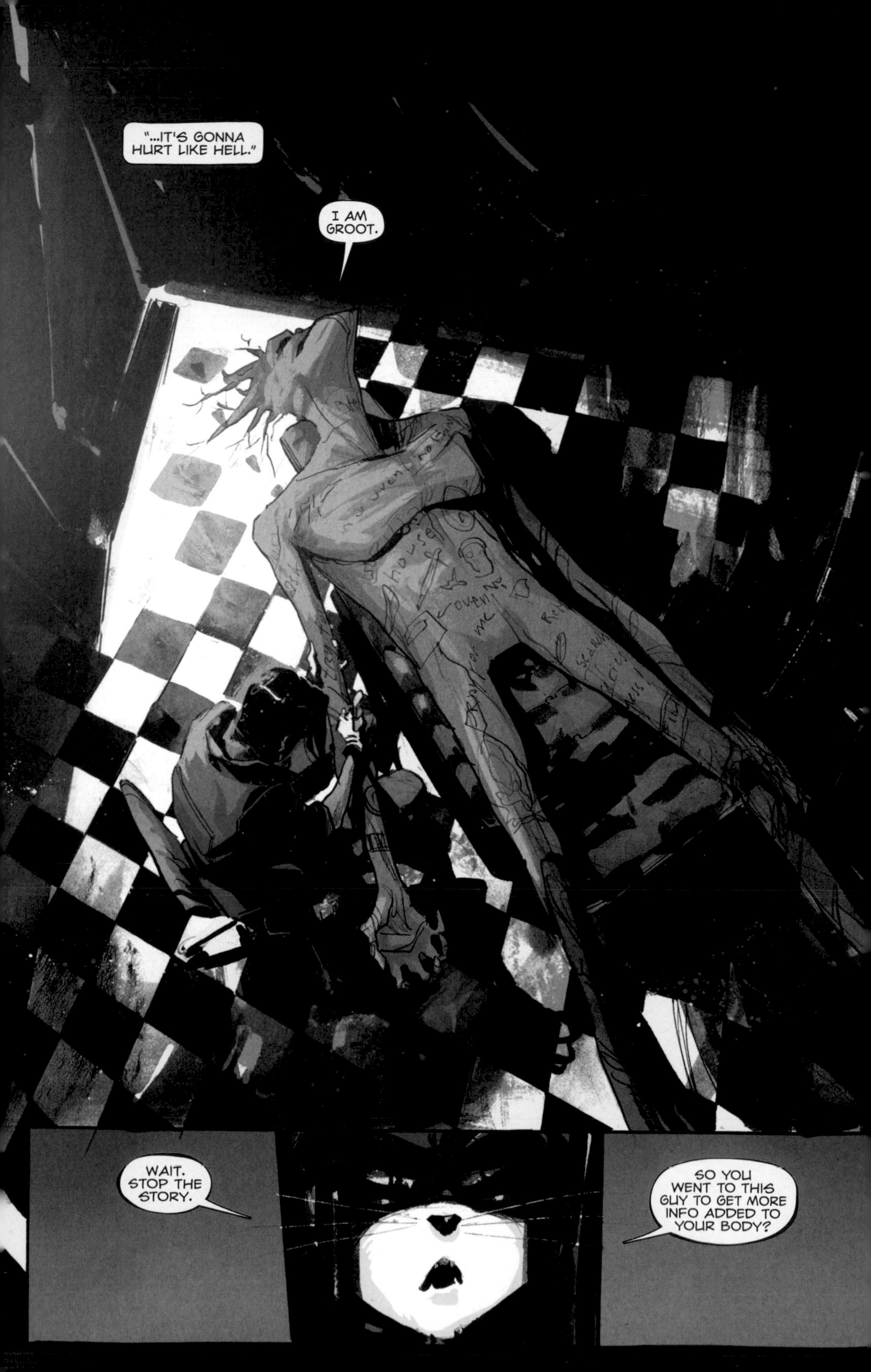
"...IT'S GONNA HURT LIKE HELL."
I AM GROOT.
WAIT. STOP THE STORY.
SO YOU WENT TO THIS GUY TO GET MORE INFO ADDED TO YOUR BODY?

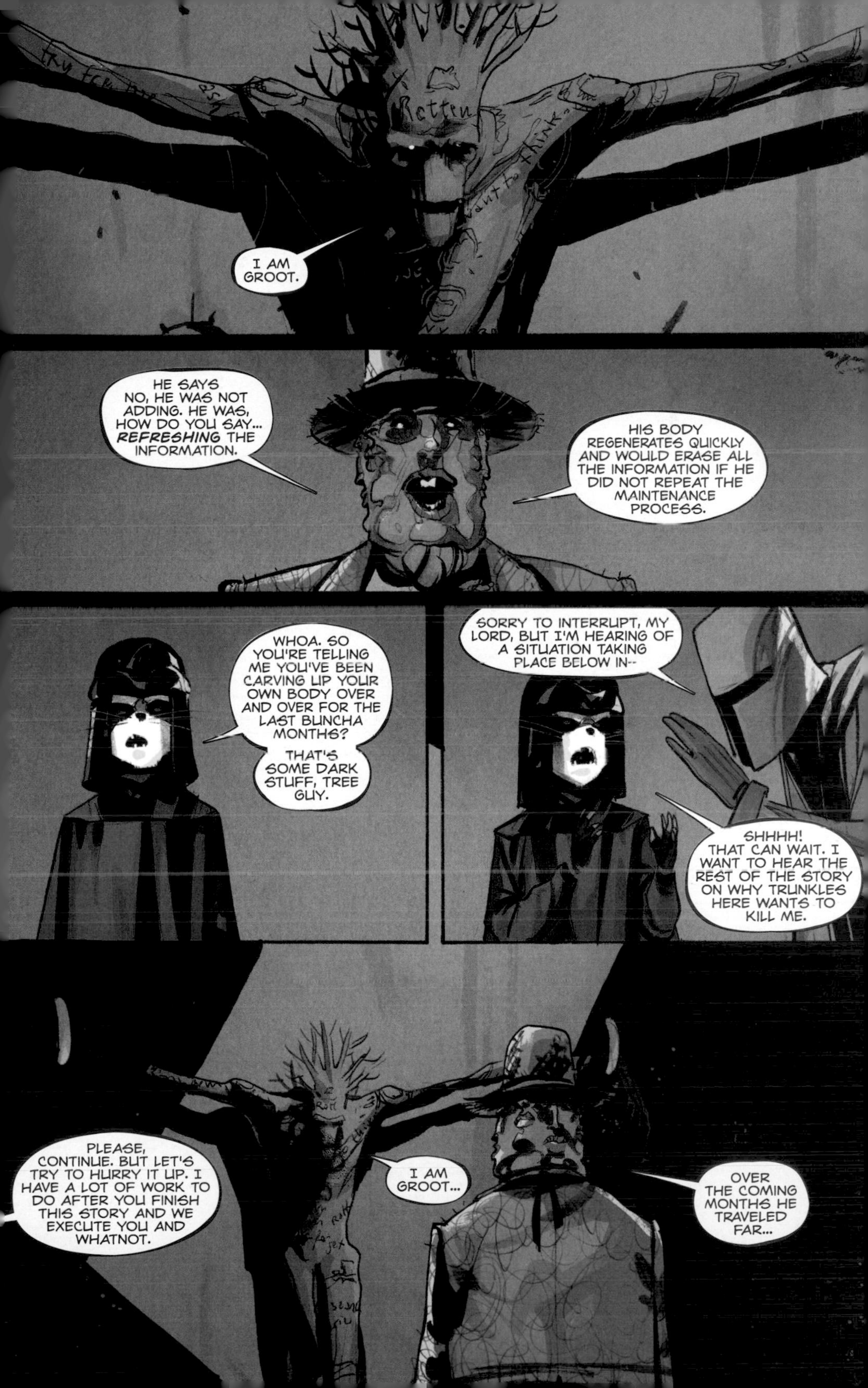

I AM GROOT.
HE SAYS NO, HE WAS NOT ADDING. HE WAS, HOW DO YOU SAY... ***REFRESHING*** THE INFORMATION.
HIS BODY REGENERATES QUICKLY AND WOULD ERASE ALL THE INFORMATION IF HE DID NOT REPEAT THE MAINTENANCE PROCESS.
WHOA. SO YOU'RE TELLING ME YOU'VE BEEN CARVING UP YOUR OWN BODY OVER AND OVER FOR THE LAST BUNCHA MONTHS?
THAT'S SOME DARK STUFF, TREE GUY.
SORRY TO INTERRUPT, MY LORD, BUT I'M HEARING OF A SITUATION TAKING PLACE BELOW IN--
SHHHH! THAT CAN WAIT. I WANT TO HEAR THE REST OF THE STORY ON WHY TRUNKLES HERE WANTS TO KILL ME.
PLEASE, CONTINUE. BUT LET'S TRY TO HURRY IT UP. I HAVE A LOT OF WORK TO DO AFTER YOU FINISH THIS STORY AND WE EXECUTE YOU AND WHATNOT.
I AM GROOT...
OVER THE COMING MONTHS HE TRAVELED FAR...

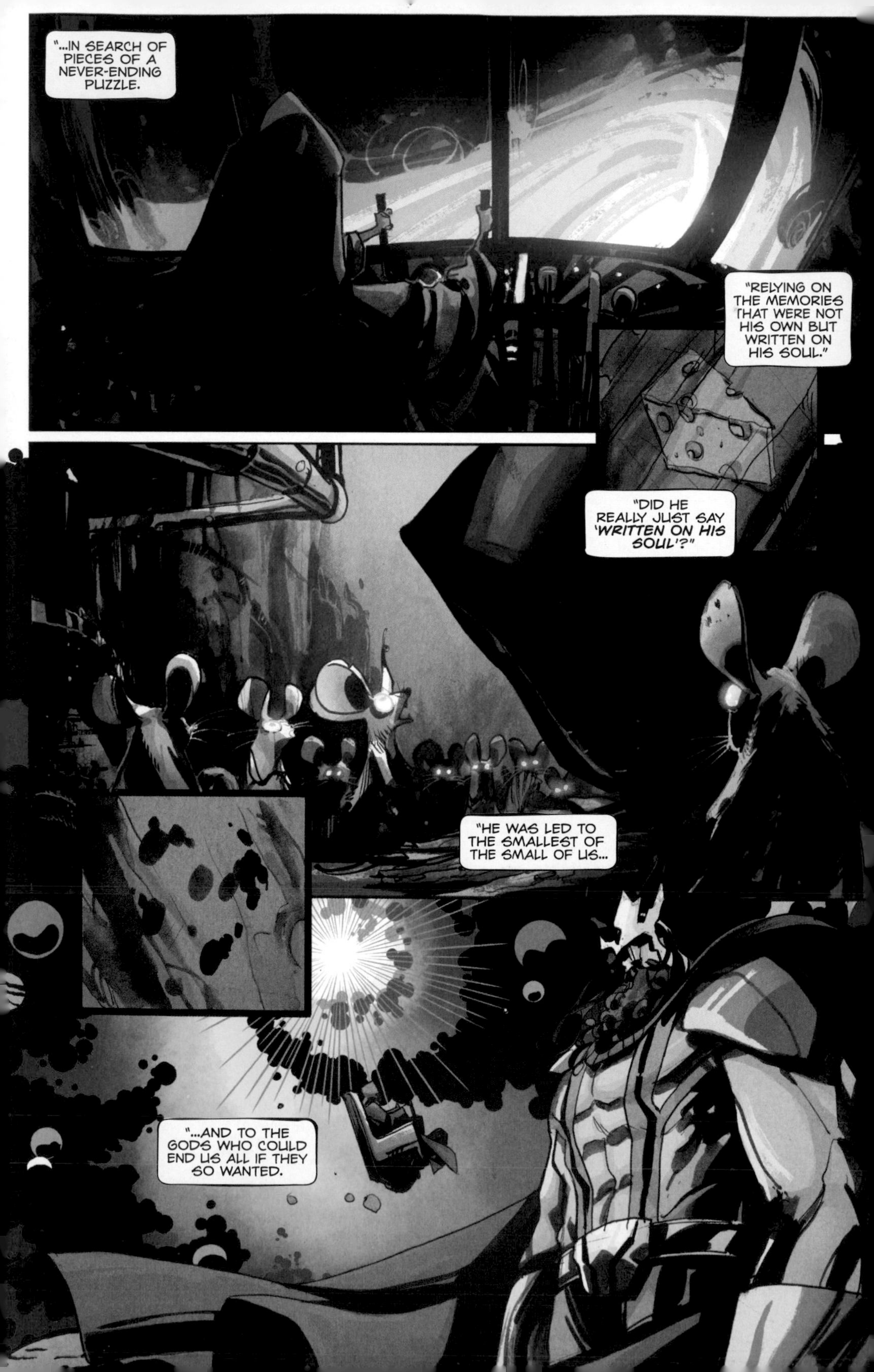
"...IN SEARCH OF PIECES OF A NEVER-ENDING PUZZLE.
"RELYING ON THE MEMORIES THAT WERE NOT HIS OWN BUT WRITTEN ON HIS SOUL."
"DID HE REALLY JUST SAY '*WRITTEN ON HIS SOUL*'?"
"HE WAS LED TO THE SMALLEST OF THE SMALL OF US...
"...AND TO THE GODS WHO COULD END US ALL IF THEY SO WANTED.

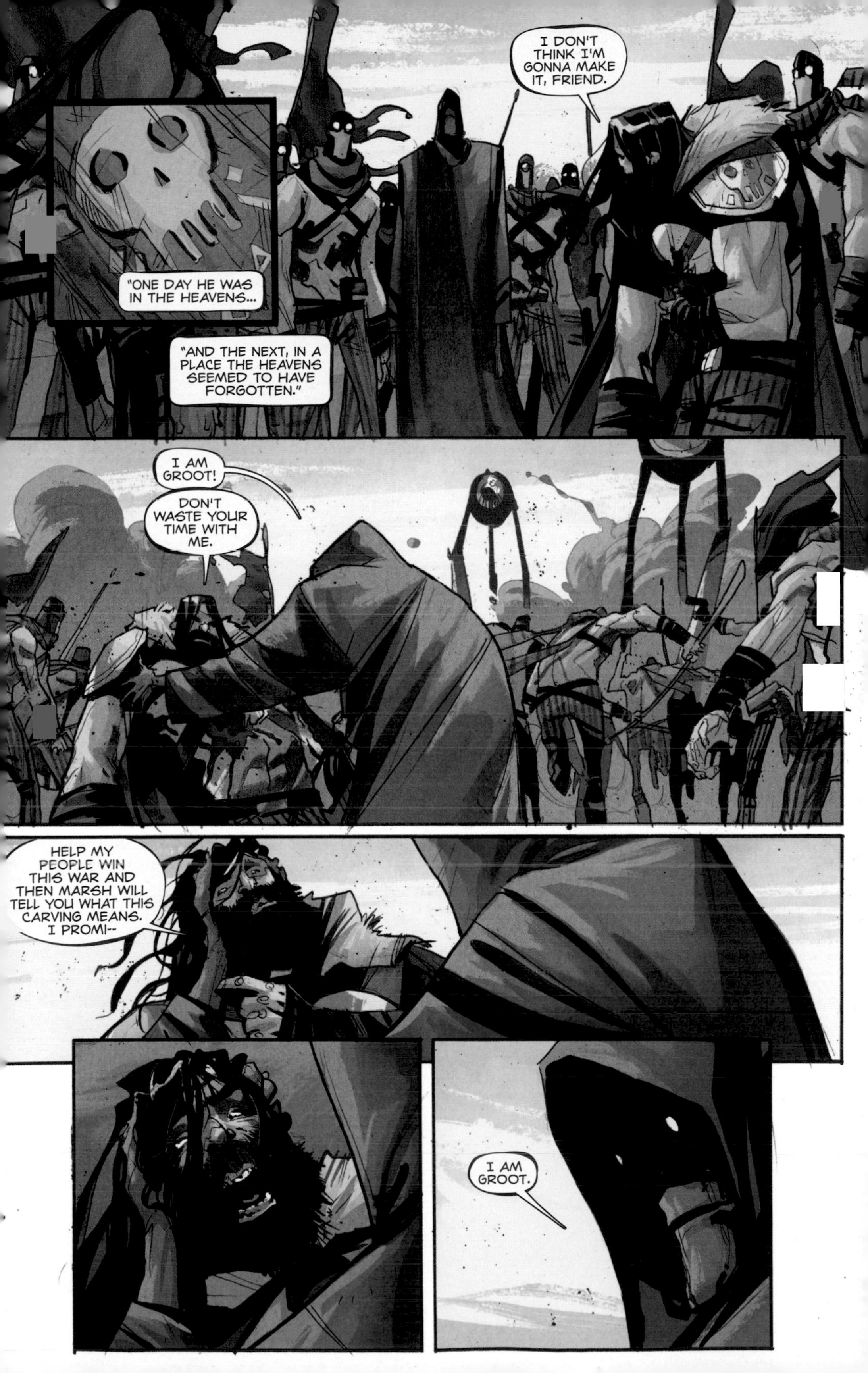
"ONE DAY HE WAS IN THE HEAVENS...
I DON'T THINK I'M GONNA MAKE IT, FRIEND.
"AND THE NEXT, IN A PLACE THE HEAVENS SEEMED TO HAVE FORGOTTEN."
I AM GROOT!
DON'T WASTE YOUR TIME WITH ME.
HELP MY PEOPLE WIN THIS WAR AND THEN MARSH WILL TELL YOU WHAT THIS CARVING MEANS. I PROMI--
I AM GROOT.

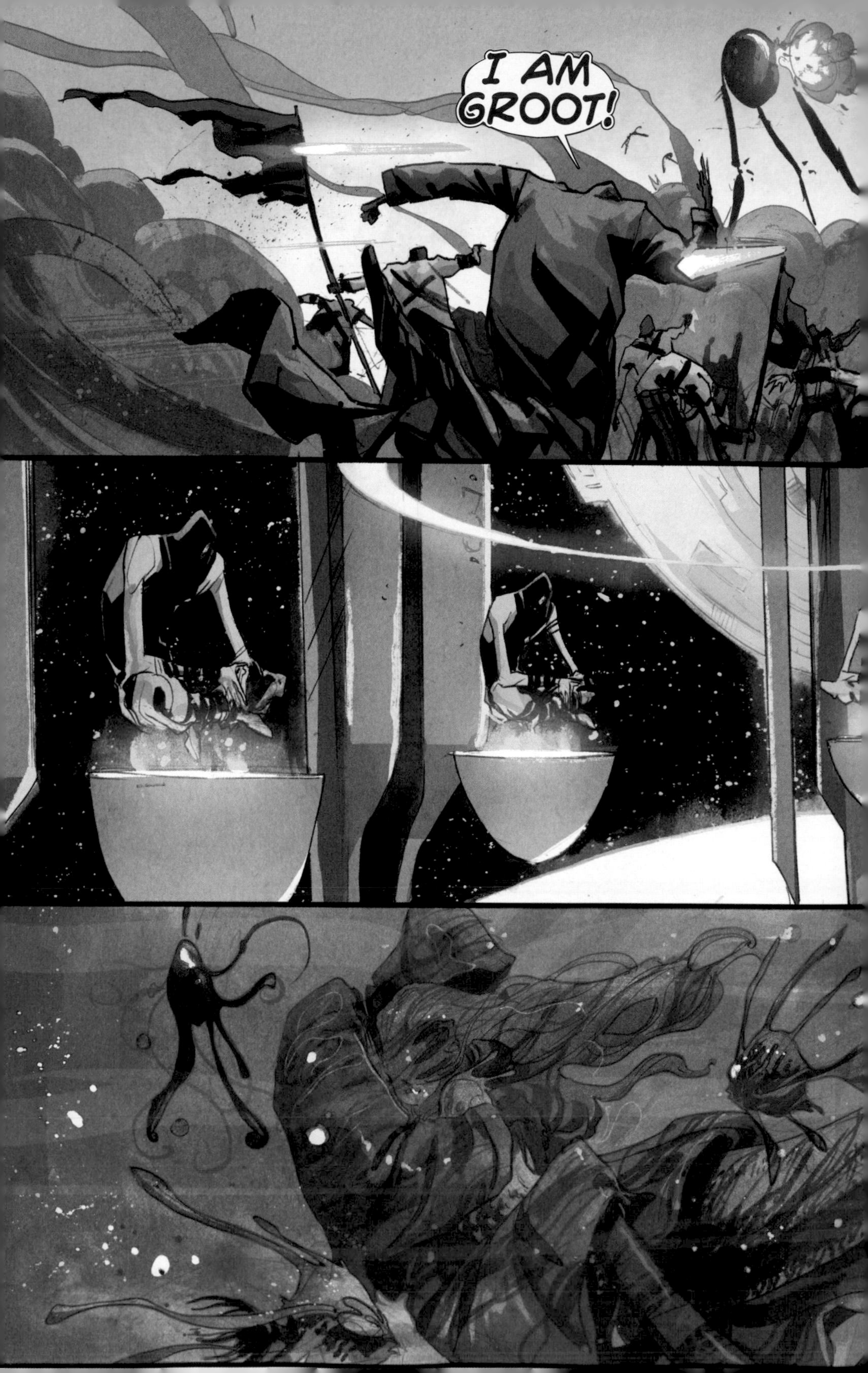
I AM GROOT!

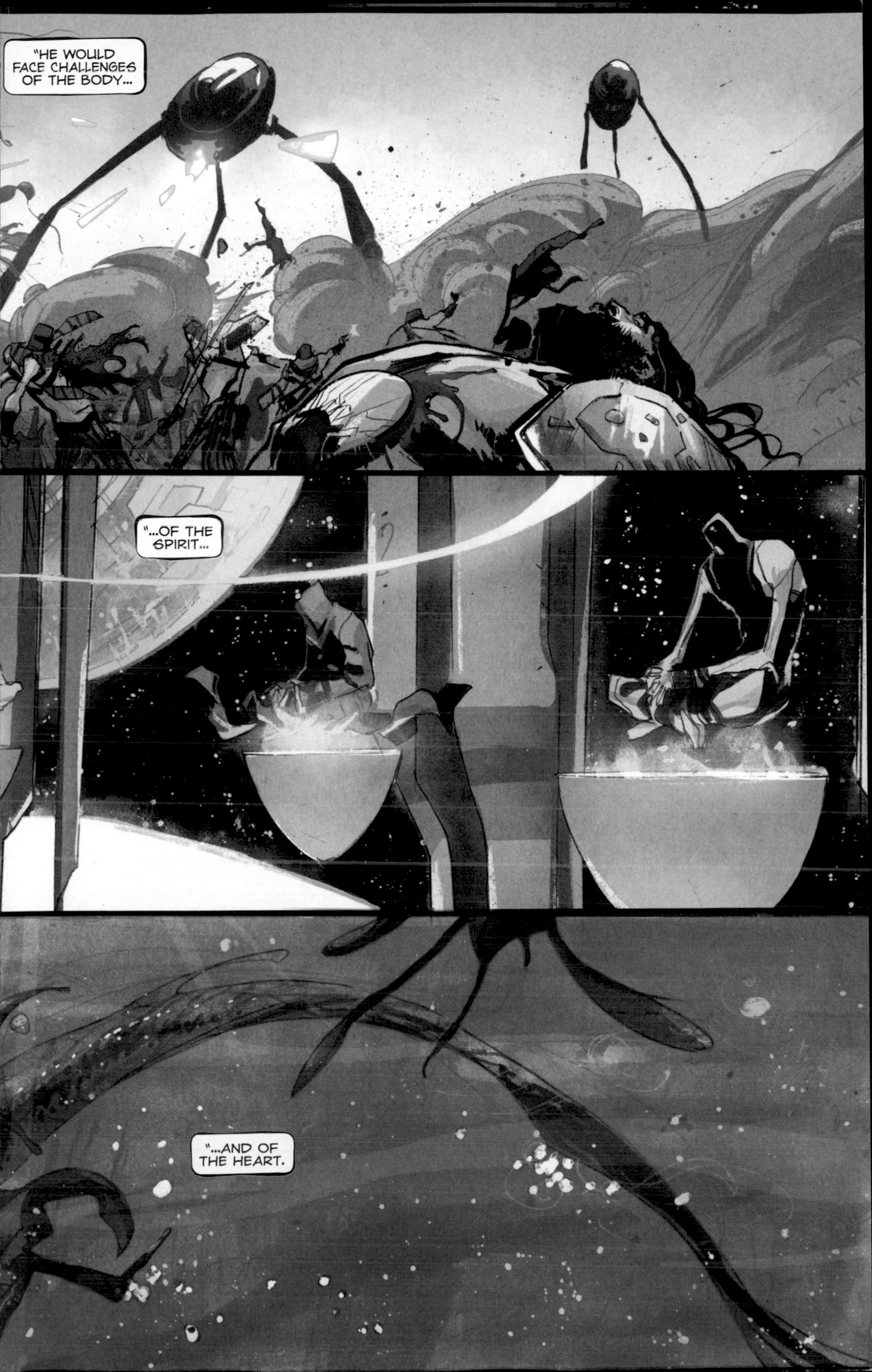
"HE WOULD FACE CHALLENGES OF THE BODY...
"...OF THE SPIRIT...
"...AND OF THE HEART.

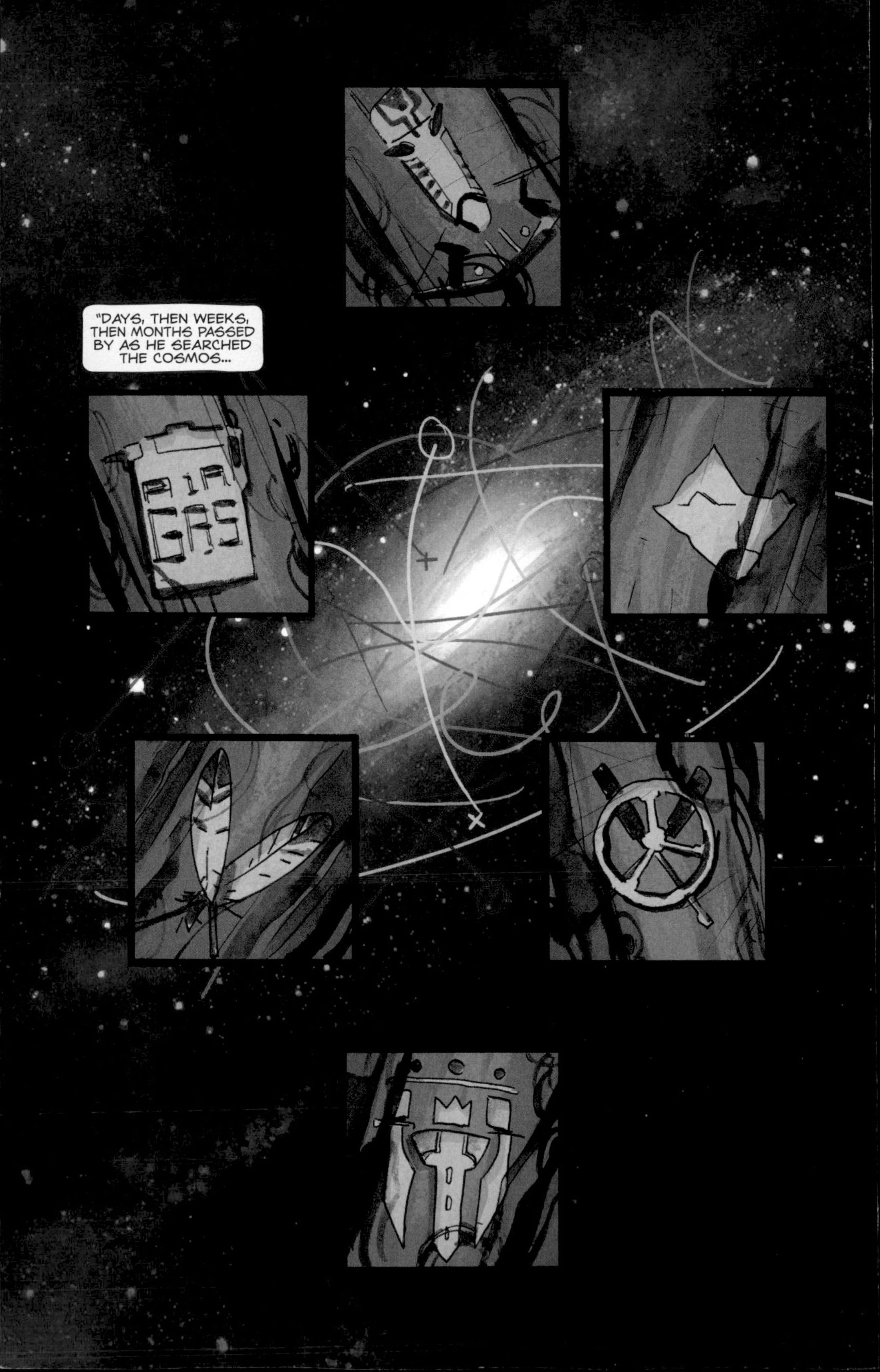
"DAYS, THEN WEEKS, THEN MONTHS PASSED BY AS HE SEARCHED THE COSMOS...

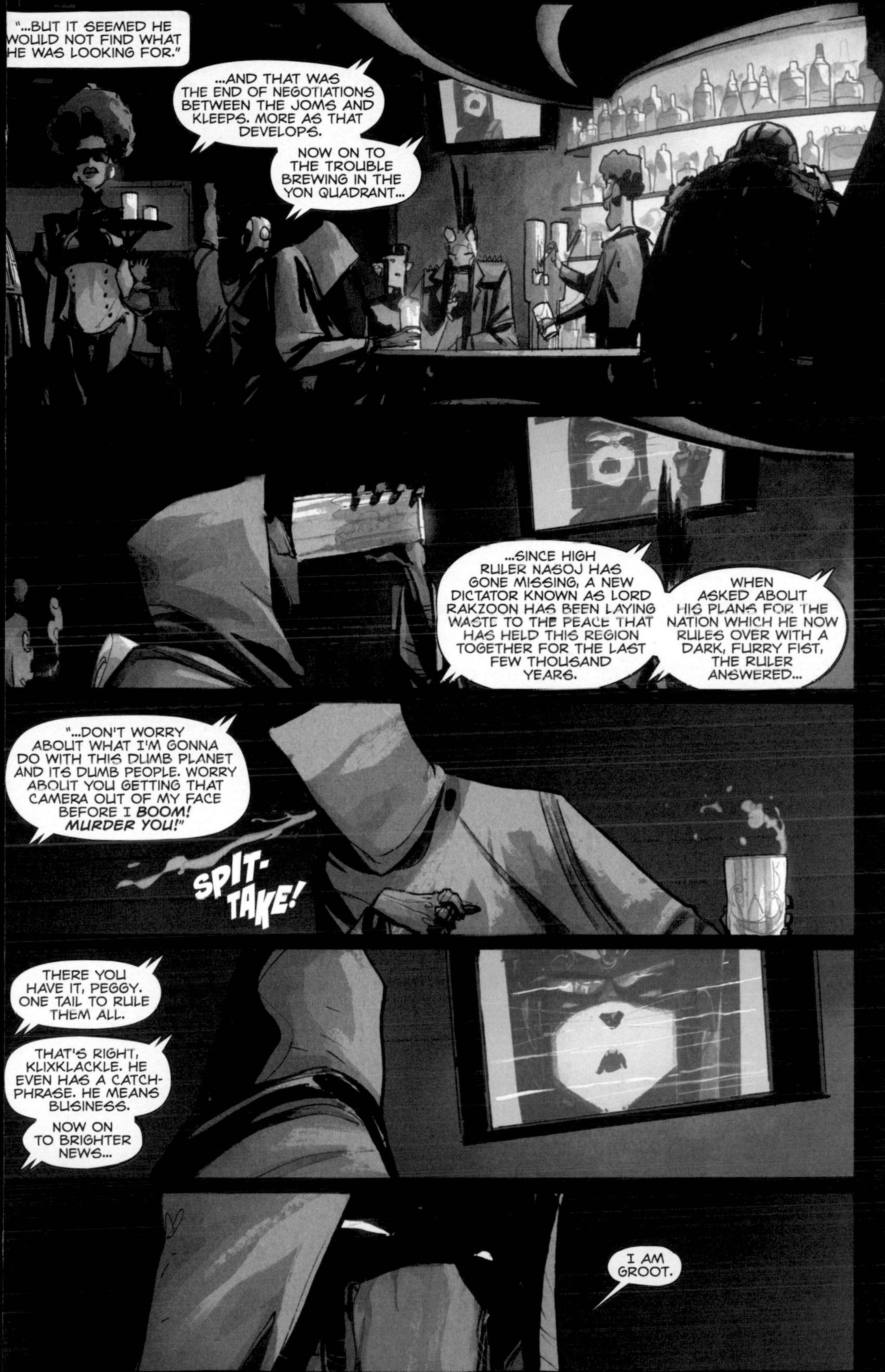
"...BUT IT SEEMED HE WOULD NOT FIND WHAT HE WAS LOOKING FOR."
...AND THAT WAS THE END OF NEGOTIATIONS BETWEEN THE JOMS AND KLEEPS. MORE AS THAT DEVELOPS.
NOW ON TO THE TROUBLE BREWING IN THE YON QUADRANT...
...SINCE HIGH RULER NASOJ HAS GONE MISSING, A NEW DICTATOR KNOWN AS LORD RAKZOON HAS BEEN LAYING WASTE TO THE PEACE THAT HAS HELD THIS REGION TOGETHER FOR THE LAST FEW THOUSAND YEARS.
WHEN ASKED ABOUT HIS PLANS FOR THE NATION WHICH HE NOW RULES OVER WITH A DARK, FURRY FIST, THE RULER ANSWERED...
"...DON'T WORRY ABOUT WHAT I'M GONNA DO WITH THIS DUMB PLANET AND ITS DUMB PEOPLE. WORRY ABOUT YOU GETTING THAT CAMERA OUT OF MY FACE BEFORE I *BOOM! MURDER YOU!*"
SPIT-TAKE!
THERE YOU HAVE IT, PEGGY. ONE TAIL TO RULE THEM ALL.
THAT'S RIGHT, KLIXKLACKLE. HE EVEN HAS A CATCH-PHRASE. HE MEANS BUSINESS.
NOW ON TO BRIGHTER NEWS...
I AM GROOT.

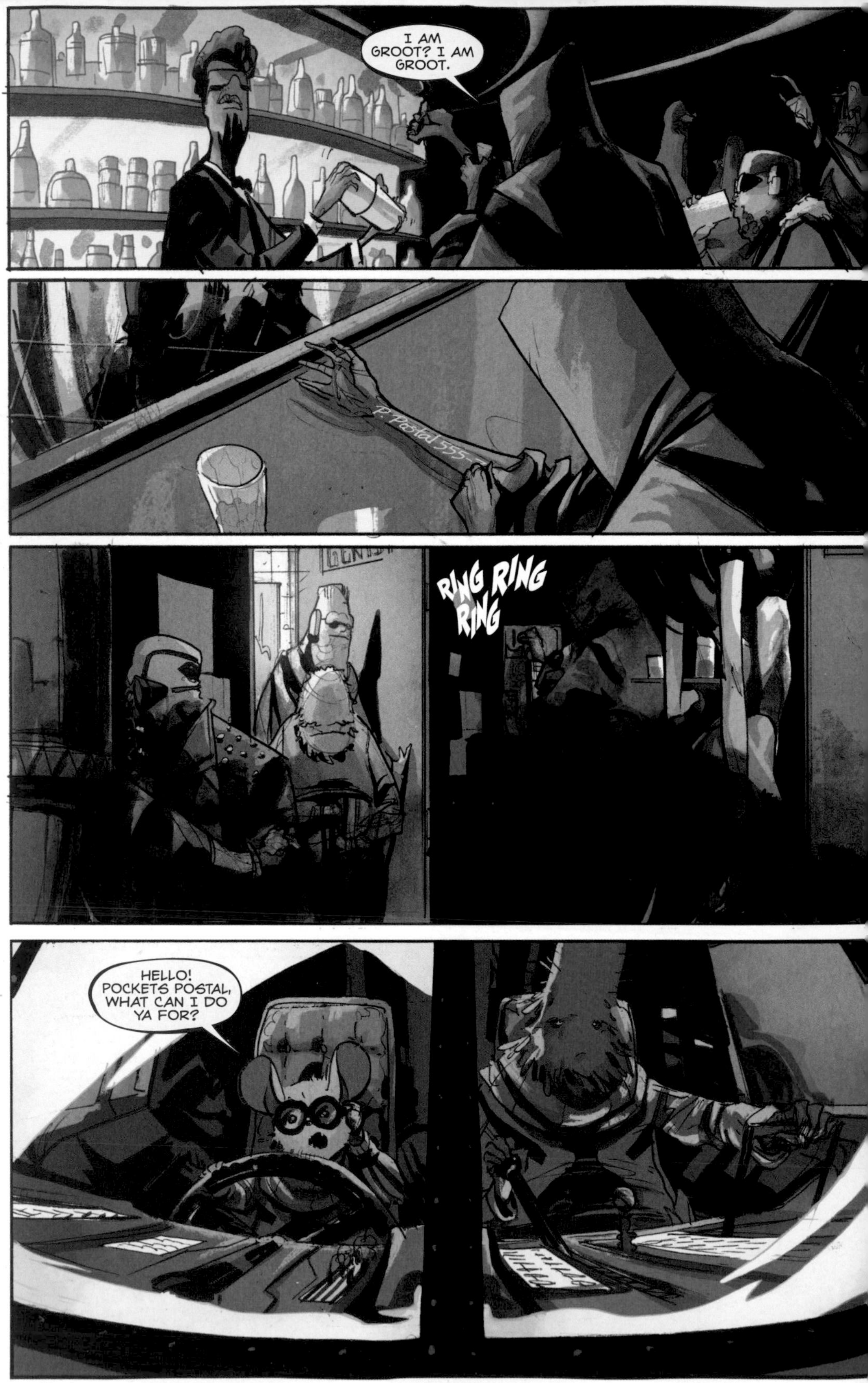
I AM GROOT? I AM GROOT.
P. Postal 555-
RING RING RING
HELLO! POCKETS POSTAL, WHAT CAN I DO YA FOR?

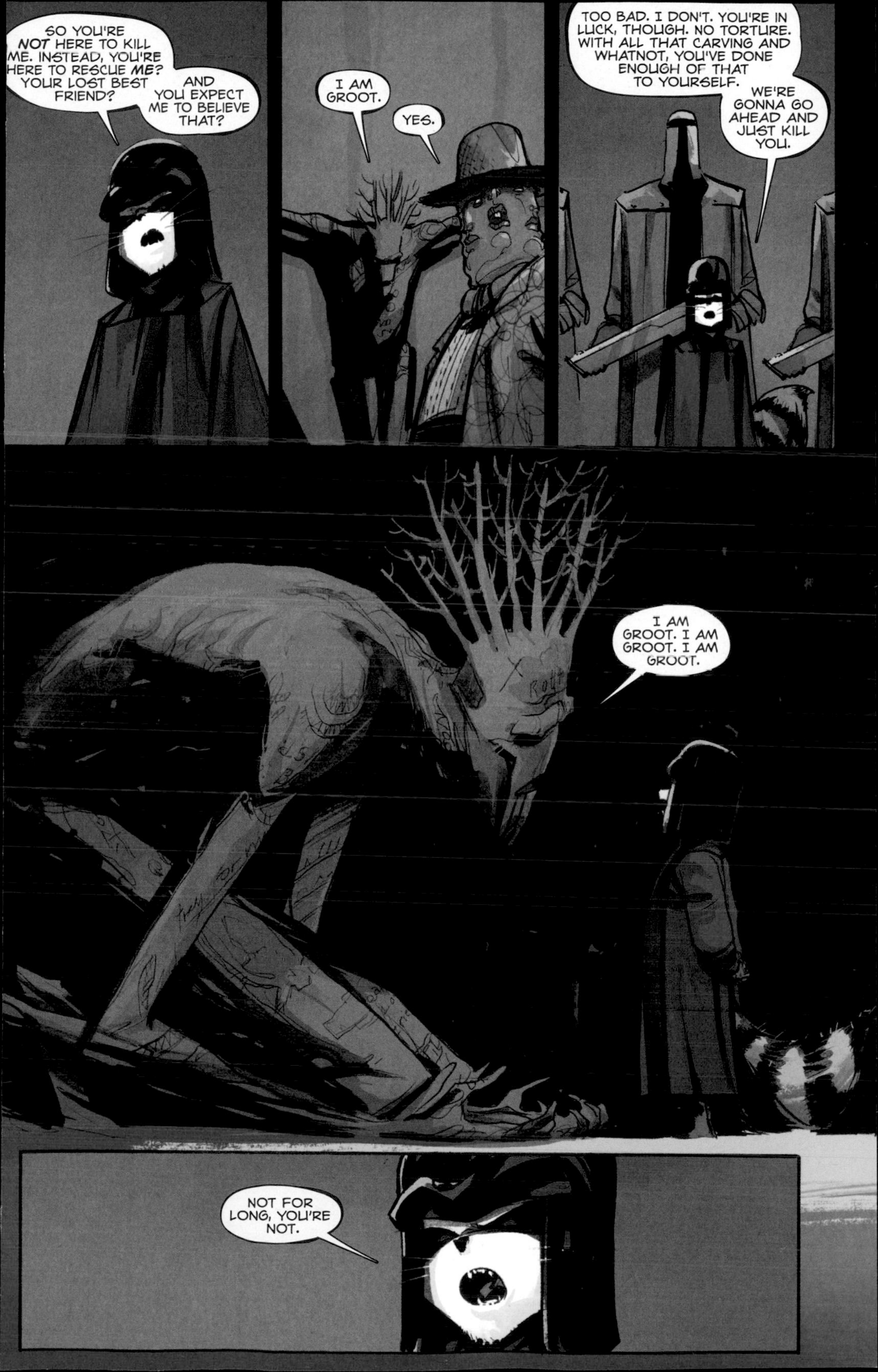

SO YOU'RE *NOT* HERE TO KILL ME. INSTEAD, YOU'RE HERE TO RESCUE *ME*? YOUR LOST BEST FRIEND?
AND YOU EXPECT ME TO BELIEVE THAT?
I AM GROOT.
YES.
TOO BAD. I DON'T. YOU'RE IN LUCK, THOUGH. NO TORTURE. WITH ALL THAT CARVING AND WHATNOT, YOU'VE DONE ENOUGH OF THAT TO YOURSELF.
WE'RE GONNA GO AHEAD AND JUST KILL YOU.
I AM GROOT. I AM GROOT. I AM GROOT.
NOT FOR LONG, YOU'RE NOT.

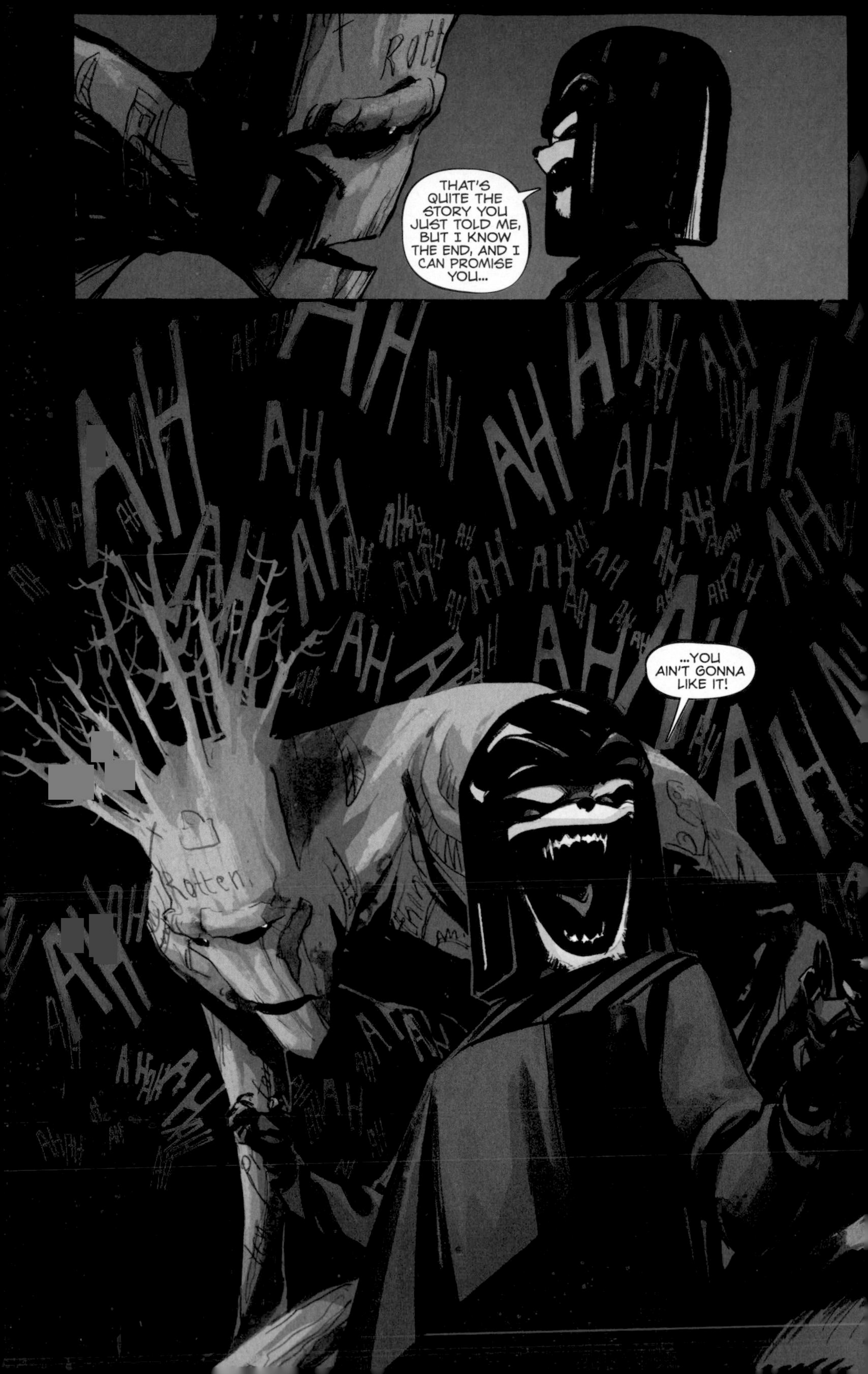
THAT'S QUITE THE STORY YOU JUST TOLD ME, BUT I KNOW THE END, AND I CAN PROMISE YOU...
...YOU AIN'T GONNA LIKE IT!

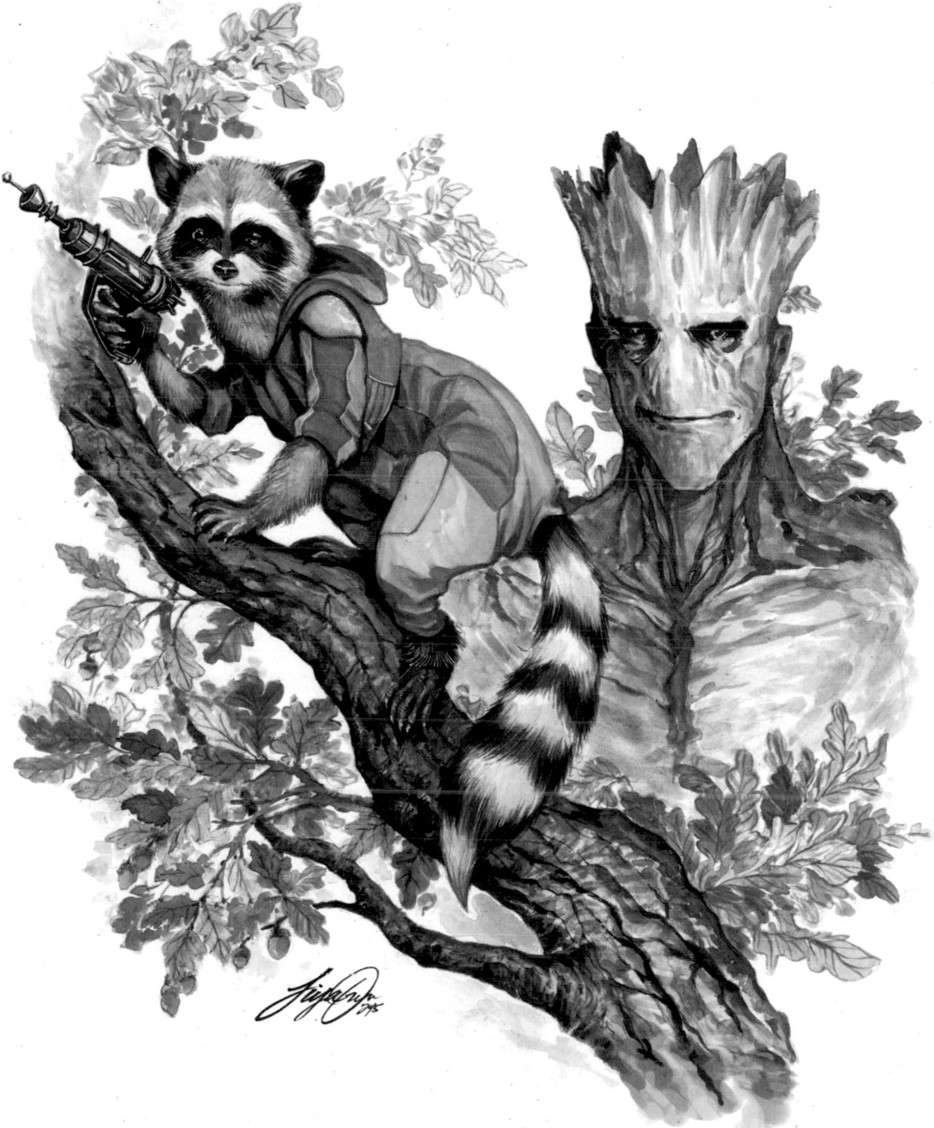

**ROCKET RACCOON & GROOT #3 VARIANT**
BY SIYA OUM

# 3

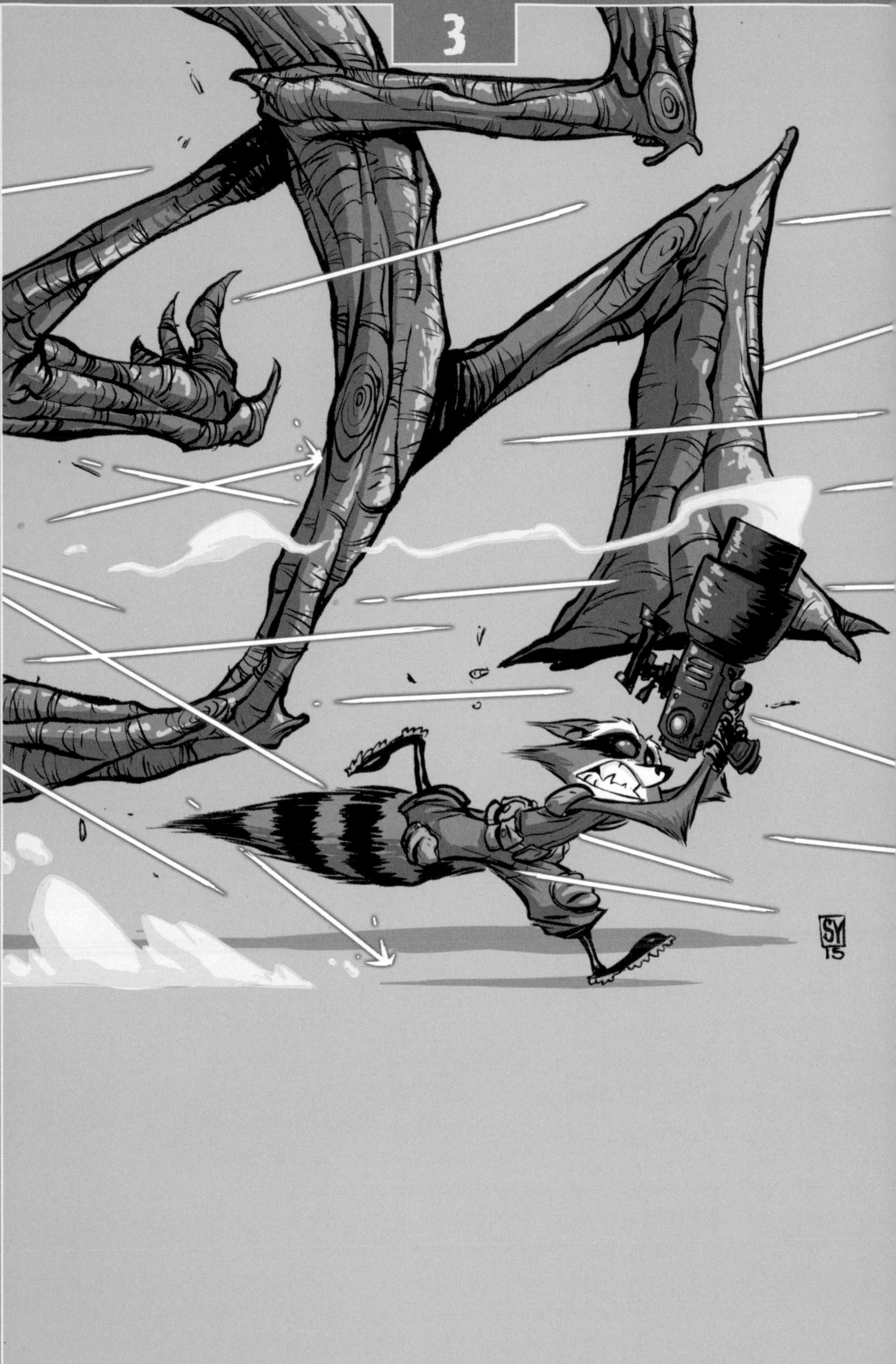
SY
15

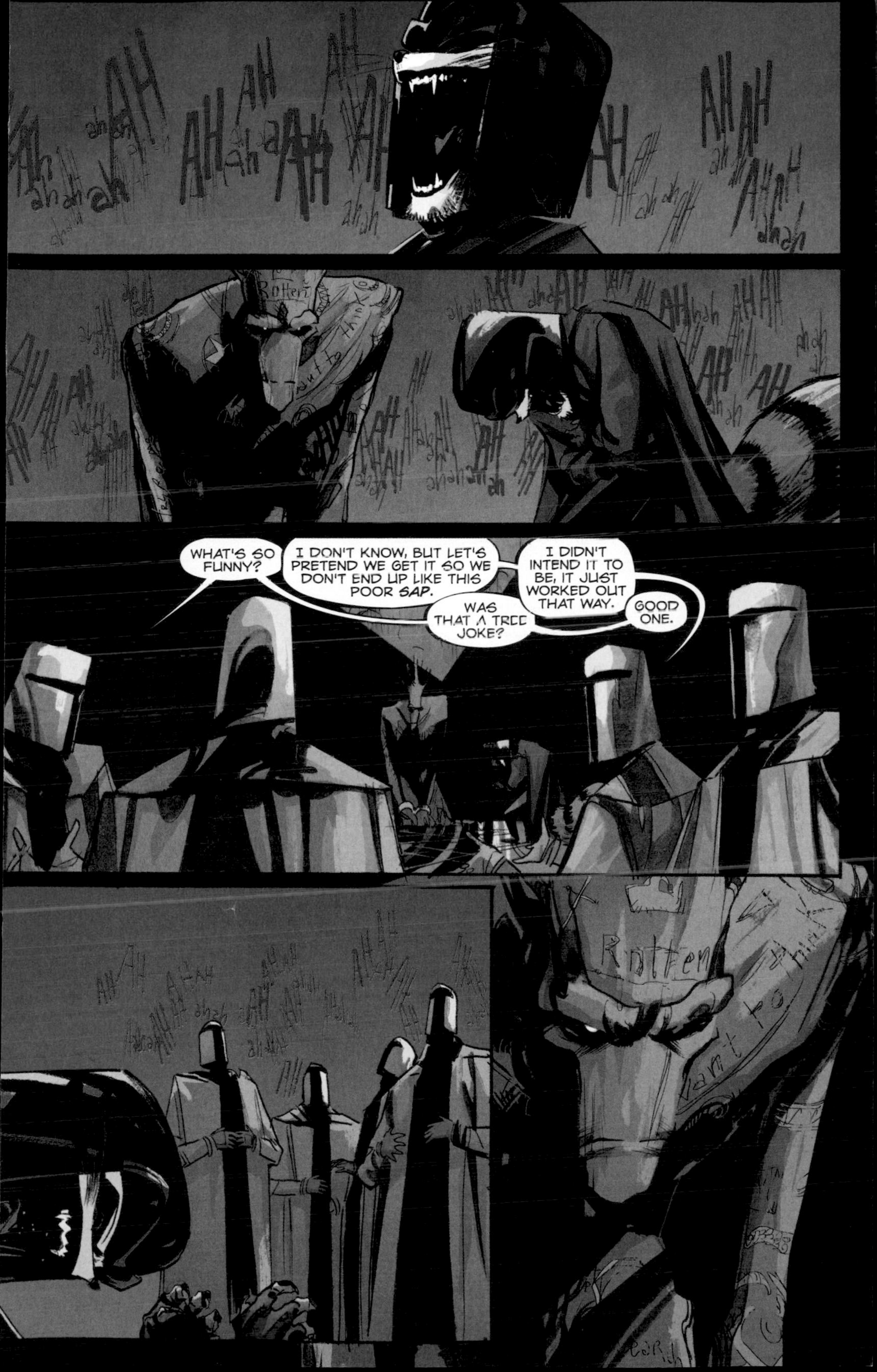
WHAT'S SO FUNNY?
I DON'T KNOW, BUT LET'S PRETEND WE GET IT SO WE DON'T END UP LIKE THIS POOR *SAP*.
WAS THAT A TREE JOKE?
I DIDN'T INTEND IT TO BE, IT JUST WORKED OUT THAT WAY.
GOOD ONE.

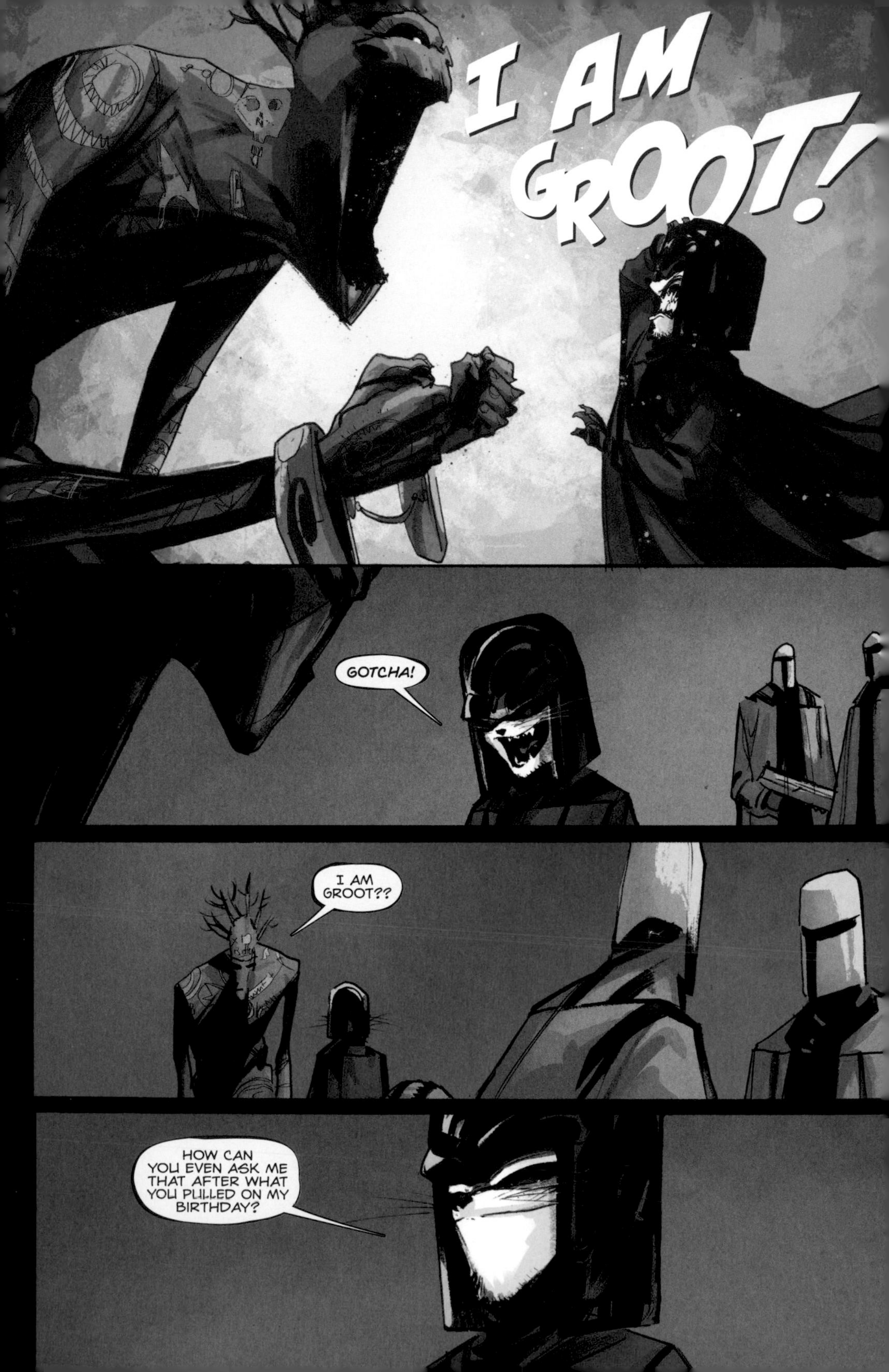
I AM GROOT!
GOTCHA!
I AM GROOT??
HOW CAN YOU EVEN ASK ME THAT AFTER WHAT YOU PULLED ON MY BIRTHDAY?

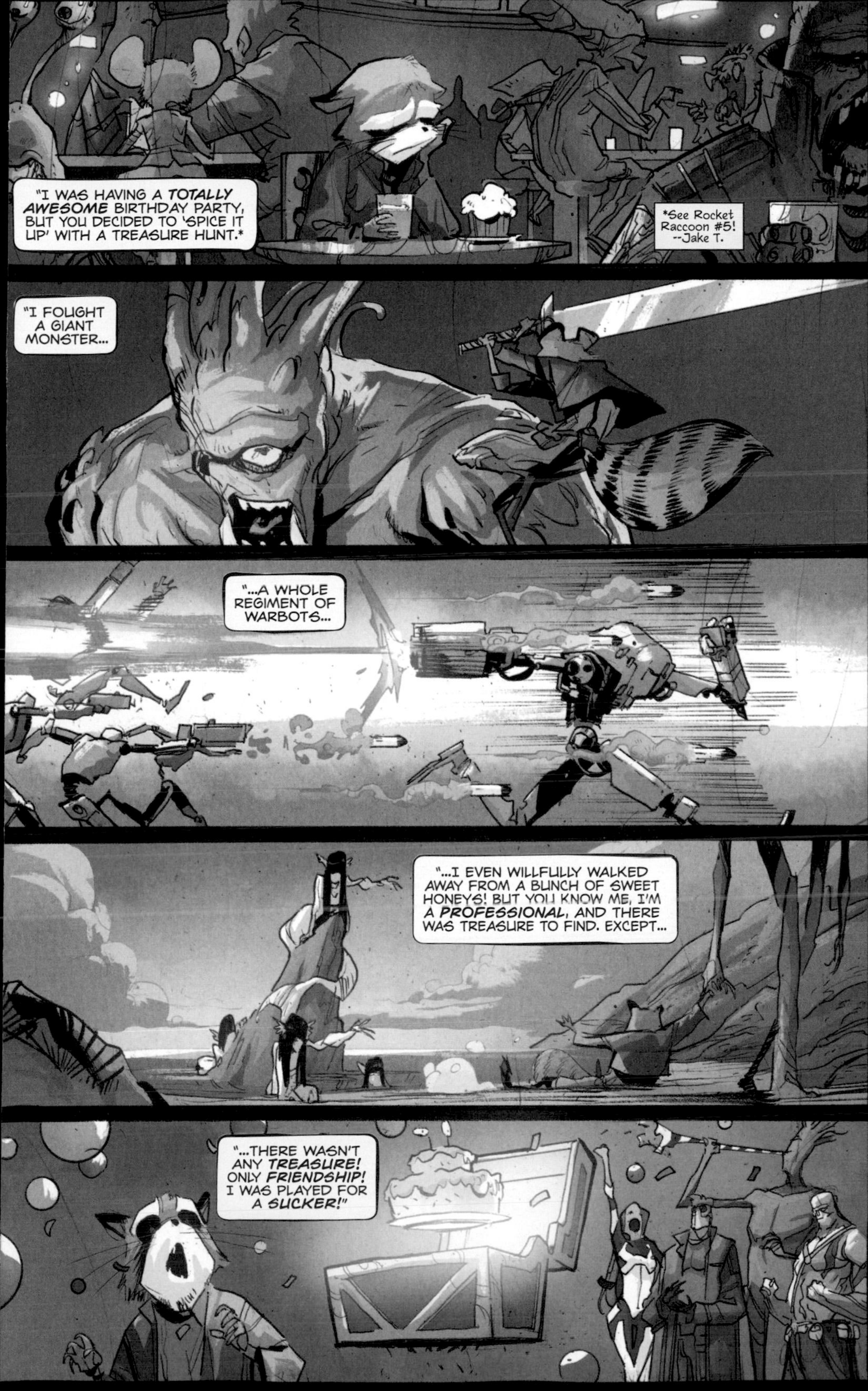
"I WAS HAVING A TOTALLY AWESOME BIRTHDAY PARTY, BUT YOU DECIDED TO 'SPICE IT UP' WITH A TREASURE HUNT.*
*See Rocket Raccoon #5! --Jake T.
"I FOUGHT A GIANT MONSTER...
"...A WHOLE REGIMENT OF WARBOTS...
"...I EVEN WILLFULLY WALKED AWAY FROM A BUNCH OF SWEET HONEYS! BUT YOU KNOW ME, I'M A PROFESSIONAL, AND THERE WAS TREASURE TO FIND. EXCEPT...
"...THERE WASN'T ANY TREASURE! ONLY FRIENDSHIP! I WAS PLAYED FOR A SUCKER!"

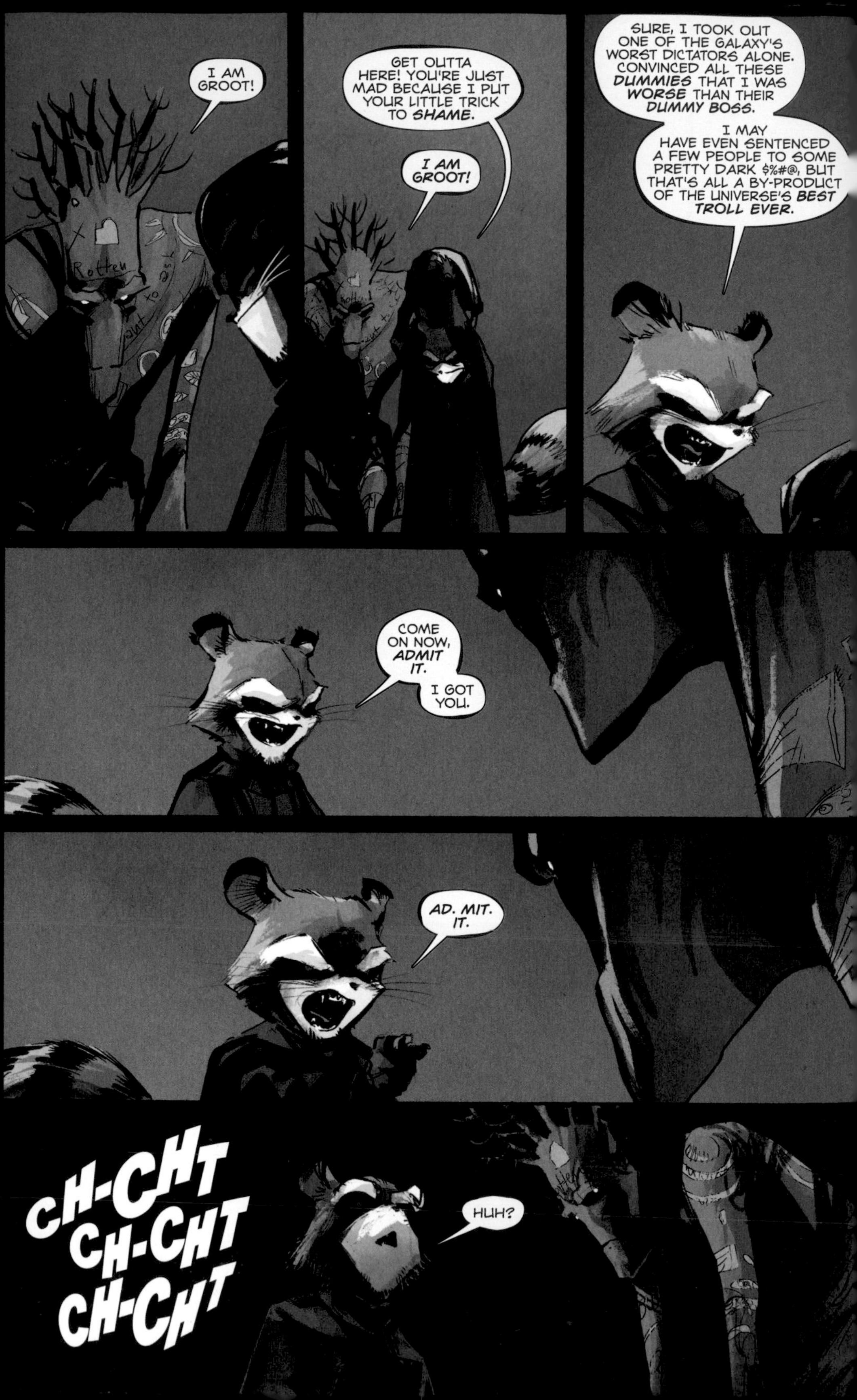
I AM GROOT!
GET OUTTA HERE! YOU'RE JUST MAD BECAUSE I PUT YOUR LITTLE TRICK TO SHAME.
I AM GROOT!
SURE, I TOOK OUT ONE OF THE GALAXY'S WORST DICTATORS ALONE. CONVINCED ALL THESE DUMMIES THAT I WAS WORSE THAN THEIR DUMMY BOSS.
I MAY HAVE EVEN SENTENCED A FEW PEOPLE TO SOME PRETTY DARK $%#@, BUT THAT'S ALL A BY-PRODUCT OF THE UNIVERSE'S BEST TROLL EVER.
COME ON NOW, ADMIT IT.
I GOT YOU.
AD. MIT. IT.
CH-CHT CH-CHT CH-CHT
HUH?

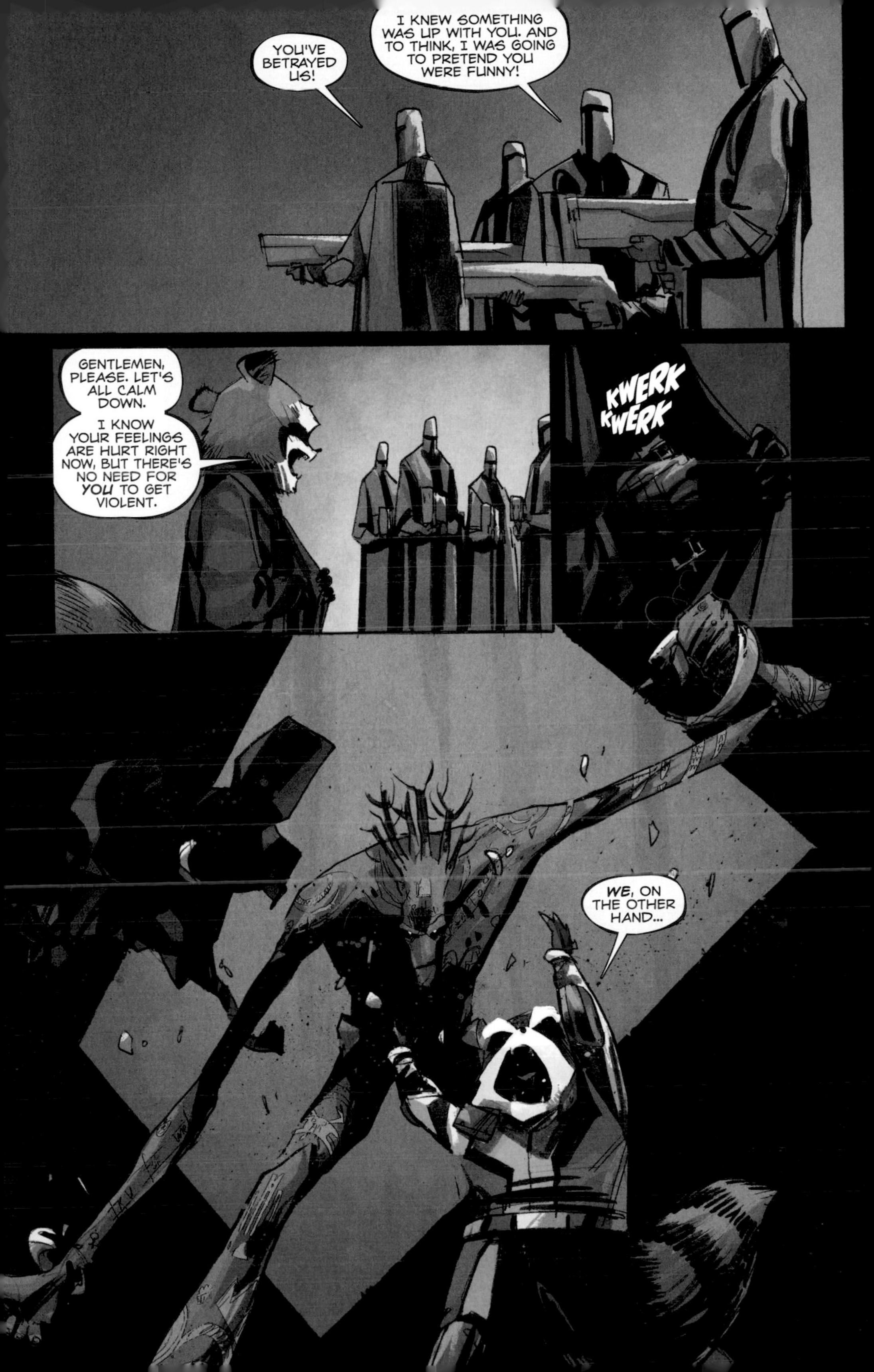
YOU'VE BETRAYED US!
I KNEW SOMETHING WAS UP WITH YOU. AND TO THINK, I WAS GOING TO PRETEND YOU WERE FUNNY!
GENTLEMEN, PLEASE. LET'S ALL CALM DOWN.
I KNOW YOUR FEELINGS ARE HURT RIGHT NOW, BUT THERE'S NO NEED FOR YOU TO GET VIOLENT.
KWERK KWERK
WE, ON THE OTHER HAND...

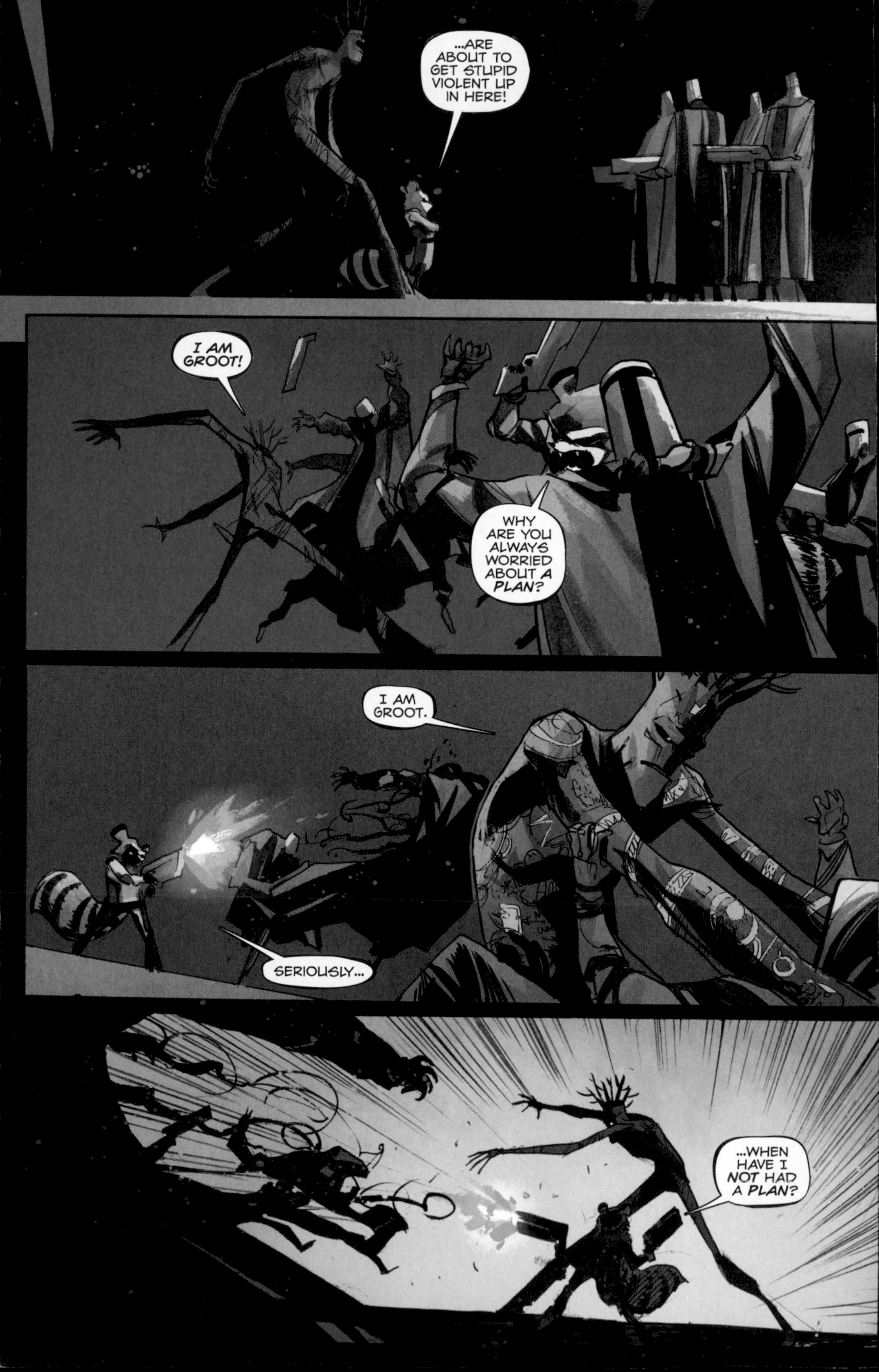
...ARE ABOUT TO GET STUPID VIOLENT UP IN HERE!
I AM GROOT!
WHY ARE YOU ALWAYS WORRIED ABOUT *A PLAN*?
I AM GROOT.
SERIOUSLY...
...WHEN HAVE I *NOT* HAD A *PLAN*?

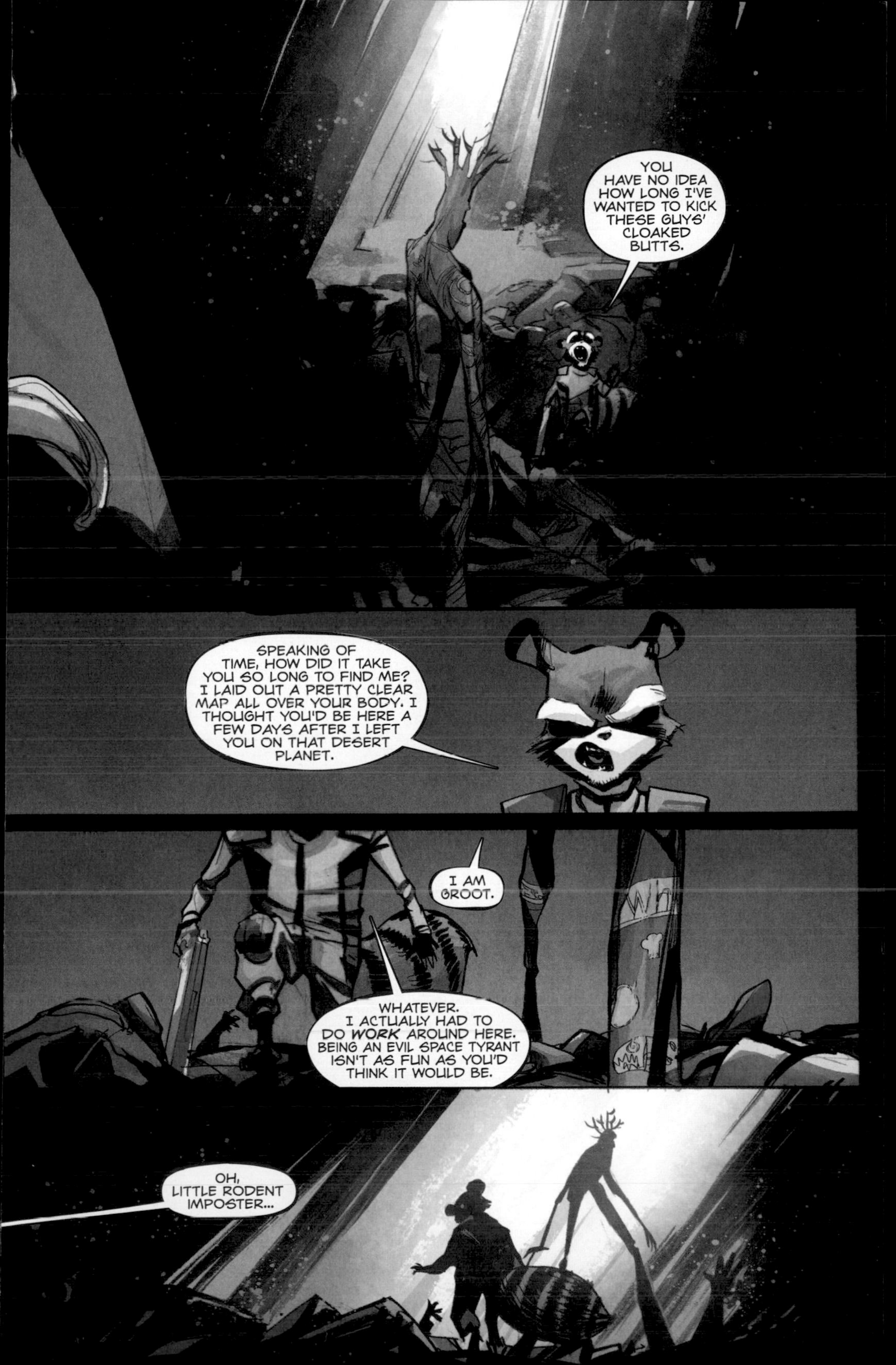
YOU HAVE NO IDEA HOW LONG I'VE WANTED TO KICK THESE GUYS' CLOAKED BUTTS.
SPEAKING OF TIME, HOW DID IT TAKE YOU SO LONG TO FIND ME? I LAID OUT A PRETTY CLEAR MAP ALL OVER YOUR BODY. I THOUGHT YOU'D BE HERE A FEW DAYS AFTER I LEFT YOU ON THAT DESERT PLANET.
I AM GROOT.
WHATEVER. I ACTUALLY HAD TO DO *WORK* AROUND HERE. BEING AN EVIL SPACE TYRANT ISN'T AS FUN AS YOU'D THINK IT WOULD BE.
OH, LITTLE RODENT IMPOSTER...

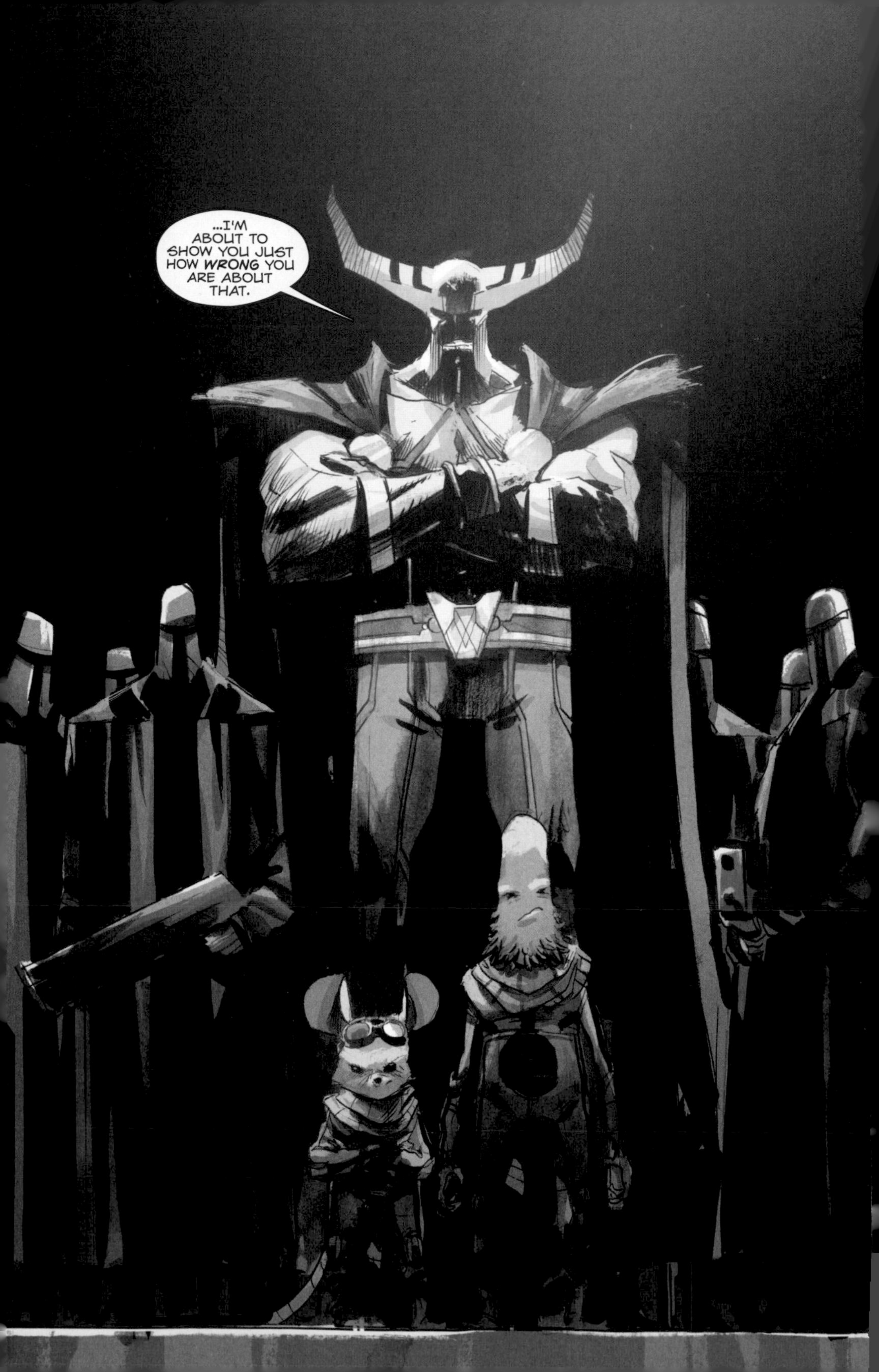
...I'M ABOUT TO SHOW YOU JUST HOW WRONG YOU ARE ABOUT THAT.

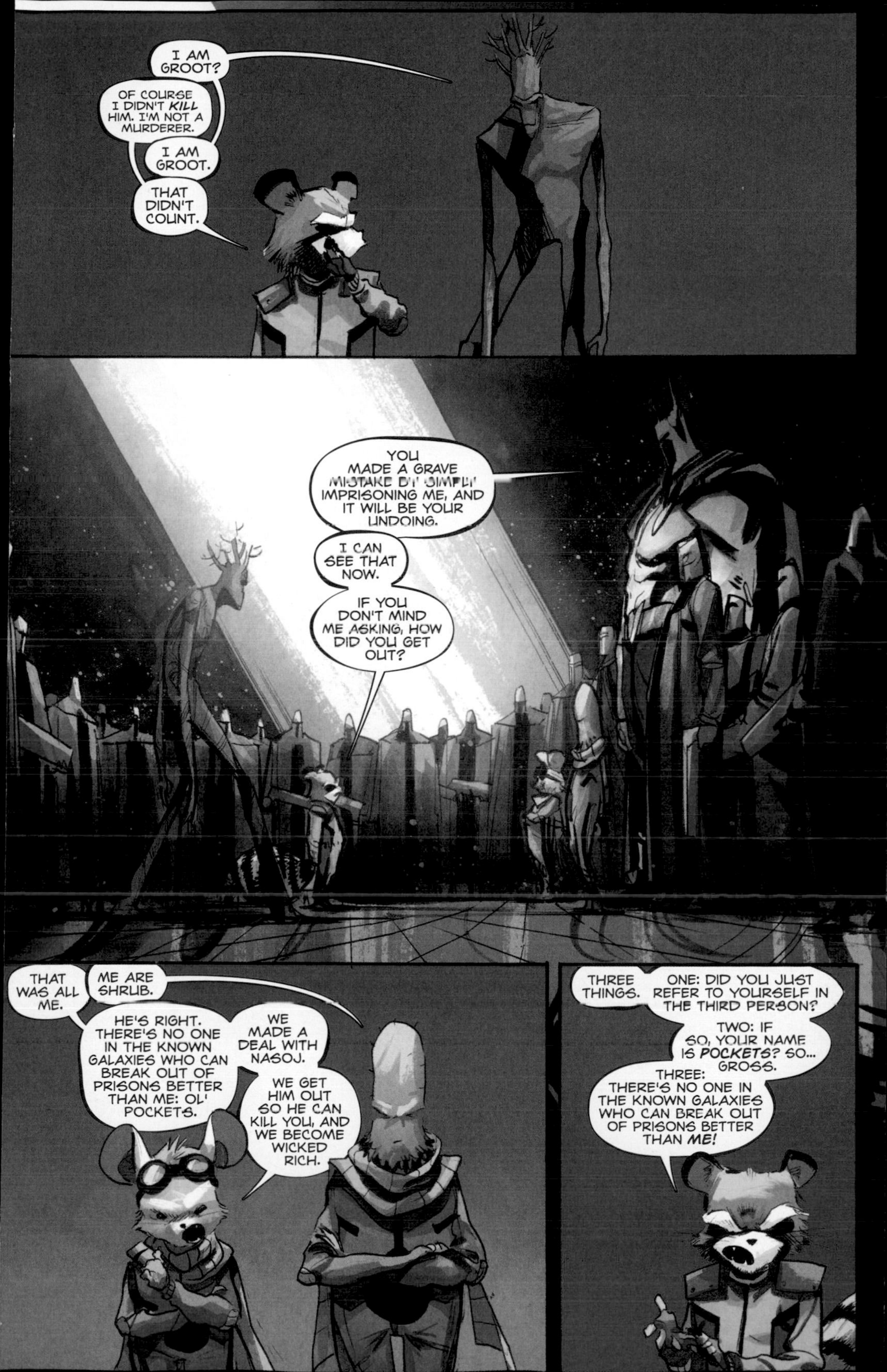
I AM GROOT?
OF COURSE I DIDN'T KILL HIM. I'M NOT A MURDERER.
I AM GROOT.
THAT DIDN'T COUNT.
YOU MADE A GRAVE MISTAKE BY SIMPLY IMPRISONING ME, AND IT WILL BE YOUR UNDOING.
I CAN SEE THAT NOW.
IF YOU DON'T MIND ME ASKING, HOW DID YOU GET OUT?
THAT WAS ALL ME.
ME ARE SHRUB.
HE'S RIGHT. THERE'S NO ONE IN THE KNOWN GALAXIES WHO CAN BREAK OUT OF PRISONS BETTER THAN ME: OL' POCKETS.
WE MADE A DEAL WITH NASOJ.
WE GET HIM OUT SO HE CAN KILL YOU, AND WE BECOME WICKED RICH.
THREE THINGS.
ONE: DID YOU JUST REFER TO YOURSELF IN THE THIRD PERSON?
TWO: IF SO, YOUR NAME IS POCKETS? SO... GROSS.
THREE: THERE'S NO ONE IN THE KNOWN GALAXIES WHO CAN BREAK OUT OF PRISONS BETTER THAN ME!

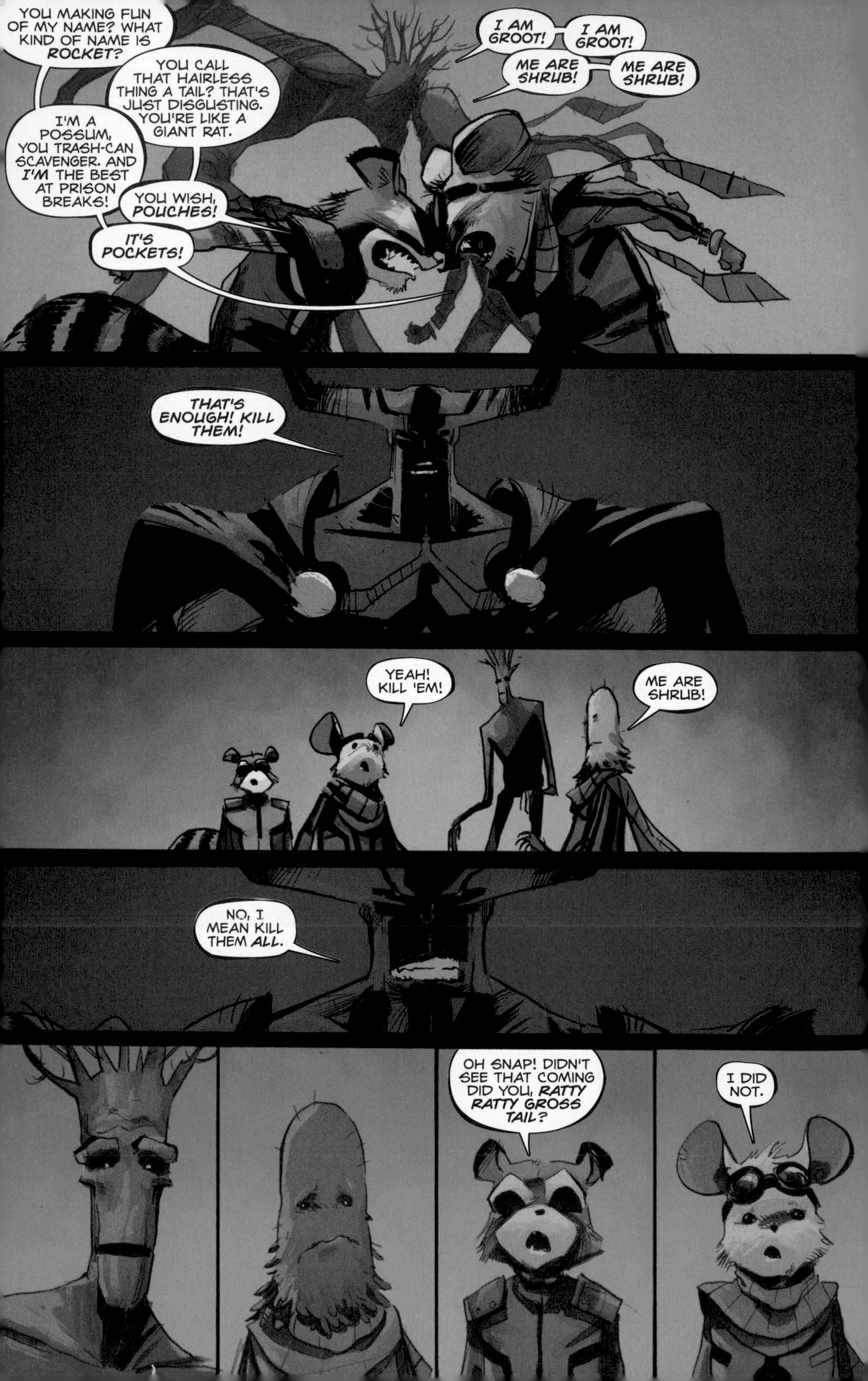
YOU MAKING FUN OF MY NAME? WHAT KIND OF NAME IS ROCKET?
YOU CALL THAT HAIRLESS THING A TAIL? THAT'S JUST DISGUSTING. YOU'RE LIKE A GIANT RAT.
I'M A POSSUM, YOU TRASH-CAN SCAVENGER. AND I'M THE BEST AT PRISON BREAKS!
YOU WISH, POUCHES!
IT'S POCKETS!
I AM GROOT!
I AM GROOT!
ME ARE SHRUB!
ME ARE SHRUB!
THAT'S ENOUGH! KILL THEM!
YEAH! KILL 'EM!
ME ARE SHRUB!
NO, I MEAN KILL THEM ALL.
OH SNAP! DIDN'T SEE THAT COMING DID YOU, RATTY RATTY GROSS TAIL?
I DID NOT.

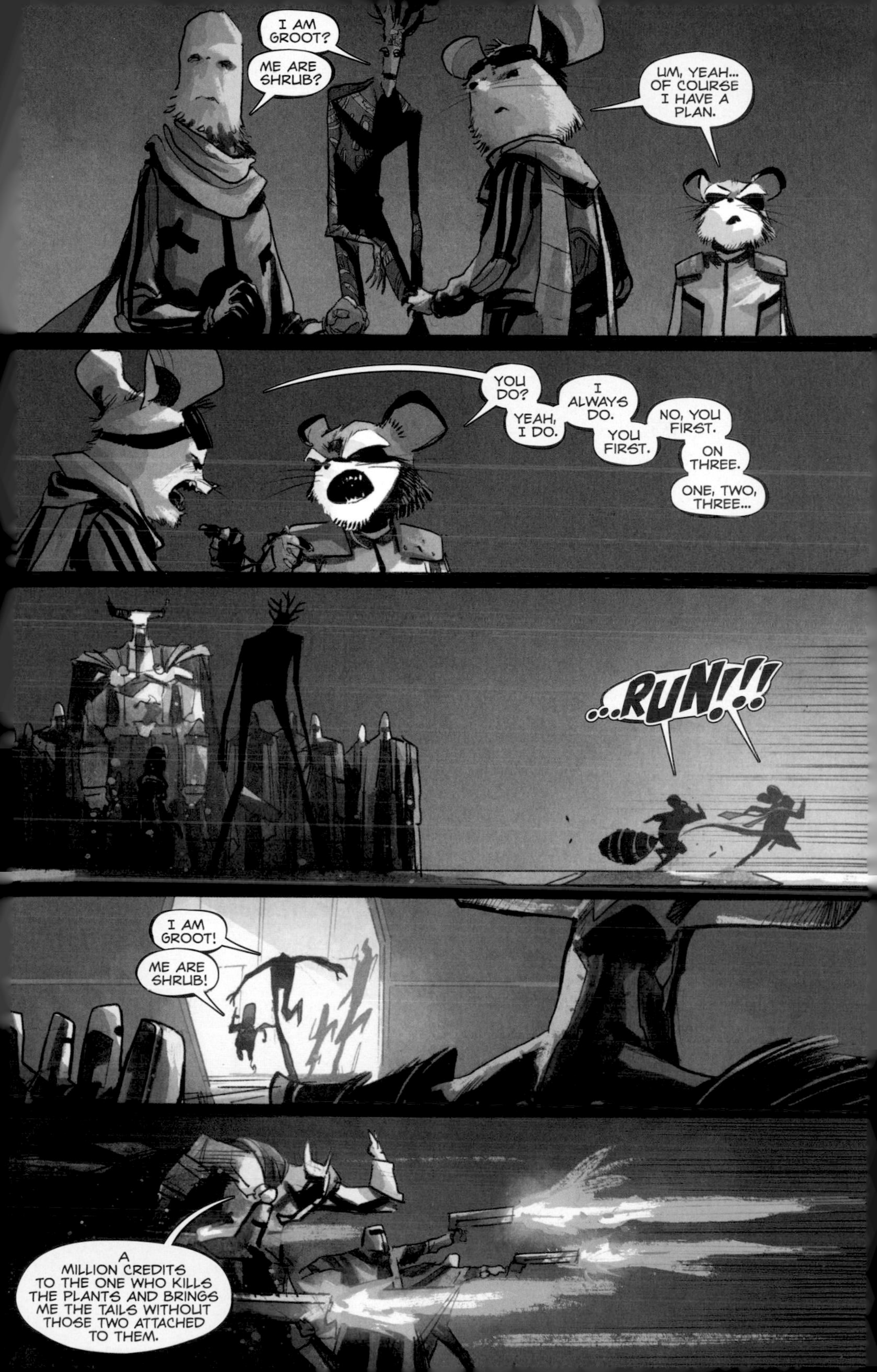
I AM GROOT?
ME ARE SHRUB?
UM, YEAH... OF COURSE I HAVE A PLAN.
YOU DO?
YEAH, I DO.
I ALWAYS DO.
YOU FIRST.
NO, YOU FIRST.
ON THREE.
ONE, TWO, THREE...
...RUN!!!
I AM GROOT!
ME ARE SHRUB!
A MILLION CREDITS TO THE ONE WHO KILLS THE PLANTS AND BRINGS ME THE TAILS WITHOUT THOSE TWO ATTACHED TO THEM.

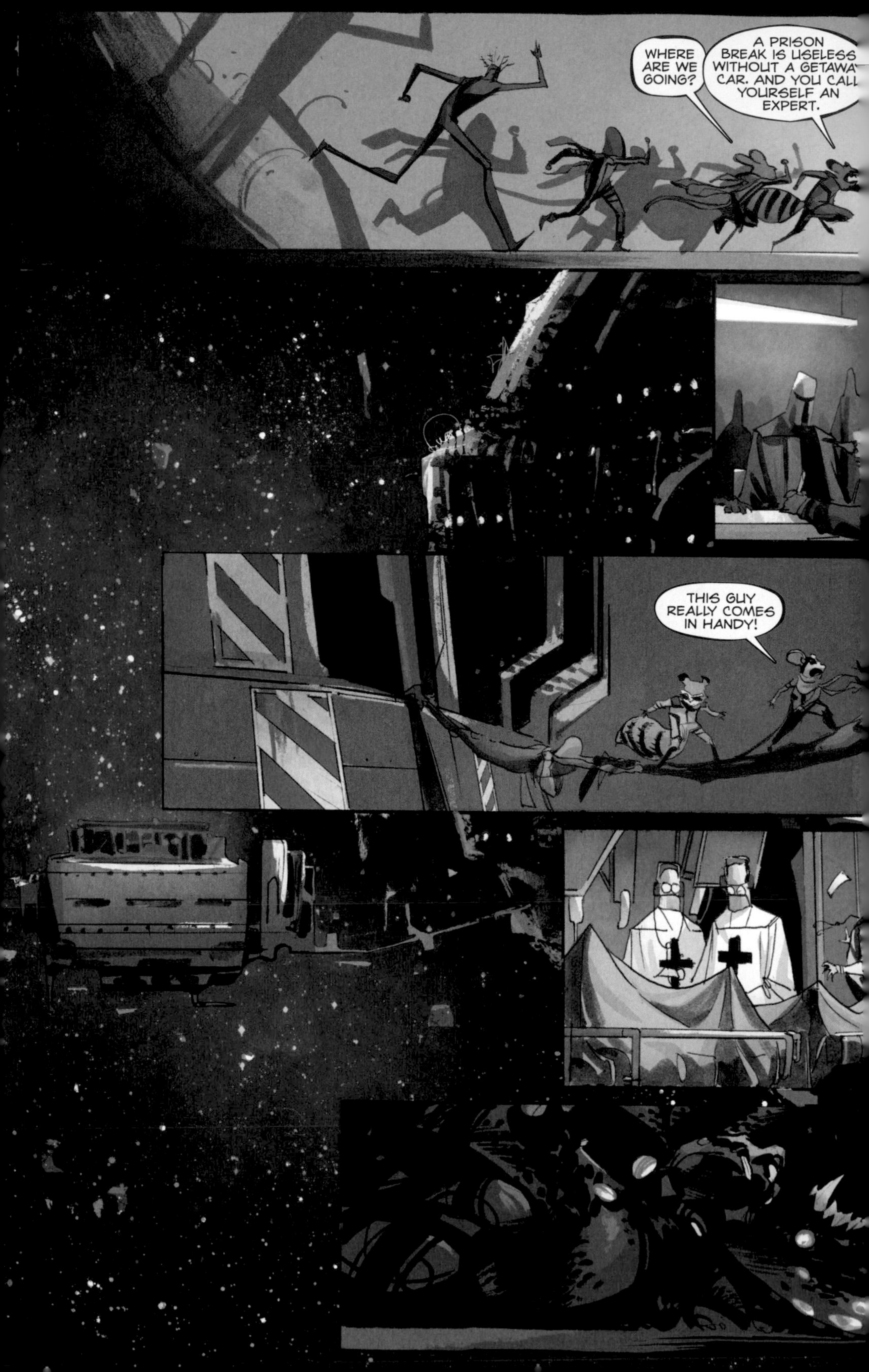
WHERE ARE WE GOING?
A PRISON BREAK IS USELESS WITHOUT A GETAWAY CAR. AND YOU CALL YOURSELF AN EXPERT.
THIS GUY REALLY COMES IN HANDY!

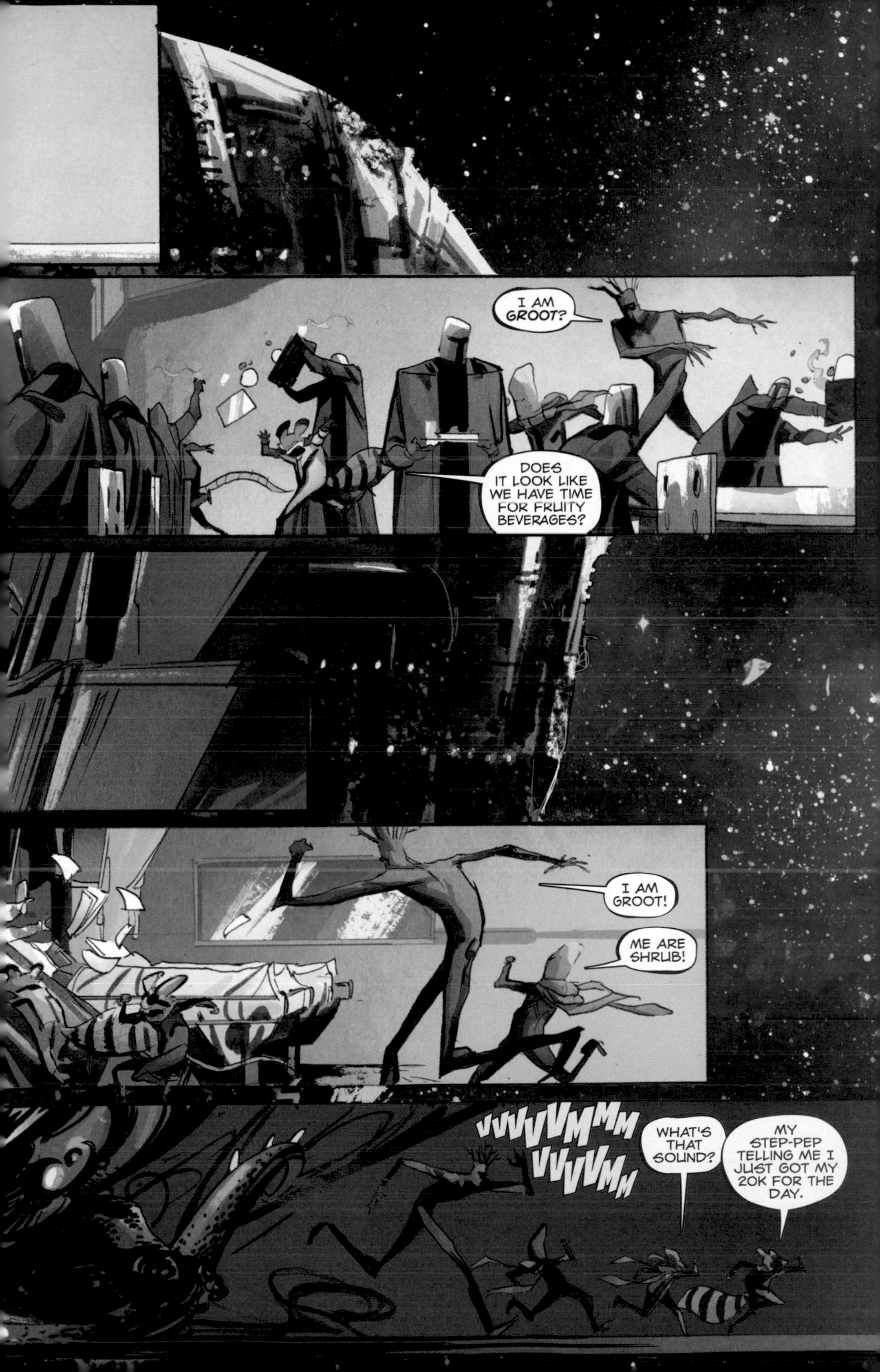

I AM GROOT?
DOES IT LOOK LIKE WE HAVE TIME FOR FRUITY BEVERAGES?
I AM GROOT!
ME ARE SHRUB!
VVVVVMMMM VVVVVMM
WHAT'S THAT SOUND?
MY STEP-PEP TELLING ME I JUST GOT MY 20K FOR THE DAY.

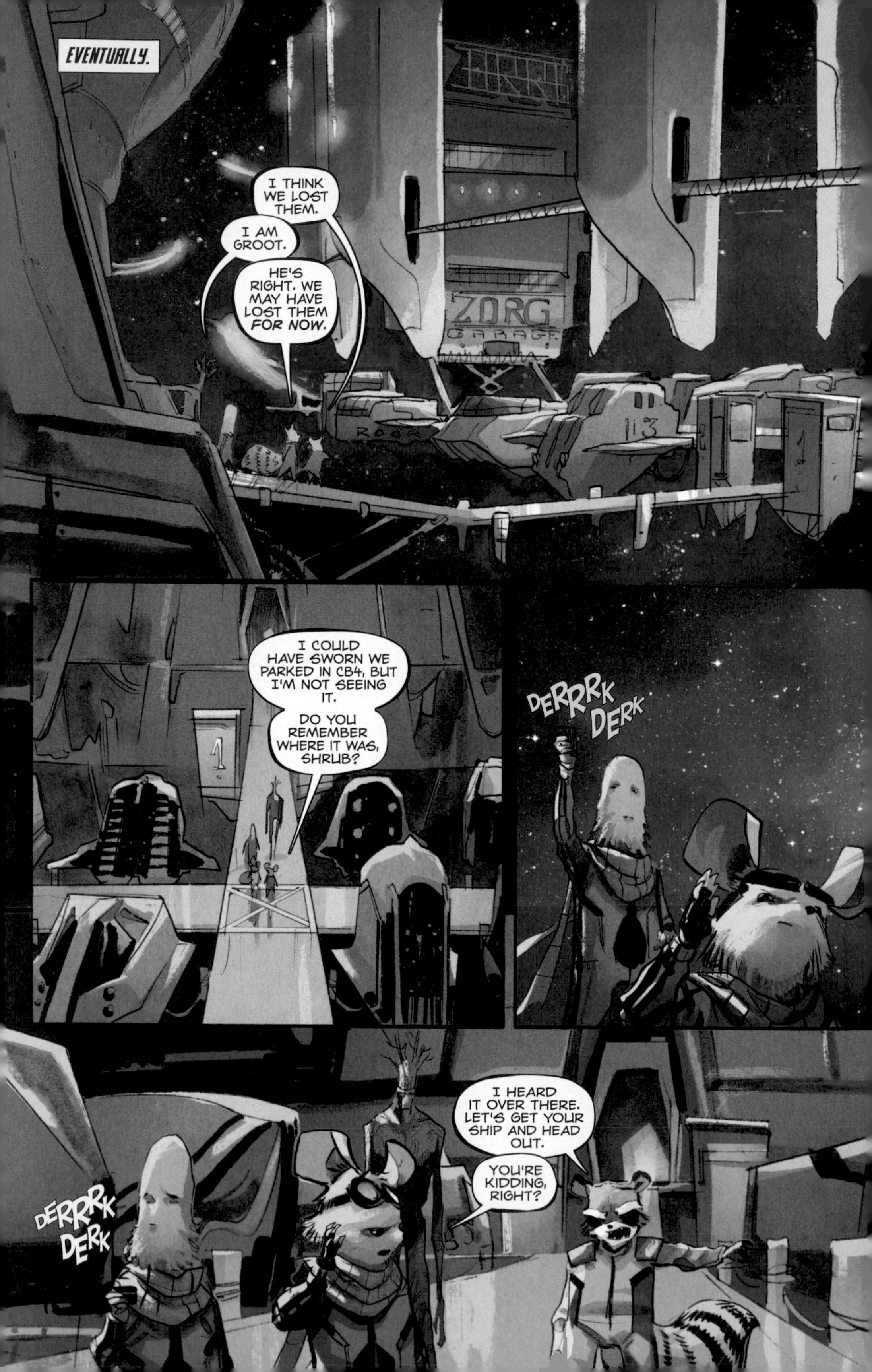
EVENTUALLY.
I THINK WE LOST THEM.
I AM GROOT.
HE'S RIGHT. WE MAY HAVE LOST THEM FOR NOW.
ZORG GARAGE
I COULD HAVE SWORN WE PARKED IN CB4, BUT I'M NOT SEEING IT.
DO YOU REMEMBER WHERE IT WAS, SHRUB?
DERRRK DERK
DERRRK DERK
I HEARD IT OVER THERE. LET'S GET YOUR SHIP AND HEAD OUT.
YOU'RE KIDDING, RIGHT?

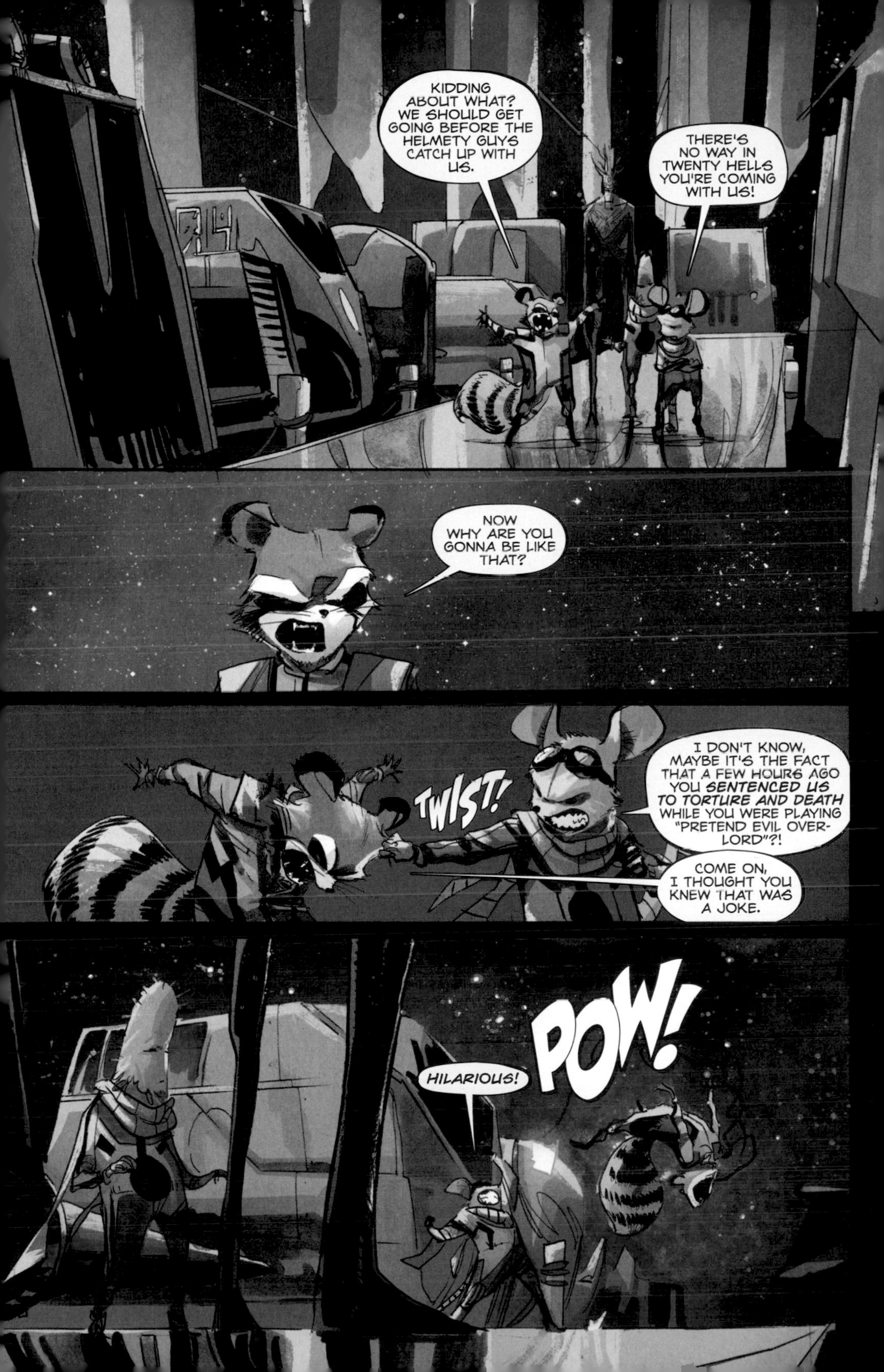
KIDDING ABOUT WHAT? WE SHOULD GET GOING BEFORE THE HELMETY GUYS CATCH UP WITH US.
THERE'S NO WAY IN TWENTY HELLS YOU'RE COMING WITH US!
NOW WHY ARE YOU GONNA BE LIKE THAT?
TWIST!
I DON'T KNOW, MAYBE IT'S THE FACT THAT A FEW HOURS AGO YOU SENTENCED US TO TORTURE AND DEATH WHILE YOU WERE PLAYING "PRETEND EVIL OVER-LORD"?!
COME ON, I THOUGHT YOU KNEW THAT WAS A JOKE.
HILARIOUS!
POW!

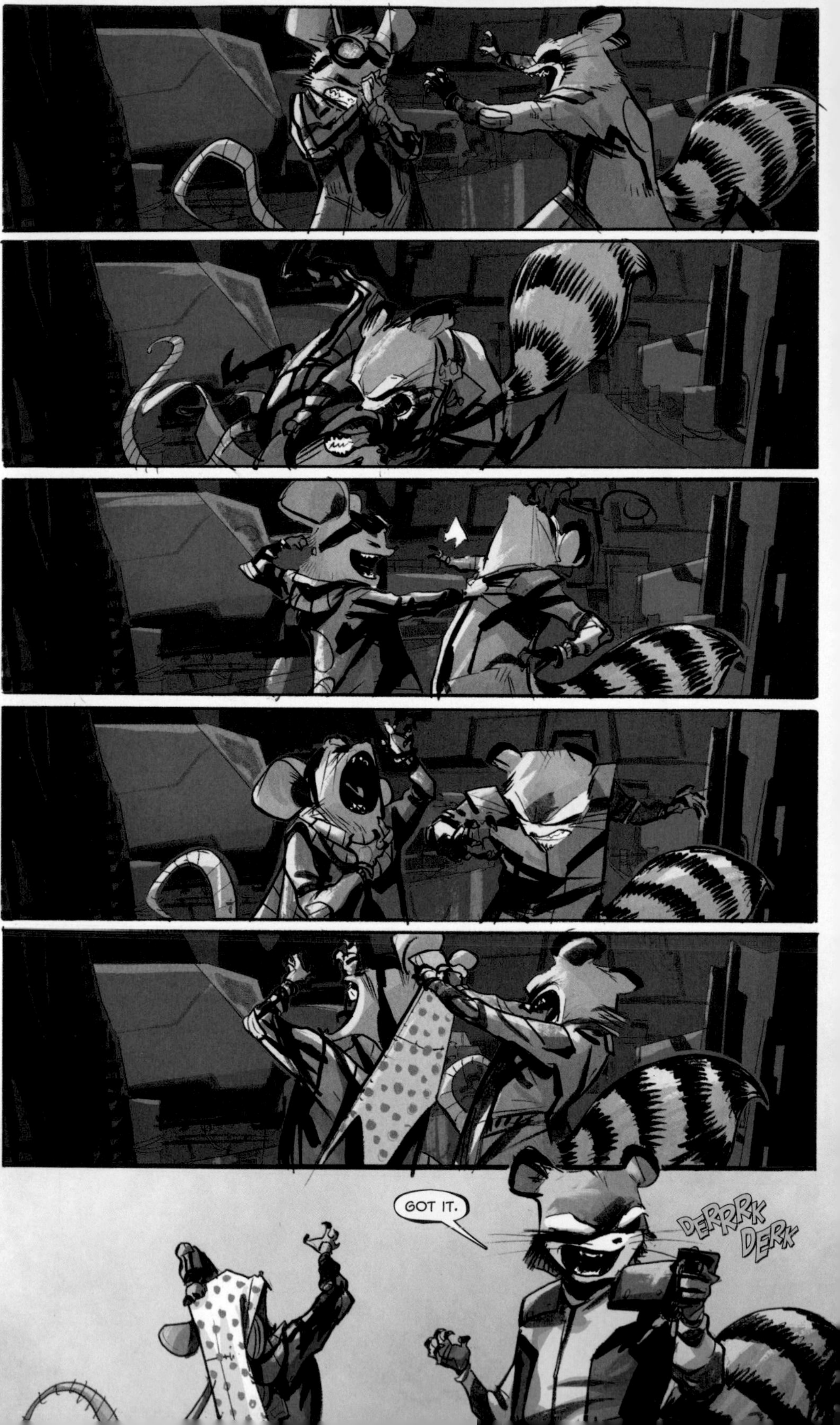
GOT IT.
DERRRK
DERK

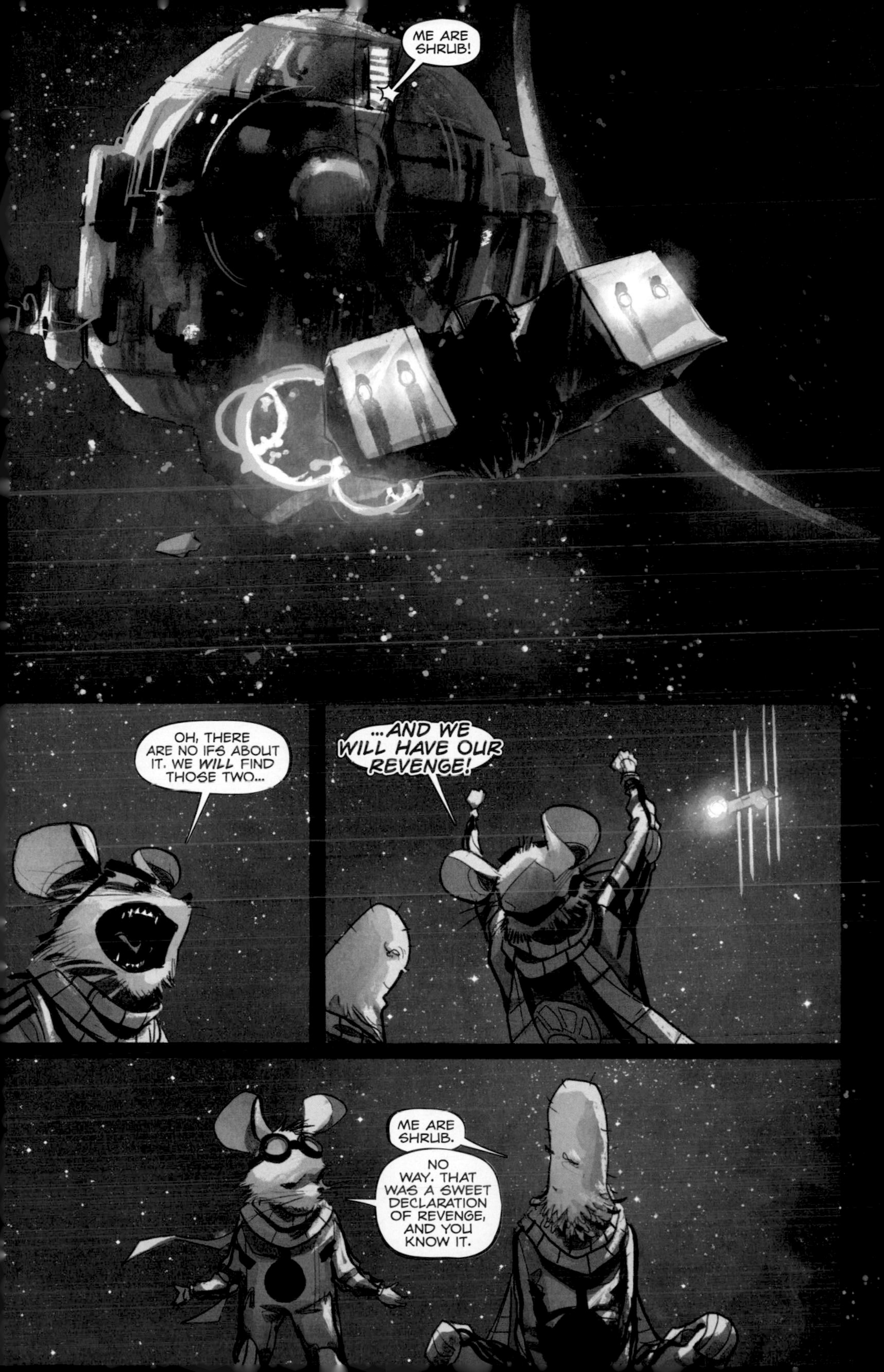
ME ARE SHRUB!
OH, THERE ARE NO IFS ABOUT IT. WE WILL FIND THOSE TWO...
...AND WE WILL HAVE OUR REVENGE!
ME ARE SHRUB.
NO WAY. THAT WAS A SWEET DECLARATION OF REVENGE, AND YOU KNOW IT.

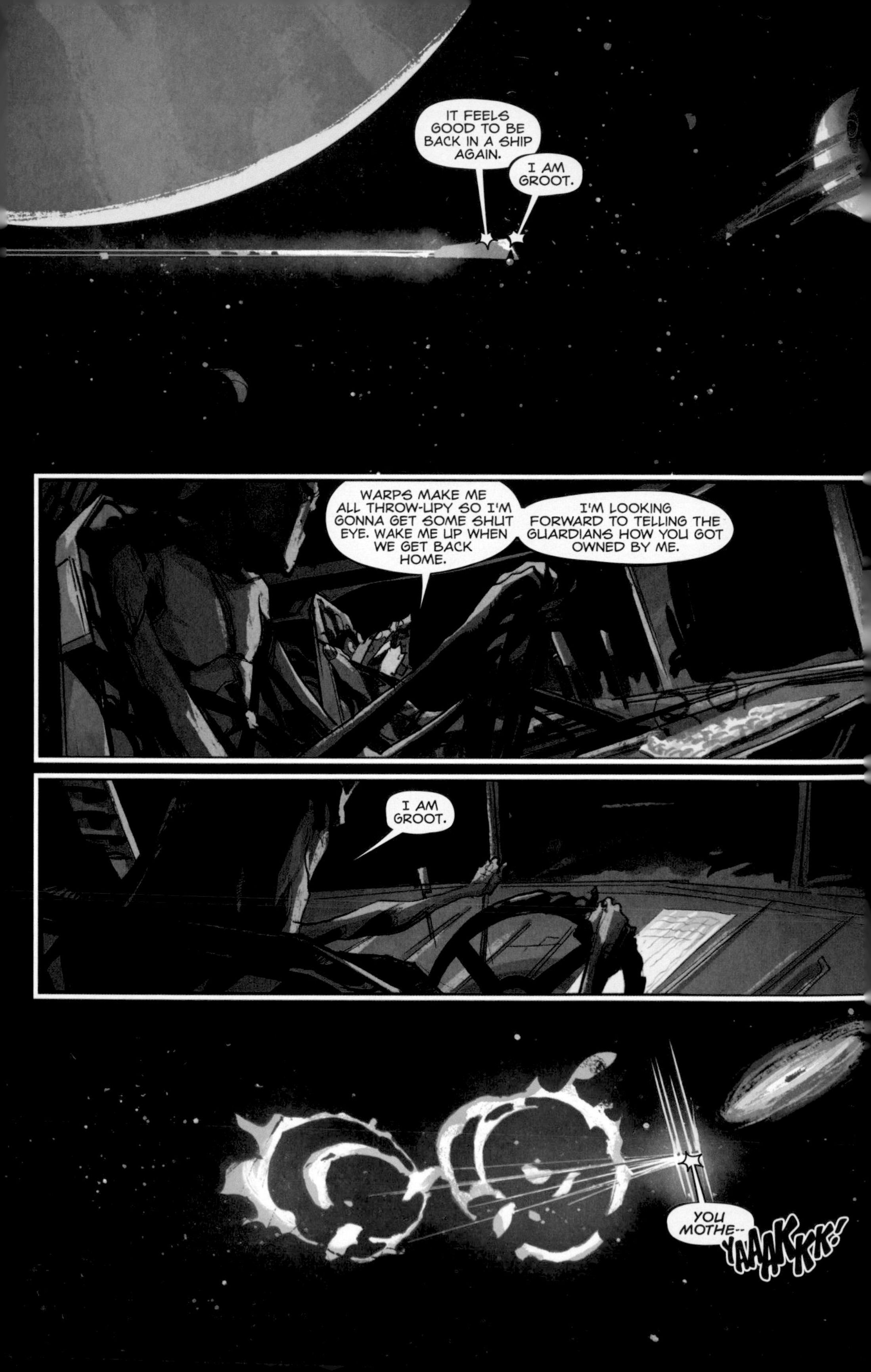
IT FEELS GOOD TO BE BACK IN A SHIP AGAIN.
I AM GROOT.
WARPS MAKE ME ALL THROW-UPY SO I'M GONNA GET SOME SHUT EYE. WAKE ME UP WHEN WE GET BACK HOME.
I'M LOOKING FORWARD TO TELLING THE GUARDIANS HOW YOU GOT OWNED BY ME.
I AM GROOT.
YOU MOTHE--
YAAAKKKK!

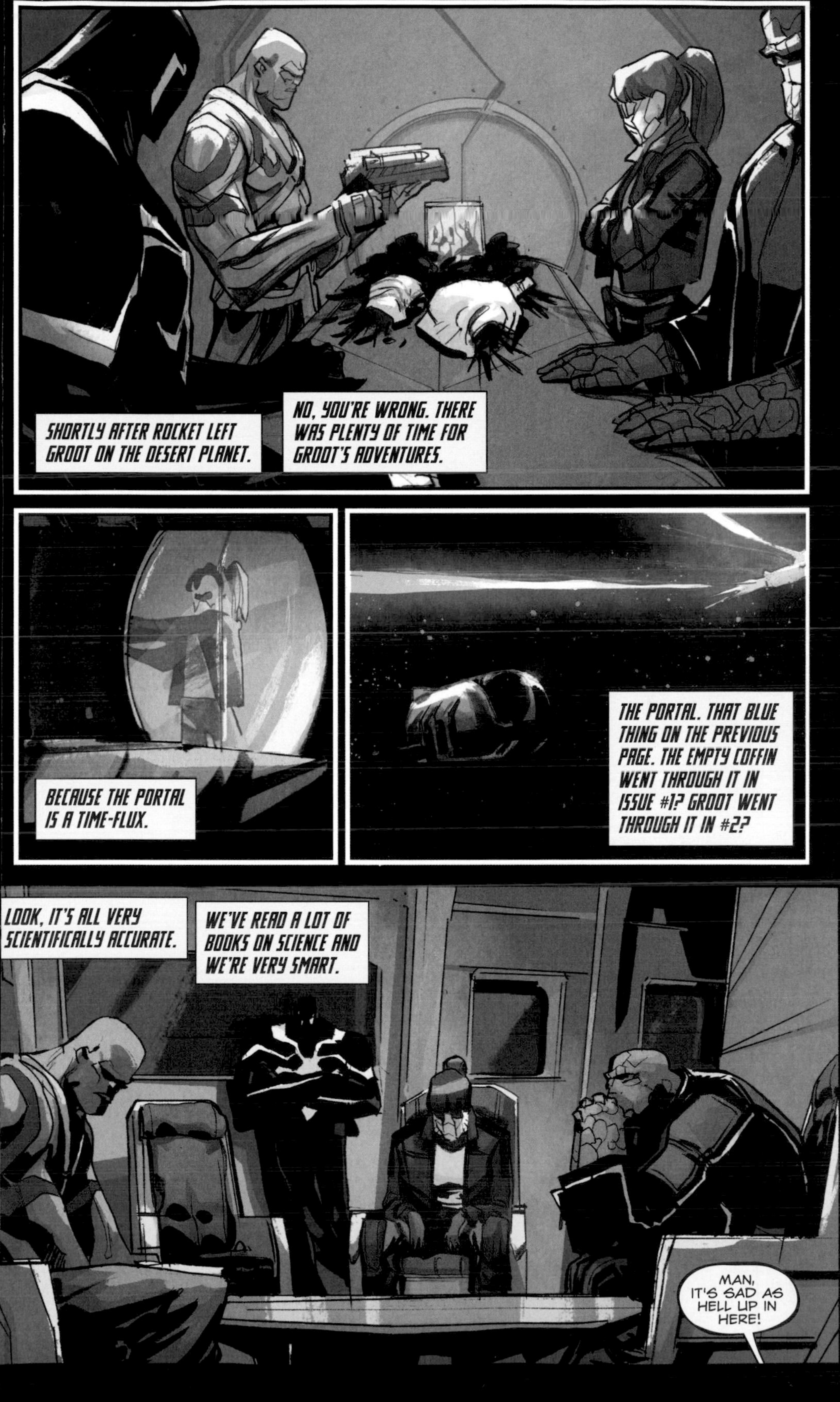
SHORTLY AFTER ROCKET LEFT GROOT ON THE DESERT PLANET.
NO, YOU'RE WRONG. THERE WAS PLENTY OF TIME FOR GROOT'S ADVENTURES.
BECAUSE THE PORTAL IS A TIME-FLUX.
THE PORTAL. THAT BLUE THING ON THE PREVIOUS PAGE. THE EMPTY COFFIN WENT THROUGH IT IN ISSUE #1? GROOT WENT THROUGH IT IN #2?
LOOK, IT'S ALL VERY SCIENTIFICALLY ACCURATE.
WE'VE READ A LOT OF BOOKS ON SCIENCE AND WE'RE VERY SMART.
MAN, IT'S SAD AS HELL UP IN HERE!

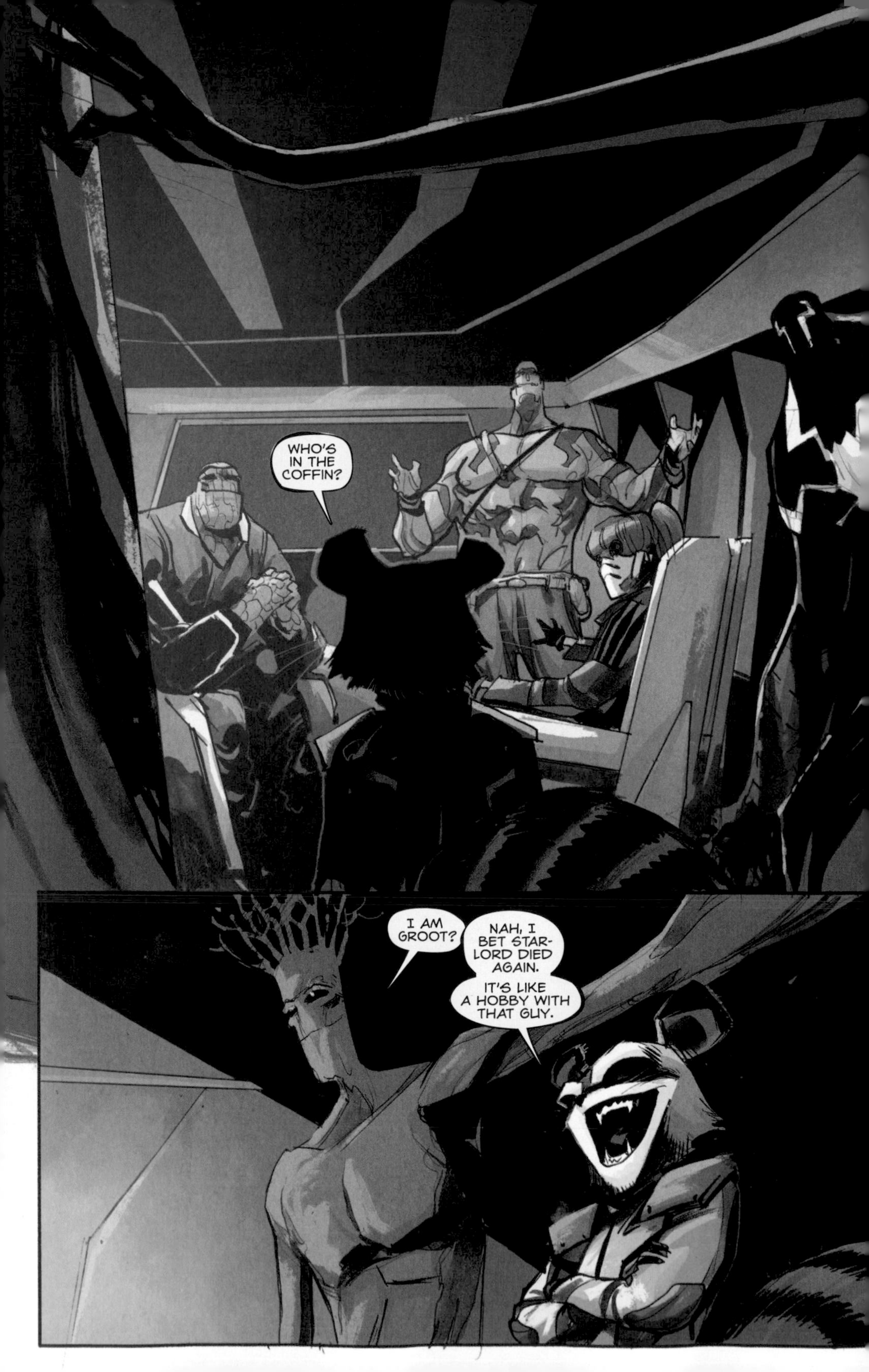
WHO'S IN THE COFFIN?
I AM GROOT?
NAH, I BET STAR-LORD DIED AGAIN.
IT'S LIKE A HOBBY WITH THAT GUY.

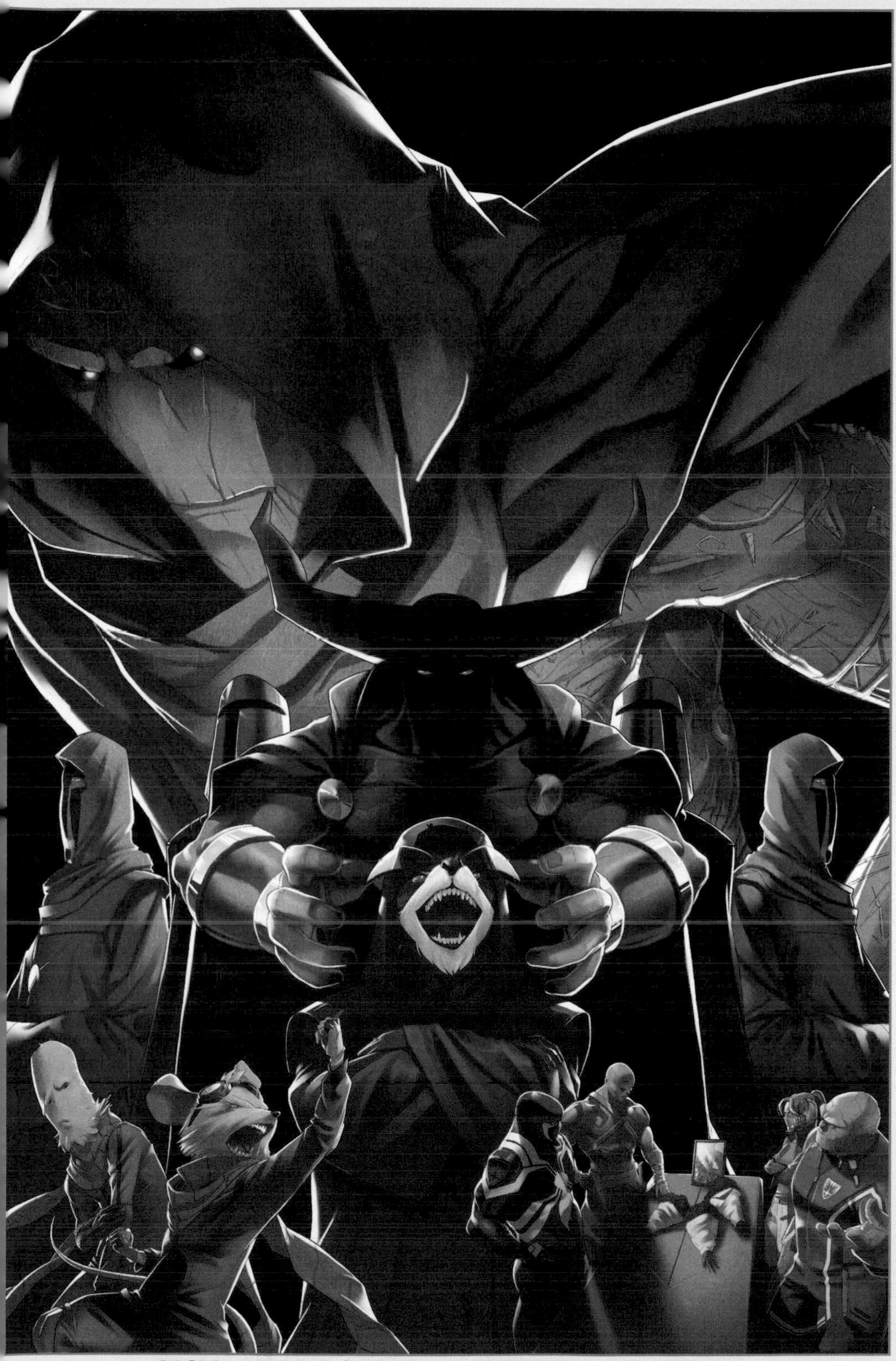

**ROCKET RACCOON & GROOT #4 STORY THUS FAR VARIANT**
BY JAMAL CAMPBELL

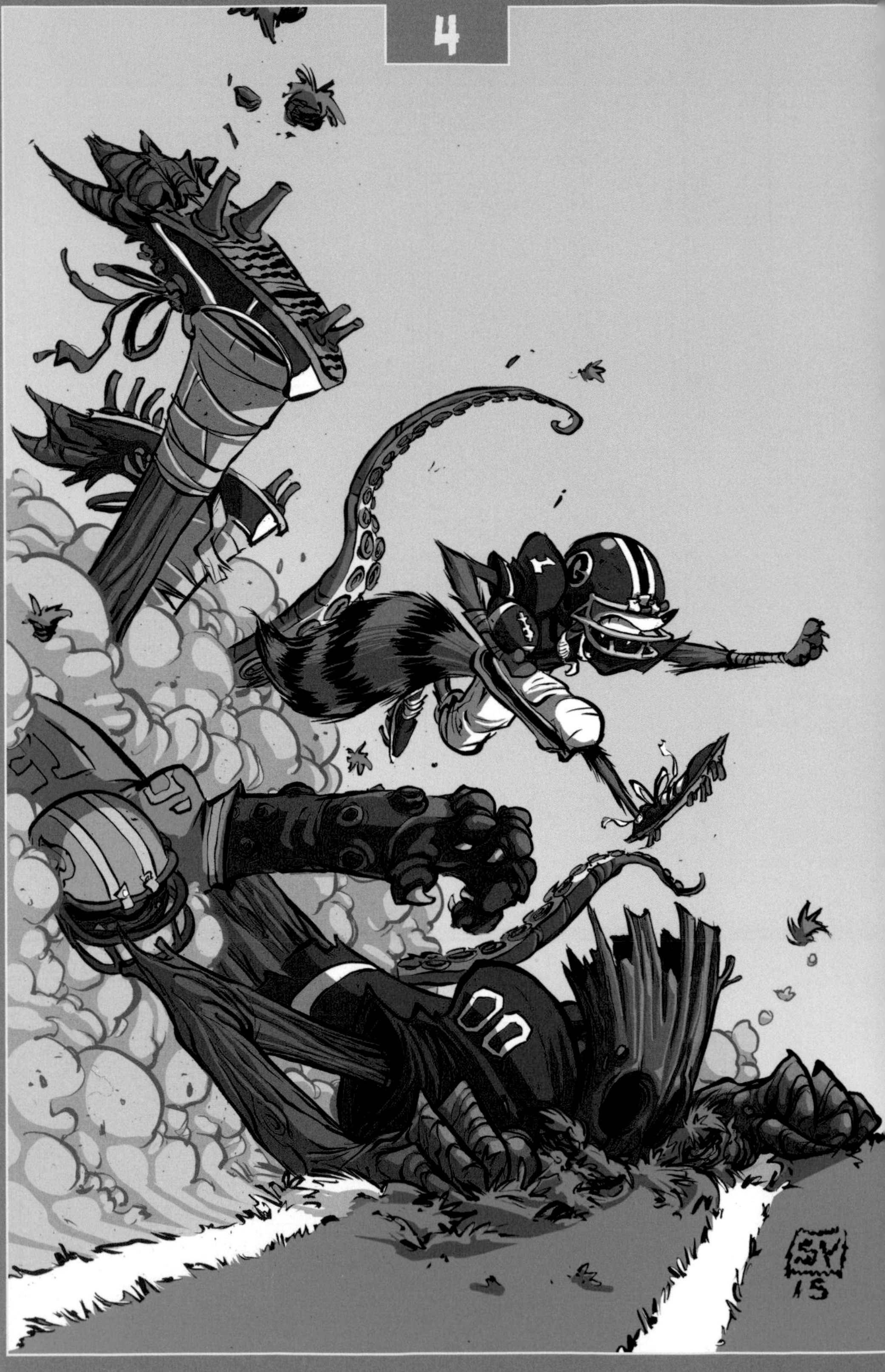
4
00
SV
15

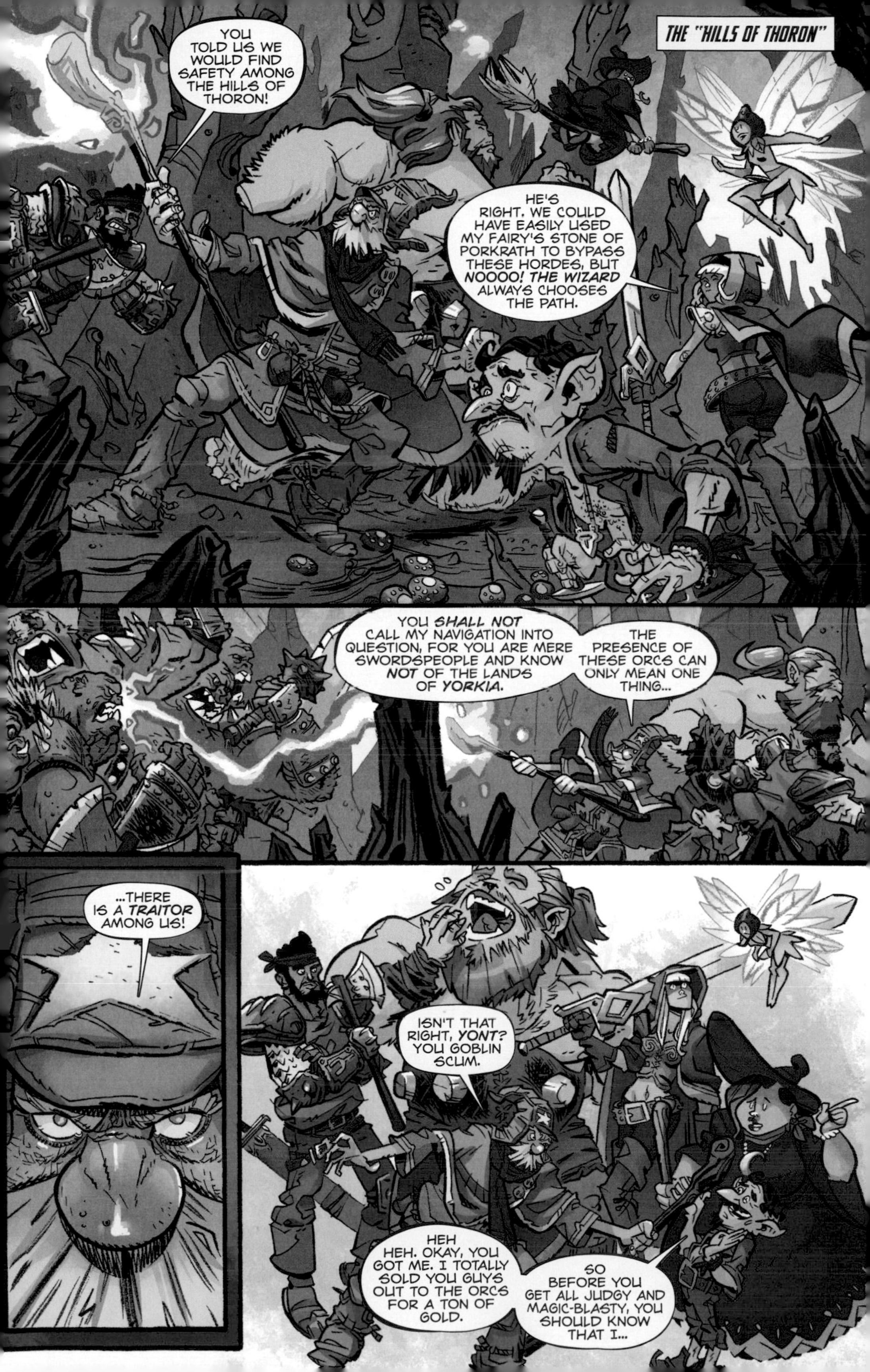
THE "HILLS OF THORON"
YOU TOLD US WE WOULD FIND SAFETY AMONG THE HILLS OF THORON!
HE'S RIGHT. WE COULD HAVE EASILY USED MY FAIRY'S STONE OF PORKRATH TO BYPASS THESE HORDES, BUT NOOOO! THE WIZARD ALWAYS CHOOSES THE PATH.
YOU SHALL NOT CALL MY NAVIGATION INTO QUESTION, FOR YOU ARE MERE SWORDSPEOPLE AND KNOW NOT OF THE LANDS OF YORKIA.
THE PRESENCE OF THESE ORCS CAN ONLY MEAN ONE THING...
...THERE IS A TRAITOR AMONG US!
ISN'T THAT RIGHT, YONT? YOU GOBLIN SCUM.
HEH HEH. OKAY, YOU GOT ME. I TOTALLY SOLD YOU GUYS OUT TO THE ORCS FOR A TON OF GOLD.
SO BEFORE YOU GET ALL JUDGY AND MAGIC-BLASTY, YOU SHOULD KNOW THAT I...

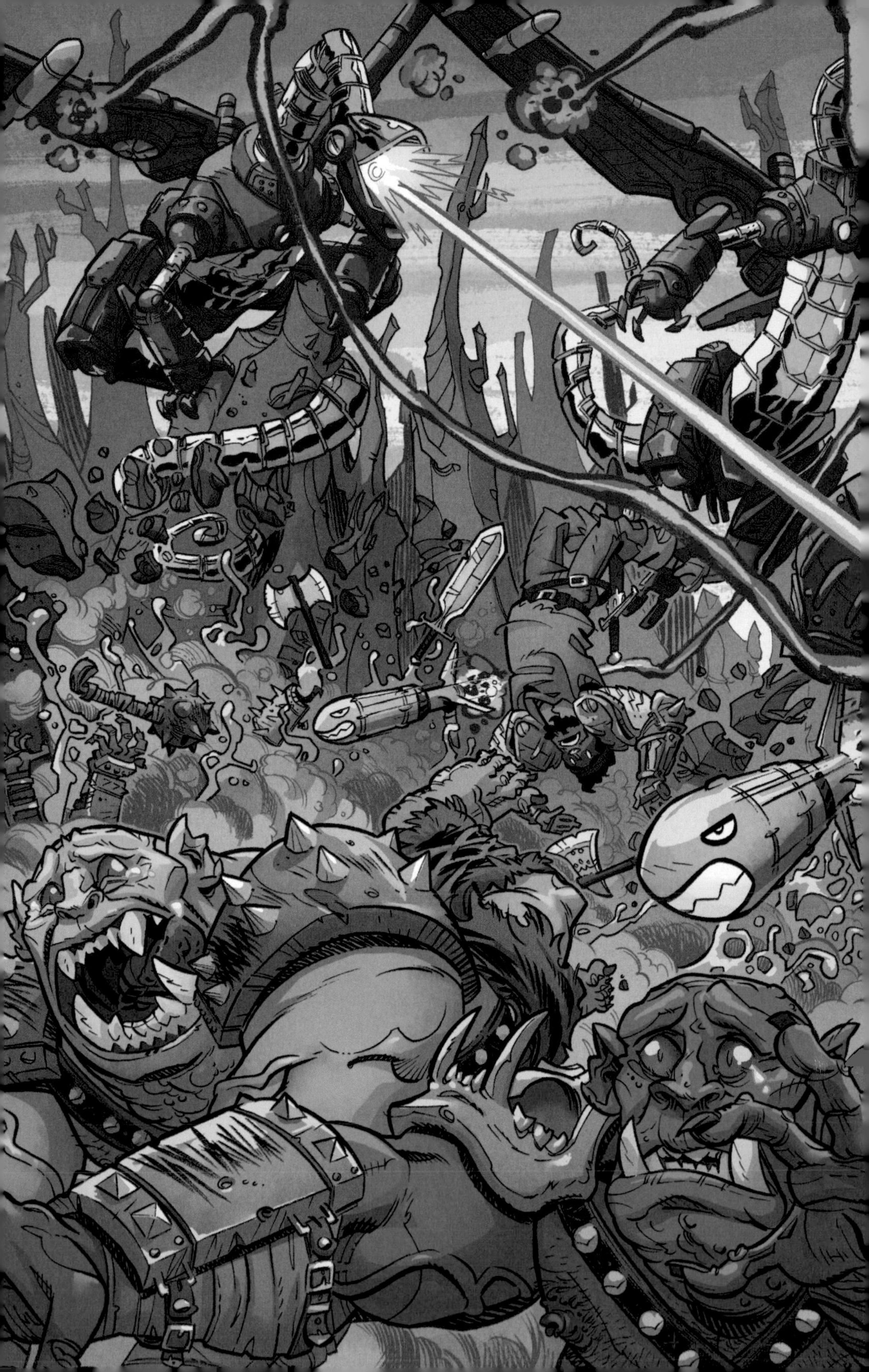

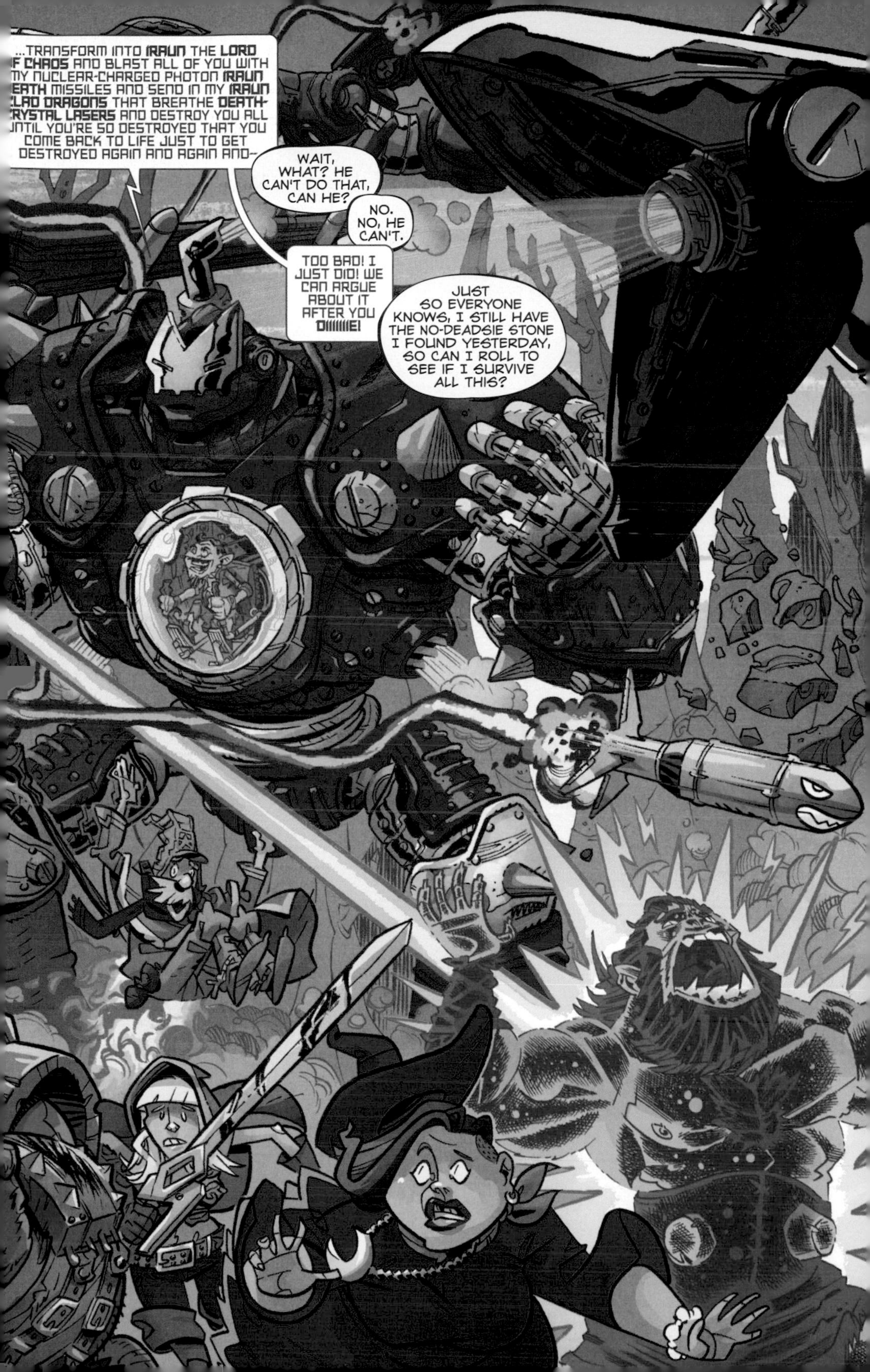
...TRANSFORM INTO IRAUN THE LORD OF CHAOS AND BLAST ALL OF YOU WITH MY NUCLEAR-CHARGED PHOTON IRAUN DEATH MISSILES AND SEND IN MY IRAUN CLAD DRAGONS THAT BREATHE DEATH-CRYSTAL LASERS AND DESTROY YOU ALL UNTIL YOU'RE SO DESTROYED THAT YOU COME BACK TO LIFE JUST TO GET DESTROYED AGAIN AND AGAIN AND--
WAIT, WHAT? HE CAN'T DO THAT, CAN HE?
NO. NO, HE CAN'T.
TOO BAD! I JUST DID! WE CAN ARGUE ABOUT IT AFTER YOU DIIIIIE!
JUST SO EVERYONE KNOWS, I STILL HAVE THE NO-DEADSIE STONE I FOUND YESTERDAY, SO CAN I ROLL TO SEE IF I SURVIVE ALL THIS?

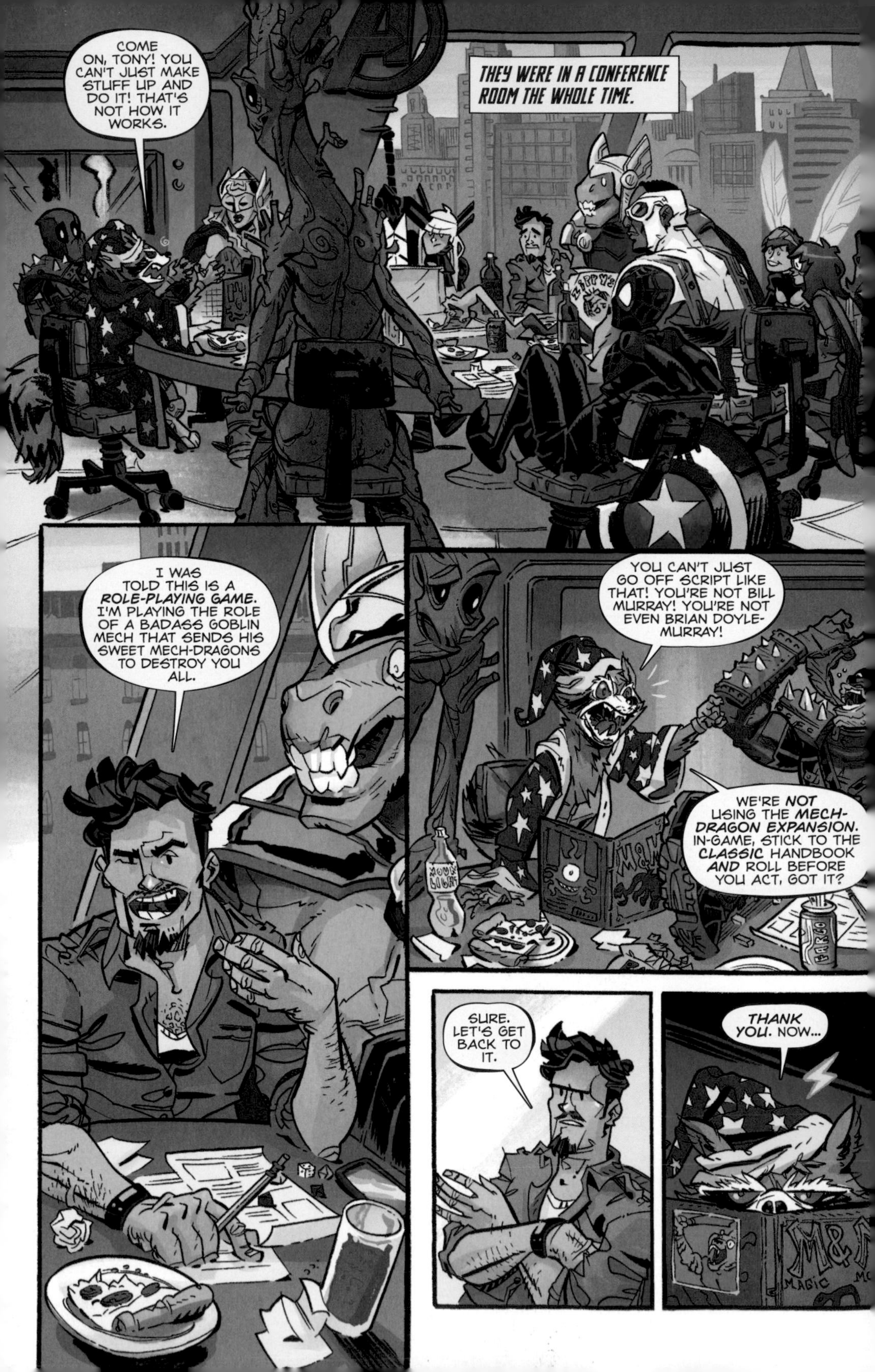
COME ON, TONY! YOU CAN'T JUST MAKE STUFF UP AND DO IT! THAT'S NOT HOW IT WORKS.
THEY WERE IN A CONFERENCE ROOM THE WHOLE TIME.
I WAS TOLD THIS IS A ROLE-PLAYING GAME. I'M PLAYING THE ROLE OF A BADASS GOBLIN MECH THAT SENDS HIS SWEET MECH-DRAGONS TO DESTROY YOU ALL.
YOU CAN'T JUST GO OFF SCRIPT LIKE THAT! YOU'RE NOT BILL MURRAY! YOU'RE NOT EVEN BRIAN DOYLE-MURRAY!
WE'RE NOT USING THE MECH-DRAGON EXPANSION. IN-GAME, STICK TO THE CLASSIC HANDBOOK AND ROLL BEFORE YOU ACT, GOT IT?
FARGO
SURE. LET'S GET BACK TO IT.
THANK YOU. NOW...
M&M
MAGIC

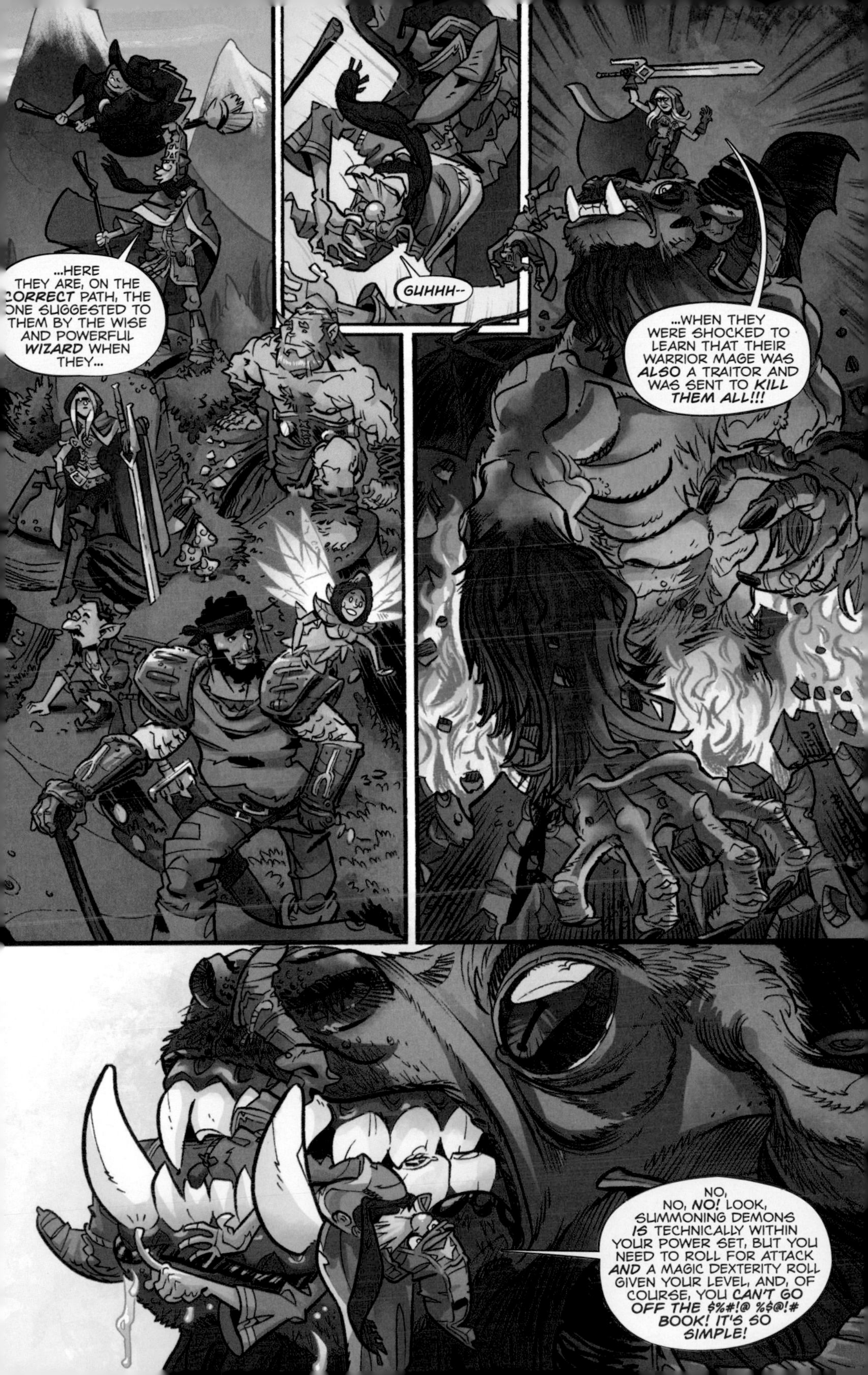
...HERE THEY ARE, ON THE CORRECT PATH, THE ONE SUGGESTED TO THEM BY THE WISE AND POWERFUL WIZARD WHEN THEY...
GUHHH--
...WHEN THEY WERE SHOCKED TO LEARN THAT THEIR WARRIOR MAGE WAS ALSO A TRAITOR AND WAS SENT TO KILL THEM ALL!!!
NO, NO, NO! LOOK, SUMMONING DEMONS IS TECHNICALLY WITHIN YOUR POWER SET, BUT YOU NEED TO ROLL FOR ATTACK AND A MAGIC DEXTERITY ROLL GIVEN YOUR LEVEL, AND, OF COURSE, YOU CAN'T GO OFF THE $%#!@ %$@!# BOOK! IT'S SO SIMPLE!

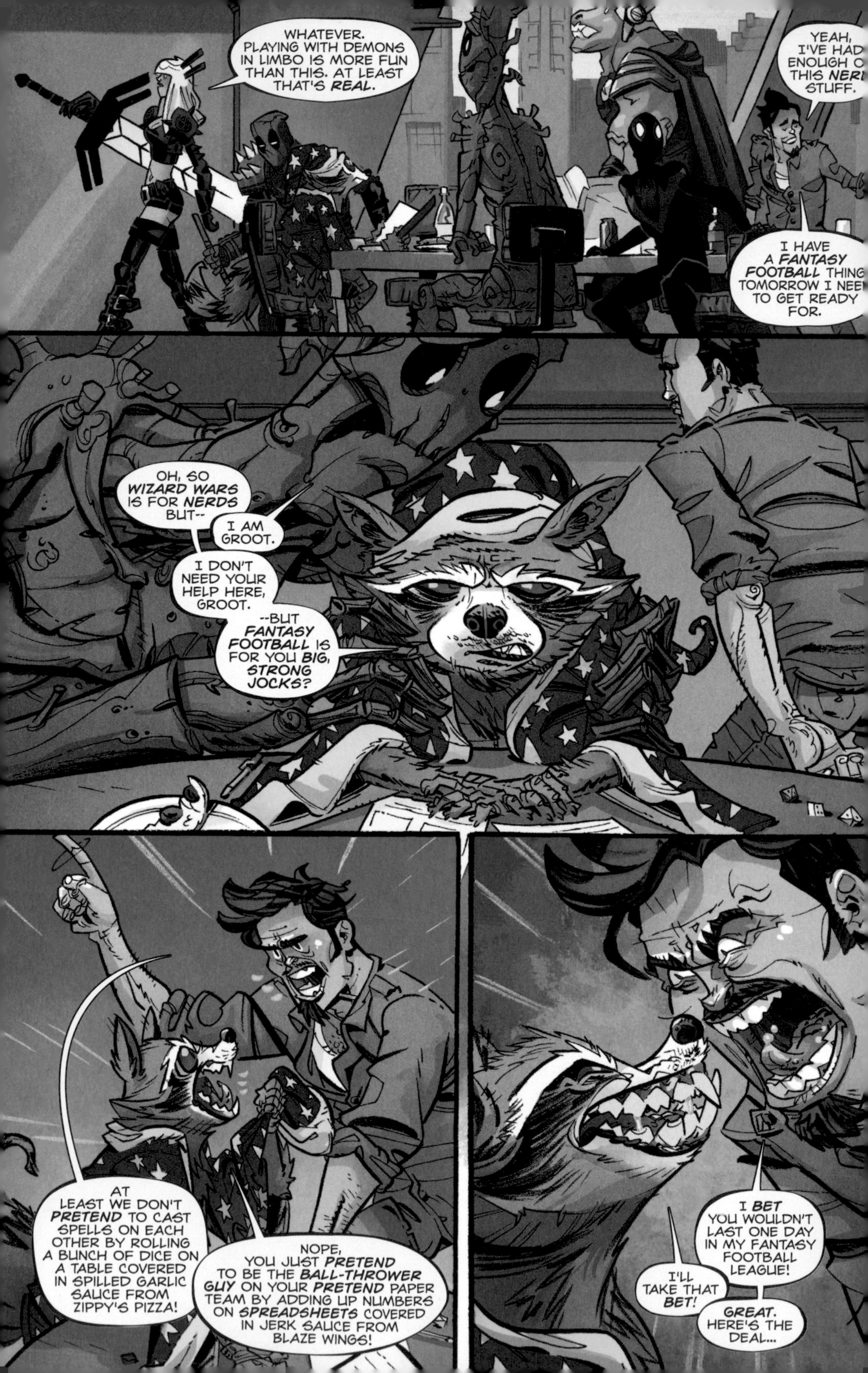

WHATEVER. PLAYING WITH DEMONS IN LIMBO IS MORE FUN THAN THIS. AT LEAST THAT'S *REAL*.
YEAH, I'VE HAD ENOUGH O THIS *NERD* STUFF.
I HAVE A *FANTASY FOOTBALL* THING TOMORROW I NEE TO GET READY FOR.
OH, SO *WIZARD WARS* IS FOR *NERDS* BUT--
I AM GROOT.
I DON'T NEED YOUR HELP HERE, GROOT.
--BUT *FANTASY FOOTBALL* IS FOR YOU *BIG, STRONG JOCKS*?
AT LEAST WE DON'T *PRETEND* TO CAST SPELLS ON EACH OTHER BY ROLLING A BUNCH OF DICE ON A TABLE COVERED IN SPILLED GARLIC SAUCE FROM ZIPPY'S PIZZA!
NOPE, YOU JUST *PRETEND* TO BE THE *BALL-THROWER GUY* ON YOUR *PRETEND* PAPER TEAM BY ADDING UP NUMBERS ON *SPREADSHEETS* COVERED IN JERK SAUCE FROM BLAZE WINGS!
I *BET* YOU WOULDN'T LAST ONE DAY IN MY FANTASY FOOTBALL LEAGUE!
I'LL TAKE THAT *BET*!
*GREAT*. HERE'S THE DEAL...

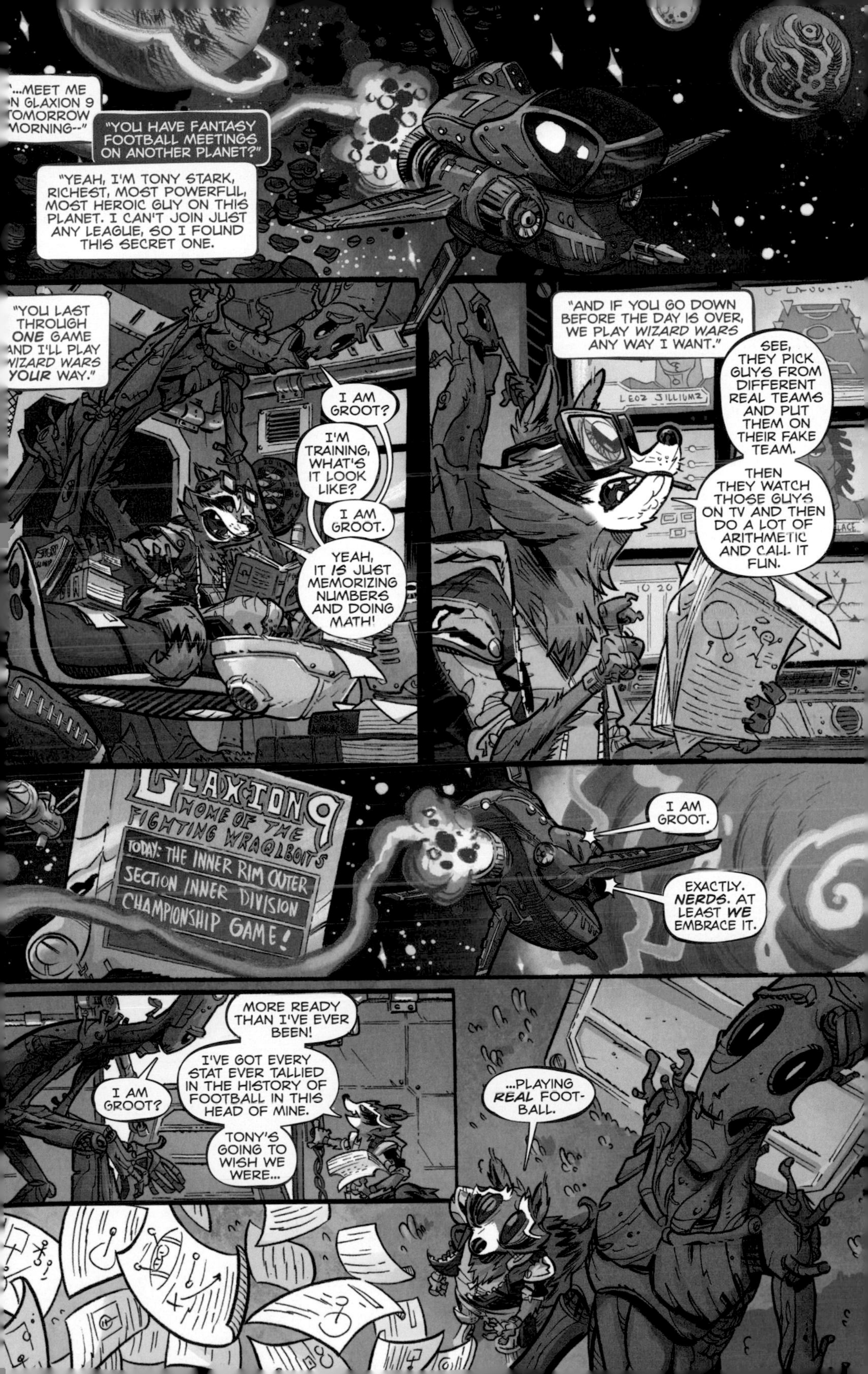
"...MEET ME ON GLAXION 9 TOMORROW MORNING--"
"YOU HAVE FANTASY FOOTBALL MEETINGS ON ANOTHER PLANET?"
"YEAH, I'M TONY STARK, RICHEST, MOST POWERFUL, MOST HEROIC GUY ON THIS PLANET. I CAN'T JOIN JUST ANY LEAGUE, SO I FOUND THIS SECRET ONE.
"YOU LAST THROUGH ONE GAME AND I'LL PLAY WIZARD WARS YOUR WAY."
I AM GROOT?
I'M TRAINING, WHAT'S IT LOOK LIKE?
I AM GROOT.
YEAH, IT IS JUST MEMORIZING NUMBERS AND DOING MATH!
"AND IF YOU GO DOWN BEFORE THE DAY IS OVER, WE PLAY WIZARD WARS ANY WAY I WANT."
SEE, THEY PICK GUYS FROM DIFFERENT REAL TEAMS AND PUT THEM ON THEIR FAKE TEAM.
THEN THEY WATCH THOSE GUYS ON TV AND THEN DO A LOT OF ARITHMETIC AND CALL IT FUN.
GLAXION 9
HOME OF THE FIGHTING WRAQLBOITS
TODAY: THE INNER RIM OUTER SECTION INNER DIVISION CHAMPIONSHIP GAME!
I AM GROOT.
EXACTLY. NERDS. AT LEAST WE EMBRACE IT.
I AM GROOT?
MORE READY THAN I'VE EVER BEEN!
I'VE GOT EVERY STAT EVER TALLIED IN THE HISTORY OF FOOTBALL IN THIS HEAD OF MINE.
TONY'S GOING TO WISH WE WERE...
...PLAYING REAL FOOT-BALL.

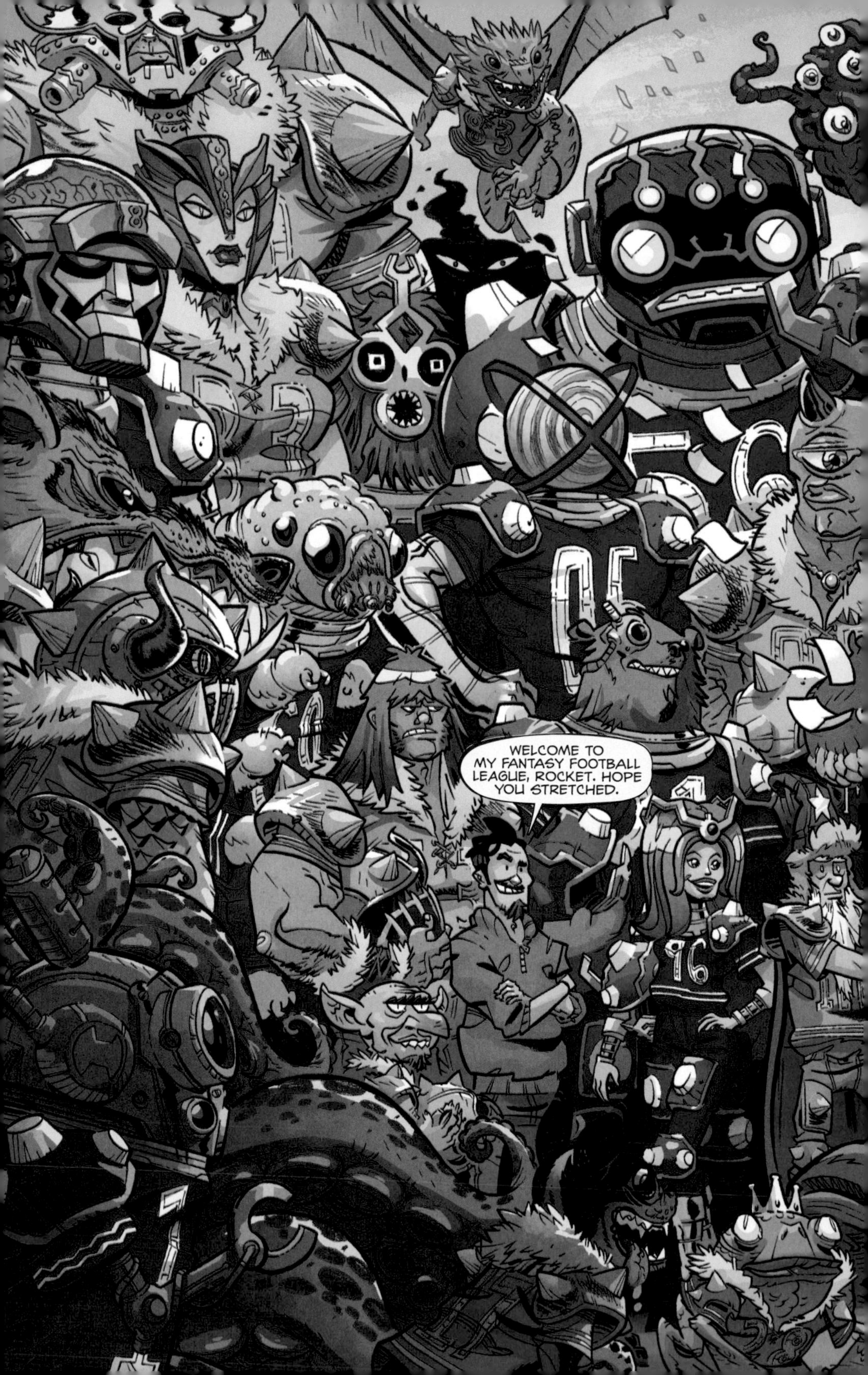
WELCOME TO MY FANTASY FOOTBALL LEAGUE, ROCKET. HOPE YOU STRETCHED.

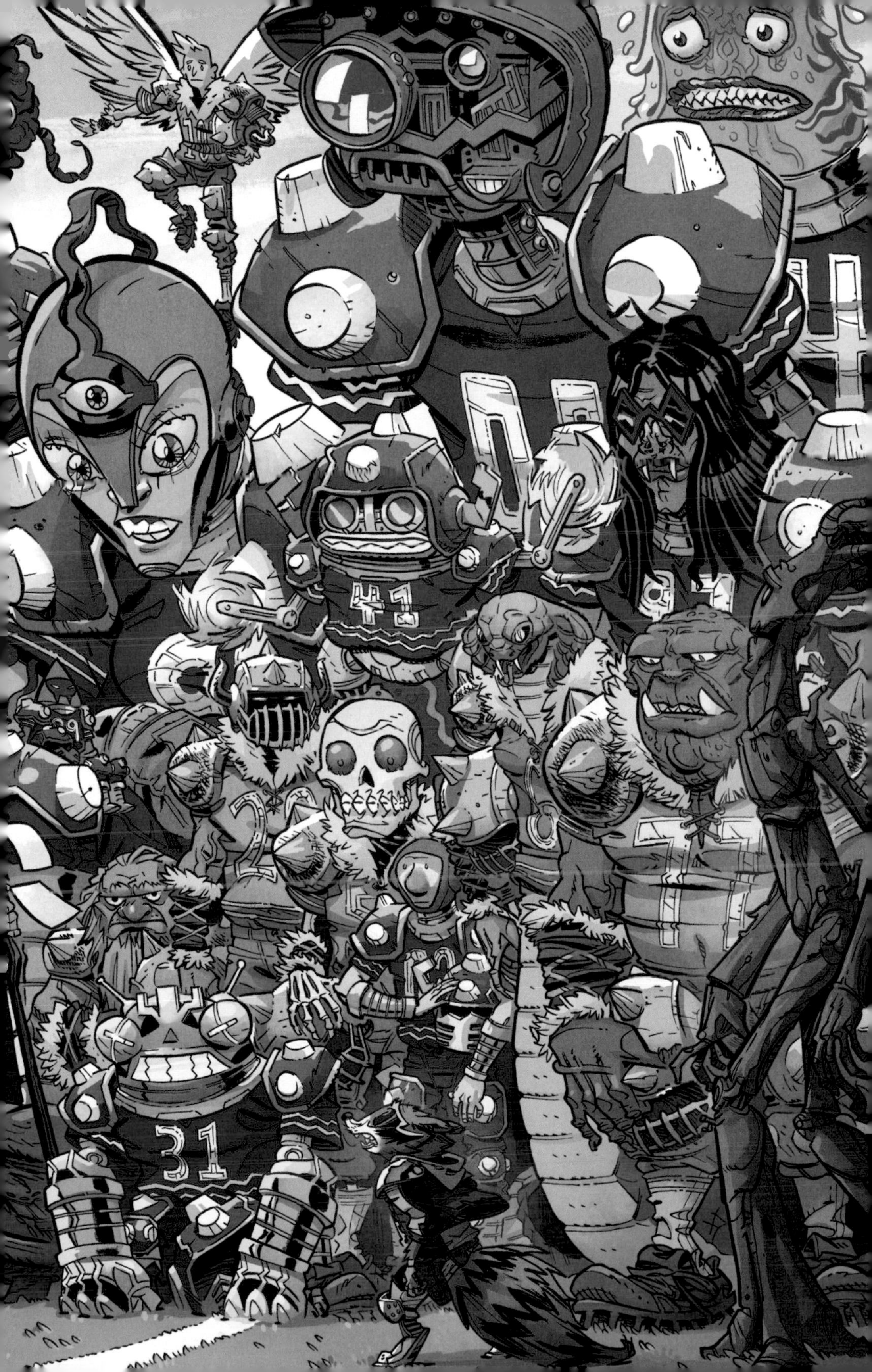
41
31

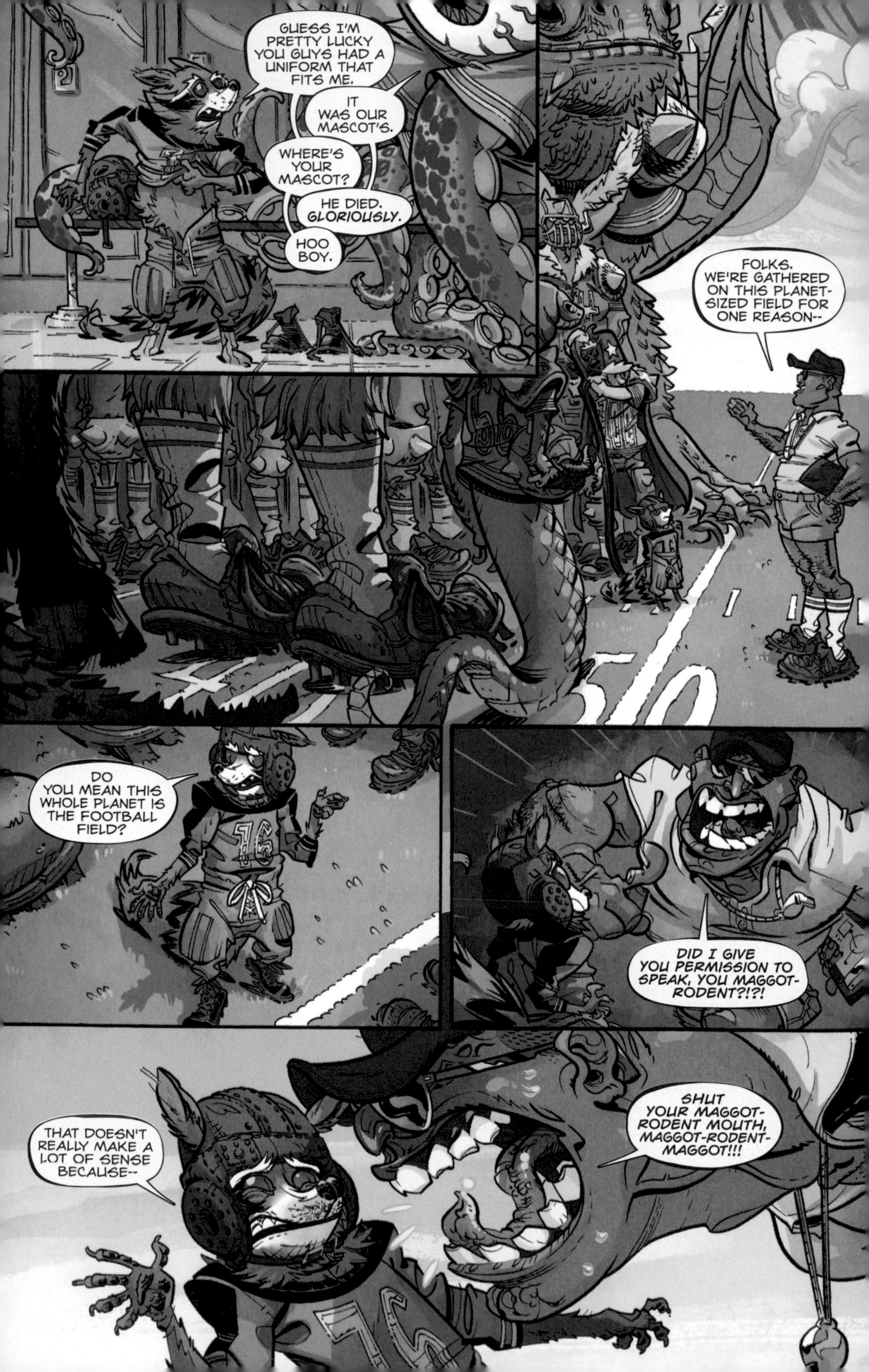
GUESS I'M PRETTY LUCKY YOU GUYS HAD A UNIFORM THAT FITS ME.
IT WAS OUR MASCOT'S.
WHERE'S YOUR MASCOT?
HE DIED. *GLORIOUSLY.*
HOO BOY.
FOLKS. WE'RE GATHERED ON THIS PLANET-SIZED FIELD FOR ONE REASON--
DO YOU MEAN THIS WHOLE PLANET IS THE FOOTBALL FIELD?
DID I GIVE YOU PERMISSION TO SPEAK, YOU MAGGOT-RODENT?!?!
THAT DOESN'T REALLY MAKE A LOT OF SENSE BECAUSE--
SHUT YOUR MAGGOT-RODENT MOUTH, MAGGOT-RODENT-MAGGOT!!!

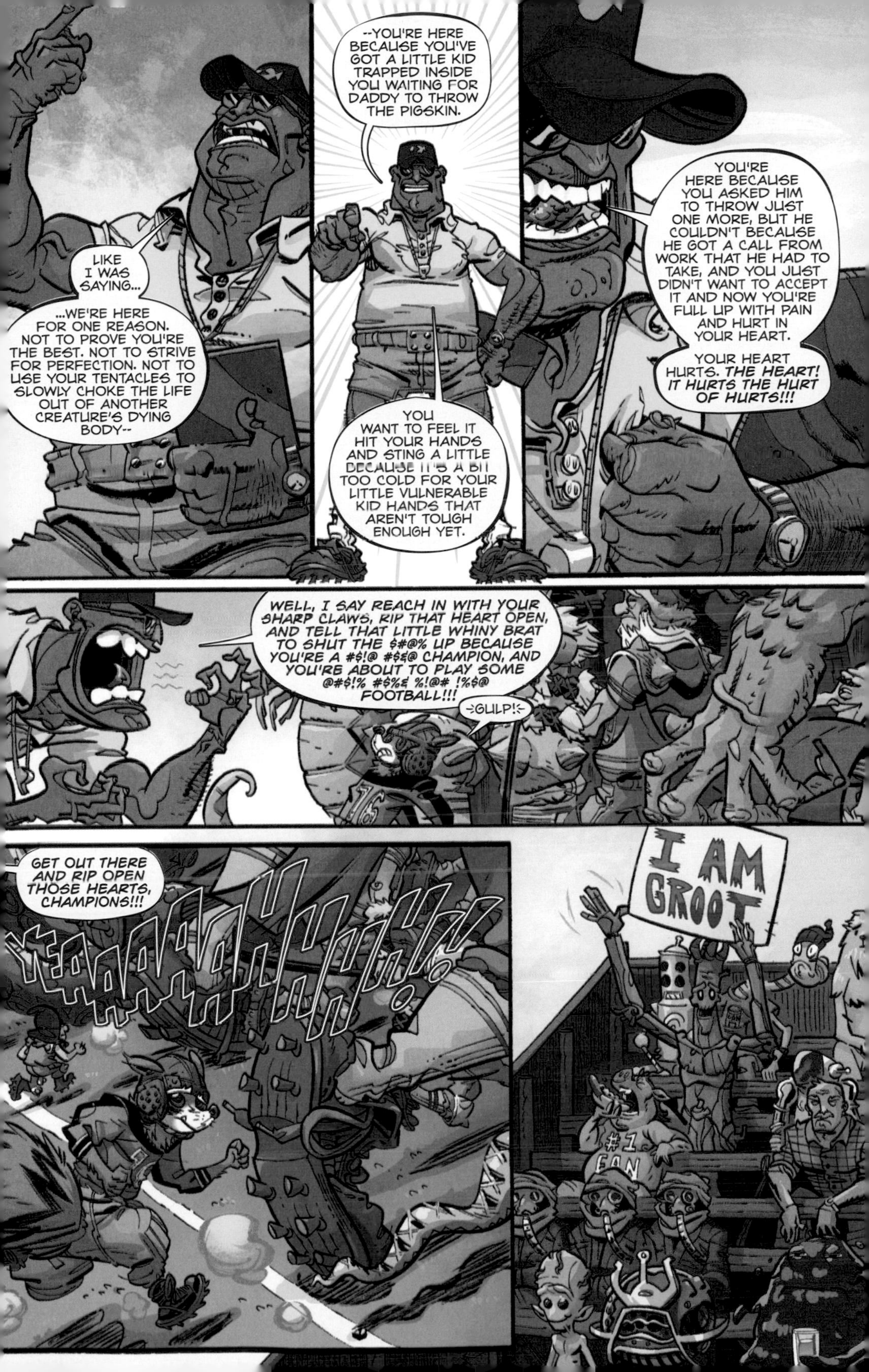
LIKE I WAS SAYING...
...WE'RE HERE FOR ONE REASON. NOT TO PROVE YOU'RE THE BEST. NOT TO STRIVE FOR PERFECTION. NOT TO USE YOUR TENTACLES TO SLOWLY CHOKE THE LIFE OUT OF ANOTHER CREATURE'S DYING BODY--
--YOU'RE HERE BECAUSE YOU'VE GOT A LITTLE KID TRAPPED INSIDE YOU WAITING FOR DADDY TO THROW THE PIGSKIN.
YOU WANT TO FEEL IT HIT YOUR HANDS AND STING A LITTLE BECAUSE IT'S A BIT TOO COLD FOR YOUR LITTLE VULNERABLE KID HANDS THAT AREN'T TOUGH ENOUGH YET.
YOU'RE HERE BECAUSE YOU ASKED HIM TO THROW JUST ONE MORE, BUT HE COULDN'T BECAUSE HE GOT A CALL FROM WORK THAT HE HAD TO TAKE, AND YOU JUST DIDN'T WANT TO ACCEPT IT AND NOW YOU'RE FULL UP WITH PAIN AND HURT IN YOUR HEART.
YOUR HEART HURTS. THE HEART! IT HURTS THE HURT OF HURTS!!!
WELL, I SAY REACH IN WITH YOUR SHARP CLAWS, RIP THAT HEART OPEN, AND TELL THAT LITTLE WHINY BRAT TO SHUT THE $#@% UP BECAUSE YOU'RE A #$!@ #$&@ CHAMPION, AND YOU'RE ABOUT TO PLAY SOME @#$!% #$%& %!@# !%$@ FOOTBALL!!!
GULP!
GET OUT THERE AND RIP OPEN THOSE HEARTS, CHAMPIONS!!!
YEAAAAAAHHHHHH!!
I AM GROOT
#1 FAN

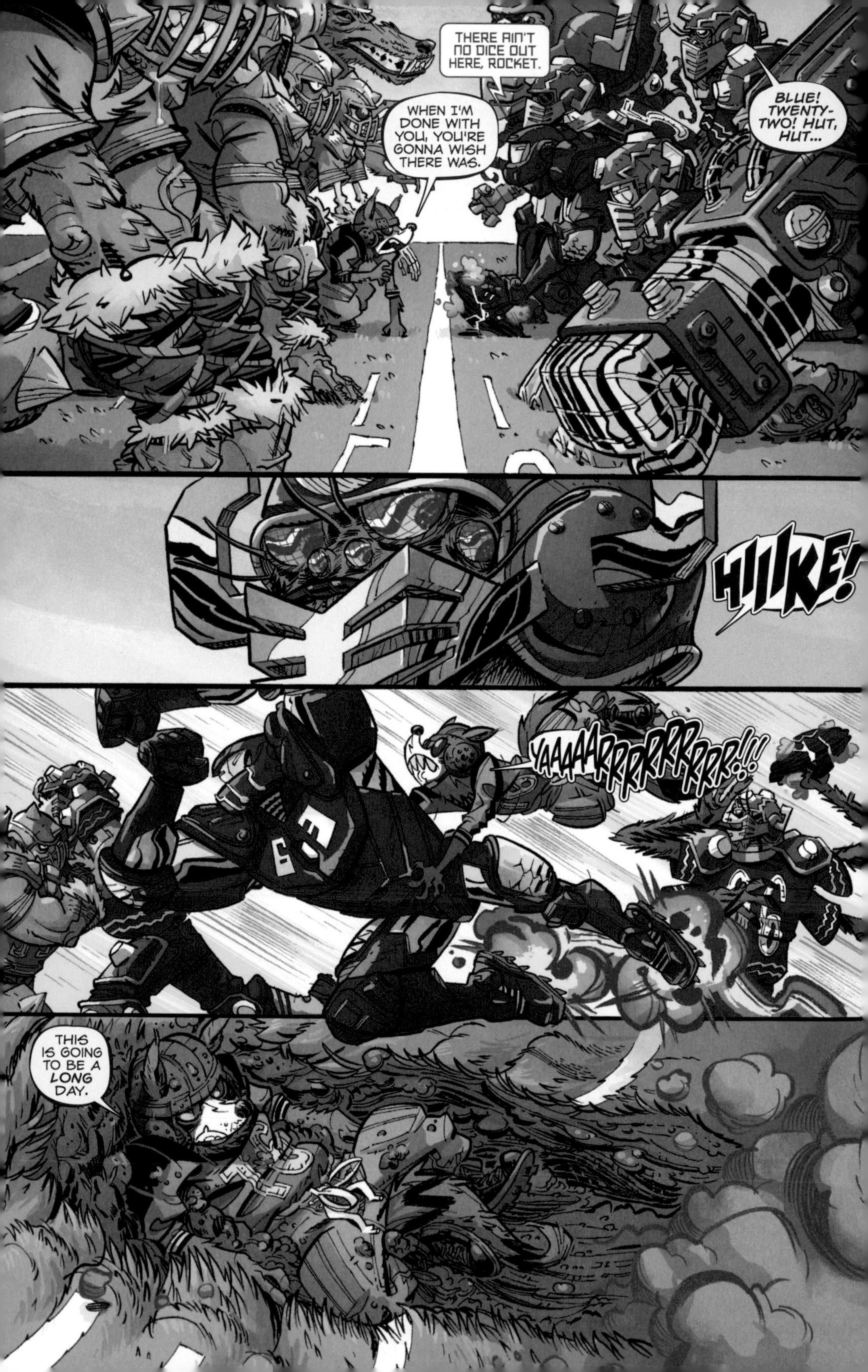
THERE AIN'T NO DICE OUT HERE, ROCKET.
WHEN I'M DONE WITH YOU, YOU'RE GONNA WISH THERE WAS.
BLUE! TWENTY-TWO! HUT, HUT...
HIIIKE!
YAAAAARRRRRRRRR!!!
THIS IS GOING TO BE A LONG DAY.

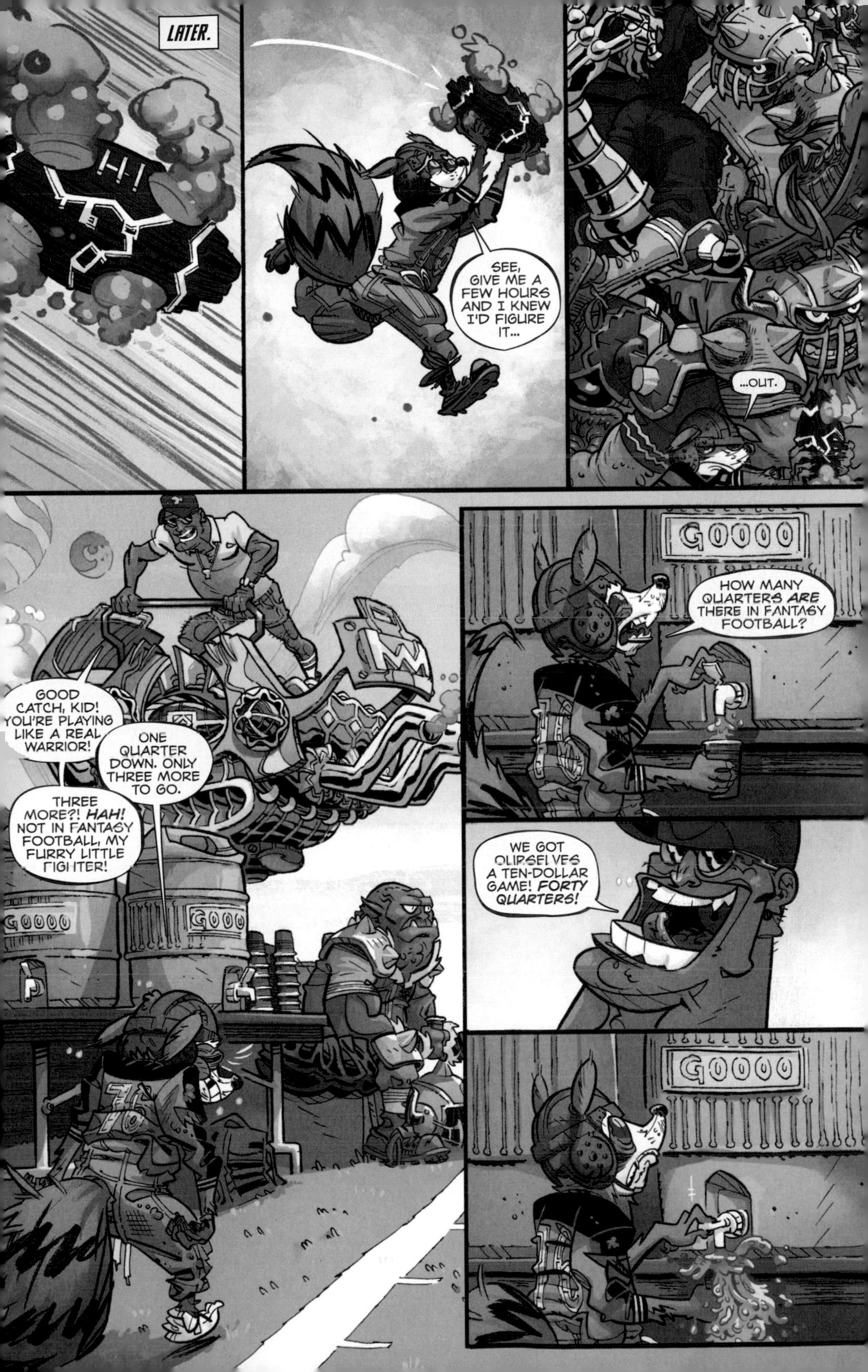
LATER.
SEE, GIVE ME A FEW HOURS AND I KNEW I'D FIGURE IT...
...OUT.
GOOD CATCH, KID! YOU'RE PLAYING LIKE A REAL WARRIOR!
ONE QUARTER DOWN. ONLY THREE MORE TO GO.
THREE MORE?! HAH! NOT IN FANTASY FOOTBALL, MY FURRY LITTLE FIGHTER!
GOOOO
HOW MANY QUARTERS ARE THERE IN FANTASY FOOTBALL?
WE GOT OURSELVES A TEN-DOLLAR GAME! FORTY QUARTERS!
GOOOO

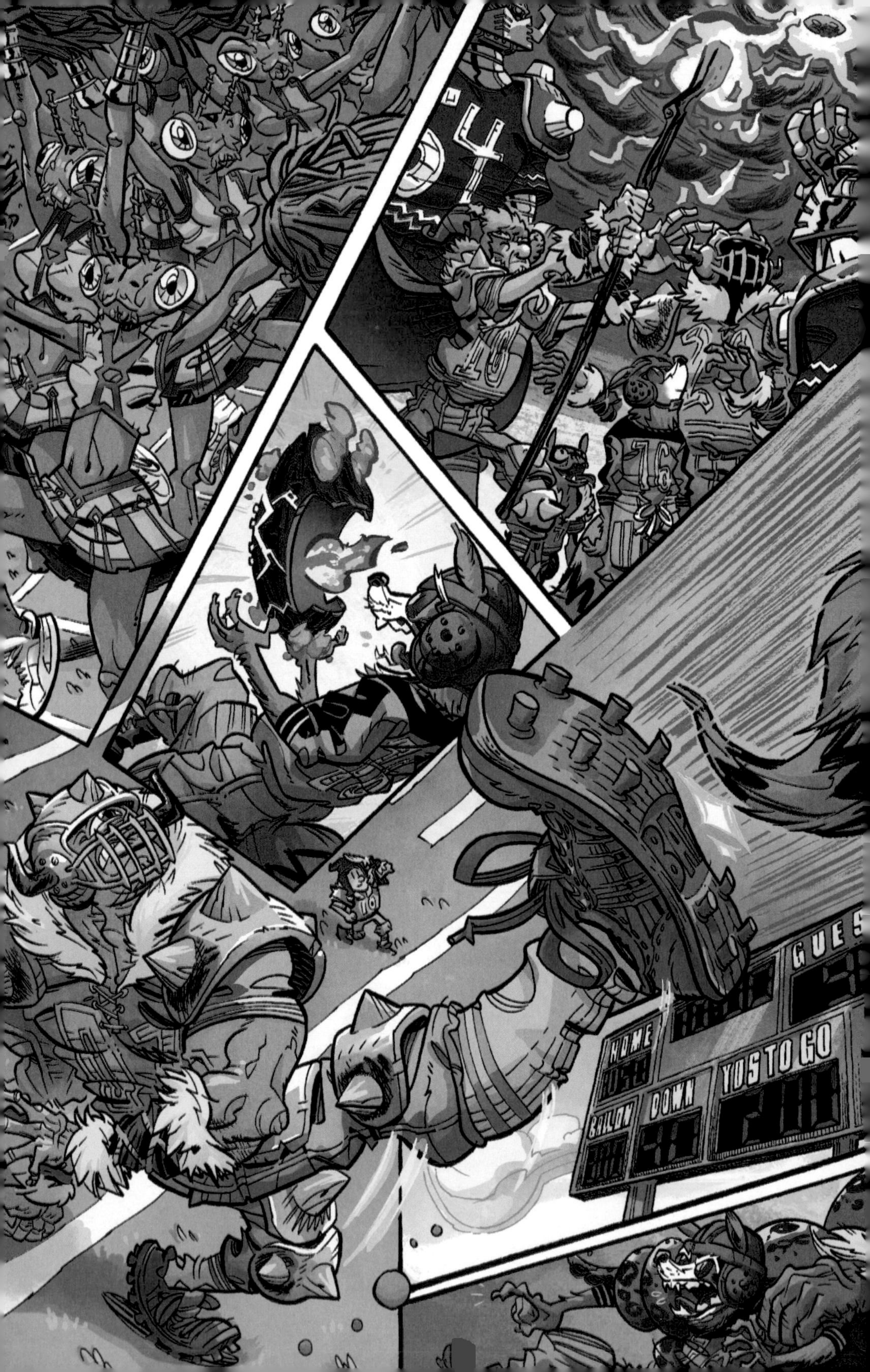
HOME
YDS TO GO
BALL ON
DOWN

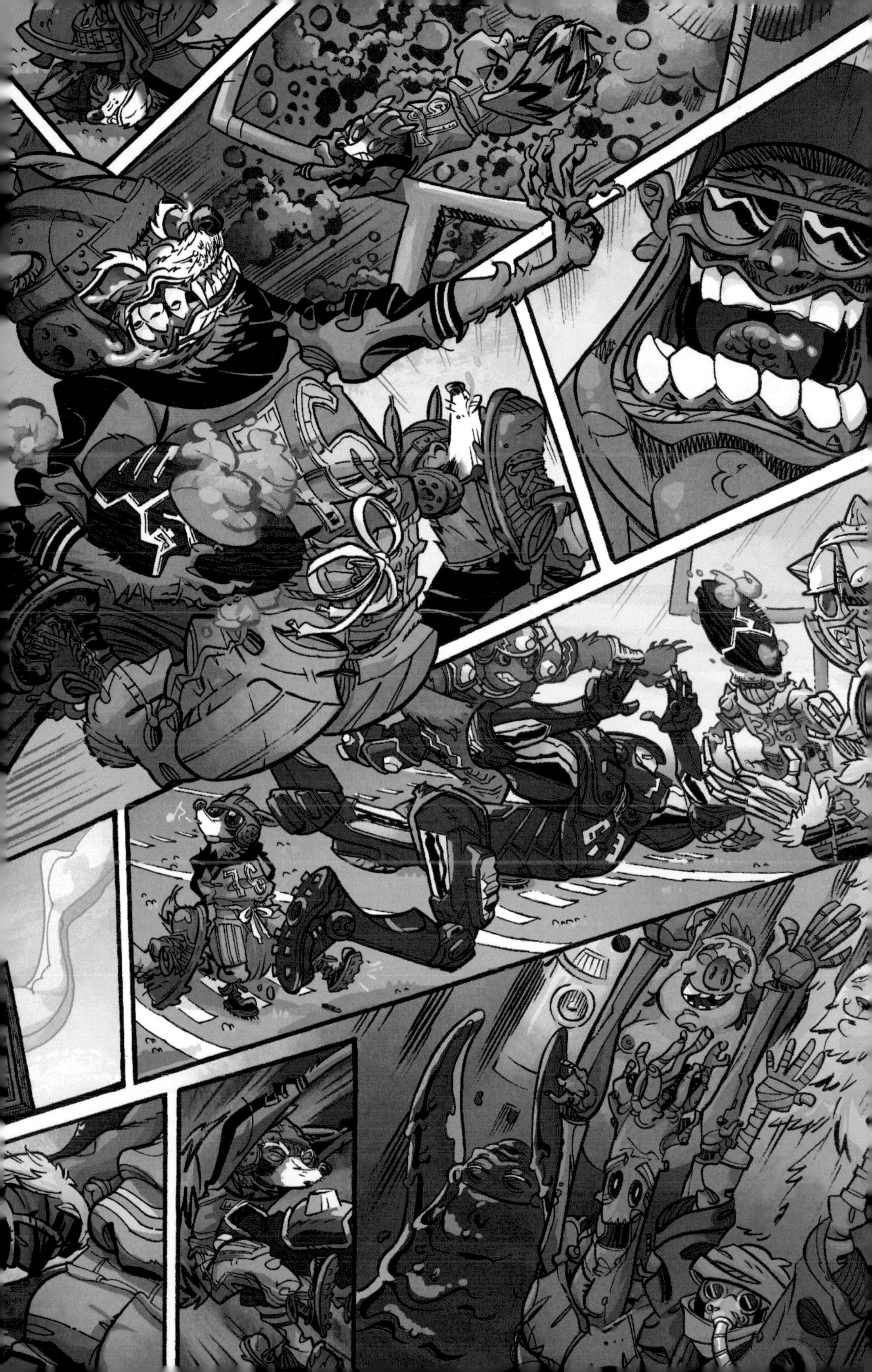

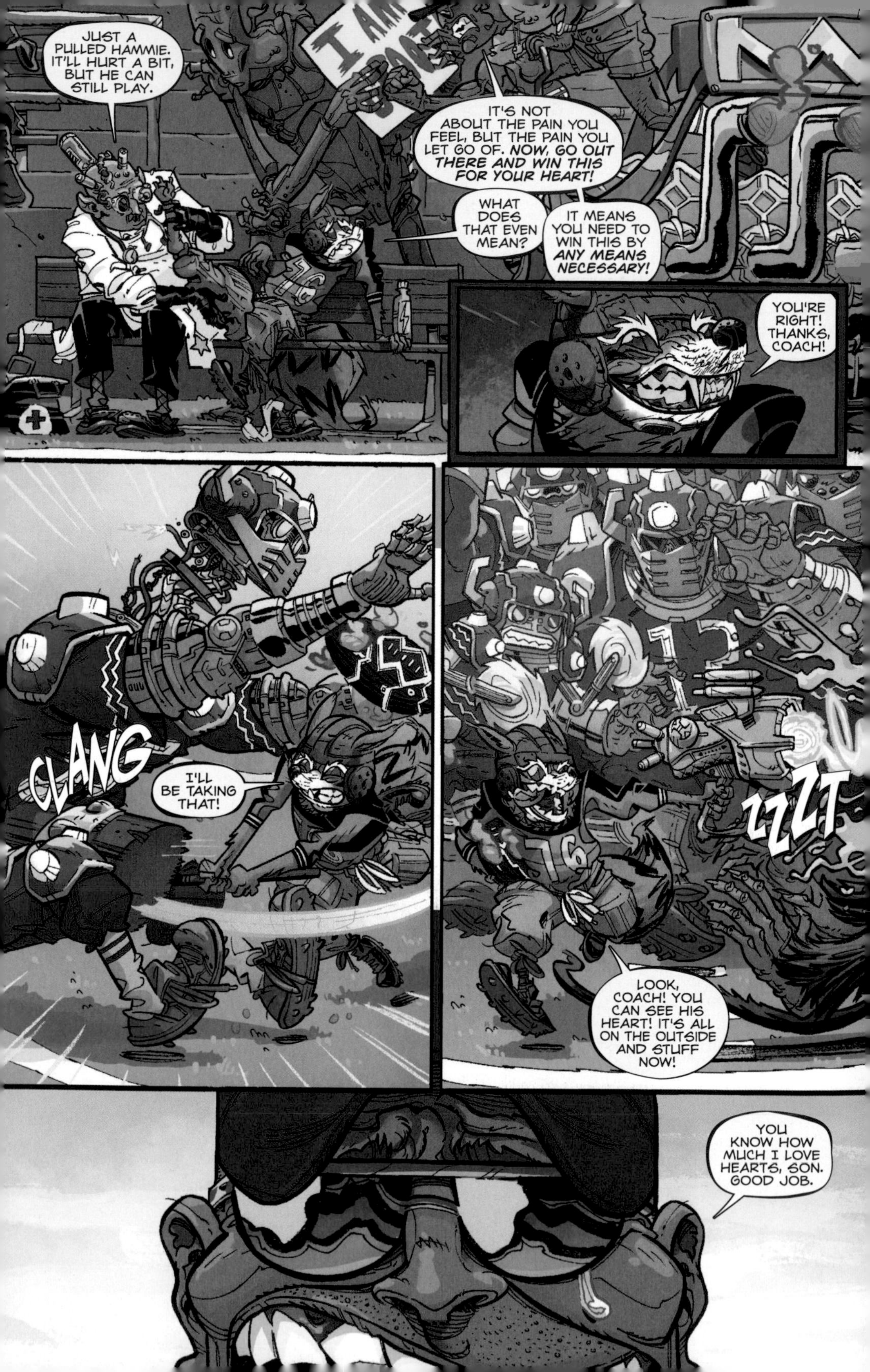

I AM
JUST A PULLED HAMMIE. IT'LL HURT A BIT, BUT HE CAN STILL PLAY.
IT'S NOT ABOUT THE PAIN YOU FEEL, BUT THE PAIN YOU LET GO OF. NOW, GO OUT THERE AND WIN THIS FOR YOUR HEART!
WHAT DOES THAT EVEN MEAN?
IT MEANS YOU NEED TO WIN THIS BY ANY MEANS NECESSARY!
YOU'RE RIGHT! THANKS, COACH!
CLANG
I'LL BE TAKING THAT!
ZZZT
LOOK, COACH! YOU CAN SEE HIS HEART! IT'S ALL ON THE OUTSIDE AND STUFF NOW!
YOU KNOW HOW MUCH I LOVE HEARTS, SON. GOOD JOB.

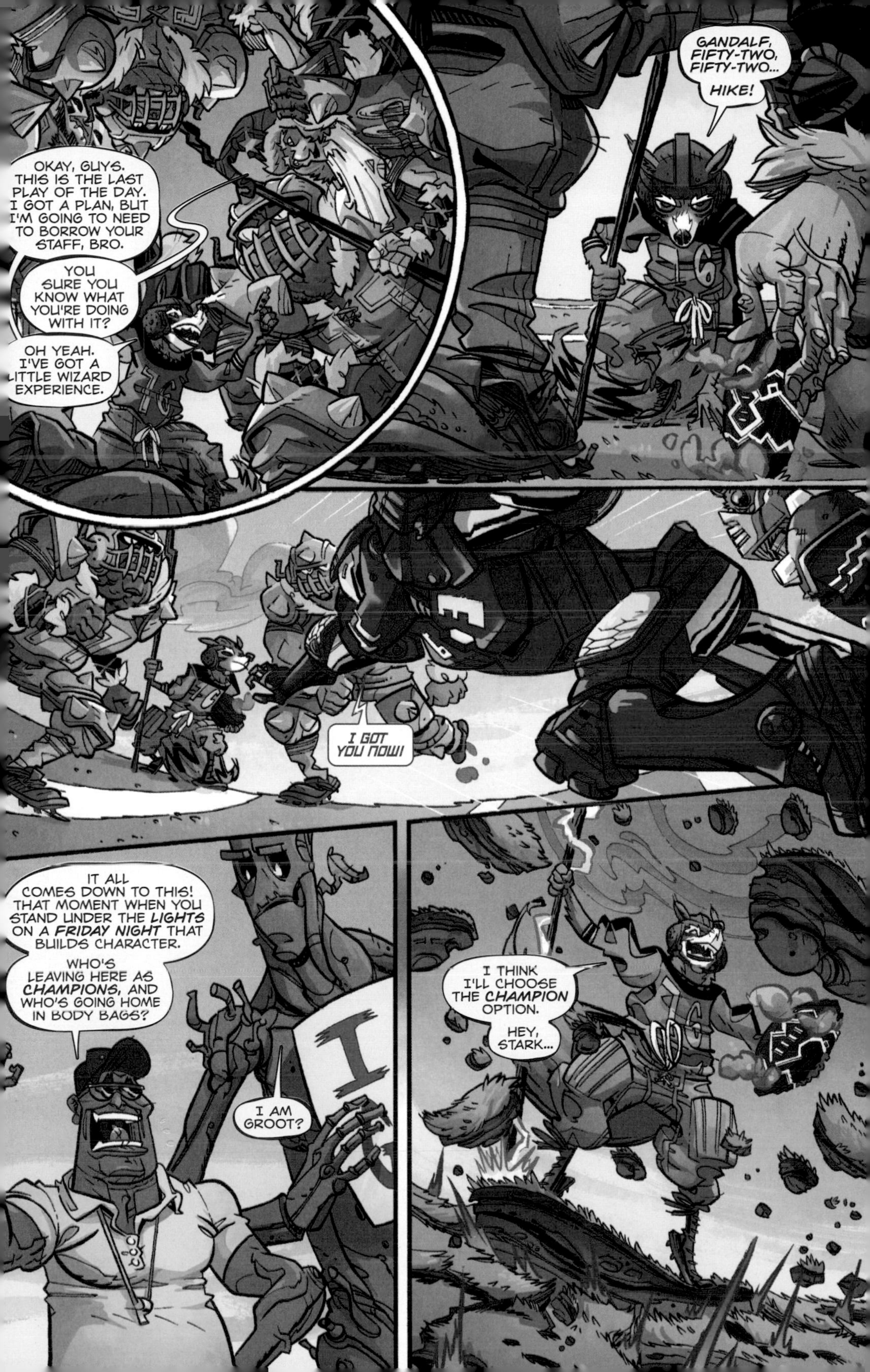

OKAY, GUYS. THIS IS THE LAST PLAY OF THE DAY. I GOT A PLAN, BUT I'M GOING TO NEED TO BORROW YOUR STAFF, BRO.
YOU SURE YOU KNOW WHAT YOU'RE DOING WITH IT?
OH YEAH. I'VE GOT A LITTLE WIZARD EXPERIENCE.
GANDALF, FIFTY-TWO, FIFTY-TWO...
HIKE!
I GOT YOU NOW!
IT ALL COMES DOWN TO THIS! THAT MOMENT WHEN YOU STAND UNDER THE LIGHTS ON A FRIDAY NIGHT THAT BUILDS CHARACTER.
WHO'S LEAVING HERE AS CHAMPIONS, AND WHO'S GOING HOME IN BODY BAGS?
I AM GROOT?
I THINK I'LL CHOOSE THE CHAMPION OPTION.
HEY, STARK...

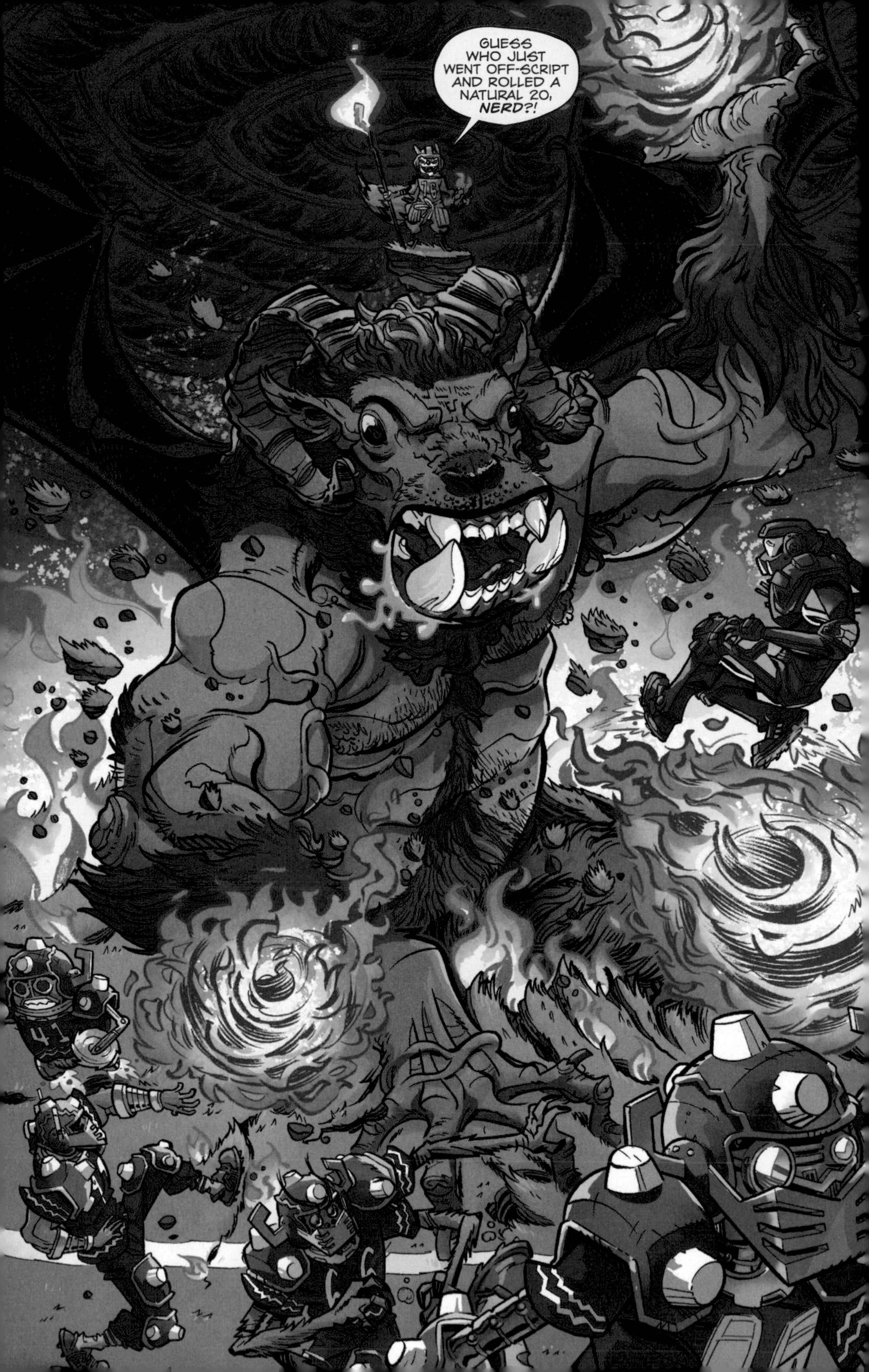
GUESS WHO JUST WENT OFF-SCRIPT AND ROLLED A NATURAL 20, NERD?!

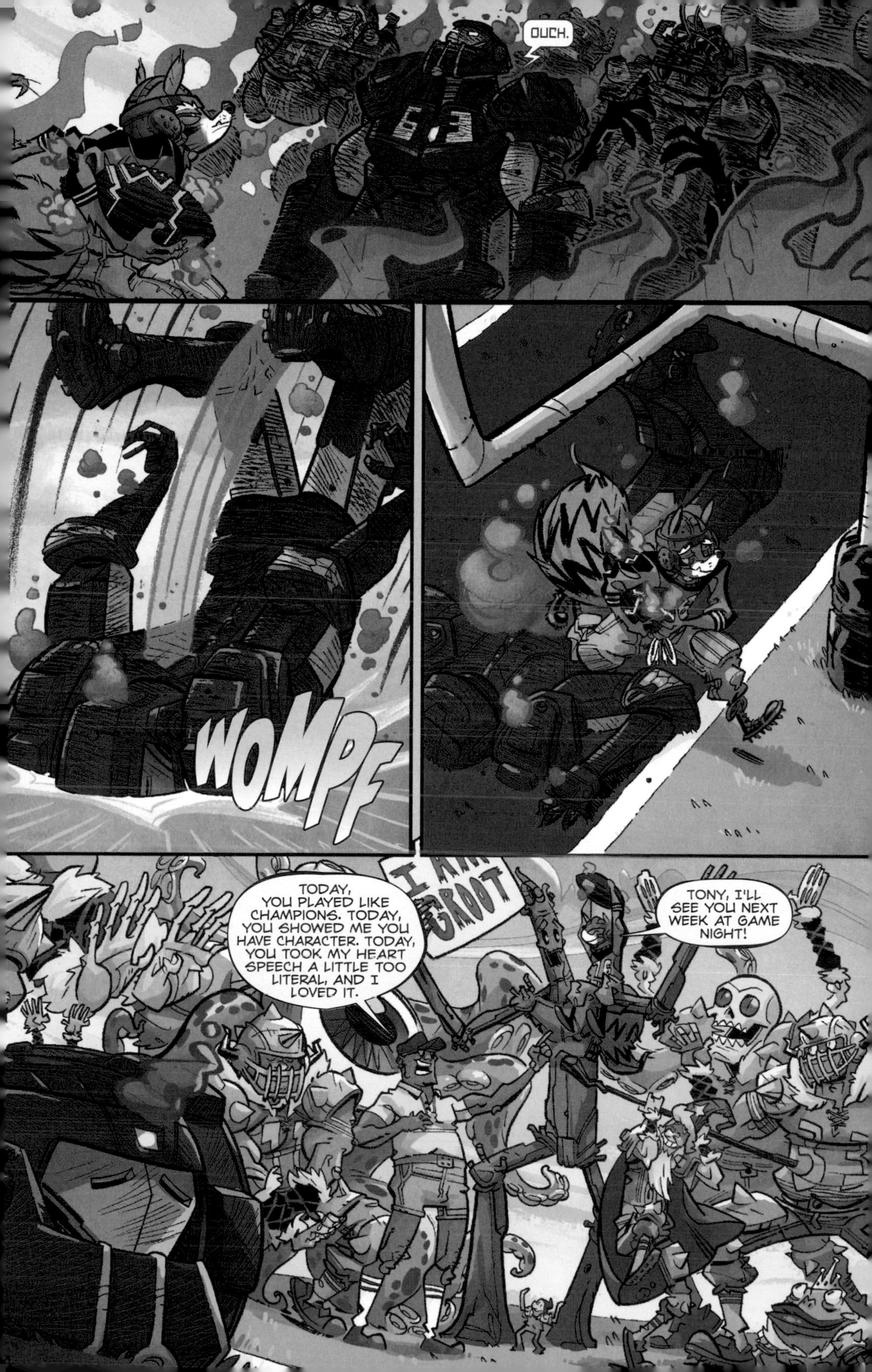
OUCH.
WOMPF
I AM GROOT
TODAY, YOU PLAYED LIKE CHAMPIONS. TODAY, YOU SHOWED ME YOU HAVE CHARACTER. TODAY, YOU TOOK MY HEART SPEECH A LITTLE TOO LITERAL, AND I LOVED IT.
TONY, I'LL SEE YOU NEXT WEEK AT GAME NIGHT!

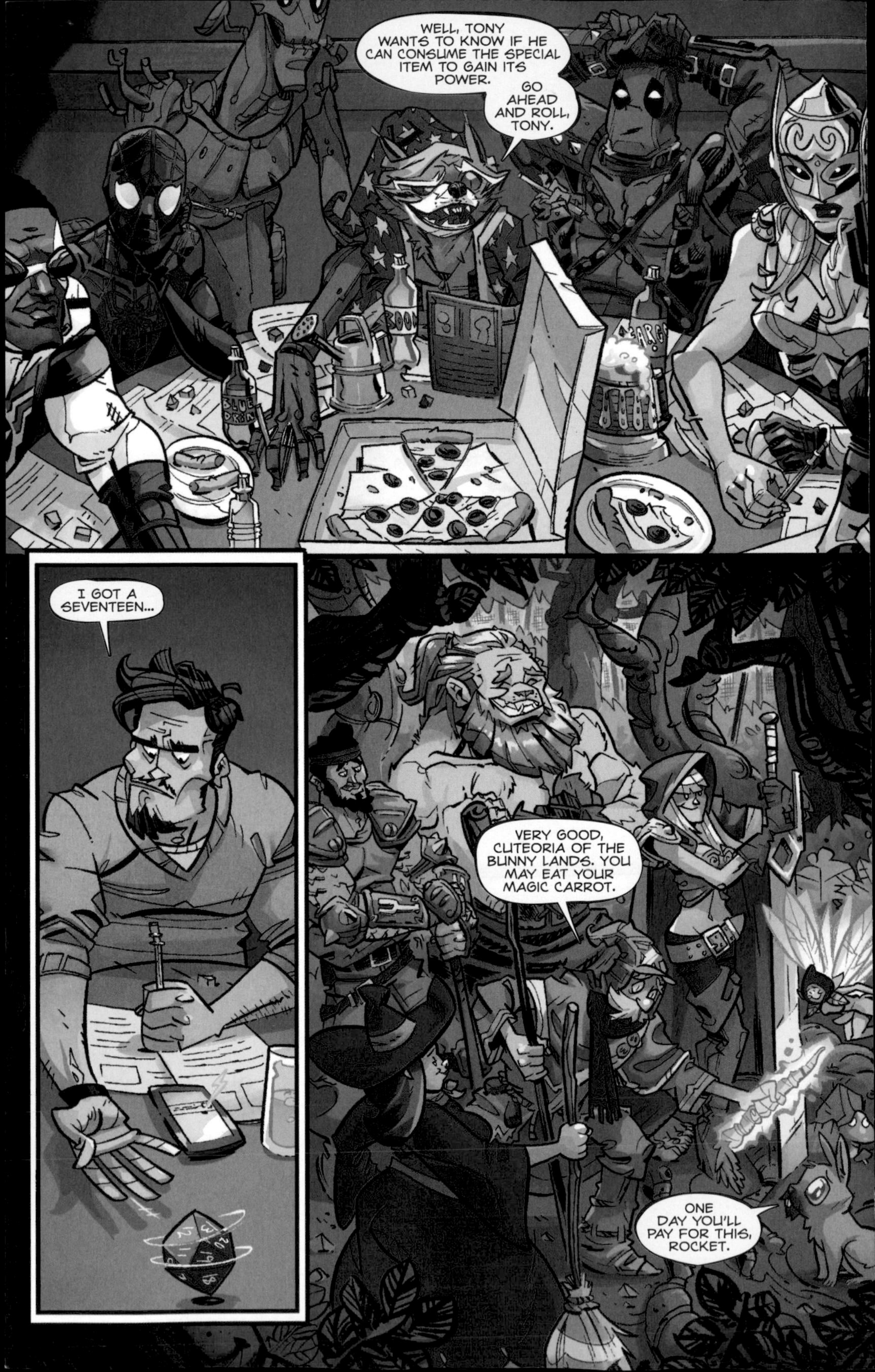
WELL, TONY WANTS TO KNOW IF HE CAN CONSUME THE SPECIAL ITEM TO GAIN ITS POWER.
GO AHEAD AND ROLL, TONY.
BOOM
BLUE DRIN
I GOT A SEVENTEEN...
VERY GOOD, CUTEORIA OF THE BUNNY LANDS. YOU MAY EAT YOUR MAGIC CARROT.
ONE DAY YOU'LL PAY FOR THIS, ROCKET.

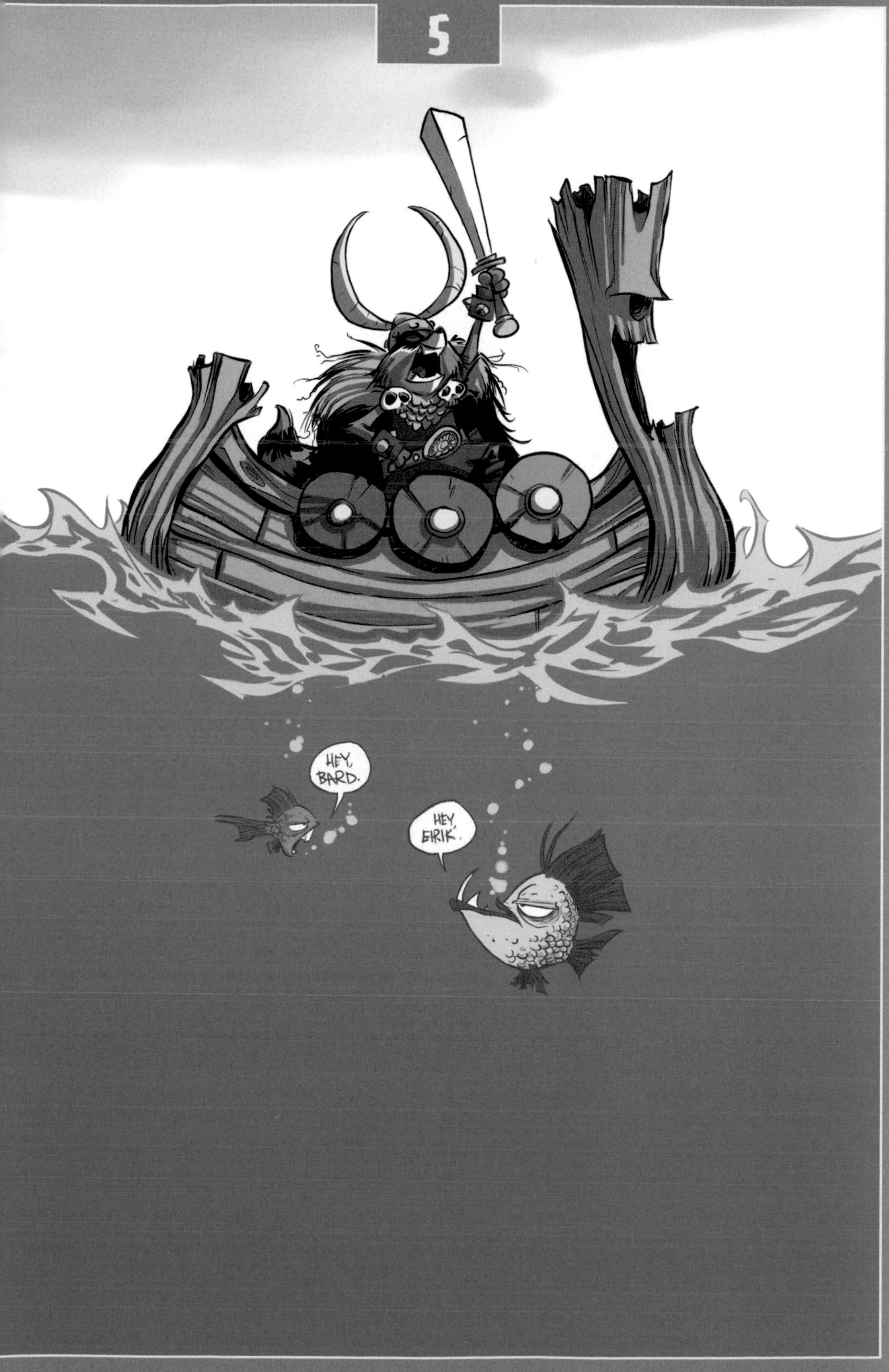
5
HEY, BARD.
HEY, EIRIK.

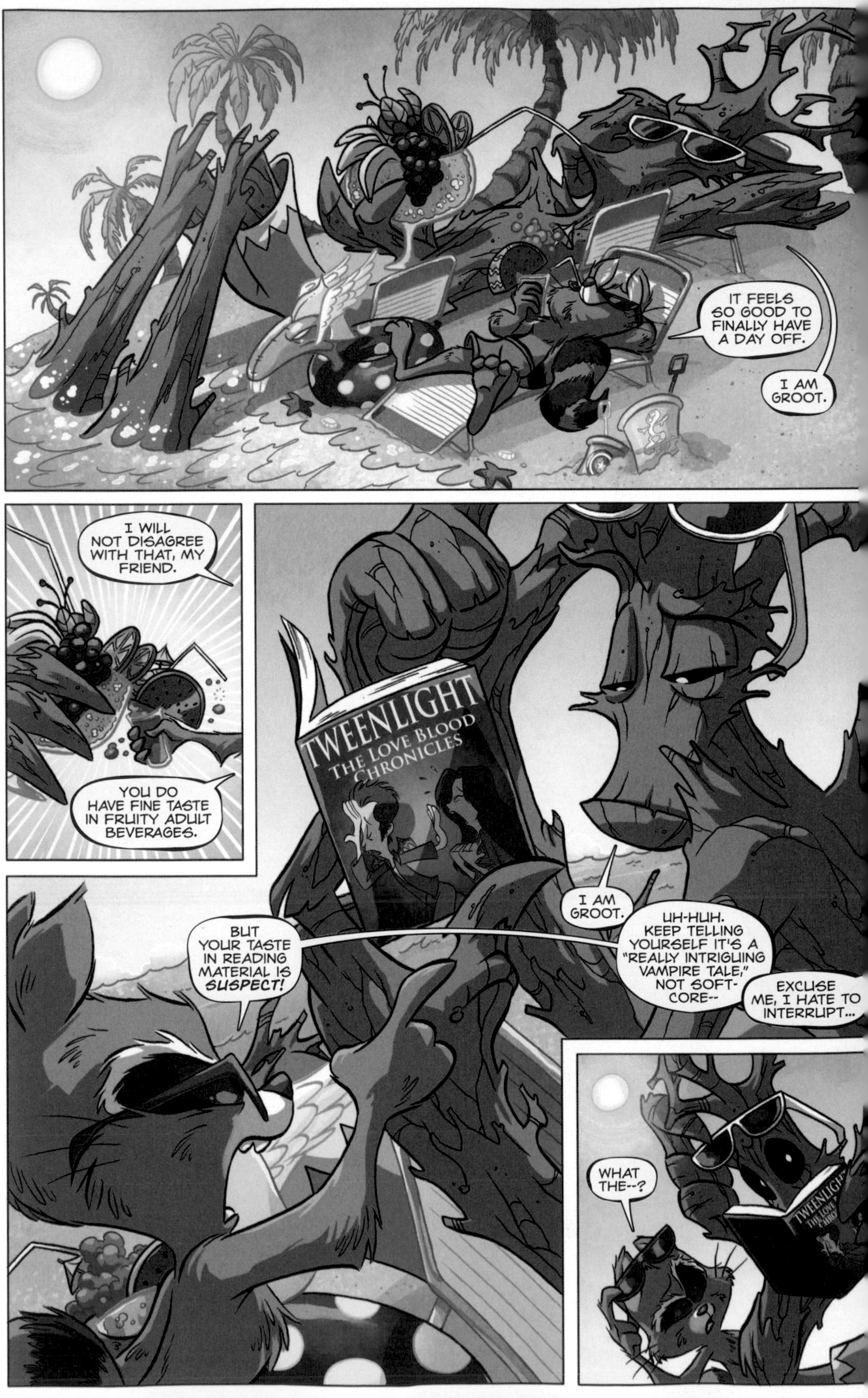
IT FEELS SO GOOD TO FINALLY HAVE A DAY OFF.
I AM GROOT.
I WILL NOT DISAGREE WITH THAT, MY FRIEND.
YOU DO HAVE FINE TASTE IN FRUITY ADULT BEVERAGES.
TWEENLIGHT
THE LOVE BLOOD CHRONICLES
BUT YOUR TASTE IN READING MATERIAL IS SUSPECT!
I AM GROOT.
UH-HUH. KEEP TELLING YOURSELF IT'S A "REALLY INTRIGUING VAMPIRE TALE," NOT SOFT-CORE--
EXCUSE ME, I HATE TO INTERRUPT...
WHAT THE--?

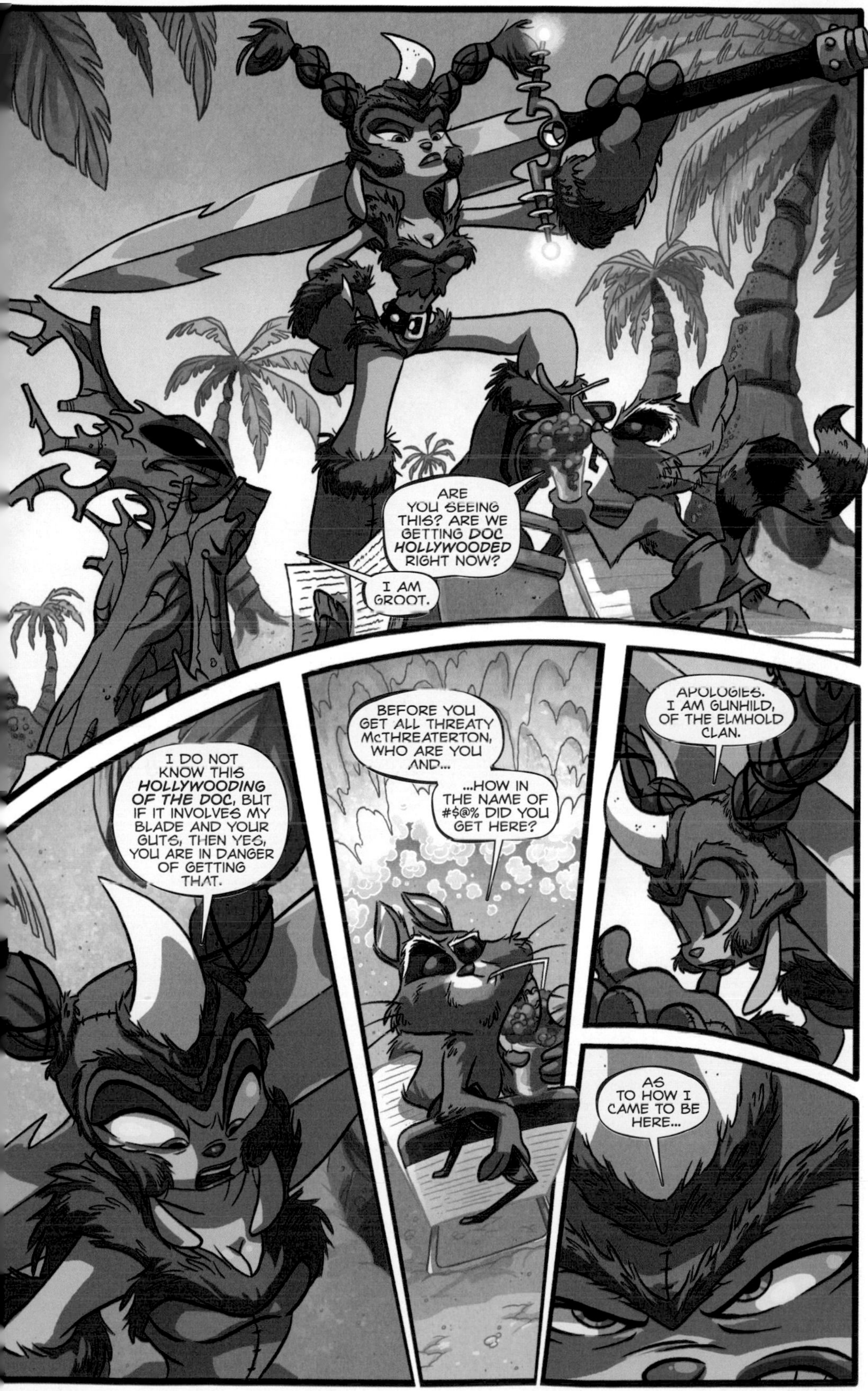
ARE YOU SEEING THIS? ARE WE GETTING *DOC HOLLYWOODED* RIGHT NOW?
I AM GROOT.
I DO NOT KNOW THIS *HOLLYWOODING OF THE DOC*, BUT IF IT INVOLVES MY BLADE AND YOUR GUTS, THEN YES, YOU ARE IN DANGER OF GETTING THAT.
BEFORE YOU GET ALL THREATY McTHREATERTON, WHO ARE YOU AND...
...HOW IN THE NAME OF #$@% DID YOU GET HERE?
APOLOGIES. I AM GUNHILD, OF THE ELMHOLD CLAN.
AS TO HOW I CAME TO BE HERE...

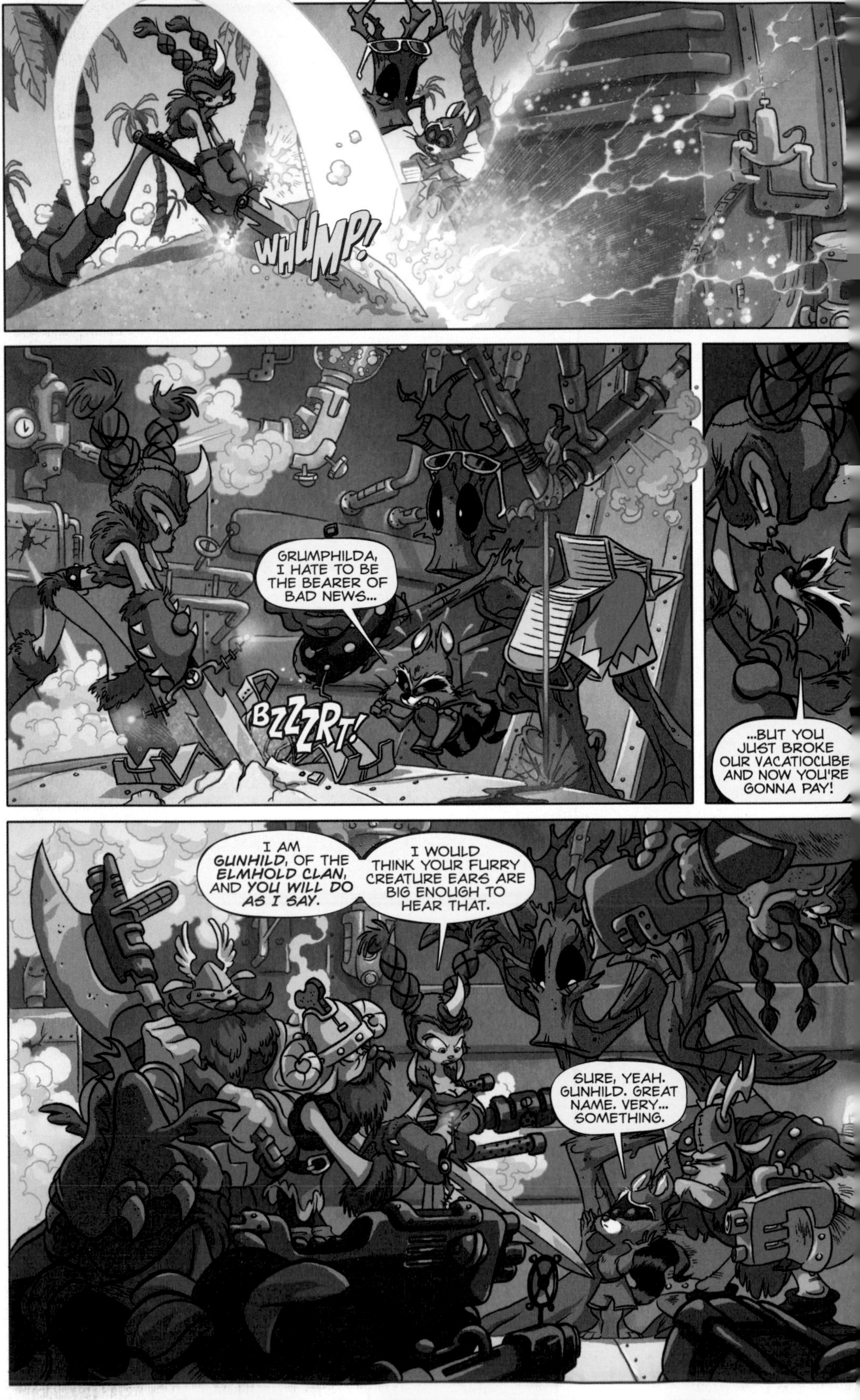
WHUMP!
GRUMPHILDA, I HATE TO BE THE BEARER OF BAD NEWS...
BZZZRT!
...BUT YOU JUST BROKE OUR VACATIOCUBE AND NOW YOU'RE GONNA PAY!
I AM GUNHILD, OF THE ELMHOLD CLAN, AND YOU WILL DO AS I SAY.
I WOULD THINK YOUR FURRY CREATURE EARS ARE BIG ENOUGH TO HEAR THAT.
SURE, YEAH. GUNHILD. GREAT NAME. VERY... SOMETHING.

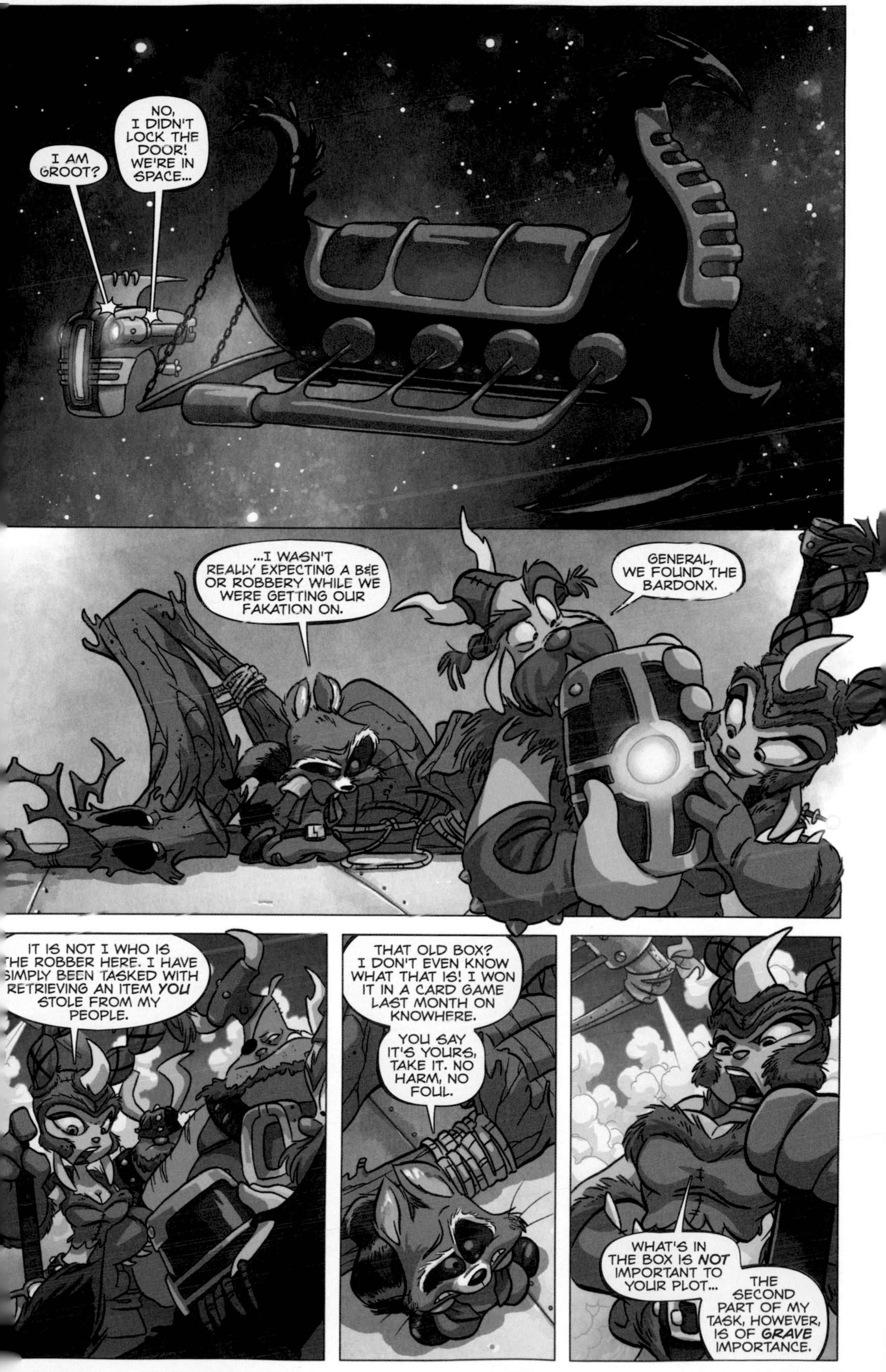
I AM GROOT?
NO, I DIDN'T LOCK THE DOOR! WE'RE IN SPACE...
...I WASN'T REALLY EXPECTING A B&E OR ROBBERY WHILE WE WERE GETTING OUR FAKATION ON.
GENERAL, WE FOUND THE BARDONX.
IT IS NOT I WHO IS THE ROBBER HERE. I HAVE SIMPLY BEEN TASKED WITH RETRIEVING AN ITEM YOU STOLE FROM MY PEOPLE.
THAT OLD BOX? I DON'T EVEN KNOW WHAT THAT IS! I WON IT IN A CARD GAME LAST MONTH ON KNOWHERE.
YOU SAY IT'S YOURS, TAKE IT. NO HARM, NO FOUL.
WHAT'S IN THE BOX IS NOT IMPORTANT TO YOUR PLOT...
THE SECOND PART OF MY TASK, HOWEVER, IS OF GRAVE IMPORTANCE.

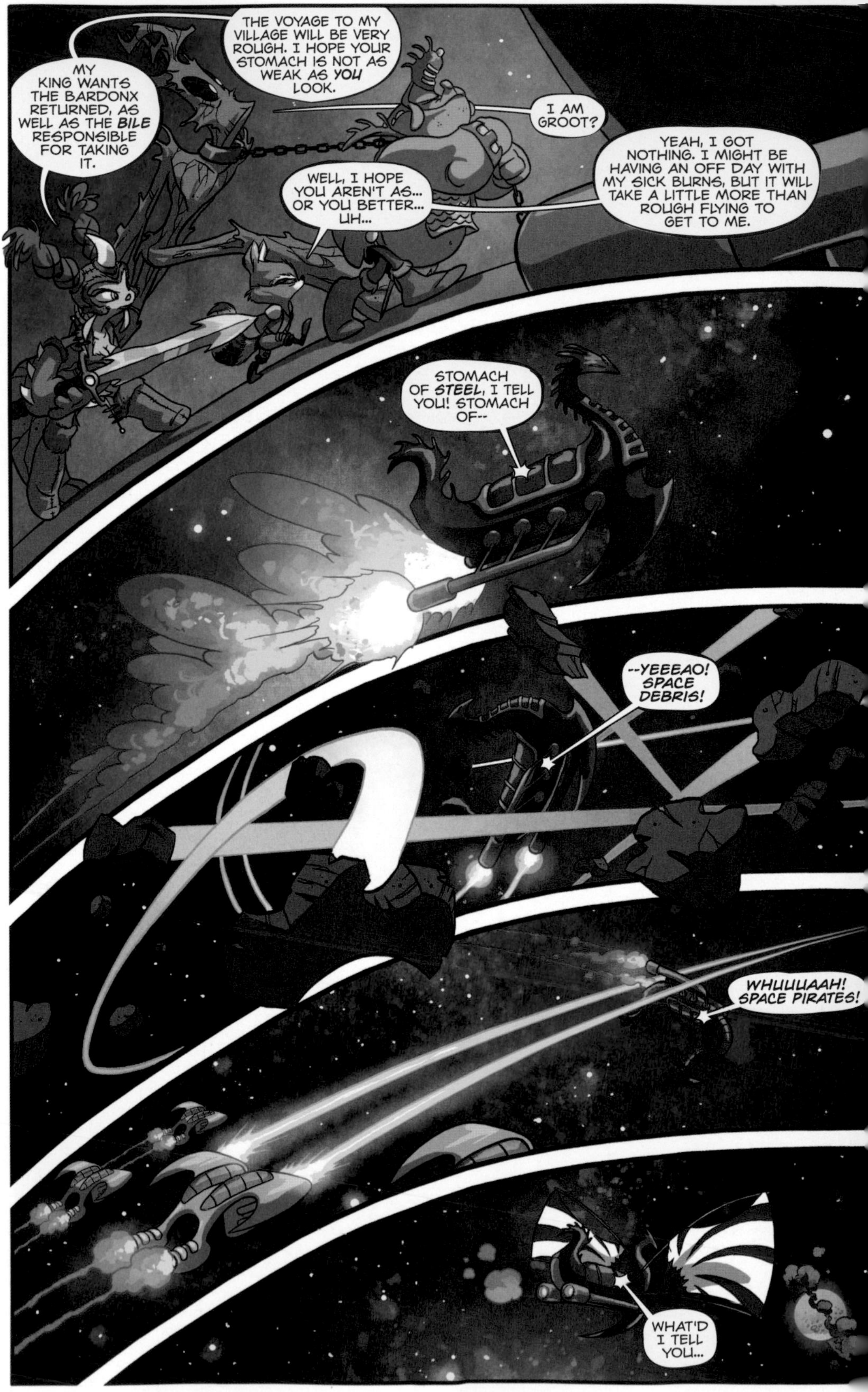
MY KING WANTS THE BARDONX RETURNED, AS WELL AS THE BILE RESPONSIBLE FOR TAKING IT.
THE VOYAGE TO MY VILLAGE WILL BE VERY ROUGH. I HOPE YOUR STOMACH IS NOT AS WEAK AS YOU LOOK.
I AM GROOT?
WELL, I HOPE YOU AREN'T AS... OR YOU BETTER... UH...
YEAH, I GOT NOTHING. I MIGHT BE HAVING AN OFF DAY WITH MY SICK BURNS, BUT IT WILL TAKE A LITTLE MORE THAN ROUGH FLYING TO GET TO ME.
STOMACH OF STEEL, I TELL YOU! STOMACH OF--
--YEEEAO! SPACE DEBRIS!
WHUUUAAH! SPACE PIRATES!
WHAT'D I TELL YOU...

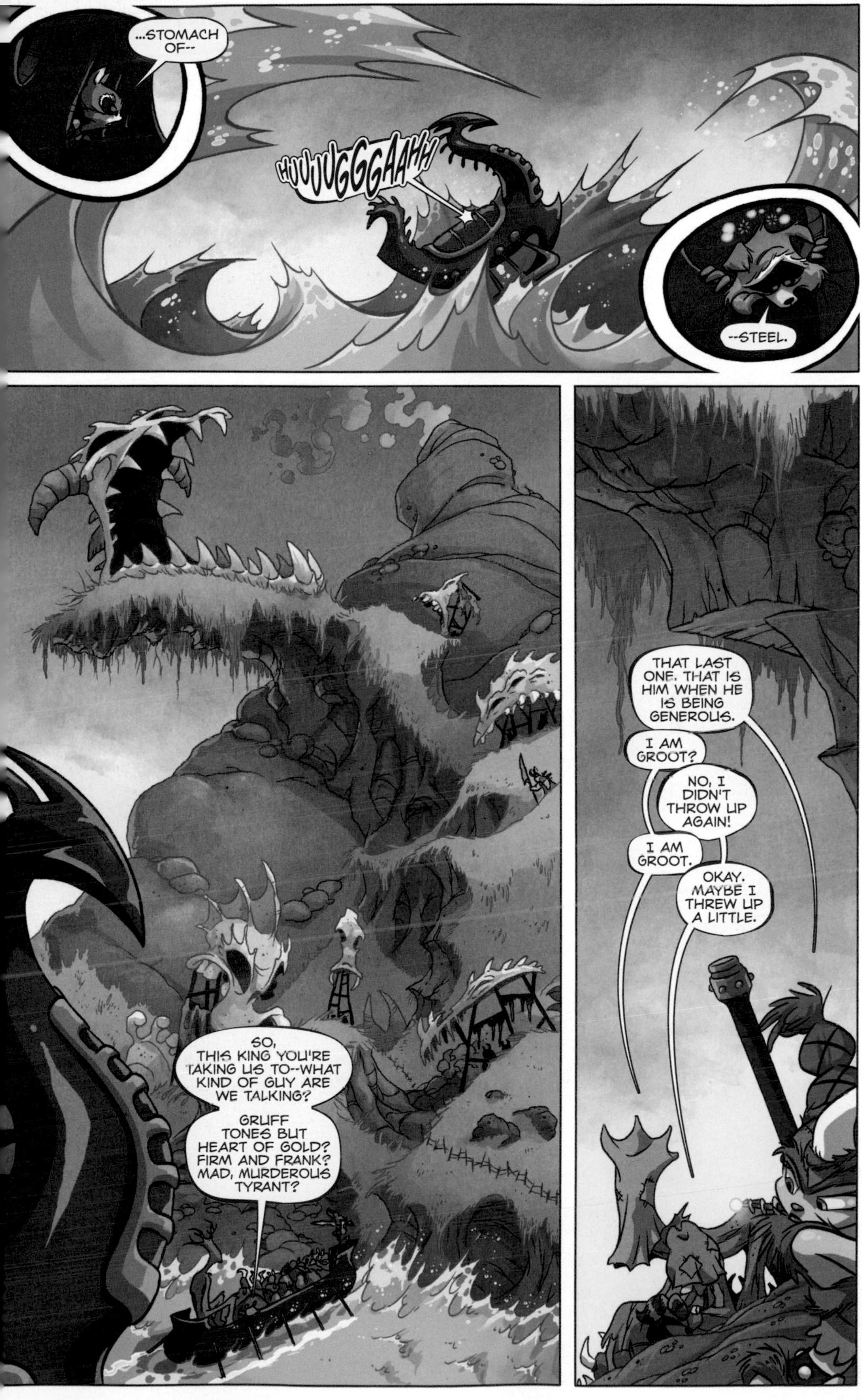
...STOMACH OF--
HUUUUGGGAAHH
--STEEL.
SO, THIS KING YOU'RE TAKING US TO--WHAT KIND OF GUY ARE WE TALKING?
GRUFF TONES BUT HEART OF GOLD? FIRM AND FRANK? MAD, MURDEROUS TYRANT?
THAT LAST ONE. THAT IS HIM WHEN HE IS BEING GENEROUS.
I AM GROOT?
NO, I DIDN'T THROW UP AGAIN!
I AM GROOT.
OKAY. MAYBE I THREW UP A LITTLE.

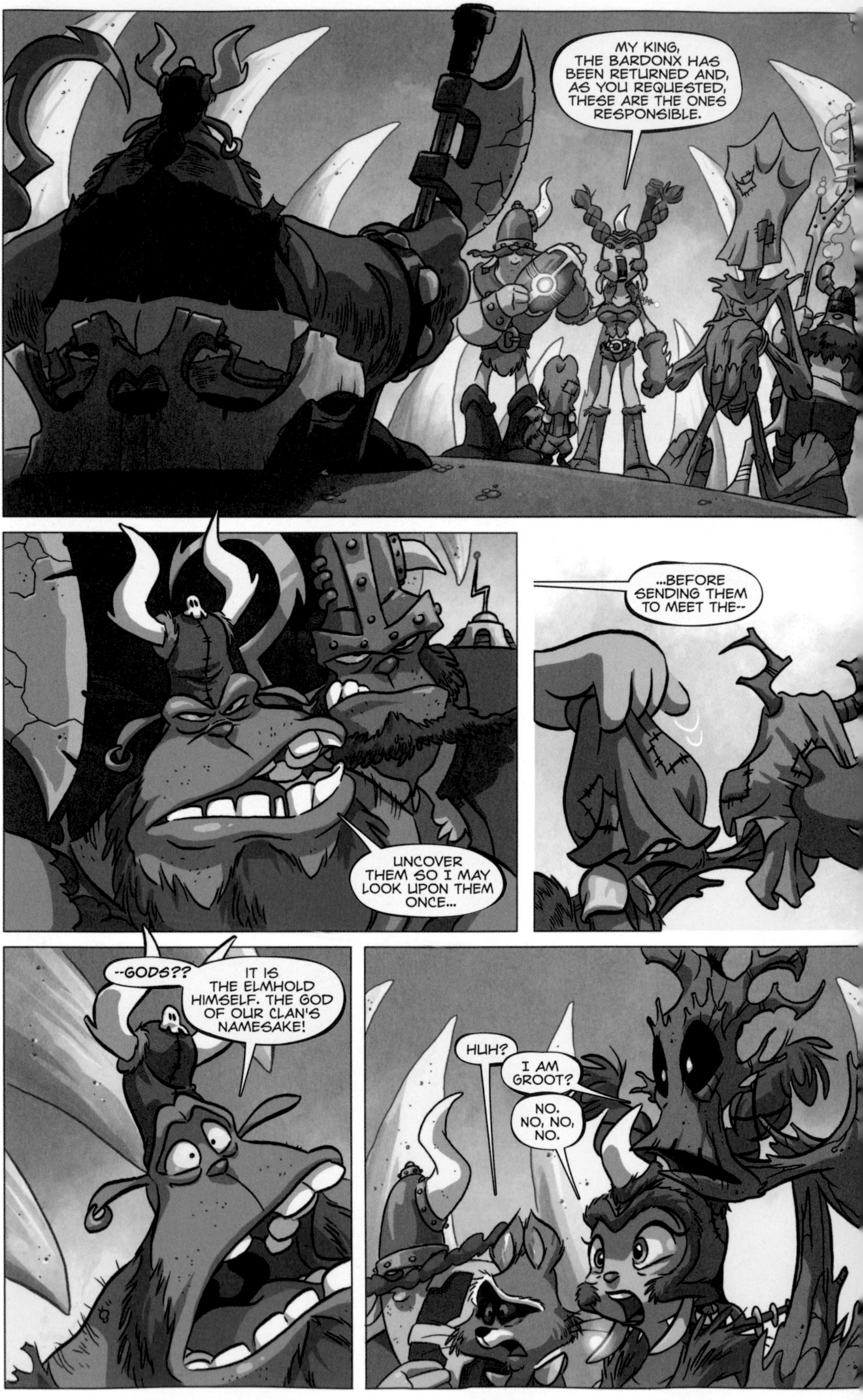
MY KING, THE BARDONX HAS BEEN RETURNED AND, AS YOU REQUESTED, THESE ARE THE ONES RESPONSIBLE.
UNCOVER THEM SO I MAY LOOK UPON THEM ONCE...
...BEFORE SENDING THEM TO MEET THE--
--GODS??
IT IS THE ELMHOLD HIMSELF. THE GOD OF OUR CLAN'S NAMESAKE!
HUH?
I AM GROOT?
NO. NO, NO, NO.

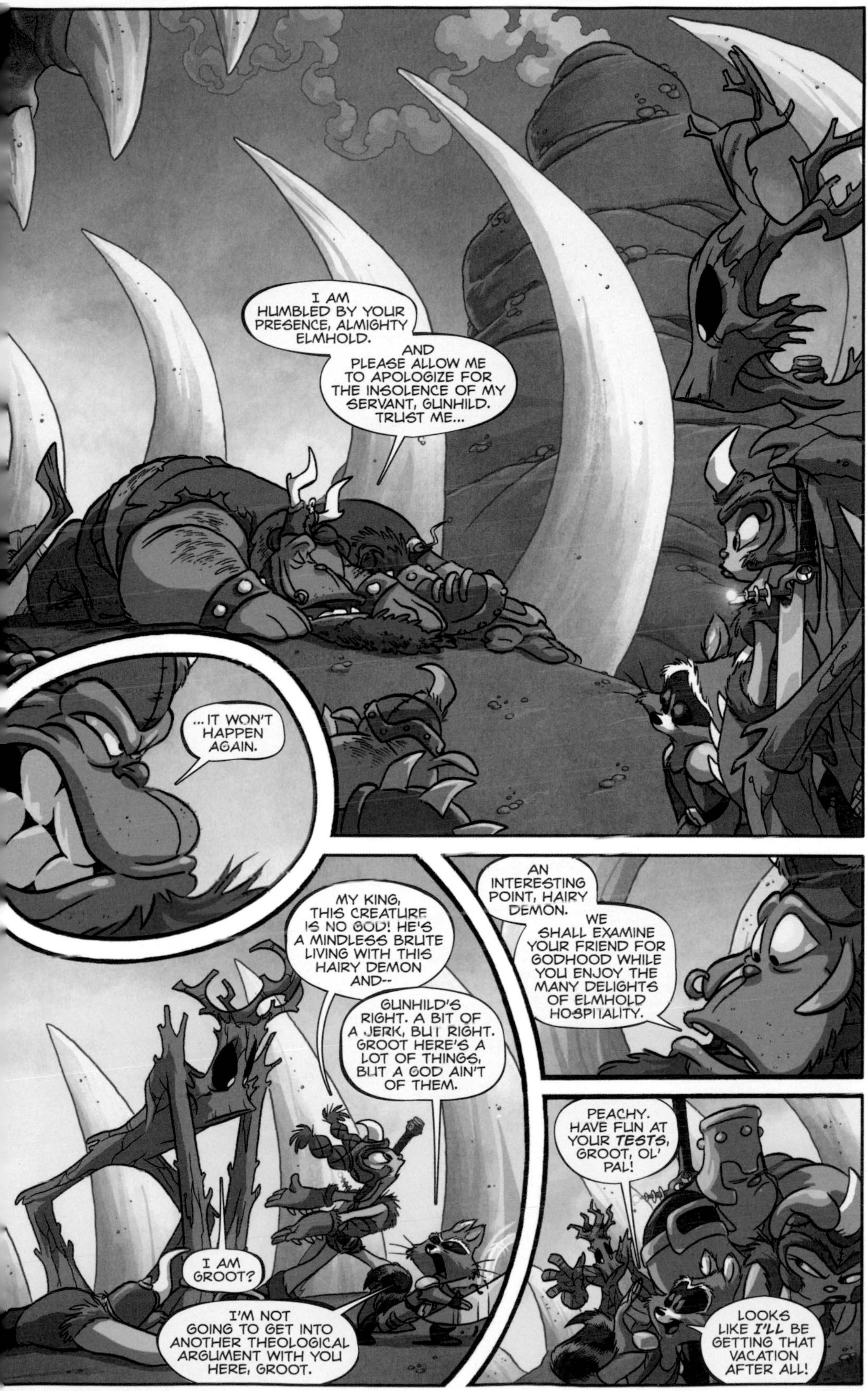
I AM HUMBLED BY YOUR PRESENCE, ALMIGHTY ELMHOLD.
AND PLEASE ALLOW ME TO APOLOGIZE FOR THE INSOLENCE OF MY SERVANT, GUNHILD. TRUST ME...
...IT WON'T HAPPEN AGAIN.
MY KING, THIS CREATURE IS NO GOD! HE'S A MINDLESS BRUTE LIVING WITH THIS HAIRY DEMON AND--
GUNHILD'S RIGHT. A BIT OF A JERK, BUT RIGHT. GROOT HERE'S A LOT OF THINGS, BUT A GOD AIN'T OF THEM.
I AM GROOT?
I'M NOT GOING TO GET INTO ANOTHER THEOLOGICAL ARGUMENT WITH YOU HERE, GROOT.
AN INTERESTING POINT, HAIRY DEMON.
WE SHALL EXAMINE YOUR FRIEND FOR GODHOOD WHILE YOU ENJOY THE MANY DELIGHTS OF ELMHOLD HOSPITALITY.
PEACHY. HAVE FUN AT YOUR TESTS, GROOT, OL' PAL!
LOOKS LIKE I'LL BE GETTING THAT VACATION AFTER ALL!

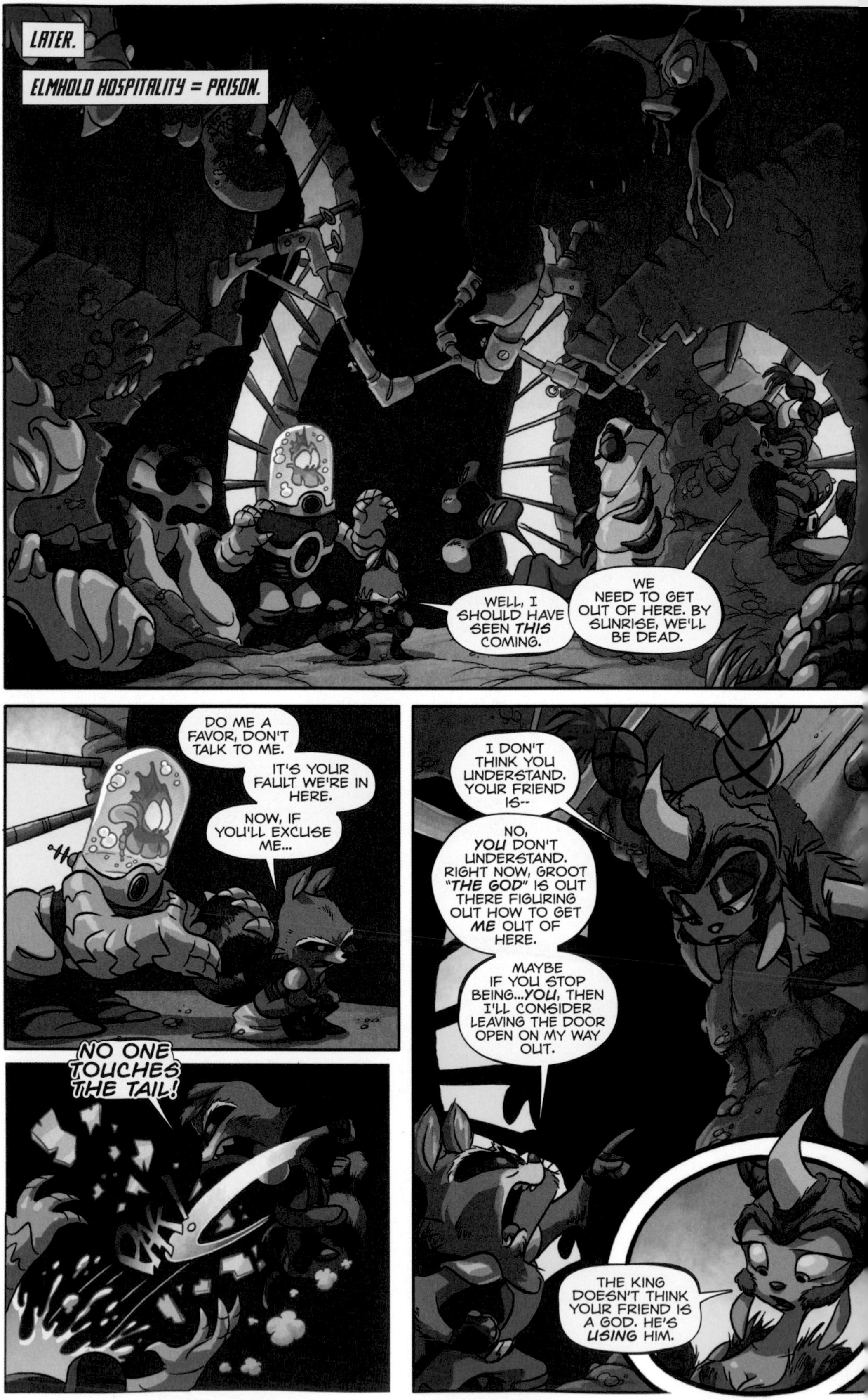
LATER.
ELMHOLD HOSPITALITY = PRISON.
WELL, I SHOULD HAVE SEEN THIS COMING.
WE NEED TO GET OUT OF HERE. BY SUNRISE, WE'LL BE DEAD.
DO ME A FAVOR, DON'T TALK TO ME.
IT'S YOUR FAULT WE'RE IN HERE.
NOW, IF YOU'LL EXCUSE ME...
I DON'T THINK YOU UNDERSTAND. YOUR FRIEND IS--
NO, YOU DON'T UNDERSTAND. RIGHT NOW, GROOT "THE GOD" IS OUT THERE FIGURING OUT HOW TO GET ME OUT OF HERE.
MAYBE IF YOU STOP BEING...YOU, THEN I'LL CONSIDER LEAVING THE DOOR OPEN ON MY WAY OUT.
NO ONE TOUCHES THE TAIL!
THE KING DOESN'T THINK YOUR FRIEND IS A GOD. HE'S USING HIM.

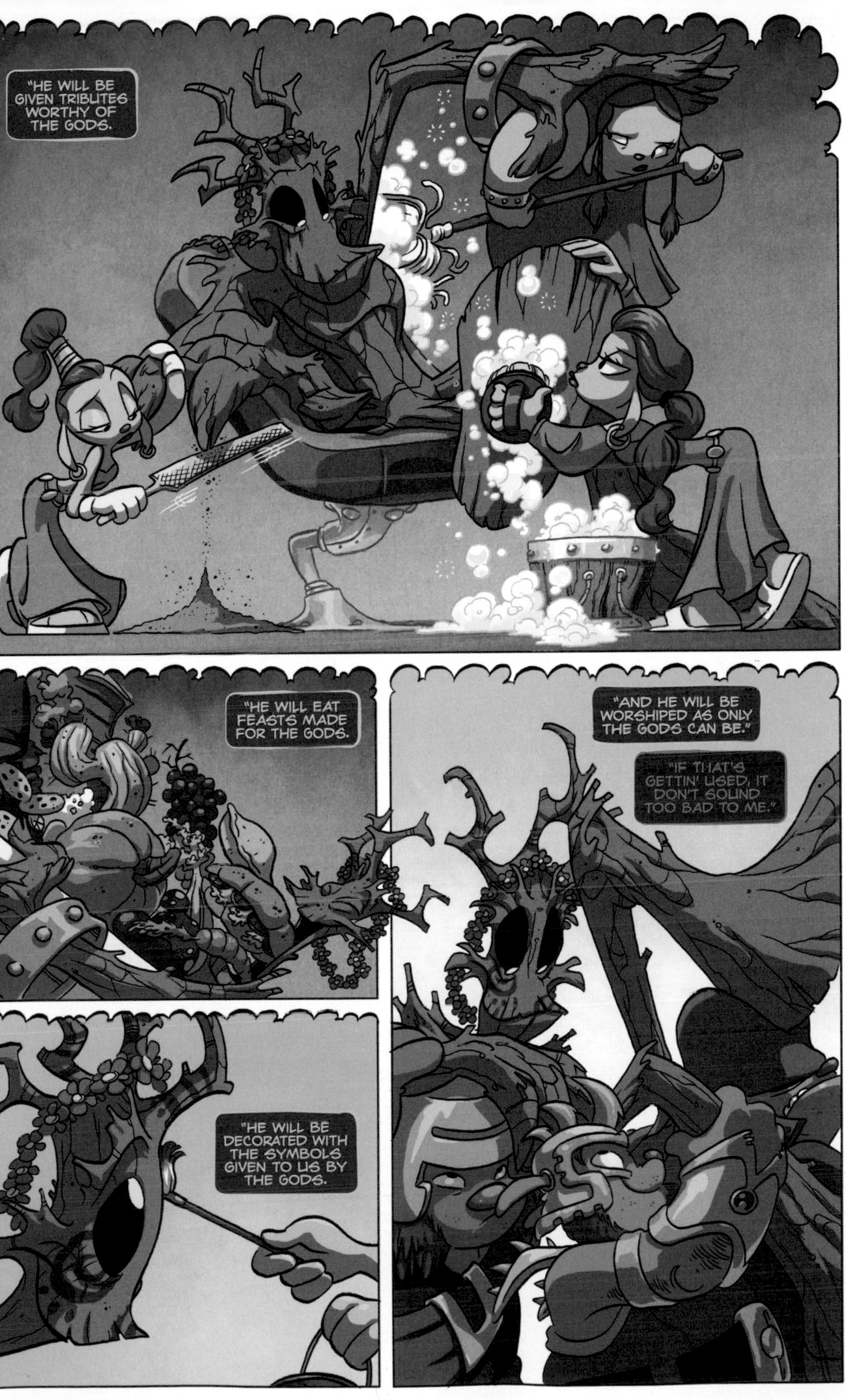
"HE WILL BE GIVEN TRIBUTES WORTHY OF THE GODS.
"HE WILL EAT FEASTS MADE FOR THE GODS.
"AND HE WILL BE WORSHIPED AS ONLY THE GODS CAN BE."
"IF THAT'S GETTIN' USED, IT DON'T SOUND TOO BAD TO ME."
"HE WILL BE DECORATED WITH THE SYMBOLS GIVEN TO US BY THE GODS.

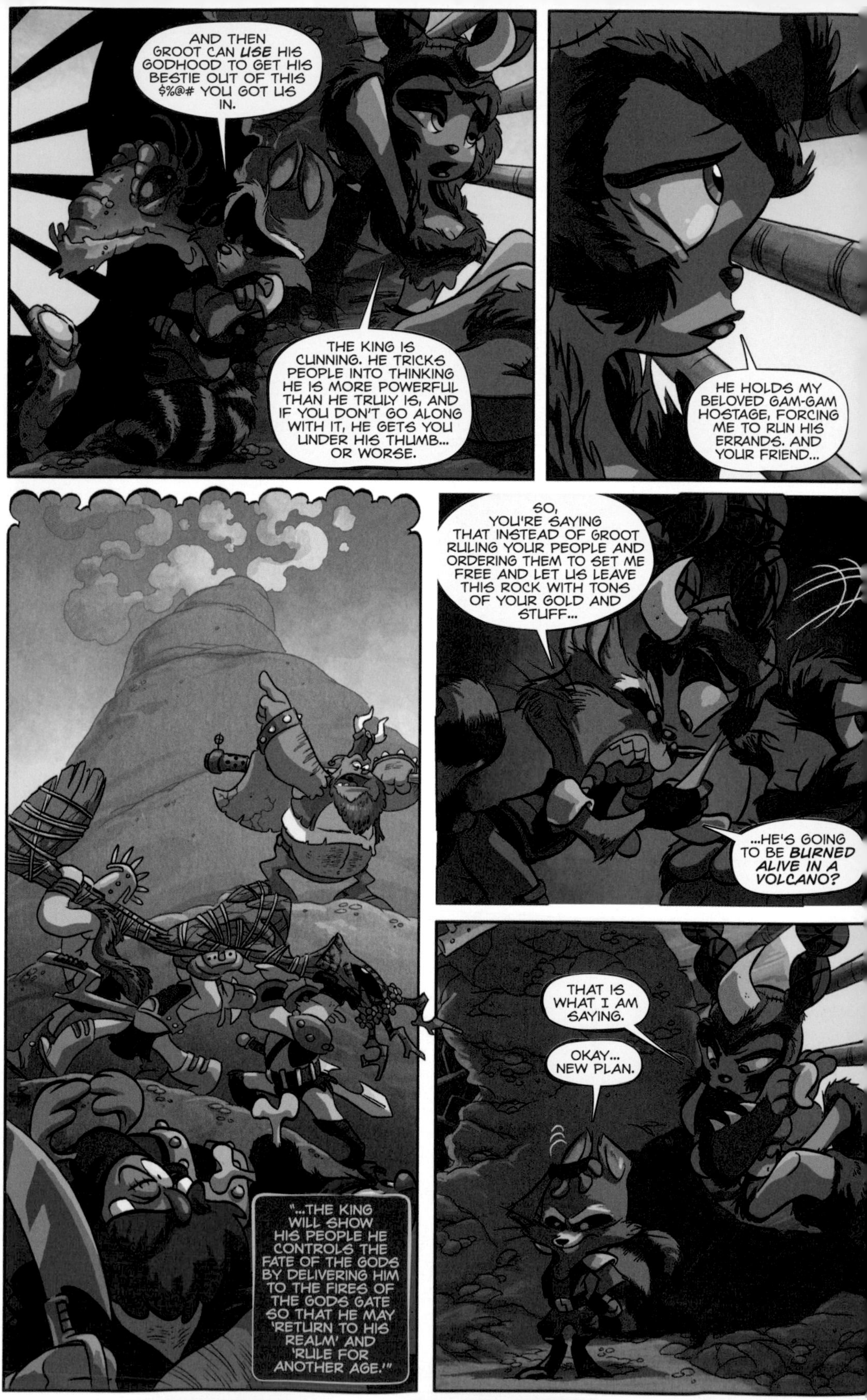
AND THEN GROOT CAN USE HIS GODHOOD TO GET HIS BESTIE OUT OF THIS $%@# YOU GOT US IN.
THE KING IS CUNNING. HE TRICKS PEOPLE INTO THINKING HE IS MORE POWERFUL THAN HE TRULY IS, AND IF YOU DON'T GO ALONG WITH IT, HE GETS YOU UNDER HIS THUMB... OR WORSE.
HE HOLDS MY BELOVED GAM-GAM HOSTAGE, FORCING ME TO RUN HIS ERRANDS. AND YOUR FRIEND...
"...THE KING WILL SHOW HIS PEOPLE HE CONTROLS THE FATE OF THE GODS BY DELIVERING HIM TO THE FIRES OF THE GODS GATE SO THAT HE MAY 'RETURN TO HIS REALM' AND 'RULE FOR ANOTHER AGE.'"
SO, YOU'RE SAYING THAT INSTEAD OF GROOT RULING YOUR PEOPLE AND ORDERING THEM TO SET ME FREE AND LET US LEAVE THIS ROCK WITH TONS OF YOUR GOLD AND STUFF...
...HE'S GOING TO BE BURNED ALIVE IN A VOLCANO?
THAT IS WHAT I AM SAYING.
OKAY... NEW PLAN.

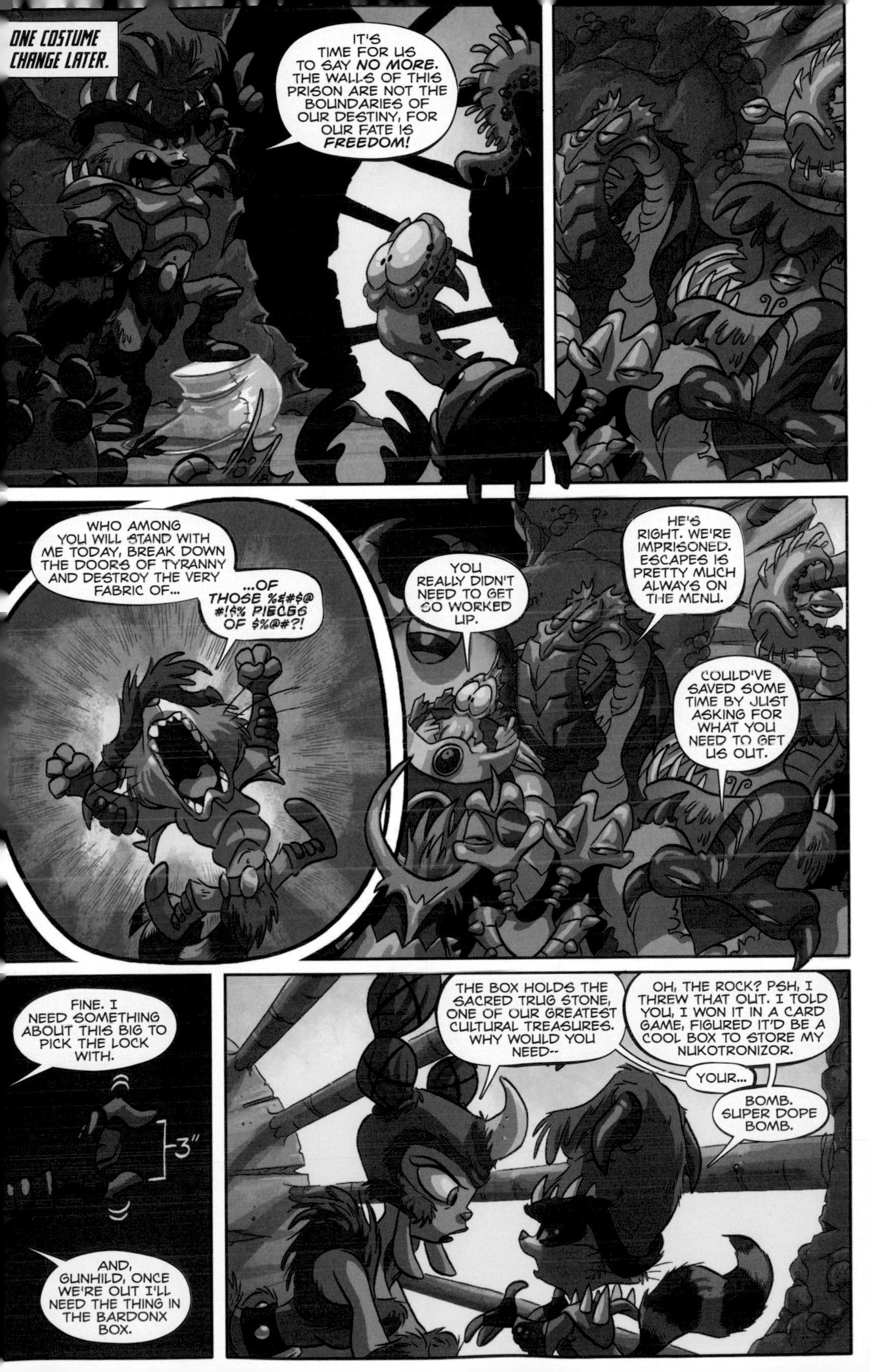
ONE COSTUME CHANGE LATER.
IT'S TIME FOR US TO SAY NO MORE. THE WALLS OF THIS PRISON ARE NOT THE BOUNDARIES OF OUR DESTINY, FOR OUR FATE IS FREEDOM!
WHO AMONG YOU WILL STAND WITH ME TODAY, BREAK DOWN THE DOORS OF TYRANNY AND DESTROY THE VERY FABRIC OF...
...OF THOSE %&#$@ #!$% PIECES OF $%@#?!
YOU REALLY DIDN'T NEED TO GET SO WORKED UP.
HE'S RIGHT. WE'RE IMPRISONED. ESCAPES IS PRETTY MUCH ALWAYS ON THE MENU.
COULD'VE SAVED SOME TIME BY JUST ASKING FOR WHAT YOU NEED TO GET US OUT.
FINE. I NEED SOMETHING ABOUT THIS BIG TO PICK THE LOCK WITH.
3"
AND, GUNHILD, ONCE WE'RE OUT I'LL NEED THE THING IN THE BARDONX BOX.
THE BOX HOLDS THE SACRED TRUG STONE, ONE OF OUR GREATEST CULTURAL TREASURES. WHY WOULD YOU NEED--
OH, THE ROCK? PSH, I THREW THAT OUT. I TOLD YOU, I WON IT IN A CARD GAME, FIGURED IT'D BE A COOL BOX TO STORE MY NUKOTRONIZOR.
YOUR...
BOMB. SUPER DOPE BOMB.

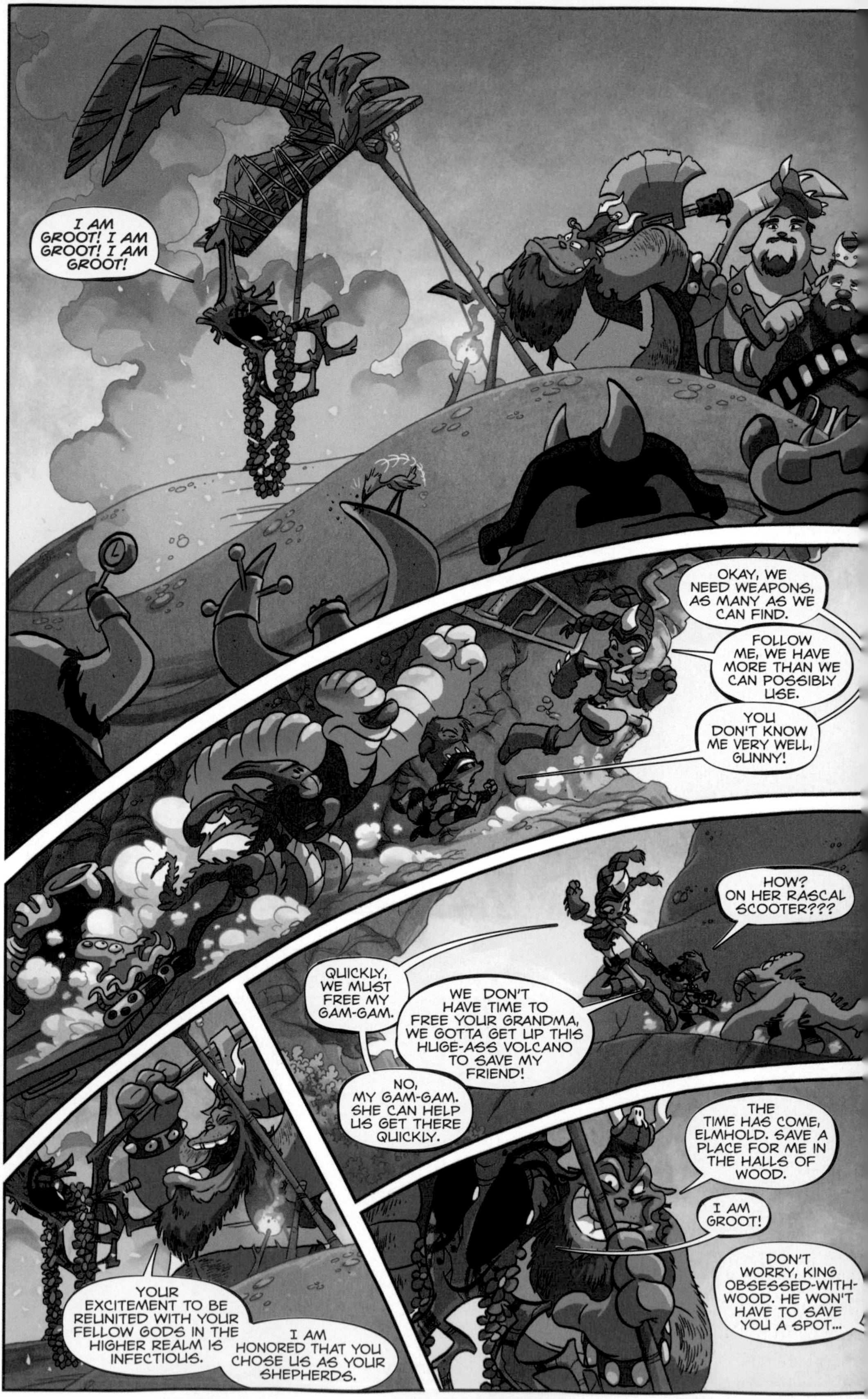
I AM GROOT! I AM GROOT! I AM GROOT!
OKAY, WE NEED WEAPONS, AS MANY AS WE CAN FIND.
FOLLOW ME, WE HAVE MORE THAN WE CAN POSSIBLY USE.
YOU DON'T KNOW ME VERY WELL, GUNNY!
QUICKLY, WE MUST FREE MY GAM-GAM.
WE DON'T HAVE TIME TO FREE YOUR GRANDMA, WE GOTTA GET UP THIS HUGE-ASS VOLCANO TO SAVE MY FRIEND!
NO, MY GAM-GAM. SHE CAN HELP US GET THERE QUICKLY.
HOW? ON HER RASCAL SCOOTER???
YOUR EXCITEMENT TO BE REUNITED WITH YOUR FELLOW GODS IN THE HIGHER REALM IS INFECTIOUS.
I AM HONORED THAT YOU CHOSE US AS YOUR SHEPHERDS.
THE TIME HAS COME, ELMHOLD. SAVE A PLACE FOR ME IN THE HALLS OF WOOD.
I AM GROOT!
DON'T WORRY, KING OBSESSED-WITH-WOOD. HE WON'T HAVE TO SAVE YOU A SPOT...

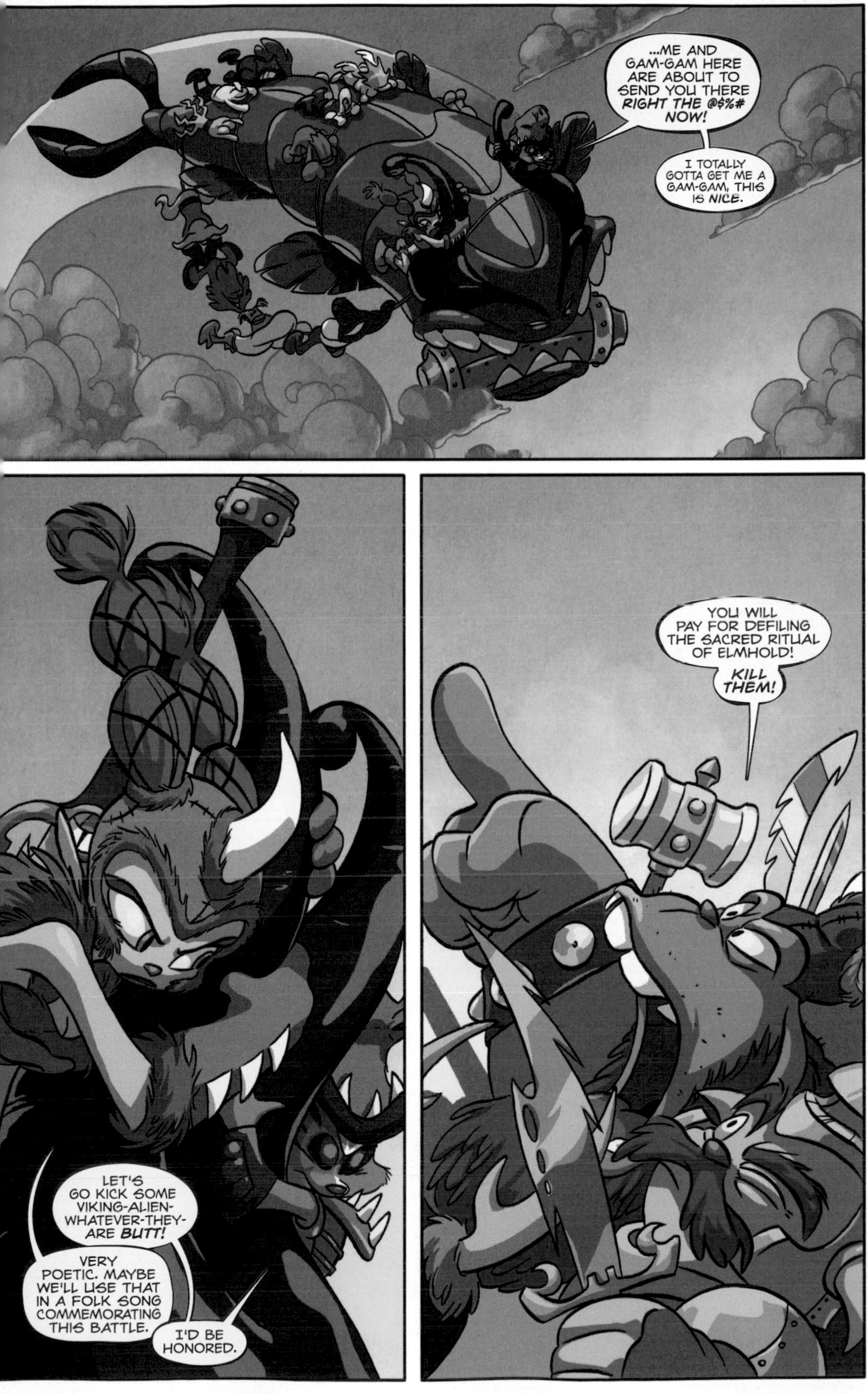
...ME AND GAM-GAM HERE ARE ABOUT TO SEND YOU THERE RIGHT THE @$%# NOW!
I TOTALLY GOTTA GET ME A GAM-GAM, THIS IS NICE.
LET'S GO KICK SOME VIKING-ALIEN-WHATEVER-THEY-ARE BUTT!
VERY POETIC. MAYBE WE'LL USE THAT IN A FOLK SONG COMMEMORATING THIS BATTLE.
I'D BE HONORED.
YOU WILL PAY FOR DEFILING THE SACRED RITUAL OF ELMHOLD!
KILL THEM!

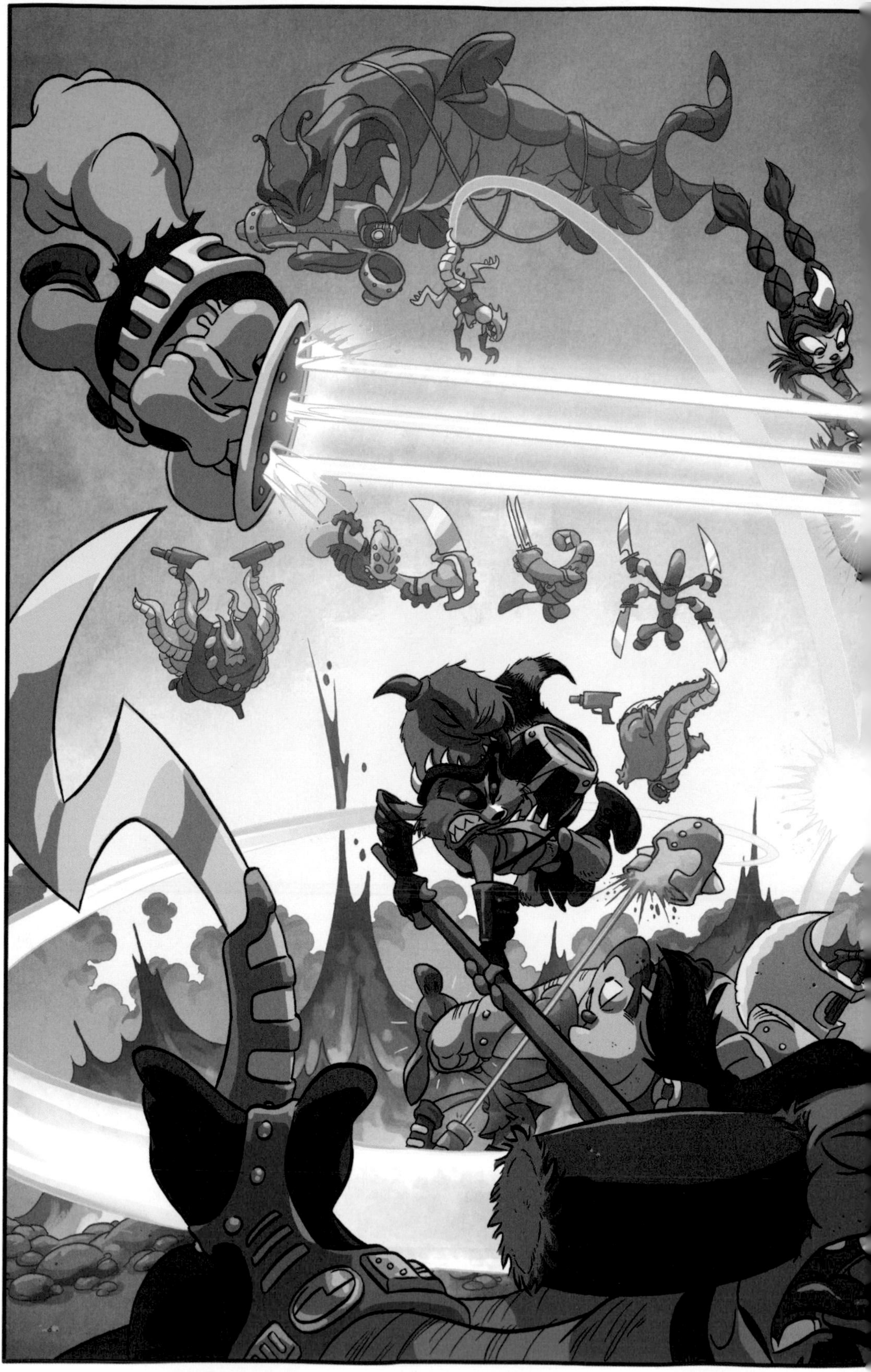

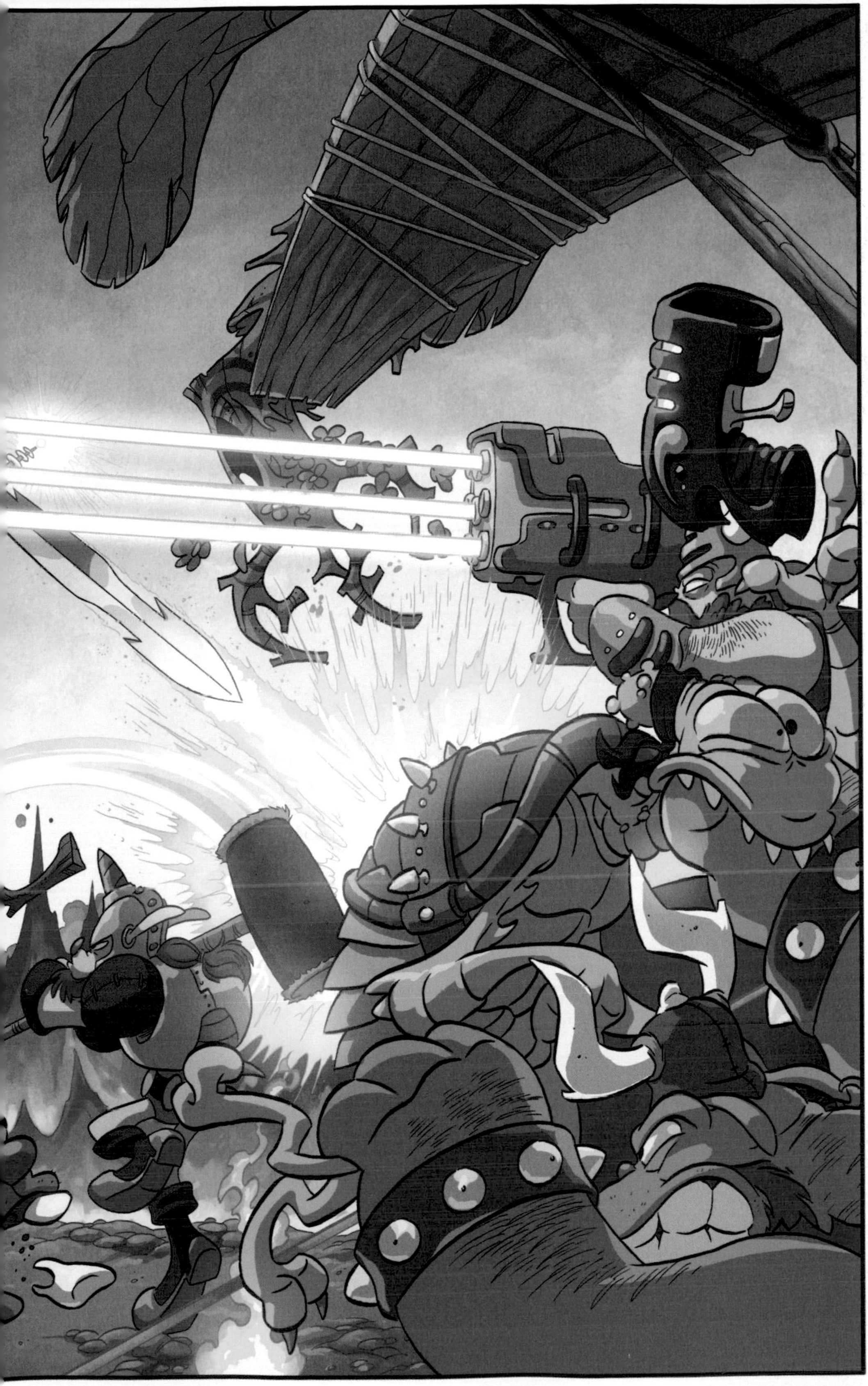

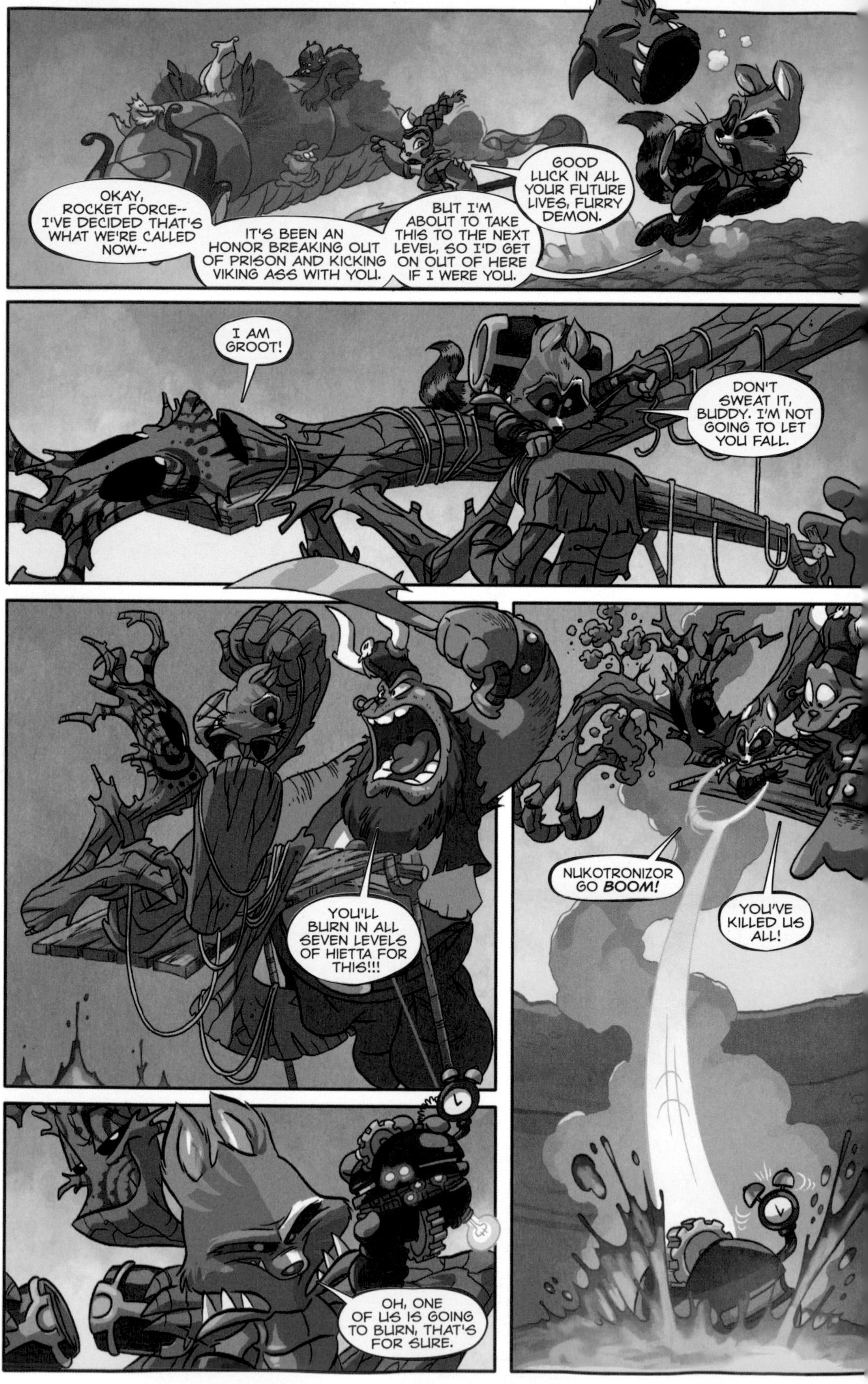
OKAY, ROCKET FORCE-- I'VE DECIDED THAT'S WHAT WE'RE CALLED NOW--
IT'S BEEN AN HONOR BREAKING OUT OF PRISON AND KICKING VIKING ASS WITH YOU.
BUT I'M ABOUT TO TAKE THIS TO THE NEXT LEVEL, SO I'D GET ON OUT OF HERE IF I WERE YOU.
GOOD LUCK IN ALL YOUR FUTURE LIVES, FURRY DEMON.
I AM GROOT!
DON'T SWEAT IT, BUDDY. I'M NOT GOING TO LET YOU FALL.
YOU'LL BURN IN ALL SEVEN LEVELS OF HIETTA FOR THIS!!!
NUKOTRONIZOR GO BOOM!
YOU'VE KILLED US ALL!
OH, ONE OF US IS GOING TO BURN, THAT'S FOR SURE.

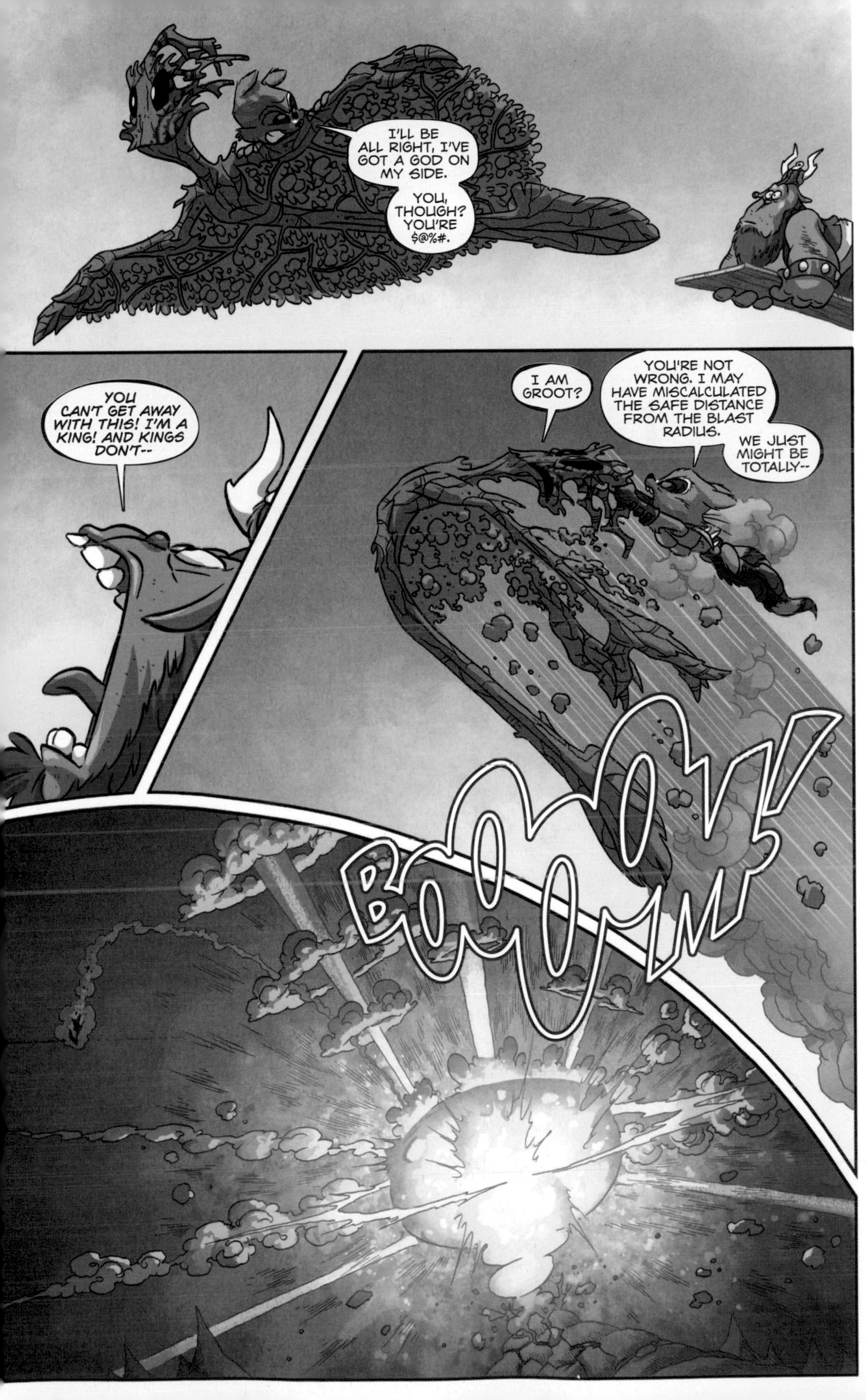
I'LL BE ALL RIGHT, I'VE GOT A GOD ON MY SIDE.
YOU, THOUGH? YOU'RE $@%#.
YOU CAN'T GET AWAY WITH THIS! I'M A KING! AND KINGS DON'T--
I AM GROOT?
YOU'RE NOT WRONG. I MAY HAVE MISCALCULATED THE SAFE DISTANCE FROM THE BLAST RADIUS.
WE JUST MIGHT BE TOTALLY--
BOOOOM!

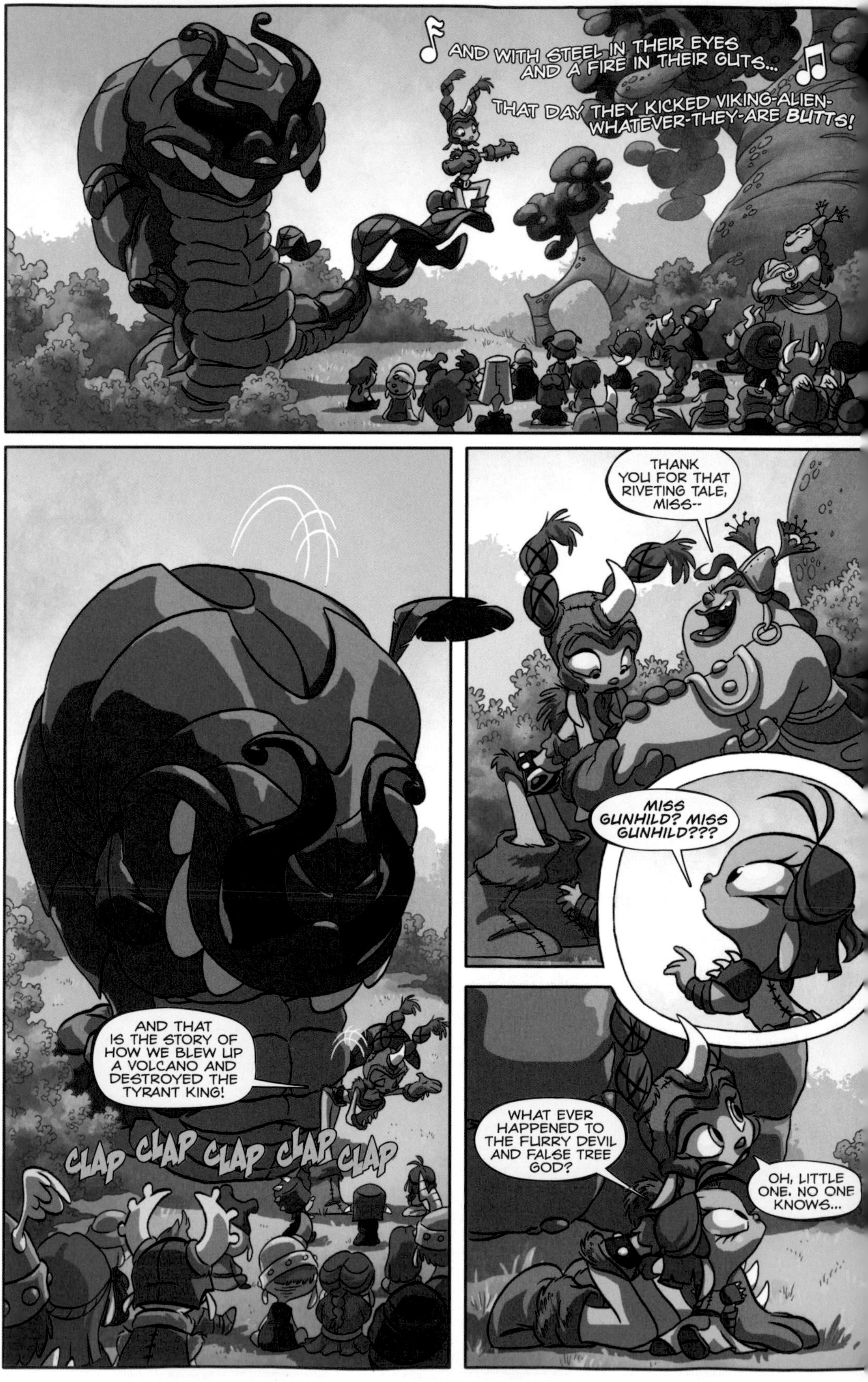
AND WITH STEEL IN THEIR EYES AND A FIRE IN THEIR GUTS...
THAT DAY THEY KICKED VIKING-ALIEN-WHATEVER-THEY-ARE BUTTS!
AND THAT IS THE STORY OF HOW WE BLEW UP A VOLCANO AND DESTROYED THE TYRANT KING!
CLAP CLAP CLAP CLAP CLAP
THANK YOU FOR THAT RIVETING TALE, MISS--
MISS GUNHILD? MISS GUNHILD???
WHAT EVER HAPPENED TO THE FURRY DEVIL AND FALSE TREE GOD?
OH, LITTLE ONE. NO ONE KNOWS...

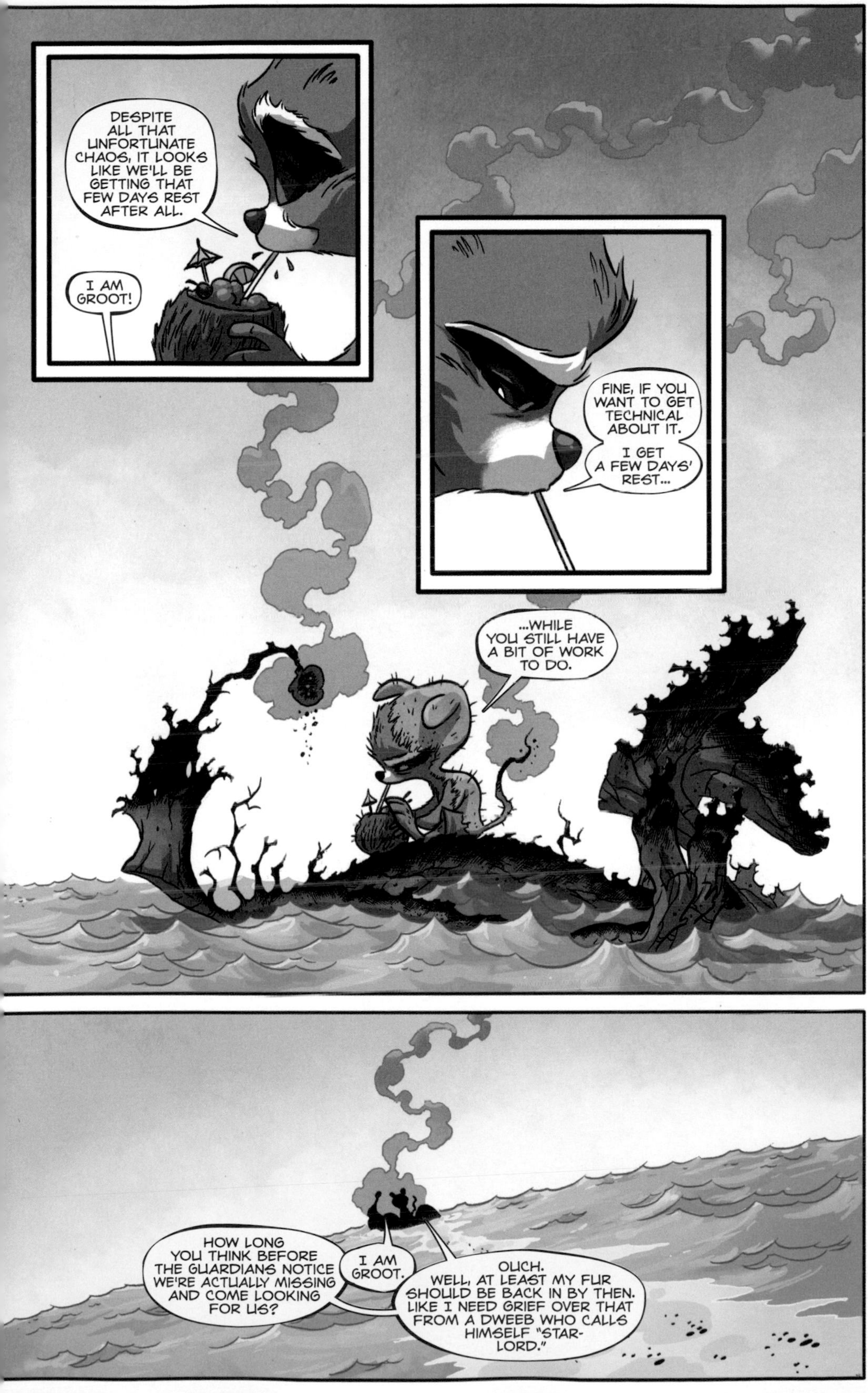
DESPITE ALL THAT UNFORTUNATE CHAOS, IT LOOKS LIKE WE'LL BE GETTING THAT FEW DAYS REST AFTER ALL.
I AM GROOT!
FINE, IF YOU WANT TO GET TECHNICAL ABOUT IT.
I GET A FEW DAYS' REST...
...WHILE YOU STILL HAVE A BIT OF WORK TO DO.
HOW LONG YOU THINK BEFORE THE GUARDIANS NOTICE WE'RE ACTUALLY MISSING AND COME LOOKING FOR US?
I AM GROOT.
OUCH. WELL, AT LEAST MY FUR SHOULD BE BACK IN BY THEN. LIKE I NEED GRIEF OVER THAT FROM A DWEEB WHO CALLS HIMSELF "STAR-LORD."

# 6

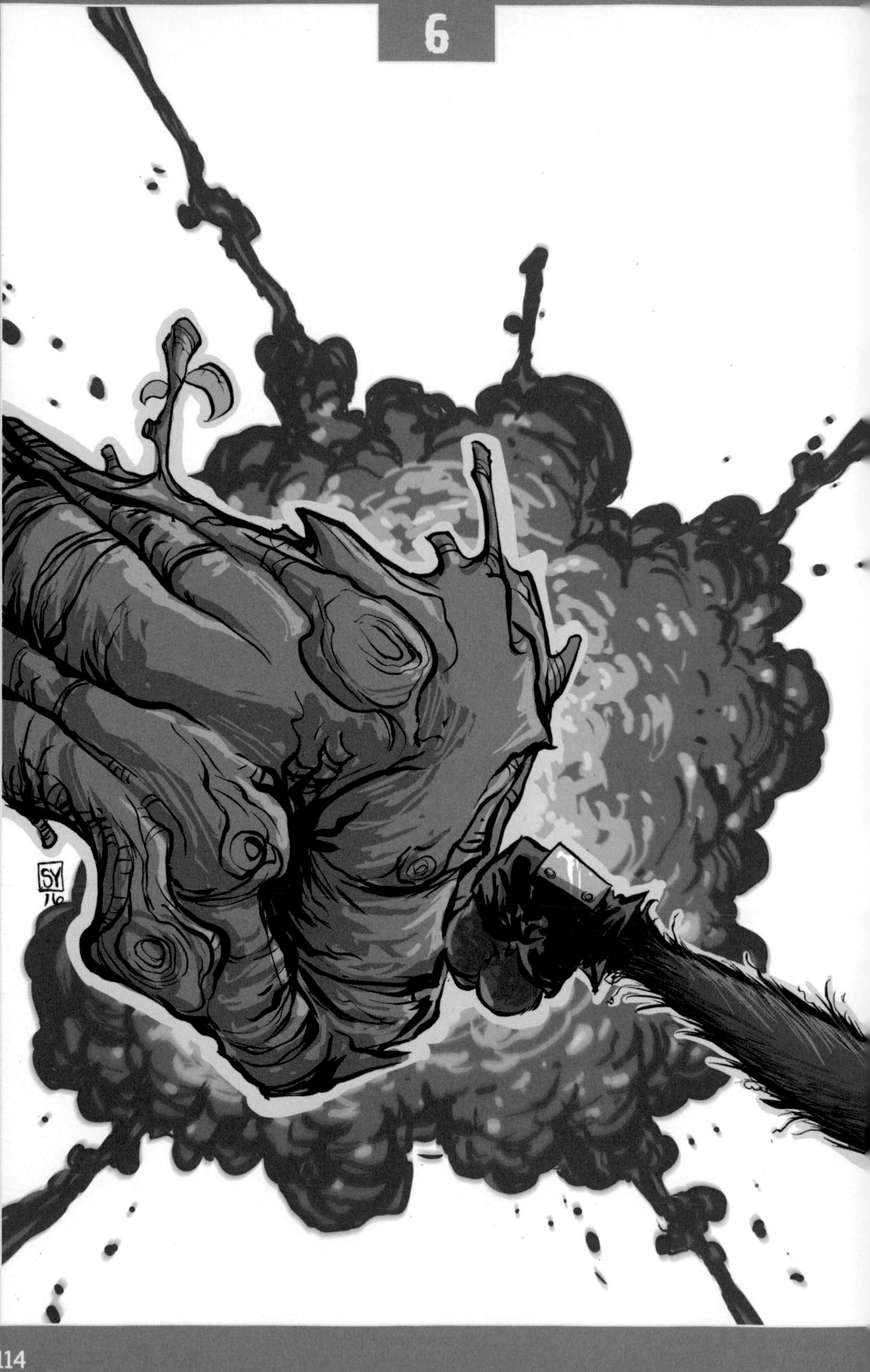

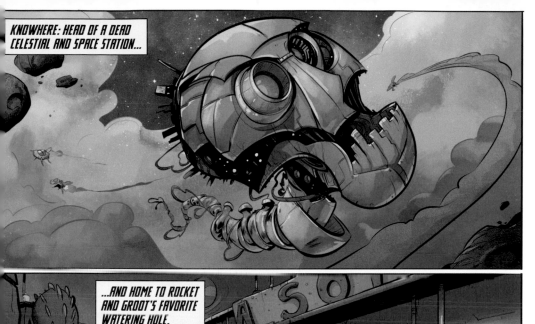

KNOWHERE: HEAD OF A DEAD CELESTIAL AND SPACE STATION...

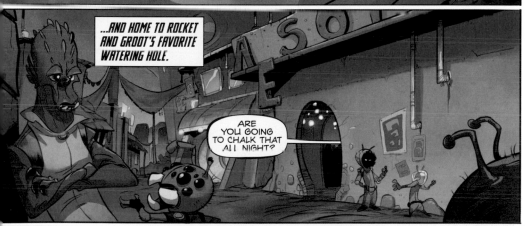

...AND HOME TO ROCKET AND GROOT'S FAVORITE WATERING HOLE.

ARE YOU GOING TO CHALK THAT ALL NIGHT?

OR CAN WE CONTINUE THIS BUTT-WHOOPING I'M IN THE PROCESS OF DELIVERING?

I AM GROOT.

SURE YOU ARE. JUST SHOOT.

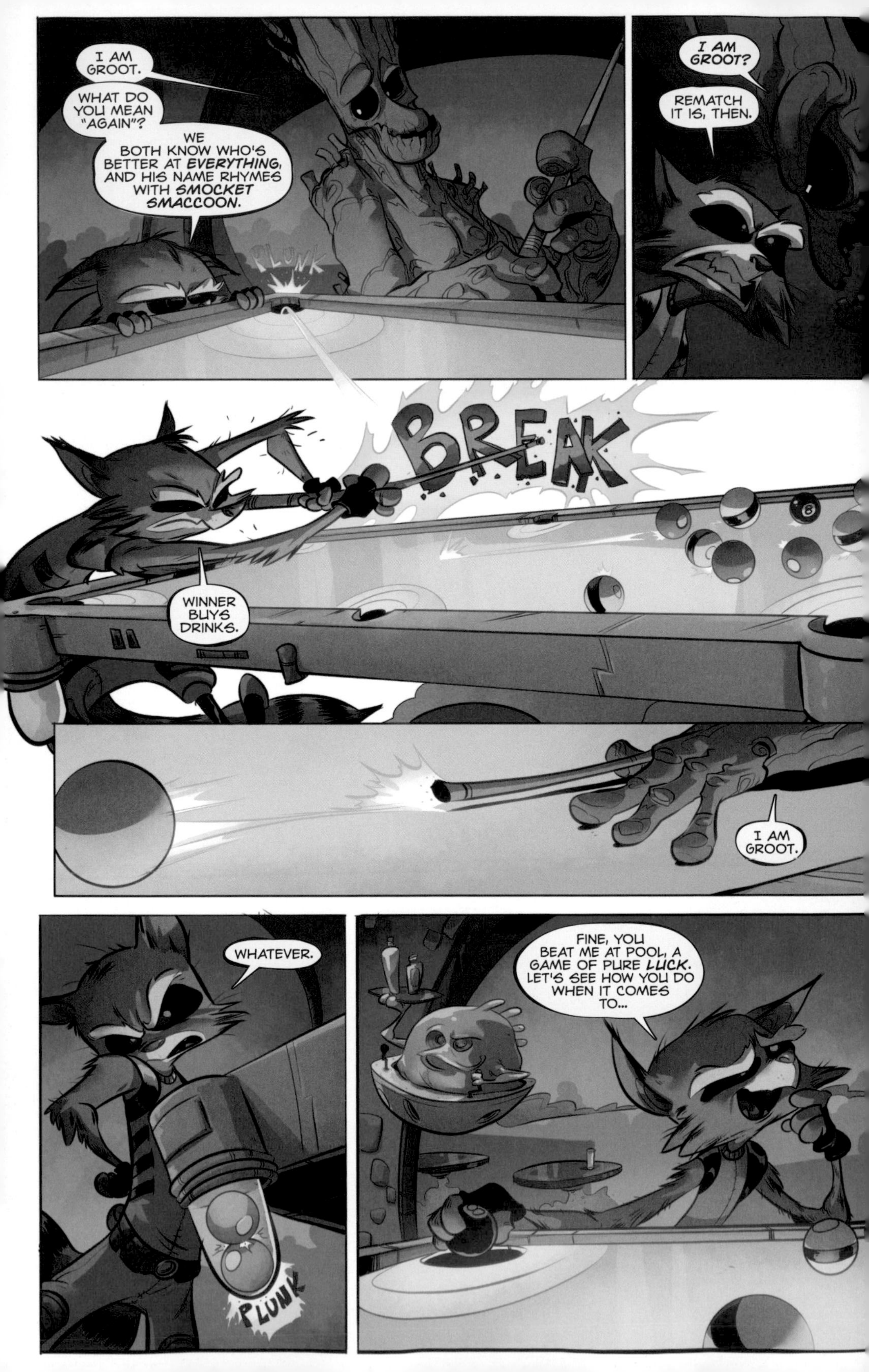
I AM GROOT.
WHAT DO YOU MEAN "AGAIN"?
WE BOTH KNOW WHO'S BETTER AT EVERYTHING, AND HIS NAME RHYMES WITH SMOCKET SMACCOON.
PLUNK
I AM GROOT?
REMATCH IT IS, THEN.
BREAK
WINNER BUYS DRINKS.
I AM GROOT.
WHATEVER.
PLUNK
FINE, YOU BEAT ME AT POOL, A GAME OF PURE LUCK. LET'S SEE HOW YOU DO WHEN IT COMES TO...

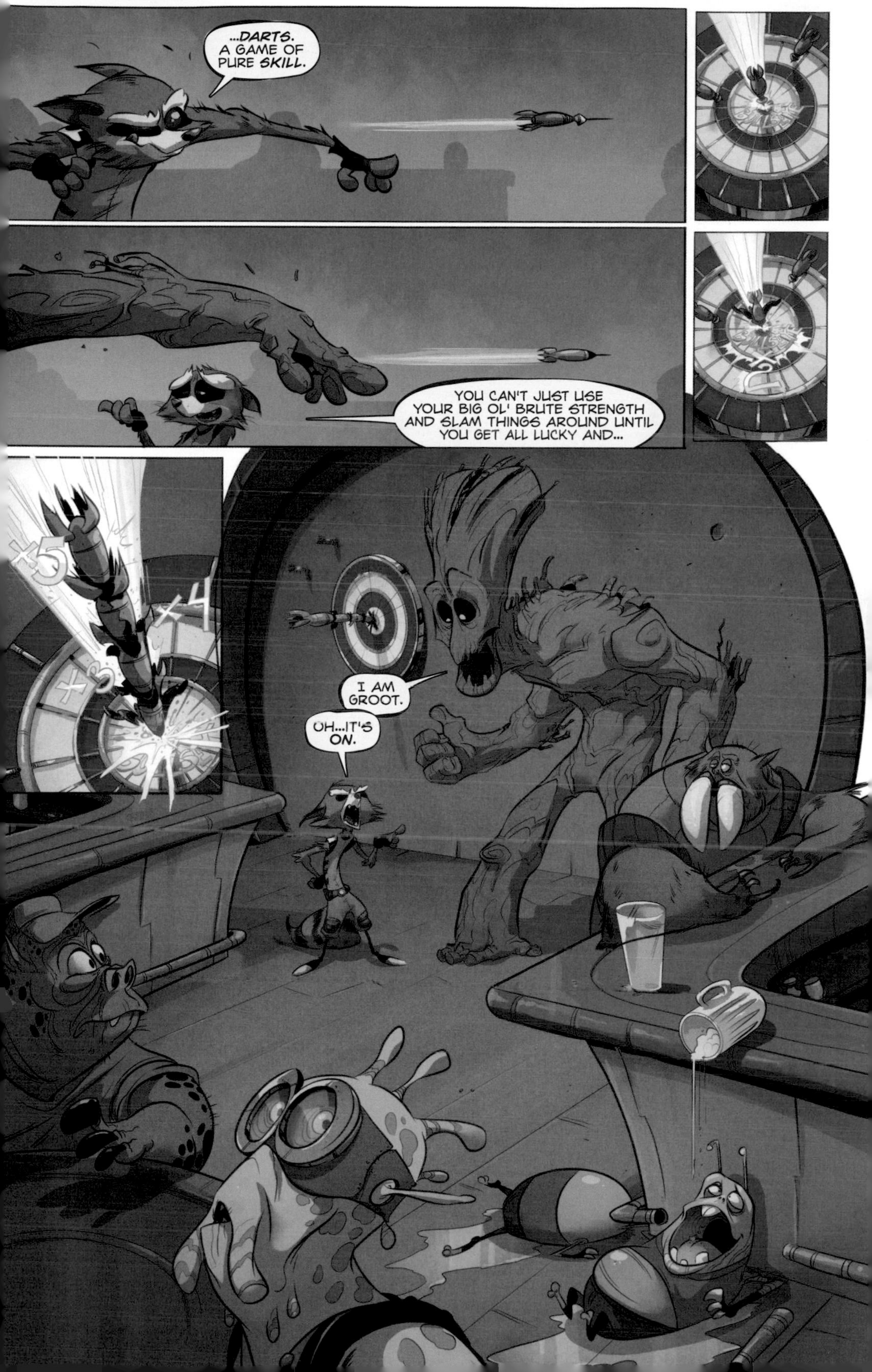
...DARTS. A GAME OF PURE SKILL.
YOU CAN'T JUST USE YOUR BIG OL' BRUTE STRENGTH AND SLAM THINGS AROUND UNTIL YOU GET ALL LUCKY AND...
I AM GROOT.
OH...IT'S ON.

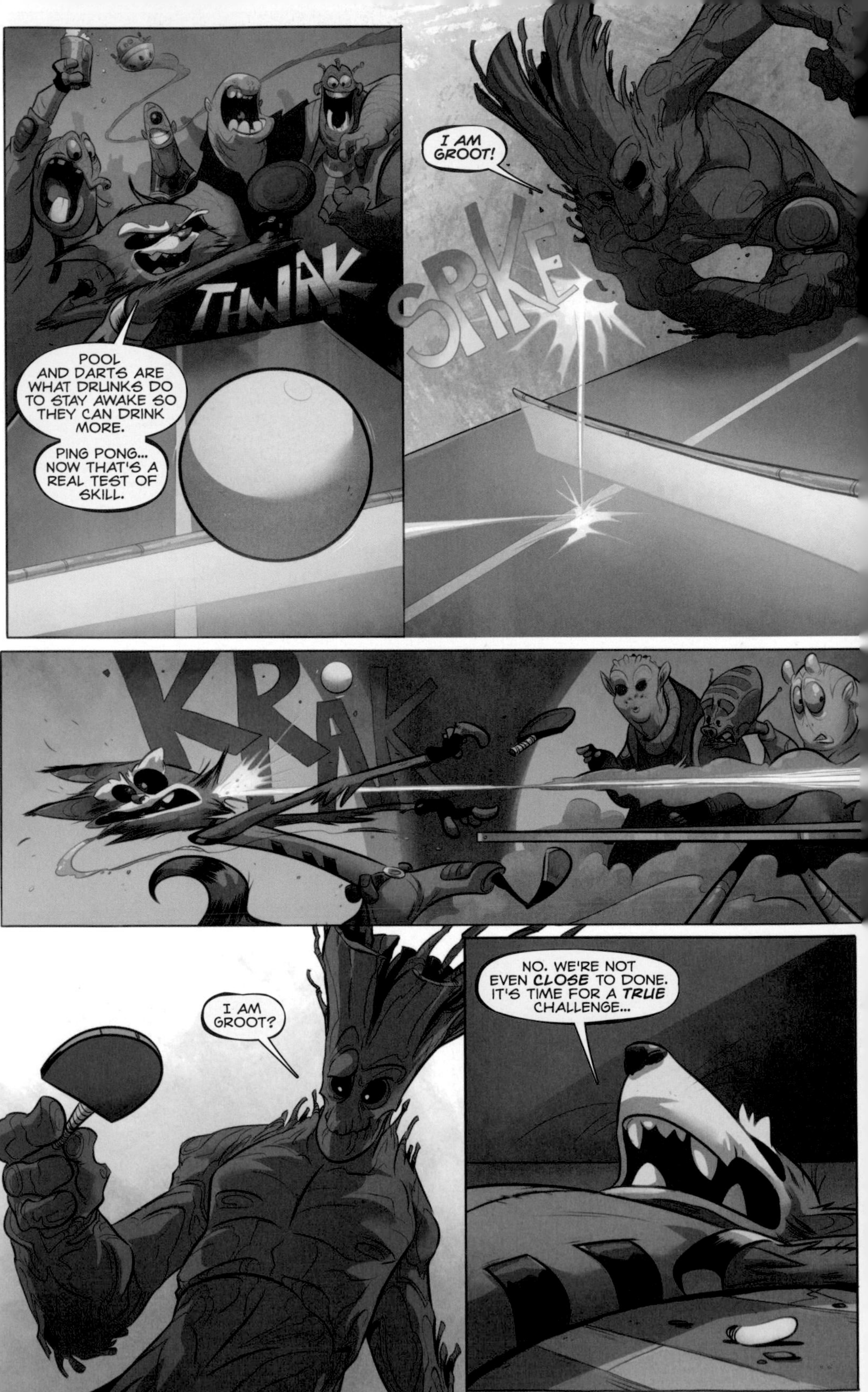
THWAK
POOL AND DARTS ARE WHAT DRUNKS DO TO STAY AWAKE SO THEY CAN DRINK MORE.
PING PONG... NOW THAT'S A REAL TEST OF SKILL.
I AM GROOT!
SPIKE
KRAK
I AM GROOT?
NO. WE'RE NOT EVEN ***CLOSE*** TO DONE. IT'S TIME FOR A ***TRUE*** CHALLENGE...

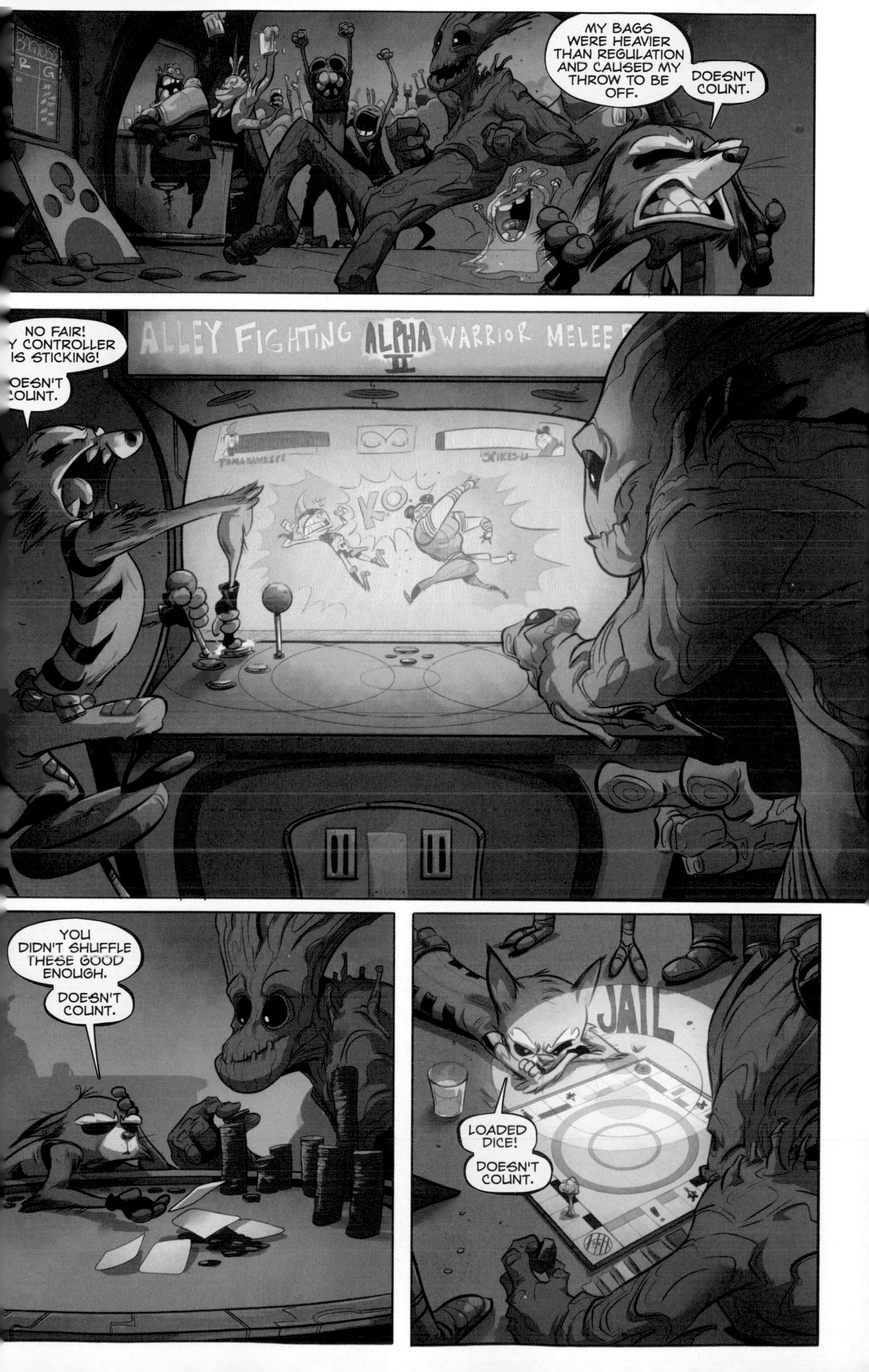
MY BAGS WERE HEAVIER THAN REGULATION AND CAUSED MY THROW TO BE OFF.
DOESN'T COUNT.
ALLEY FIGHTING ALPHA II WARRIOR MELEE
NO FAIR! Y CONTROLLER IS STICKING!
OESN'T COUNT.
K.O.
YOU DIDN'T SHUFFLE THESE GOOD ENOUGH.
DOESN'T COUNT.
JAIL
LOADED DICE!
DOESN'T COUNT.

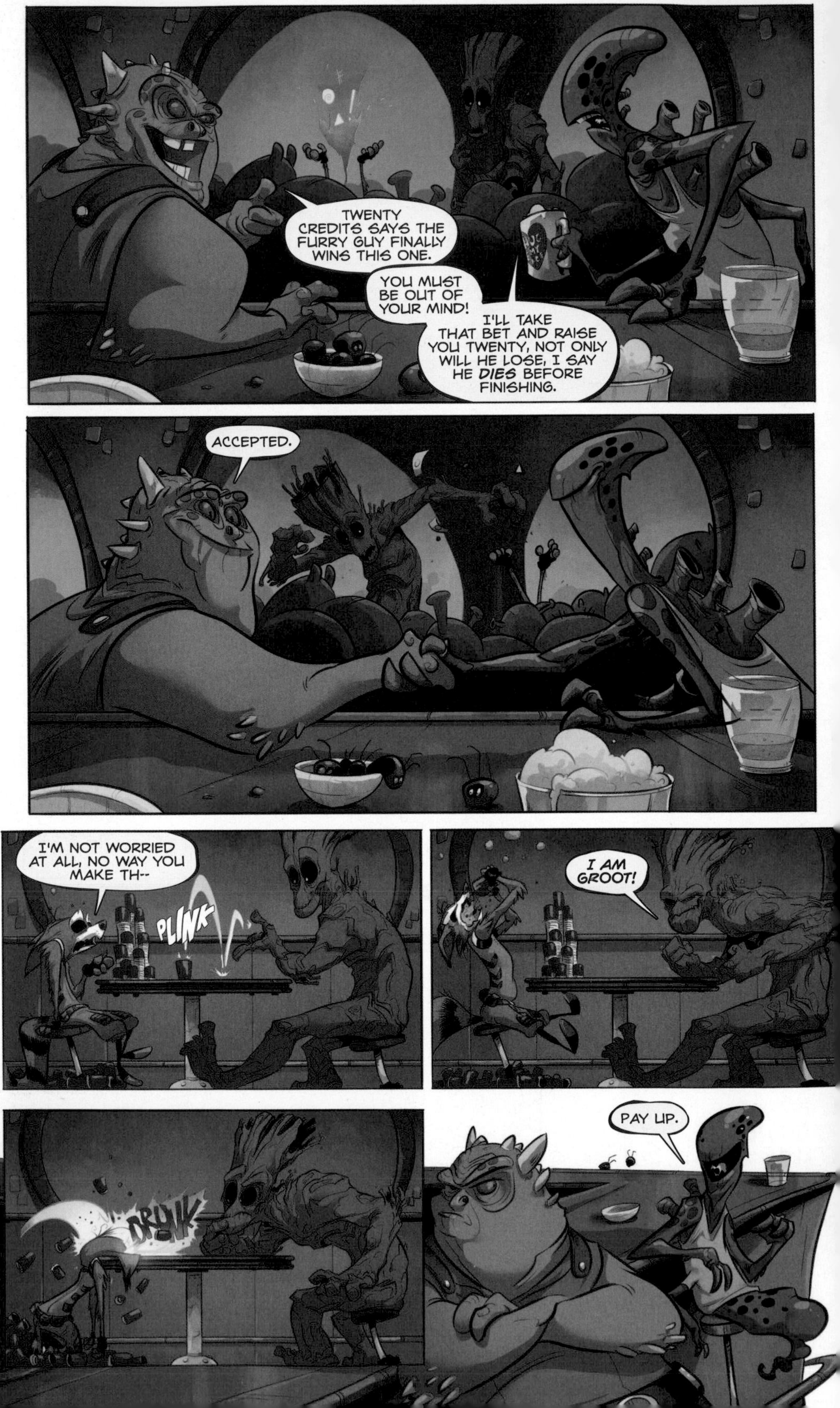
TWENTY CREDITS SAYS THE FURRY GUY FINALLY WINS THIS ONE.
YOU MUST BE OUT OF YOUR MIND!
I'LL TAKE THAT BET AND RAISE YOU TWENTY, NOT ONLY WILL HE LOSE, I SAY HE DIES BEFORE FINISHING.
ACCEPTED.
I'M NOT WORRIED AT ALL, NO WAY YOU MAKE TH--
PLINK
I AM GROOT!
DRUNK
PAY UP.

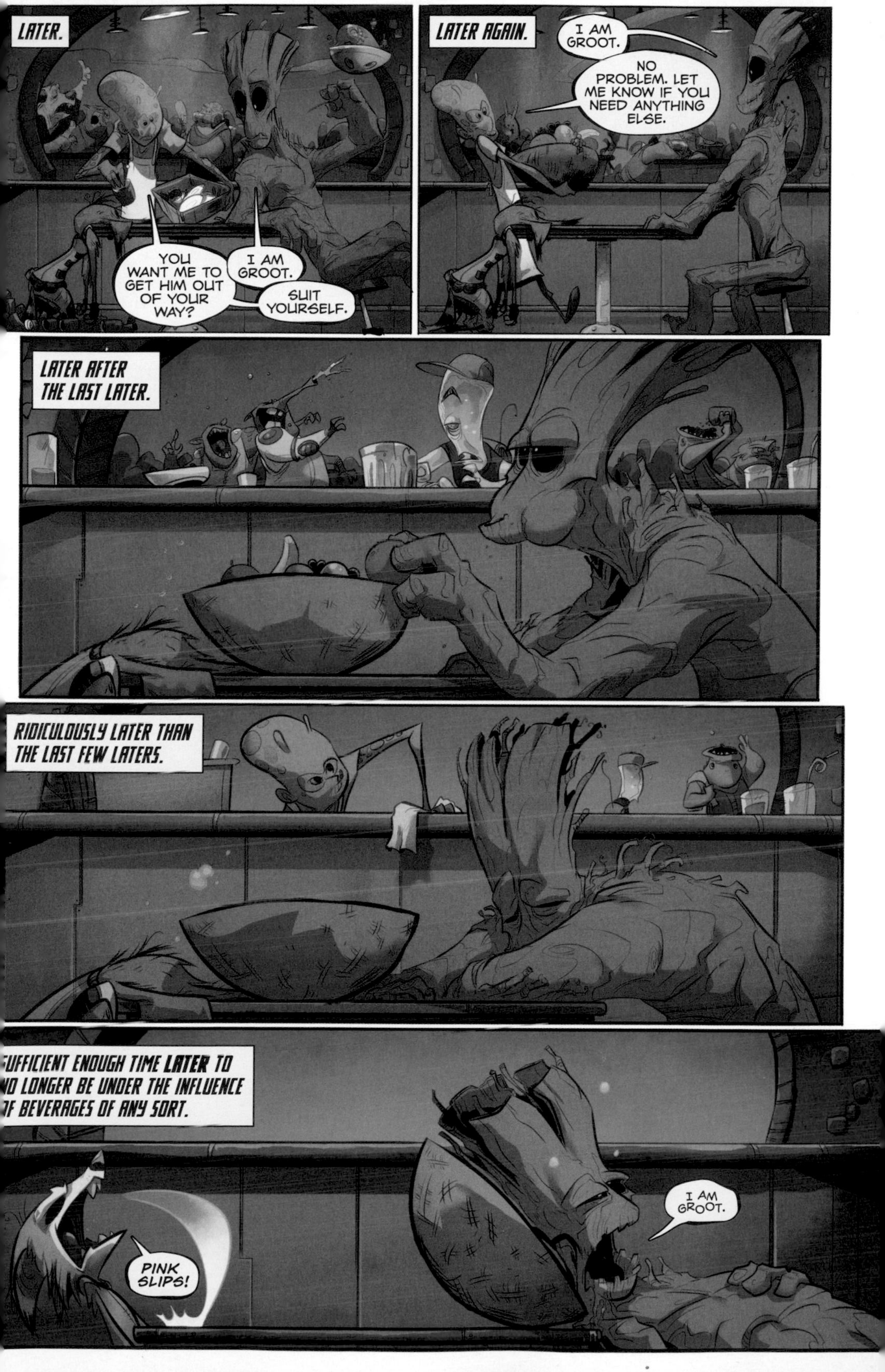
LATER.
YOU WANT ME TO GET HIM OUT OF YOUR WAY?
I AM GROOT.
SUIT YOURSELF.
LATER AGAIN.
I AM GROOT.
NO PROBLEM. LET ME KNOW IF YOU NEED ANYTHING ELSE.
LATER AFTER THE LAST LATER.
RIDICULOUSLY LATER THAN THE LAST FEW LATERS.
SUFFICIENT ENOUGH TIME LATER TO NO LONGER BE UNDER THE INFLUENCE OF BEVERAGES OF ANY SORT.
PINK SLIPS!
I AM GROOT.

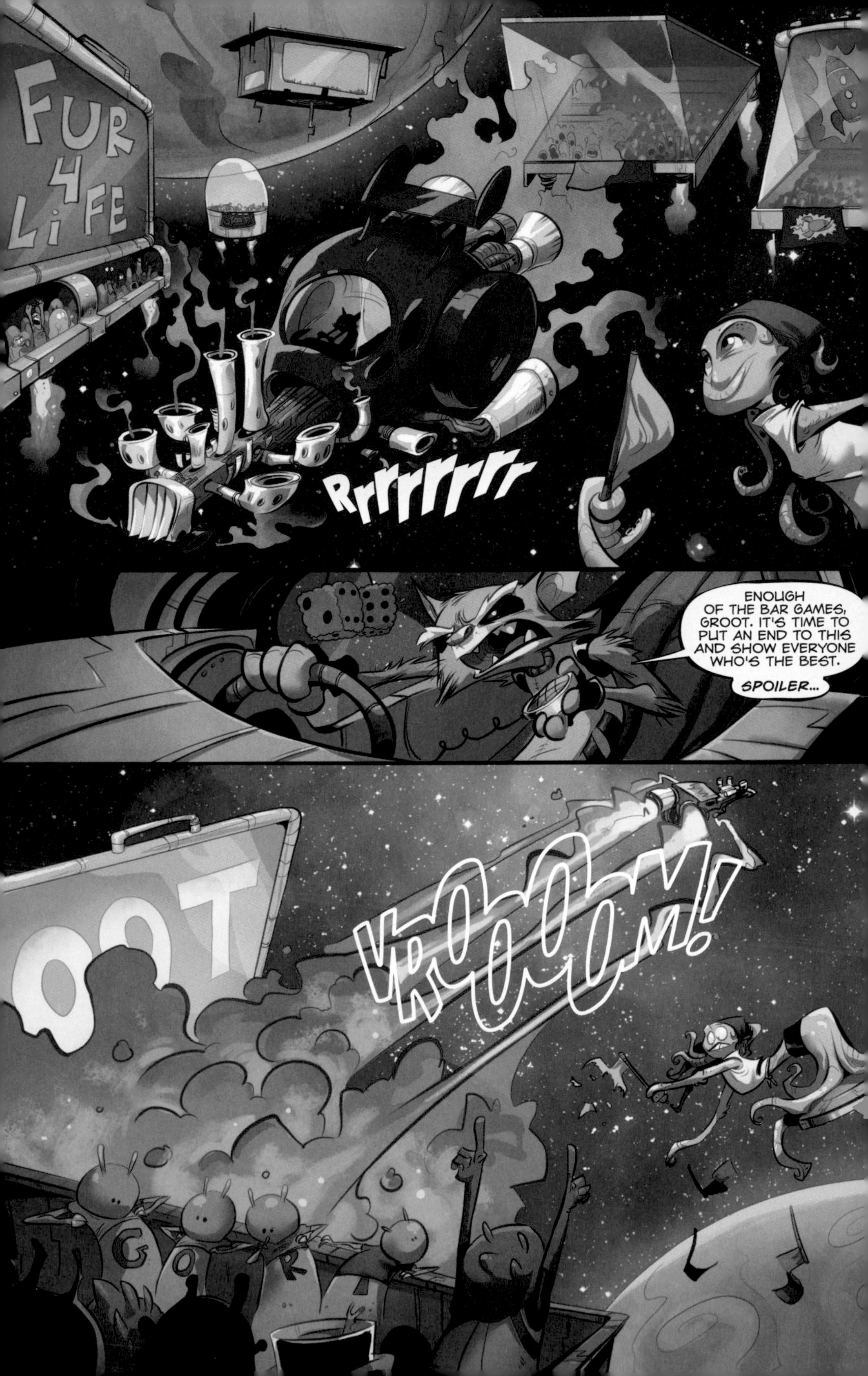
FUR 4 LiFE
Rrrrrrrr
ENOUGH OF THE BAR GAMES, GROOT. IT'S TIME TO PUT AN END TO THIS AND SHOW EVERYONE WHO'S THE BEST.
SPOILER...
VROOOOM!

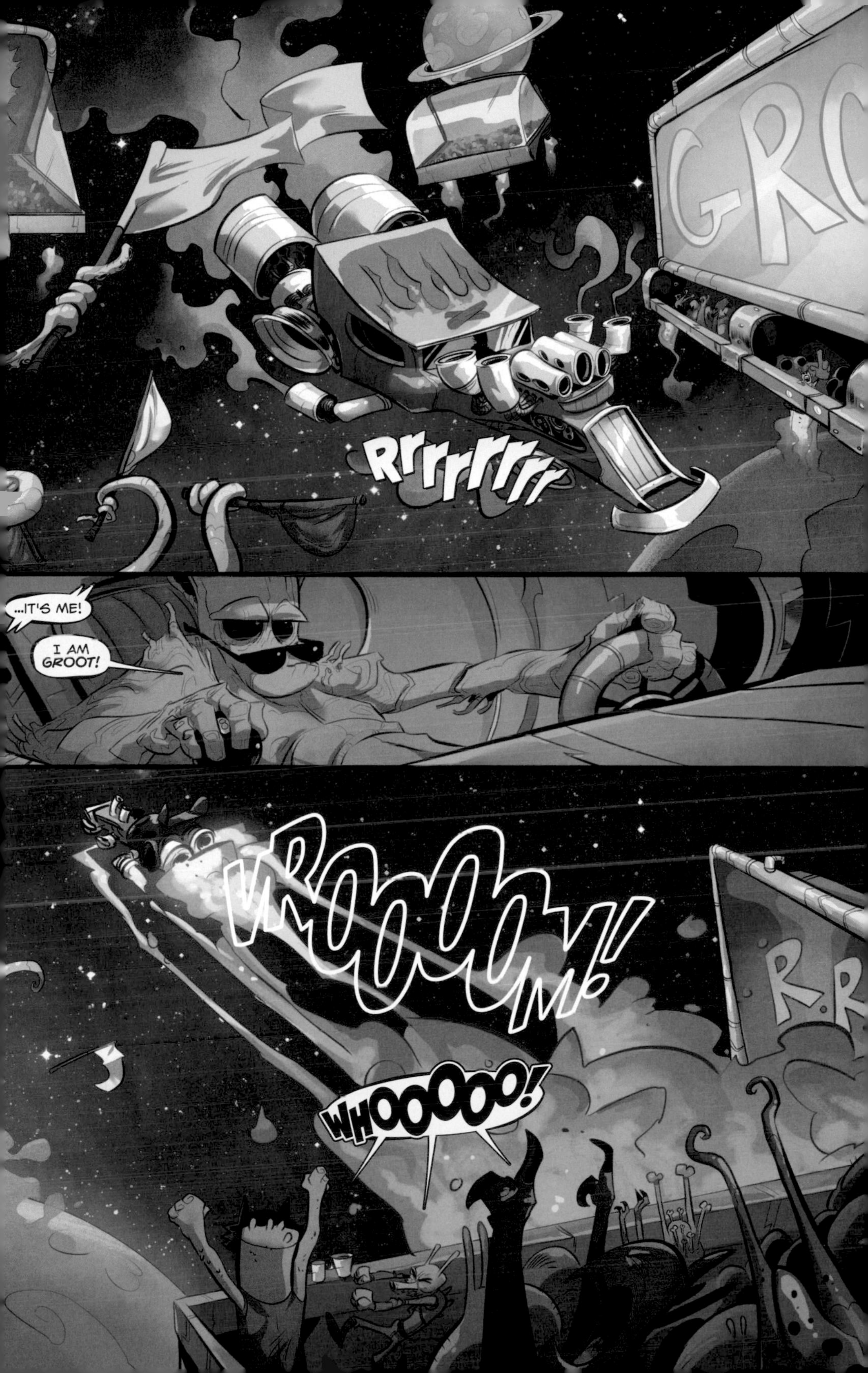
GRO
Rrrrrrrr
...IT'S ME!
I AM GROOT!
VROOOOM!
R.R
WHOOOOO!

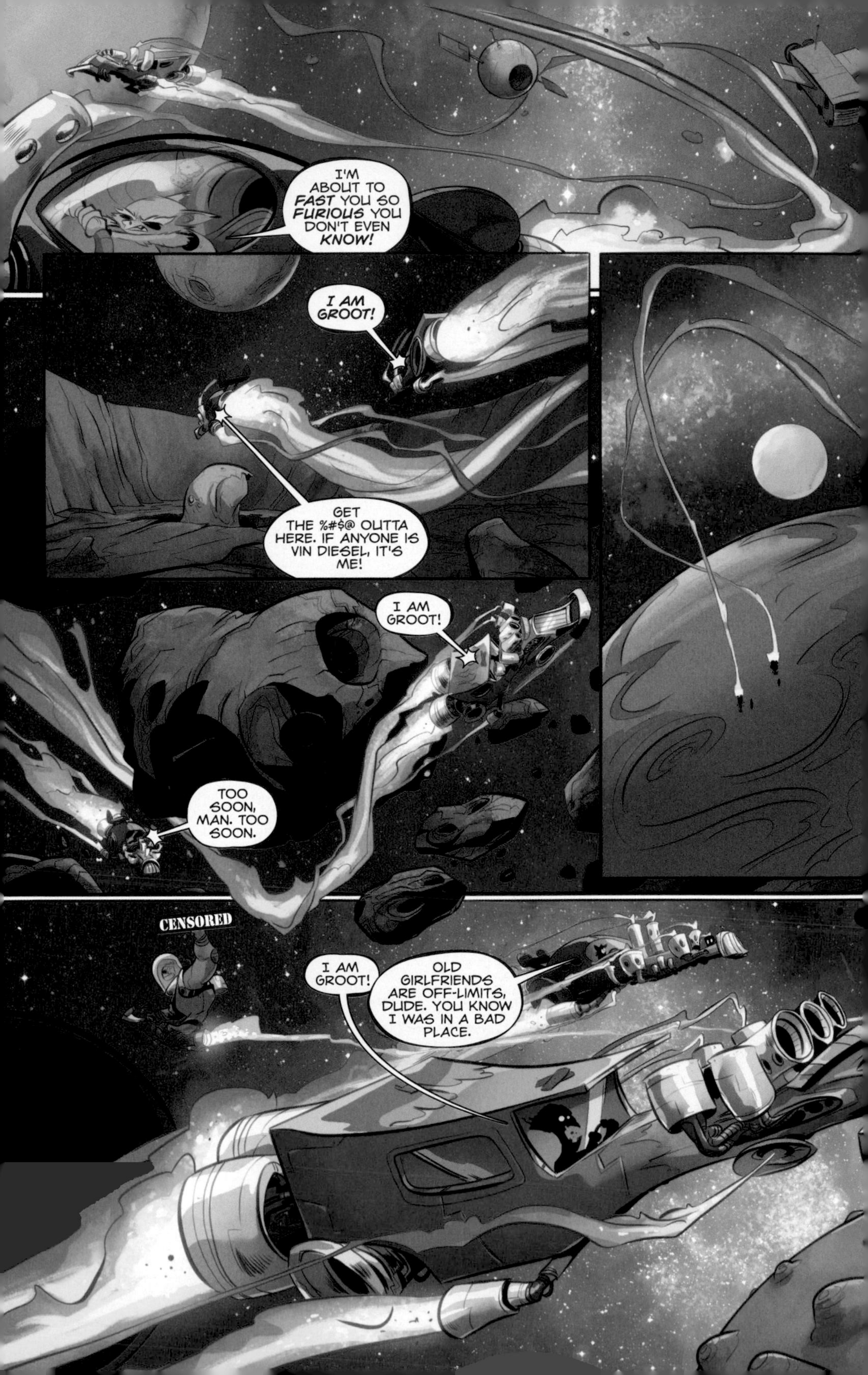
I'M ABOUT TO FAST YOU SO FURIOUS YOU DON'T EVEN KNOW!
I AM GROOT!
GET THE %#$@ OUTTA HERE. IF ANYONE IS VIN DIESEL, IT'S ME!
I AM GROOT!
TOO SOON, MAN. TOO SOON.
CENSORED
I AM GROOT!
OLD GIRLFRIENDS ARE OFF-LIMITS, DUDE. YOU KNOW I WAS IN A BAD PLACE.

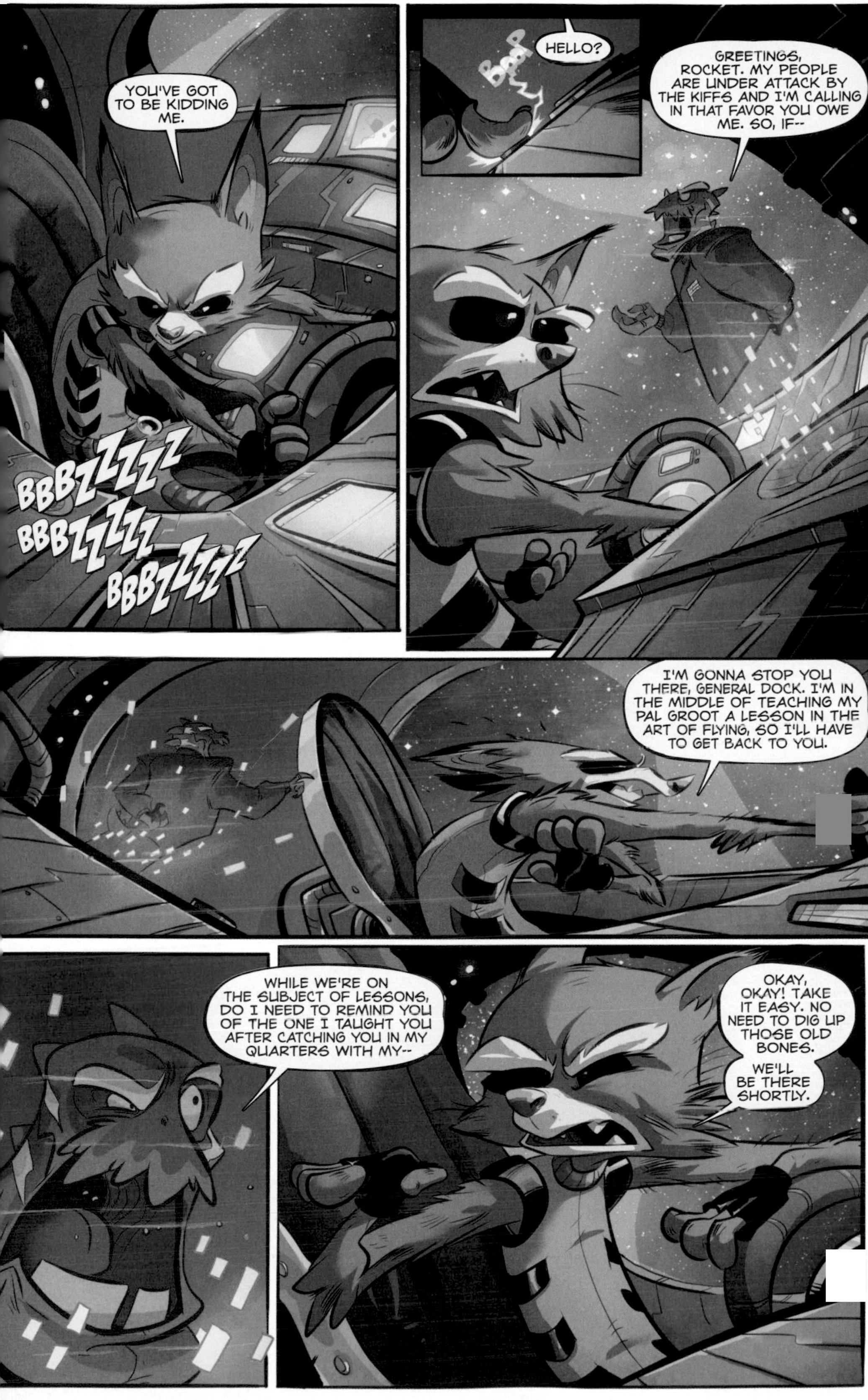
YOU'VE GOT TO BE KIDDING ME.
BBBZZZZZZ
BBBZZZZZZ
BBBZZZZZZ
BOOP
HELLO?
GREETINGS, ROCKET. MY PEOPLE ARE UNDER ATTACK BY THE KIFFS AND I'M CALLING IN THAT FAVOR YOU OWE ME. SO, IF--
I'M GONNA STOP YOU THERE, GENERAL DOCK. I'M IN THE MIDDLE OF TEACHING MY PAL GROOT A LESSON IN THE ART OF FLYING, SO I'LL HAVE TO GET BACK TO YOU.
WHILE WE'RE ON THE SUBJECT OF LESSONS, DO I NEED TO REMIND YOU OF THE ONE I TAUGHT YOU AFTER CATCHING YOU IN MY QUARTERS WITH MY--
OKAY, OKAY! TAKE IT EASY. NO NEED TO DIG UP THOSE OLD BONES.
WE'LL BE THERE SHORTLY.

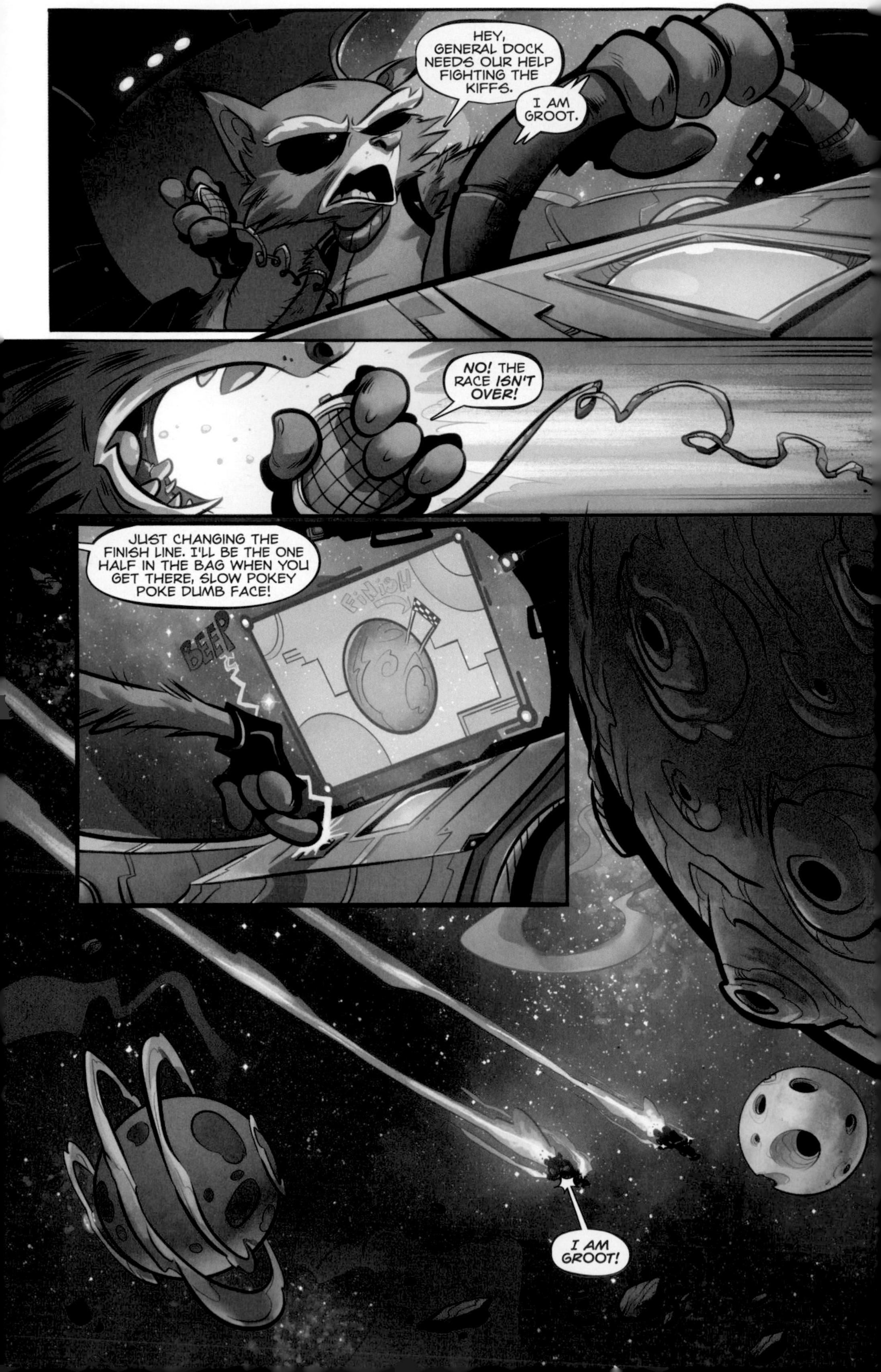
HEY, GENERAL DOCK NEEDS OUR HELP FIGHTING THE KIFFS.
I AM GROOT.
NO! THE RACE ISN'T OVER!
JUST CHANGING THE FINISH LINE. I'LL BE THE ONE HALF IN THE BAG WHEN YOU GET THERE, SLOW POKEY POKE DUMB FACE!
FINISH
BEEP
I AM GROOT!

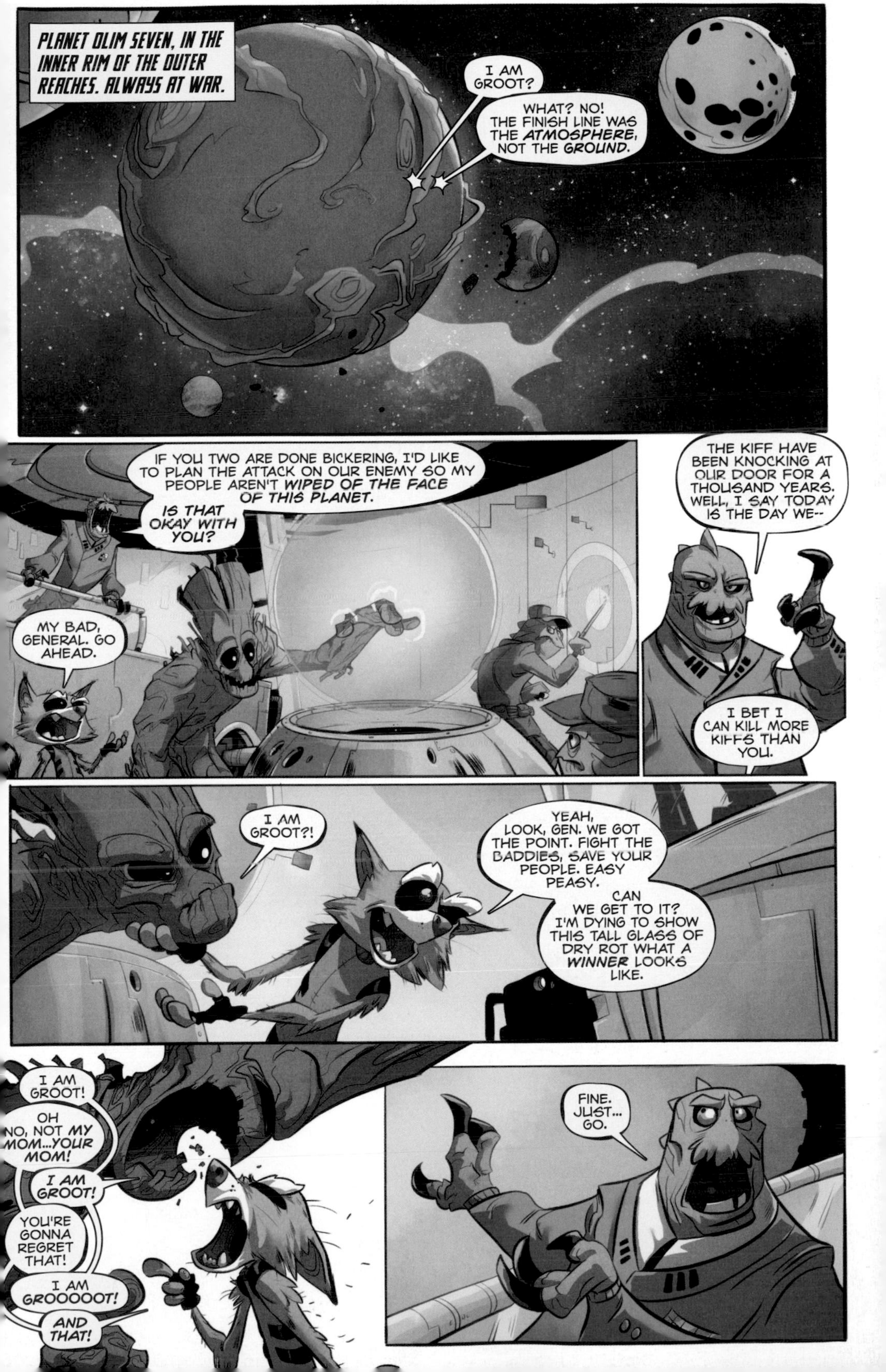
PLANET OLIM SEVEN, IN THE INNER RIM OF THE OUTER REACHES. ALWAYS AT WAR.
I AM GROOT?
WHAT? NO! THE FINISH LINE WAS THE ATMOSPHERE, NOT THE GROUND.
IF YOU TWO ARE DONE BICKERING, I'D LIKE TO PLAN THE ATTACK ON OUR ENEMY SO MY PEOPLE AREN'T WIPED OF THE FACE OF THIS PLANET.
IS THAT OKAY WITH YOU?
MY BAD, GENERAL. GO AHEAD.
THE KIFF HAVE BEEN KNOCKING AT OUR DOOR FOR A THOUSAND YEARS. WELL, I SAY TODAY IS THE DAY WE--
I BET I CAN KILL MORE KIFFS THAN YOU.
I AM GROOT?!
YEAH, LOOK, GEN. WE GOT THE POINT. FIGHT THE BADDIES, SAVE YOUR PEOPLE. EASY PEASY.
CAN WE GET TO IT? I'M DYING TO SHOW THIS TALL GLASS OF DRY ROT WHAT A WINNER LOOKS LIKE.
I AM GROOT!
OH NO, NOT MY MOM...YOUR MOM!
I AM GROOT!
YOU'RE GONNA REGRET THAT!
I AM GROOOOOT!
AND THAT!
FINE. JUST... GO.

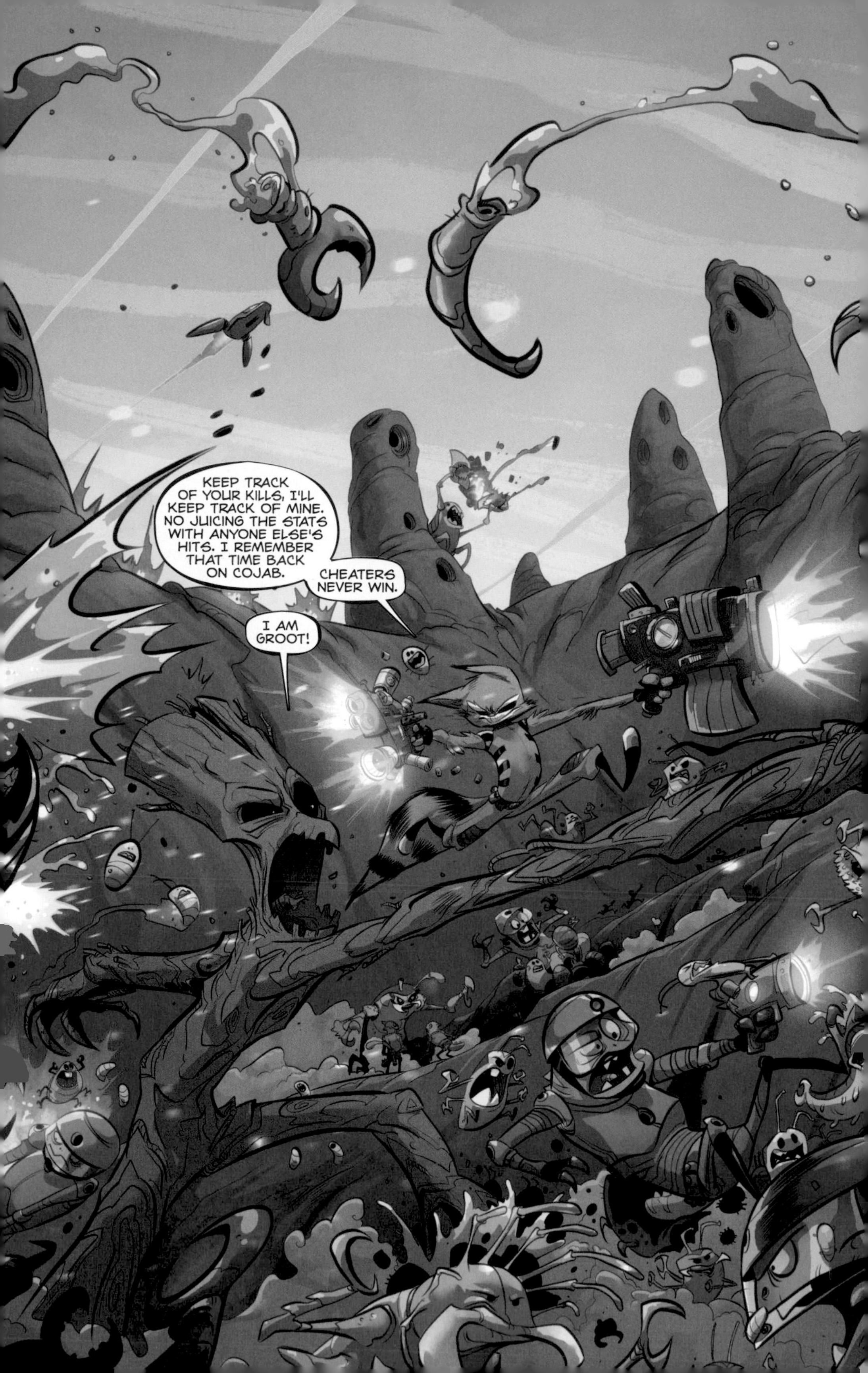
KEEP TRACK OF YOUR KILLS, I'LL KEEP TRACK OF MINE. NO JUICING THE STATS WITH ANYONE ELSE'S HITS. I REMEMBER THAT TIME BACK ON COJAB.
CHEATERS NEVER WIN.
I AM GROOT!

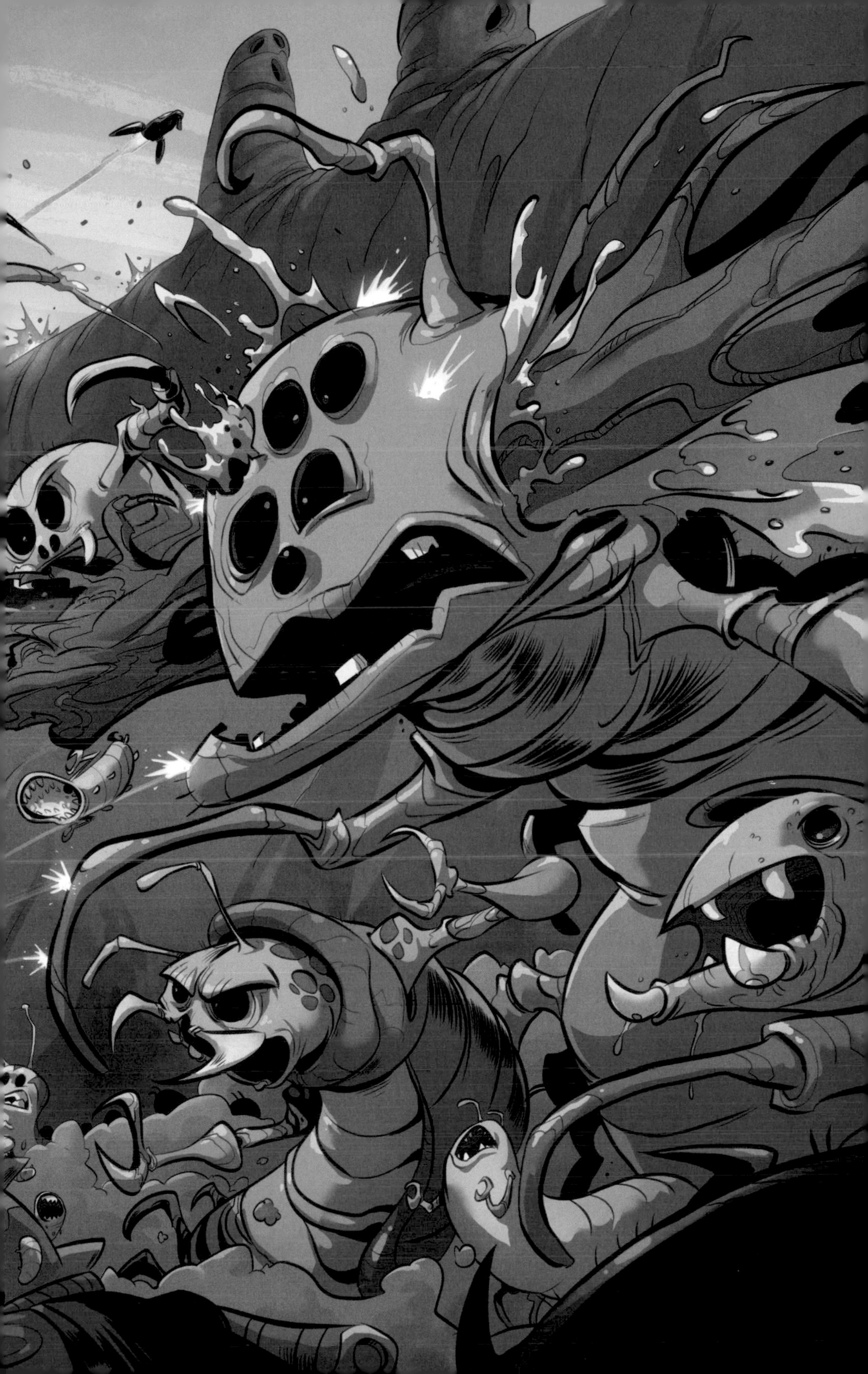

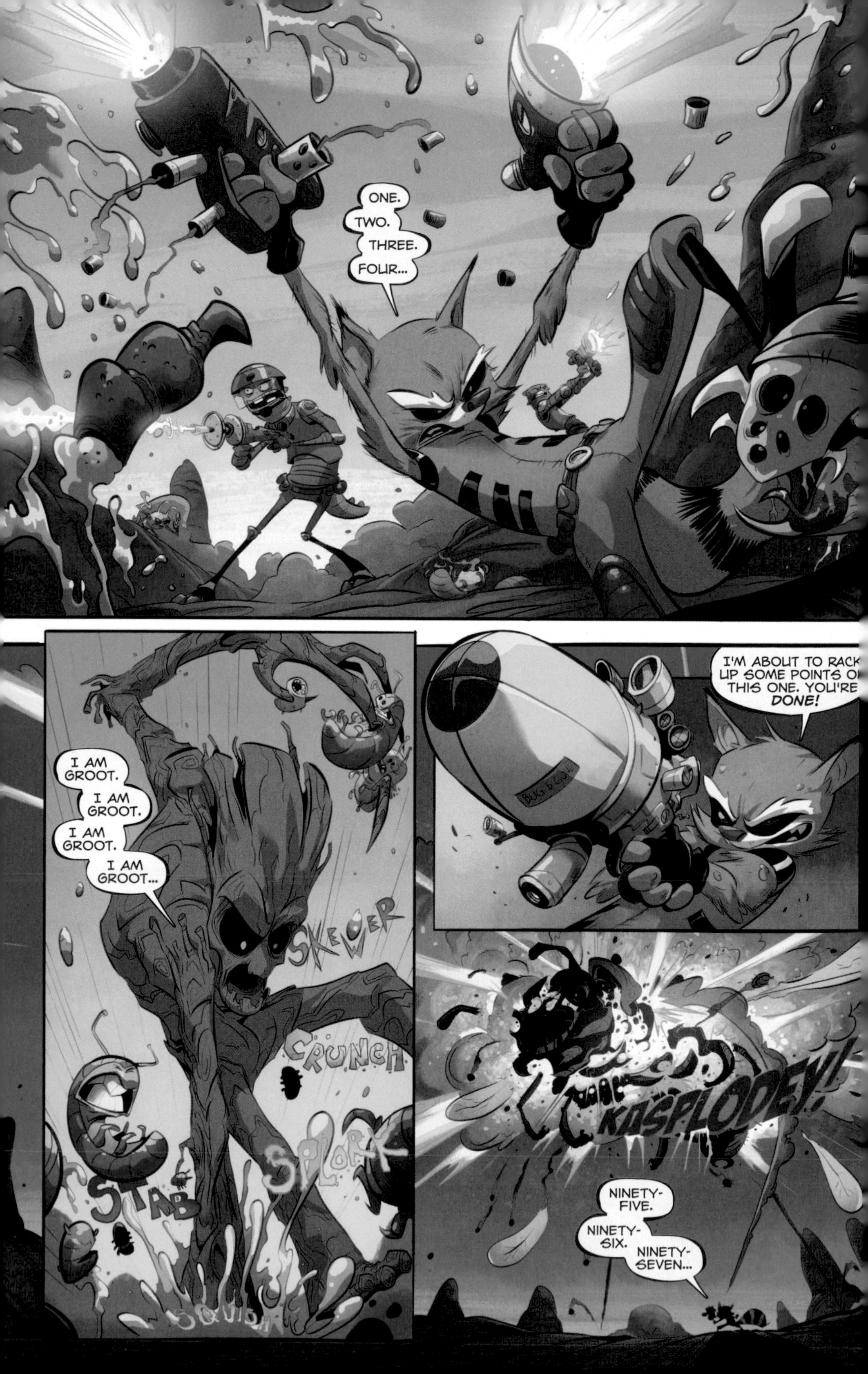
ONE.
TWO.
THREE.
FOUR...
I AM GROOT.
I AM GROOT.
I AM GROOT.
I AM GROOT...
SKEWER
CRUNCH
SPLORK
STAB
SQUISH
I'M ABOUT TO RACK UP SOME POINTS ON THIS ONE. YOU'RE *DONE!*
KASPLODEY!!
NINETY-FIVE.
NINETY-SIX.
NINETY-SEVEN...

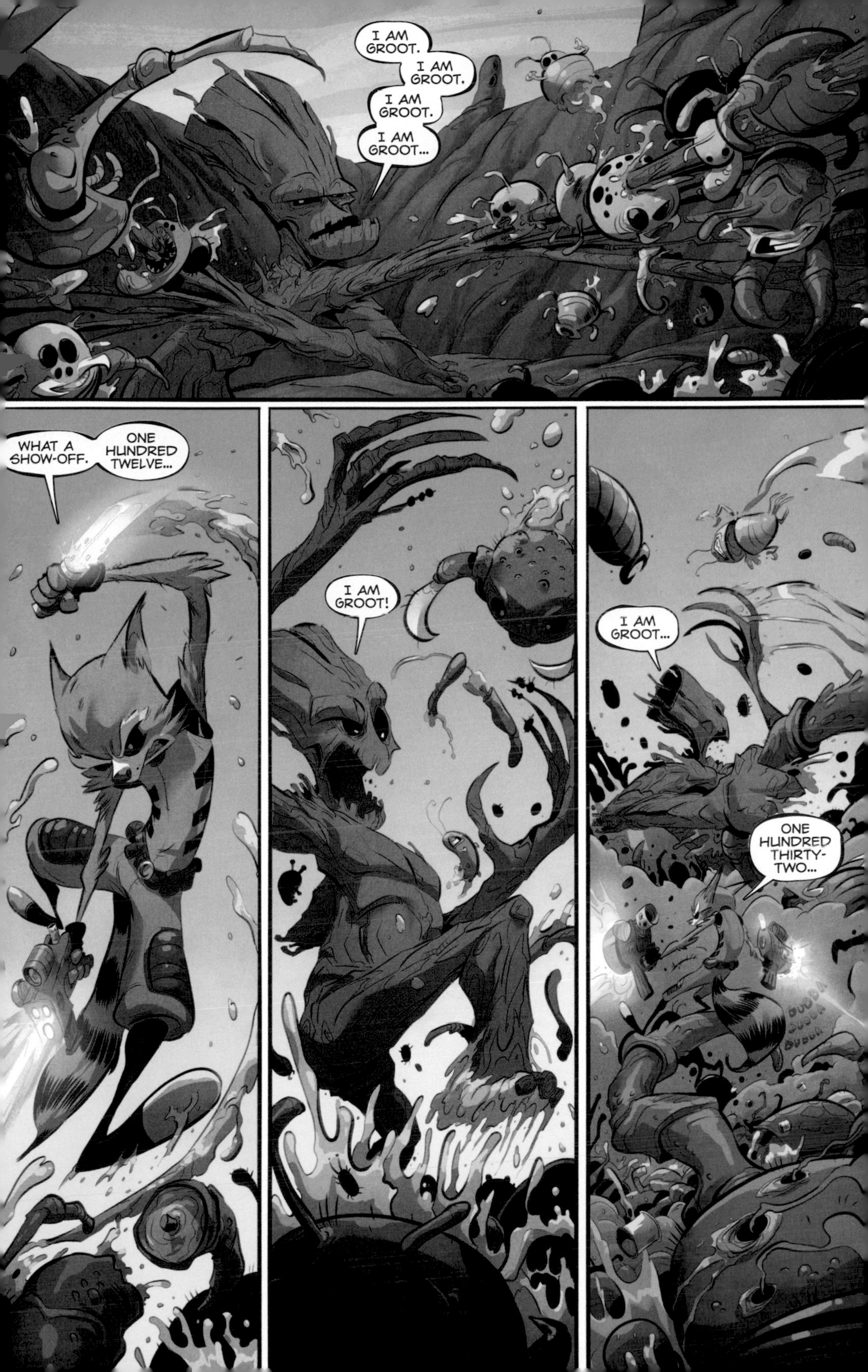
I AM GROOT.
I AM GROOT.
I AM GROOT.
I AM GROOT...
WHAT A SHOW-OFF.
ONE HUNDRED TWELVE...
I AM GROOT!
I AM GROOT...
ONE HUNDRED THIRTY-TWO...
BUDDA BUDDA BUDDA

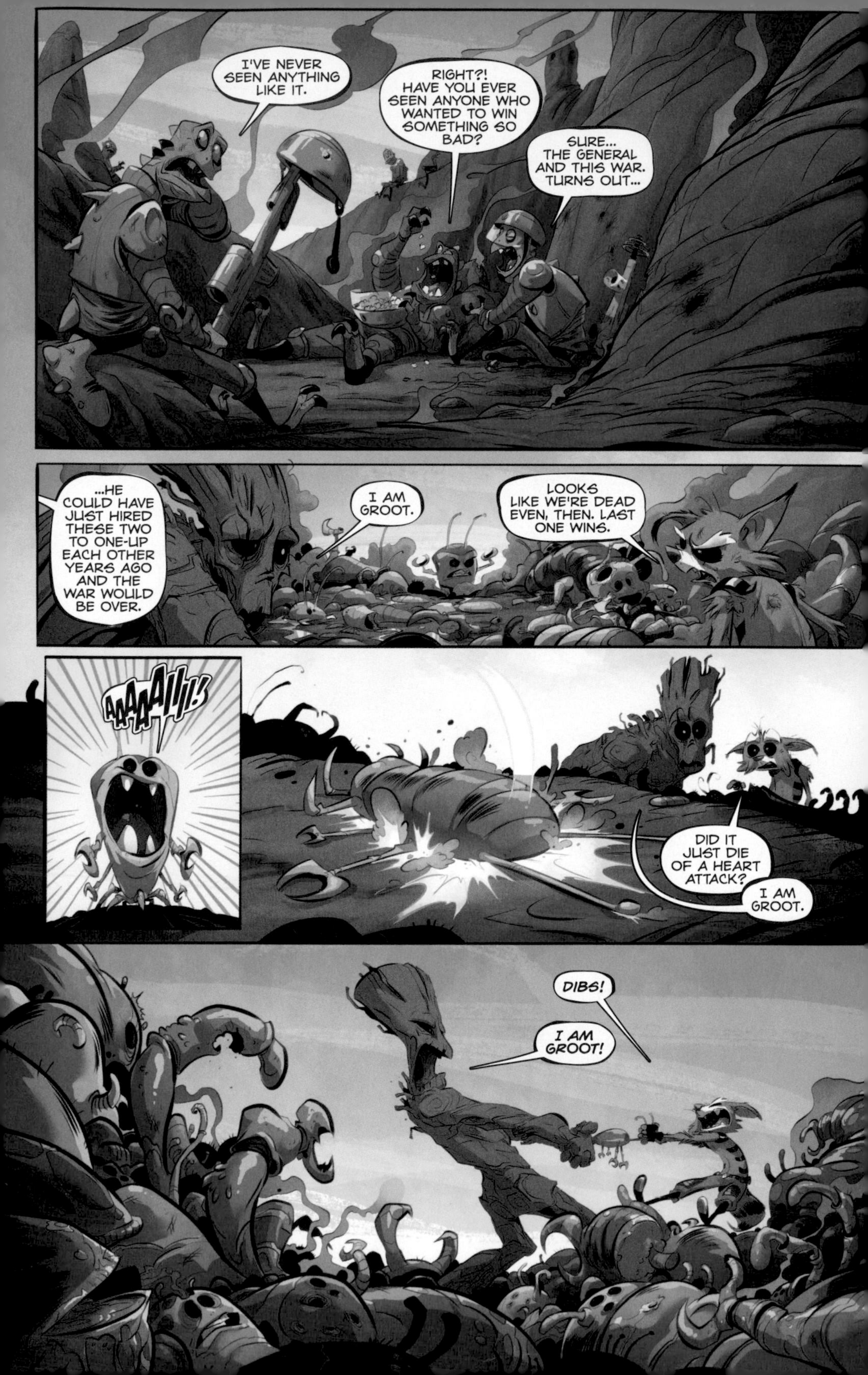
I'VE NEVER SEEN ANYTHING LIKE IT.
RIGHT?! HAVE YOU EVER SEEN ANYONE WHO WANTED TO WIN SOMETHING SO BAD?
SURE... THE GENERAL AND THIS WAR. TURNS OUT...
...HE COULD HAVE JUST HIRED THESE TWO TO ONE-UP EACH OTHER YEARS AGO AND THE WAR WOULD BE OVER.
I AM GROOT.
LOOKS LIKE WE'RE DEAD EVEN, THEN. LAST ONE WINS.
AAAAAIIII!
DID IT JUST DIE OF A HEART ATTACK?
I AM GROOT.
DIBS!
I AM GROOT!

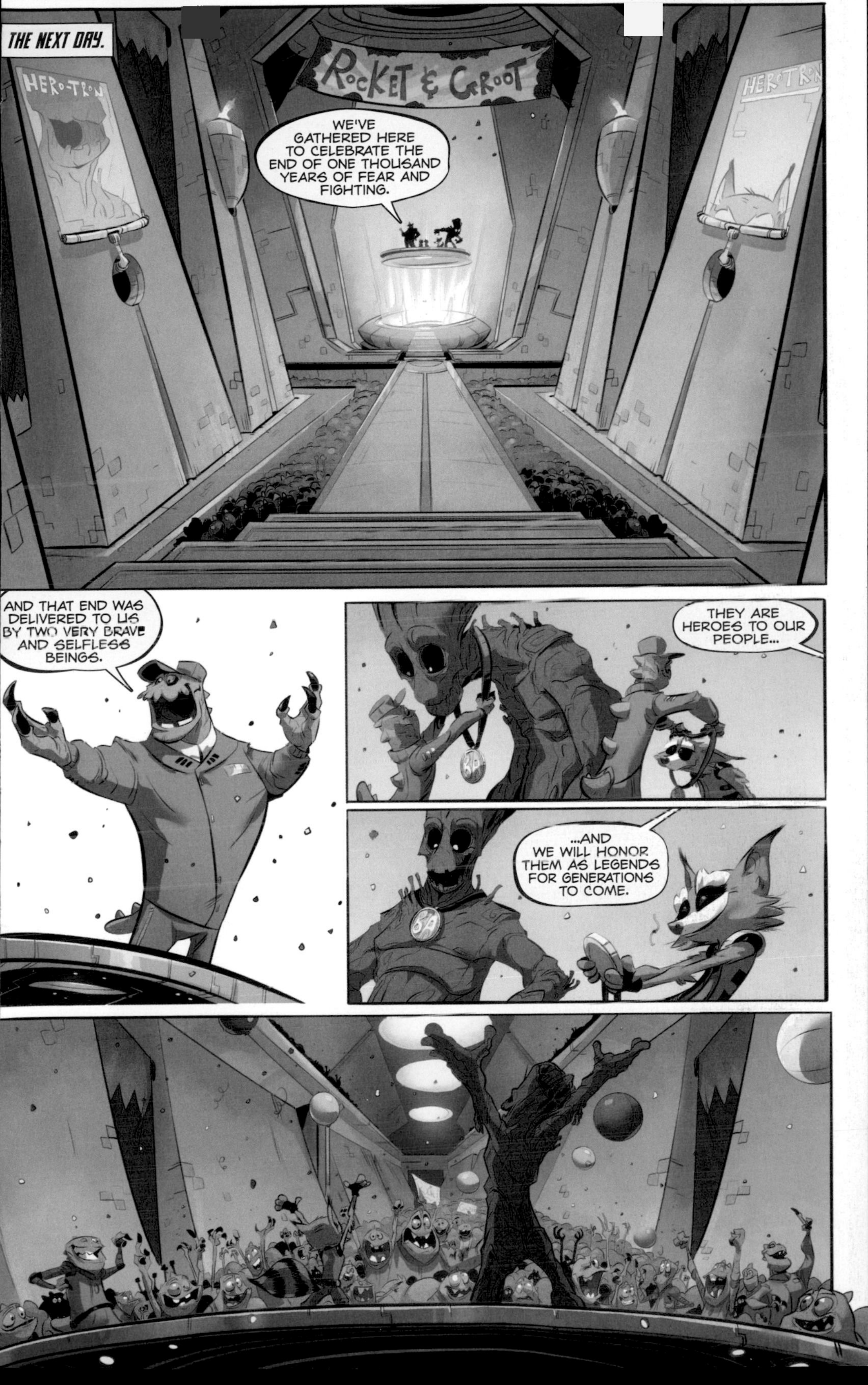
THE NEXT DAY.
ROCKET & GROOT
HERO-TRON
HERO-TRON
WE'VE GATHERED HERE TO CELEBRATE THE END OF ONE THOUSAND YEARS OF FEAR AND FIGHTING.
AND THAT END WAS DELIVERED TO US BY TWO VERY BRAVE AND SELFLESS BEINGS.
THEY ARE HEROES TO OUR PEOPLE...
...AND WE WILL HONOR THEM AS LEGENDS FOR GENERATIONS TO COME.

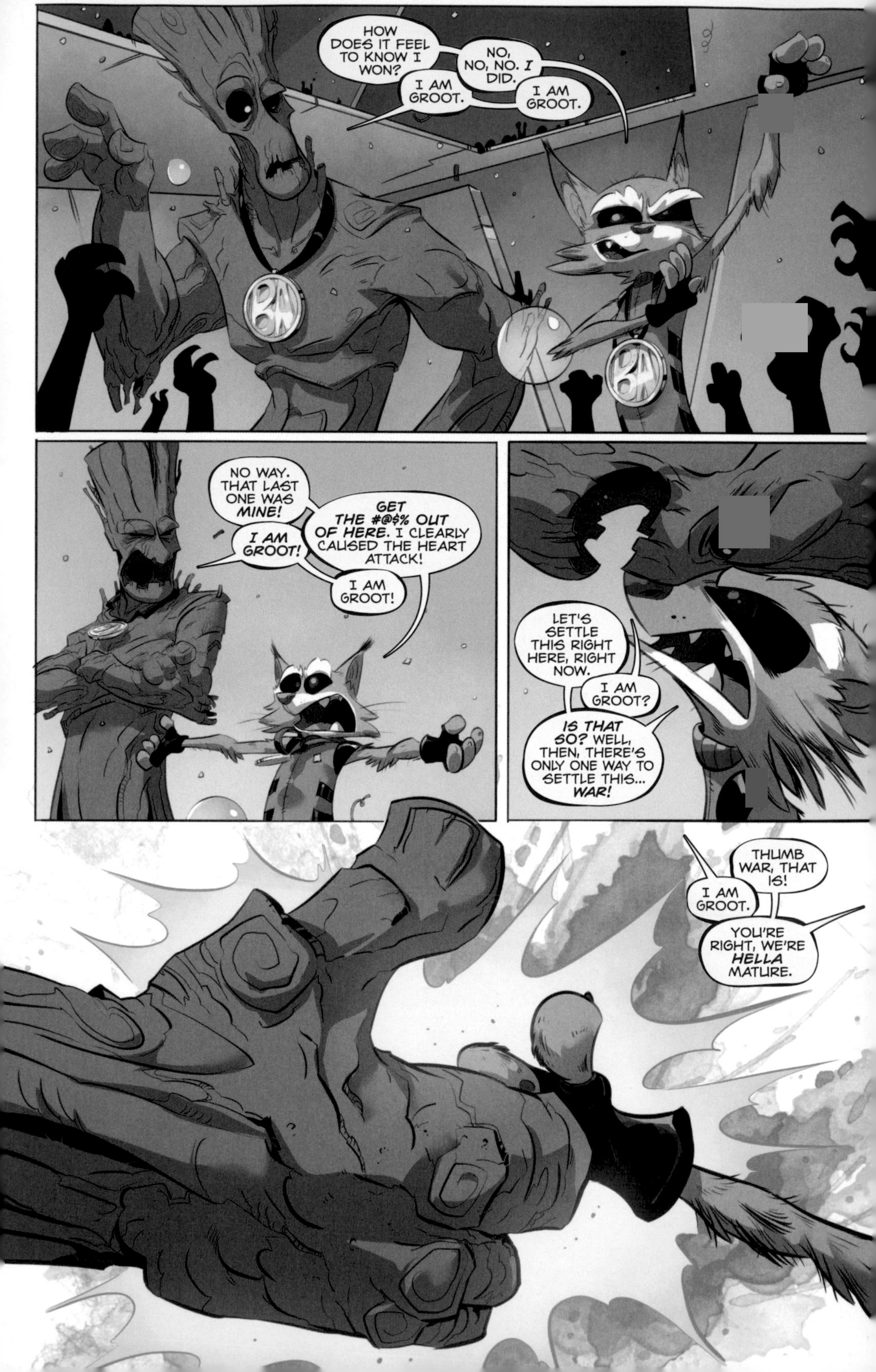
HOW DOES IT FEEL TO KNOW I WON?
I AM GROOT.
NO, NO, NO. *I* DID.
I AM GROOT.
NO WAY. THAT LAST ONE WAS *MINE!*
*I AM GROOT!*
*GET THE #@$% OUT OF HERE.* I CLEARLY CAUSED THE HEART ATTACK!
I AM GROOT!
LET'S SETTLE THIS RIGHT HERE, RIGHT NOW.
I AM GROOT?
*IS THAT SO?* WELL, THEN, THERE'S ONLY ONE WAY TO SETTLE THIS... *WAR!*
THUMB WAR, THAT IS!
I AM GROOT.
YOU'RE RIGHT, WE'RE *HELLA* MATURE.

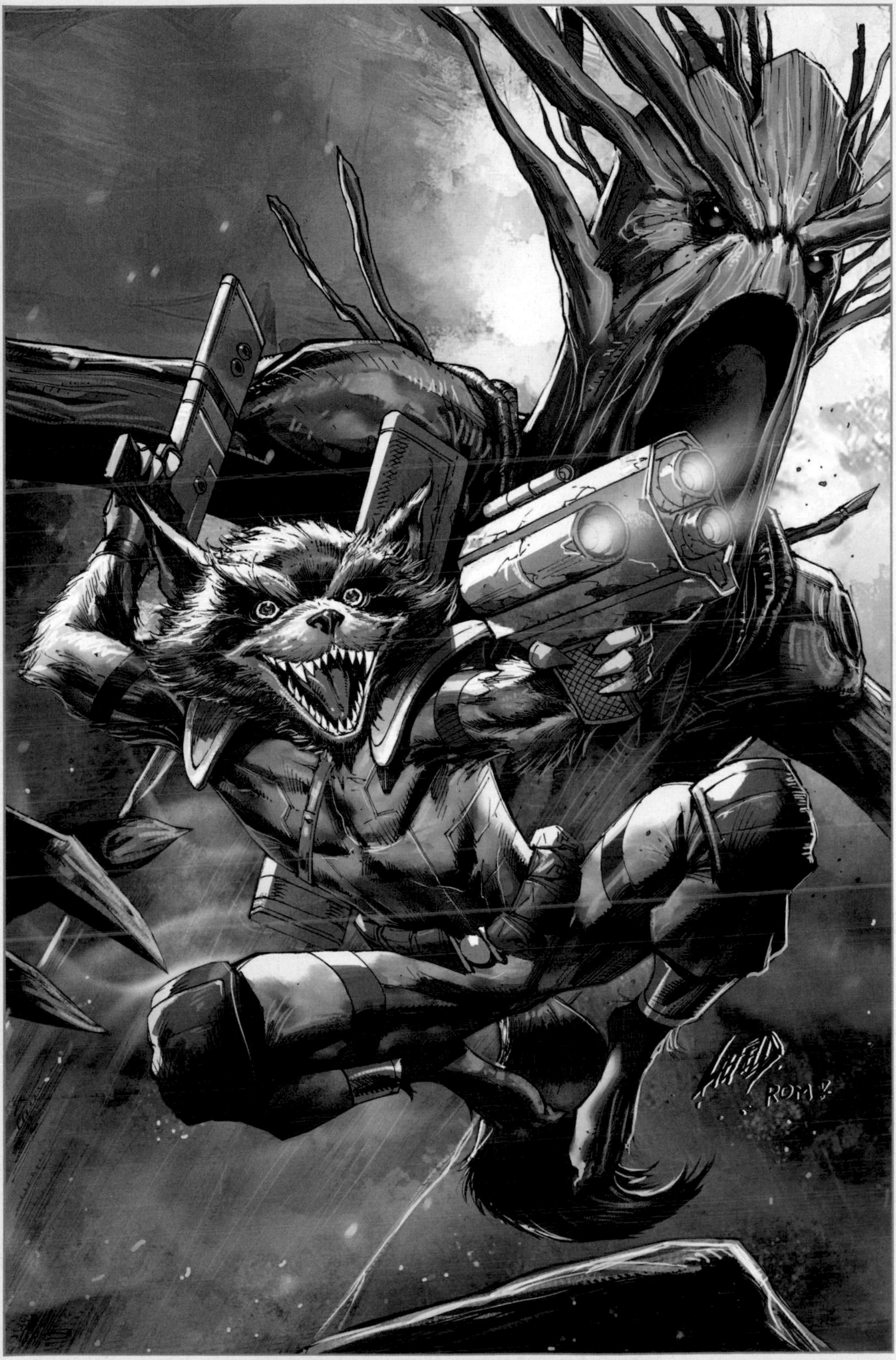

**ROCKET RACCOON & GROOT #4 VARIANT**
BY ROB LIEFELD & ROMULO FAJARDO JR.

# 7

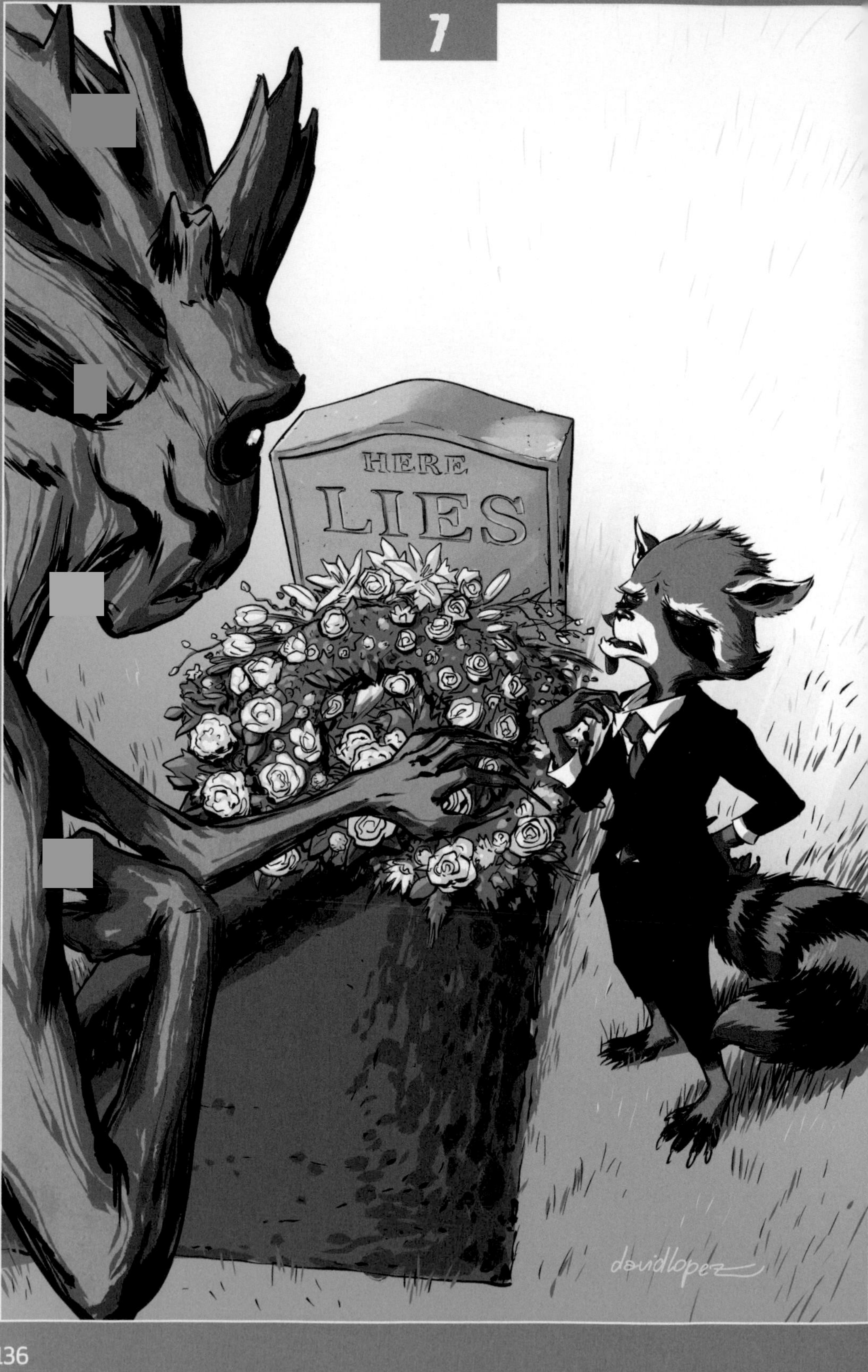
HERE
LIES
davidlopez

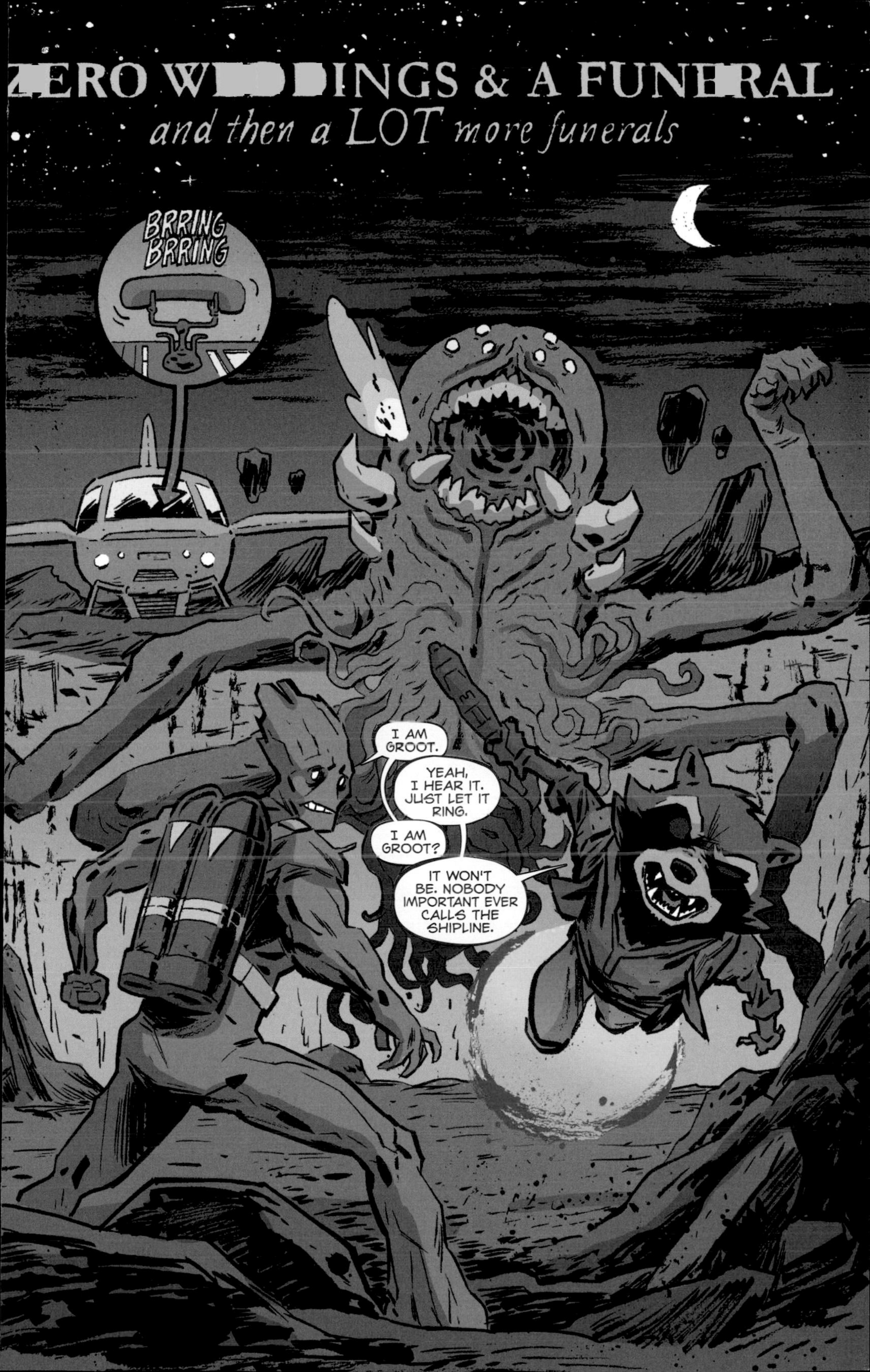
ZERO WEDDINGS & A FUNERAL
and then a LOT more funerals
BRRING BRRING
I AM GROOT.
YEAH, I HEAR IT. JUST LET IT RING.
I AM GROOT?
IT WON'T BE. NOBODY IMPORTANT EVER CALLS THE SHIPLINE.

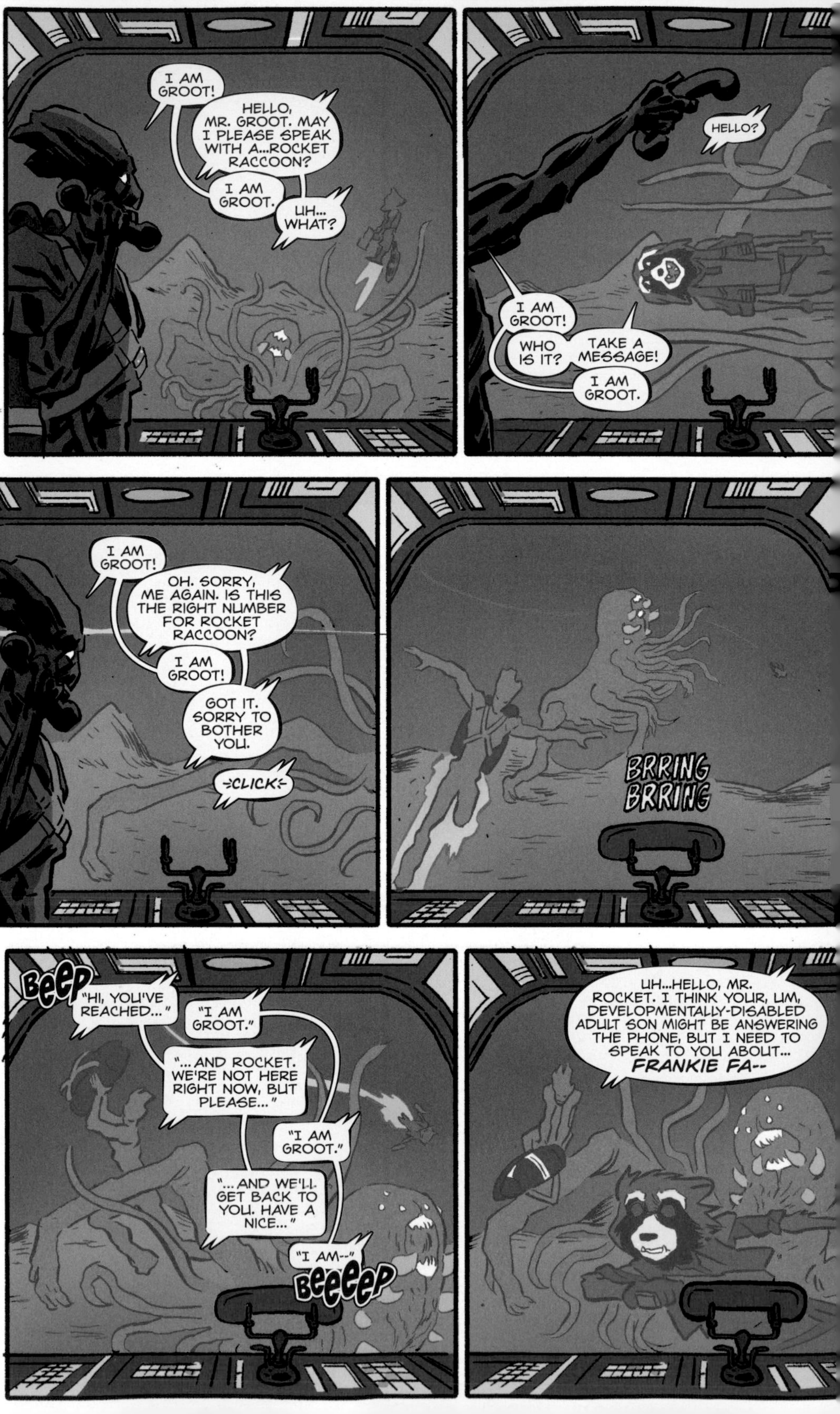
I AM GROOT!
HELLO, MR. GROOT. MAY I PLEASE SPEAK WITH A...ROCKET RACCOON?
I AM GROOT.
UH... WHAT?
HELLO?
I AM GROOT!
WHO IS IT?
TAKE A MESSAGE!
I AM GROOT.
I AM GROOT!
OH. SORRY, ME AGAIN. IS THIS THE RIGHT NUMBER FOR ROCKET RACCOON?
I AM GROOT!
GOT IT. SORRY TO BOTHER YOU.
CLICK
BRRING BRRING
BEEP
"HI, YOU'VE REACHED..."
"I AM GROOT."
"... AND ROCKET. WE'RE NOT HERE RIGHT NOW, BUT PLEASE..."
"I AM GROOT."
"... AND WE'LL GET BACK TO YOU. HAVE A NICE..."
"I AM--"
BEEEEP
UH...HELLO, MR. ROCKET. I THINK YOUR, UM, DEVELOPMENTALLY-DISABLED ADULT SON MIGHT BE ANSWERING THE PHONE, BUT I NEED TO SPEAK TO YOU ABOUT... FRANKIE FA--

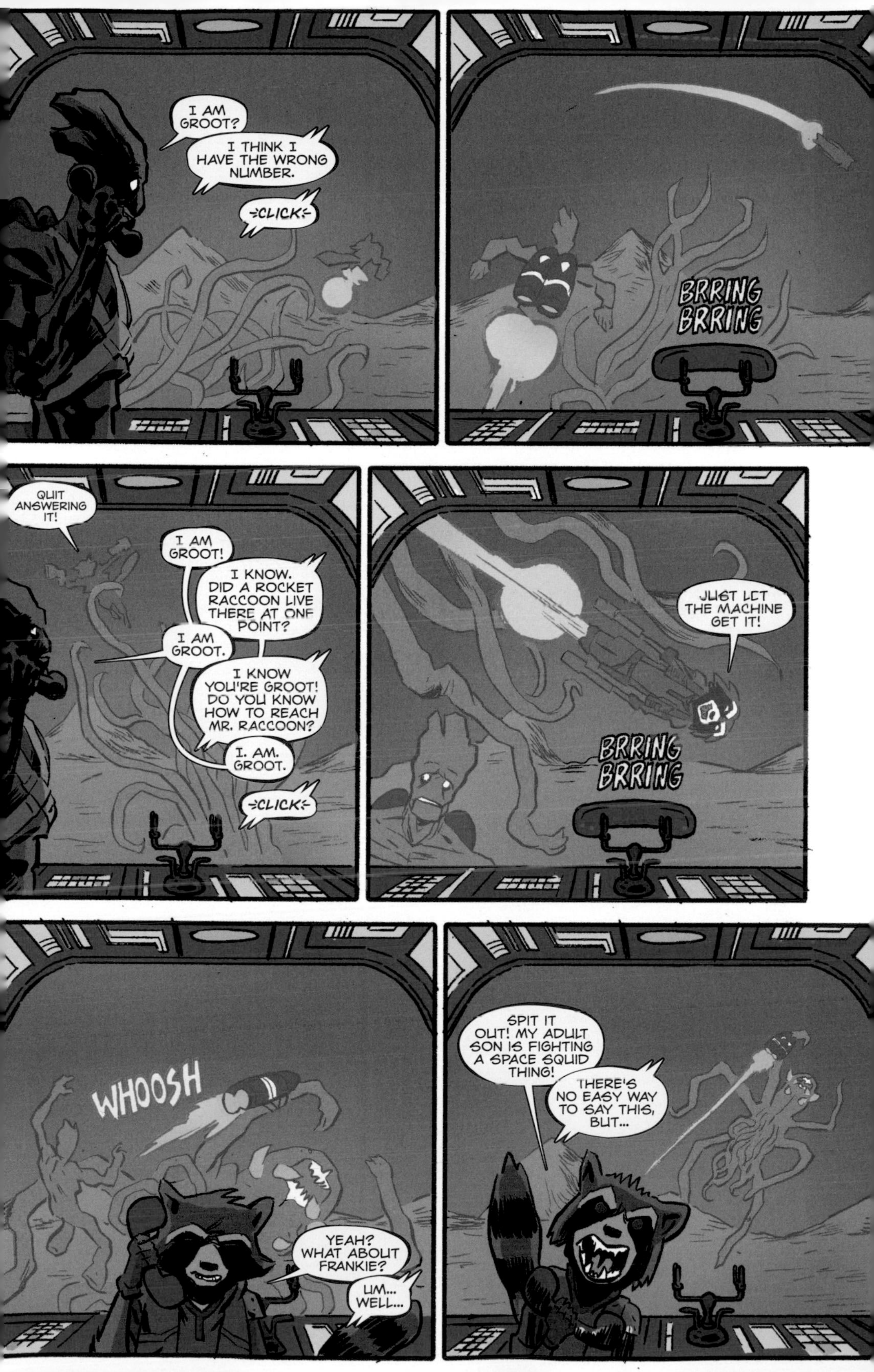
I AM GROOT?
I THINK I HAVE THE WRONG NUMBER.
=CLICK=
BRRING BRRING
QUIT ANSWERING IT!
I AM GROOT!
I KNOW. DID A ROCKET RACCOON LIVE THERE AT ONE POINT?
I AM GROOT.
I KNOW YOU'RE GROOT! DO YOU KNOW HOW TO REACH MR. RACCOON?
I. AM. GROOT.
=CLICK=
JUST LET THE MACHINE GET IT!
BRRING BRRING
WHOOSH
YEAH? WHAT ABOUT FRANKIE?
UM... WELL...
SPIT IT OUT! MY ADULT SON IS FIGHTING A SPACE SQUID THING!
THERE'S NO EASY WAY TO SAY THIS, BUT...

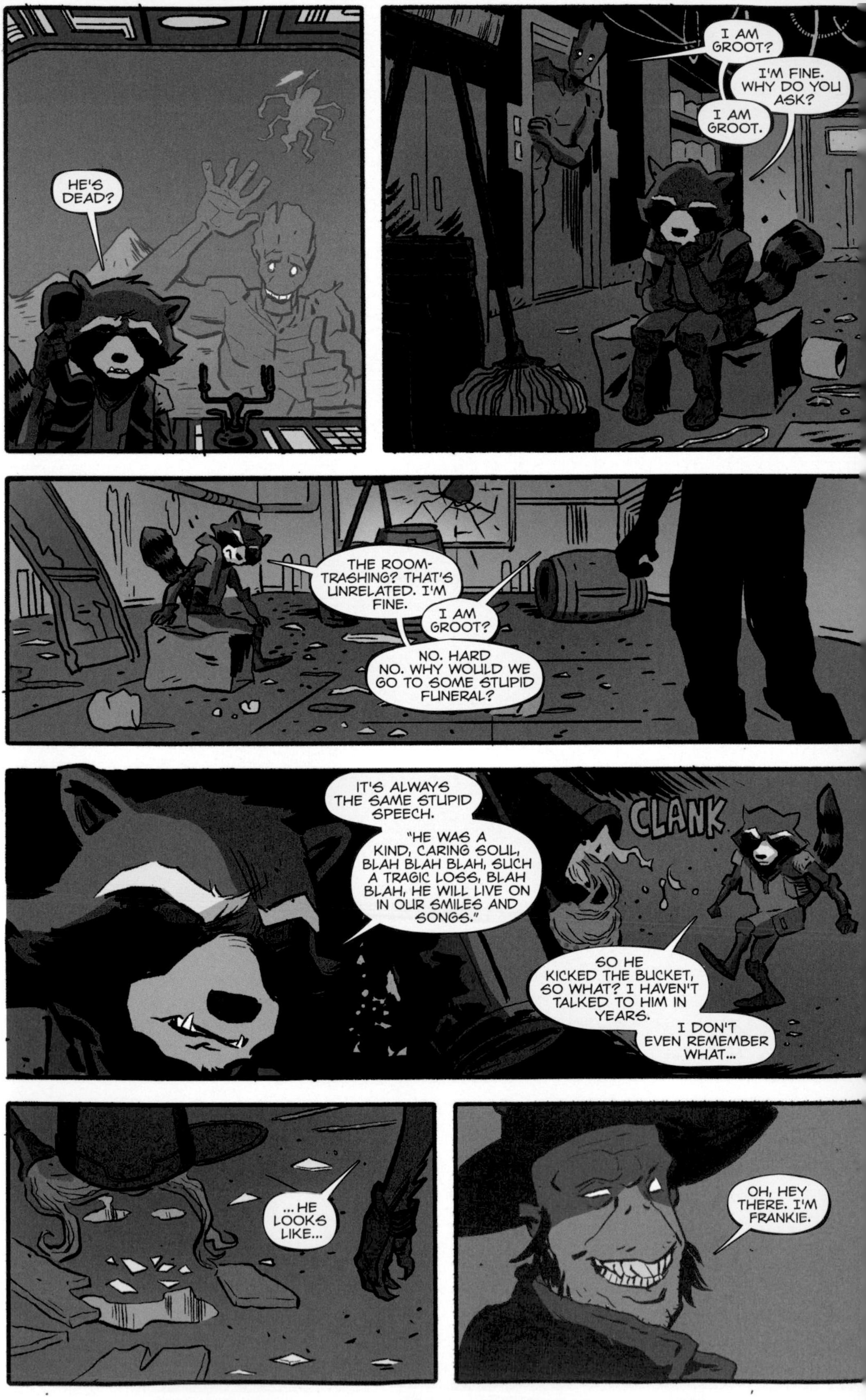
HE'S DEAD?
I AM GROOT?
I'M FINE. WHY DO YOU ASK?
I AM GROOT.
THE ROOM-TRASHING? THAT'S UNRELATED. I'M FINE.
I AM GROOT?
NO. HARD NO. WHY WOULD WE GO TO SOME STUPID FUNERAL?
IT'S ALWAYS THE SAME STUPID SPEECH.
"HE WAS A KIND, CARING SOUL, BLAH BLAH BLAH, SUCH A TRAGIC LOSS, BLAH BLAH, HE WILL LIVE ON IN OUR SMILES AND SONGS."
CLANK
SO HE KICKED THE BUCKET, SO WHAT? I HAVEN'T TALKED TO HIM IN YEARS.
I DON'T EVEN REMEMBER WHAT...
...HE LOOKS LIKE...
OH, HEY THERE. I'M FRANKIE.

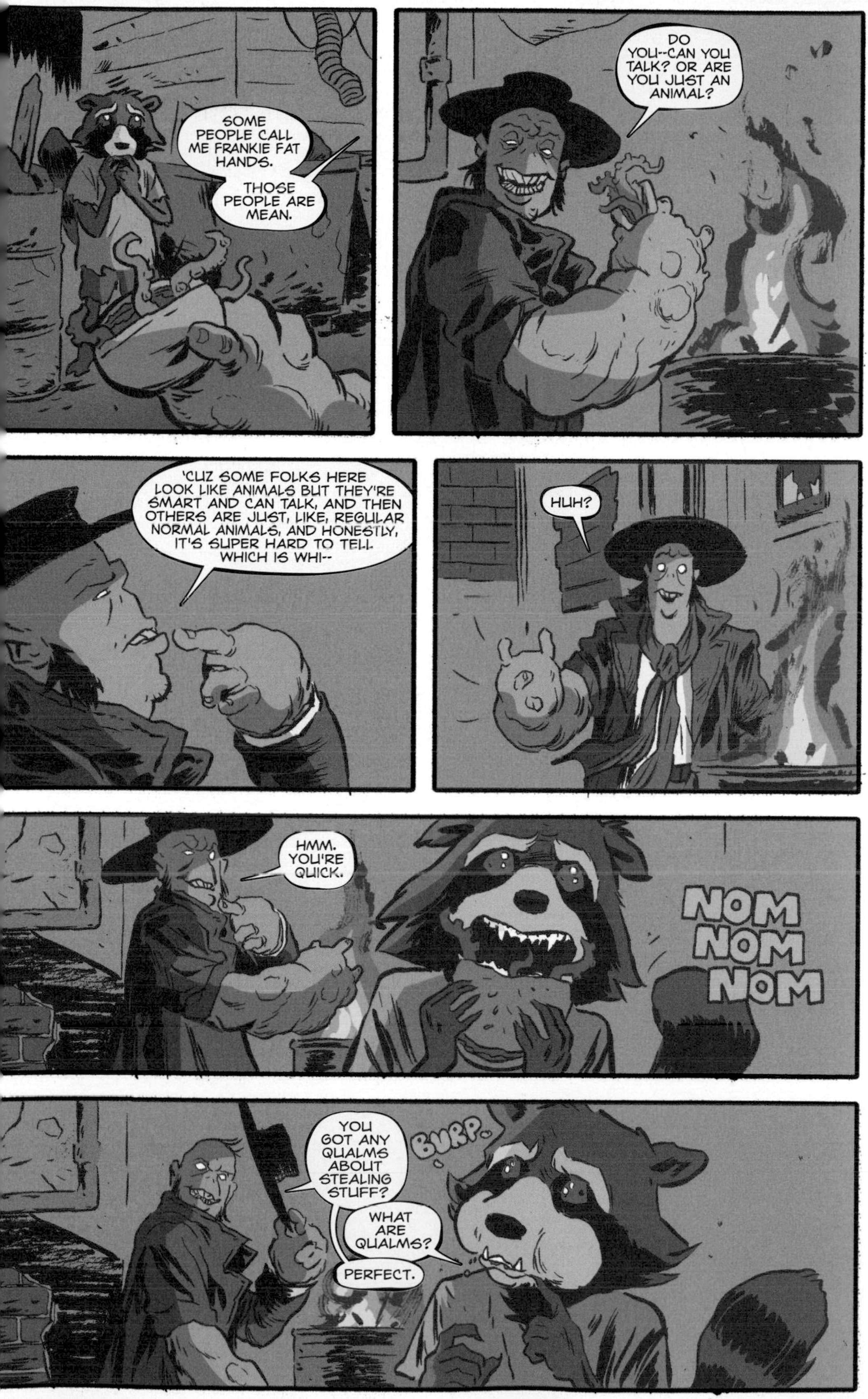
SOME PEOPLE CALL ME FRANKIE FAT HANDS.
THOSE PEOPLE ARE MEAN.
DO YOU--CAN YOU TALK? OR ARE YOU JUST AN ANIMAL?
'CUZ SOME FOLKS HERE LOOK LIKE ANIMALS BUT THEY'RE SMART AND CAN TALK, AND THEN OTHERS ARE JUST, LIKE, REGULAR NORMAL ANIMALS, AND HONESTLY, IT'S SUPER HARD TO TELL WHICH IS WHI--
HUH?
HMM. YOU'RE QUICK.
NOM NOM NOM
YOU GOT ANY QUALMS ABOUT STEALING STUFF?
BURP.
WHAT ARE QUALMS?
PERFECT.

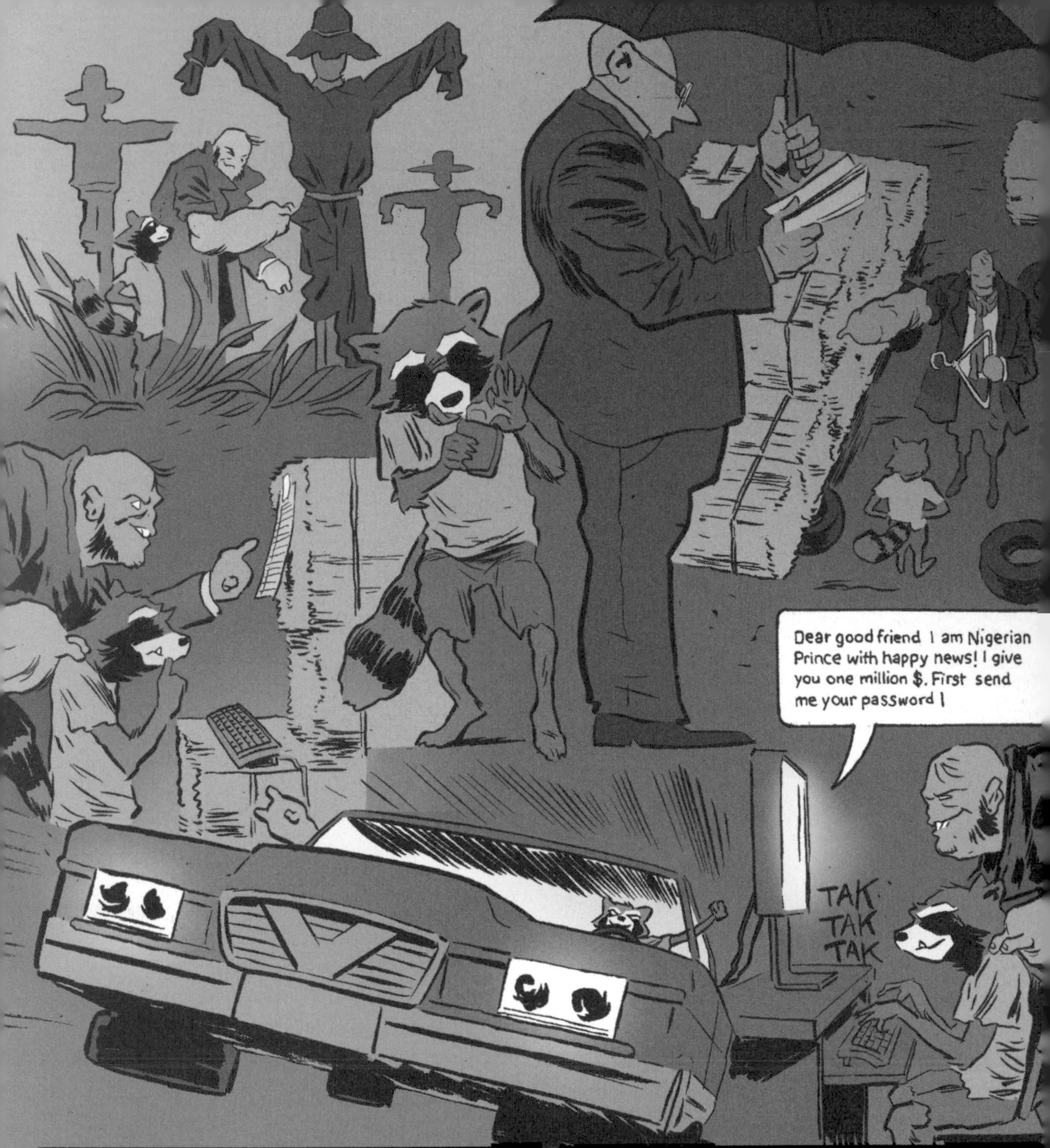
Dear good friend I am Nigerian Prince with happy news! I give you one million $. First send me your password!
TAK TAK TAK

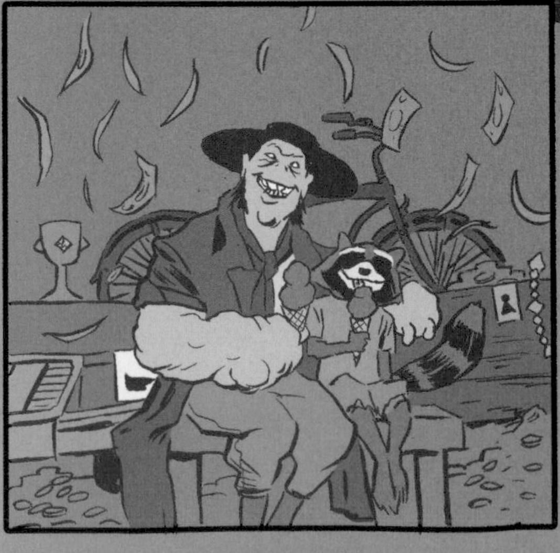

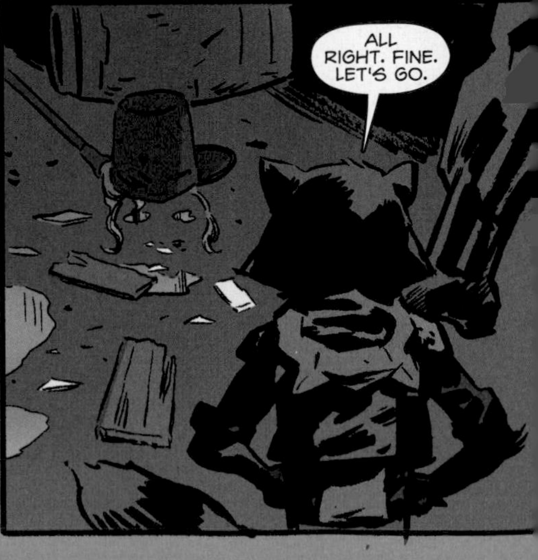
ALL RIGHT. FINE. LET'S GO.

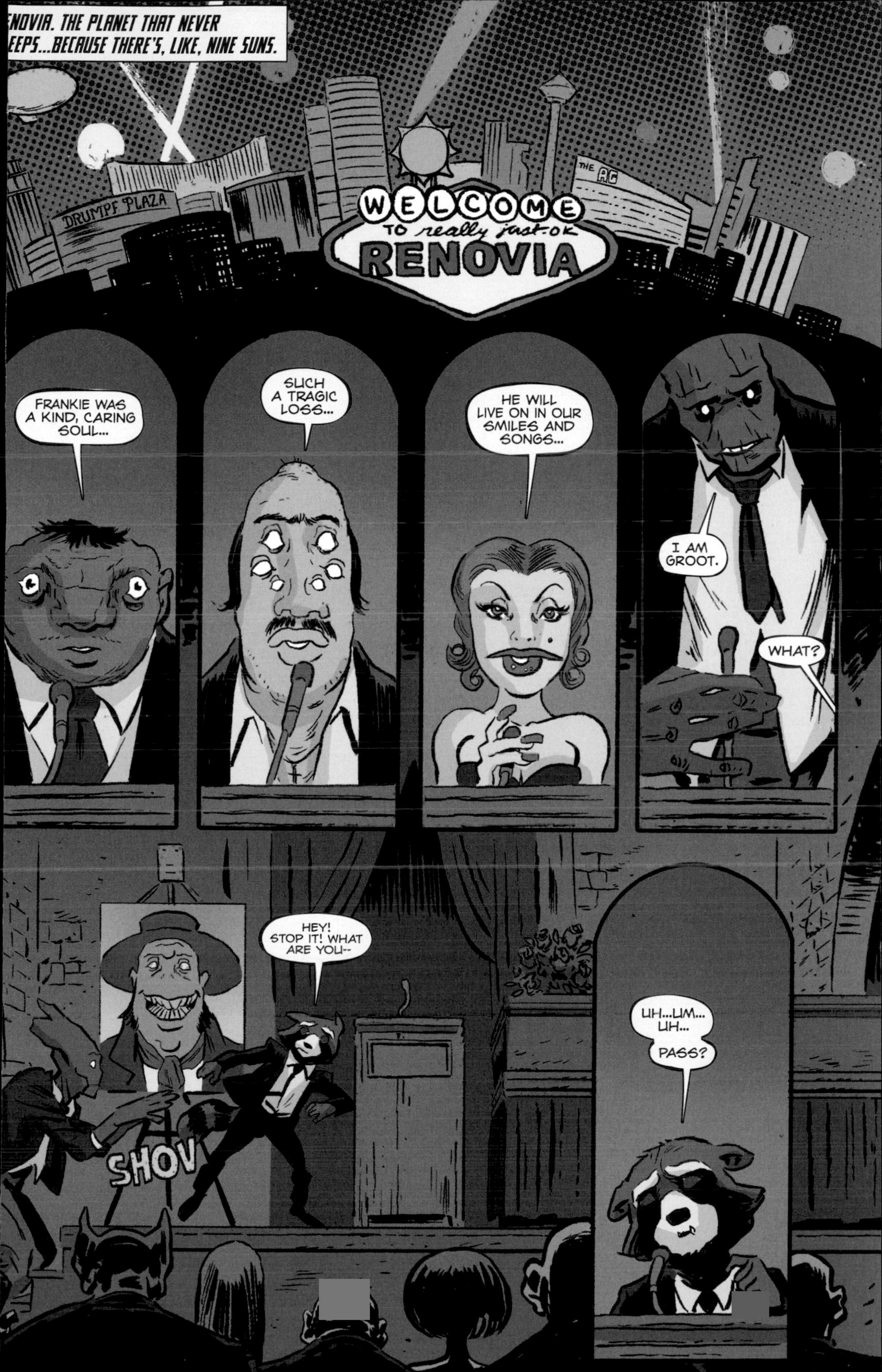
ENOVIA. THE PLANET THAT NEVER
EEPS...BECAUSE THERE'S, LIKE, NINE SUNS.
DRUMPF PLAZA
THE AG
WELCOME
TO really just-OK
RENOVIA
FRANKIE WAS A KIND, CARING SOUL...
SUCH A TRAGIC LOSS...
HE WILL LIVE ON IN OUR SMILES AND SONGS...
I AM GROOT.
WHAT?
HEY! STOP IT! WHAT ARE YOU--
SHOV
UH...UM... UH...
PASS?

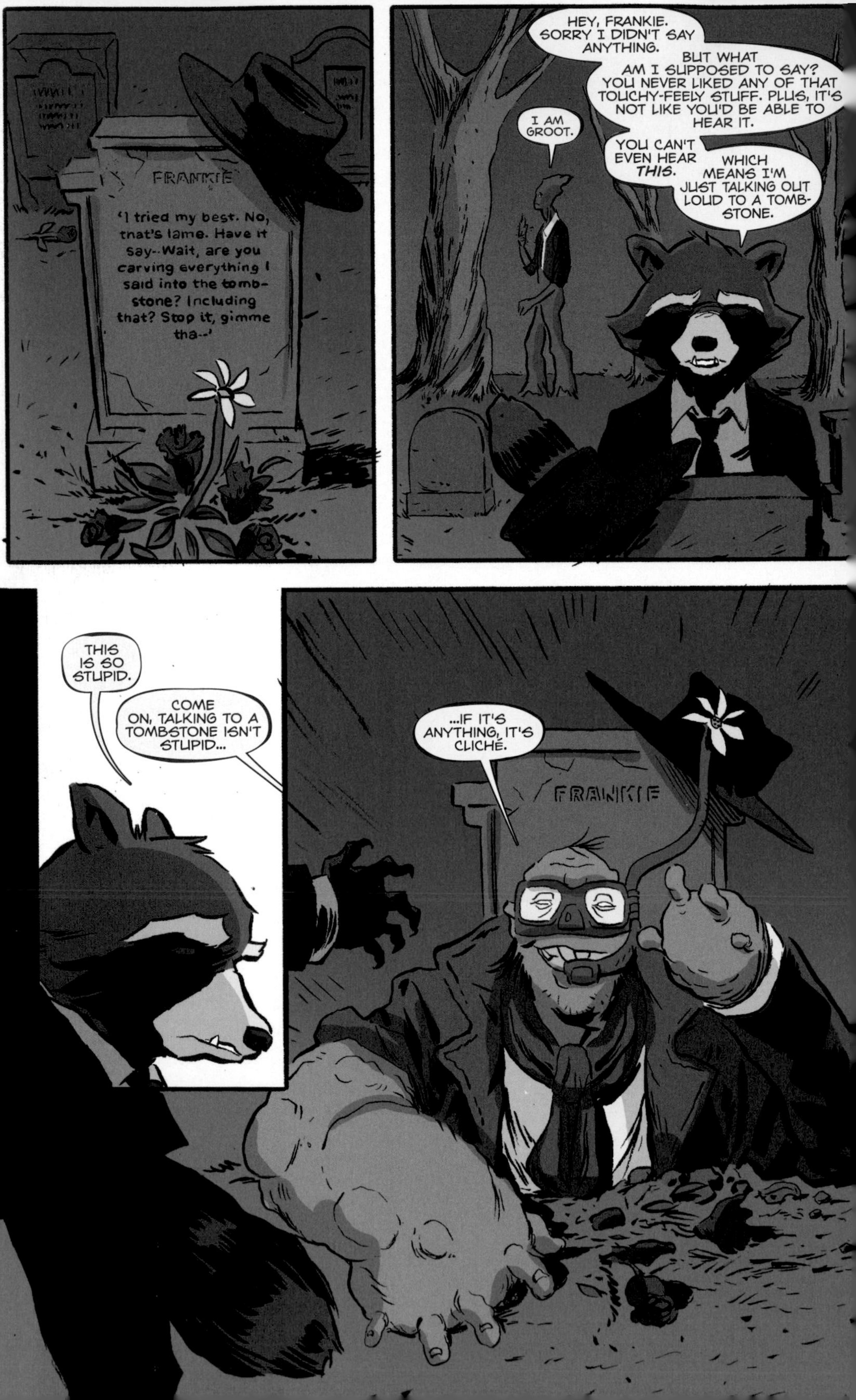
FRANKIE
'I tried my best. No, that's lame. Have it say--Wait, are you carving everything I said into the tomb-stone? Including that? Stop it, gimme tha--'
HEY, FRANKIE. SORRY I DIDN'T SAY ANYTHING.
BUT WHAT AM I SUPPOSED TO SAY? YOU NEVER LIKED ANY OF THAT TOUCHY-FEELY STUFF. PLUS, IT'S NOT LIKE YOU'D BE ABLE TO HEAR IT.
I AM GROOT.
YOU CAN'T EVEN HEAR *THIS*.
WHICH MEANS I'M JUST TALKING OUT LOUD TO A TOMB-STONE.
THIS IS SO STUPID.
COME ON, TALKING TO A TOMBSTONE ISN'T STUPID...
...IF IT'S ANYTHING, IT'S CLICHÉ.
FRANKIE

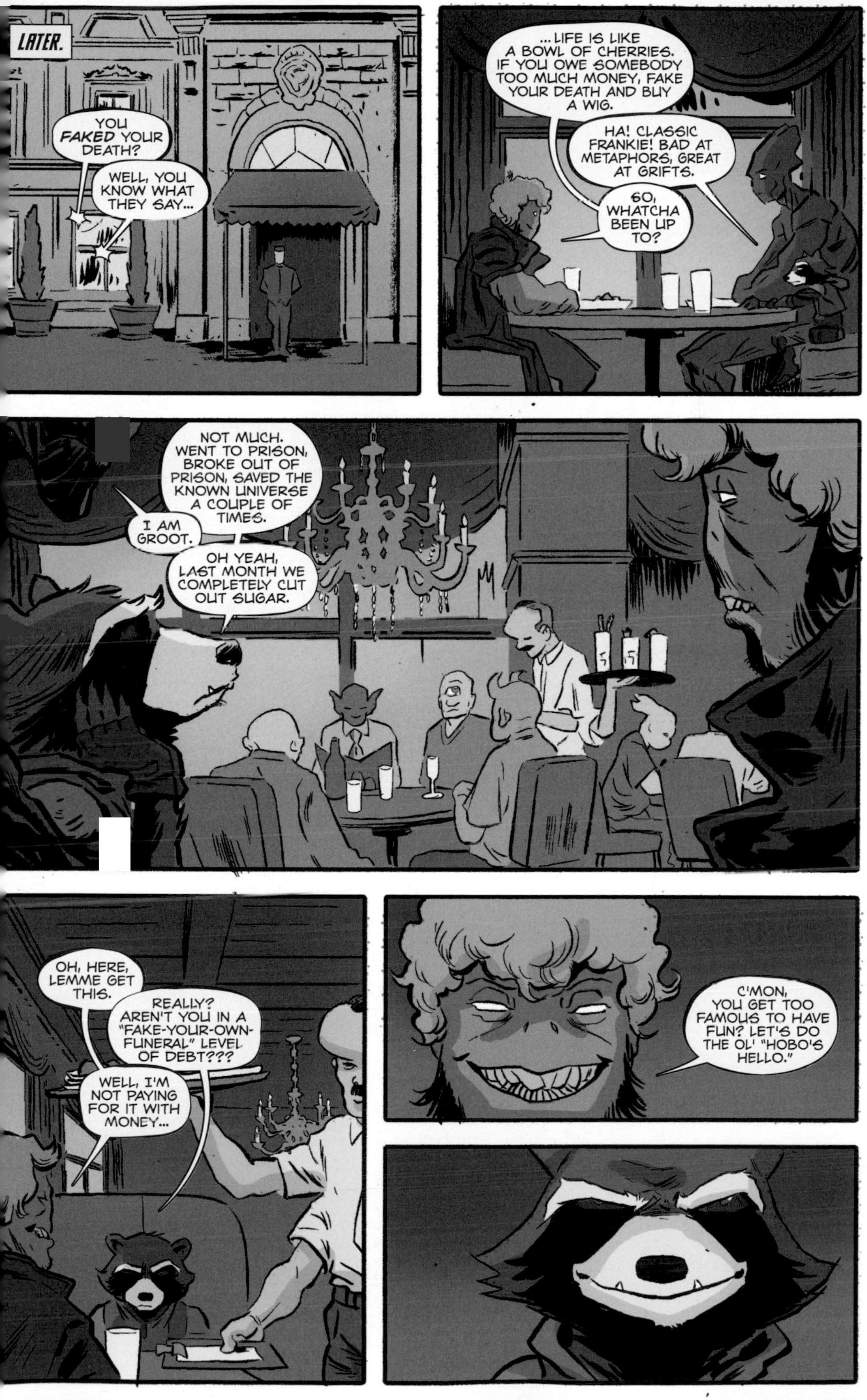
LATER.
YOU FAKED YOUR DEATH?
WELL, YOU KNOW WHAT THEY SAY...
...LIFE IS LIKE A BOWL OF CHERRIES. IF YOU OWE SOMEBODY TOO MUCH MONEY, FAKE YOUR DEATH AND BUY A WIG.
HA! CLASSIC FRANKIE! BAD AT METAPHORS, GREAT AT GRIFTS.
SO, WHATCHA BEEN UP TO?
NOT MUCH. WENT TO PRISON, BROKE OUT OF PRISON, SAVED THE KNOWN UNIVERSE A COUPLE OF TIMES.
I AM GROOT.
OH YEAH, LAST MONTH WE COMPLETELY CUT OUT SUGAR.
OH, HERE, LEMME GET THIS.
REALLY? AREN'T YOU IN A "FAKE-YOUR-OWN-FUNERAL" LEVEL OF DEBT???
WELL, I'M NOT PAYING FOR IT WITH MONEY...
C'MON, YOU GET TOO FAMOUS TO HAVE FUN? LET'S DO THE OL' "HOBO'S HELLO."

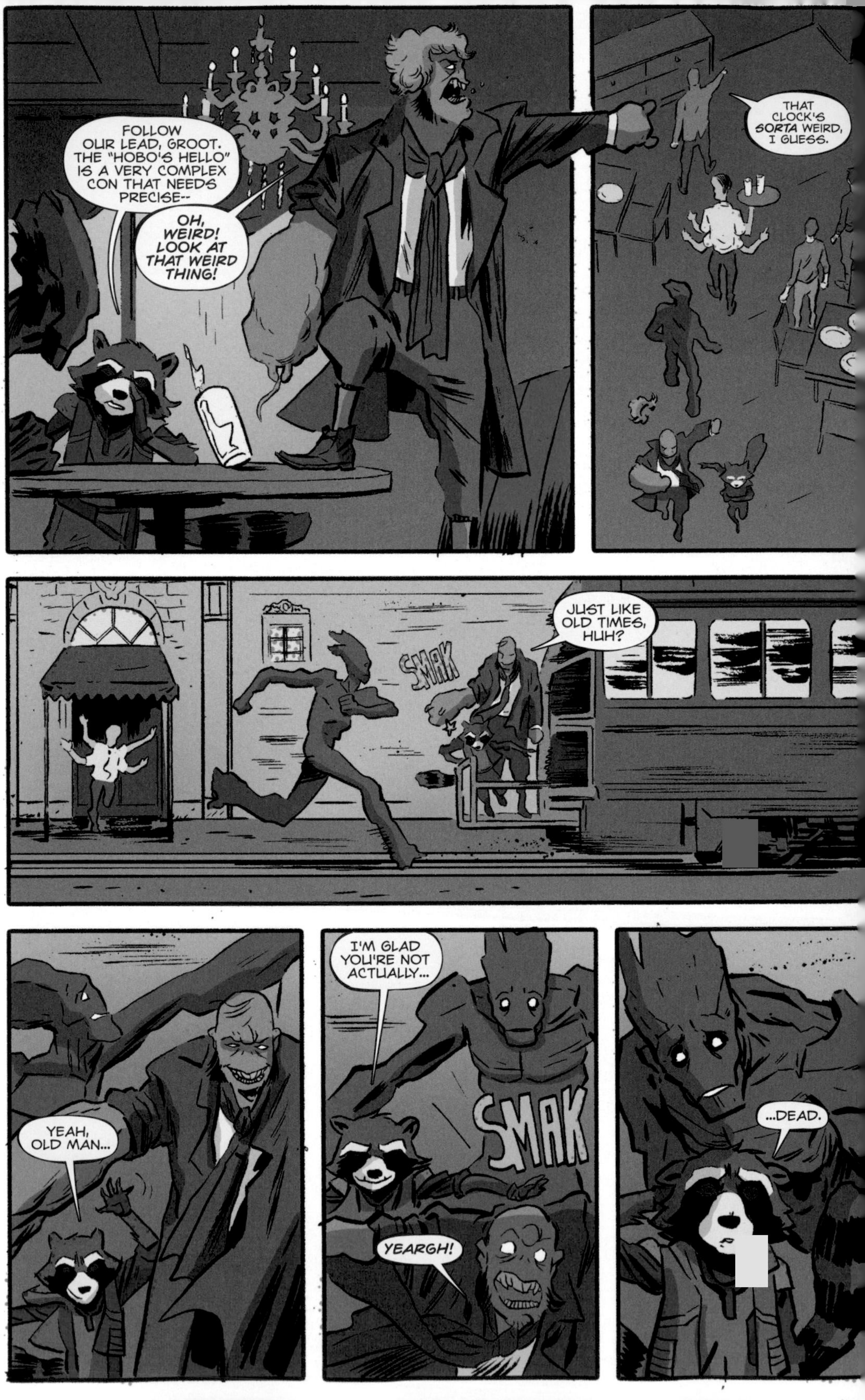
FOLLOW OUR LEAD, GROOT. THE "HOBO'S HELLO" IS A VERY COMPLEX CON THAT NEEDS PRECISE--
OH, WEIRD! LOOK AT THAT WEIRD THING!
THAT CLOCK'S SORTA WEIRD, I GUESS.
SMAK
JUST LIKE OLD TIMES, HUH?
YEAH, OLD MAN...
I'M GLAD YOU'RE NOT ACTUALLY...
SMAK
YEARGH!
...DEAD.

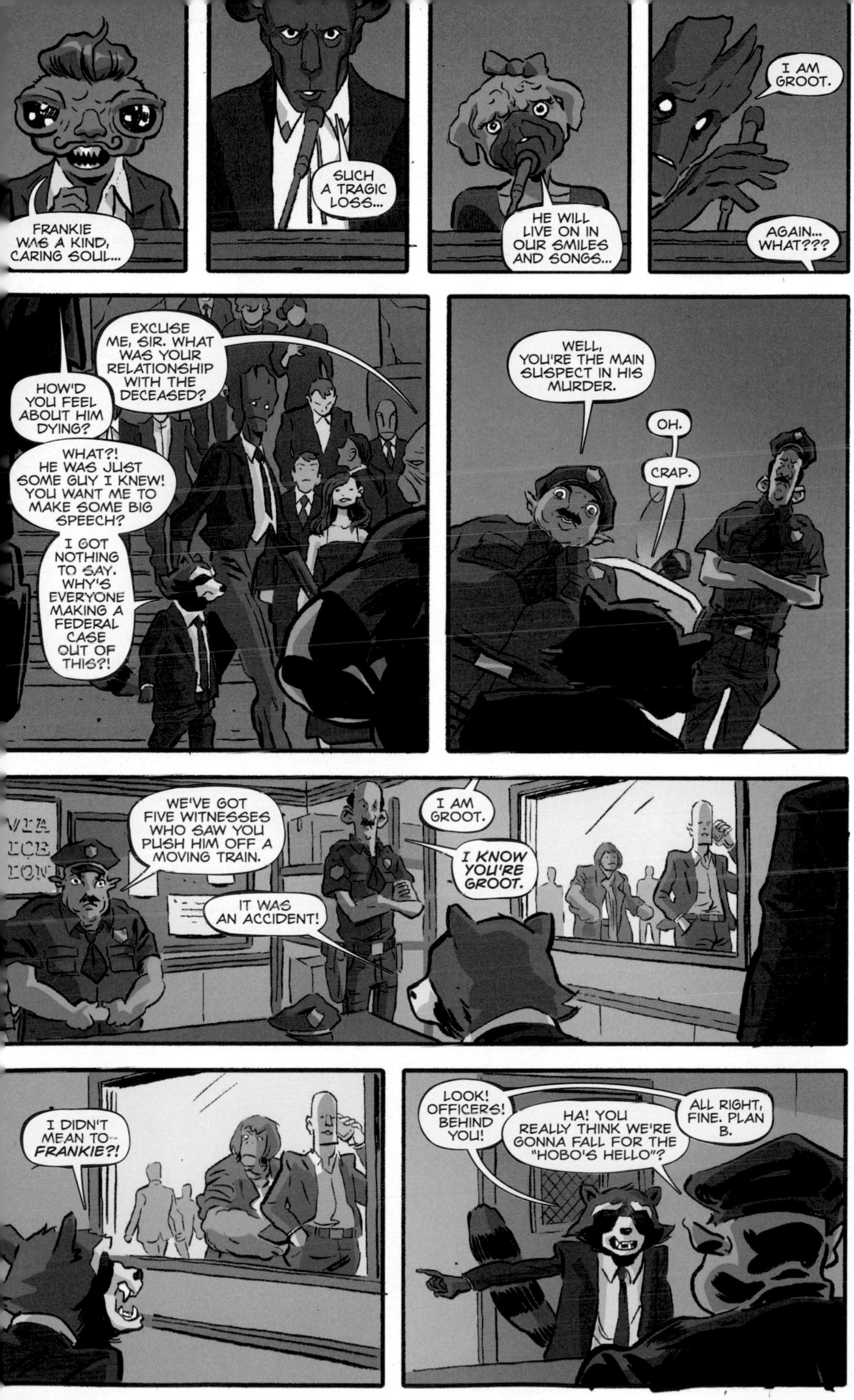
FRANKIE WAS A KIND, CARING SOUL...
SUCH A TRAGIC LOSS...
HE WILL LIVE ON IN OUR SMILES AND SONGS...
I AM GROOT.
AGAIN... WHAT???
EXCUSE ME, SIR. WHAT WAS YOUR RELATIONSHIP WITH THE DECEASED?
HOW'D YOU FEEL ABOUT HIM DYING?
WHAT?! HE WAS JUST SOME GUY I KNEW! YOU WANT ME TO MAKE SOME BIG SPEECH?
I GOT NOTHING TO SAY. WHY'S EVERYONE MAKING A FEDERAL CASE OUT OF THIS?!
WELL, YOU'RE THE MAIN SUSPECT IN HIS MURDER.
OH.
CRAP.
WE'VE GOT FIVE WITNESSES WHO SAW YOU PUSH HIM OFF A MOVING TRAIN.
IT WAS AN ACCIDENT!
I AM GROOT.
I KNOW YOU'RE GROOT.
I DIDN'T MEAN TO-- FRANKIE?!
LOOK! OFFICERS! BEHIND YOU!
HA! YOU REALLY THINK WE'RE GONNA FALL FOR THE "HOBO'S HELLO"?
ALL RIGHT, FINE. PLAN B.

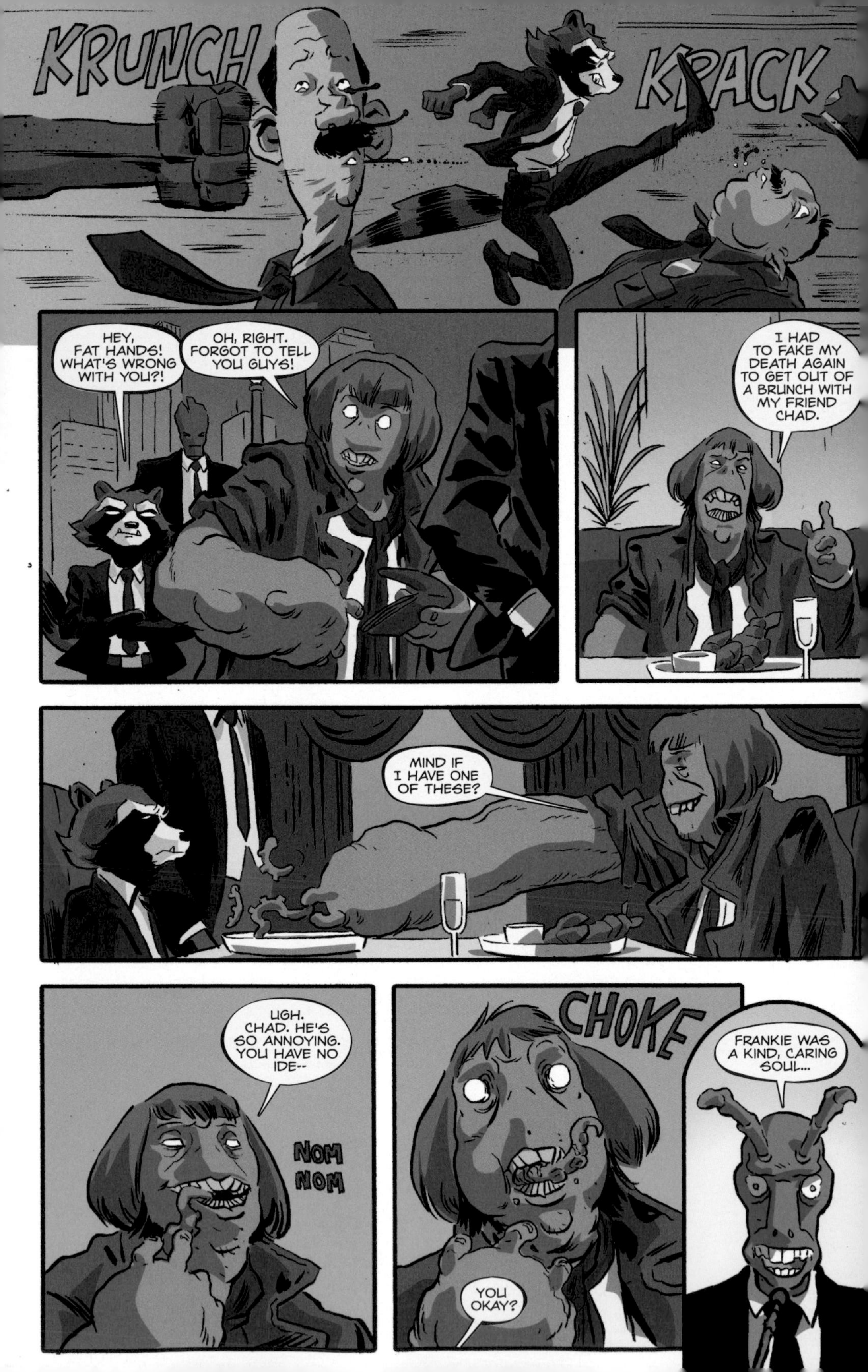
KRUNCH
KRACK
HEY, FAT HANDS! WHAT'S WRONG WITH YOU?!
OH, RIGHT. FORGOT TO TELL YOU GUYS!
I HAD TO FAKE MY DEATH AGAIN TO GET OUT OF A BRUNCH WITH MY FRIEND CHAD.
MIND IF I HAVE ONE OF THESE?
UGH. CHAD. HE'S SO ANNOYING. YOU HAVE NO IDE--
NOM NOM
CHOKE
YOU OKAY?
FRANKIE WAS A KIND, CARING SOUL...

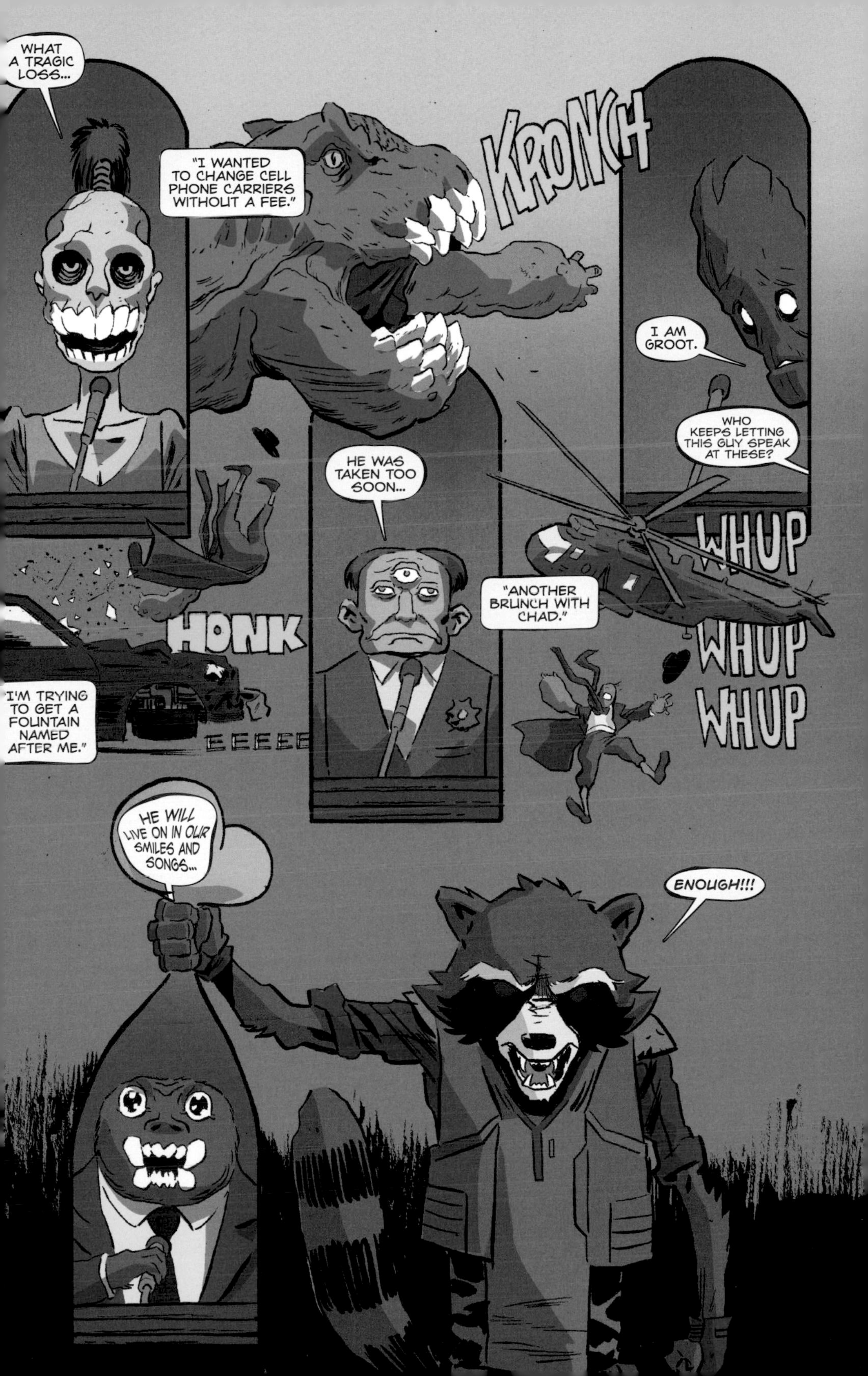
WHAT A TRAGIC LOSS...
"I WANTED TO CHANGE CELL PHONE CARRIERS WITHOUT A FEE."
KRONCH
I AM GROOT.
WHO KEEPS LETTING THIS GUY SPEAK AT THESE?
HE WAS TAKEN TOO SOON...
"ANOTHER BRUNCH WITH CHAD."
WHUP
WHUP
WHUP
HONK
"I'M TRYING TO GET A FOUNTAIN NAMED AFTER ME."
EEEEE
HE WILL LIVE ON IN OUR SMILES AND SONGS...
ENOUGH!!!

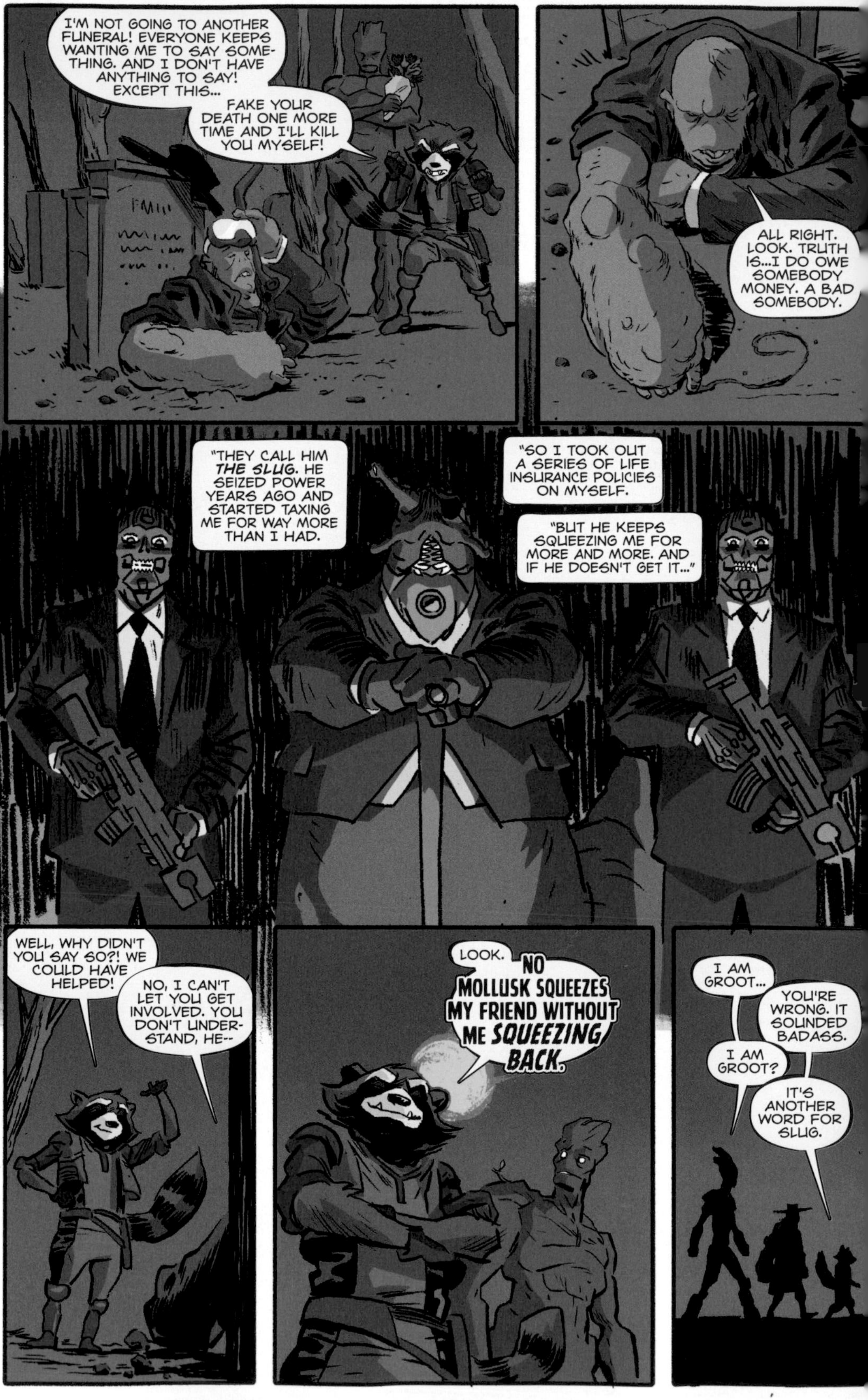
I'M NOT GOING TO ANOTHER FUNERAL! EVERYONE KEEPS WANTING ME TO SAY SOMETHING. AND I DON'T HAVE ANYTHING TO SAY! EXCEPT THIS...
FAKE YOUR DEATH ONE MORE TIME AND I'LL KILL YOU MYSELF!
ALL RIGHT. LOOK. TRUTH IS...I DO OWE SOMEBODY MONEY. A BAD SOMEBODY.
"THEY CALL HIM *THE SLUG*. HE SEIZED POWER YEARS AGO AND STARTED TAXING ME FOR WAY MORE THAN I HAD.
"SO I TOOK OUT A SERIES OF LIFE INSURANCE POLICIES ON MYSELF.
"BUT HE KEEPS SQUEEZING ME FOR MORE AND MORE. AND IF HE DOESN'T GET IT..."
WELL, WHY DIDN'T YOU SAY SO?! WE COULD HAVE HELPED!
NO, I CAN'T LET YOU GET INVOLVED. YOU DON'T UNDERSTAND, HE--
LOOK.
NO MOLLUSK SQUEEZES MY FRIEND WITHOUT ME *SQUEEZING* BACK.
I AM GROOT...
YOU'RE WRONG. IT SOUNDED BADASS.
I AM GROOT?
IT'S ANOTHER WORD FOR SLUG.

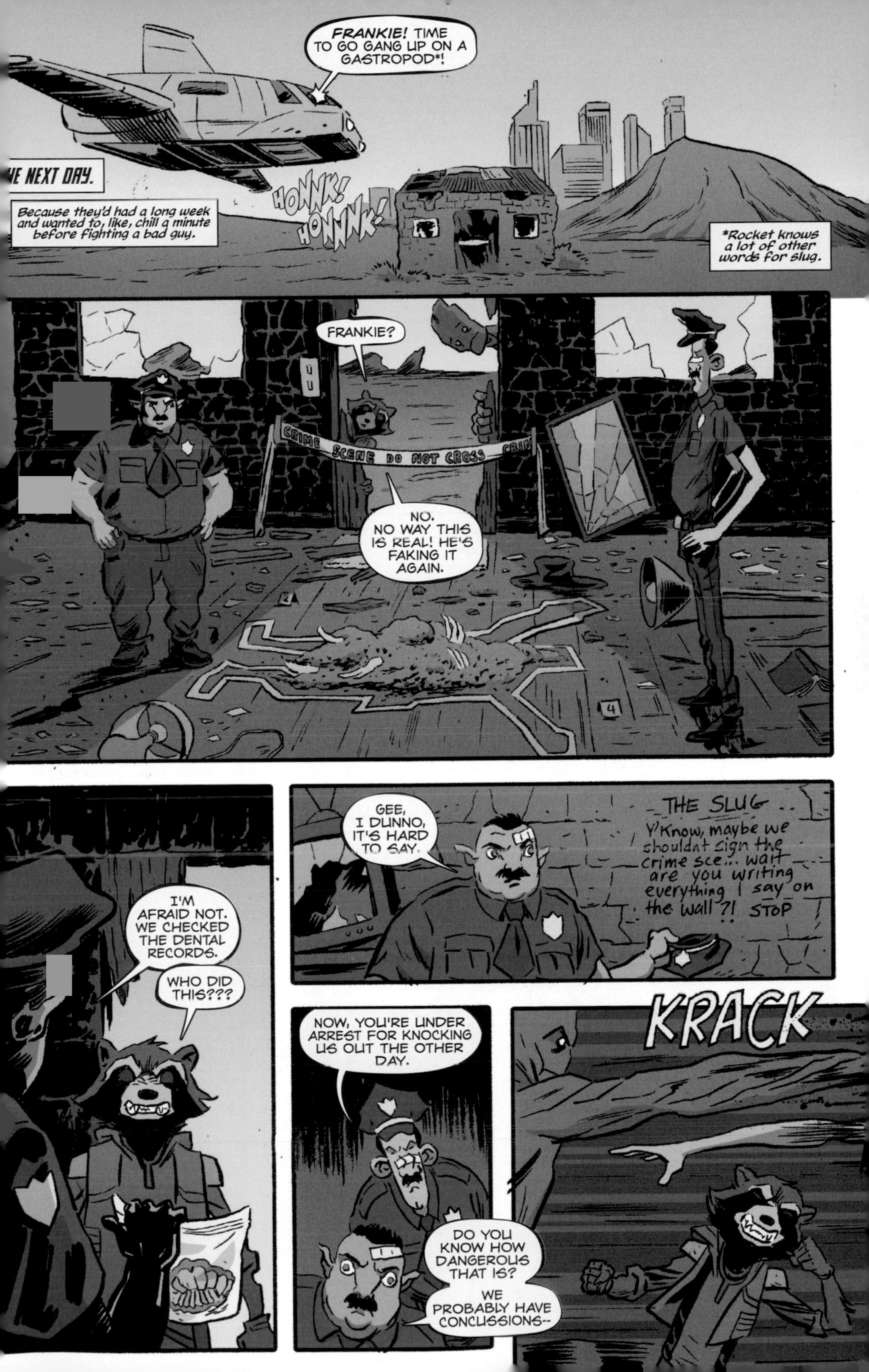
FRANKIE! TIME TO GO GANG UP ON A GASTROPOD*!
HE NEXT DAY.
Because they'd had a long week and wanted to, like, chill a minute before fighting a bad guy.
HONNK! HONNNK!
*Rocket knows a lot of other words for slug.
FRANKIE?
CRIME SCENE DO NOT CROSS
NO. NO WAY THIS IS REAL! HE'S FAKING IT AGAIN.
I'M AFRAID NOT. WE CHECKED THE DENTAL RECORDS.
WHO DID THIS???
GEE, I DUNNO, IT'S HARD TO SAY.
THE SLUG
Y'Know, maybe we shouldnt sign the crime sce... wait are you writing everything I say on the wall?! STOP
NOW, YOU'RE UNDER ARREST FOR KNOCKING US OUT THE OTHER DAY.
DO YOU KNOW HOW DANGEROUS THAT IS?
WE PROBABLY HAVE CONCUSSIONS--
KRACK

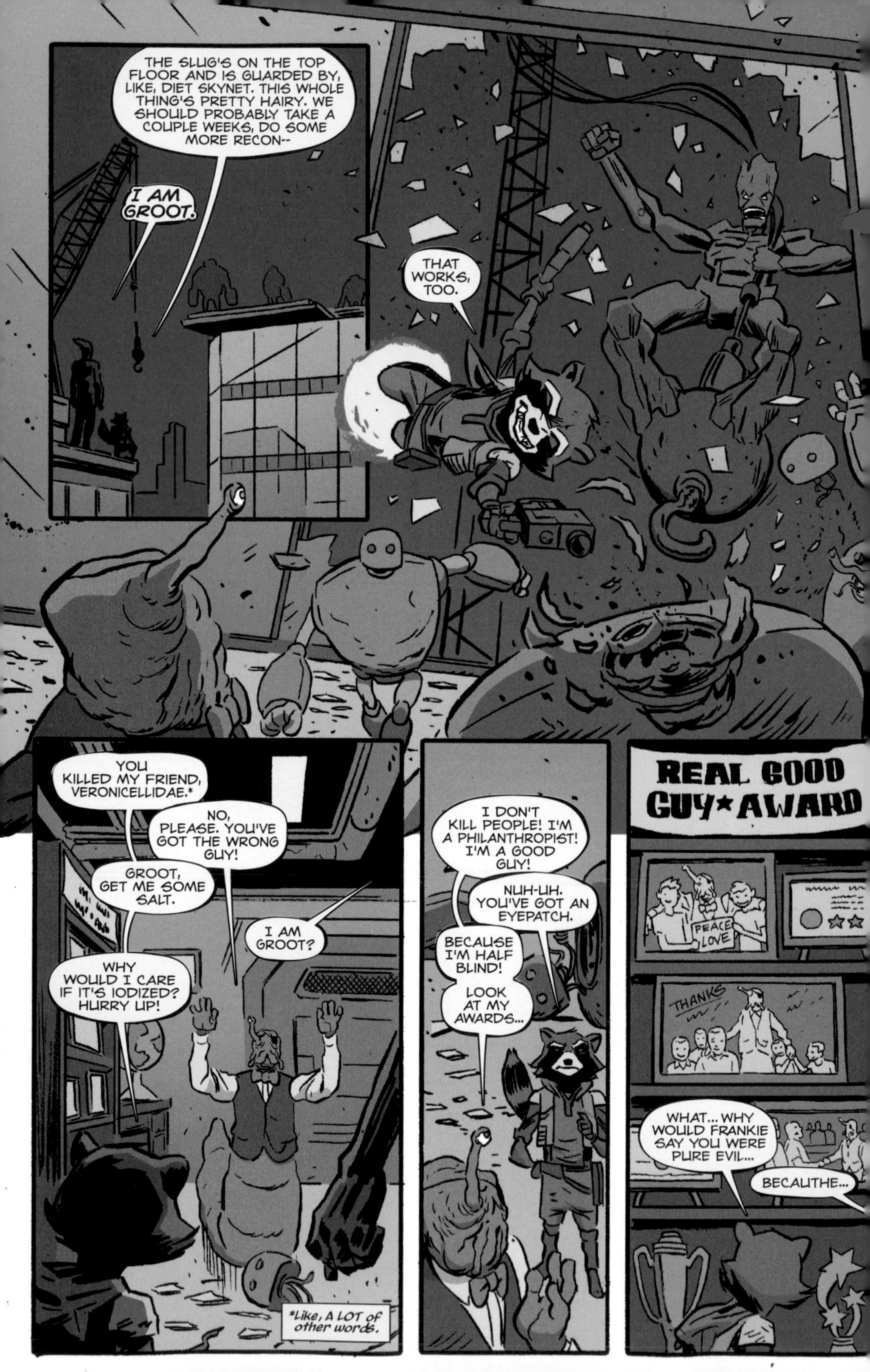
THE SLUG'S ON THE TOP FLOOR AND IS GUARDED BY, LIKE, DIET SKYNET. THIS WHOLE THING'S PRETTY HAIRY. WE SHOULD PROBABLY TAKE A COUPLE WEEKS, DO SOME MORE RECON--
I AM GROOT.
THAT WORKS, TOO.
YOU KILLED MY FRIEND, VERONICELLIDAE.*
NO, PLEASE. YOU'VE GOT THE WRONG GUY!
GROOT, GET ME SOME SALT.
I AM GROOT?
WHY WOULD I CARE IF IT'S IODIZED? HURRY UP!
*Like, A LOT of other words.
I DON'T KILL PEOPLE! I'M A PHILANTHROPIST! I'M A GOOD GUY!
NUH-UH. YOU'VE GOT AN EYEPATCH.
BECAUSE I'M HALF BLIND!
LOOK AT MY AWARDS...
REAL GOOD GUY★AWARD
PEACE LOVE
THANKS
WHAT... WHY WOULD FRANKIE SAY YOU WERE PURE EVIL...
BECAUTHE...

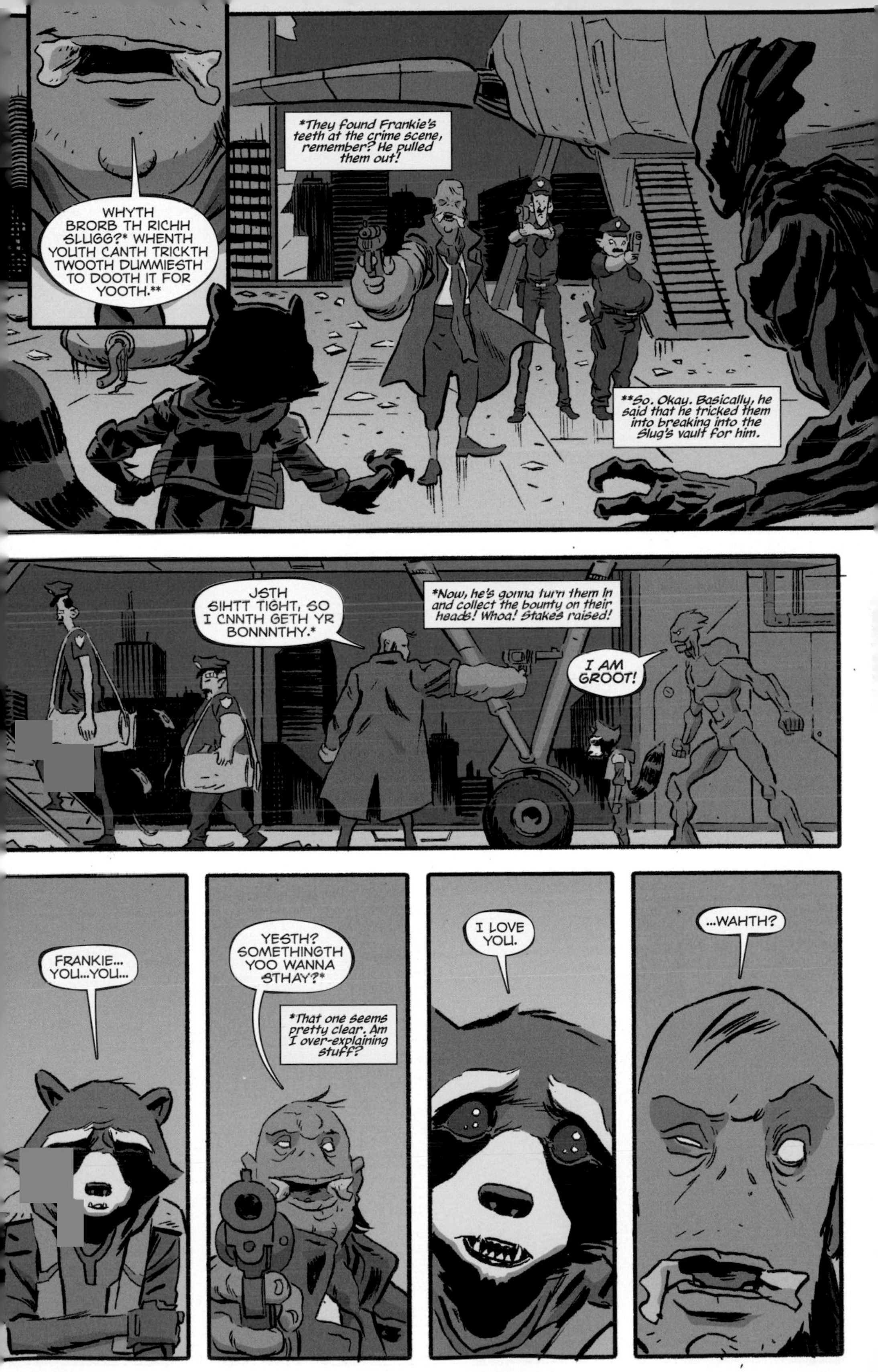
WHYTH BRORB TH RICHH SLUGG?* WHENTH YOUTH CANTH TRICKTH TWOOTH DUMMIESTH TO DOOTH IT FOR YOOTH.**
*They found Frankie's teeth at the crime scene, remember? He pulled them out!
**So. Okay. Basically, he said that he tricked them into breaking into the Slug's vault for him.
JSTH SIHTT TIGHT, SO I CNNTH GETH YR BONNNTHY.*
*Now, he's gonna turn them in and collect the bounty on their heads! Whoa! Stakes raised!
I AM GROOT!
FRANKIE... YOU...YOU...
YESTH? SOMETHINGTH YOO WANNA STHAY?*
*That one seems pretty clear. Am I over-explaining stuff?
I LOVE YOU.
...WAHTH?

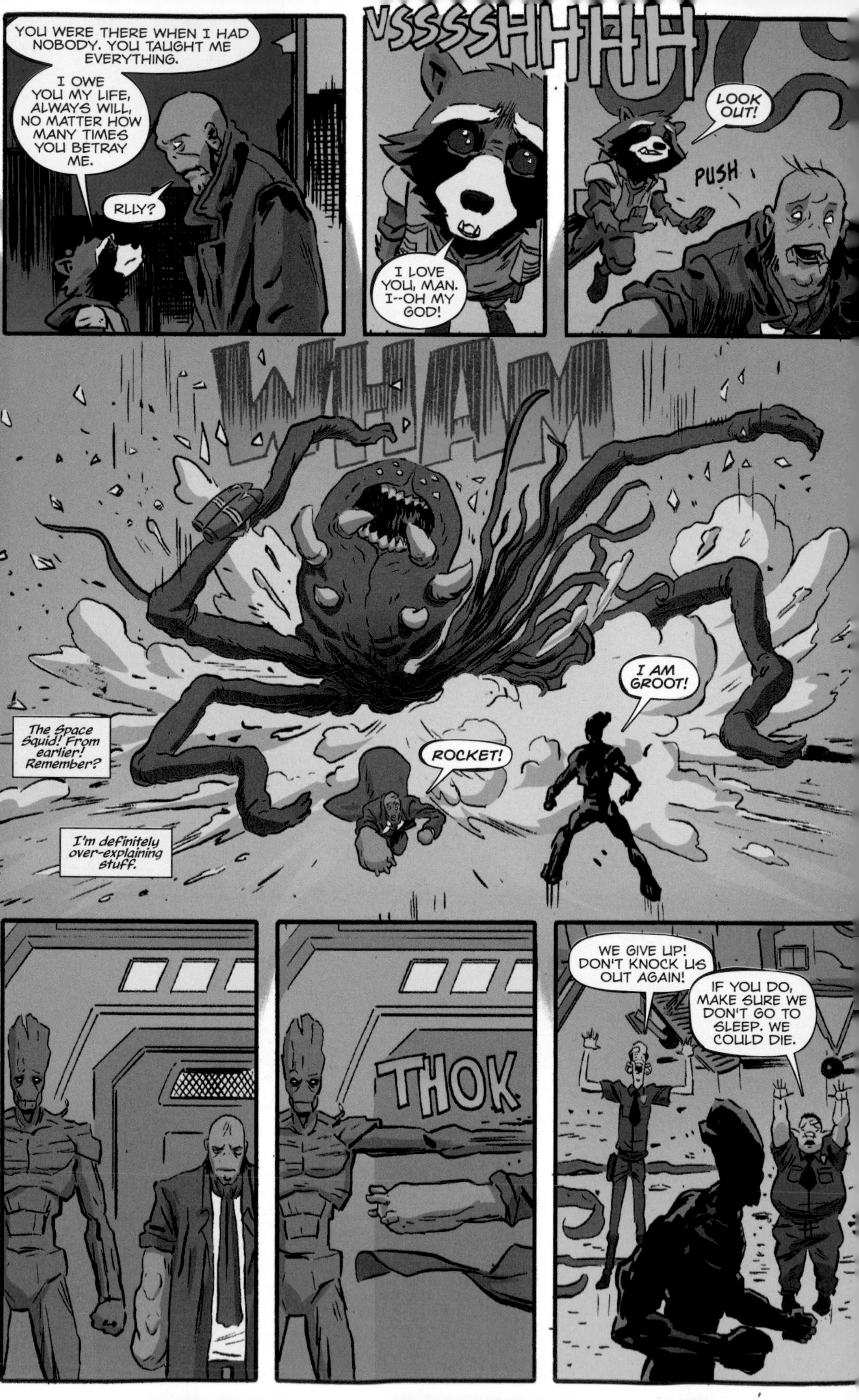
YOU WERE THERE WHEN I HAD NOBODY. YOU TAUGHT ME EVERYTHING.
I OWE YOU MY LIFE, ALWAYS WILL, NO MATTER HOW MANY TIMES YOU BETRAY ME.
RLLY?
VSSSSHHHH
I LOVE YOU, MAN. I--OH MY GOD!
LOOK OUT!
PUSH
WHAM
The Space Squid! From earlier! Remember?
I'm definitely over-explaining stuff.
ROCKET!
I AM GROOT!
THOK
WE GIVE UP! DON'T KNOCK US OUT AGAIN!
IF YOU DO, MAKE SURE WE DON'T GO TO SLEEP. WE COULD DIE.

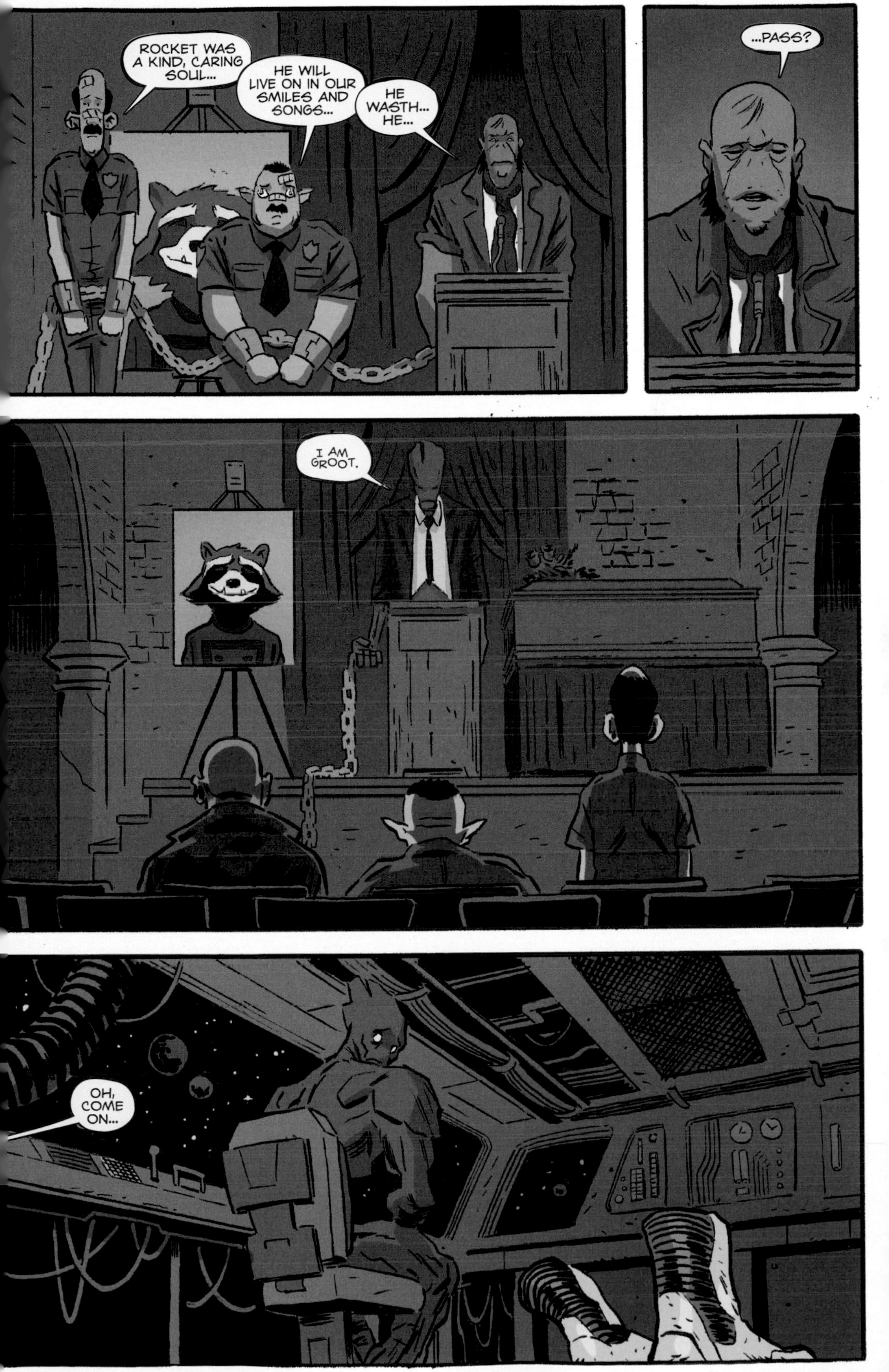
ROCKET WAS A KIND, CARING SOUL...
HE WILL LIVE ON IN OUR SMILES AND SONGS...
HE WASTH... HE...
...PASS?
I AM GROOT.
OH, COME ON...

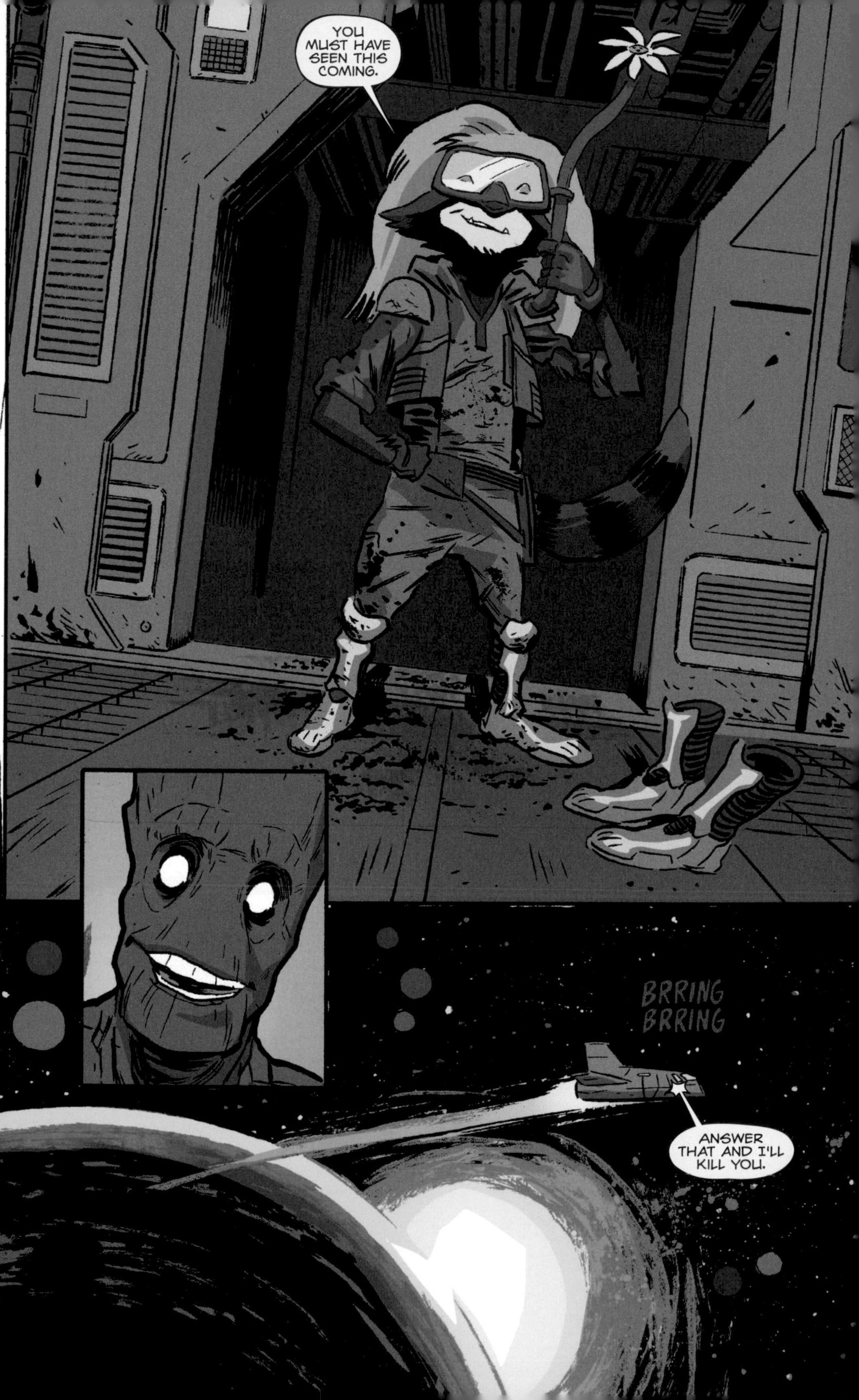
YOU MUST HAVE SEEN THIS COMING.
BRRING BRRING
ANSWER THAT AND I'LL KILL YOU.

# 8

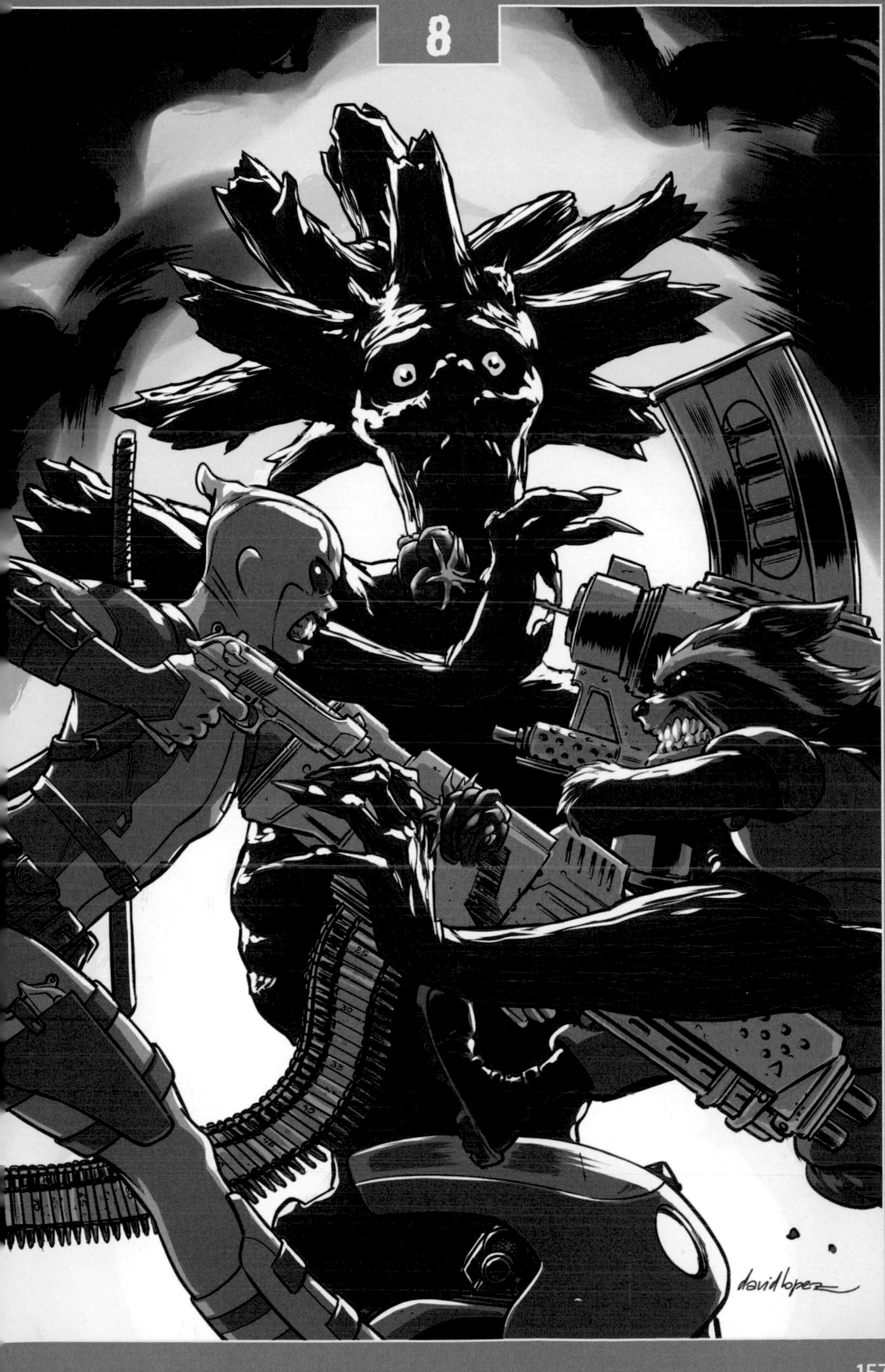

EARTH'S HEROES PREVENTED A CATACLYSMIC EVENT
THANKS TO A NEW INHUMAN NAMED ULYSSES, WHO
SEEMS TO BE ABLE TO PREDICT THE FUTURE. NOW,
EARTH'S GREATEST CHAMPIONS ARE FORCED TO MAKE A
CHOICE: **PROTECT** THE FUTURE...OR **CHANGE** IT?

FORMER GUARDIANS OF THE GALAXY TEAMMATE AND
CURRENT COMMANDER OF ALPHA FLIGHT CAPTAIN
MARVEL WANTS TO **CHANGE** THE FUTURE TO **PROTECT**
THE STUFF IN IT. SHE'S ASKED ALL HER ALLIES TO HELP
RESPOND TO ULYSSES' PREDICTIONS, INCLUDING THE
GUARDIANS. ROCKET PILOTS THEIR SHIP, AND CAROL
COULDN'T JUST ASK HIM AND GROOT TO WAIT OUTSIDE.

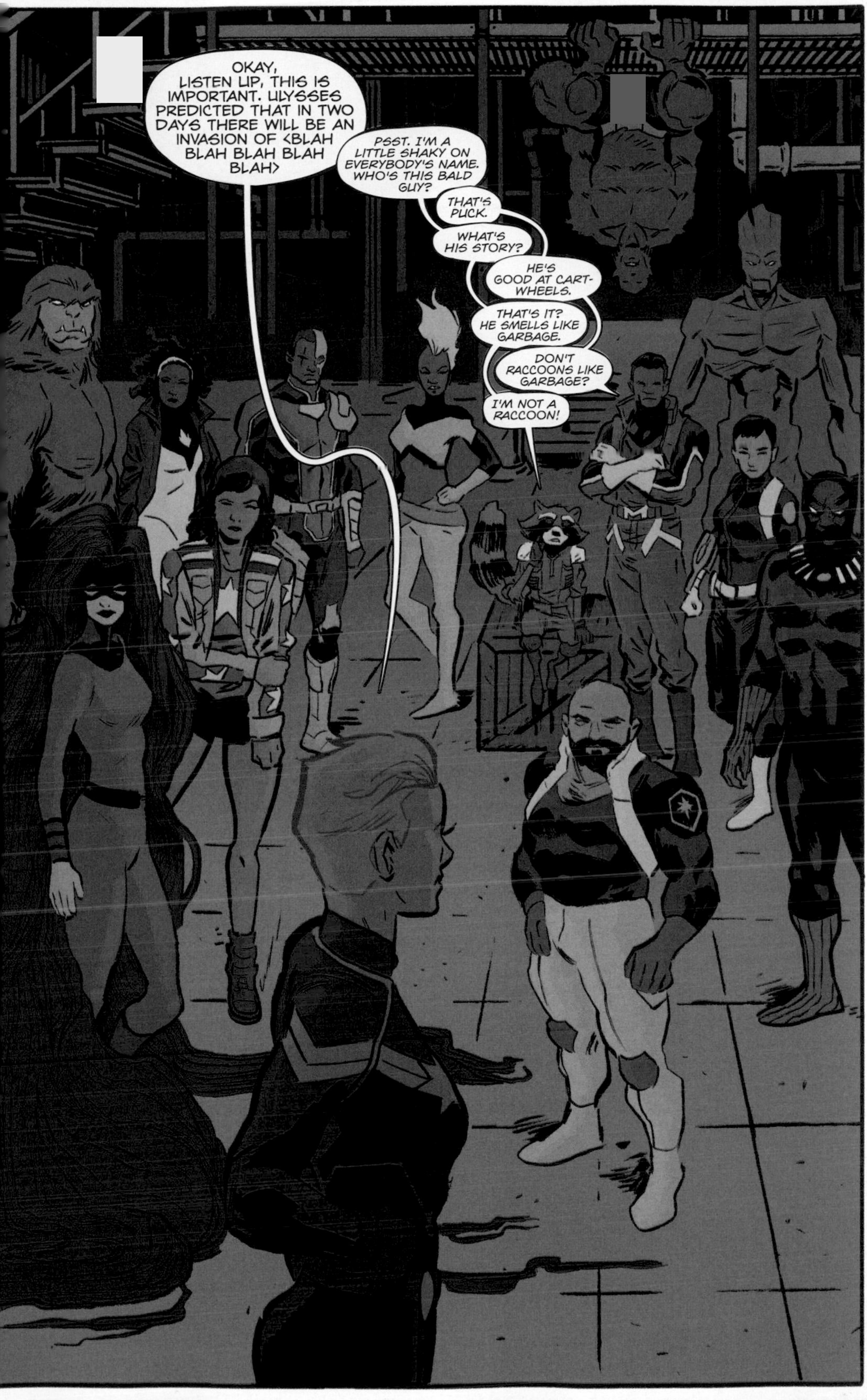
OKAY, LISTEN UP, THIS IS IMPORTANT. ULYSSES PREDICTED THAT IN TWO DAYS THERE WILL BE AN INVASION OF <BLAH BLAH BLAH BLAH BLAH>
PSST. I'M A LITTLE SHAKY ON EVERYBODY'S NAME. WHO'S THIS BALD GUY?
THAT'S PUCK.
WHAT'S HIS STORY?
HE'S GOOD AT CART-WHEELS.
THAT'S IT? HE SMELLS LIKE GARBAGE.
DON'T RACCOONS LIKE GARBAGE?
I'M NOT A RACCOON!

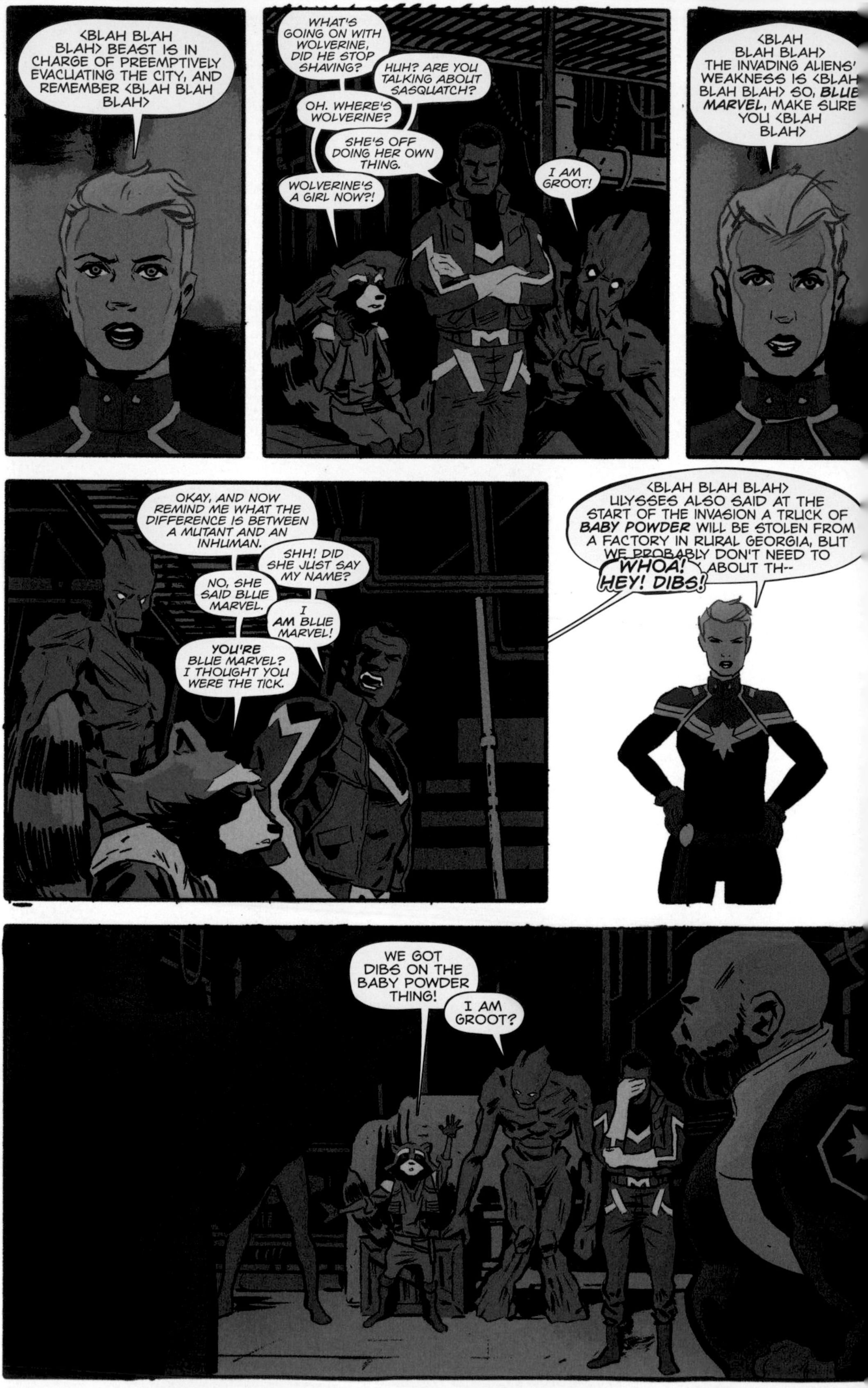

<BLAH BLAH BLAH> BEAST IS IN CHARGE OF PREEMPTIVELY EVACUATING THE CITY, AND REMEMBER <BLAH BLAH BLAH>
WHAT'S GOING ON WITH WOLVERINE, DID HE STOP SHAVING?
HUH? ARE YOU TALKING ABOUT SASQUATCH?
OH. WHERE'S WOLVERINE?
SHE'S OFF DOING HER OWN THING.
WOLVERINE'S A GIRL NOW?!
I AM GROOT!
<BLAH BLAH BLAH> THE INVADING ALIENS' WEAKNESS IS <BLAH BLAH BLAH> SO, BLUE MARVEL, MAKE SURE YOU <BLAH BLAH>
OKAY, AND NOW REMIND ME WHAT THE DIFFERENCE IS BETWEEN A MUTANT AND AN INHUMAN.
SHH! DID SHE JUST SAY MY NAME?
NO, SHE SAID BLUE MARVEL.
I AM BLUE MARVEL!
YOU'RE BLUE MARVEL? I THOUGHT YOU WERE THE TICK.
<BLAH BLAH BLAH> ULYSSES ALSO SAID AT THE START OF THE INVASION A TRUCK OF BABY POWDER WILL BE STOLEN FROM A FACTORY IN RURAL GEORGIA, BUT WE PROBABLY DON'T NEED TO ABOUT TH--
WHOA! HEY! DIBS!
WE GOT DIBS ON THE BABY POWDER THING!
I AM GROOT?

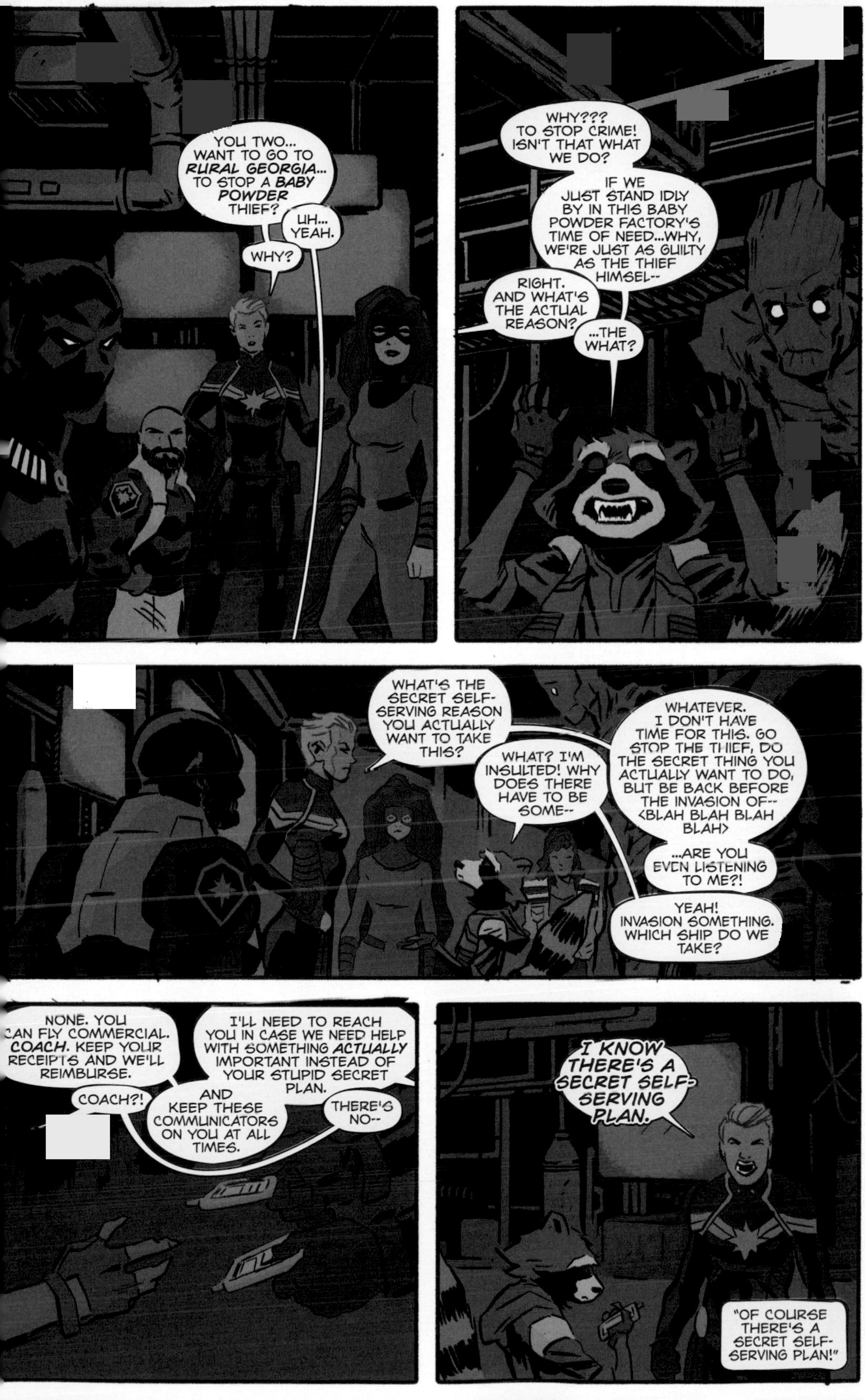
YOU TWO... WANT TO GO TO RURAL GEORGIA... TO STOP A BABY POWDER THIEF?
UH... YEAH.
WHY?
WHY??? TO STOP CRIME! ISN'T THAT WHAT WE DO?
IF WE JUST STAND IDLY BY IN THIS BABY POWDER FACTORY'S TIME OF NEED...WHY, WE'RE JUST AS GUILTY AS THE THIEF HIMSEL--
RIGHT. AND WHAT'S THE ACTUAL REASON?
...THE WHAT?
WHAT'S THE SECRET SELF-SERVING REASON YOU ACTUALLY WANT TO TAKE THIS?
WHAT? I'M INSULTED! WHY DOES THERE HAVE TO BE SOME--
WHATEVER. I DON'T HAVE TIME FOR THIS. GO STOP THE THIEF, DO THE SECRET THING YOU ACTUALLY WANT TO DO, BUT BE BACK BEFORE THE INVASION OF-- <BLAH BLAH BLAH BLAH>
...ARE YOU EVEN LISTENING TO ME?!
YEAH! INVASION SOMETHING. WHICH SHIP DO WE TAKE?
NONE. YOU CAN FLY COMMERCIAL. COACH. KEEP YOUR RECEIPTS AND WE'LL REIMBURSE.
COACH?!
I'LL NEED TO REACH YOU IN CASE WE NEED HELP WITH SOMETHING ACTUALLY IMPORTANT INSTEAD OF YOUR STUPID SECRET PLAN.
AND KEEP THESE COMMUNICATORS ON YOU AT ALL TIMES.
THERE'S NO--
I KNOW THERE'S A SECRET SELF-SERVING PLAN.
"OF COURSE THERE'S A SECRET SELF-SERVING PLAN!"

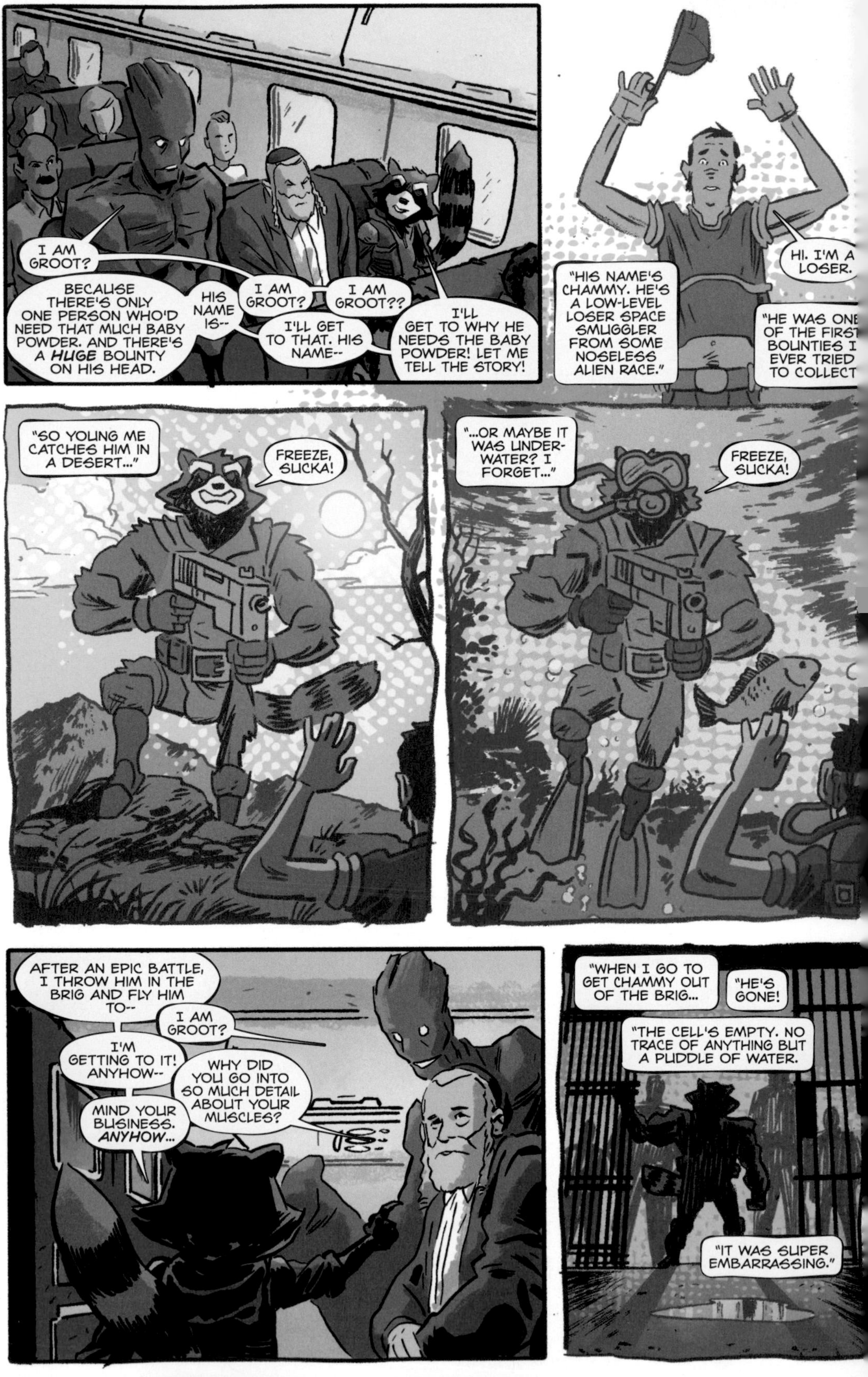
I AM GROOT?
BECAUSE THERE'S ONLY ONE PERSON WHO'D NEED THAT MUCH BABY POWDER. AND THERE'S A *HUGE* BOUNTY ON HIS HEAD.
I AM GROOT?
HIS NAME IS--
I AM GROOT??
I'LL GET TO THAT. HIS NAME--
I'LL GET TO WHY HE NEEDS THE BABY POWDER! LET ME TELL THE STORY!
"HIS NAME'S CHAMMY. HE'S A LOW-LEVEL LOSER SPACE SMUGGLER FROM SOME NOSELESS ALIEN RACE."
HI. I'M A LOSER.
"HE WAS ONE OF THE FIRST BOUNTIES I EVER TRIED TO COLLECT.
"SO YOUNG ME CATCHES HIM IN A DESERT..."
FREEZE, SUCKA!
"...OR MAYBE IT WAS UNDER-WATER? I FORGET..."
FREEZE, SUCKA!
AFTER AN EPIC BATTLE, I THROW HIM IN THE BRIG AND FLY HIM TO--
I AM GROOT?
I'M GETTING TO IT! ANYHOW--
WHY DID YOU GO INTO SO MUCH DETAIL ABOUT YOUR MUSCLES?
MIND YOUR BUSINESS. *ANYHOW*...
"WHEN I GO TO GET CHAMMY OUT OF THE BRIG...
"HE'S GONE!
"THE CELL'S EMPTY. NO TRACE OF ANYTHING BUT A PUDDLE OF WATER.
"IT WAS SUPER EMBARRASSING."

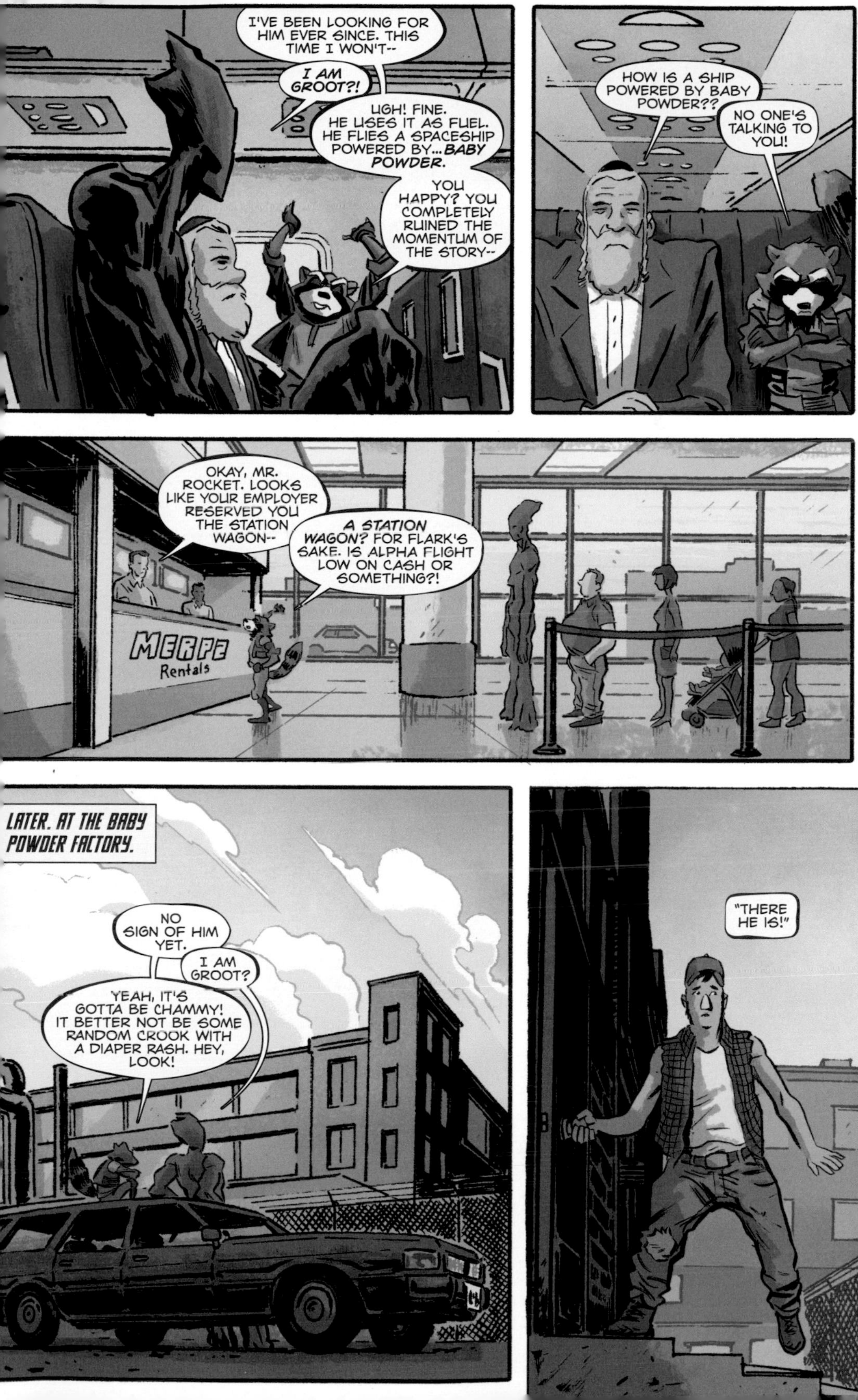
I'VE BEEN LOOKING FOR HIM EVER SINCE. THIS TIME I WON'T--
I AM GROOT?!
UGH! FINE. HE USES IT AS FUEL. HE FLIES A SPACESHIP POWERED BY... BABY POWDER.
YOU HAPPY? YOU COMPLETELY RUINED THE MOMENTUM OF THE STORY--
HOW IS A SHIP POWERED BY BABY POWDER??
NO ONE'S TALKING TO YOU!
OKAY, MR. ROCKET. LOOKS LIKE YOUR EMPLOYER RESERVED YOU THE STATION WAGON--
A STATION WAGON? FOR FLARK'S SAKE. IS ALPHA FLIGHT LOW ON CASH OR SOMETHING?!
MERPZ Rentals
LATER. AT THE BABY POWDER FACTORY.
NO SIGN OF HIM YET.
I AM GROOT?
YEAH, IT'S GOTTA BE CHAMMY! IT BETTER NOT BE SOME RANDOM CROOK WITH A DIAPER RASH. HEY, LOOK!
"THERE HE IS!"

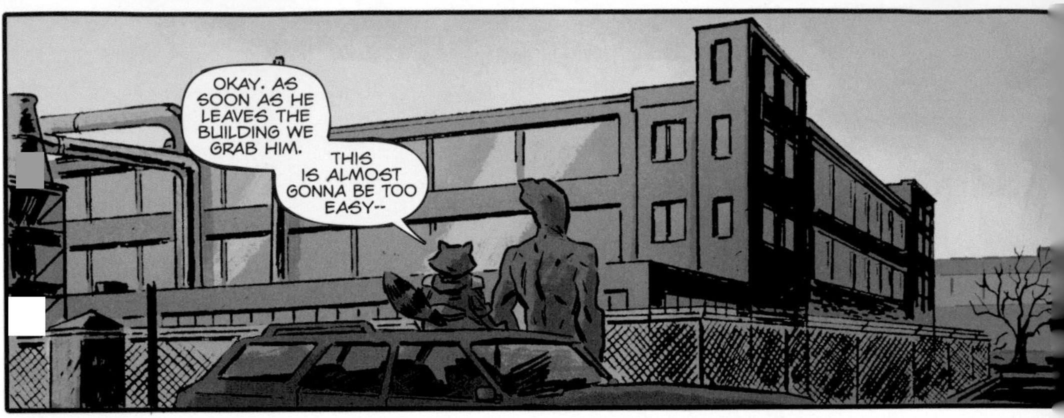
OKAY. AS SOON AS HE LEAVES THE BUILDING WE GRAB HIM.
THIS IS ALMOST GONNA BE TOO EASY--

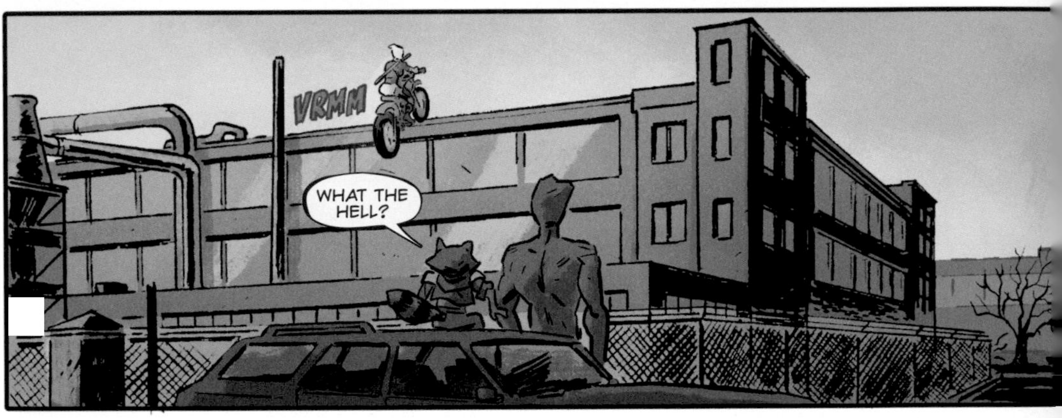
VRMM
WHAT THE HELL?

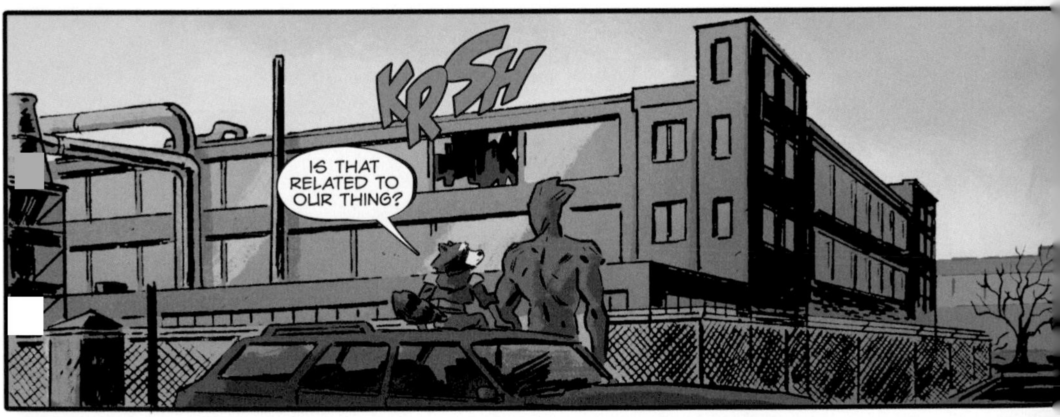
KRSH
IS THAT RELATED TO OUR THING?

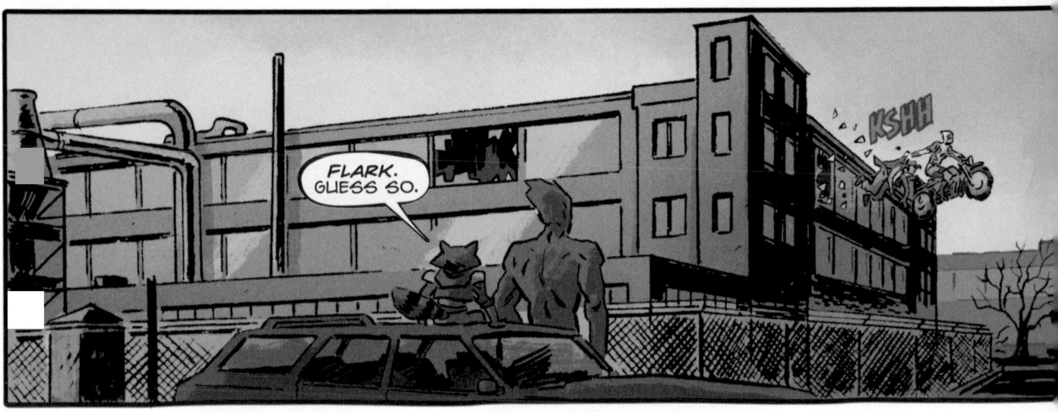
KSHH
*FLARK.* GUESS SO.

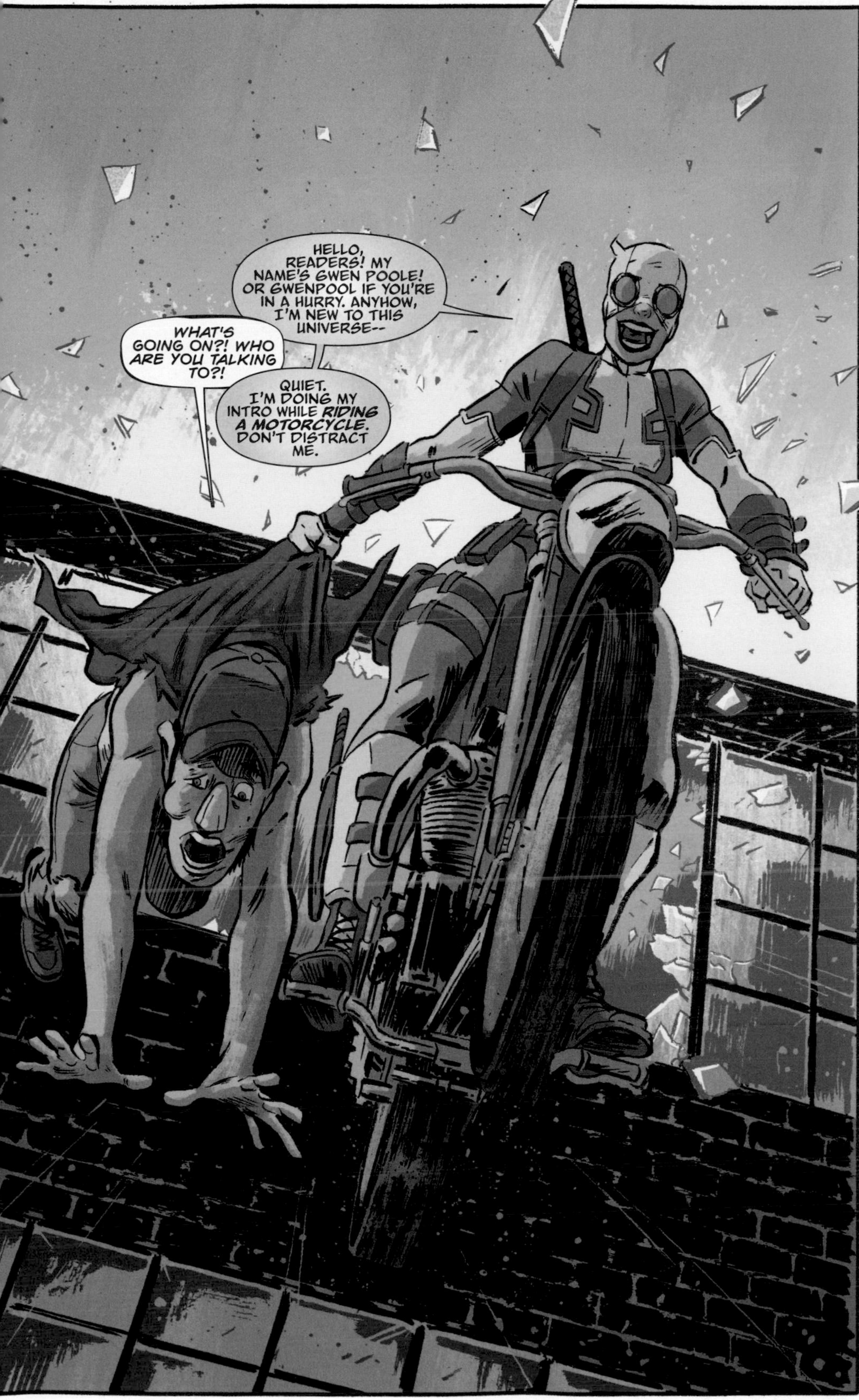
HELLO, READERS! MY NAME'S GWEN POOLE! OR GWENPOOL IF YOU'RE IN A HURRY. ANYHOW, I'M NEW TO THIS UNIVERSE--
WHAT'S GOING ON?! WHO ARE YOU TALKING TO?!
QUIET. I'M DOING MY INTRO WHILE *RIDING A MOTORCYCLE.* DON'T DISTRACT ME.

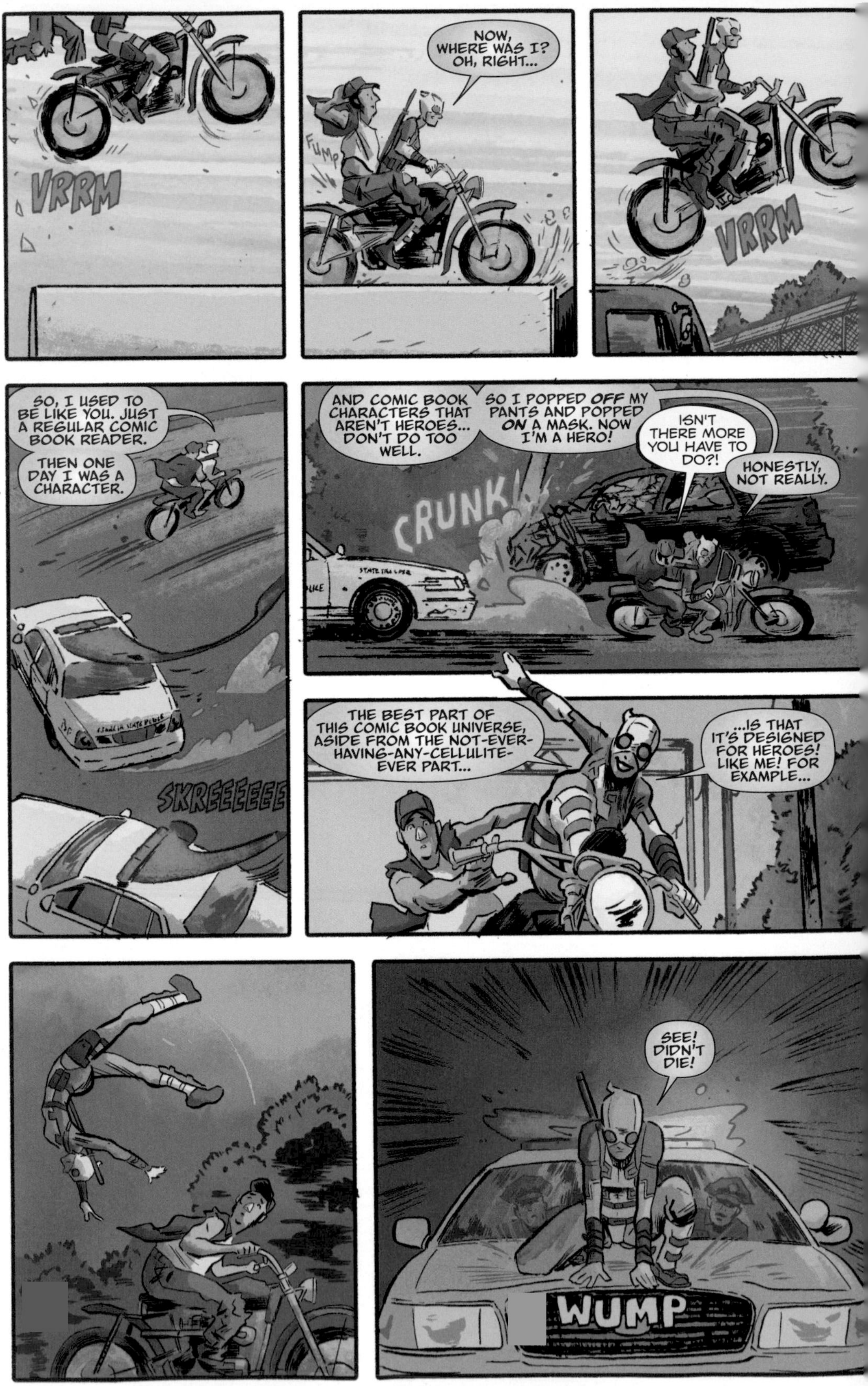
VRRM
NOW, WHERE WAS I? OH, RIGHT...
FUMP
VRRM
SO, I USED TO BE LIKE YOU. JUST A REGULAR COMIC BOOK READER.
THEN ONE DAY I WAS A CHARACTER.
SKREEEEEEE
AND COMIC BOOK CHARACTERS THAT AREN'T HEROES... DON'T DO TOO WELL.
SO I POPPED OFF MY PANTS AND POPPED ON A MASK. NOW I'M A HERO!
ISN'T THERE MORE YOU HAVE TO DO?!
HONESTLY, NOT REALLY.
CRUNK!
STATE TROOPER
THE BEST PART OF THIS COMIC BOOK UNIVERSE, ASIDE FROM THE NOT-EVER-HAVING-ANY-CELLULITE-EVER PART...
...IS THAT IT'S DESIGNED FOR HEROES! LIKE ME! FOR EXAMPLE...
SEE! DIDN'T DIE!
WUMP

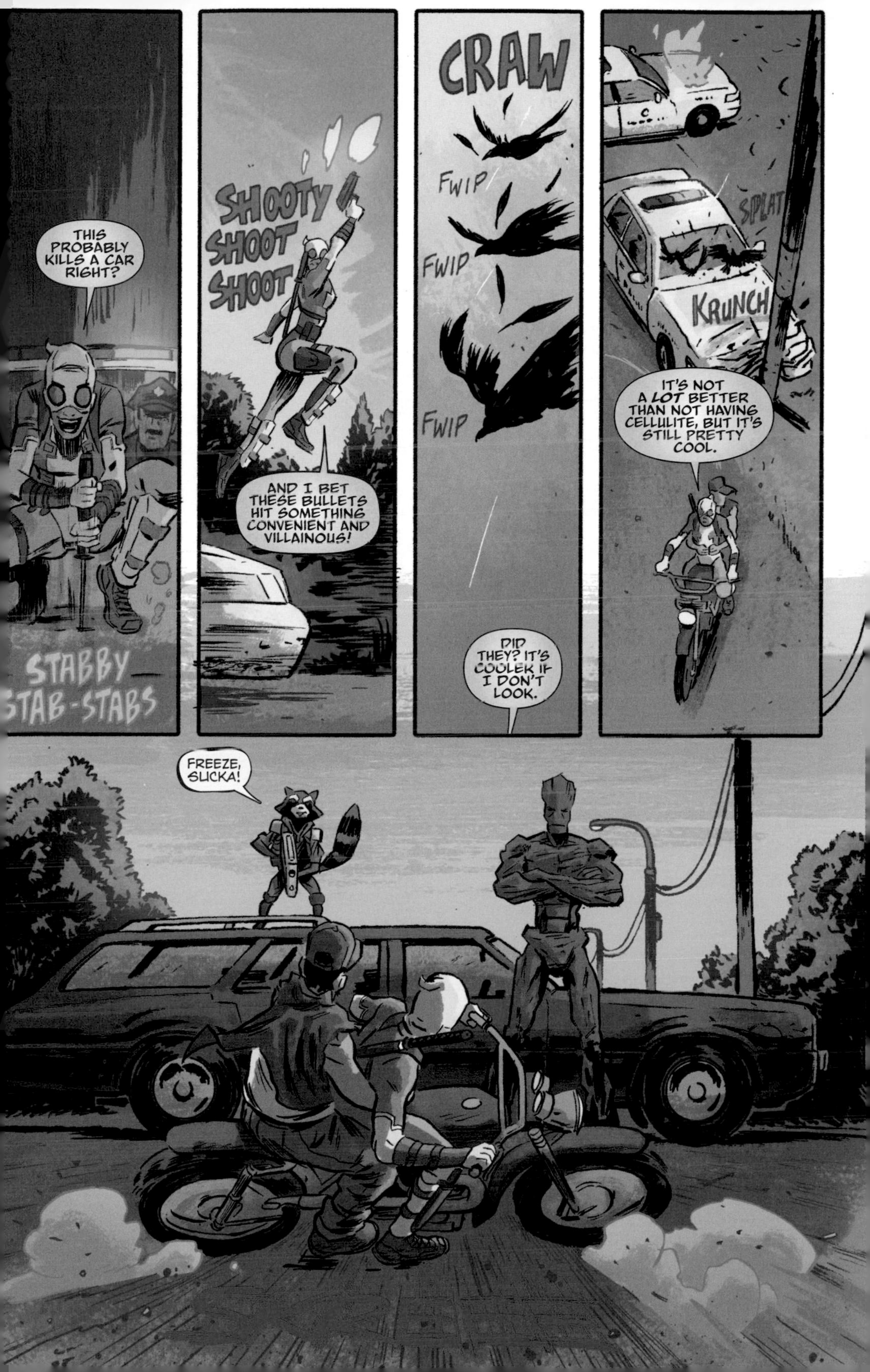
THIS PROBABLY KILLS A CAR RIGHT?
STABBY STAB-STABS
SHOOTY SHOOT SHOOT
AND I BET THESE BULLETS HIT SOMETHING CONVENIENT AND VILLAINOUS!
CRAW
FWIP
FWIP
FWIP
DID THEY? IT'S COOLER IF I DON'T LOOK.
SPLAT
KRUNCH
IT'S NOT A LOT BETTER THAN NOT HAVING CELLULITE, BUT IT'S STILL PRETTY COOL.
FREEZE, SUCKA!

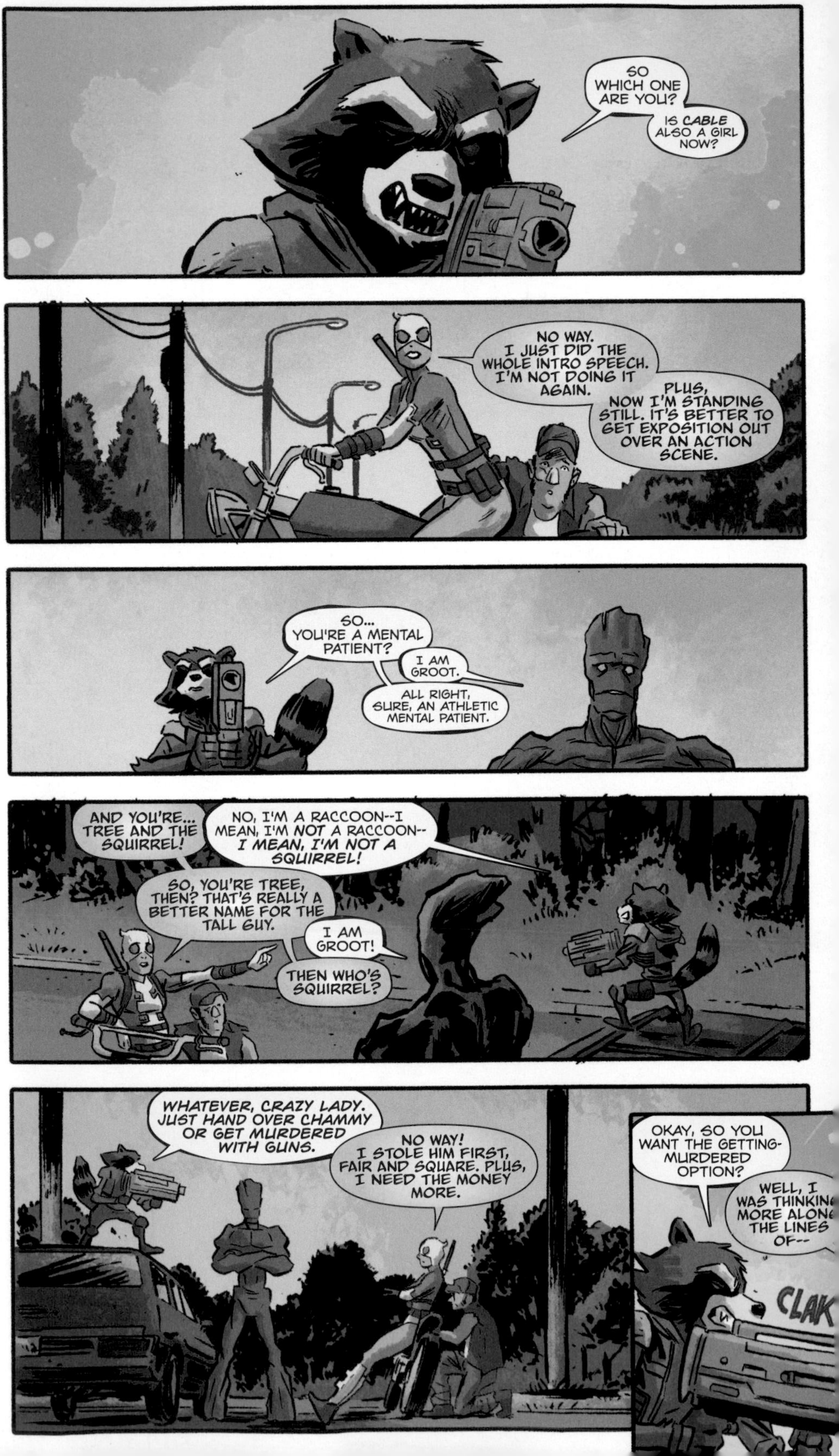
SO WHICH ONE ARE YOU?
IS CABLE ALSO A GIRL NOW?
NO WAY. I JUST DID THE WHOLE INTRO SPEECH. I'M NOT DOING IT AGAIN.
PLUS, NOW I'M STANDING STILL. IT'S BETTER TO GET EXPOSITION OUT OVER AN ACTION SCENE.
SO... YOU'RE A MENTAL PATIENT?
I AM GROOT.
ALL RIGHT, SURE, AN ATHLETIC MENTAL PATIENT.
AND YOU'RE... TREE AND THE SQUIRREL!
NO, I'M A RACCOON--I MEAN, I'M NOT A RACCOON-- I MEAN, I'M NOT A SQUIRREL!
SO, YOU'RE TREE, THEN? THAT'S REALLY A BETTER NAME FOR THE TALL GUY.
I AM GROOT!
THEN WHO'S SQUIRREL?
WHATEVER, CRAZY LADY. JUST HAND OVER CHAMMY OR GET MURDERED WITH GUNS.
NO WAY! I STOLE HIM FIRST, FAIR AND SQUARE. PLUS, I NEED THE MONEY MORE.
OKAY, SO YOU WANT THE GETTING-MURDERED OPTION?
WELL, I WAS THINKING MORE ALONG THE LINES OF--
CLAK

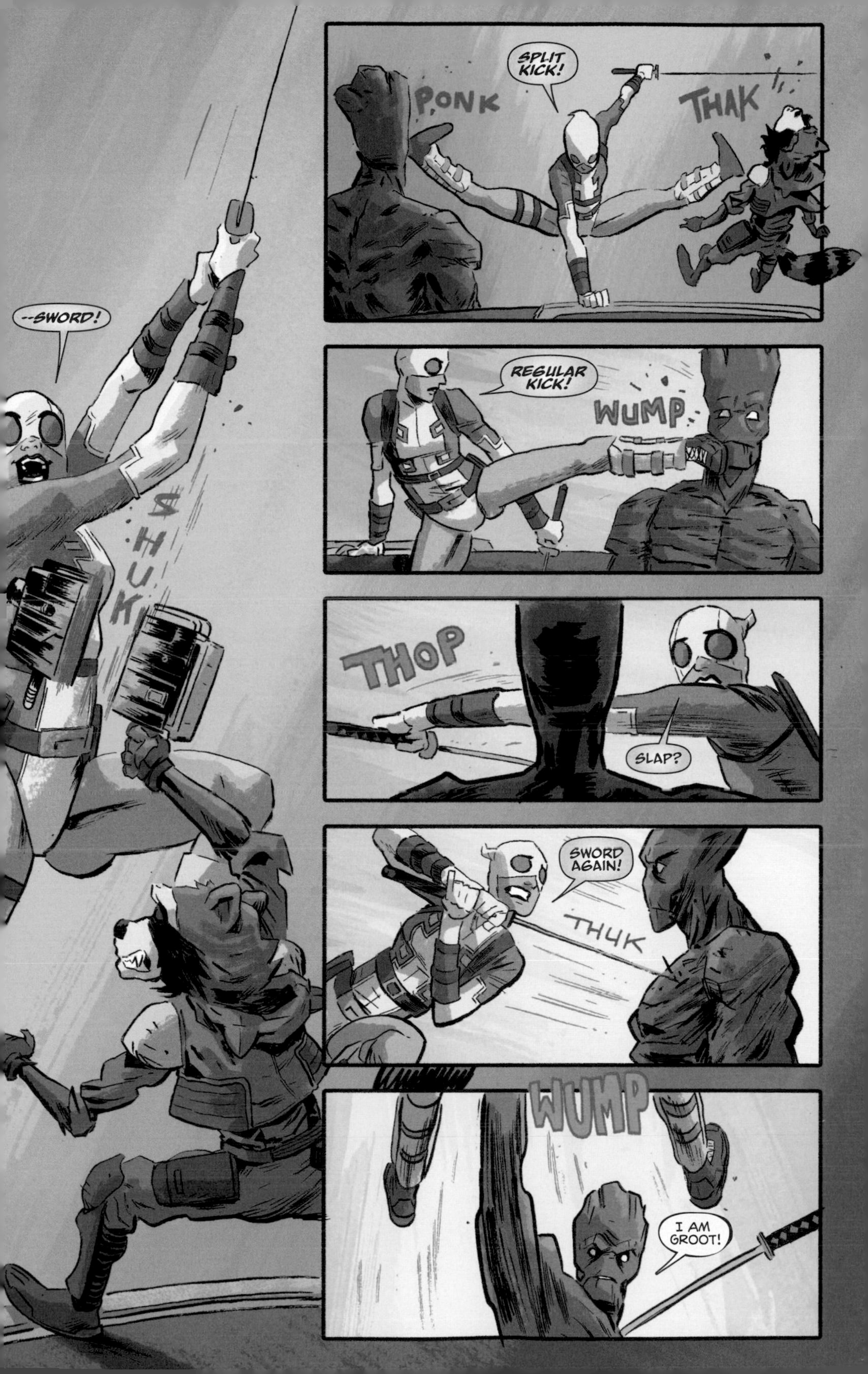
--SWORD!
SHUK
SPLIT KICK!
PONK
THAK
REGULAR KICK!
WUMP
THOP
SLAP?
SWORD AGAIN!
THUK
WUMP
I AM GROOT!

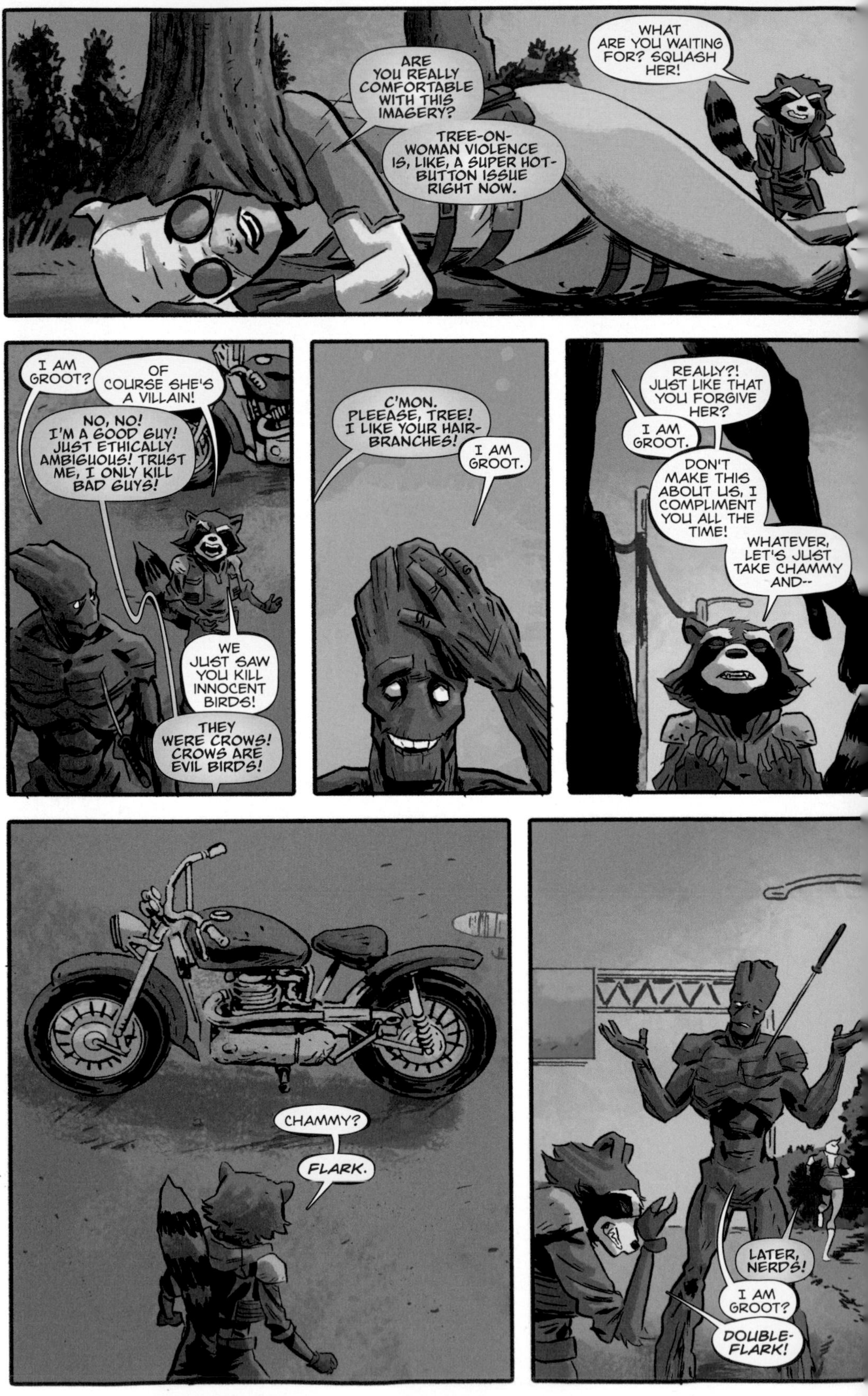
ARE YOU REALLY COMFORTABLE WITH THIS IMAGERY?
TREE-ON-WOMAN VIOLENCE IS, LIKE, A SUPER HOT-BUTTON ISSUE RIGHT NOW.
WHAT ARE YOU WAITING FOR? SQUASH HER!
I AM GROOT?
OF COURSE SHE'S A VILLAIN!
NO, NO! I'M A GOOD GUY! JUST ETHICALLY AMBIGUOUS! TRUST ME, I ONLY KILL BAD GUYS!
WE JUST SAW YOU KILL INNOCENT BIRDS!
THEY WERE CROWS! CROWS ARE EVIL BIRDS!
C'MON. PLEEASE, TREE! I LIKE YOUR HAIR-BRANCHES!
I AM GROOT.
REALLY?! JUST LIKE THAT YOU FORGIVE HER?
I AM GROOT.
DON'T MAKE THIS ABOUT US, I COMPLIMENT YOU ALL THE TIME!
WHATEVER, LET'S JUST TAKE CHAMMY AND--
CHAMMY?
FLARK.
LATER, NERDS!
I AM GROOT?
DOUBLE-FLARK!

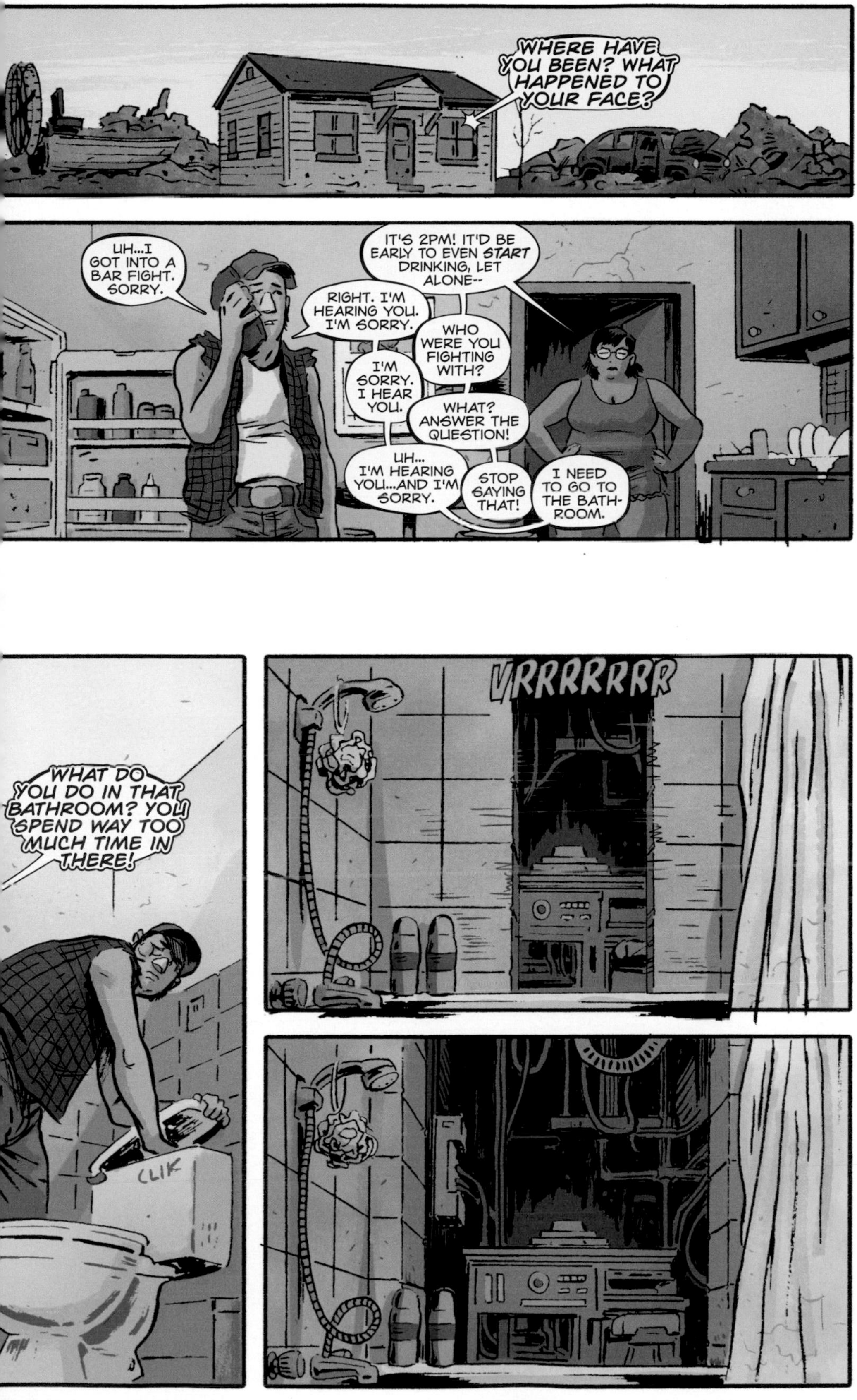
WHERE HAVE YOU BEEN? WHAT HAPPENED TO YOUR FACE?
UH...I GOT INTO A BAR FIGHT. SORRY.
IT'S 2PM! IT'D BE EARLY TO EVEN START DRINKING, LET ALONE--
RIGHT. I'M HEARING YOU. I'M SORRY.
WHO WERE YOU FIGHTING WITH?
I'M SORRY. I HEAR YOU.
WHAT? ANSWER THE QUESTION!
UH... I'M HEARING YOU...AND I'M SORRY.
STOP SAYING THAT!
I NEED TO GO TO THE BATH-ROOM.
WHAT DO YOU DO IN THAT BATHROOM? YOU SPEND WAY TOO MUCH TIME IN THERE!
CLIK
VRRRRRRR

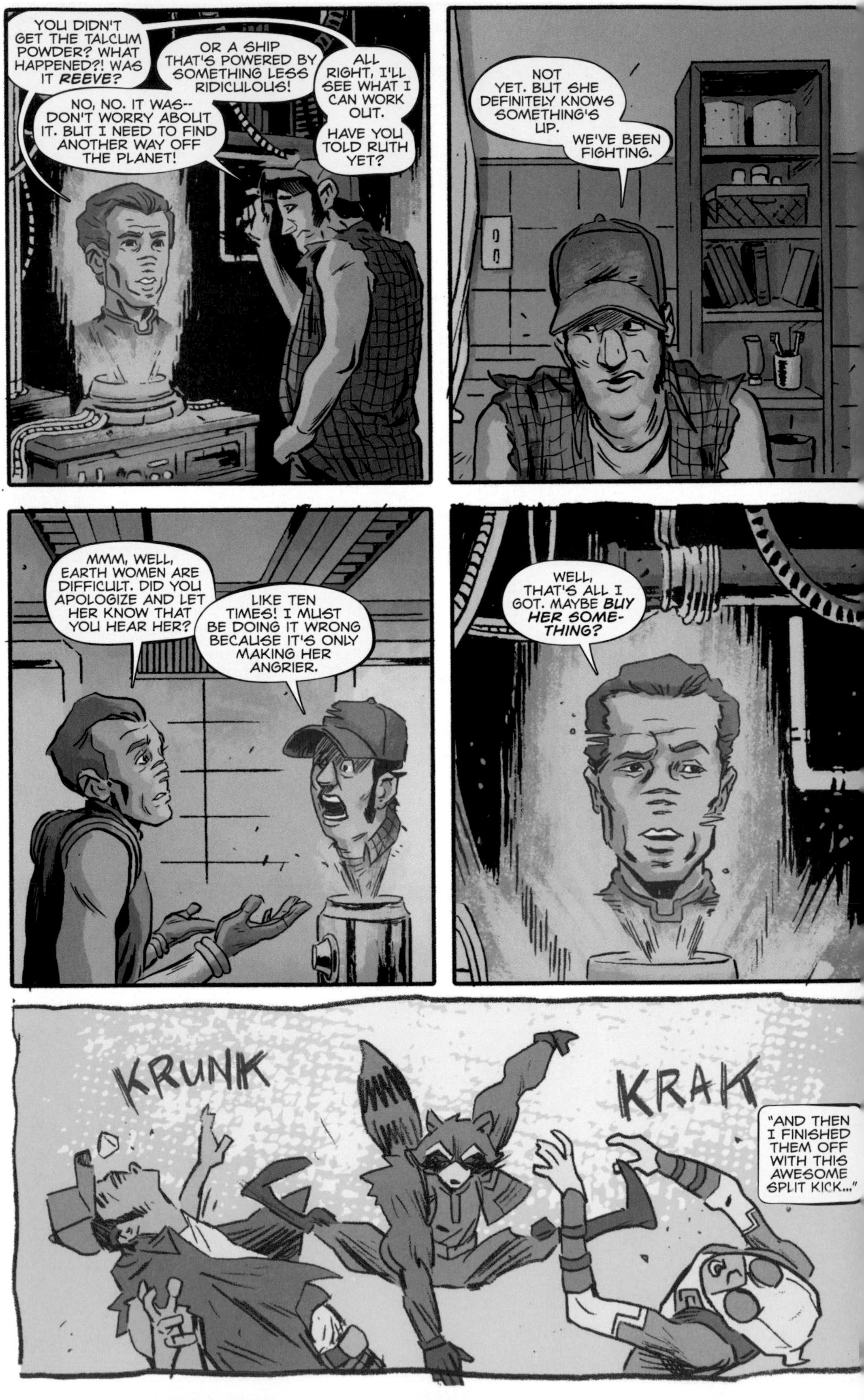
YOU DIDN'T GET THE TALCUM POWDER? WHAT HAPPENED?! WAS IT REEVE?
NO, NO. IT WAS-- DON'T WORRY ABOUT IT. BUT I NEED TO FIND ANOTHER WAY OFF THE PLANET!
OR A SHIP THAT'S POWERED BY SOMETHING LESS RIDICULOUS!
ALL RIGHT, I'LL SEE WHAT I CAN WORK OUT.
HAVE YOU TOLD RUTH YET?
NOT YET. BUT SHE DEFINITELY KNOWS SOMETHING'S UP.
WE'VE BEEN FIGHTING.
MMM, WELL, EARTH WOMEN ARE DIFFICULT. DID YOU APOLOGIZE AND LET HER KNOW THAT YOU HEAR HER?
LIKE TEN TIMES! I MUST BE DOING IT WRONG BECAUSE IT'S ONLY MAKING HER ANGRIER.
WELL, THAT'S ALL I GOT. MAYBE BUY HER SOMETHING?
KRUNK
KRAK
"AND THEN I FINISHED THEM OFF WITH THIS AWESOME SPLIT KICK..."

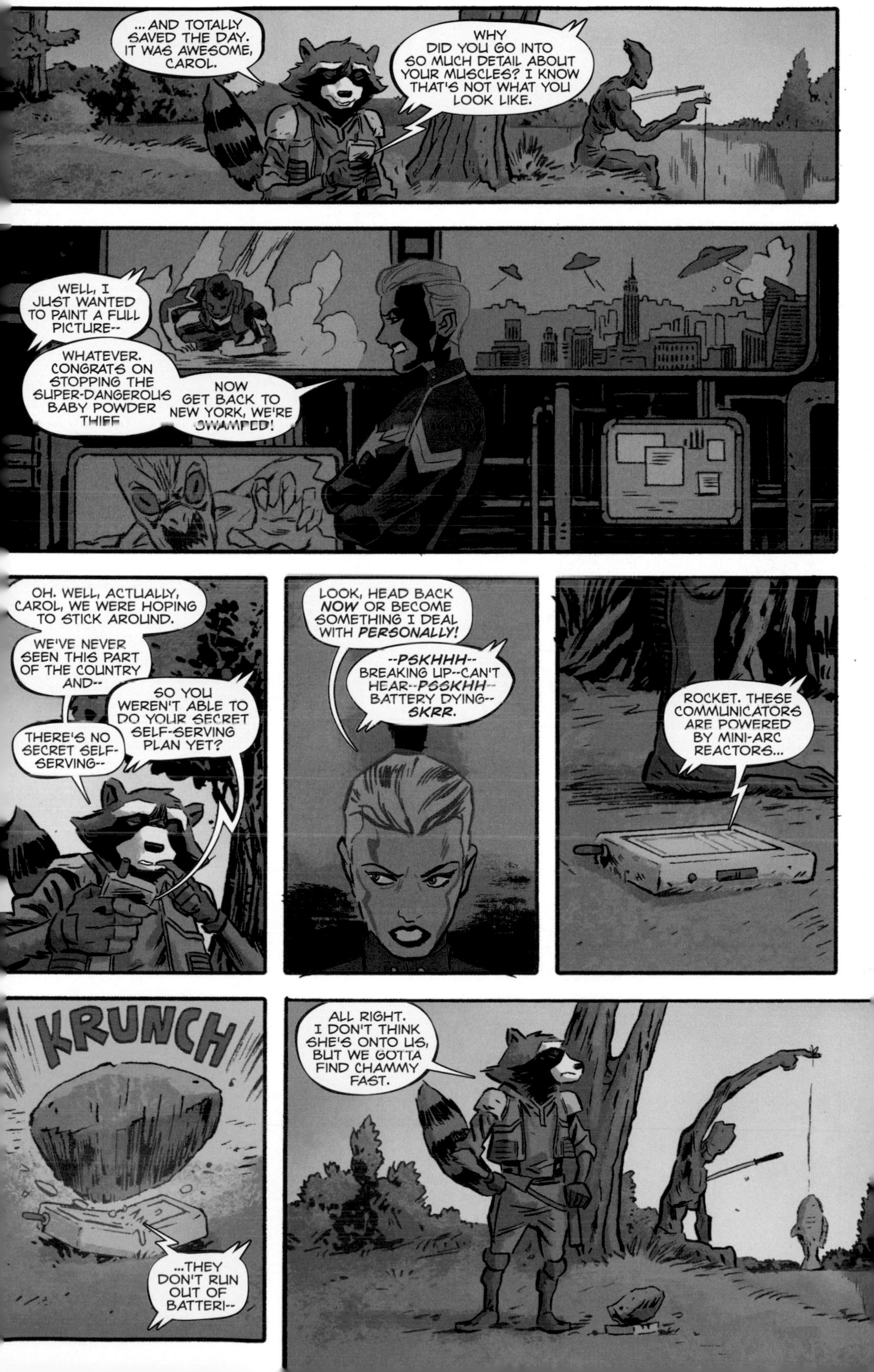
...AND TOTALLY SAVED THE DAY. IT WAS AWESOME, CAROL.
WHY DID YOU GO INTO SO MUCH DETAIL ABOUT YOUR MUSCLES? I KNOW THAT'S NOT WHAT YOU LOOK LIKE.
WELL, I JUST WANTED TO PAINT A FULL PICTURE--
WHATEVER. CONGRATS ON STOPPING THE SUPER-DANGEROUS BABY POWDER THIEF.
NOW GET BACK TO NEW YORK, WE'RE SWAMPED!
OH. WELL, ACTUALLY, CAROL, WE WERE HOPING TO STICK AROUND.
WE'VE NEVER SEEN THIS PART OF THE COUNTRY AND--
SO YOU WEREN'T ABLE TO DO YOUR SECRET SELF-SERVING PLAN YET?
THERE'S NO SECRET SELF-SERVING--
LOOK, HEAD BACK NOW OR BECOME SOMETHING I DEAL WITH PERSONALLY!
--PSKHHH-- BREAKING UP--CAN'T HEAR--PSSKHH-- BATTERY DYING-- SKRR.
ROCKET. THESE COMMUNICATORS ARE POWERED BY MINI-ARC REACTORS...
KRUNCH
...THEY DON'T RUN OUT OF BATTERI--
ALL RIGHT. I DON'T THINK SHE'S ONTO US, BUT WE GOTTA FIND CHAMMY FAST.

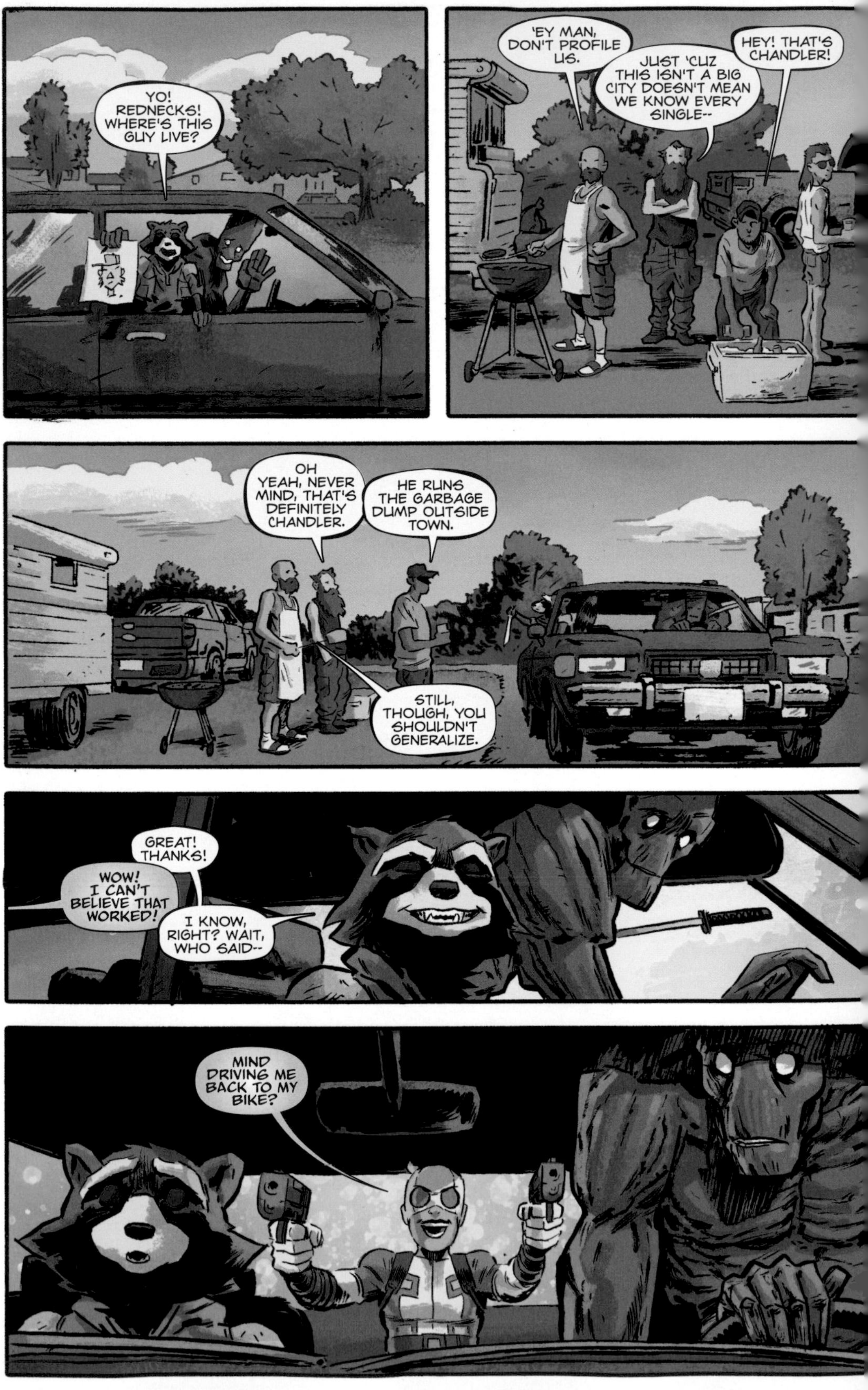

YO! REDNECKS! WHERE'S THIS GUY LIVE?
'EY MAN, DON'T PROFILE US.
JUST 'CUZ THIS ISN'T A BIG CITY DOESN'T MEAN WE KNOW EVERY SINGLE--
HEY! THAT'S CHANDLER!
OH YEAH, NEVER MIND, THAT'S DEFINITELY CHANDLER.
HE RUNS THE GARBAGE DUMP OUTSIDE TOWN.
STILL, THOUGH, YOU SHOULDN'T GENERALIZE.
GREAT! THANKS!
WOW! I CAN'T BELIEVE THAT WORKED!
I KNOW, RIGHT? WAIT, WHO SAID--
MIND DRIVING ME BACK TO MY BIKE?

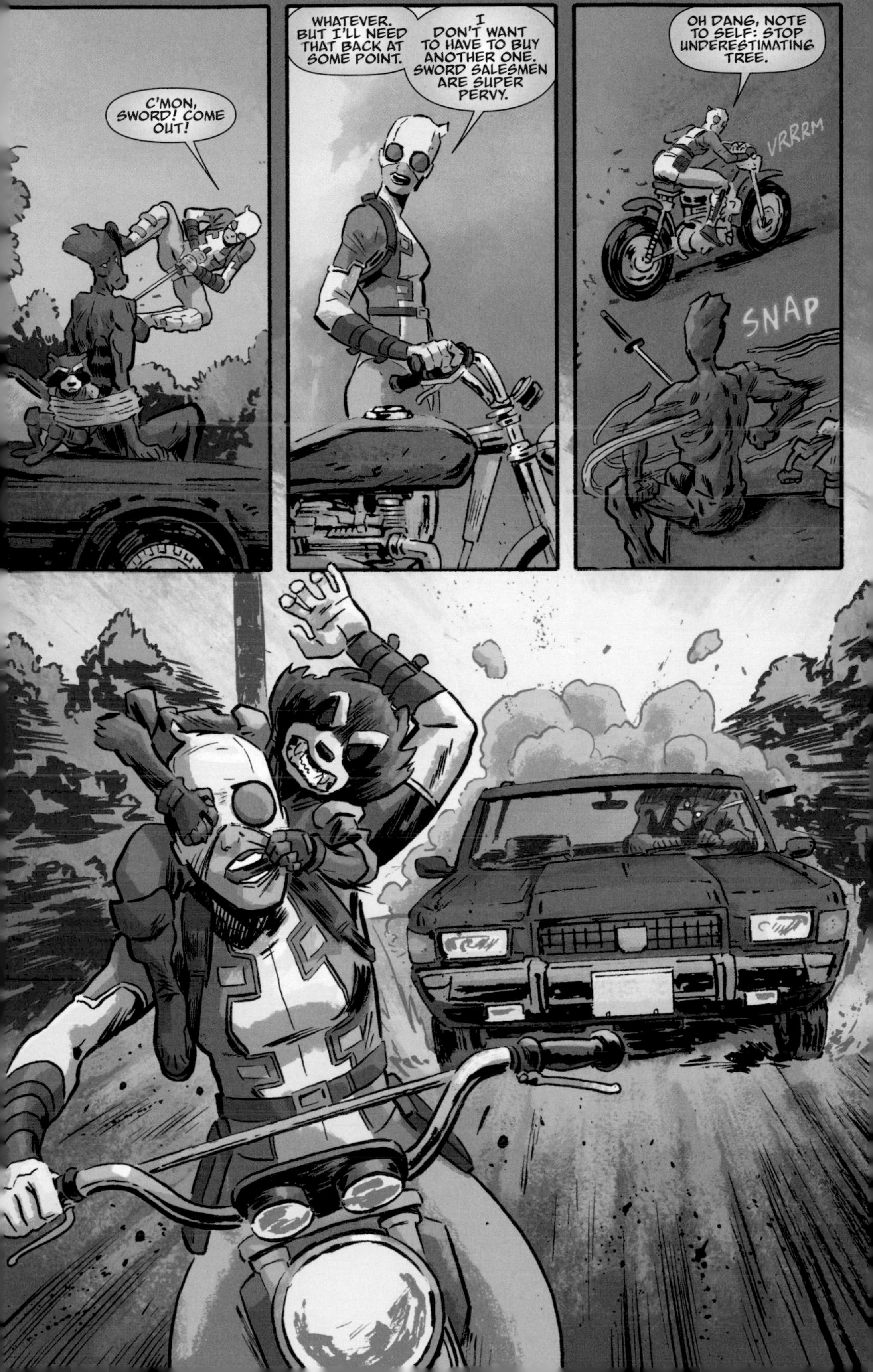
C'MON, SWORD! COME OUT!
WHATEVER. BUT I'LL NEED THAT BACK AT SOME POINT.
I DON'T WANT TO HAVE TO BUY ANOTHER ONE. SWORD SALESMEN ARE SUPER PERVY.
OH DANG, NOTE TO SELF: STOP UNDERESTIMATING TREE.
VRRRM
SNAP

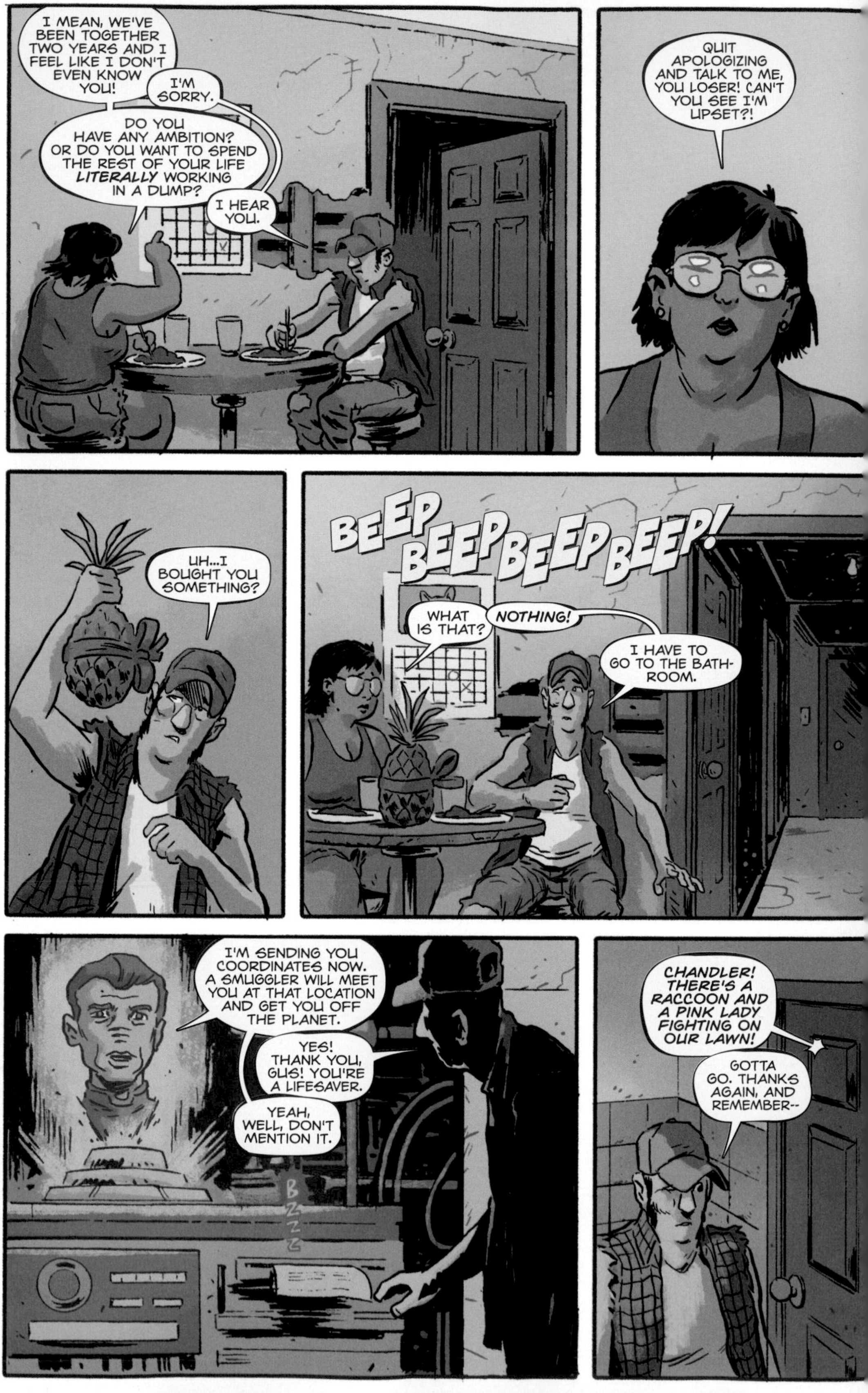
I MEAN, WE'VE BEEN TOGETHER TWO YEARS AND I FEEL LIKE I DON'T EVEN KNOW YOU!
I'M SORRY.
DO YOU HAVE ANY AMBITION? OR DO YOU WANT TO SPEND THE REST OF YOUR LIFE *LITERALLY* WORKING IN A DUMP?
I HEAR YOU.
QUIT APOLOGIZING AND TALK TO ME, YOU LOSER! CAN'T YOU SEE I'M UPSET?!
UH...I BOUGHT YOU SOMETHING?
BEEP BEEP BEEP BEEP!
WHAT IS THAT?
*NOTHING!*
I HAVE TO GO TO THE BATH-ROOM.
I'M SENDING YOU COORDINATES NOW. A SMUGGLER WILL MEET YOU AT THAT LOCATION AND GET YOU OFF THE PLANET.
YES! THANK YOU, GUS! YOU'RE A LIFESAVER.
YEAH, WELL, DON'T MENTION IT.
BZZZ
*CHANDLER! THERE'S A RACCOON AND A PINK LADY FIGHTING ON OUR LAWN!*
GOTTA GO. THANKS AGAIN, AND REMEMBER--

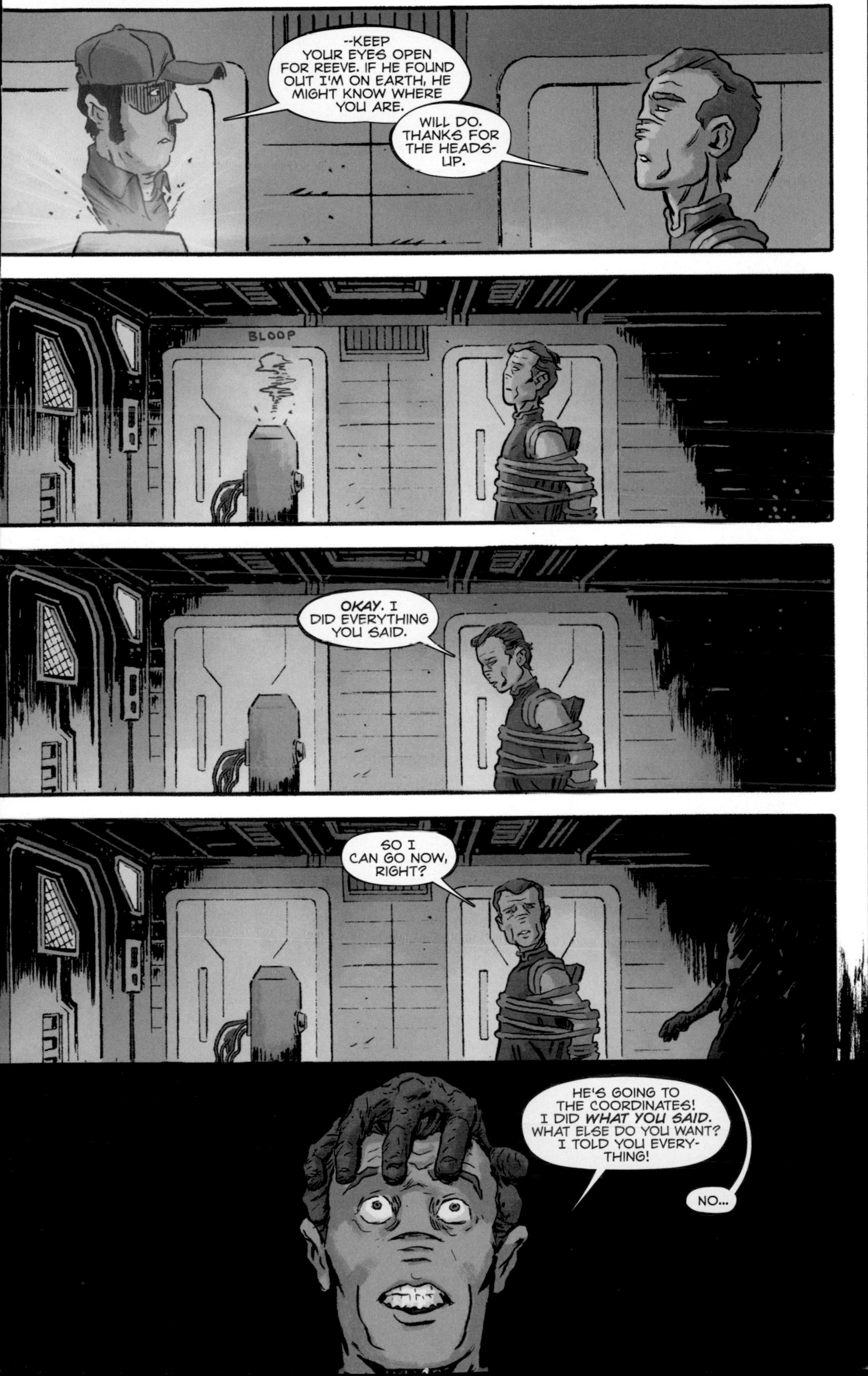
--KEEP YOUR EYES OPEN FOR REEVE. IF HE FOUND OUT I'M ON EARTH, HE MIGHT KNOW WHERE YOU ARE.
WILL DO. THANKS FOR THE HEADS-UP.
BLOOP
OKAY. I DID EVERYTHING YOU SAID.
SO I CAN GO NOW, RIGHT?
HE'S GOING TO THE COORDINATES! I DID WHAT YOU SAID. WHAT ELSE DO YOU WANT? I TOLD YOU EVERY-THING!
NO...

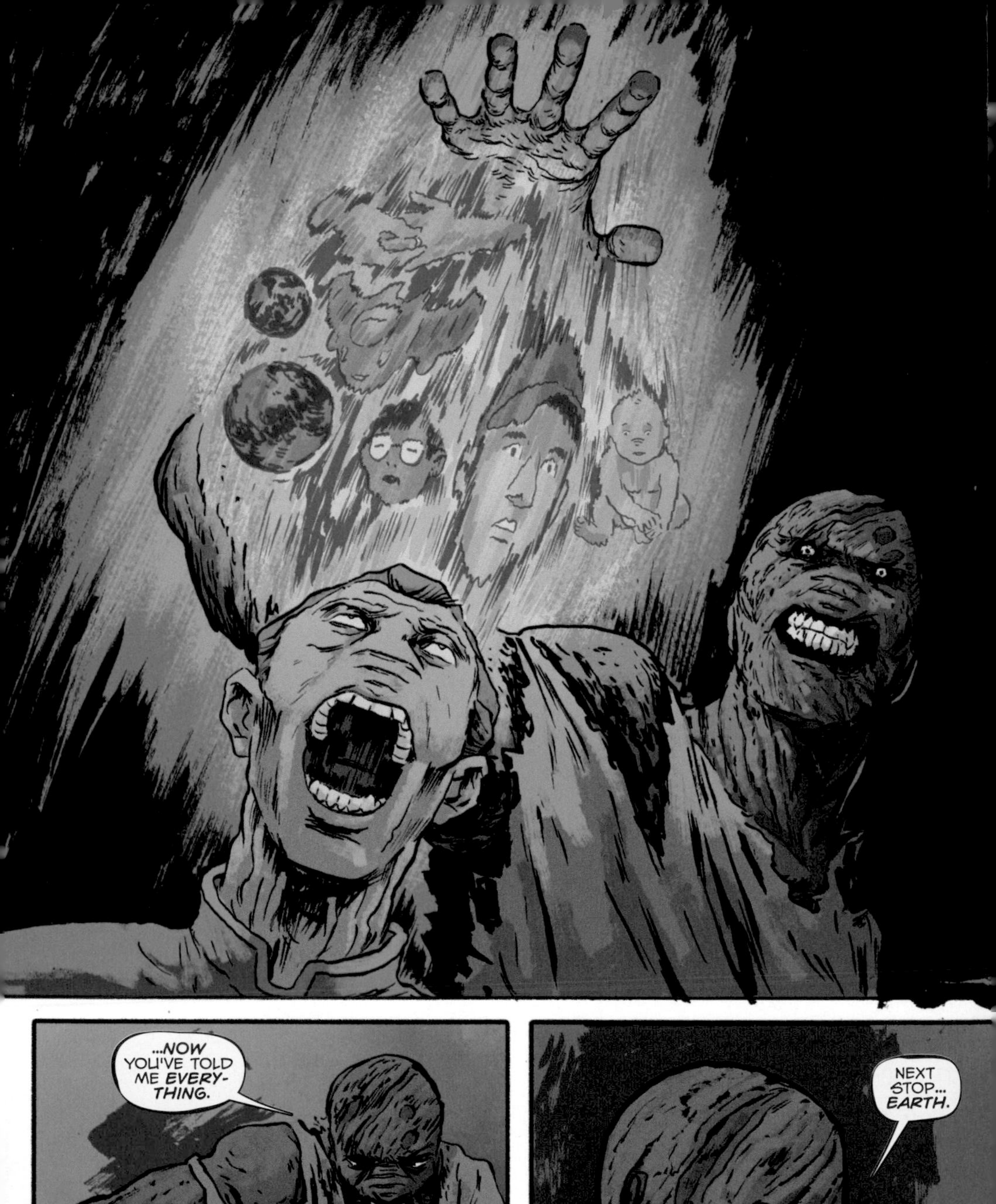

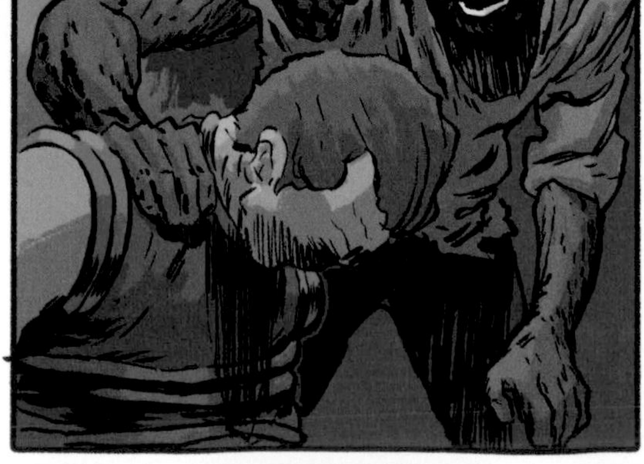
...NOW YOU'VE TOLD ME EVERYTHING.

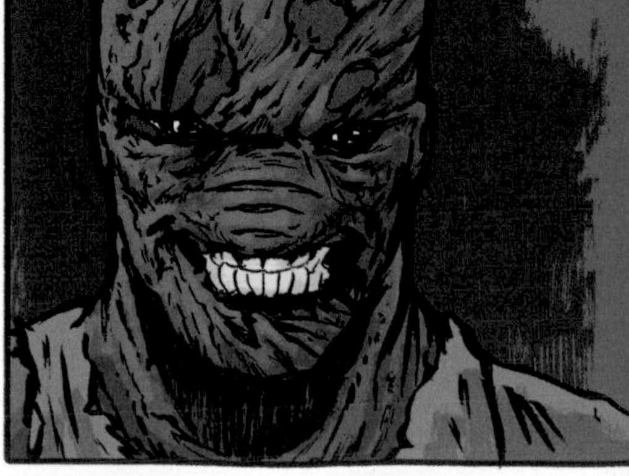
NEXT STOP... EARTH.

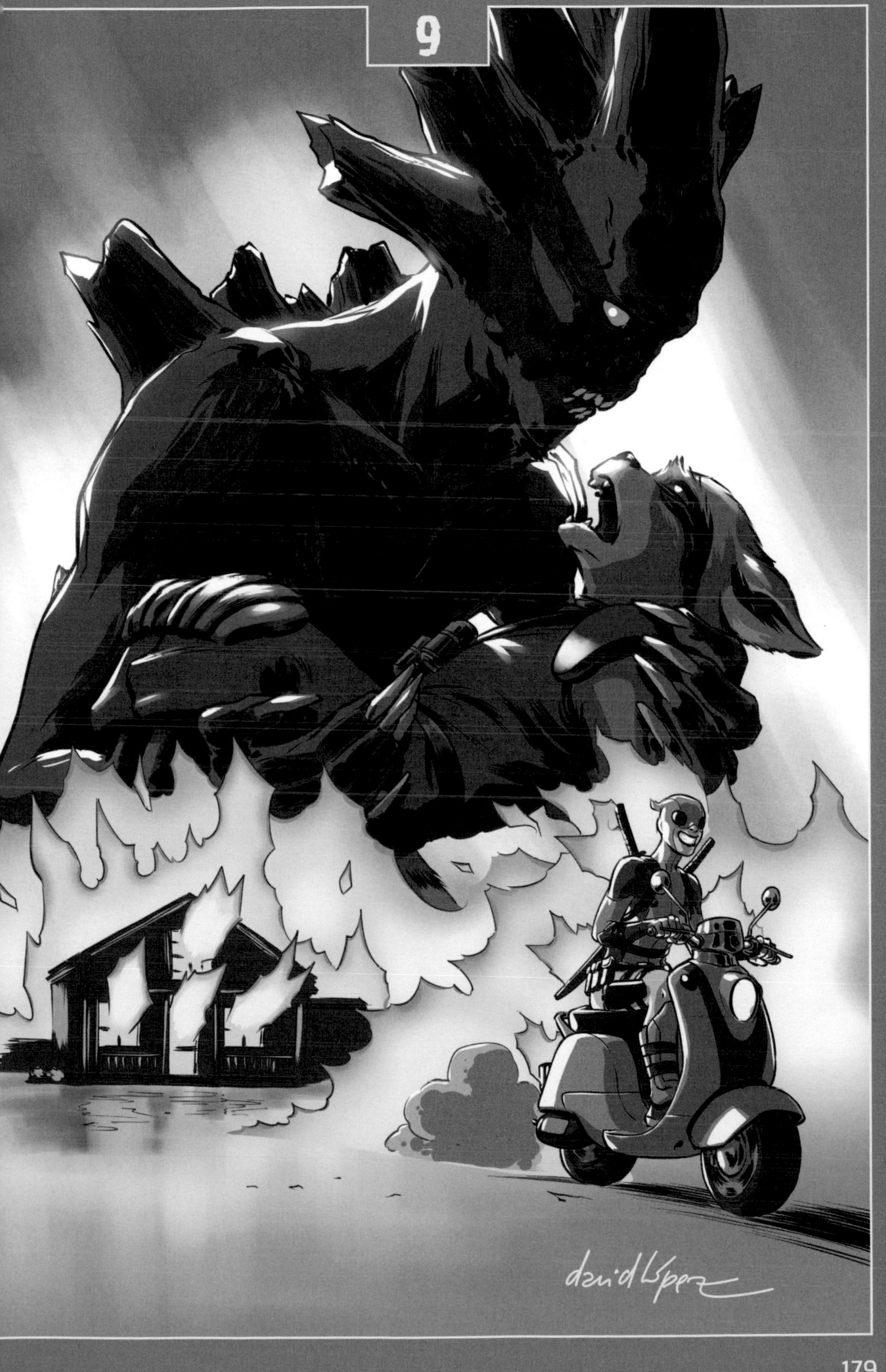
9
david lópez

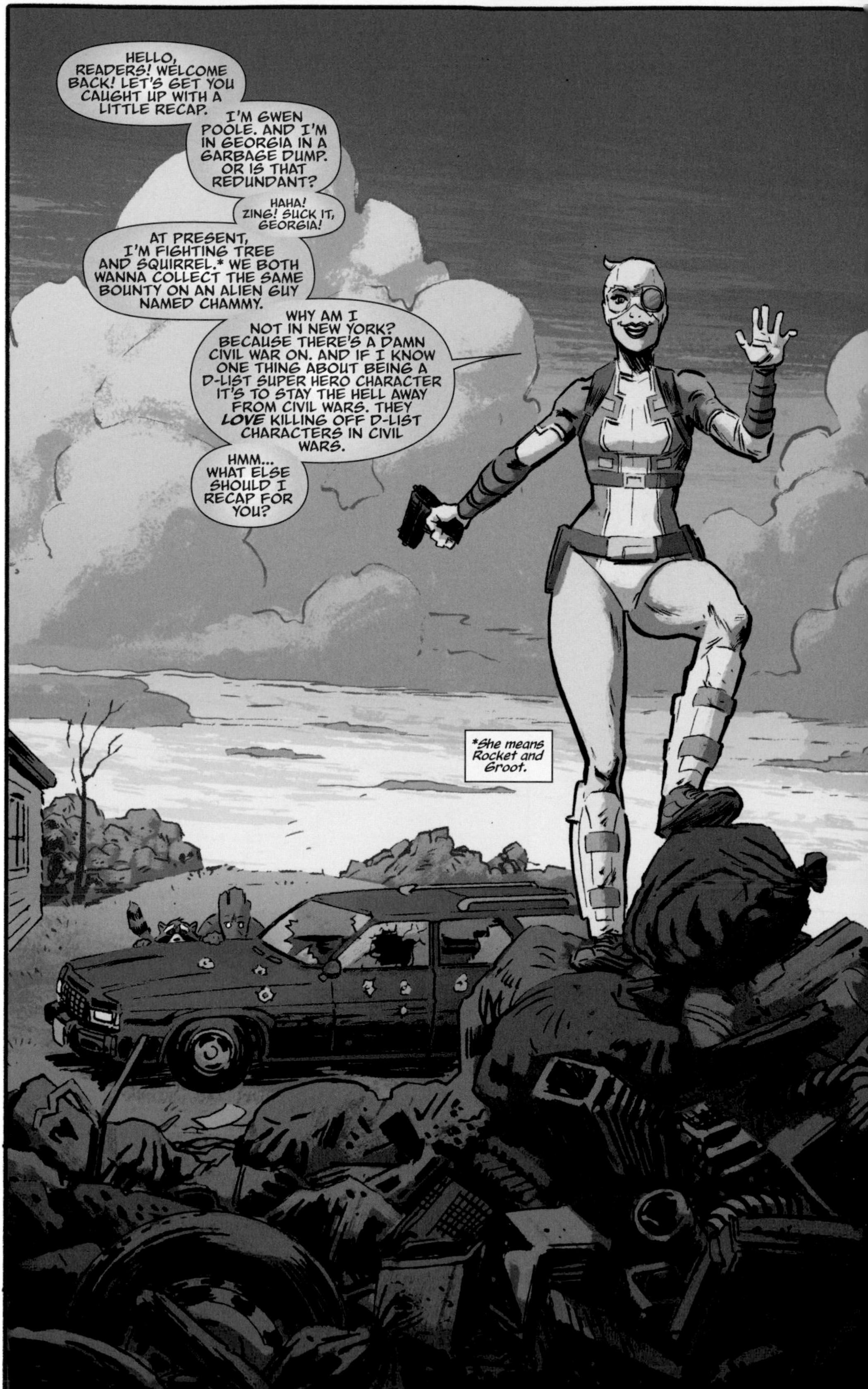
HELLO, READERS! WELCOME BACK! LET'S GET YOU CAUGHT UP WITH A LITTLE RECAP.
I'M GWEN POOLE. AND I'M IN GEORGIA IN A GARBAGE DUMP. OR IS THAT REDUNDANT?
HAHA! ZING! SUCK IT, GEORGIA!
AT PRESENT, I'M FIGHTING TREE AND SQUIRREL.* WE BOTH WANNA COLLECT THE SAME BOUNTY ON AN ALIEN GUY NAMED CHAMMY.
WHY AM I NOT IN NEW YORK? BECAUSE THERE'S A DAMN CIVIL WAR ON. AND IF I KNOW ONE THING ABOUT BEING A D-LIST SUPER HERO CHARACTER IT'S TO STAY THE HELL AWAY FROM CIVIL WARS. THEY LOVE KILLING OFF D-LIST CHARACTERS IN CIVIL WARS.
HMM... WHAT ELSE SHOULD I RECAP FOR YOU?
*She means Rocket and Groot.

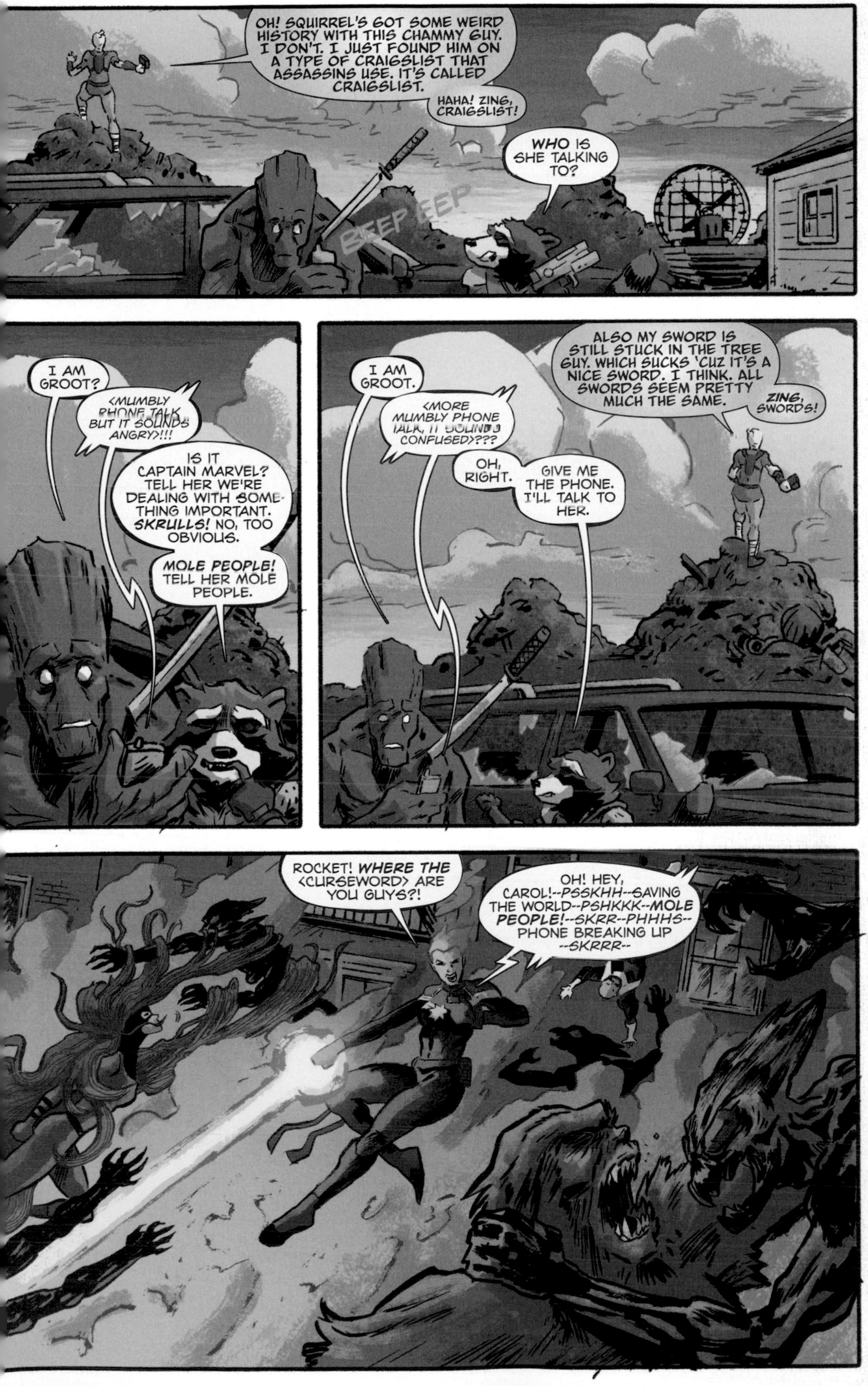
OH! SQUIRREL'S GOT SOME WEIRD HISTORY WITH THIS CHAMMY GUY. I DON'T. I JUST FOUND HIM ON A TYPE OF CRAIGSLIST THAT ASSASSINS USE. IT'S CALLED CRAIGSLIST.
HAHA! ZING, CRAIGSLIST!
BEEP EEP
WHO IS SHE TALKING TO?
I AM GROOT?
<MUMBLY PHONE TALK BUT IT SOUNDS ANGRY>!!!
IS IT CAPTAIN MARVEL? TELL HER WE'RE DEALING WITH SOMETHING IMPORTANT. SKRULLS! NO, TOO OBVIOUS.
MOLE PEOPLE! TELL HER MOLE PEOPLE.
I AM GROOT.
<MORE MUMBLY PHONE TALK, IT SOUNDS CONFUSED>???
OH, RIGHT.
GIVE ME THE PHONE. I'LL TALK TO HER.
ALSO MY SWORD IS STILL STUCK IN THE TREE GUY. WHICH SUCKS 'CUZ IT'S A NICE SWORD. I THINK. ALL SWORDS SEEM PRETTY MUCH THE SAME.
ZING, SWORDS!
ROCKET! WHERE THE <CURSEWORD> ARE YOU GUYS?!
OH! HEY, CAROL!--PSSKHH--SAVING THE WORLD--PSHKKK--MOLE PEOPLE!--SKRR--PHHHS--PHONE BREAKING UP --SKRRR--

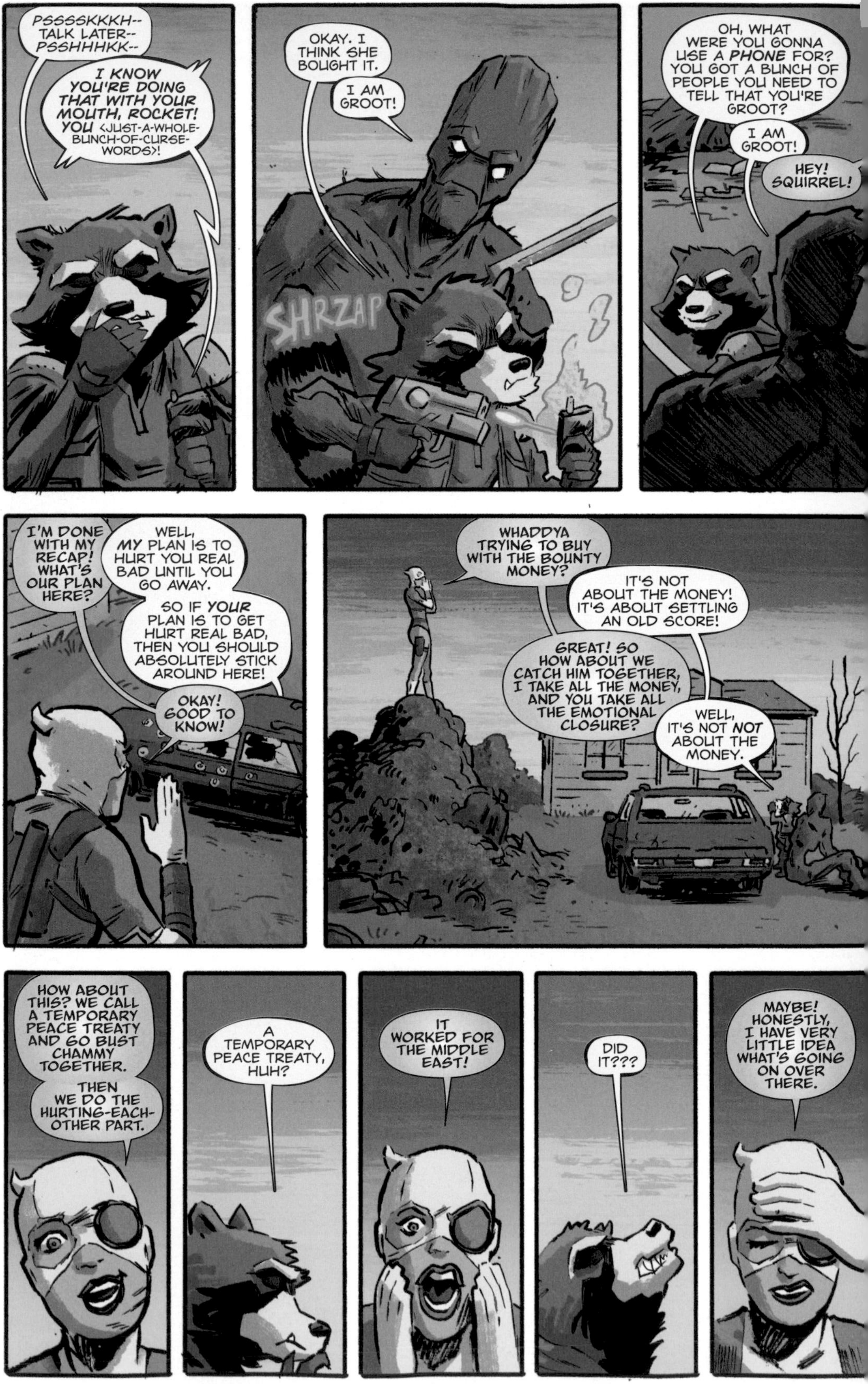
PSSSSKKKH-- TALK LATER-- PSSHHHKK--
I KNOW YOU'RE DOING THAT WITH YOUR MOUTH, ROCKET! YOU <JUST-A-WHOLE-BUNCH-OF-CURSE-WORDS>!
OKAY. I THINK SHE BOUGHT IT.
I AM GROOT!
SHRZAP
OH, WHAT WERE YOU GONNA USE A PHONE FOR? YOU GOT A BUNCH OF PEOPLE YOU NEED TO TELL THAT YOU'RE GROOT?
I AM GROOT!
HEY! SQUIRREL!
I'M DONE WITH MY RECAP! WHAT'S OUR PLAN HERE?
WELL, MY PLAN IS TO HURT YOU REAL BAD UNTIL YOU GO AWAY.
SO IF YOUR PLAN IS TO GET HURT REAL BAD, THEN YOU SHOULD ABSOLUTELY STICK AROUND HERE!
OKAY! GOOD TO KNOW!
WHADDYA TRYING TO BUY WITH THE BOUNTY MONEY?
IT'S NOT ABOUT THE MONEY! IT'S ABOUT SETTLING AN OLD SCORE!
GREAT! SO HOW ABOUT WE CATCH HIM TOGETHER, I TAKE ALL THE MONEY, AND YOU TAKE ALL THE EMOTIONAL CLOSURE?
WELL, IT'S NOT NOT ABOUT THE MONEY.
HOW ABOUT THIS? WE CALL A TEMPORARY PEACE TREATY AND GO BUST CHAMMY TOGETHER.
THEN WE DO THE HURTING-EACH-OTHER PART.
A TEMPORARY PEACE TREATY, HUH?
IT WORKED FOR THE MIDDLE EAST!
DID IT???
MAYBE! HONESTLY, I HAVE VERY LITTLE IDEA WHAT'S GOING ON OVER THERE.

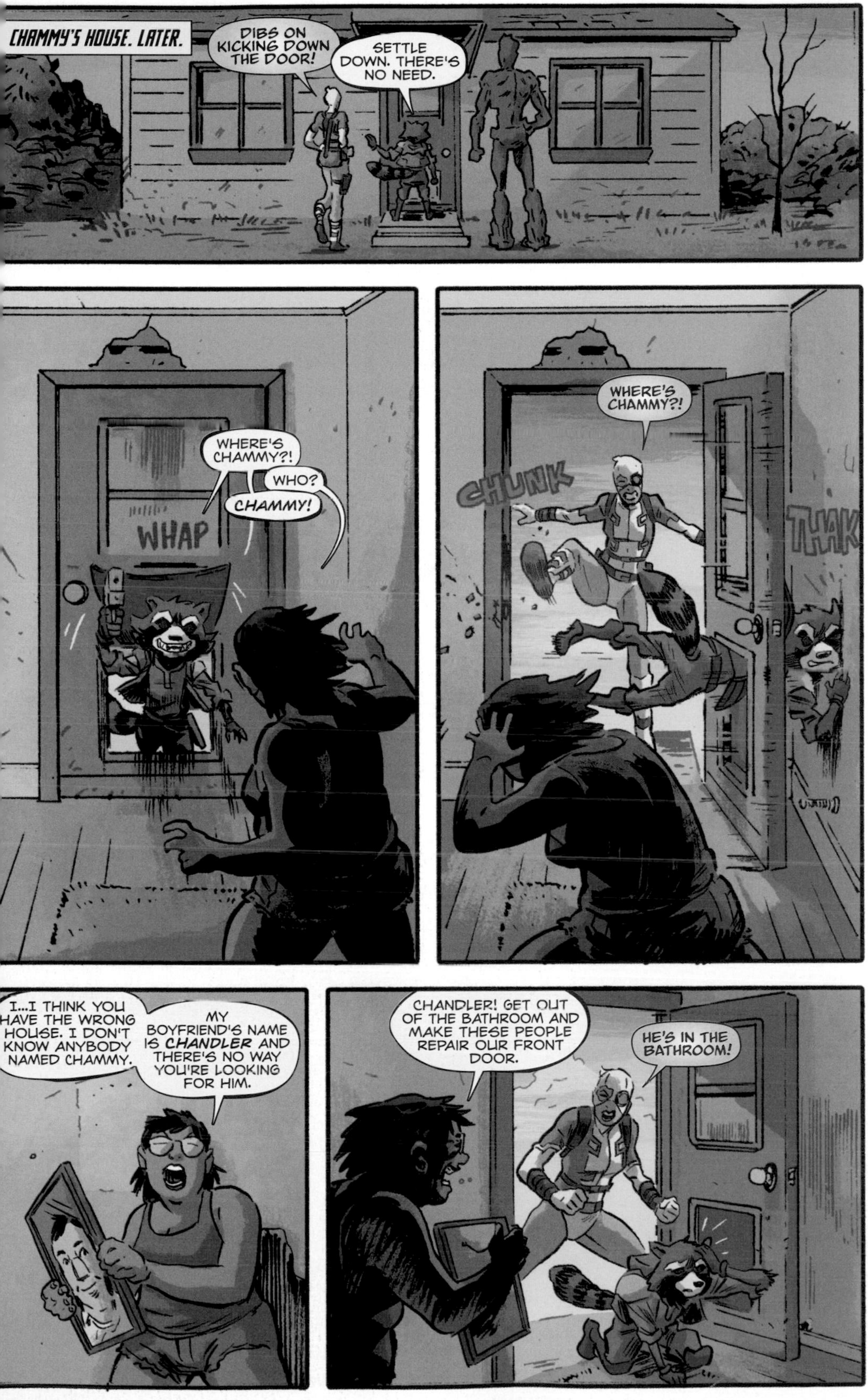
CHAMMY'S HOUSE. LATER.
DIBS ON KICKING DOWN THE DOOR!
SETTLE DOWN. THERE'S NO NEED.
WHERE'S CHAMMY?!
WHO?
CHAMMY!
WHAP
WHERE'S CHAMMY?!
CHUNK
THAK
I...I THINK YOU HAVE THE WRONG HOUSE. I DON'T KNOW ANYBODY NAMED CHAMMY.
MY BOYFRIEND'S NAME IS CHANDLER AND THERE'S NO WAY YOU'RE LOOKING FOR HIM.
CHANDLER! GET OUT OF THE BATHROOM AND MAKE THESE PEOPLE REPAIR OUR FRONT DOOR.
HE'S IN THE BATHROOM!

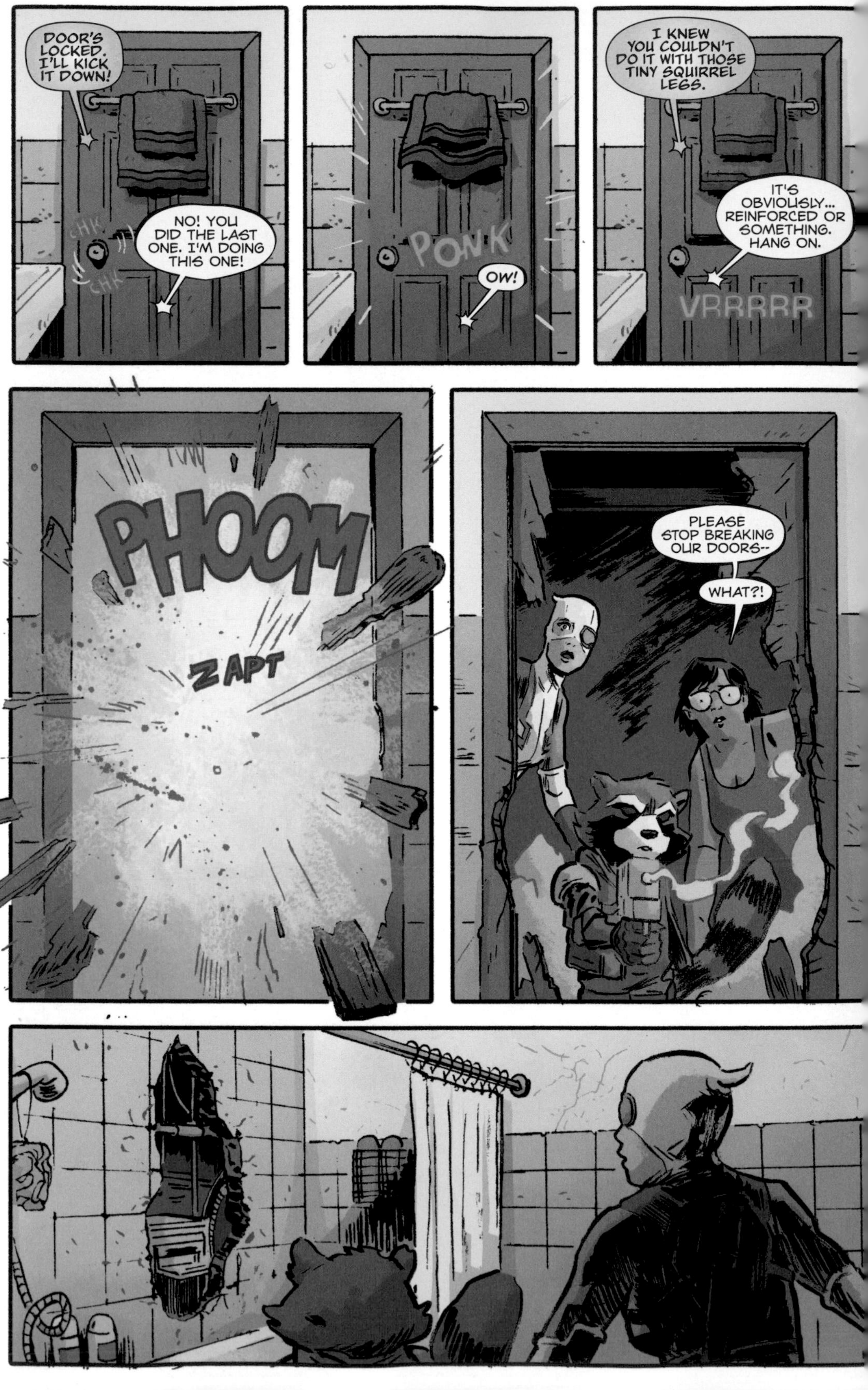
DOOR'S LOCKED. I'LL KICK IT DOWN!
CHK
CHK
NO! YOU DID THE LAST ONE. I'M DOING THIS ONE!
PONK
OW!
I KNEW YOU COULDN'T DO IT WITH THOSE TINY SQUIRREL LEGS.
IT'S OBVIOUSLY... REINFORCED OR SOMETHING. HANG ON.
VRRRRR
PHOOM
ZAPT
PLEASE STOP BREAKING OUR DOORS--
WHAT?!

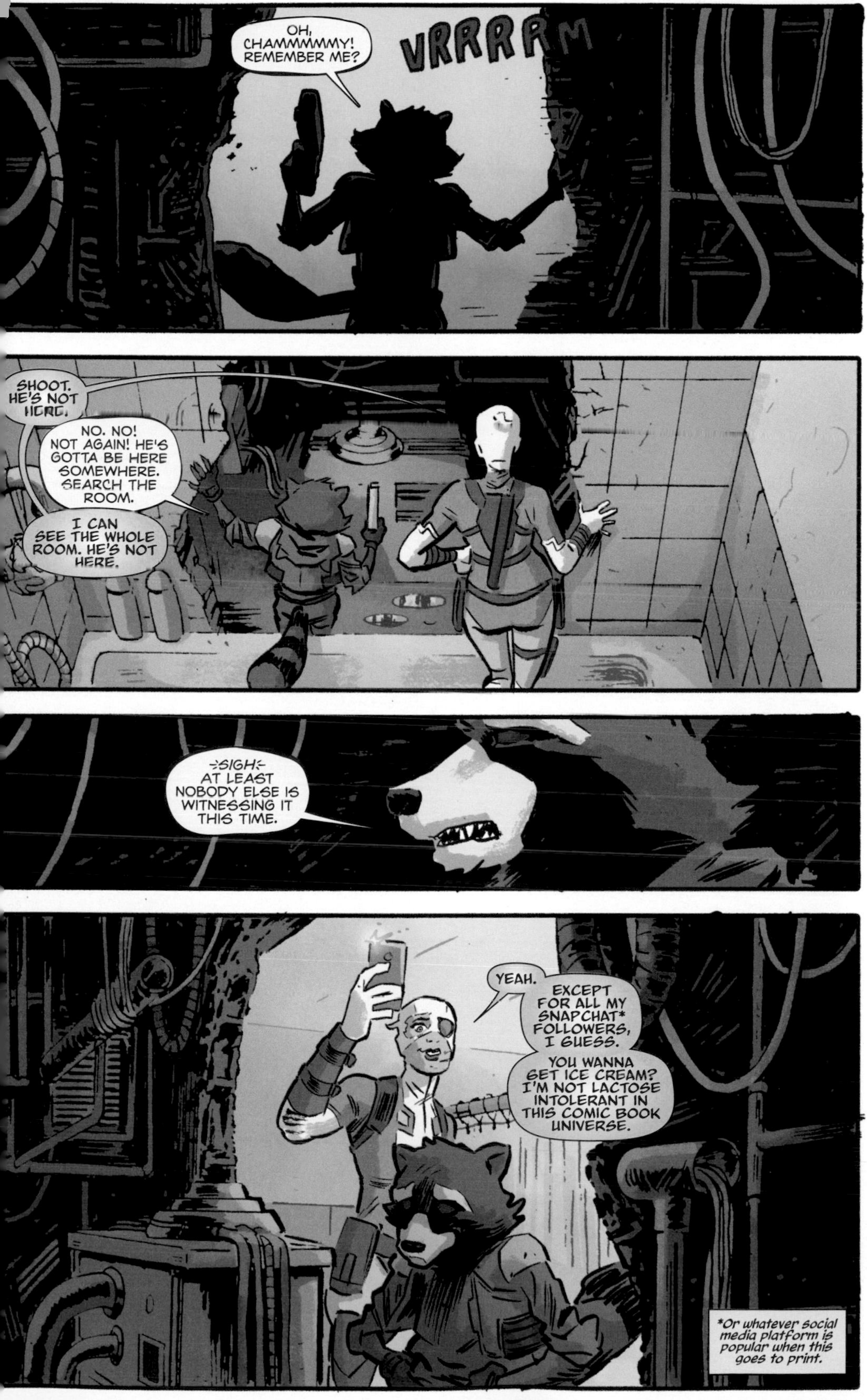
OH, CHAMMMMMY! REMEMBER ME?
VRRRRM
SHOOT. HE'S NOT HERE.
NO. NO! NOT AGAIN! HE'S GOTTA BE HERE SOMEWHERE. SEARCH THE ROOM.
I CAN SEE THE WHOLE ROOM. HE'S NOT HERE.
SIGH AT LEAST NOBODY ELSE IS WITNESSING IT THIS TIME.
YEAH.
EXCEPT FOR ALL MY SNAPCHAT* FOLLOWERS, I GUESS.
YOU WANNA GET ICE CREAM? I'M NOT LACTOSE INTOLERANT IN THIS COMIC BOOK UNIVERSE.
*Or whatever social media platform is popular when this goes to print.

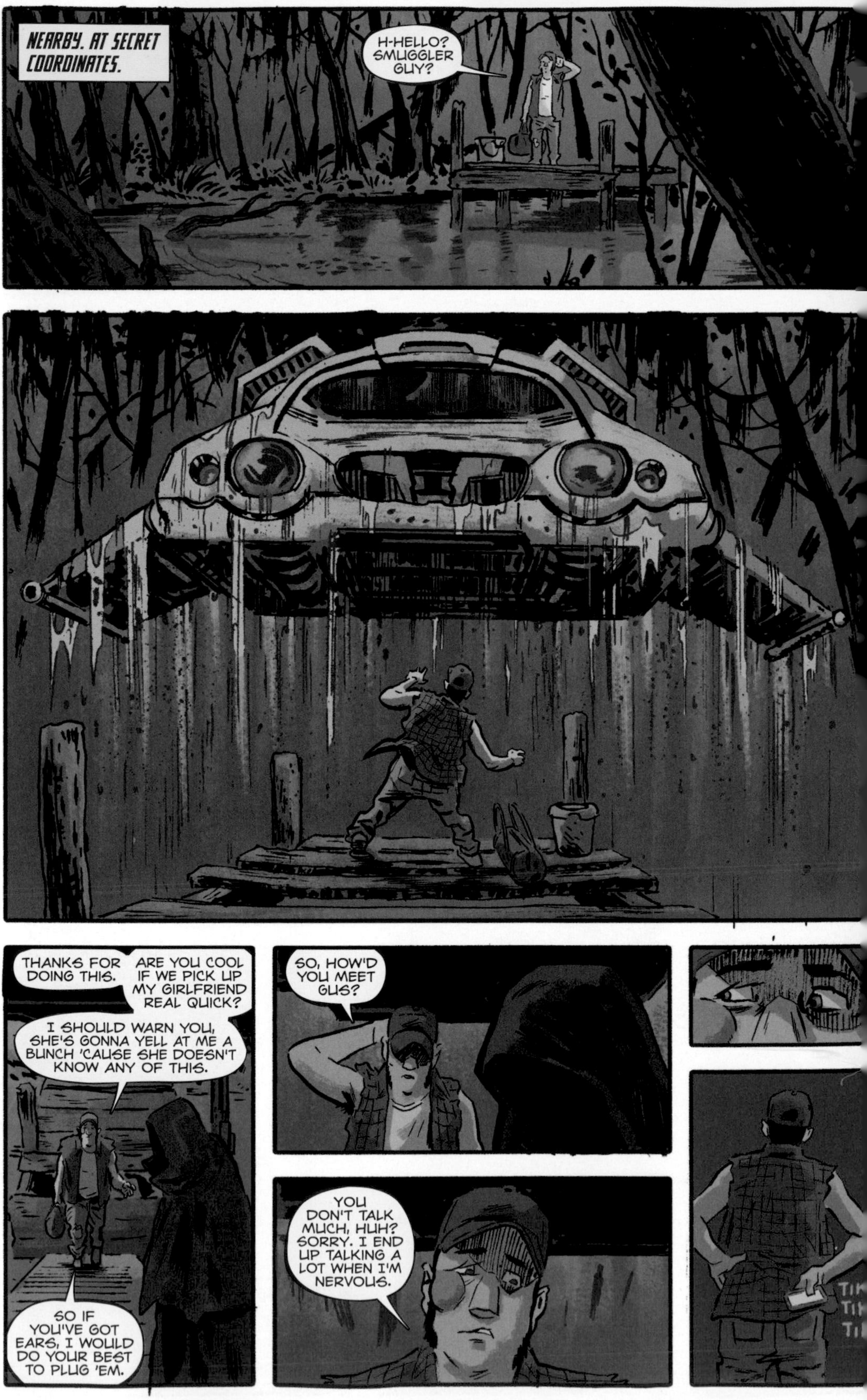
NEARBY. AT SECRET COORDINATES.
H-HELLO? SMUGGLER GUY?
THANKS FOR DOING THIS.
ARE YOU COOL IF WE PICK UP MY GIRLFRIEND REAL QUICK?
I SHOULD WARN YOU, SHE'S GONNA YELL AT ME A BUNCH 'CAUSE SHE DOESN'T KNOW ANY OF THIS.
SO IF YOU'VE GOT EARS, I WOULD DO YOUR BEST TO PLUG 'EM.
SO, HOW'D YOU MEET GUS?
YOU DON'T TALK MUCH, HUH? SORRY. I END UP TALKING A LOT WHEN I'M NERVOUS.

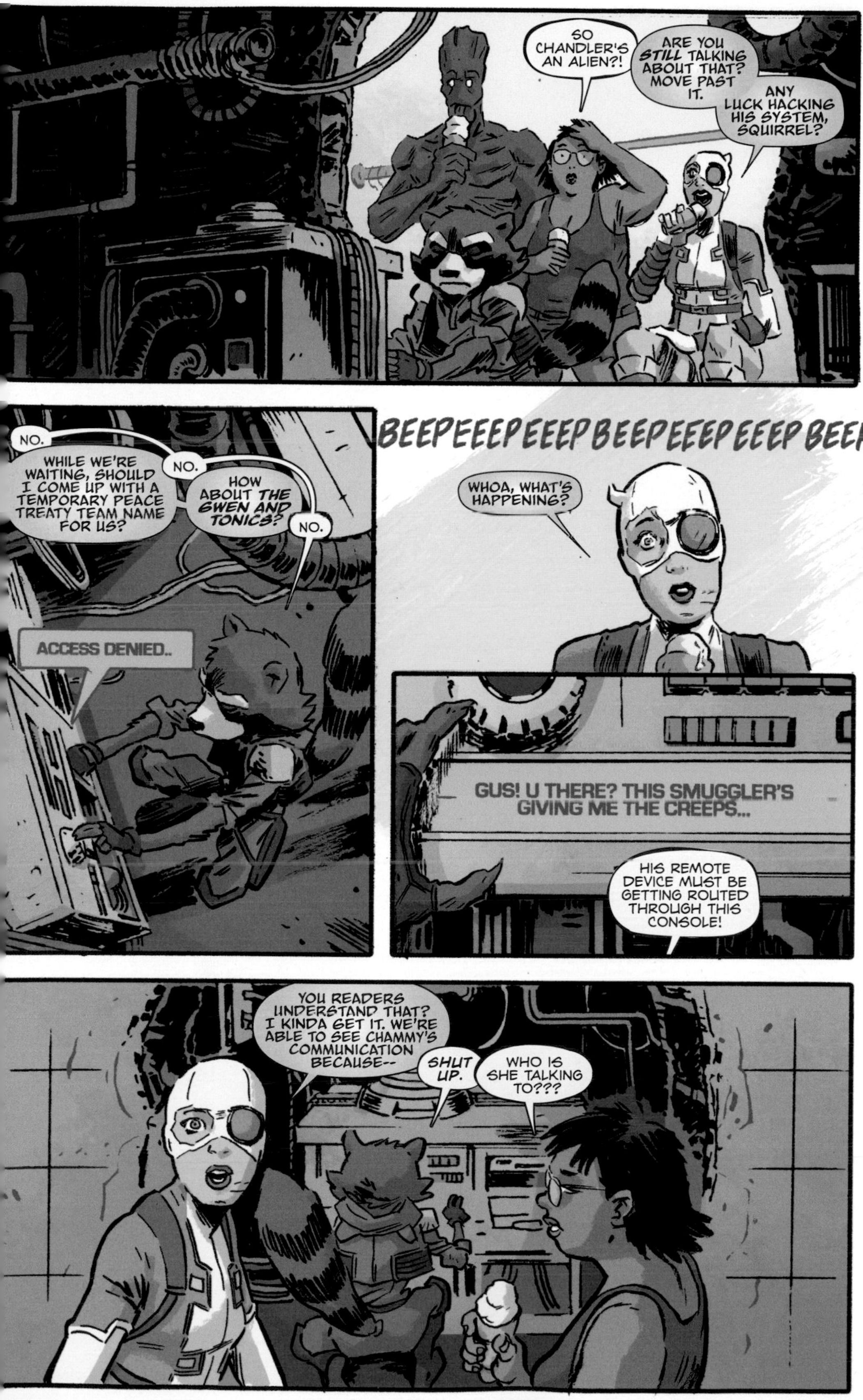
SO CHANDLER'S AN ALIEN?!
ARE YOU STILL TALKING ABOUT THAT? MOVE PAST IT.
ANY LUCK HACKING HIS SYSTEM, SQUIRREL?
NO.
WHILE WE'RE WAITING, SHOULD I COME UP WITH A TEMPORARY PEACE TREATY TEAM NAME FOR US?
NO.
HOW ABOUT THE GWEN AND TONICS?
NO.
ACCESS DENIED..
BEEPEEEPEEEPBEEPEEEPEEEPBEEPE
WHOA, WHAT'S HAPPENING?
GUS! U THERE? THIS SMUGGLER'S GIVING ME THE CREEPS...
HIS REMOTE DEVICE MUST BE GETTING ROUTED THROUGH THIS CONSOLE!
YOU READERS UNDERSTAND THAT? I KINDA GET IT. WE'RE ABLE TO SEE CHAMMY'S COMMUNICATION BECAUSE--
SHUT UP.
WHO IS SHE TALKING TO???

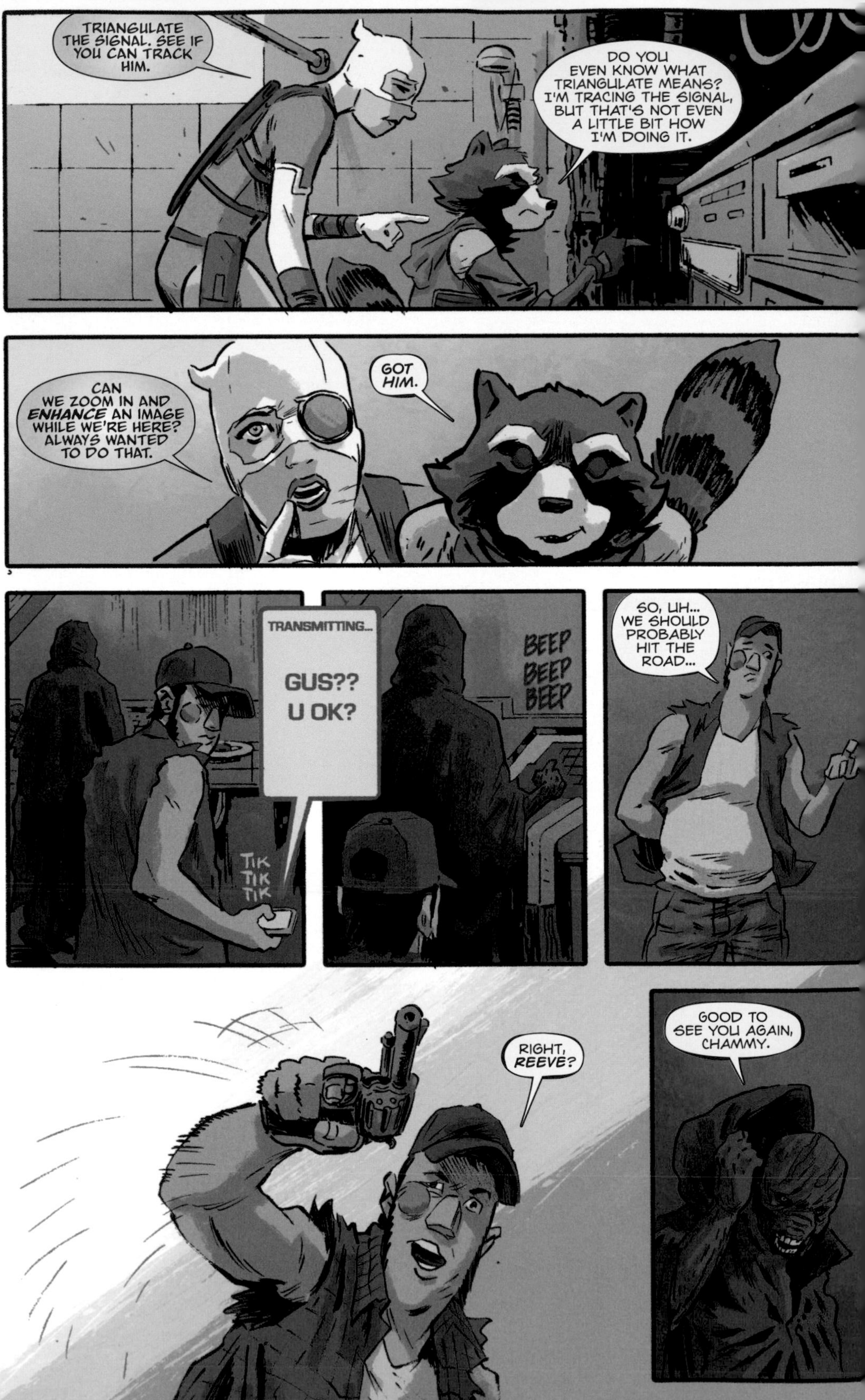
TRIANGULATE THE SIGNAL. SEE IF YOU CAN TRACK HIM.
DO YOU EVEN KNOW WHAT TRIANGULATE MEANS? I'M TRACING THE SIGNAL, BUT THAT'S NOT EVEN A LITTLE BIT HOW I'M DOING IT.
CAN WE ZOOM IN AND ENHANCE AN IMAGE WHILE WE'RE HERE? ALWAYS WANTED TO DO THAT.
GOT HIM.
TRANSMITTING...
GUS?? U OK?
TIK TIK TIK
BEEP BEEP BEEP
SO, UH... WE SHOULD PROBABLY HIT THE ROAD...
RIGHT, REEVE?
GOOD TO SEE YOU AGAIN, CHAMMY.

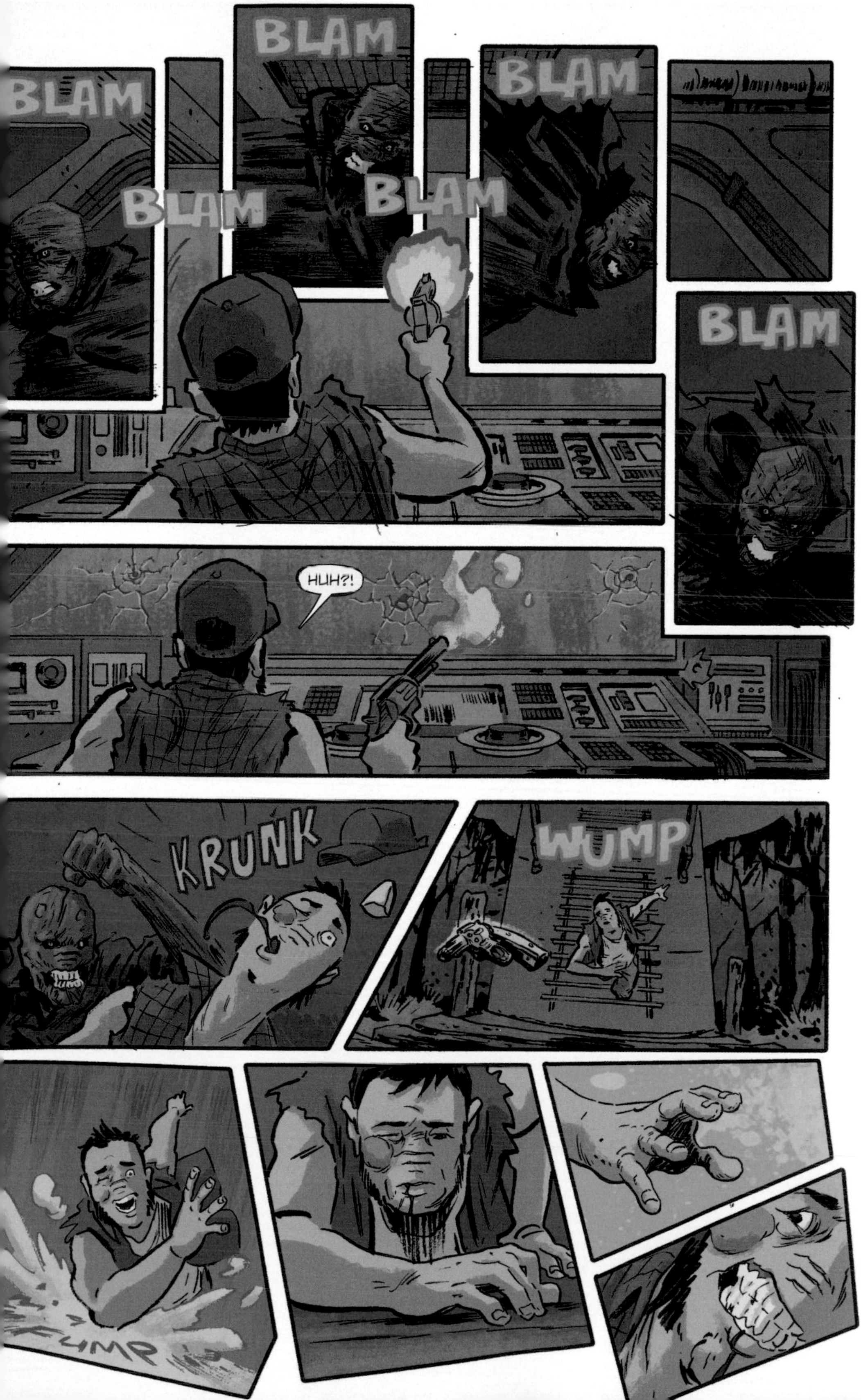
BLAM
BLAM
BLAM
BLAM
BLAM
BLAM
HUH?!
KRUNK
WUMP
FUMP

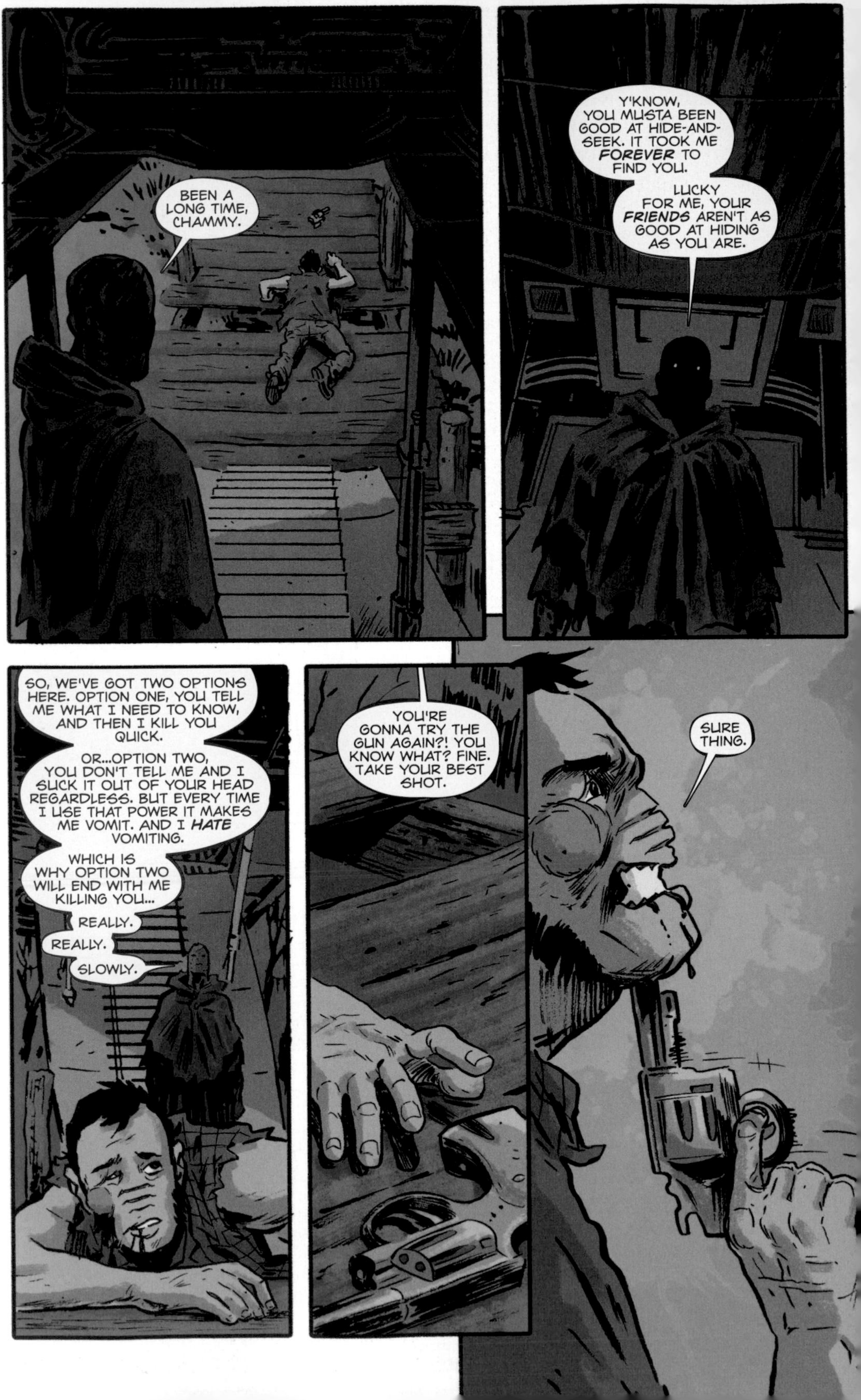
BEEN A LONG TIME, CHAMMY.
Y'KNOW, YOU MUSTA BEEN GOOD AT HIDE-AND-SEEK. IT TOOK ME FOREVER TO FIND YOU.
LUCKY FOR ME, YOUR FRIENDS AREN'T AS GOOD AT HIDING AS YOU ARE.
SO, WE'VE GOT TWO OPTIONS HERE. OPTION ONE, YOU TELL ME WHAT I NEED TO KNOW, AND THEN I KILL YOU QUICK.
OR...OPTION TWO, YOU DON'T TELL ME AND I SUCK IT OUT OF YOUR HEAD REGARDLESS. BUT EVERY TIME I USE THAT POWER IT MAKES ME VOMIT. AND I HATE VOMITING.
WHICH IS WHY OPTION TWO WILL END WITH ME KILLING YOU...
REALLY.
REALLY.
SLOWLY.
YOU'RE GONNA TRY THE GUN AGAIN?! YOU KNOW WHAT? FINE. TAKE YOUR BEST SHOT.
SURE THING.

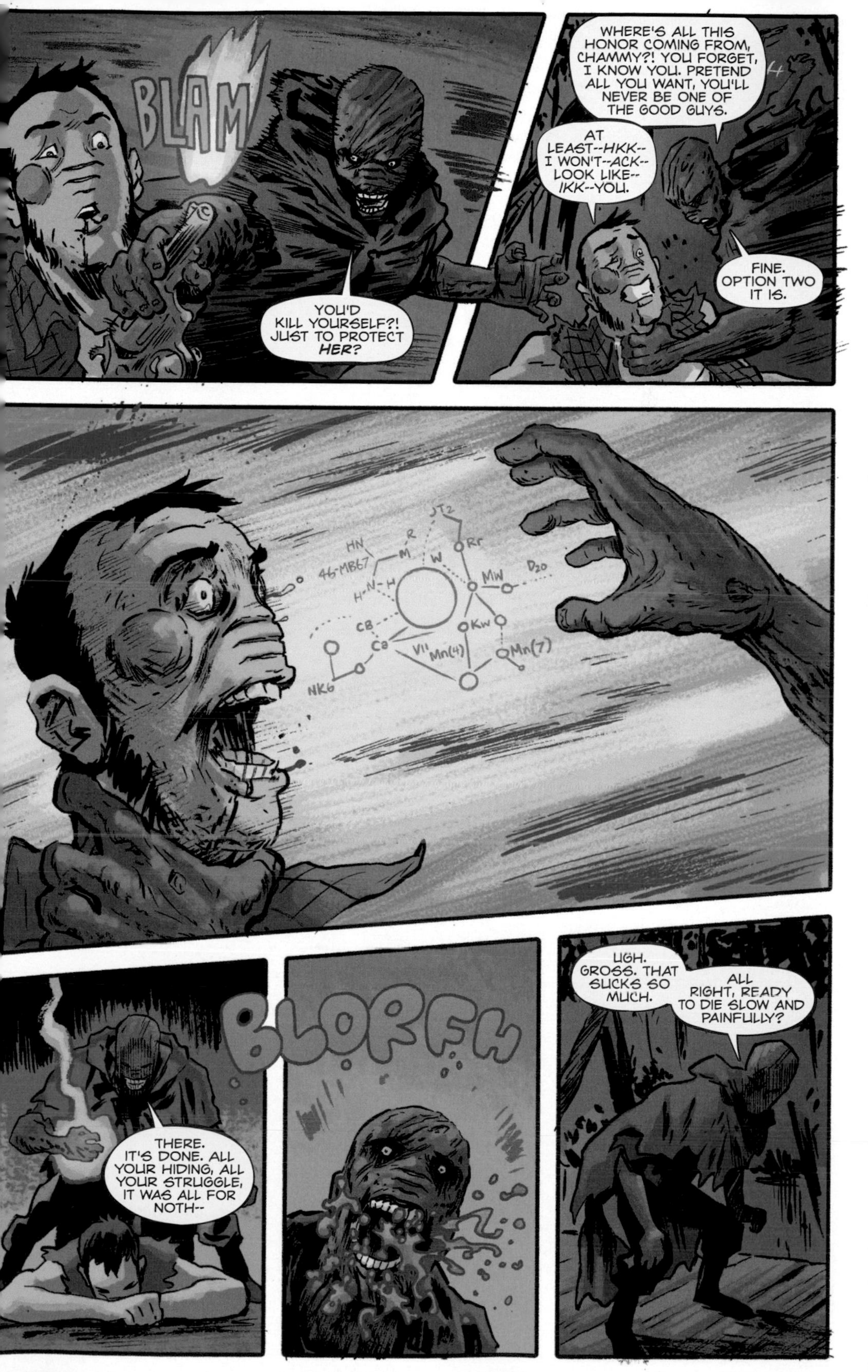
BLAM
YOU'D KILL YOURSELF?! JUST TO PROTECT HER?
WHERE'S ALL THIS HONOR COMING FROM, CHAMMY?! YOU FORGET, I KNOW YOU. PRETEND ALL YOU WANT, YOU'LL NEVER BE ONE OF THE GOOD GUYS.
AT LEAST--HKK-- I WON'T--ACK-- LOOK LIKE-- IKK--YOU.
FINE. OPTION TWO IT IS.
THERE. IT'S DONE. ALL YOUR HIDING, ALL YOUR STRUGGLE, IT WAS ALL FOR NOTH--
BLORFH
UGH. GROSS. THAT SUCKS SO MUCH.
ALL RIGHT, READY TO DIE SLOW AND PAINFULLY?

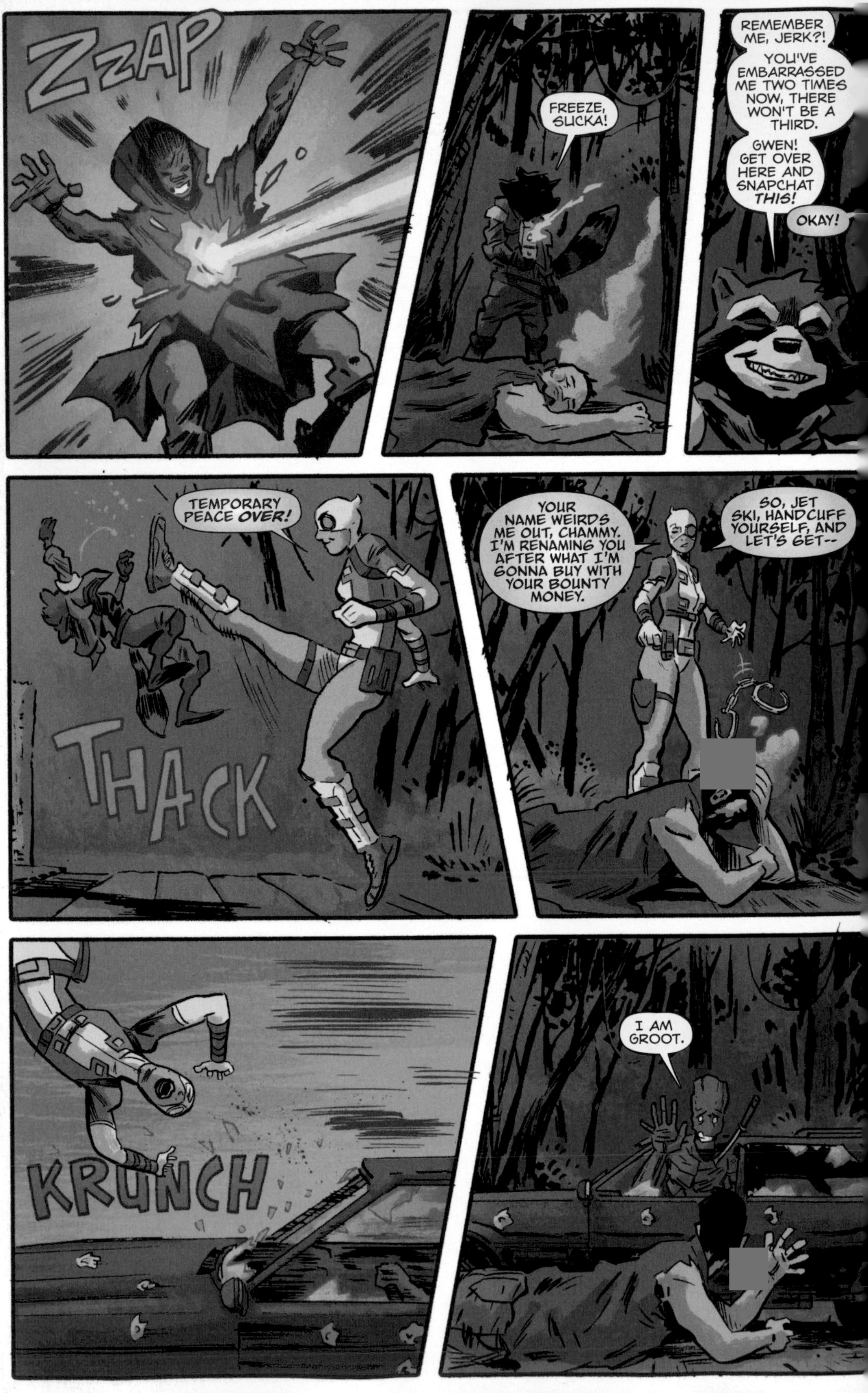
ZZAP
FREEZE, SUCKA!
REMEMBER ME, JERK?!
YOU'VE EMBARRASSED ME TWO TIMES NOW, THERE WON'T BE A THIRD.
GWEN! GET OVER HERE AND SNAPCHAT THIS!
OKAY!
TEMPORARY PEACE OVER!
THACK
YOUR NAME WEIRDS ME OUT, CHAMMY. I'M RENAMING YOU AFTER WHAT I'M GONNA BUY WITH YOUR BOUNTY MONEY.
SO, JET SKI, HANDCUFF YOURSELF, AND LET'S GET--
KRUNCH
I AM GROOT.

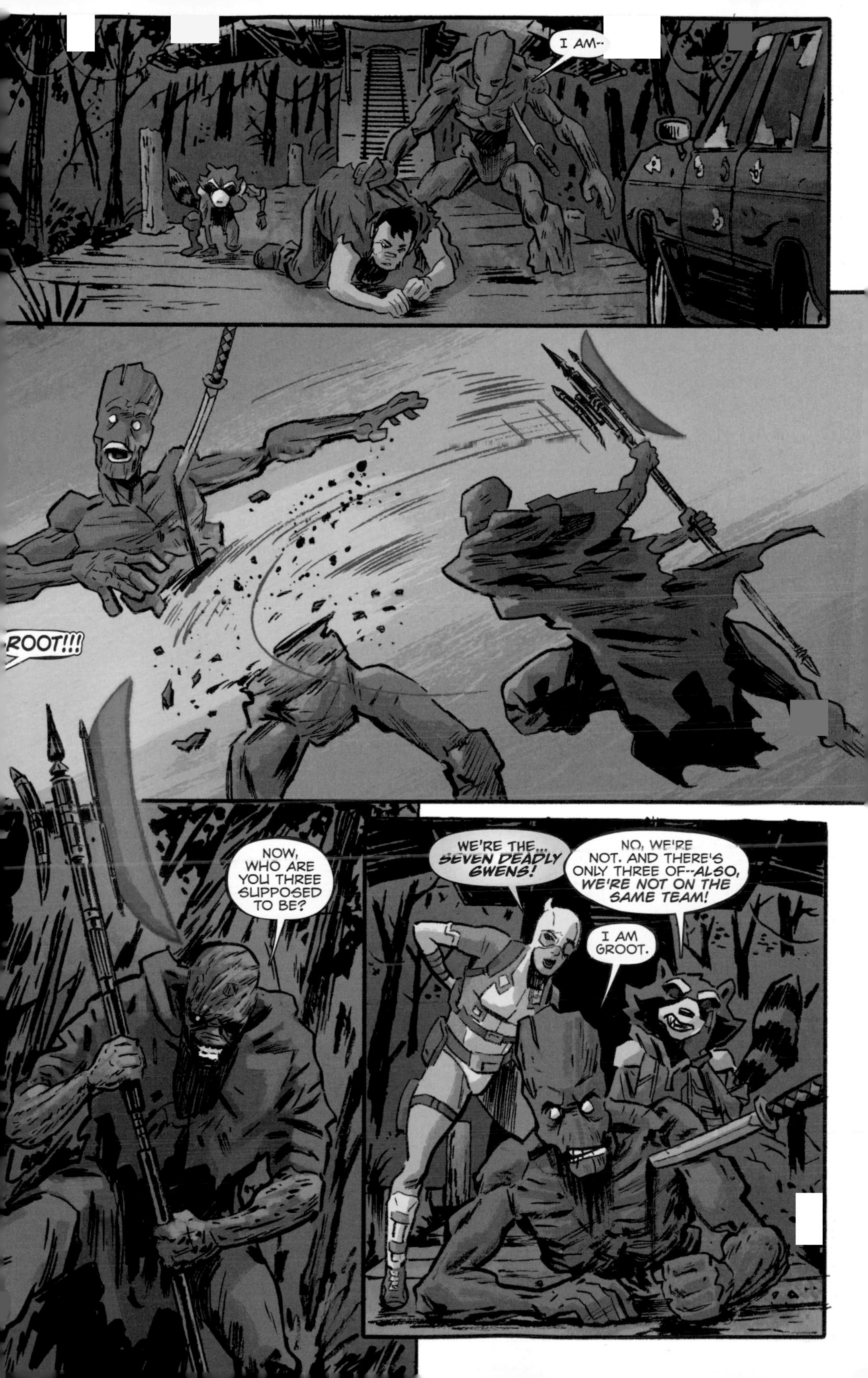
I AM--
GROOT!!!
NOW, WHO ARE YOU THREE SUPPOSED TO BE?
WE'RE THE... SEVEN DEADLY GWENS!
NO, WE'RE NOT. AND THERE'S ONLY THREE OF--ALSO, WE'RE NOT ON THE SAME TEAM!
I AM GROOT.

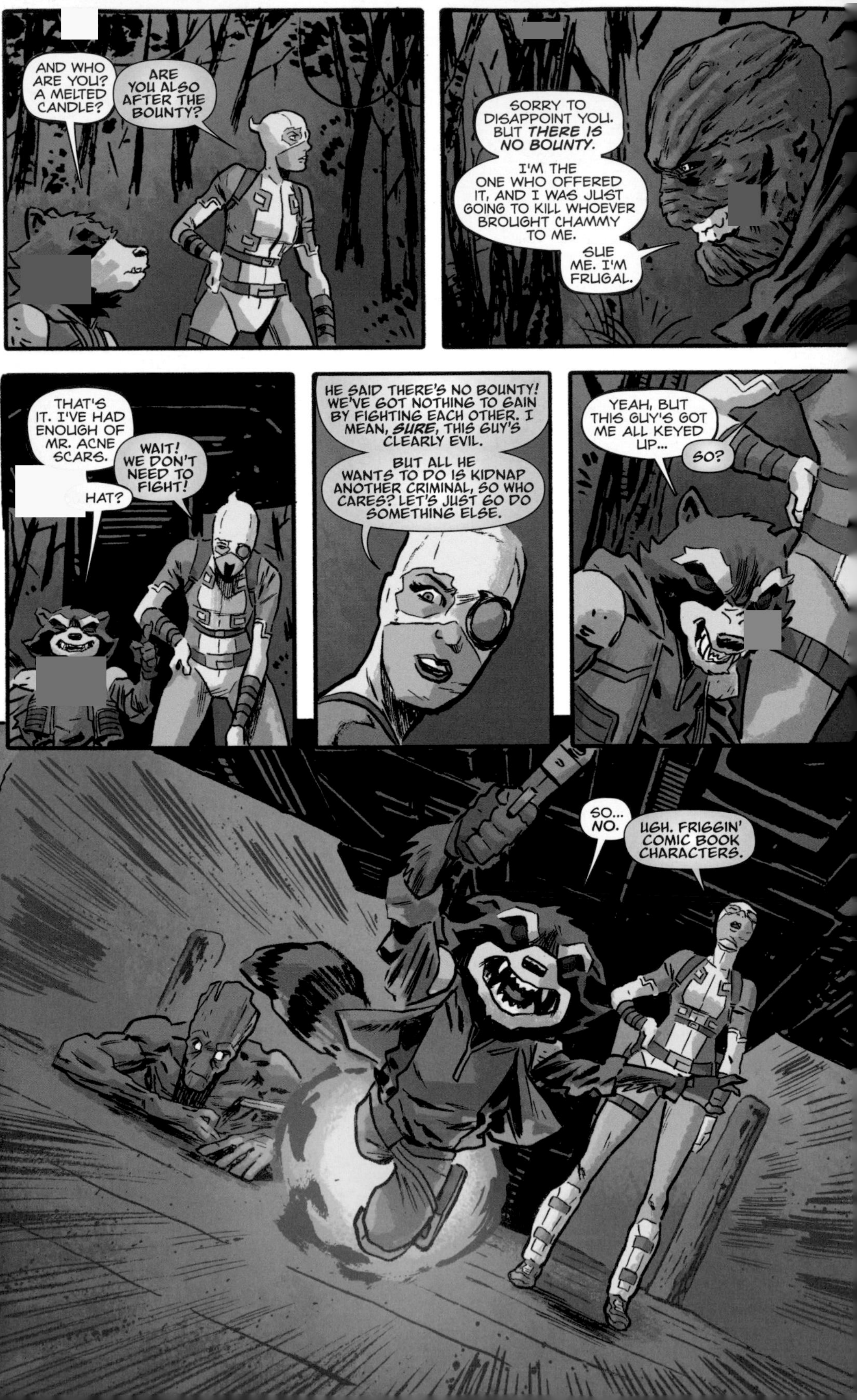
AND WHO ARE YOU? A MELTED CANDLE?
ARE YOU ALSO AFTER THE BOUNTY?
SORRY TO DISAPPOINT YOU. BUT *THERE IS NO BOUNTY.*
I'M THE ONE WHO OFFERED IT, AND I WAS JUST GOING TO KILL WHOEVER BROUGHT CHAMMY TO ME.
SUE ME. I'M FRUGAL.
THAT'S IT. I'VE HAD ENOUGH OF MR. ACNE SCARS.
WAIT! WE DON'T NEED TO FIGHT!
HAT?
HE SAID THERE'S NO BOUNTY! WE'VE GOT NOTHING TO GAIN BY FIGHTING EACH OTHER. I MEAN, *SURE*, THIS GUY'S CLEARLY EVIL.
BUT ALL HE WANTS TO DO IS KIDNAP ANOTHER CRIMINAL, SO WHO CARES? LET'S JUST GO DO SOMETHING ELSE.
YEAH, BUT THIS GUY'S GOT ME ALL KEYED UP...
SO?
SO... NO.
UGH. FRIGGIN' COMIC BOOK CHARACTERS.

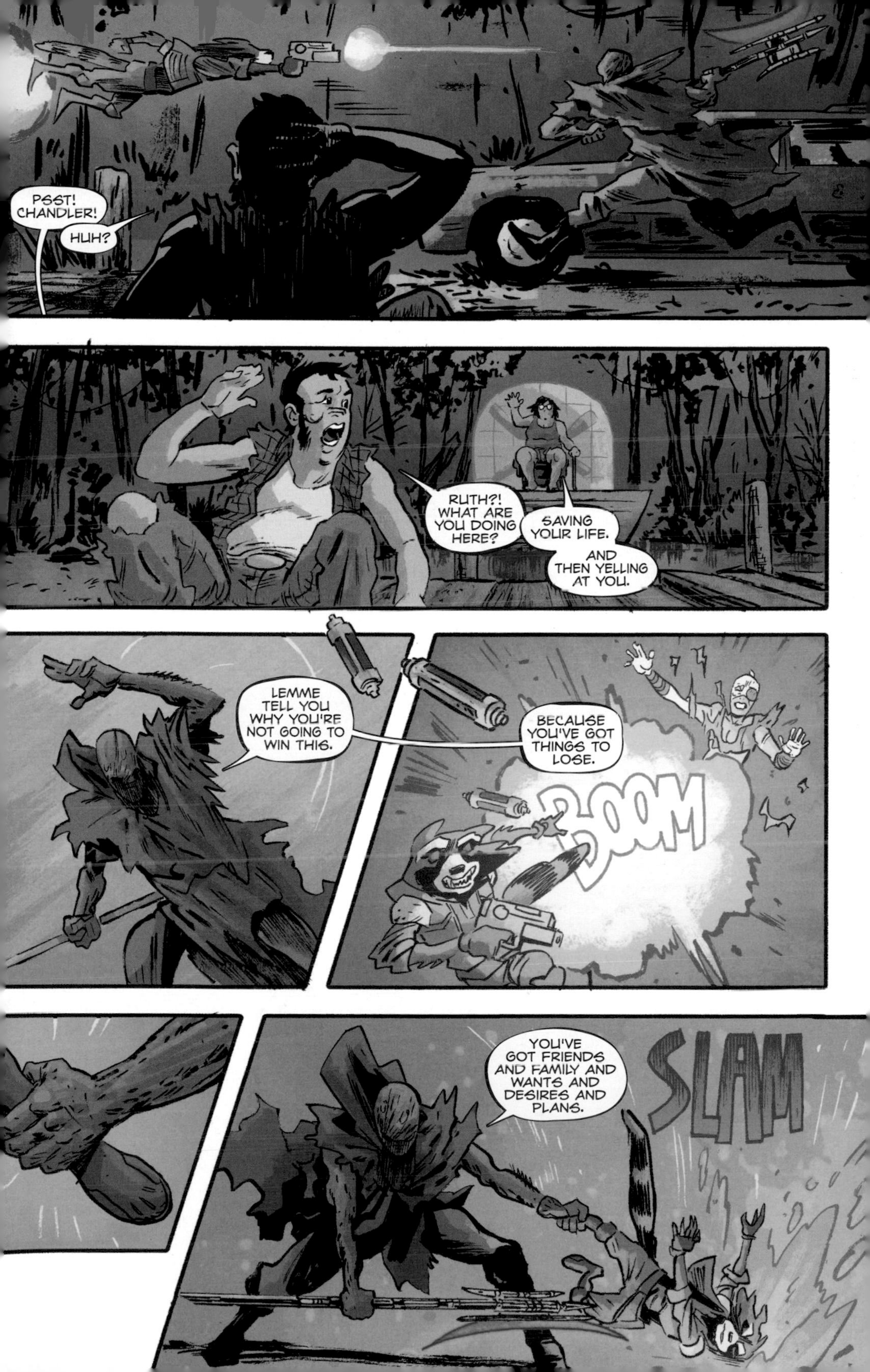
PSST! CHANDLER!
HUH?
RUTH?! WHAT ARE YOU DOING HERE?
SAVING YOUR LIFE.
AND THEN YELLING AT YOU.
LEMME TELL YOU WHY YOU'RE NOT GOING TO WIN THIS.
BECAUSE YOU'VE GOT THINGS TO LOSE.
BOOM
YOU'VE GOT FRIENDS AND FAMILY AND WANTS AND DESIRES AND PLANS.
SLAM

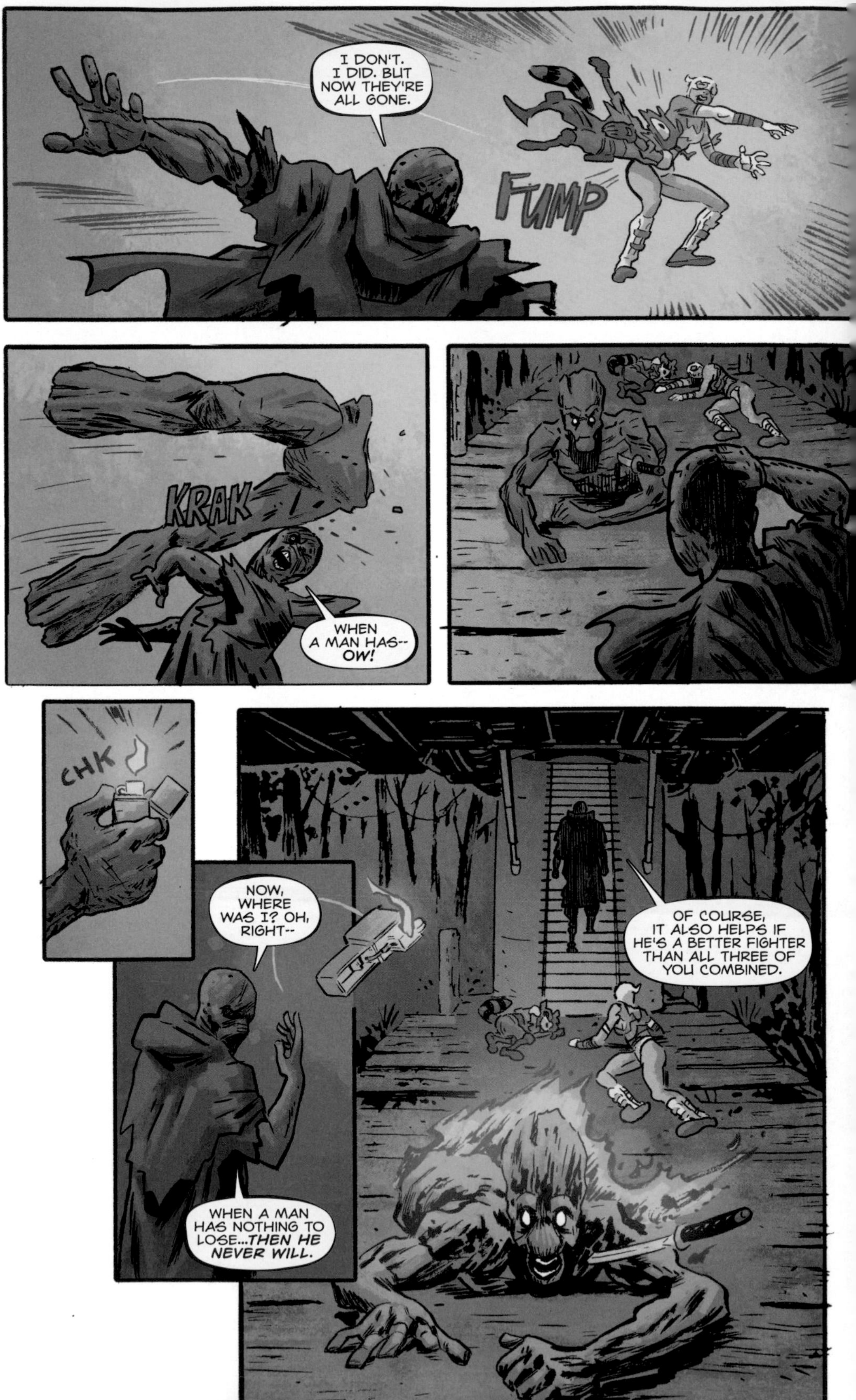
I DON'T. I DID. BUT NOW THEY'RE ALL GONE.
FUMP
KRAK
WHEN A MAN HAS-- OW!
CHK
NOW, WHERE WAS I? OH, RIGHT--
WHEN A MAN HAS NOTHING TO LOSE...THEN HE NEVER WILL.
OF COURSE, IT ALSO HELPS IF HE'S A BETTER FIGHTER THAN ALL THREE OF YOU COMBINED.

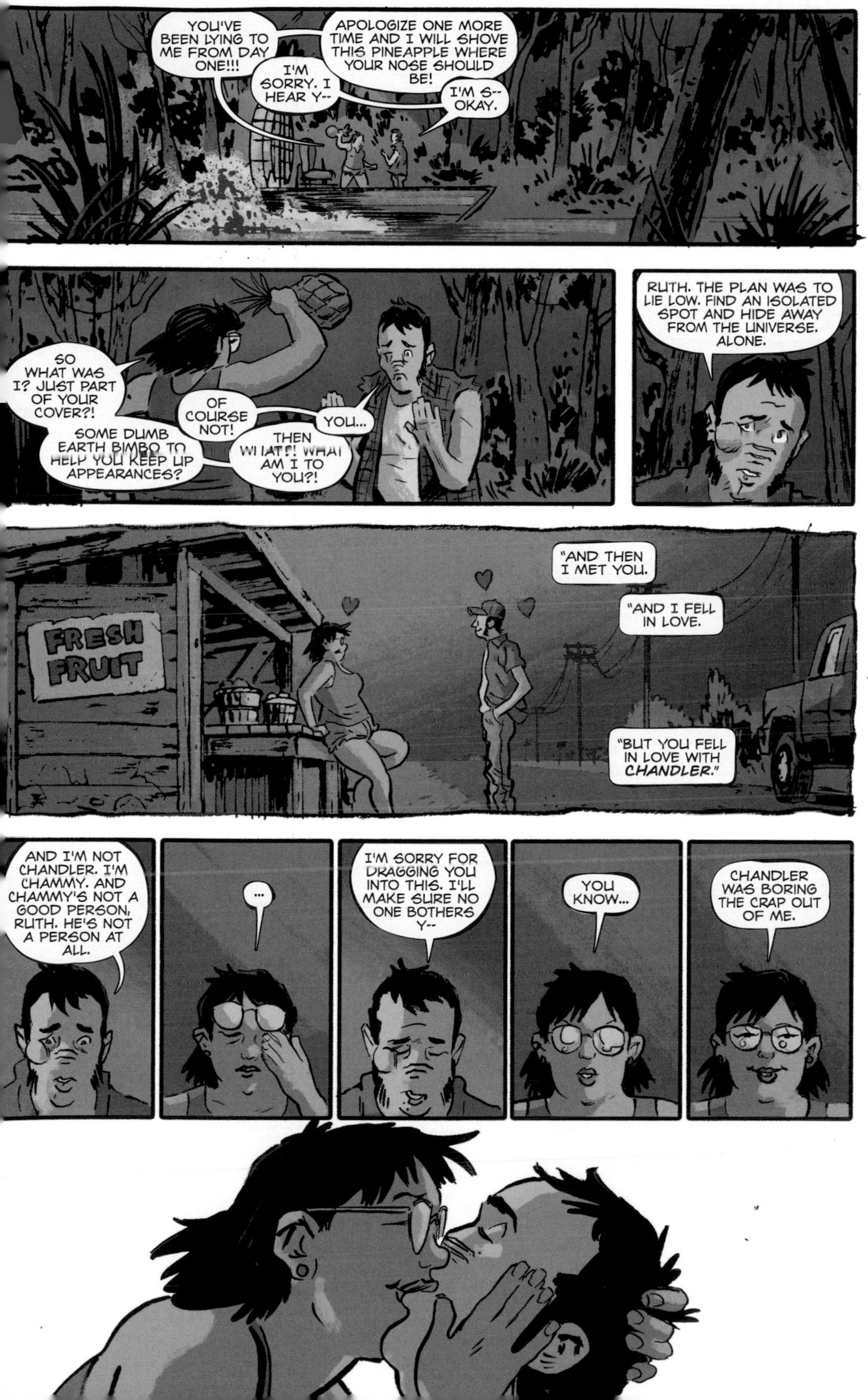
YOU'VE BEEN LYING TO ME FROM DAY ONE!!!
APOLOGIZE ONE MORE TIME AND I WILL SHOVE THIS PINEAPPLE WHERE YOUR NOSE SHOULD BE!
I'M SORRY. I HEAR Y--
I'M S-- OKAY.
SO WHAT WAS I? JUST PART OF YOUR COVER?!
SOME DUMB EARTH BIMBO TO HELP YOU KEEP UP APPEARANCES?
OF COURSE NOT!
YOU...
THEN WHAT?! WHAT AM I TO YOU?!
RUTH. THE PLAN WAS TO LIE LOW. FIND AN ISOLATED SPOT AND HIDE AWAY FROM THE UNIVERSE. ALONE.
FRESH FRUIT
"AND THEN I MET YOU.
"AND I FELL IN LOVE.
"BUT YOU FELL IN LOVE WITH CHANDLER."
AND I'M NOT CHANDLER. I'M CHAMMY. AND CHAMMY'S NOT A GOOD PERSON, RUTH. HE'S NOT A PERSON AT ALL.
...
I'M SORRY FOR DRAGGING YOU INTO THIS. I'LL MAKE SURE NO ONE BOTHERS Y--
YOU KNOW...
CHANDLER WAS BORING THE CRAP OUT OF ME.

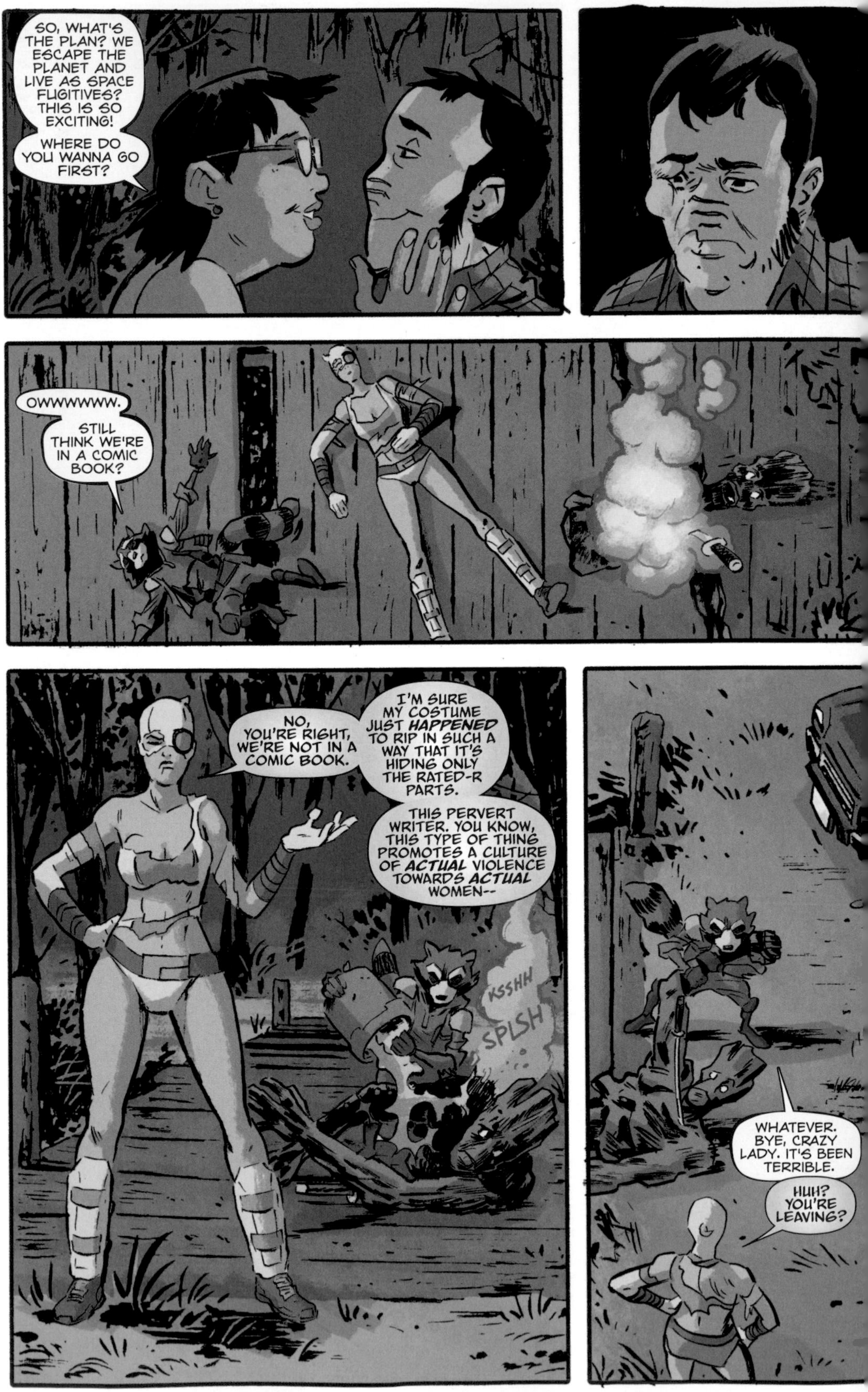
SO, WHAT'S THE PLAN? WE ESCAPE THE PLANET AND LIVE AS SPACE FUGITIVES? THIS IS SO EXCITING!
WHERE DO YOU WANNA GO FIRST?
OWWWWWW.
STILL THINK WE'RE IN A COMIC BOOK?
NO, YOU'RE RIGHT, WE'RE NOT IN A COMIC BOOK.
I'M SURE MY COSTUME JUST HAPPENED TO RIP IN SUCH A WAY THAT IT'S HIDING ONLY THE RATED-R PARTS.
THIS PERVERT WRITER. YOU KNOW, THIS TYPE OF THING PROMOTES A CULTURE OF ACTUAL VIOLENCE TOWARDS ACTUAL WOMEN--
KSSHH
SPLSH
WHATEVER. BYE, CRAZY LADY. IT'S BEEN TERRIBLE.
HUH? YOU'RE LEAVING?

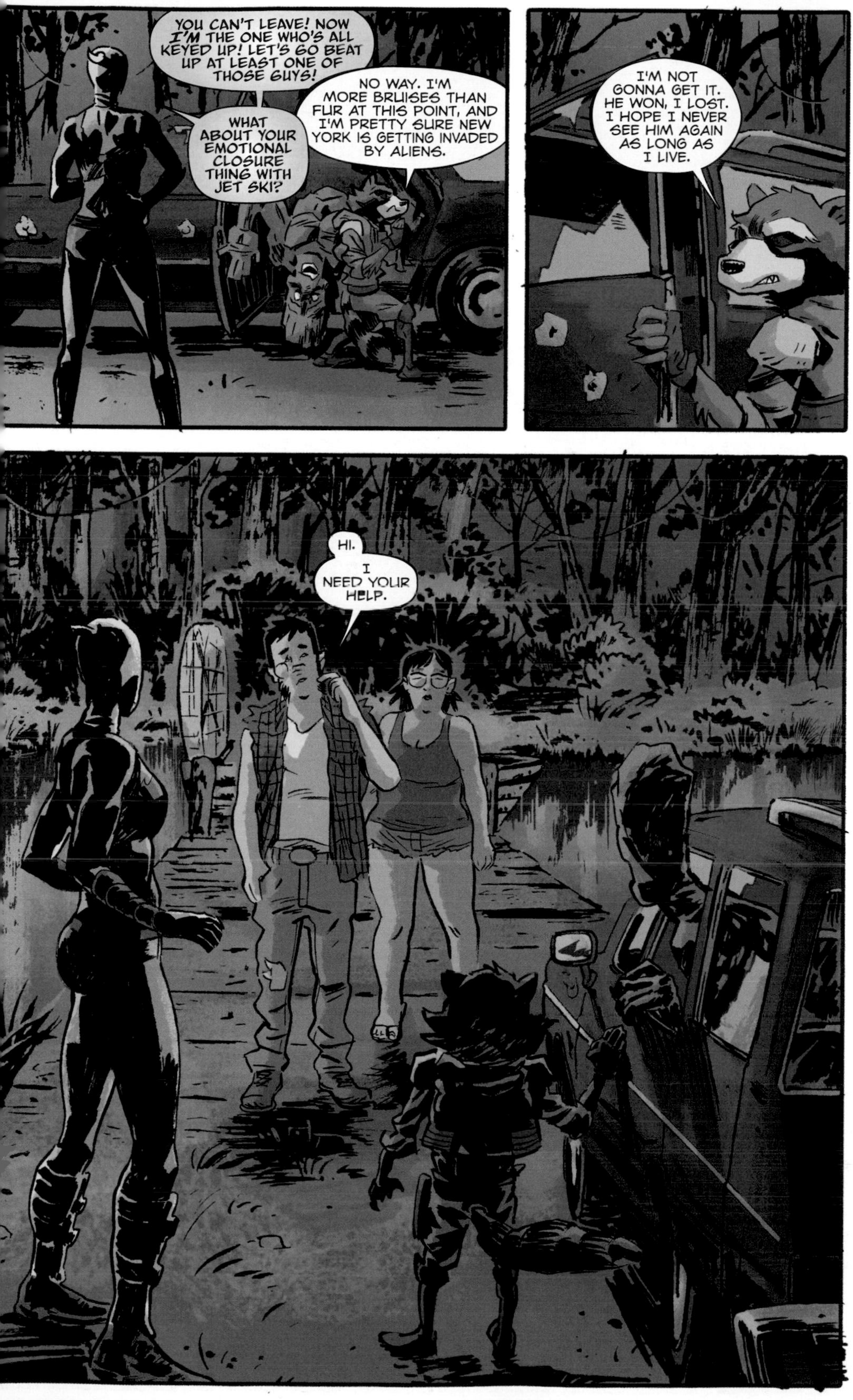
YOU CAN'T LEAVE! NOW I'M THE ONE WHO'S ALL KEYED UP! LET'S GO BEAT UP AT LEAST ONE OF THOSE GUYS!
WHAT ABOUT YOUR EMOTIONAL CLOSURE THING WITH JET SKI?
NO WAY. I'M MORE BRUISES THAN FUR AT THIS POINT, AND I'M PRETTY SURE NEW YORK IS GETTING INVADED BY ALIENS.
I'M NOT GONNA GET IT. HE WON, I LOST. I HOPE I NEVER SEE HIM AGAIN AS LONG AS I LIVE.
HI.
I NEED YOUR HELP.

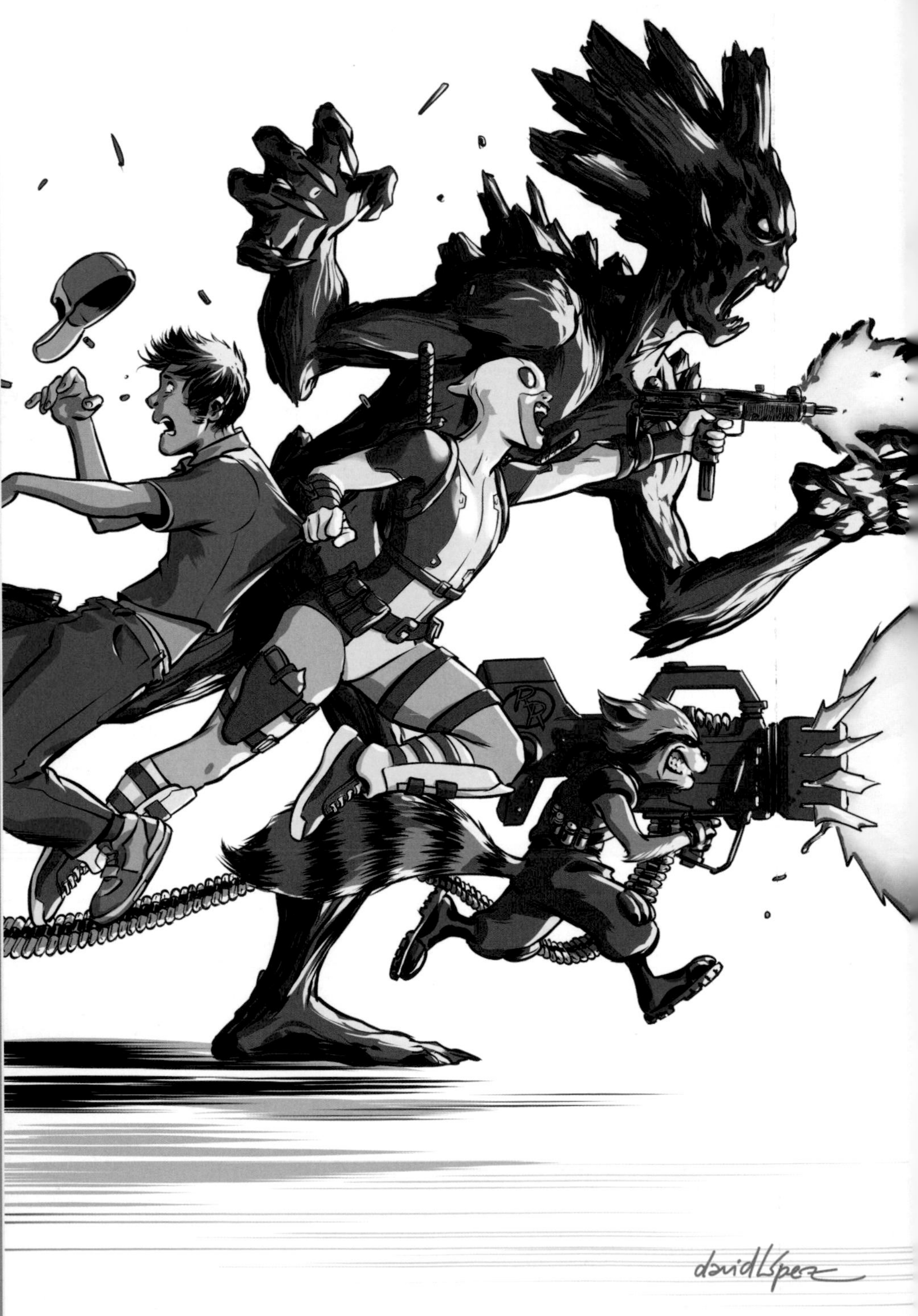
RR
davidLópez

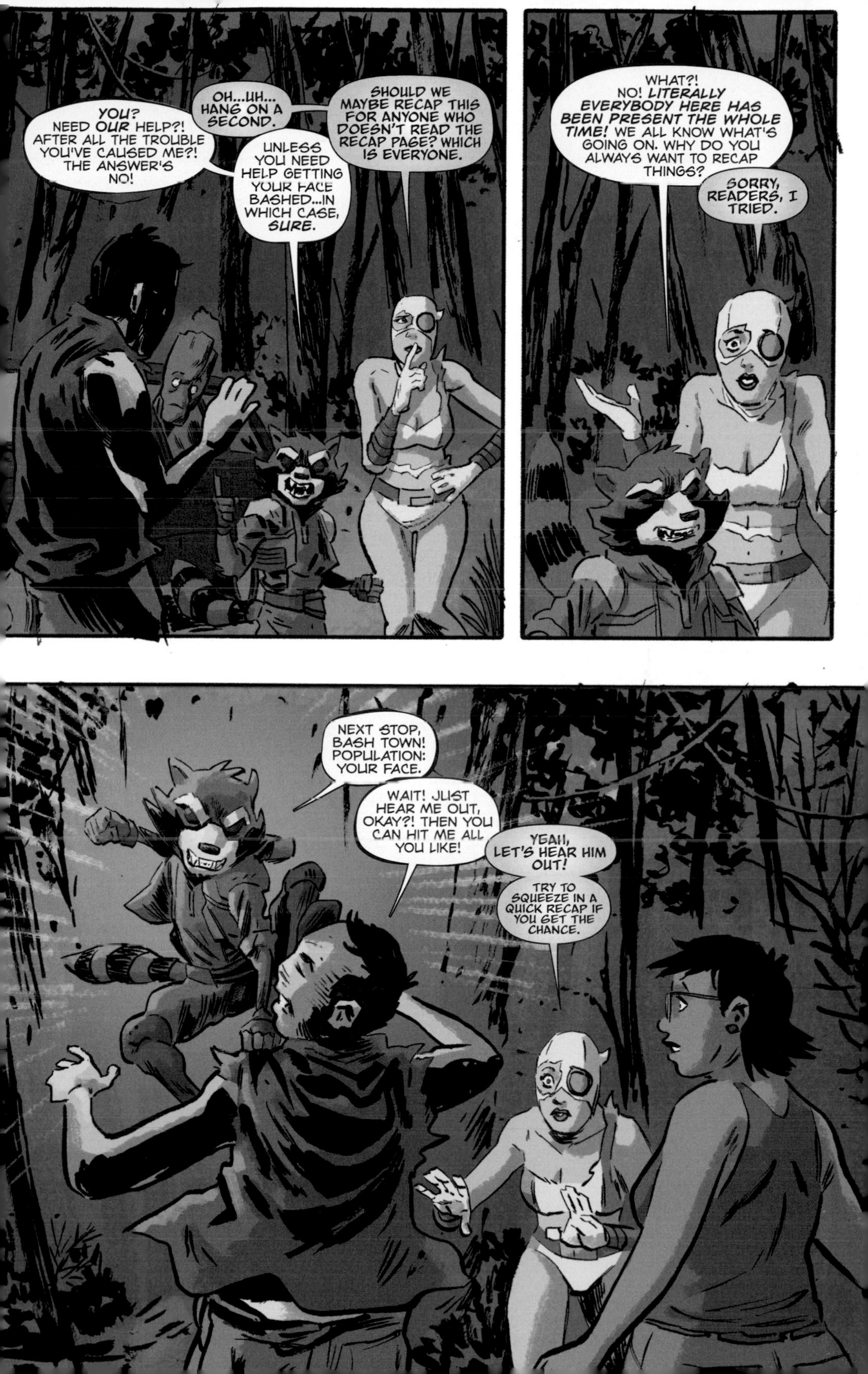
YOU? NEED OUR HELP?! AFTER ALL THE TROUBLE YOU'VE CAUSED ME?! THE ANSWER'S NO!
OH...UH... HANG ON A SECOND.
SHOULD WE MAYBE RECAP THIS FOR ANYONE WHO DOESN'T READ THE RECAP PAGE? WHICH IS EVERYONE.
UNLESS YOU NEED HELP GETTING YOUR FACE BASHED...IN WHICH CASE, SURE.
WHAT?! NO! LITERALLY EVERYBODY HERE HAS BEEN PRESENT THE WHOLE TIME! WE ALL KNOW WHAT'S GOING ON. WHY DO YOU ALWAYS WANT TO RECAP THINGS?
SORRY, READERS, I TRIED.
NEXT STOP, BASH TOWN! POPULATION: YOUR FACE.
WAIT! JUST HEAR ME OUT, OKAY?! THEN YOU CAN HIT ME ALL YOU LIKE!
YEAH, LET'S HEAR HIM OUT!
TRY TO SQUEEZE IN A QUICK RECAP IF YOU GET THE CHANCE.

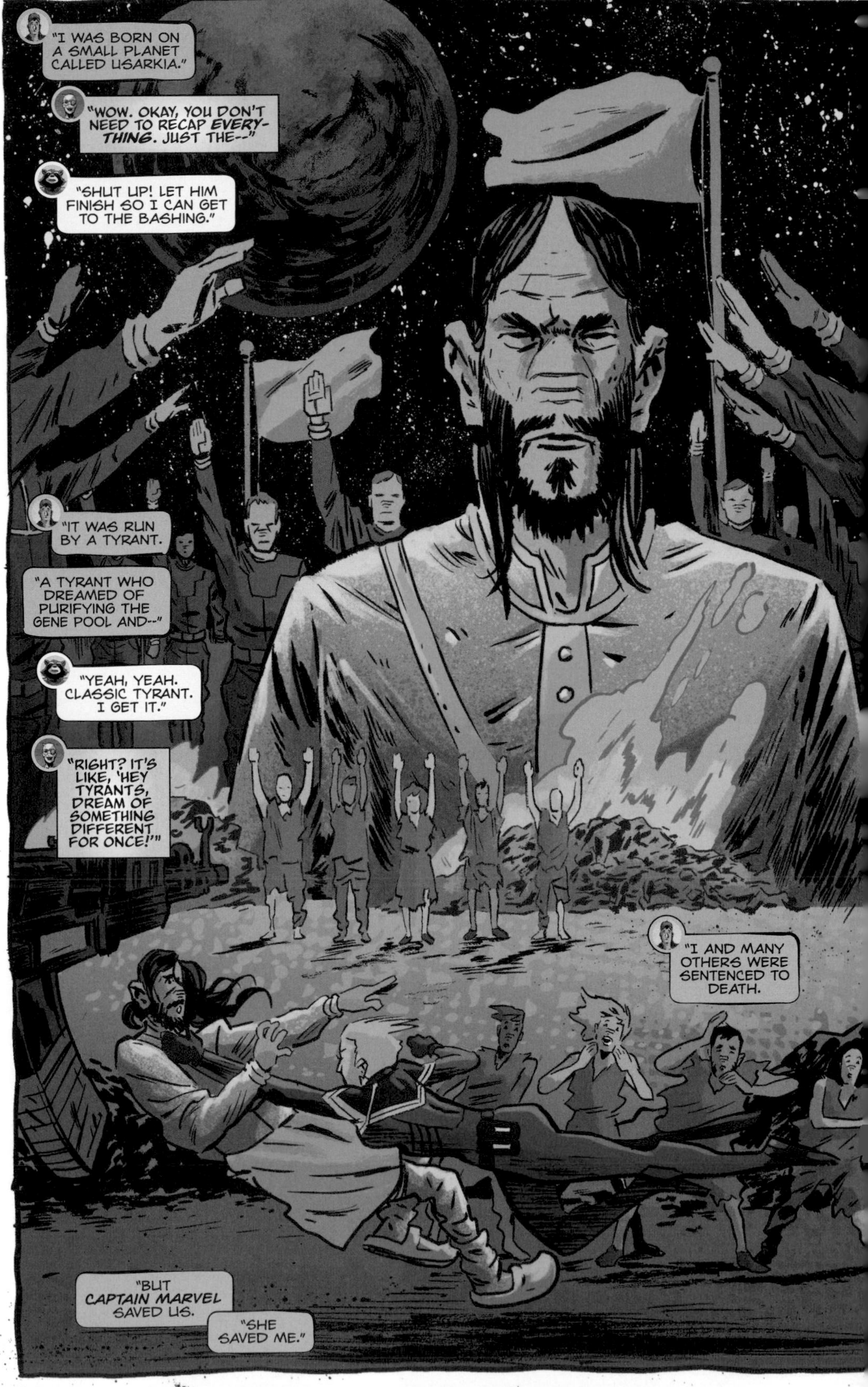
"I WAS BORN ON A SMALL PLANET CALLED USARKIA."
"WOW. OKAY, YOU DON'T NEED TO RECAP EVERYTHING. JUST THE--"
"SHUT UP! LET HIM FINISH SO I CAN GET TO THE BASHING."
"IT WAS RUN BY A TYRANT.
"A TYRANT WHO DREAMED OF PURIFYING THE GENE POOL AND--"
"YEAH, YEAH. CLASSIC TYRANT. I GET IT."
"RIGHT? IT'S LIKE, 'HEY TYRANTS, DREAM OF SOMETHING DIFFERENT FOR ONCE!'"
"I AND MANY OTHERS WERE SENTENCED TO DEATH.
"BUT CAPTAIN MARVEL SAVED US.
"SHE SAVED ME."

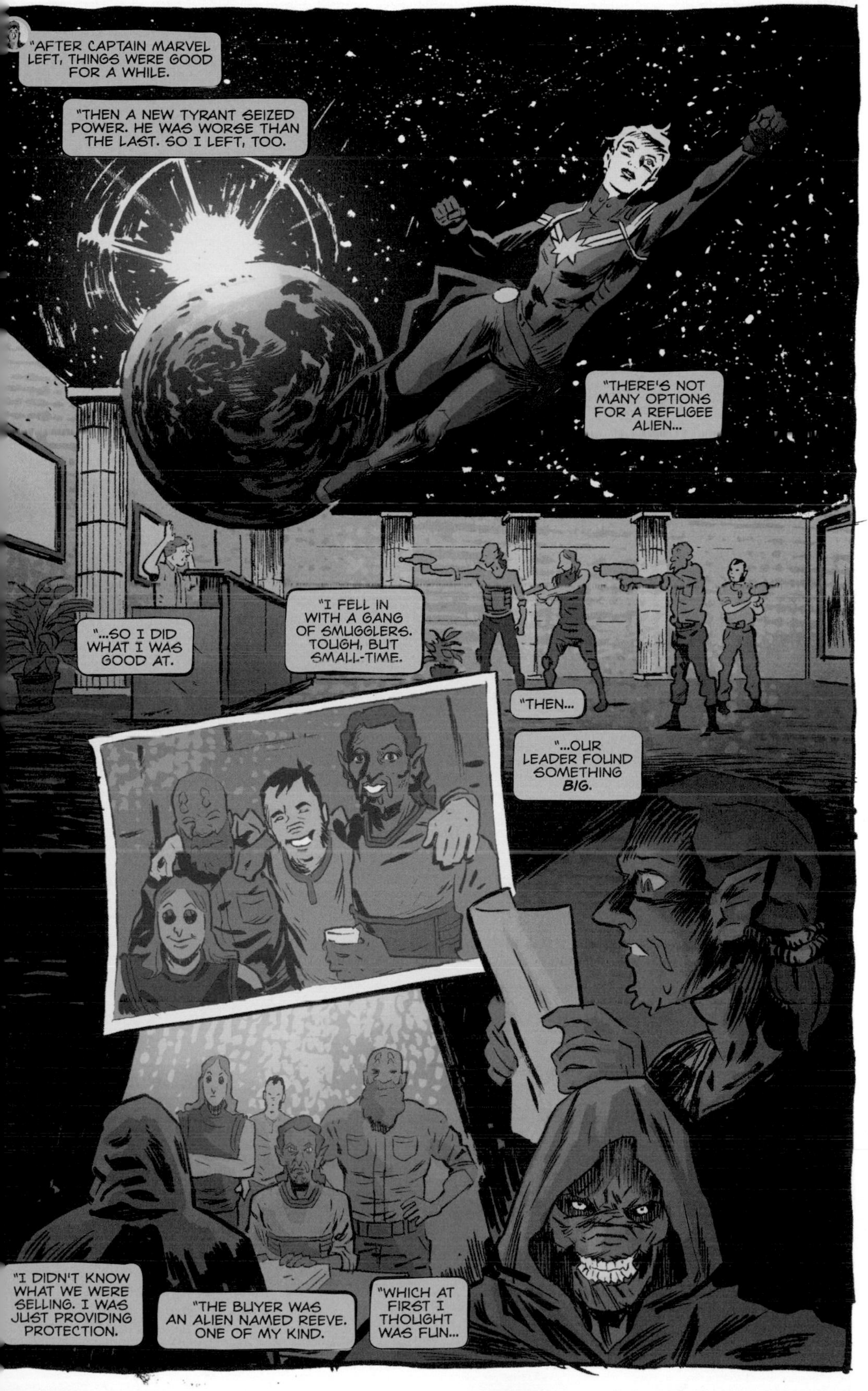
"AFTER CAPTAIN MARVEL LEFT, THINGS WERE GOOD FOR A WHILE.
"THEN A NEW TYRANT SEIZED POWER. HE WAS WORSE THAN THE LAST. SO I LEFT, TOO.
"THERE'S NOT MANY OPTIONS FOR A REFUGEE ALIEN...
"...SO I DID WHAT I WAS GOOD AT.
"I FELL IN WITH A GANG OF SMUGGLERS. TOUGH, BUT SMALL-TIME.
"THEN...
"...OUR LEADER FOUND SOMETHING BIG.
"I DIDN'T KNOW WHAT WE WERE SELLING. I WAS JUST PROVIDING PROTECTION.
"THE BUYER WAS AN ALIEN NAMED REEVE. ONE OF MY KIND.
"WHICH AT FIRST I THOUGHT WAS FUN...

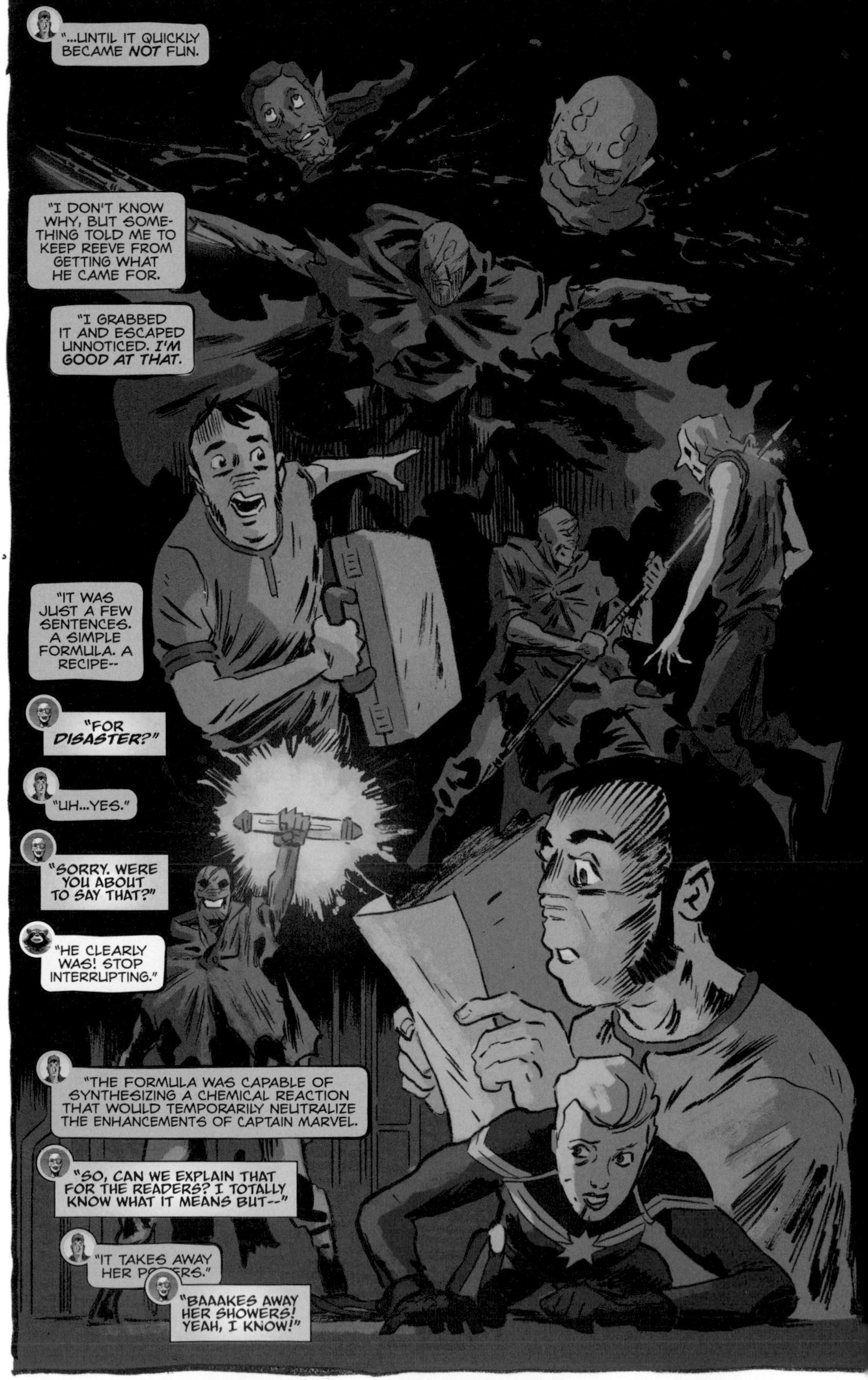
"...UNTIL IT QUICKLY BECAME *NOT* FUN.
"I DON'T KNOW WHY, BUT SOMETHING TOLD ME TO KEEP REEVE FROM GETTING WHAT HE CAME FOR.
"I GRABBED IT AND ESCAPED UNNOTICED. *I'M GOOD AT THAT*.
"IT WAS JUST A FEW SENTENCES. A SIMPLE FORMULA. A RECIPE--
"FOR *DISASTER?*"
"UH...YES."
"SORRY. WERE YOU ABOUT TO SAY THAT?"
"HE CLEARLY WAS! STOP INTERRUPTING."
"THE FORMULA WAS CAPABLE OF SYNTHESIZING A CHEMICAL REACTION THAT WOULD TEMPORARILY NEUTRALIZE THE ENHANCEMENTS OF CAPTAIN MARVEL.
"SO, CAN WE EXPLAIN THAT FOR THE READERS? I TOTALLY KNOW WHAT IT MEANS BUT--"
"IT TAKES AWAY HER POWERS."
"BAAAKES AWAY HER SHOWERS! YEAH, I KNOW!"

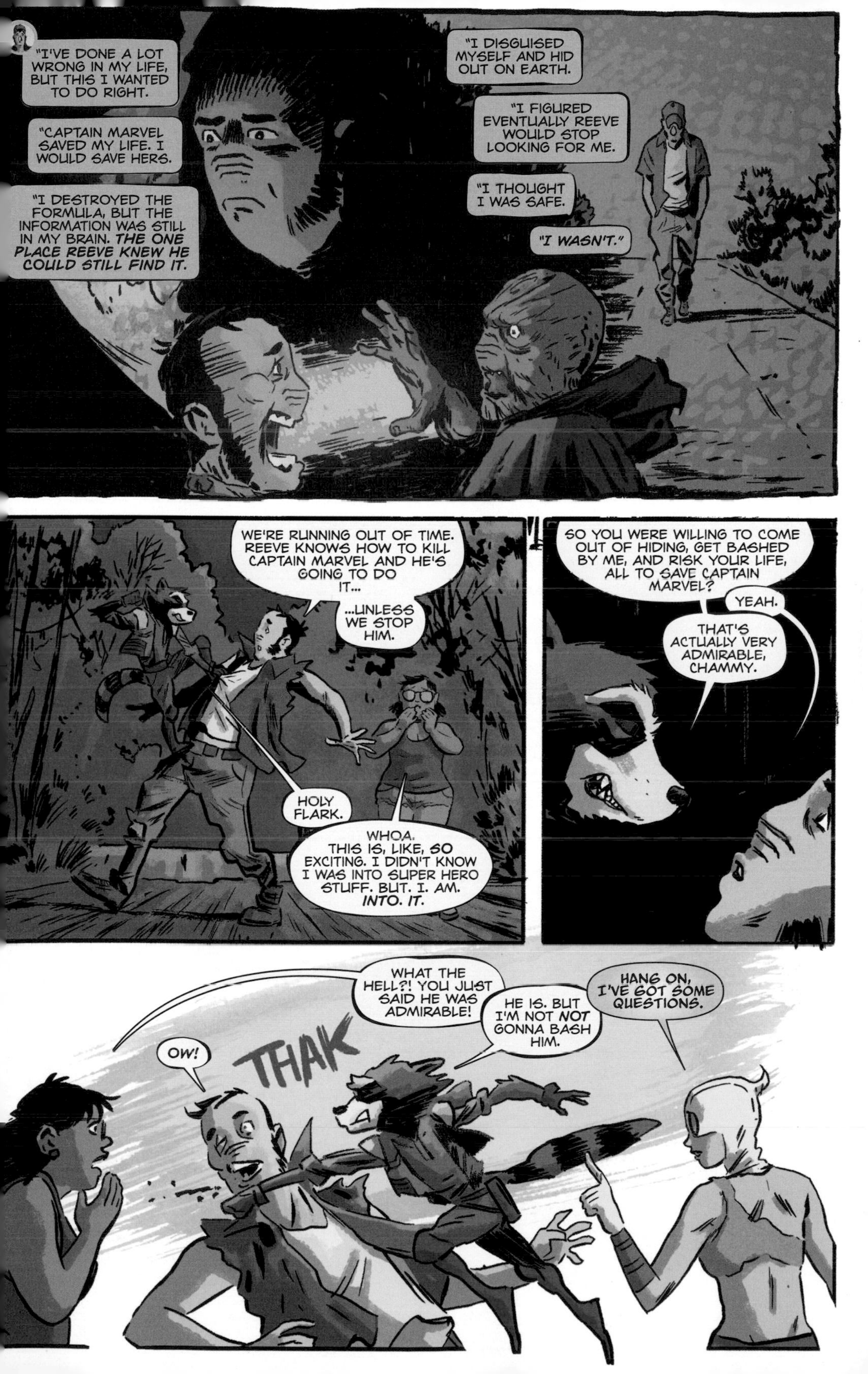
"I'VE DONE A LOT WRONG IN MY LIFE, BUT THIS I WANTED TO DO RIGHT.
"CAPTAIN MARVEL SAVED MY LIFE. I WOULD SAVE HERS.
"I DESTROYED THE FORMULA, BUT THE INFORMATION WAS STILL IN MY BRAIN. THE ONE PLACE REEVE KNEW HE COULD STILL FIND IT.
"I DISGUISED MYSELF AND HID OUT ON EARTH.
"I FIGURED EVENTUALLY REEVE WOULD STOP LOOKING FOR ME.
"I THOUGHT I WAS SAFE.
"I WASN'T."
WE'RE RUNNING OUT OF TIME. REEVE KNOWS HOW TO KILL CAPTAIN MARVEL AND HE'S GOING TO DO IT...
...UNLESS WE STOP HIM.
HOLY FLARK.
WHOA. THIS IS, LIKE, SO EXCITING. I DIDN'T KNOW I WAS INTO SUPER HERO STUFF. BUT. I. AM. INTO. IT.
SO YOU WERE WILLING TO COME OUT OF HIDING, GET BASHED BY ME, AND RISK YOUR LIFE, ALL TO SAVE CAPTAIN MARVEL?
YEAH.
THAT'S ACTUALLY VERY ADMIRABLE, CHAMMY.
OW!
THAK
WHAT THE HELL?! YOU JUST SAID HE WAS ADMIRABLE!
HE IS. BUT I'M NOT NOT GONNA BASH HIM.
HANG ON, I'VE GOT SOME QUESTIONS.

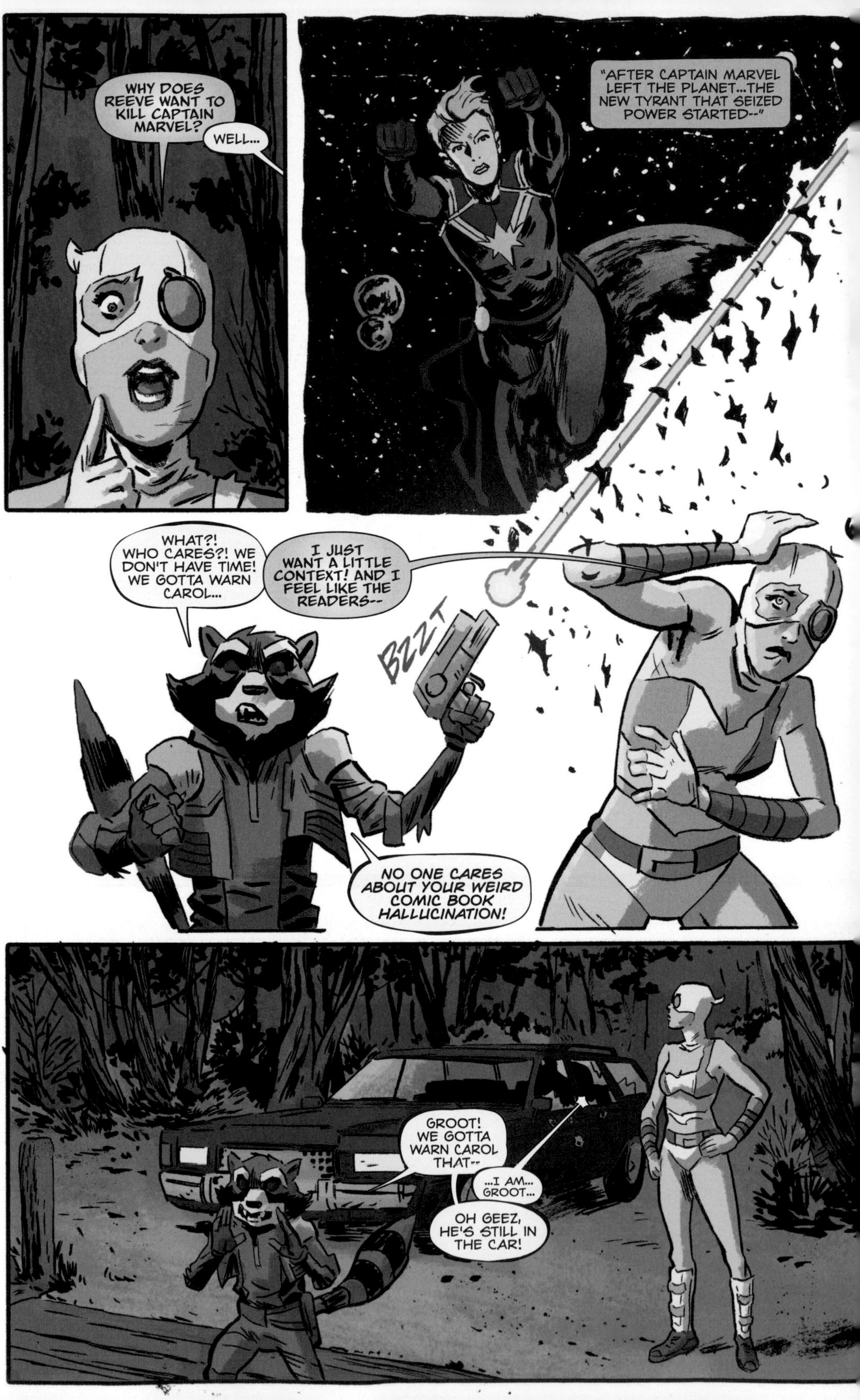

WHY DOES REEVE WANT TO KILL CAPTAIN MARVEL?
WELL...
"AFTER CAPTAIN MARVEL LEFT THE PLANET...THE NEW TYRANT THAT SEIZED POWER STARTED--"
WHAT?! WHO CARES?! WE DON'T HAVE TIME! WE GOTTA WARN CAROL...
I JUST WANT A LITTLE CONTEXT! AND I FEEL LIKE THE READERS--
BZZT
NO ONE CARES ABOUT YOUR WEIRD COMIC BOOK HALLUCINATION!
GROOT! WE GOTTA WARN CAROL THAT--
...I AM... GROOT...
OH GEEZ, HE'S STILL IN THE CAR!

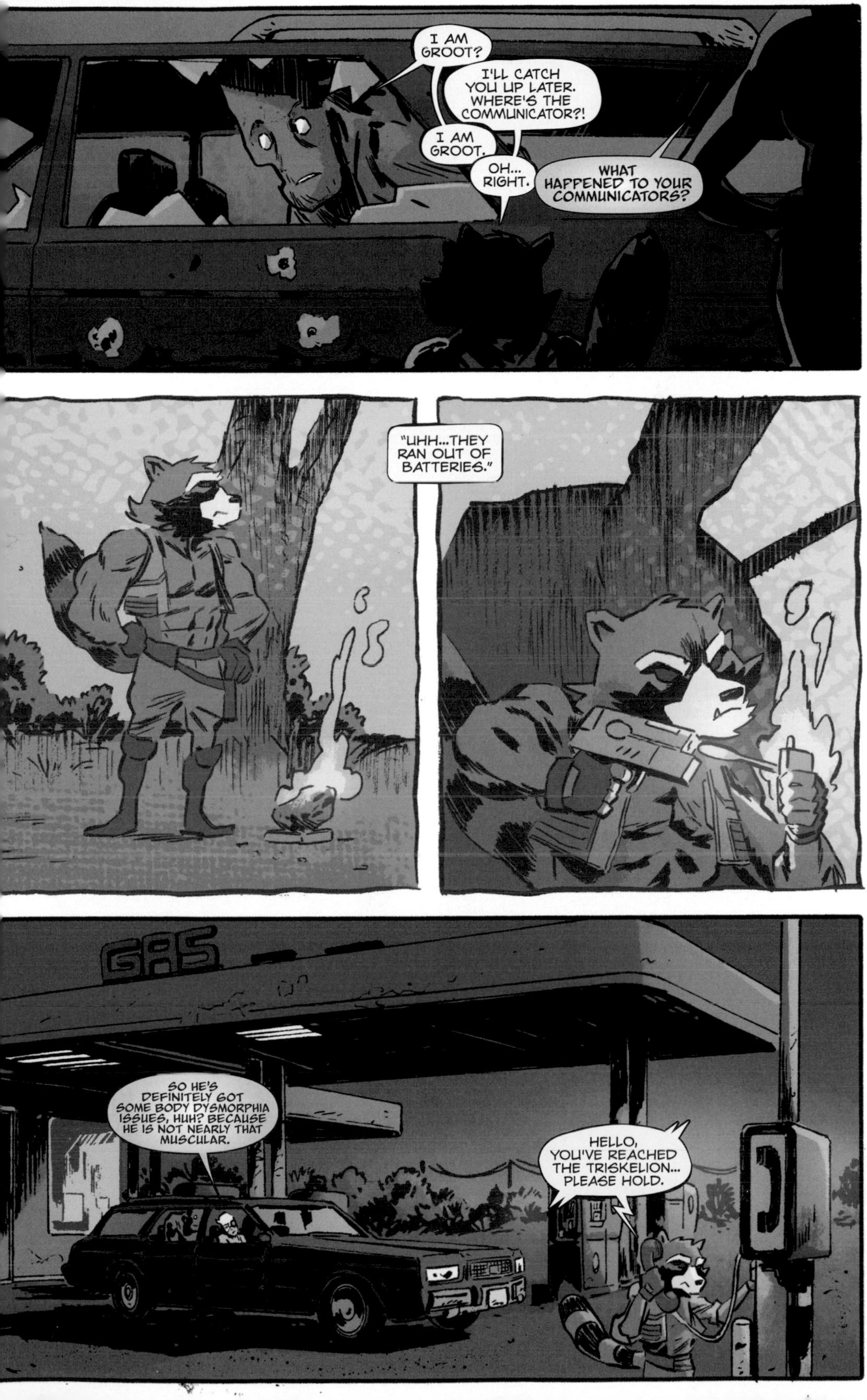
I AM GROOT?
I'LL CATCH YOU UP LATER. WHERE'S THE COMMUNICATOR?!
I AM GROOT.
OH... RIGHT.
WHAT HAPPENED TO YOUR COMMUNICATORS?
"UHH...THEY RAN OUT OF BATTERIES."
GAS
SO HE'S DEFINITELY GOT SOME BODY DYSMORPHIA ISSUES, HUH? BECAUSE HE IS NOT NEARLY THAT MUSCULAR.
HELLO, YOU'VE REACHED THE TRISKELION... PLEASE HOLD.

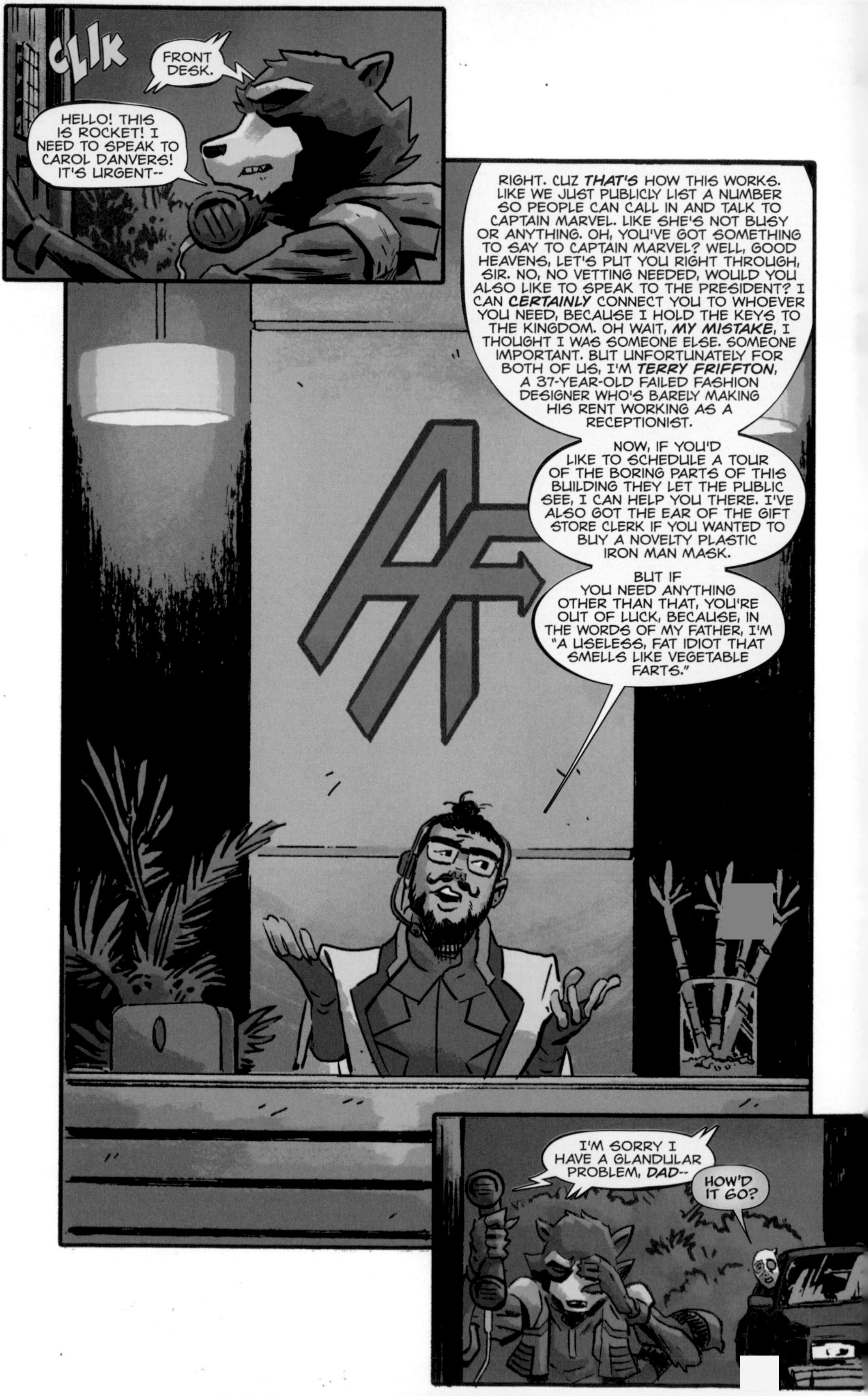
CLIK
FRONT DESK.
HELLO! THIS IS ROCKET! I NEED TO SPEAK TO CAROL DANVERS! IT'S URGENT--
RIGHT. CUZ THAT'S HOW THIS WORKS. LIKE WE JUST PUBLICLY LIST A NUMBER SO PEOPLE CAN CALL IN AND TALK TO CAPTAIN MARVEL. LIKE SHE'S NOT BUSY OR ANYTHING. OH, YOU'VE GOT SOMETHING TO SAY TO CAPTAIN MARVEL? WELL, GOOD HEAVENS, LET'S PUT YOU RIGHT THROUGH, SIR. NO, NO VETTING NEEDED, WOULD YOU ALSO LIKE TO SPEAK TO THE PRESIDENT? I CAN CERTAINLY CONNECT YOU TO WHOEVER YOU NEED, BECAUSE I HOLD THE KEYS TO THE KINGDOM. OH WAIT, MY MISTAKE, I THOUGHT I WAS SOMEONE ELSE. SOMEONE IMPORTANT. BUT UNFORTUNATELY FOR BOTH OF US, I'M TERRY FRIFFTON, A 37-YEAR-OLD FAILED FASHION DESIGNER WHO'S BARELY MAKING HIS RENT WORKING AS A RECEPTIONIST.
NOW, IF YOU'D LIKE TO SCHEDULE A TOUR OF THE BORING PARTS OF THIS BUILDING THEY LET THE PUBLIC SEE, I CAN HELP YOU THERE. I'VE ALSO GOT THE EAR OF THE GIFT STORE CLERK IF YOU WANTED TO BUY A NOVELTY PLASTIC IRON MAN MASK.
BUT IF YOU NEED ANYTHING OTHER THAN THAT, YOU'RE OUT OF LUCK, BECAUSE, IN THE WORDS OF MY FATHER, I'M "A USELESS, FAT IDIOT THAT SMELLS LIKE VEGETABLE FARTS."
I'M SORRY I HAVE A GLANDULAR PROBLEM, DAD--
HOW'D IT GO?

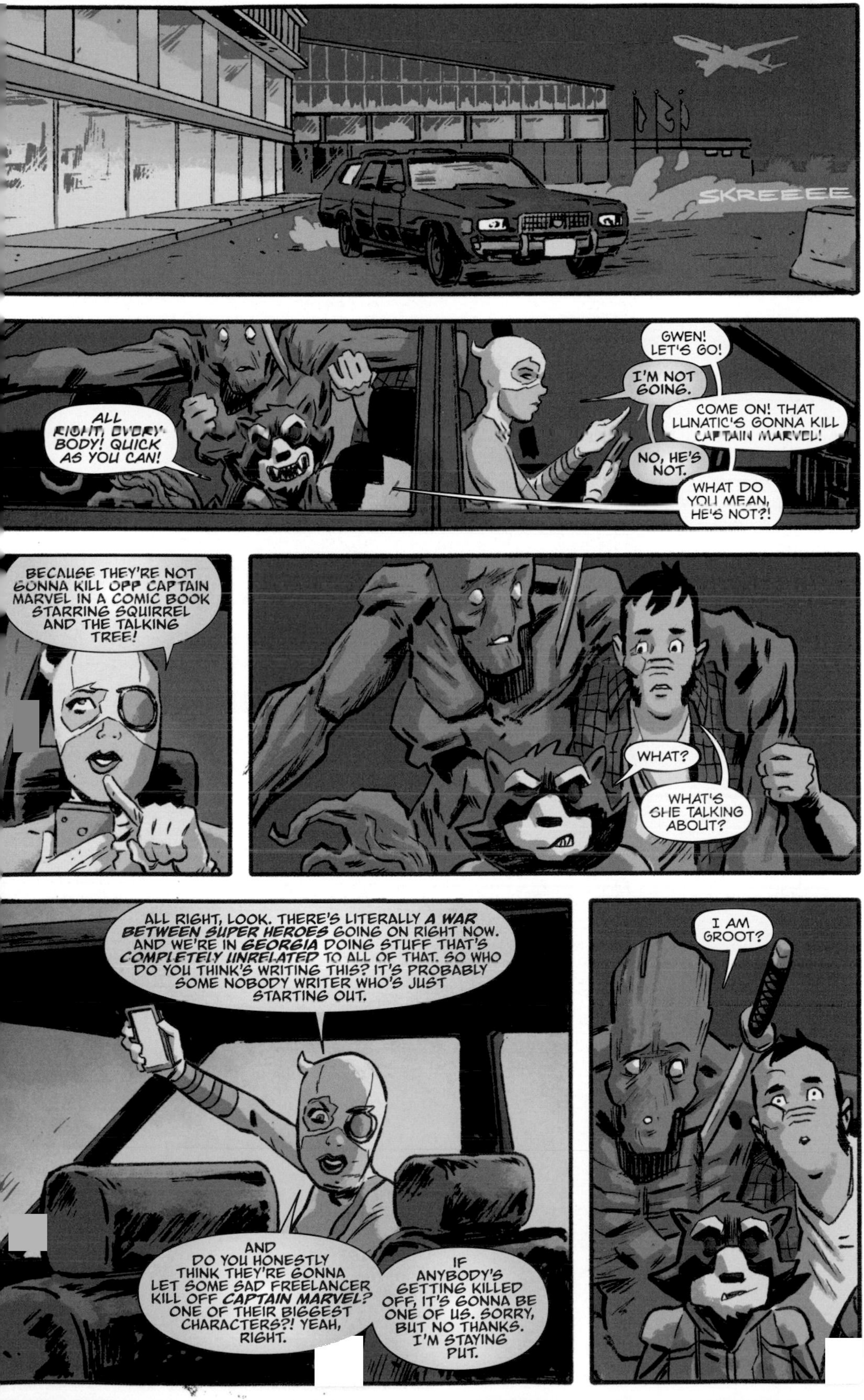
SKREEEEE
ALL RIGHT, EVERY-BODY! QUICK AS YOU CAN!
GWEN! LET'S GO!
I'M NOT GOING.
COME ON! THAT LUNATIC'S GONNA KILL CAPTAIN MARVEL!
NO, HE'S NOT.
WHAT DO YOU MEAN, HE'S NOT?!
BECAUSE THEY'RE NOT GONNA KILL OFF CAPTAIN MARVEL IN A COMIC BOOK STARRING SQUIRREL AND THE TALKING TREE!
WHAT?
WHAT'S SHE TALKING ABOUT?
ALL RIGHT, LOOK. THERE'S LITERALLY A WAR BETWEEN SUPER HEROES GOING ON RIGHT NOW. AND WE'RE IN GEORGIA DOING STUFF THAT'S COMPLETELY UNRELATED TO ALL OF THAT. SO WHO DO YOU THINK'S WRITING THIS? IT'S PROBABLY SOME NOBODY WRITER WHO'S JUST STARTING OUT.
AND DO YOU HONESTLY THINK THEY'RE GONNA LET SOME SAD FREELANCER KILL OFF CAPTAIN MARVEL? ONE OF THEIR BIGGEST CHARACTERS?! YEAH, RIGHT.
IF ANYBODY'S GETTING KILLED OFF, IT'S GONNA BE ONE OF US. SORRY, BUT NO THANKS. I'M STAYING PUT.
I AM GROOT?

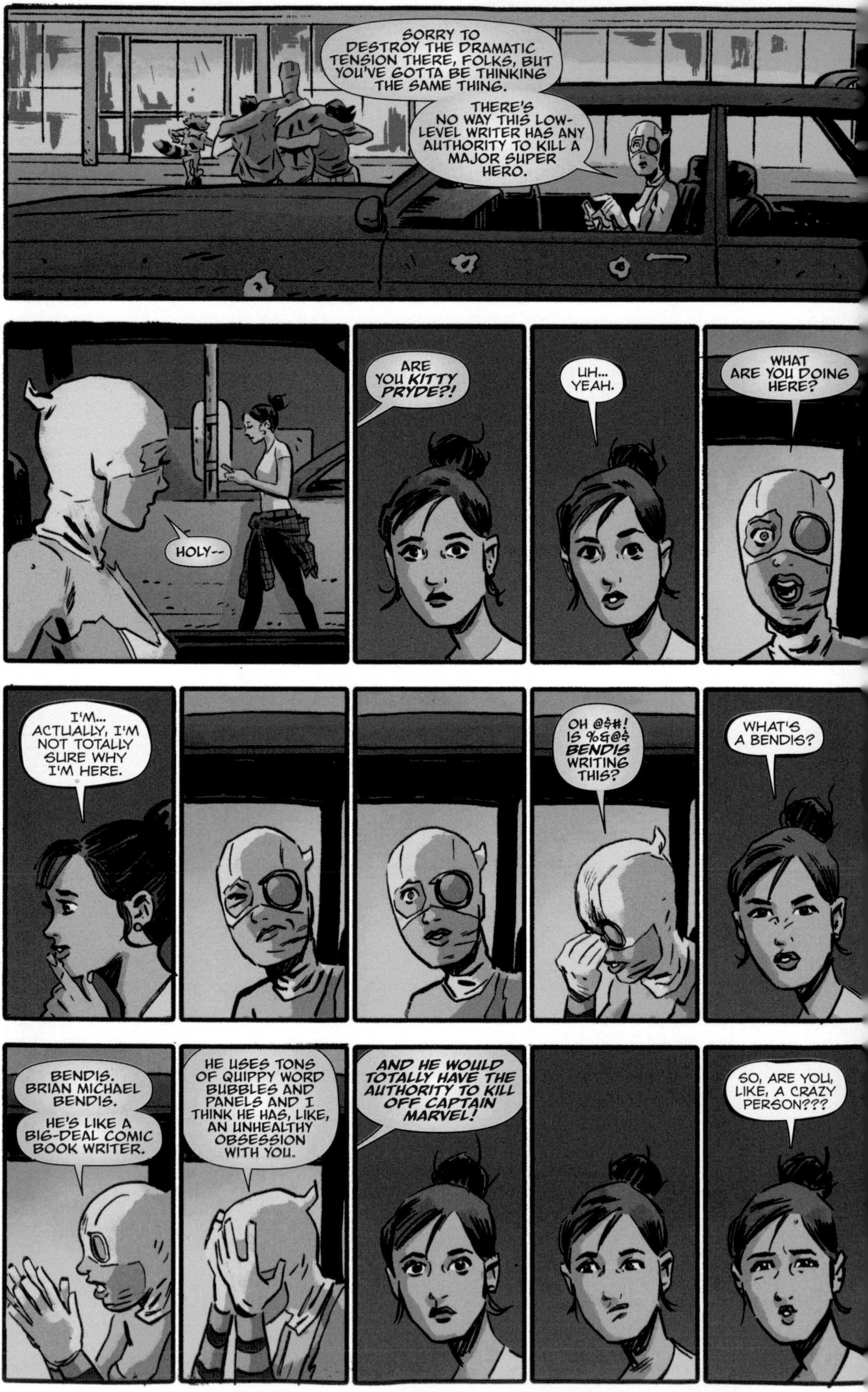

SORRY TO DESTROY THE DRAMATIC TENSION THERE, FOLKS, BUT YOU'VE GOTTA BE THINKING THE SAME THING.
THERE'S NO WAY THIS LOW-LEVEL WRITER HAS ANY AUTHORITY TO KILL A MAJOR SUPER HERO.
HOLY--
ARE YOU KITTY PRYDE?!
UH... YEAH.
WHAT ARE YOU DOING HERE?
I'M... ACTUALLY, I'M NOT TOTALLY SURE WHY I'M HERE.
OH @$#! IS %&@$ BENDIS WRITING THIS?
WHAT'S A BENDIS?
BENDIS. BRIAN MICHAEL BENDIS.
HE'S LIKE A BIG-DEAL COMIC BOOK WRITER.
HE USES TONS OF QUIPPY WORD BUBBLES AND PANELS AND I THINK HE HAS, LIKE, AN UNHEALTHY OBSESSION WITH YOU.
AND HE WOULD TOTALLY HAVE THE AUTHORITY TO KILL OFF CAPTAIN MARVEL!
SO, ARE YOU, LIKE, A CRAZY PERSON???

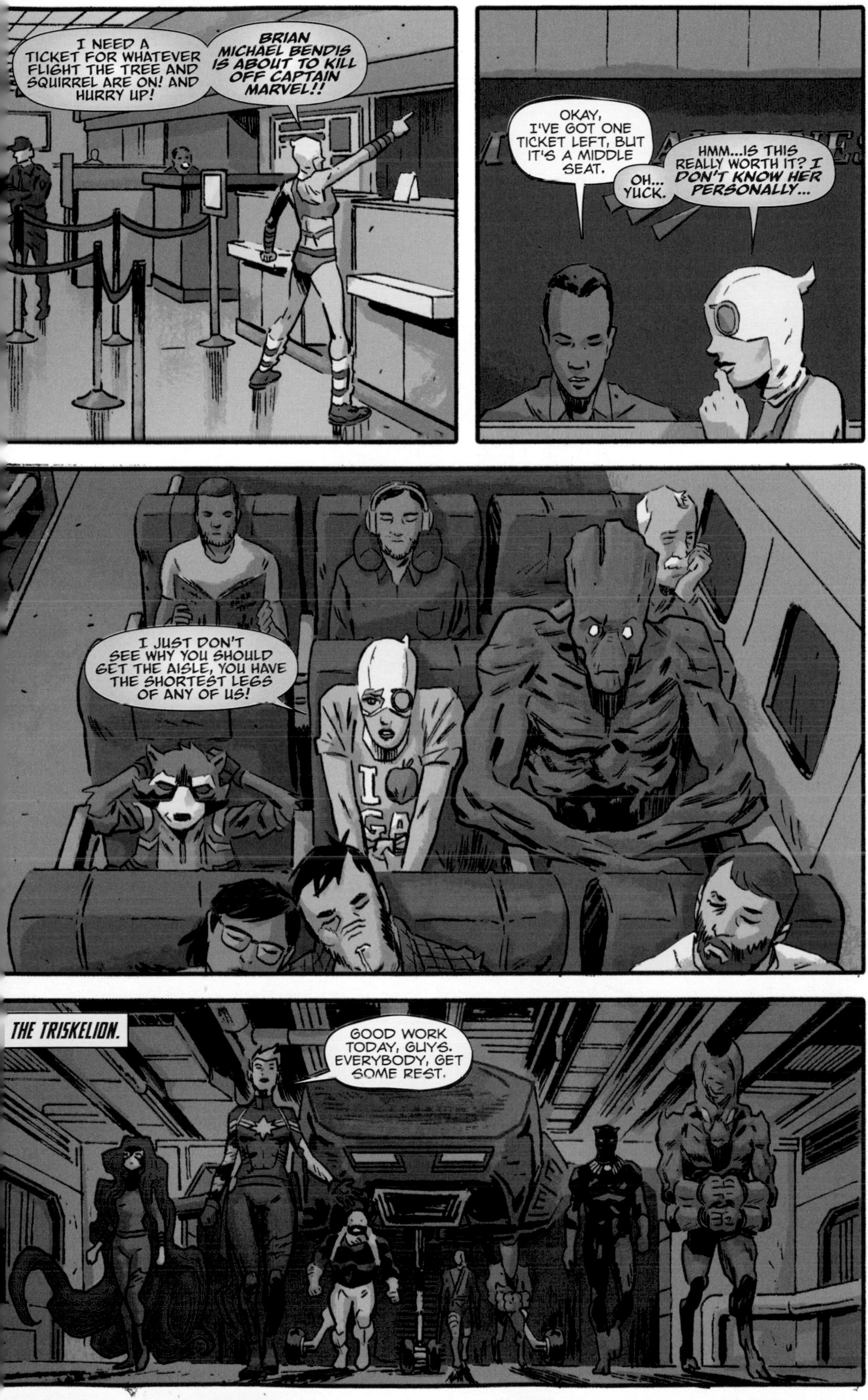
I NEED A TICKET FOR WHATEVER FLIGHT THE TREE AND SQUIRREL ARE ON! AND HURRY UP!
BRIAN MICHAEL BENDIS IS ABOUT TO KILL OFF CAPTAIN MARVEL!!
OKAY, I'VE GOT ONE TICKET LEFT, BUT IT'S A MIDDLE SEAT.
OH... YUCK.
HMM...IS THIS REALLY WORTH IT? I DON'T KNOW HER PERSONALLY...
I JUST DON'T SEE WHY YOU SHOULD GET THE AISLE, YOU HAVE THE SHORTEST LEGS OF ANY OF US!
THE TRISKELION.
GOOD WORK TODAY, GUYS. EVERYBODY, GET SOME REST.

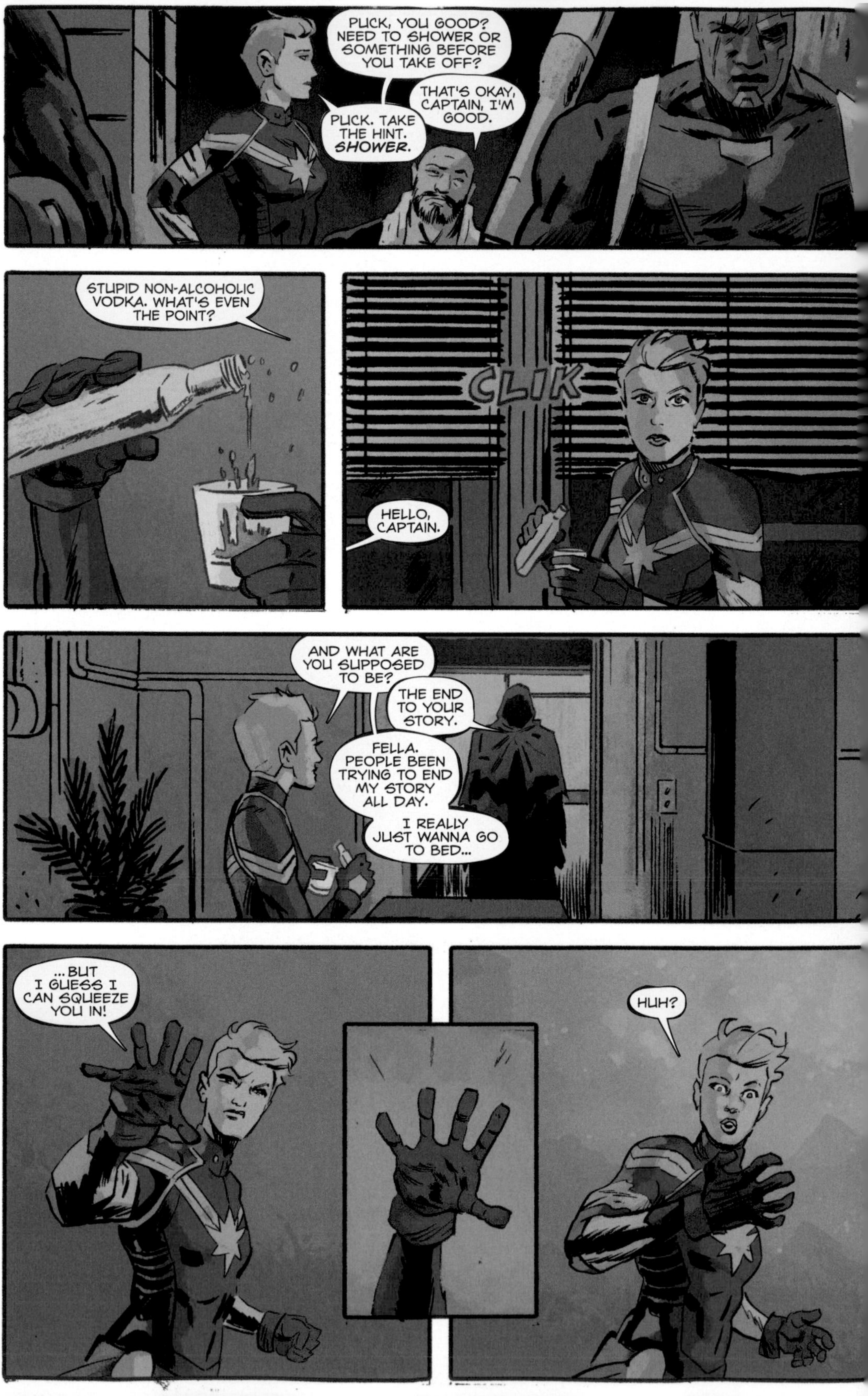
PUCK, YOU GOOD? NEED TO SHOWER OR SOMETHING BEFORE YOU TAKE OFF?
PUCK. TAKE THE HINT. SHOWER.
THAT'S OKAY, CAPTAIN, I'M GOOD.
STUPID NON-ALCOHOLIC VODKA. WHAT'S EVEN THE POINT?
CLIK
HELLO, CAPTAIN.
AND WHAT ARE YOU SUPPOSED TO BE?
THE END TO YOUR STORY.
FELLA. PEOPLE BEEN TRYING TO END MY STORY ALL DAY.
I REALLY JUST WANNA GO TO BED...
...BUT I GUESS I CAN SQUEEZE YOU IN!
HUH?

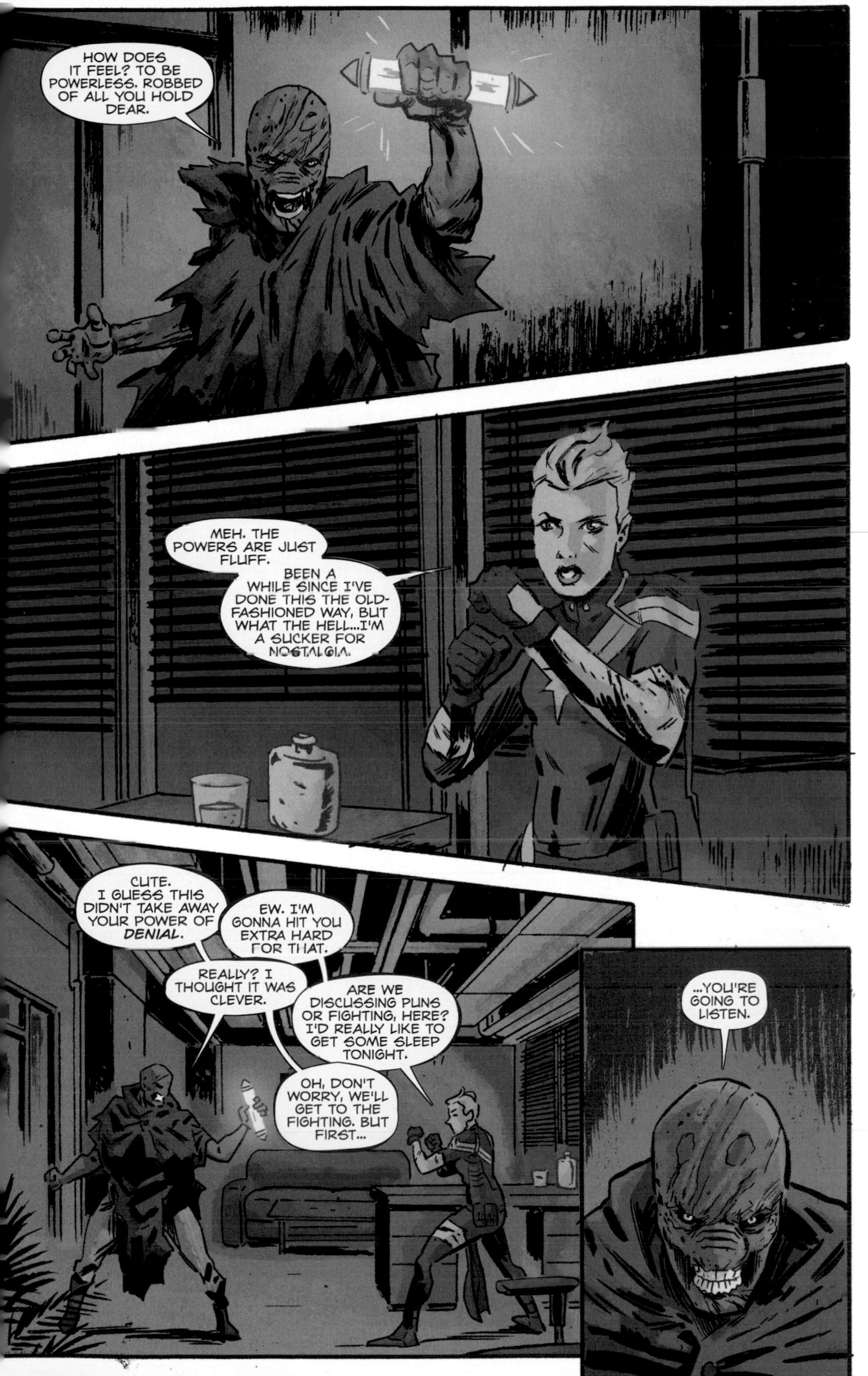
HOW DOES IT FEEL? TO BE POWERLESS. ROBBED OF ALL YOU HOLD DEAR.
MEH. THE POWERS ARE JUST FLUFF.
BEEN A WHILE SINCE I'VE DONE THIS THE OLD-FASHIONED WAY, BUT WHAT THE HELL...I'M A SUCKER FOR NOSTALGIA.
CUTE. I GUESS THIS DIDN'T TAKE AWAY YOUR POWER OF *DENIAL*.
EW. I'M GONNA HIT YOU EXTRA HARD FOR THAT.
REALLY? I THOUGHT IT WAS CLEVER.
ARE WE DISCUSSING PUNS OR FIGHTING, HERE? I'D REALLY LIKE TO GET SOME SLEEP TONIGHT.
OH, DON'T WORRY, WE'LL GET TO THE FIGHTING. BUT FIRST...
...YOU'RE GOING TO LISTEN.

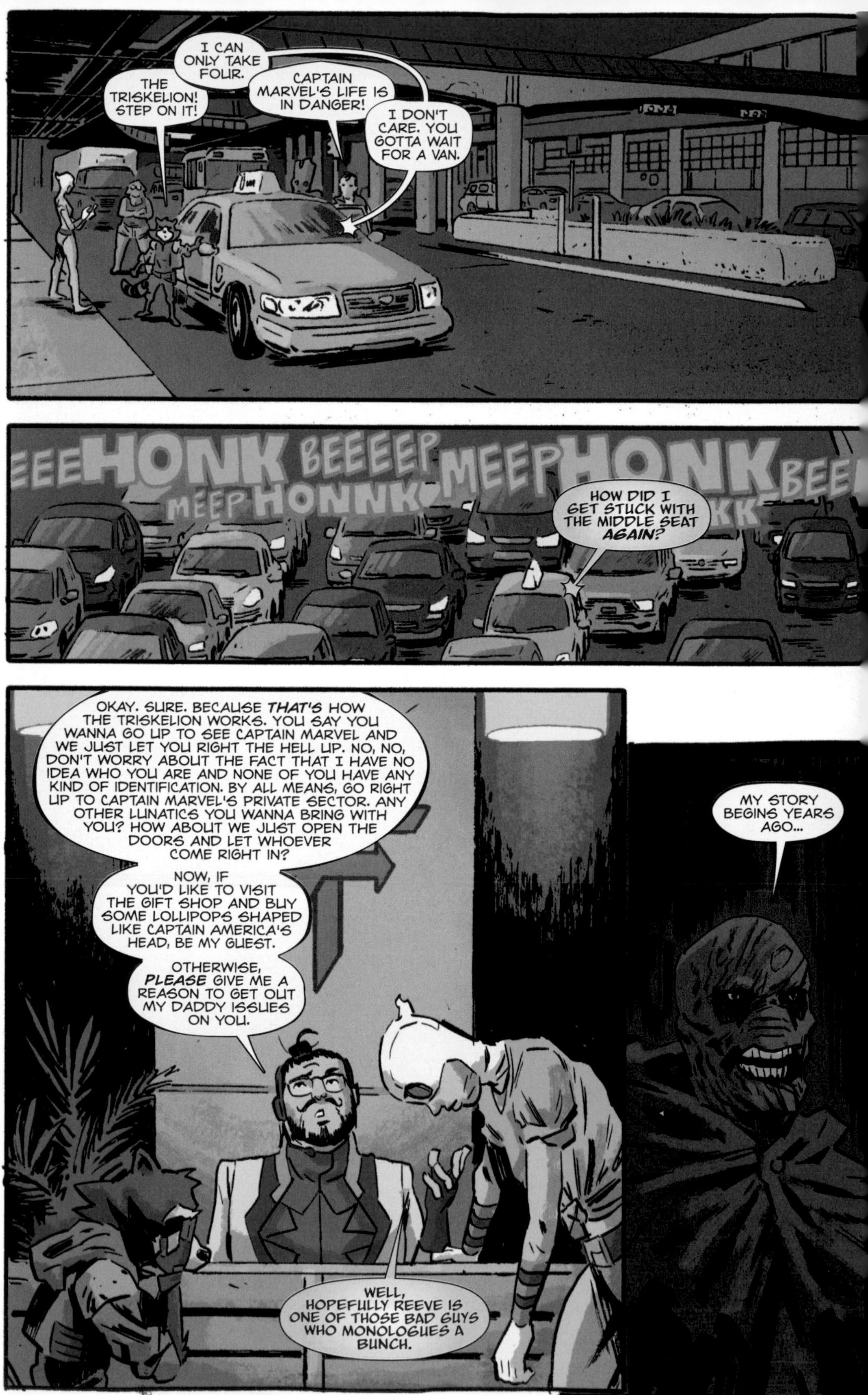
THE TRISKELION! STEP ON IT!
I CAN ONLY TAKE FOUR.
CAPTAIN MARVEL'S LIFE IS IN DANGER!
I DON'T CARE. YOU GOTTA WAIT FOR A VAN.
EEEHONK BEEEEP MEEPHONK BEE
MEEP HONNK
HOW DID I GET STUCK WITH THE MIDDLE SEAT AGAIN?
OKAY. SURE. BECAUSE THAT'S HOW THE TRISKELION WORKS. YOU SAY YOU WANNA GO UP TO SEE CAPTAIN MARVEL AND WE JUST LET YOU RIGHT THE HELL UP. NO, NO, DON'T WORRY ABOUT THE FACT THAT I HAVE NO IDEA WHO YOU ARE AND NONE OF YOU HAVE ANY KIND OF IDENTIFICATION. BY ALL MEANS, GO RIGHT UP TO CAPTAIN MARVEL'S PRIVATE SECTOR. ANY OTHER LUNATICS YOU WANNA BRING WITH YOU? HOW ABOUT WE JUST OPEN THE DOORS AND LET WHOEVER COME RIGHT IN?
NOW, IF YOU'D LIKE TO VISIT THE GIFT SHOP AND BUY SOME LOLLIPOPS SHAPED LIKE CAPTAIN AMERICA'S HEAD, BE MY GUEST.
OTHERWISE, PLEASE GIVE ME A REASON TO GET OUT MY DADDY ISSUES ON YOU.
WELL, HOPEFULLY REEVE IS ONE OF THOSE BAD GUYS WHO MONOLOGUES A BUNCH.
MY STORY BEGINS YEARS AGO...

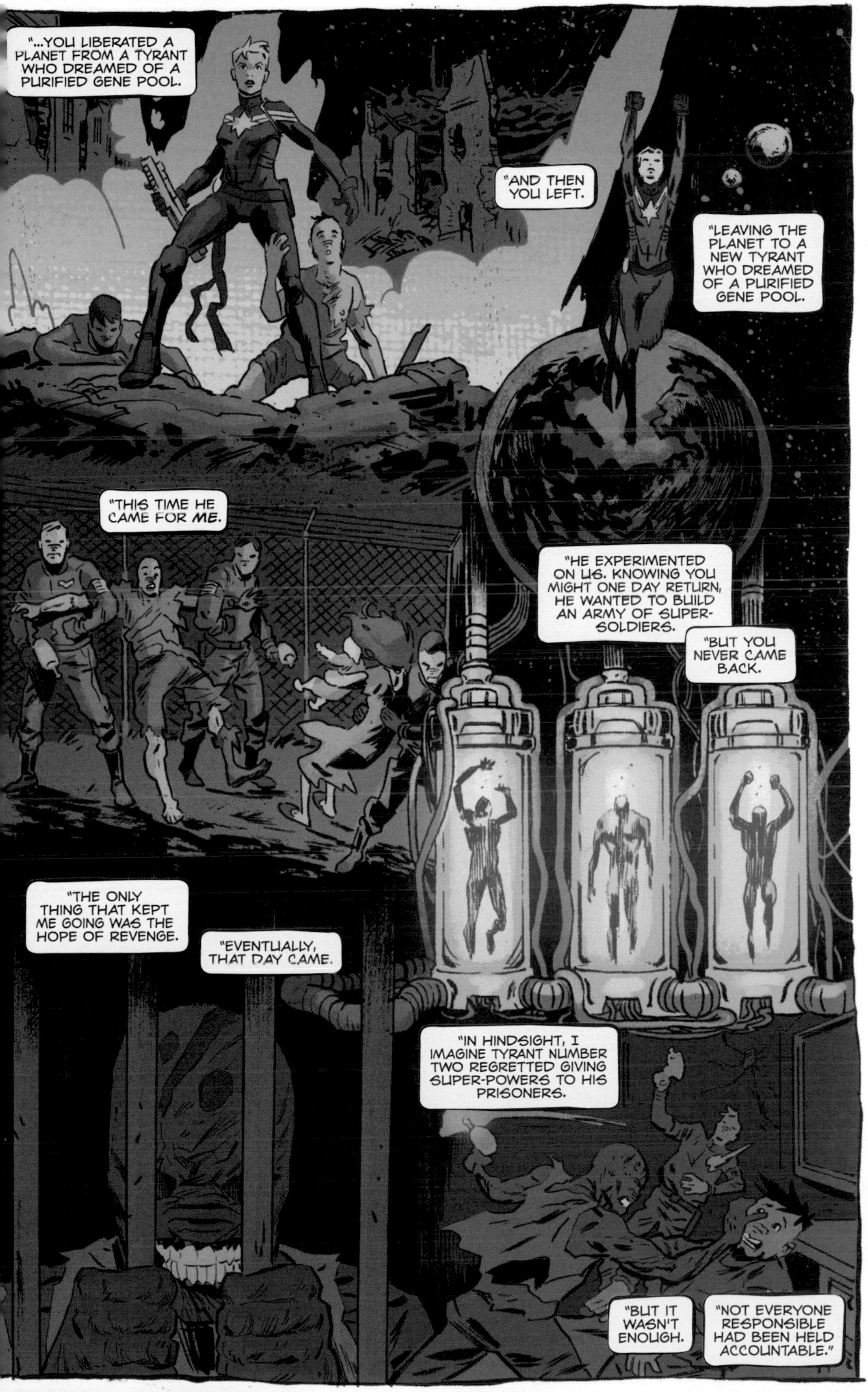
"...YOU LIBERATED A PLANET FROM A TYRANT WHO DREAMED OF A PURIFIED GENE POOL.
"AND THEN YOU LEFT.
"LEAVING THE PLANET TO A NEW TYRANT WHO DREAMED OF A PURIFIED GENE POOL.
"THIS TIME HE CAME FOR ME.
"HE EXPERIMENTED ON US. KNOWING YOU MIGHT ONE DAY RETURN, HE WANTED TO BUILD AN ARMY OF SUPER-SOLDIERS.
"BUT YOU NEVER CAME BACK.
"THE ONLY THING THAT KEPT ME GOING WAS THE HOPE OF REVENGE.
"EVENTUALLY, THAT DAY CAME.
"IN HINDSIGHT, I IMAGINE TYRANT NUMBER TWO REGRETTED GIVING SUPER-POWERS TO HIS PRISONERS.
"BUT IT WASN'T ENOUGH.
"NOT EVERYONE RESPONSIBLE HAD BEEN HELD ACCOUNTABLE."

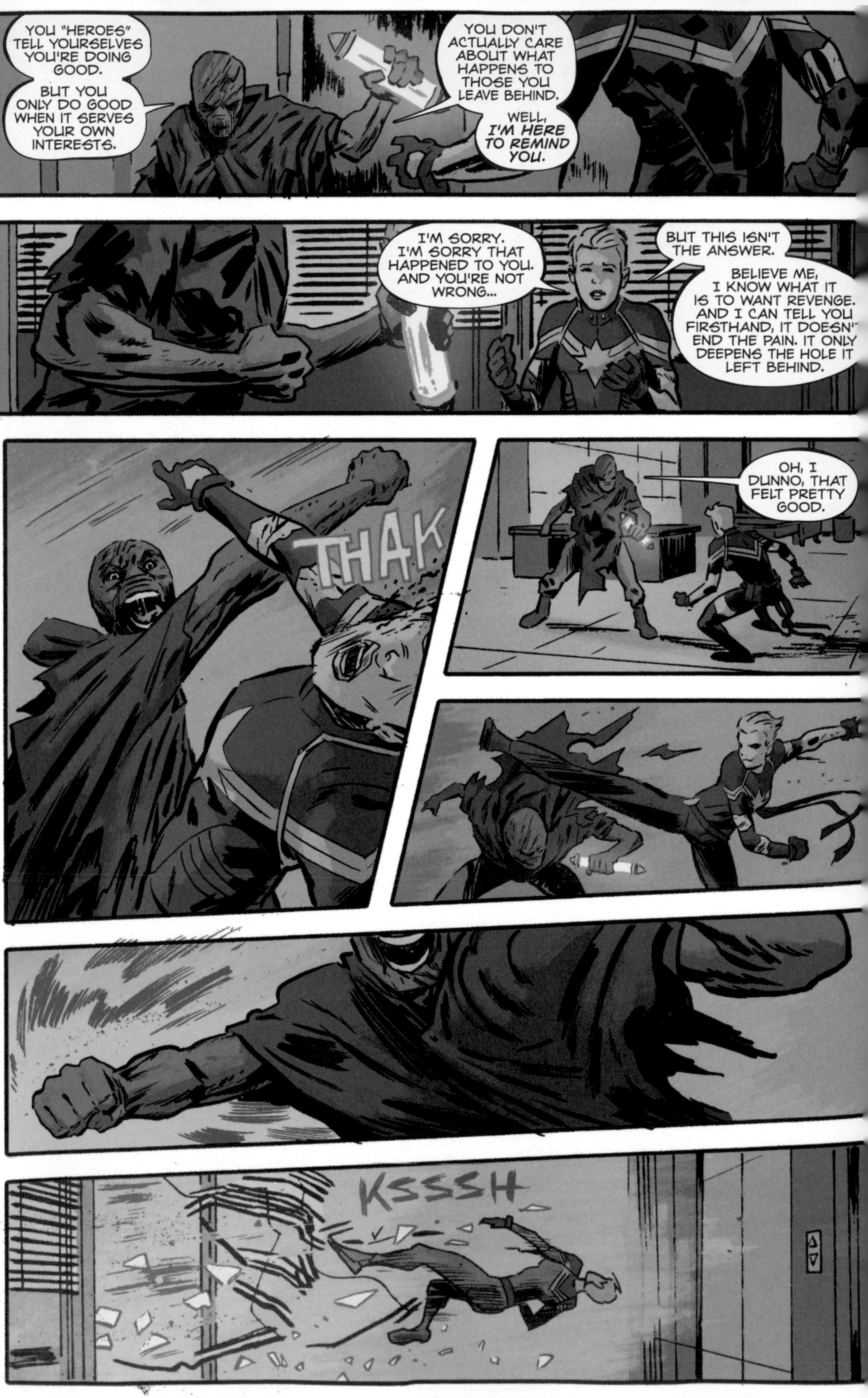
YOU "HEROES" TELL YOURSELVES YOU'RE DOING GOOD.
BUT YOU ONLY DO GOOD WHEN IT SERVES YOUR OWN INTERESTS.
YOU DON'T ACTUALLY CARE ABOUT WHAT HAPPENS TO THOSE YOU LEAVE BEHIND.
WELL, I'M HERE TO REMIND YOU.
I'M SORRY. I'M SORRY THAT HAPPENED TO YOU. AND YOU'RE NOT WRONG...
BUT THIS ISN'T THE ANSWER.
BELIEVE ME, I KNOW WHAT IT IS TO WANT REVENGE. AND I CAN TELL YOU FIRSTHAND, IT DOESN'T END THE PAIN. IT ONLY DEEPENS THE HOLE IT LEFT BEHIND.
THAK
OH, I DUNNO, THAT FELT PRETTY GOOD.
KSSSH

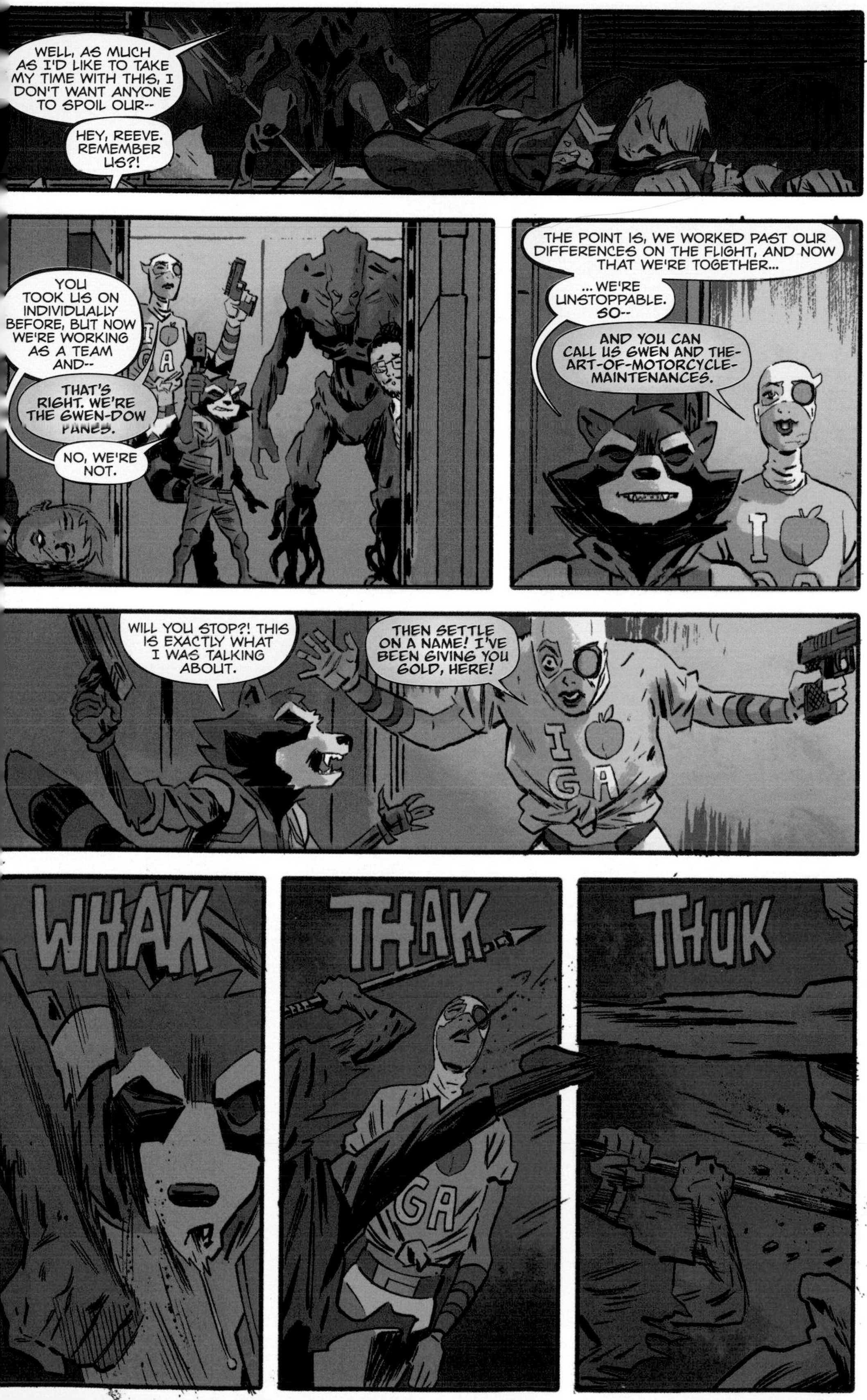
WELL, AS MUCH AS I'D LIKE TO TAKE MY TIME WITH THIS, I DON'T WANT ANYONE TO SPOIL OUR--
HEY, REEVE. REMEMBER US?!
YOU TOOK US ON INDIVIDUALLY BEFORE, BUT NOW WE'RE WORKING AS A TEAM AND--
THAT'S RIGHT. WE'RE THE GWEN-DOW PANES.
NO, WE'RE NOT.
THE POINT IS, WE WORKED PAST OUR DIFFERENCES ON THE FLIGHT, AND NOW THAT WE'RE TOGETHER...
...WE'RE UNSTOPPABLE. SO--
AND YOU CAN CALL US GWEN AND THE-ART-OF-MOTORCYCLE-MAINTENANCES.
WILL YOU STOP?! THIS IS EXACTLY WHAT I WAS TALKING ABOUT.
THEN SETTLE ON A NAME! I'VE BEEN GIVING YOU GOLD, HERE!
WHAK
THAK
THUK

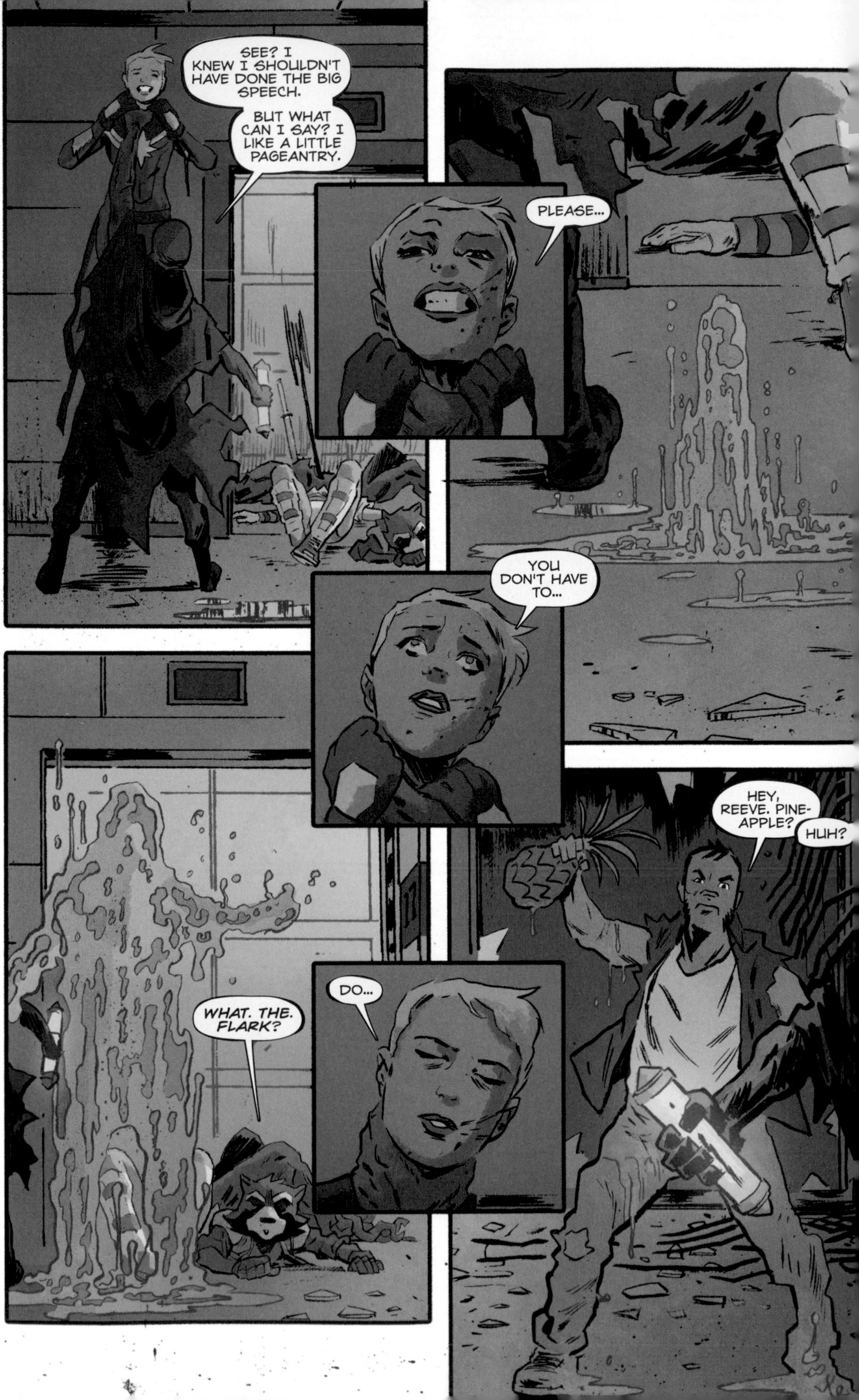
SEE? I KNEW I SHOULDN'T HAVE DONE THE BIG SPEECH.
BUT WHAT CAN I SAY? I LIKE A LITTLE PAGEANTRY.
PLEASE...
YOU DON'T HAVE TO...
DO...
WHAT. THE. FLARK?
HEY, REEVE. PINE-APPLE?
HUH?

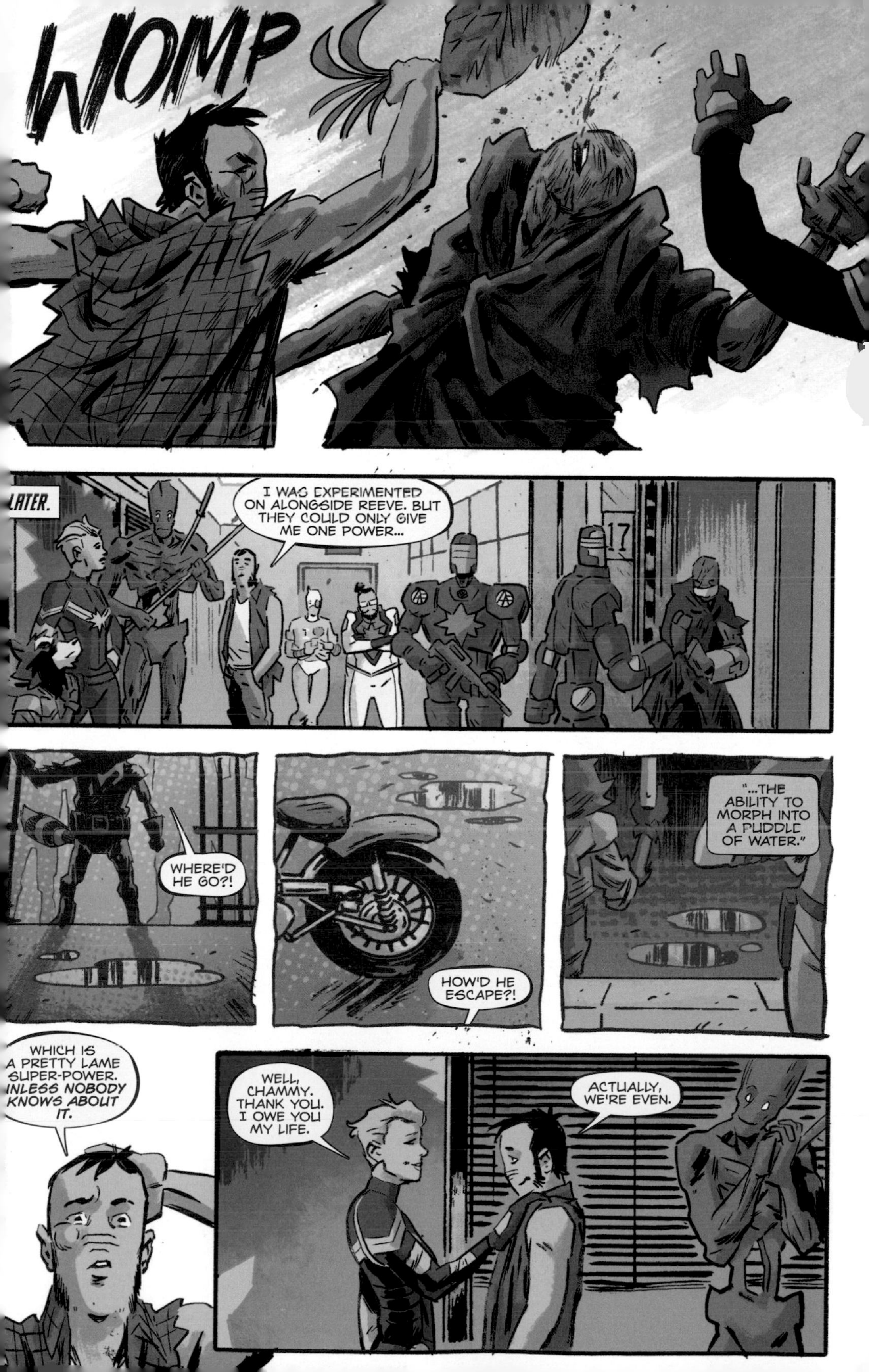
WOMP
LATER.
I WAS EXPERIMENTED ON ALONGSIDE REEVE. BUT THEY COULD ONLY GIVE ME ONE POWER...
17
WHERE'D HE GO?!
HOW'D HE ESCAPE?!
"...THE ABILITY TO MORPH INTO A PUDDLE OF WATER."
WHICH IS A PRETTY LAME SUPER-POWER. UNLESS NOBODY KNOWS ABOUT IT.
WELL, CHAMMY. THANK YOU. I OWE YOU MY LIFE.
ACTUALLY, WE'RE EVEN.

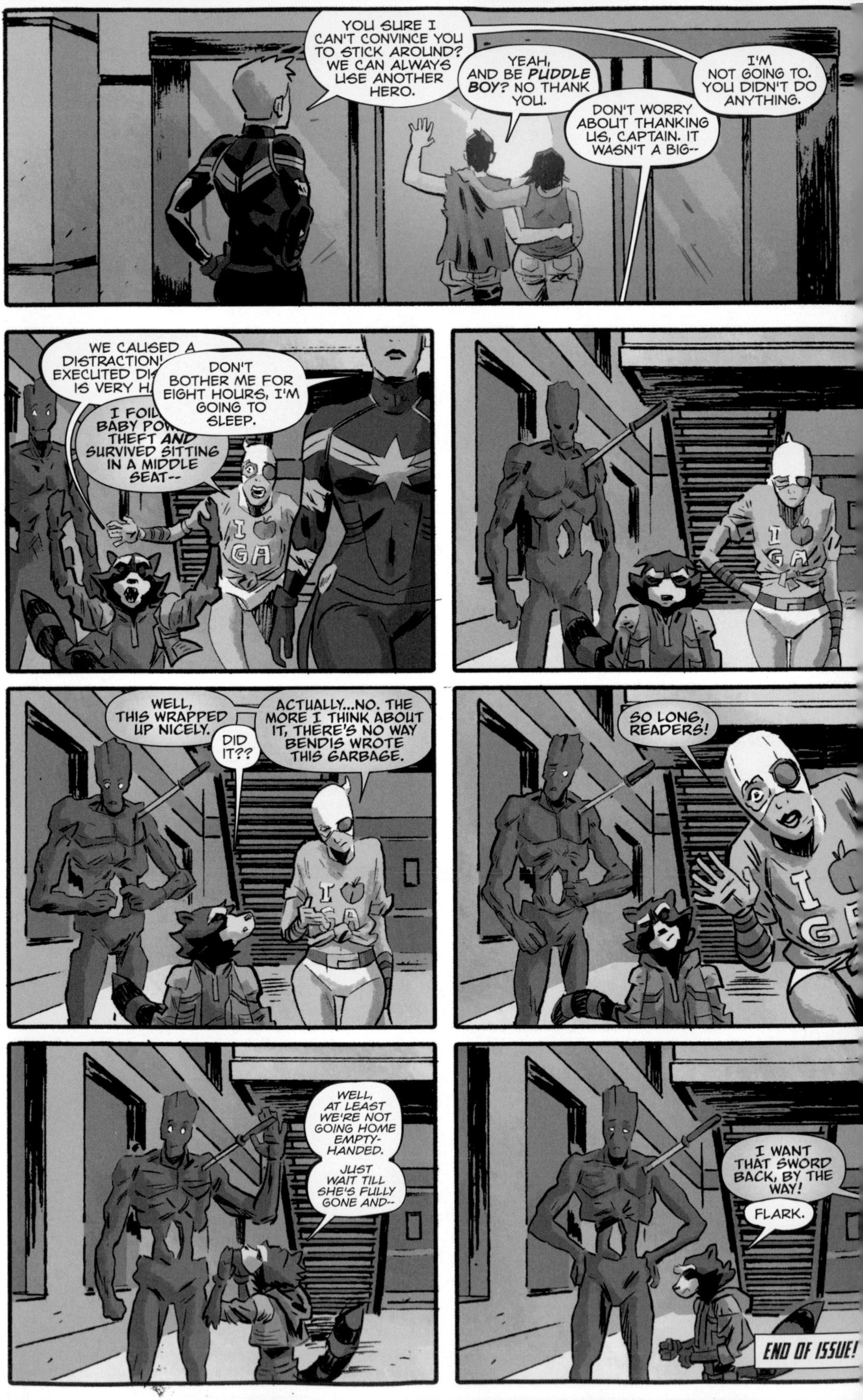
YOU SURE I CAN'T CONVINCE YOU TO STICK AROUND? WE CAN ALWAYS USE ANOTHER HERO.
YEAH, AND BE PUDDLE BOY? NO THANK YOU.
I'M NOT GOING TO. YOU DIDN'T DO ANYTHING.
DON'T WORRY ABOUT THANKING US, CAPTAIN. IT WASN'T A BIG--
WE CAUSED A DISTRACTION! EXECUTED DI... IS VERY HA...
DON'T BOTHER ME FOR EIGHT HOURS, I'M GOING TO SLEEP.
I FOIL... BABY POW... THEFT AND SURVIVED SITTING IN A MIDDLE SEAT--
WELL, THIS WRAPPED UP NICELY.
DID IT??
ACTUALLY...NO. THE MORE I THINK ABOUT IT, THERE'S NO WAY BENDIS WROTE THIS GARBAGE.
SO LONG, READERS!
WELL, AT LEAST WE'RE NOT GOING HOME EMPTY-HANDED.
JUST WAIT TILL SHE'S FULLY GONE AND--
I WANT THAT SWORD BACK, BY THE WAY!
FLARK.
END OF ISSUE!

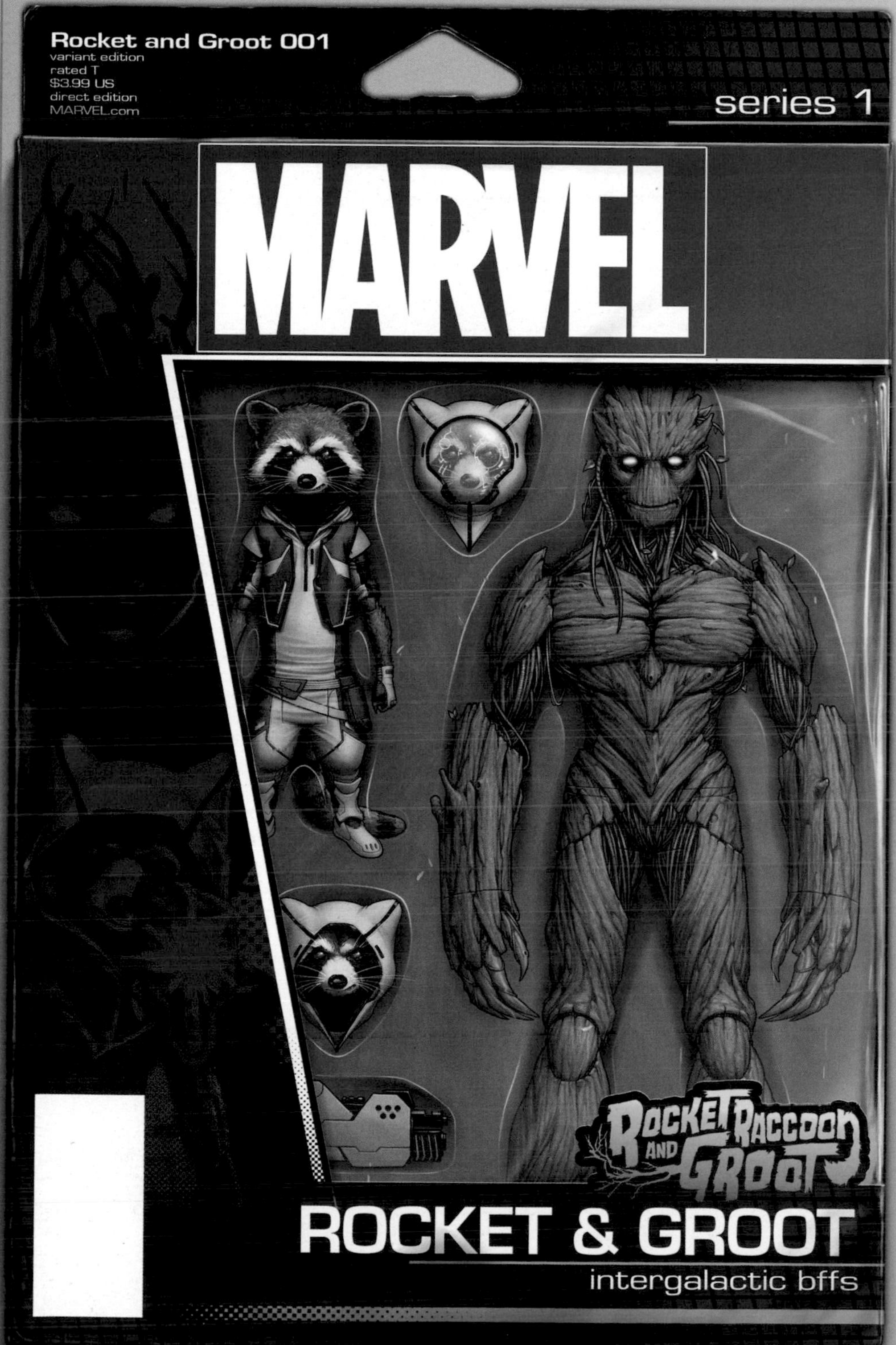
Rocket and Groot 001
variant edition
rated T
$3.99 US
direct edition
MARVEL.com
series 1
MARVEL
ROCKET RACCOON AND GROOT
ROCKET & GROOT
intergalactic bffs

ROCKET RACCOON & GROOT #1 ACTION FIGURE VARIANT
BY JOHN TYLER CHRISTOPHER

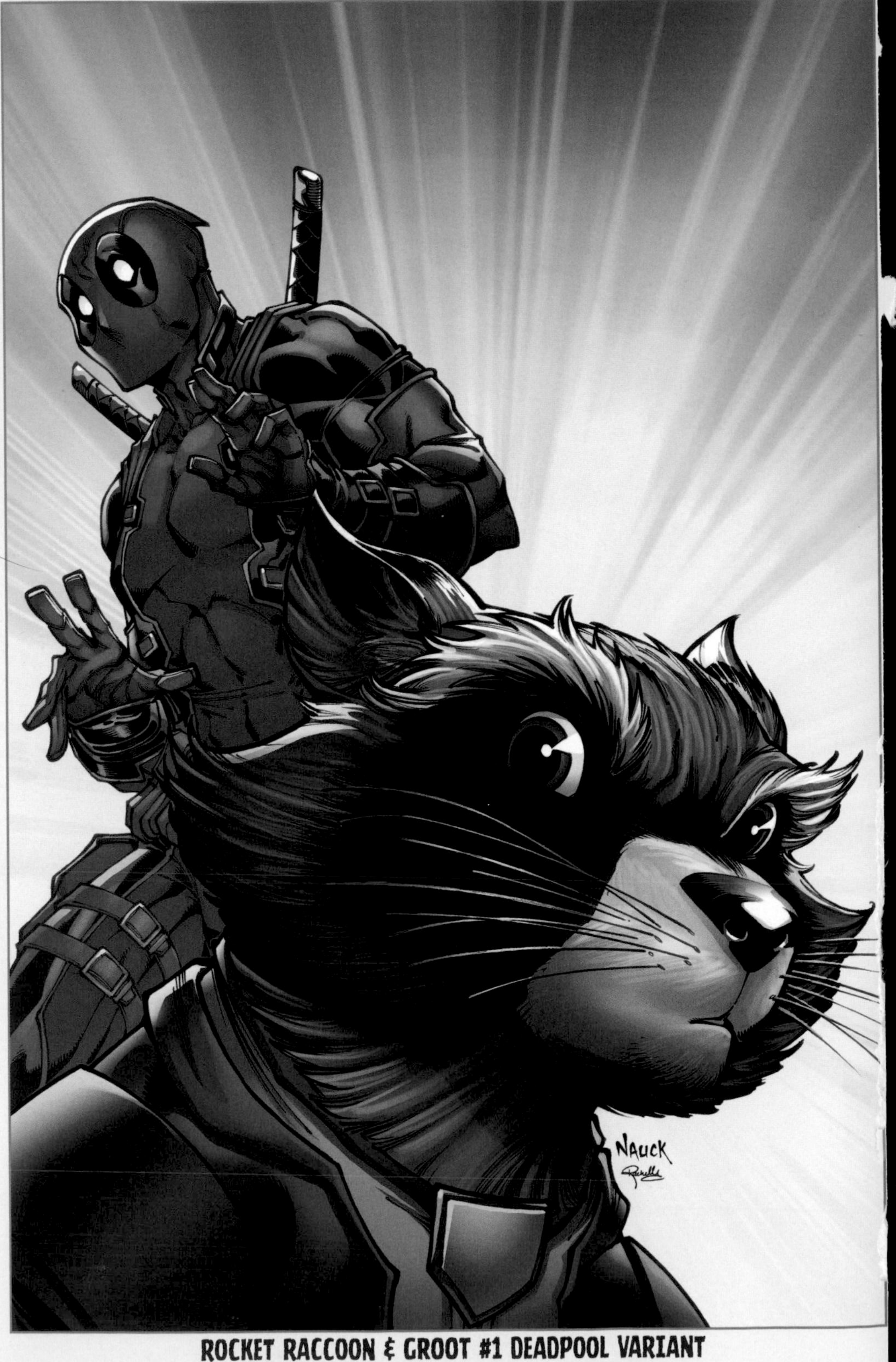
NAUCK

ROCKET RACCOON & GROOT #1 DEADPOOL VARIANT
BY TODD NAUCK & RACHELLE ROSENBERG

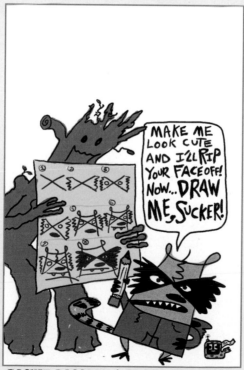

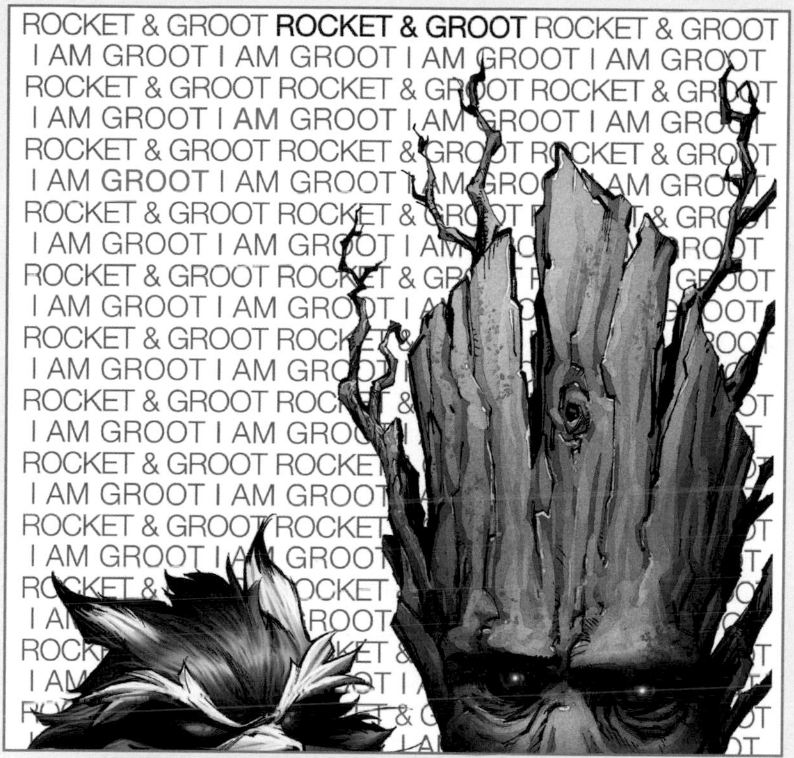
ROCKET & GROOT ROCKET & GROOT ROCKET & GROOT
I AM GROOT I AM GROOT I AM GROOT I AM GROOT

**ROCKET RACCOON & GROOT #1 HIP-HOP VARIANT**
BY KHARY RANDOLPH

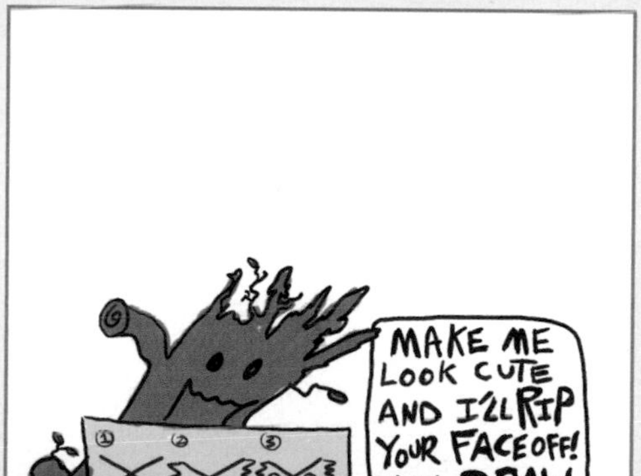
MAKE ME LOOK CUTE AND I'LL RIP YOUR FACE OFF! NOW... DRAW ME, SUCKER!

**ROCKET RACCOON & GROOT #6 VARIANT**
BY TOM ANGLEBERGER

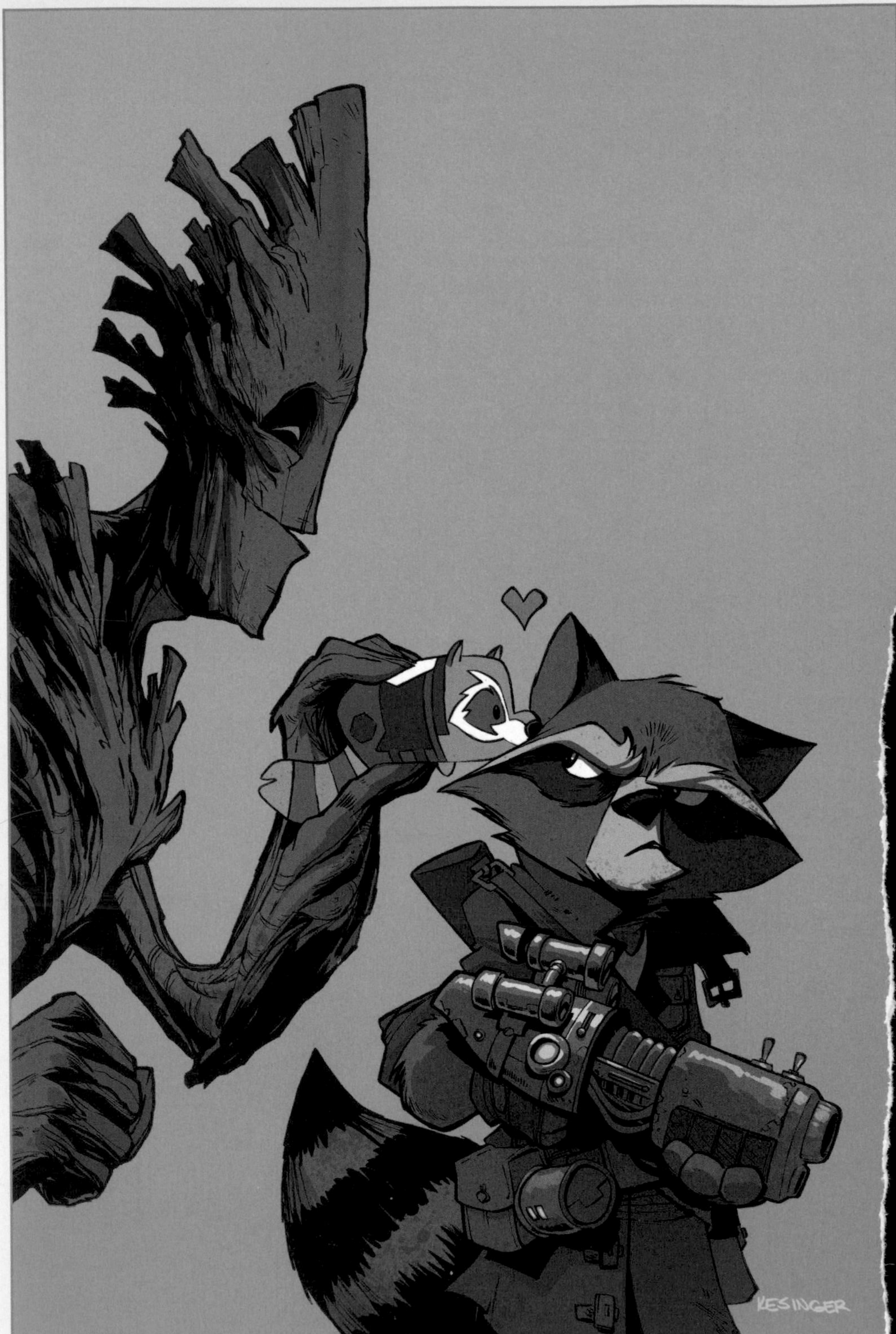
KESINGER

ROCKET RACCOON & GROOT #8 MARVEL TSUM TSUM TAKEOVER VARIANT
BY BRIAN KESINGER